The
Cottage
of
Curiosities

Celia Anderson is now living the dream as a full-time writer. She was a teacher and assistant head in her previous life, but other jobs have included barmaid, library assistant and cycling proficiency tutor. Pulling pints and sorting books are two of the most useful life skills she's acquired over the years. Cycling ... just isn't.

An enthusiastic member of the Romantic Novelists' Association, Celia currently organizes the judging for their Romantic Novel of the Year awards, spends far too much time on Facebook and posts increasingly random photographs on Instagram. Her interests include cooking, eating, walking, reading and drinking wine, usually with her husband, except for the cooking bit and not necessarily in that order. Celia feels very lucky to have two daughters who have not only presented her with two equally lovely sons-in-law, but are also very keen on putting apostrophes in the right places. Such a relief.

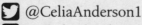 @CeliaAnderson1
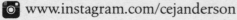 www.facebook.com/CeliaAndersonAuthor
www.instagram.com/cejanderson

Also by Celia Anderson
59 Memory Lane

The
Cottage
of
Curiosities

CELIA ANDERSON

HarperCollins*Publishers*

HarperCollins*Publishers*
The News Building,
1 London Bridge Street,
London SE1 9GF

www.harpercollins.co.uk

A Paperback Original 2020

1

A catalogue record for this book
is available from the British Library

ISBN: 978-0-00-831282-4

Set in Birka by Palimpsest Book Production Limited, Falkirk, Stirlingshire

Printed and bound in Great Britain by CPI Group (UK) Ltd, Croydon CR0 4YY

MIX
Paper from
responsible sources
FSC™ C007454
www.fsc.org

This book is produced from independently certified FSC™ paper
to ensure responsible forest management.

For more information visit: www.harpercollins.co.uk/green

In loving memory of Tracey Stasaitis
9/9/1967 – 23/4/2020
Into the Mystic

We'll live in birds and flowers and dragonflies and pine trees and in clouds and in those little specks of light you see floating in sunbeams …

PHILIP PULLMAN: *THE AMBER SPYGLASS*

1966

May Rosevere looks down at the cosily wrapped bundle in her arms. The baby's small snubbed nose reminds her of a button mushroom and the thought occurs to her that if she had opted to keep this little daughter, at some point in the future the nose might have given rise to one of those pet names that parents everywhere seem to love.

'I expect I would have called you Button,' May whispers to the sleeping child, 'and you would probably have hated it.'

The baby stirs and opens her eyes. They are a brilliant shade of blue and the gaze is startlingly piercing. May remembers somebody once telling her that a baby's eyes change colour as they get older, but she will never know if this is true. She hears the door open, and wishes that time would stand still, if only for a little while.

'Well, we can't just sit here looking at each other,' May murmurs, as the couple enter the room. 'You're going on a big adventure now, and I can't come with you, I'm afraid.'

1

Getting to her feet, she passes the baby into the waiting arms of the woman who stands in front of her. They exchange a long look.

'Are you absolutely sure about this, Mrs Rosevere?' the man asks. 'You know there's no going back, don't you? I won't have my Audrey upset. We'll take great care of the child, that goes without saying. She'll be well loved,' he adds hastily, when he sees the expression on May's face.

May tries to smile but it's too difficult, so she settles for making certain she's not going to cry.

'I'm sure,' she says, 'but I really think I'd better go now. My train leaves in half an hour. The taxi's waiting. I know you'll be the best possible parents for Barbara.'

'She's Grace now. Grace Hope Clarke.' The woman's voice is husky as she speaks for the first time. 'We decided to give her a fresh start. She needs to feel like our baby right from the beginning. You do understand, don't you?'

'Of course I understand. She's your daughter now.' May steels herself and bends forward for one last look at the baby, who has fallen asleep again in her new mother's embrace.

'Goodbye, Barbara,' she says, so quietly that even the other woman can't hear her. 'Perhaps we'll meet again one day. I hope so, I really do. Be good for these kind people, and have a wonderful life, my poppet.'

Turning, she makes her way out of the room without speaking to the couple again. It's impossible to think of anything useful to say. This parting was planned before the child entered the world and all the necessary arrangements have been made, if rather hurriedly.

As May climbs into the taxi, avoiding the driver's curious glance, she takes one last look over her shoulder. She can see the couple clearly through the window. They don't pay any attention to her because their eyes are firmly fixed on their brand-new daughter. The scene swims before May's eyes and she blinks hard.

'It's for the best,' she tells herself. 'What else could I have done? Living under the same roof as Charles Rosevere is no place for a child to be growing up, and I'm not cut out for motherhood. I'm just not.'

The taxi pulls away from the kerb and the driver clears his throat noisily. 'So, we're off to the train station, love?' he says. 'Going anywhere nice today?'

'I'm going to Cornwall,' May answers, 'I'm going home.'

Chapter One

April

Train travel has always been difficult for Grace Clarke, and today she's stuck right inside one of her worst nightmares. When passengers stare out of the windows on public transport their minds often spiral out of control, flitting from thought to thought with breath-taking speed as their memories are jogged by the scenery flashing past, a snatch of overheard conversation or the happy rustle of a crisp packet being opened. Being forced to listen in to the memories all around her is something Grace lives with on a day-to-day basis, and has done as far back as she can remember, but speeding south on the overcrowded train to Penzance, she feels as if she's drowning in them.

The girl in the next seat is clutching her phone like a lifeline. She snorts quietly to herself as she reads the latest message that's landed with a loud ping. A sudden vivid picture flashes into Grace's mind, and she blushes. The memory the text has sparked isn't one she wants to share. Who knew golden syrup had so many uses?

'My mother's in that retirement home near the sock factory now,' says a clear voice from the seat in front, 'but she still refuses to be parted from her can of squirty cream. Always has one tucked away in her handbag, just in case somebody gives her a cake, or a dish of apple crumble. Then she whips it out, and Bob's your uncle.'

The girl next to Grace looks up from her phone at last and raises her eyebrows. Then she begins typing out a new message at great speed.

Grace sighs and makes a huge effort to block out any more stray recollections that might come her way. This is a work in progress. Over the years she's tried yoga, meditation and sheer bloody-mindedness, but the only sure-fire method of stopping other people's random memories entering her brain is to instantly conjure up a more vivid one of her own as a kind of shield, and that's not always possible if your energy levels are down. Sometimes chocolate is the only answer.

The travellers who drop asleep as soon as the station is behind them and snore gently until an announcement jolts them into life again are the easiest to handle. They're no trouble at all. Their souls must be either full to the brim of good memories, or maybe it's just that they won't let the bad ones out. This morning, nearly everyone around Grace is wide awake. The spring sunshine is warm on her face and her coffee is hot and strong, but neither of these comforts is helping. There's at least another hour to kill.

Desperate to distract herself, Grace pulls out the now-tattered letter to read yet again.

Dear Barbara,

This is the last time you'll ever be addressed by that name. I've asked Audrey and Harry to give you this letter when you're old enough to understand that your new life as Grace Clarke was chosen with care. The alternative would have been much, much worse, but you'll have to trust me on that one. Motherhood isn't one of my talents.

The meeting with Audrey in that grim Midlands hospital as she grieved for yet another miscarriage was nothing short of a miracle in my eyes. A lucky chance for both of us, and hopefully for you too. I discharged myself as soon as I was strong enough to escape that nasty place of rules, routines and disinfectant. I never could bear being told what to do. By then, our secret adoption pact was made.

I will think of you with every day that passes and wonder how you are, what you're doing and what talents we share. It seems highly likely that you'll have discovered what I mean for yourself by the time this letter gets to you. I'm fifty-seven years old now, and I thought I was long past the risk of an unplanned pregnancy. Foolishly, I hadn't taken into account my unusual gift, if you can call it that. Of course, the other way of looking at the situation is that if I had been more aware, you wouldn't exist, would you? There will be difficult questions you'll want to ask me, I'm sure of it, and I'll answer most of them if ever you decide to come and find me. A big part of me hopes you will, although I don't deserve it.

I was never going to be a good mother. This way is best, but you will always be in my heart.

May Frances Rosevere,

Seagulls, 22 The Level, Pengelly, Cornwall

What talents we share. The words echo around Grace's weary brain. Is she jumping to conclusions? The only thing she can think of as a talent is this ridiculous ability to experience other people's memories the instant they have them, and it's more of a curse than a gift. From an early age, Grace knew she was different from other children. Vague memories of playing on her own at school and feeling all at sea in company haunt her.

Grace grew to learn she had to be very careful and keep her thoughts to herself. People didn't like different. Friendships were never easy, and it soon became a habit to be solitary. She tried to tell her father about all this once or twice but, although kind-hearted, Harry wasn't one for what he called *fanciful ideas,* and so Grace resolved to make sure she was never in such a fragile position again. Self-preservation became the main aim of her childhood.

Was that what this May Frances Rosevere person meant in her letter, though? Could May have shared her difficulties? The shattering news that her mother was alive and in Cornwall all through her growing-up years has rocked Grace's world. May was there, just waiting for her to get in touch, when she believed her birth mother to be long dead.

Grace glances at her watch and puts the letter away again, willing the time to pass more quickly. Her head is already pounding and she feels short of breath. Unable to bear sitting still any longer, she retrieves her travel bag from the rack and makes her unsteady way down the carriage to where she's stowed her case. It might be easier to pass the time by the doors, where there's a better view from the window.

The carriage makes a violent lurch and Grace is forced to pause and hang on to a seat for a moment. The man sitting there is white-faced, gripping his newspaper tightly. Before she can try to put up her usual thought block, his frantic memories flood her mind. In his head, he's on another train and this time the jolt is much more drastic. People are screaming and reaching for their phones.

Grace puts a hand on his shoulder and he flinches. 'It's okay, we're off again now,' she says reassuringly.

The man looks up, and the fear in his eyes starts to fade away. 'It just reminded me ...' he begins.

'I know,' says Grace, giving him a quick pat and moving on. She's learnt to be strong in these situations. If she let people go into detail when they pick up on her sympathy, she'd never get anything done.

She moves on as swiftly as possible, feeling a tingle of second-hand excitement as she passes a young mother with a toddler on her knee. The woman is talking softly to the little boy, almost crooning. 'Soon be with your Nana,' she says softly, cuddling him close, 'and then we'll have one of her special stews and some lovely fluffy dumplings with it. You don't know about dumplings yet, do you, sweetheart?'

The rush of happy childhood memories flowing from the woman goes some way to cancelling out the other man's panic, but by the time Grace reaches the relative safety of the space near the doors, she's grumpy and jaded.

It's a good time to change places, as it happens. The train line has just started to follow the coast, and the sight of waves breaking on the shore takes Grace's breath away. Although spring is well under way, the air is chilly. Weak sunshine illuminates an almost-empty beach. Grace itches to be out there, wrapped up warmly and making fresh footprints as she heads for the waterline. Brought up in the heart of the Midlands, she has always longed to spend more time by the sea, with flat, firm sands to walk on every day and sea breezes to blow the cobwebs away. Well, there's no reason why she shouldn't now.

It's high time to take stock. The death of both of her adoptive parents and the decision to take early retirement mean Grace can travel wherever and whenever she likes. She's saved hard and invested her money well over the years. Audrey and Harry don't need her care any more. The bitterness when she remembers their years of deception about her start in life ebbs slightly. She is completely free. It's an exhilarating thought.

The plan of coming to Cornwall to stay so near to the water in Pengelly has kept Grace sane over the past month, making funeral arrangements and finishing the clearing of her parents' house. Audrey's heart attack only six months previously was a shock, and it wasn't long before Harry followed her. It's taking Grace a while to handle the backlash. Her unwieldy thoughts flit again to those last moments with Harry, while his mind was still reasonably clear.

'Dad?' she said. 'Can you hear me? Why on earth didn't you give me this letter years ago? It's mine. I should have had it.'

'Your ma ...' He shook his head. A tear ran down

his cheek and Grace automatically reached to wipe it away.

She leant closer. 'Are you trying to say Mum didn't want me to know?'

A nod this time, and a second tear.

'But ... why not? And who's my real father? There's no clue in the letter. I need to know, Dad. Please ...'

Harry was clearly making a huge effort to speak now, and Grace held his hand more tightly, willing him to get the words out but flinching as his tortured memories crowded her brain.

'I ... we ... we weren't never told who your father was. He weren't the man she were married to, love, I do know that.'

'Really? You're sure?'

'We ... didn't want no details. It was best that way.'

As the train to Penzance rattles and sways, bringing Grace nearer and nearer to her only chance of finding out the truth about her start in life, exhaustion fights with alarm. An unaccustomed fear of the unknown hits her with a force that makes her pulse race.

'I'm going to find her, Dad,' she whispers, with her back to the rest of the carriage, 'I'm going to track May Rosevere down. There's just a tiny chance she might still be alive. People are living longer and longer these days. Whatever happens, at least I'll have tried.'

Chapter Two

As Grace murmurs the words, this whole adventure suddenly seems crazy and she's glad she hasn't told anyone the real reason for it. Finding out more about Seagulls, the house mentioned in May's letter, was easier than she'd expected. Her enquiry, posing as an old family friend, resulted in a speedy reply from the new owner.

Dear Grace,

I'm not sure how well your mum and dad knew May, but I'm very sorry to have to tell you she died a few months ago. By that time she had moved to 59 Memory Lane, because she was a very old lady and she needed a place to live that had no stairs. We were more than happy to buy this house. Seagulls was May's family home, much too big for her by then, but not for us! My husband Dominic and I have two sets of twins and another baby on the way.

I can give you details of the person who lives in May's final home now. Her name is Emily Lovell, and she could possibly fill you in on any other details you would like. I'm afraid I don't have a phone number for her. If you'd like me to contact Emily for you, my email address is at the top of the page. I've heard she's opening up her home as holiday accommodation for people who need some peace and quiet for whatever reason. A lovely idea. I'm tempted to check in myself!

Hoping this helps,

Cassie Featherstone

Leaning forwards to get a better view of the beach bathed in sunlight, Grace resolves that whatever comes next, it won't be more of the same. Changes are afoot. Big changes. Her phone pings with an incoming message and, glad of the distraction, she fishes it out of her bag. It's a message from Kat, one of her ex-colleagues and the nearest thing she's got to a friend, although even Kat has no idea of the real root of her problems.

Are you there yet? Hope this is the magical cure for the migraines. Keep in touch. All at the hellhole send love. K x

Grace is catapulted back to the crowded staff room for a moment, the air full of the smell of instant coffee and cheap biscuits. The migraine story was her fallback excuse when the memories from all the others had threatened to swamp her. In the end, she'd had to resort to her own kettle in the art studio. It was her domain, and peaceful at break time. A reputation for being stuck-up was a small price to pay for the relief of a quiet space. She texts back.

Not far now. Hoping for great things from Pengelly. Will send you a postcard! G x

There is nobody else likely to ask how she's doing. Kat will probably soon forget Grace if the promised postcard isn't followed up by an email or a phone call. The thought isn't as cheering as she thought it would be. Cutting all ties seemed the best way forward, although the work family have been part of her life for so long.

It's a lot to leave behind, but the rest of her work-mates can't really be classed as close to Grace. People who make and keep friends need to be able to open up to them, at least some of the time. Being so vulner-able to random memories flying around is often painful and sometimes deeply embarrassing. The phrase *too much information* often pops into Grace's mind.

For the past few years, Grace has had the uncomfort-able feeling that she should be able to do something with this strange gift, if you can call it that. How can she be a vessel for all these random recollections but be unable to do anything with them? It must surely be possible to give some back. But how? The only possible use for her talent must be in cases of people who are losing memories too quickly. Where to

begin, though? She can hardly just walk into a retirement home and say, 'Is anyone here forgetting things
they ought to remember?' It's a tricky one.

'Hot drinks, crisps, beer and wine, chocolate. Can I
get you anything?' The man with the snack trolley
almost runs over Grace's foot, and she shakes her head.

'No, thanks. I'm not hungry.' This is not strictly true,
but she is too full of anticipation to eat.

'Are you sure? Got some nice egg and cress sarnies
on here. Got to be honest, they pong a bit, but they
taste good. Go on, treat yourself. Remind me of parties
as a kid, they do ...'

'Really, I don't need anything.' In the nick of time,
Grace conjures up her current fallback image of a tiny
courtyard in an Italian village and immerses herself
in the warm sunshine and fragrant flowers. She can
feel the edges of the man's nostalgic party thoughts
swirling around her but this time she's been quick
enough to avoid plunging head-first into them. It's a
tactic she's painstakingly developed with varying
degrees of success, and today her protective shield
works perfectly.

The trolley rattles away down the train and Grace
turns back to the window with relief, wondering for
what seems like the hundredth time who or what is
lying in wait for her. May's cottage is advertised as a
kind of retreat. It's the only link to her birth mother

apart from the explosive letter that Audrey and Harry never saw fit to share with her.

The train is slowing down for a station now and it rocks alarmingly. The other occupant of Grace's temporary refuge by the door lurches and swears under his breath. He rolls his eyes at Grace and grins.

'Sorry. Forgot myself for a minute.'

Startled out of her reverie, Grace puts on her best teacher face and glares, causing the man to open his eyes wide and take a step backwards.

'I really am embarrassed about my language,' he says. 'I wasn't holding on tightly enough.'

'No harm done,' Grace answers, mollified. She looks at him more closely. Long and lean, he's probably around sixty, but hasn't worn nearly as well as she has. The lines on his face are appealing, though – he looks as if he's smiled a lot in his lifetime so far. His salt-and-pepper hair is cropped short and his blue eyes are friendly. A well-worn tweed jacket and baggy cords give the impression of an off-duty lecturer or the owner of an exclusive antiquarian bookshop.

'Don't you have a reserved seat?' Grace asks, wishing he would go away. His presence is a distraction from the view, now that she's noticed him, and his eyes are disturbingly melancholy even though he's smiling.

'Yes, but I'd rather stand, given the choice,' he says. 'How about you?'

The man's accent is northern, well-modulated and easy on the ear. Grace isn't in the mood for conversation, but she swallows her irritation and prepares to be sociable, if only briefly. They'll soon be arriving in Penzance, so she can't possibly be stuck with him for long.

'I moved because I was fidgety. I couldn't sit still any longer,' she says.

'Me too. I get terrible cramp if I haven't got enough leg room. These seats aren't designed for anyone over six feet tall.'

'Well, never mind, we'll be out of here soon, with a bit of luck,' Grace says, turning away to find that the train line has moved away from the coast and the landscape isn't nearly so interesting now. She sighs.

'Let's hope so. Well, I'd better go and round up my granddaughter. It was good to bump into you. I'm James.' He beams at her, raising his eyebrows enquiringly, and Grace feels a jolt of something unexpected and rather delicious.

'My name's Grace,' she says, smiling back despite herself.

She watches him walk between the rows of seats, shoulders back, holding on lightly every now and again when the train rocks. He stops near the end of the carriage and a fragile-looking girl looks up at him, raising her eyebrows. Even at this distance, Grace can see that the granddaughter is striking. She has short, spiky black hair and her make-up is vivid, making her eyes look huge in her small, pointed face. She must be in her late teens, Grace thinks, feeling a pang for all the girls who have passed through her art classes, some as individual as this one, others trying hard to blend in.

The train slows down for the station, groaning and hissing as the brakes grip. Grace picks up her travel bag and retrieves her case on wheels before the hordes descend. The suitcase is a veteran of many trips in the UK and abroad, with a shiny red surface that's scratched and dented in places now. It's a solid, almost bulletproof affair.

Everything she needs is stowed away here. Grace can pack for anything up to six weeks in this combination of luggage if she rolls and folds carefully. Who knows how long she'll need to stay if she wants to find out all about her real mother and solve the mystery of who might be her father? Although in reality, she tells herself, if he was in May's age range, he'll probably have gone the same way.

If all this comes to nothing much and Grace decides not to extend her visit to Pengelly, she can take off anywhere she chooses. Her passport is in the pocket of her bag and the world, as they say, is her oyster. What a lovely thought – a world made of oysters.

The train lurches to a halt with a scream of brakes.

Grace is off the train before anyone else, minding the gap as instructed, being careful not to trip over her hem. It might have been a mistake wearing the almost floor-length camel coat with the fur collar to travel in, but Grace wants to make a good impression in her mother's home village, even if she isn't intending to reveal the true purpose of her visit just yet, at least not until she's discovered what sort of person May was. Anyway, there's no need to look like a bag lady just because you're on a train, is there?

The bustle is bewildering for a few minutes, but the platform clears quickly, leaving only Grace and the man from the doorway who is looking around vaguely. His granddaughter has vanished.

'Are you waiting for someone too?' he asks, when he spots Grace doing the same.

Grace shivers. Surely it should be warmer than this in the south of England? 'Yes, I'm being collected. How about you?' There doesn't seem any option to avoid this small talk without being rude. The rather forlorn-looking man has such kind eyes that she regrets her earlier frostiness. Hunger always makes Grace grumpy, and it's not his fault she's got a thumping head from the journey.

'A lift was supposed to be booked for us. Hope they haven't forgotten. Robyn's gone to find out what's happening. I'm ready for a shower, a glass of wine and an early night.' He reaches into his pocket and pulls out a card. 'The name of the place keeps escaping me. Ah yes, I've got it now. Curiosity Cottage, here we come.'

'You're not staying at fifty-nine Memory Lane too, are you?'

'Yes, I am. Oh ... don't say you're at the same house? That's a turn-up for the books.'

Grace can hardly believe it. So much for a retreat full of peace and quiet. 'Yes, isn't it?' she says resignedly. 'Let's go and look for your granddaughter. If I stand here for many more minutes I'll take root and also if our lift doesn't arrive soon, we'll need to find a taxi.'

She grabs her case by the handle with more force than is strictly necessary. Today has gone on far too long already.

Chapter Three

Cornish Comforts is delighted to bring you a brand-new listing today, hot off the press:

Visit Curiosity Cottage – a unique holiday experience that could change your life.

Is your head bursting with the stresses and strains of modern life? Are your memories trying to escape you? Do you find it hard to hold a thought in your head?

This ancient granite dwelling is tucked away at the end of Memory Lane, a steep cobbled street in the tranquil Cornish village of Pengelly. Your hosts, writer and publisher Emily Lovell, her grandmother Julia (whose scones are legendary) and local restaurateur Tristram Brookes, believe that finding a temporary breathing space in beautiful surroundings can be a positive step towards a more relaxed future.

Curiosity Cottage is a comfortable self-catering

23

home full of quirky treasures and artefacts, with extensive sea views and a deep sense of peace. Local restaurants, a village shop and a welcoming public house make catering easy, and direct access to the beach and the quaint working harbour brings the soothing benefits of nature right to your doorstep.

The accommodation consists of three bedrooms, all en suite, a shared living area and a sun terrace with views to ease the most troubled of minds. Come and join us for as long as it takes to make a difference.

Contact e.lovell@mainstream.co.uk for details and a brochure. Early booking recommended.

Four o'clock in the morning is the time for red-wine hangovers and regrets. Julia, in bed at 60 Memory Lane, gives up on sleep after an hour or two of feverish thoughts about her future. She shivers as she reaches for her thickest dressing gown. Julia isn't much of a drinker. A small frame and lack of practice mean she gets tipsy quite quickly so she usually sticks to one glass, but last night was a celebration. New beginnings call for claret and rare fillet steaks, according to her fiancé, Tristram, who, at eighty years old to Julia's eighty-six, still knows how to party.

Julia crunches a couple of indigestion tablets, pads barefoot across the bedroom and opens her curtains to look at the moonlit beach. The tide is out, and the glimmering light on the water moves gently with the motion of the waves. It's been a clear, cold night, unusually cloudless. The sanded boards are smooth beneath her bare feet and she stands in her old familiar place, feeling the familiar knots in the wood under her toes.

Opening the window a crack, Julia hears the distant crash of the waves and smells the tang of salt on the wind. A Cornish cove in the early hours of the morning is a beautiful sight, she thinks, squinting as she notices what look like faint footprints leading to the water's edge. Surely they're not Emily's, at this hour? Julia sighs. If her granddaughter can't sleep either, maybe Julia's right to be worried about their joint business venture.

The sight of a slender figure sitting hunched on the rocks over to the right near the harbour confirms her suspicions. Emily's bright blonde hair catches the moonbeams as it's lifted by the breeze. It can't be as cold out there as it looks, although Emily looks well-padded with a heavy coat. Her arms are wrapped around her raised knees and she's gazing out to sea. Julia feels a pang of sympathy. She knows the girl has more than enough to occupy her mind. Like Julia and Tristram, Emily is on the brink of a new relationship, with Andy who lives opposite to Julia. His house is next door to the cottage that Emily has inherited. He's a complicated man with a young daughter and plenty of painful history of his own to deal with. Julia closes the window and heads for warmth again. Emily will be safe enough on Pengelly beach at any time of day or night.

Shivering, Julia climbs back into bed, wishing she'd thought to put her slippers on. Her feet are icy now. Making a heap of pillows at the head of the crumpled bed and reaching for her bedsocks, she reflects that it's hard enough to nod off when she's alone, so how on earth is she going to rest when she and Tristram are married? Will her fluffy socks offend him?

So far, she's kept her independence and her own space, but there's often a worrying sparkle in Tristram's eyes. That thought is exciting and terrifying in equal measure. It's been a while since her husband Don died. Their last years together were deeply loving but not what you might call passionate. Tristram has already been married four times and he's a live wire, with a lot more vitality than most men half his age. What if ... but surely he won't still want to ...

She forces herself to think about their joint project instead. Curiosity Cottage, formerly Shangri-La, is (or was, she corrects herself sadly) the final home of her old friend and sparring partner, May Rosevere. These last months have been a crazy whirlwind of building work, plumbing hiccups, meetings with their solicitor and frantic planning sessions with Tristram, Emily and Andy.

Emily, the new owner of the place, is adamant that a holiday cottage called Shangri-La won't set the right tone, so, based on the fact that the place is full of the previous owner's collections of random items, she's rechristened it accordingly. Julia agrees that a fresh start needs a brand-new name, and the sign that Emily has commissioned from Angelina, their local artist, is beautiful. It shows seven magpies in a semi-circle surrounding the words *Curiosity Cottage*. 'Why magpies, and why seven?' Julia asked Emily when the sign was delivered and installed next to the yellow front door, flanked by huge pots of succulents either side of the step.

'You remember the old rhyme, don't you? *One for sorrow, two for joy, three for a girl and four for a boy …*'

'*Five for silver, six for gold, seven for a secret never to be told,*' finishes Julia, 'but what's the secret?'

Her granddaughter smiled. 'I don't know yet. I've got a feeling that there are still some of May's secrets in here waiting to be discovered.'

Emily's moved upstairs into the newly converted loft apartment only this week. Julia has been in a prime position to oversee the work and nag the builders while Emily dashes back and forth to London to keep up with her part-time publishing career. Now the alterations are done at last. It's really happening, and today's the big day.

Julia reaches for the emergency tin of digestives on the bedside table and begins to munch. A scalding hot cup of tea would be wonderful but going downstairs to make it is too much bother, so she gulps down two painkillers with some water instead. It's no wonder sleep won't come, she thinks, brushing crumbs off her chest. The last year has been eventful. There have been at least as many downs as ups, but does she really regret anything other than too much red wine last night? Apart from learning to live without dear Don, the only other really bad thing has been the loss of May. The knowledge that the two of them wasted a very long time in pointless animosity when they could have spent the time being friends still haunts her.

Everyone in Pengelly was stunned when May died, especially when she left her home to Emily. In the minds of the villagers, May was going to live forever – fresh-faced, mischievous and quirky. She'd looked so much younger than her years, and acted it too.

As they so often do, Julia's thoughts travel back over the recent months. Most startling of all has been the blossoming of her love for Tristram. She knows that there are some folk in the village who have muttered that it didn't take her long to replace poor Don. There have been rumbles about Emily too, as if she winkled the cottage out of May as the old lady lay feebly dying, which is very far from the case. May was a law unto herself and completely on the ball until the very last moment. Some people can be very small-minded, especially Vera at the village shop, who gives the term *sharp-tongued* a whole new meaning.

Julia reaches into her bedside cabinet and brings out a leather writing case. She opens it on her lap and studies the contents by the light of the lamp. There are several rather battered-looking envelopes in there, each one with an ancient stamp and a jagged tear where Don impatiently ripped them open. He was always keen to get the latest news from the Midlands, Julia reflects with a sad smile.

These faded remnants of Don's family archives were the letters that got missed when she gave the bulk of them to Emily for safekeeping. The only others still here are safely inside the packet that Julia never opens. The bad ones. She'd intended to pass these last few on too, but something held her back. It's good to have just a small reminder of how much Don had loved his mother, sisters and brother, even if their never-ending interest in his life sometimes seemed a little intense. She pulls the top one out of its envelope and re-reads the familiar words. This is Elsie speaking – she and Kathryn kept a close eye on Don and their younger brother Will, although as the letter points out, Will wasn't living up to their expectations, as usual.

So anyway, other than the crisis with the lost ring, my most important news is that I've managed to change my holiday week, and so has Kathryn. Will can't come with us this time but he sends his love. He's been a bit peaky lately, moping around like a dog that's lost its bone. I wish he'd get himself a girlfriend. Mother thinks he's just waiting for the right one to come along.

With a sharp pang of loss, Julia thinks about glamorous, enigmatic Will, so different from most of the other young men in his town. She wonders where he is. He's probably still in Ireland but it's so long since he was in touch that she's almost given him up for dead.

Looking down at the remaining letters, Julia picks another one out. This one's from the man himself. At the end of the short but newsy sheets, Will writes, in a delicate copperplate:

Don't forget to give my love to Julia, Don. I think she's cross with me for some reason, but I'm not sure why. Is it because the girls told her I've been going to the Catholic Church instead of our Methodist Chapel? They're all well and truly fed up with me at the moment! Mind you, your dear wife doesn't usually try and tell people what to do, so it must be something else. You're a very lucky man, do you know that? I'd have married Julia myself if I'd got there first.

Your affectionate brother, Will x

PS Tell J the Catholics don't sing like we do. They don't belt the old hymn tunes out like us.

Julia pulls a wry face. 'Oh no, you would never have married me, Will,' she tells the paper in her hand, 'and you know it as well as I do. I wish you were here, though. I want you to tell me about what happened with your mother's opal ring. Lost and found, but what went on in between? I think you know, don't you?'

Julia looks down at her left hand. She seldom takes the ring off unless there's a danger of it getting wet. It glows in the semi-darkness, and she touches it like the talisman it's become to her. She's read about many different ways in which opals are significant, but her favourite in the long list of their properties involves a problem close to her heart. Julia firmly believes that these precious, iridescent stones can halt forgetfulness. 'Hold on to my memories for me,' she whispers. 'I don't want to lose them.'

Finishing her second biscuit, Julia packs the writing case away, throws the covers back and goes to check the bay again. That's a relief, Emily must have gone home. The sand is empty of all but a couple of early morning gulls digging for sandworms. Exhausted, she leaves the curtains open and climbs back into bed, plumping up her pillows. She tries to calm her busy mind with pleasant thoughts of deserted beaches and the rippling golden hair of her granddaughter, but nothing seems to help today. Julia stares at the ceiling as the sky is gradually striped with salmon pink and a delicate shade of turquoise and the first rays of the morning sun begin to creep across the sea. It's no good. There's too much going on in her head for the much-needed oblivion to come.

What might the first guests be like? Will they slot easily into village life? Emily has deliberately allowed this part of the venture to be open-ended to see how it turns out, and it sounds as if James Pevensie might be with them for quite some time although his granddaughter Robyn is only staying one night, just to make sure he's safely settled.

When Julia spoke to Robyn on the phone, she got the impression that James is having quite serious memory issues but doesn't want to admit it. She hopes he won't need watching all the time in case he wanders off.

The other woman is more of a puzzle. Why would a fifty-four-year-old retired teacher need to get away from the rat race? To be able to finish working by that age is a luxury most people don't have. Grace Clarke.

Julia has a funny feeling she's heard that name before, or at least seen it written down somewhere, but she can't remember where.

Maybe I need to stay in the cottage and work on remembering things as much as anyone else does, Julia reflects somewhat anxiously, *because I can't for the life of me recall why the name Grace Clarke seems so significant.*

As is its wont, the sun continues to rise. Julia wrestles with her sluggish memory until a glance at the clock on her bedside table tells her it's time to get moving. Today is going to be the start of a whole new chapter.

Chapter Four

Bleary from lack of sleep, Julia's still in the shower when she hears Emily calling up the stairs. 'Gran? Are you decent yet? I want you to have a last look over the cottage to see if it's up to scratch before the Pevensies and Miss Clarke arrive,' she yells.

Julia turns the water off and steps onto the bath mat, wrapping herself in her most luxurious towel. There's nothing like top quality Egyptian cotton for starting the day off well. This is one of the things she's insisted on during her part in the refurbishment of May's old home. The two new shower rooms and revamped bathroom must have plenty of soft, fluffy bath sheets in jewel colours to match the selection of glass bottles on the windowsills and the vibrant ethnic rugs chosen by Emily and Andy. There should be refillable dispensers of exotic bubble bath, organic sponges, the very best scented soaps in china dishes and the radiators must be turned up high. A luxurious bathroom is a must if you're not feeling quite yourself, she's told Emily repeatedly.

'Give me five minutes,' she shouts back, 'Put the kettle on, darling.'

When Julia arrives in the kitchen, dressed in a warm but classy red woollen dress and leather boots (she's got no intention of letting standards slip just because she's had a bad night) Emily has made a pot of coffee and a plate of toast. She's sitting at the table, spreading butter and honey generously and reading the local newspaper that's just popped through the letter box. Her wild hair is loose down her back, giving her the air of a sea nymph ready for action, and her face is scrubbed clean of her sophisticated London make-up.

'You look gorgeous – like a holly berry on legs,' she says, grinning up at her grandmother. 'Hey, guess what? We're on the front page. I sent them that ad from Cornish Comforts.'

Julia comes over to stand behind Emily, putting both hands on her granddaughter's shoulders as she reads the article.

Curiosity Cottage, Pengelly: A True Taste of Cornwall
Brand-new holiday venue opens, ready for the start of the tourist season.

Local entrepreneur and restaurant owner Tristram Brookes has joined forces with Pengelly residents Julia and Emily Lovell and landscape gardener Andy Fleetwood to create an innovative bolt hole for those suffering from the stresses and strains of modern life. Providing comfortable, single-storied accommodation with a seaside theme, our cottage is situated right next to the beach at the bottom of Pengelly's oldest cobbled street; residents of Pengelly will remember it as Shangri-La, one-time home of our oldest local treasure, May Rosevere, and before that, The Beach Café. The Southern Echo *would like to wish the team the very best of luck with their new project, due to open its doors any day now.*

'That's a great photo of you, Gran,' says Emily. 'And Tris looks dapper too. Some men just suit beards, don't they? He looks a bit like an up-market politician with a good tailor.'

Julia laughs. 'Don't mention that to him,' she says. 'He models himself on one of the older James Bonds, I think. Imagine Tris in politics?'

They giggle. Tristram would never be able to hold his tongue long enough to avoid causing mayhem. He's never rude, but sticking up for the underdog has got him into trouble more times than Julia can remember.

She looks at the photograph again. 'You look lovely too, sweetheart. Shame Andy and Tamsin couldn't be there when the *Echo* photographer came to call.'

'Huh,' Emily's face clouds over. 'It wasn't that they couldn't be there, exactly. Tamsin was having one of her moments. D'you know, Gran, sometimes she seems to go against everything I'd like her to do, just for devilment.'

'She's only seven. She'll come around eventually. Just be patient.'

'Patient? For how long? She's turning into a monster. Andy hasn't spent any time on his own with me for three whole weeks.'

'You're exaggerating, surely?'

'No, I'm not. Everything we plan either includes Tam, which is fine, of course, when she's in a good mood, or it gets cancelled at the last minute because she doesn't want to let me see him without her to supervise. Or to see him at all, really. Where did I go wrong? It was all going so well to start with.'

'Hmm. I suppose when you first got together, Tamsin didn't get the message that it'd be a long-term arrangement. When you're seven, you don't look very far ahead as a rule.'

'But we had such fun, me and Tam. I built some great dens with her. We went camping on the beach ... swimming ... we started a scrapbook of cat pictures, and everything ...'

'You were just friends then. Now you're moving on to something bigger.'

'Are we? It doesn't feel like that to me.'

'Well, it probably does to Tamsin. And it's gradually dawned on her that you're sticking around and she'll have to share her dad permanently. She's had him all to herself almost since the day she was born, hasn't she? He's had to be both mother and father since Allie died.'

'You don't need to tell me that. I'm not completely insensitive, Gran.'

Emily rubs her eyes crossly, smearing newsprint across her cheeks in the process. She reminds Julia of the grumpy teenager who used to come and stay with her grandparents several times a year, spending large chunks of her holiday stomping across the beach thinking everyone hated her and moaning about wanting a tattoo.

'But if Andy's really going to be a part of running the holiday accommodation,' she continues, 'he's going to have to be a bit more available. I need him to do more than just keep the garden tidy. The financial side of it's important too. We've got to make it pay. I want to offer extras, like trips out ... maybe workshops of different kinds. And anyway, I just want to see him!' she ends on a wail.

'Give him time, darling. I know patience isn't your strong point, but you really can't rush these things.'

'Says the woman who got engaged again ten minutes after her husband died.'

Julia flinches and Emily puts her hand up to her mouth. 'I'm sorry, Gran, I didn't mean ...'

'But you must have been thinking something along those lines for it to slip out so easily.' Julia swallows hard. She's taken resistance and mild backbiting from Vera and some of the other villagers in her stride, but from Emily, it stings like salt on a cut finger. Another unexpected longing to talk to Will washes over her although she has no idea why he's been on her mind so much lately after all these years of absence and no communication. Maybe it's because she knows he'd understand. Even if he *was* Don's brother, Will won't see her relationship with Tris as a betrayal, she's sure. How she knows this with so much certainty, Julia has no idea, but know it she does, even though in her heart of hearts, she's aware that there was an animosity between Tristram and Will that was never explained.

'No, honestly I haven't,' Emily babbles. 'Not at all. Not even a little bit, really, Gran. I was just being a misery. Probably sour grapes because you and Tris can have as much time together as you like. I'm so sorry ... I really am ...'

There's a long pause as Julia wonders where to go from here. Her instincts tell her they need a break from each other to get over this crisis, but that's impossible today. There's too much to do.

'Drink your coffee and then we'll go across the road to the cottage,' she says eventually, 'and don't say another word about Tristram or me, please.' This last is as Emily starts to say sorry again. 'We'll discuss it again when we're not so tired, if we must.'

Emily nods, not meeting her grandmother's eyes. A loud rapping of knuckles against wood announces Tristram's arrival and the kitchen door swings open, breaking the uncomfortable silence and bringing in a waft of chilly air. Julia hears the dogs barking and Tristram's familiar voice with mixed feelings. His twinkling eyes take in the scene as Bruno and Buster burst into the kitchen after him and do a couple of quick circuits of the table.

'Heel, boys! Do we need to go out and come in again?' he asks, grinning at Emily.

'*You* don't, but I think *I* do.'

'Surely not? There's nobody more welcome in this house than you, Em.'

'Not today. I'm a liability. Gran will be glad when I've gone back over the road, I reckon. I think I've got out of the wrong side of the bed. Which isn't easy when you sleep in a corner under the eaves. You can give yourself concussion.'

Julia feels her shoulders tense as Tristram comes over to kiss her cheek, Bruno gooses her with enthusiasm and Buster knocks over a stool. A kitchen full of Labrador and Puggle-love is loud and a bit smelly. Her granddaughter looks as if she's been sucking a lemon and a headache is forming over Julia's right eye. At this rate, bedtime tonight can't come soon enough.

Chapter Five

Grace is just about to lead the hunt for a taxi when her spirits lift. James's granddaughter is hurrying towards them, desperately trying to keep pace with a tall, muscular man who has a small girl in tow. The three of them are loping along as if they're out on the moors rather than rushing along a cramped station platform.

The man's hair is wild and curly, matched by the halo of curls on the small girl's head. She's skipping along, trying to keep up. Grace thinks she can hear her singing.

'Hurry up, Tamsin, we're late enough as it is,' Grace hears the man say, increasing his speed even more.

'Dad,' she shouts, tugging on his hand, 'slow down. Our legs can't go that fast.'

'I'm so sorry,' the man says, as they come to a halt and try to get their breath back. 'I had a flat tyre on the way here.' He holds out oil-stained hands as if to prove it, and Grace has a sudden disconcerting image of him stripped to the waist, heaving the wheel from his car as admiring ladies lean out of passing vehicles, whistling. She gives herself a mental shake.

'Are you for Pengelly too, then? We're off to Memory Lane. Ironic, really, with the state of mine. Memory, I mean,' Grace's train companion says.

'I'm Andy, and I'm here to collect James and Robyn Pevensie and Grace Clarke. I'm guessing that's you three?'

Grace's attention is caught by the unusual surname. 'Is that Pevensie as in the family from *The Lion, the Witch and the Wardrobe?*' she asks.

'Well, yes,' James says, 'but you're the first person to spot that connection for ages.'

Their eyes meet, and Grace feels a ridiculous sense of pride. '*The Dawn Treader*'s my favourite,' she says. 'Mind you, *The Silver Chair* is ...'

Andy puts his hand on the little girl's shoulder and gently moves her into Grace's line of vision, effectively silencing this intriguing diversion. 'And this is my daughter Tamsin. They've got a teacher training day at the school so I said she could come with me.'

'Hello,' says Tamsin. 'I expect you're hungry. I am.' She looks at her father pointedly.

'You had a sandwich before we left home, stop grumbling,' he says, ruffling her curls. 'Come on then, Julia's expecting all of you over at her place for scones soon, then Emily's cooking for you later as it's the first day. She's made a lasagne. In between, you'll be able to explore the village and decide what you're going to do about catering for the rest of your stay.'

'Lasagne? That's got meat in it, right?'

'It's okay, Robyn, we got the memo,' Andy says, smiling down at the girl. 'You're vegetarian but not vegan, aren't you? Emily uses Quorn for her lasagne anyway, because Tamsin hates mince. She calls it mashed-up cow and she won't touch it.'

'I'm totally with you on that one, Tamsin,' says Robyn, shuddering. 'Why would you?'

'I know. Yuck.'

Andy ignores the gruesome face his daughter is pulling at him and picks up Robyn's rucksack, despite her protests that she's perfectly capable of carrying her own bag. He leads the way as Grace and James trundle their suitcases after him and Tamsin brings up the rear with a lot of hopping and jumping. When they reach the car – an ancient Land Rover, but recently cleaned by the look of it – Andy scratches his head.

'I don't know what the pecking order is here, guys,' he says. 'Who wants the front seat? Tam needs to go in the back.'

'Depends on what your driving's like,' says Robyn, taking her small rucksack and stowing it in the boot. 'I'm not risking it.'

'Can I sit in the front?' Grace asks. 'I'm not the world's best traveller in cars, especially if the roads are winding.'

James gives a courtly bow and opens the passenger door for her. Soon they're bowling along ever narrowing lanes with Tamsin singing a random song about a pig that likes to jump in puddles. Grace gives silent thanks for James's good manners. She would be green in the face by now if she'd been swaying around in the back.

It's a huge relief to be off the train at last. With a bit of luck, she can avoid public transport while she's here. Grace's worst travelling experience ever was on a packed flight to Rome ten years ago, when she had the bad luck to sit next to a man who must have watched every disaster movie about planes ever made. His mind was so bursting with anxiety that Grace had a crushing migraine for two days afterwards and was almost sick in her handbag as she left the plane.

Although this journey is way better than being on the train, the crowded car seems full of memories. Grace tries to block the barrage of them coming from the back seat but Andy has other ideas.

'Emily made me hoover the car out specially for this trip,' he says brightly. 'It took me ages.'

'Really?' Robyn holds up a chocolate wrapper.

'Where was that?'

'Under the seat. Are you a secret chocaholic, Tamsin?'

'That's not mine, Dad,' says the little girl, narrowing her eyes.

'I think it is, sweetheart.'

'No, it's ...'

Andy holds up a hand to silence her and she subsides into her corner, mumbling.

'Tamsin loves food of any sort, apart from beef, but sweet things are her favourite,' he says. 'She's rationed, though, because if I let her, she'd gorge herself. I'm a strict dad when I need to be.'

'I'm with you on that one,' says James. 'You've got to have rules. Our old next-door neighbour always said it's best to ban children from having sweets until they're old enough to clean their teeth properly afterwards, and then only every now and again. Now, what was her name? Something beginning with M. Can you remember, Robyn?'

His granddaughter doesn't hear him because she's intent on sending a WhatsApp message. His frown deepens and suddenly Grace can feel James's pain, as piercing as a child's shriek. The urge to help him is overwhelming. What if she was able to give this man a memory back? This could be the opportunity she's been waiting for and after all, she's going to have to start somewhere. She searches her mind for any useful information that's filtered in from James but there's nothing there. This one's gone forever, she fears. Not an auspicious beginning for her hopes of putting her talent to good use. Grace sighs.

There's a silence, which begins to feel uncomfortable. The jumbled snippets from the car's other three occupants begin to jangle in Grace's head again. She tries to shut them out but a new wave of anguish is coming from somewhere.

She glances sideways at their driver, but his eyes are on the road. After a few moments, he says, 'It's just me making the rules with Tamsin.'

'I've got no mummy,' says Tamsin, helpfully.

There's an awkward silence. Andy seems to feel the need to fill it, glancing at Tamsin in his rear-view mirror. She's staring out of the window and humming tunelessly now.

'My wife died seven years ago,' Andy says quietly, 'just after Tam was born. I look after her on my own, mostly. Emily helps, of course, and Julia and Tristram. They're the other three involved in the holiday project.'

'Oh. I'm sorry.' Grace senses the sadness in the car getting stronger. She's starting to feel dizzy.

'No need. It's a long time ago. We're fine.'

'Emily doesn't help much,' adds Tamsin.

'Oh Tam, you know she does. We'd be lost without our gang, wouldn't we?'

There seems to be nothing else to say on this subject. Grace casts around for a safer topic. 'Emily mentioned on the phone that you're starting to get some activities going for the older residents in the village. How's that going? I'm only asking because I used to volunteer for that sort of thing at my local church.'

'Hey, are you a church-goer too?' asks James, leaning forward to see Grace better.

She shakes her head. 'My parents were, so I got involved that way.'

'Oh.' The sadness is back in force, and Grace can now tell that most of it has been flowing from James.

'We've been talking about starting a drop-in group at the village hall, actually,' says Andy. 'There's a great Adopt-a-Granny scheme going on in Pengelly now, but people still get lonely.'

'Tell me more.'

'Well, it all started with the redoubtable Ida Carnell rounding a gang of residents up and telling them all quite forcefully that they should take one of the more vulnerable villagers under their wing. It didn't go down too brilliantly at the start but now it's up and running, we can see she was right.'

'She sounds a fearsome lady,' says Grace, remembering a couple of similar characters at her parents' church who ruled the roost, kindly but with a style that didn't allow for arguments.

'Not fearsome exactly, just determined. You'll meet her soon, I expect. She's away on a coach tour with her long-suffering husband at the moment. She's lived here for years. We couldn't manage without our Ida.'

'So what's the drop-in group all about?'

Andy grins across at Grace as he negotiates a tight

bend, narrowly avoiding a tractor coming the other way, and she closes her eyes for a moment, wondering how much further they've got to go.

'It's going to be for anyone who fancies a good natter and some cake, not just for the over sixties. I'll do my best to explain,' Andy says, 'but I leave all that to the boss as a rule. Ida reckons that to get the most out of life as you get older, you need to look after the whole shebang; your lifestyle, your choice of friends, any toxic acquaintances, that sort of stuff.'

'That's interesting.' Grace begins a quick mental checklist of her own pitifully small circle at home, but stops when it becomes obvious that Andy hasn't finished talking.

'Ida says she's done a lot of research about this and all sorts of outside influences affect how we function. Her point is that if we looked after ourselves and each other better, a lot less people would end up at the GP's surgery.'

'That seems to be a problem everywhere,' says James. 'My family frog-marched me to see my doctor a little while ago but he just tried to give me pills for depression. I'm not in the least bit depressed.'

Robyn looks at him sideways. 'Maybe a rest will do you good,' she says. 'Curiosity Cottage could do the trick.'

'Well, I guess that's true enough,' says James. 'And

my lot will be glad to have me off their backs.' He laughs, but Grace can't detect much humour in it.

'That's *so* not true, Gramps.'

Tamsin turns to Robyn. 'Do you want to hear my song properly?' she asks. 'I've practised now, so I'm ready.'

'Maybe later, love,' says Andy. 'Let's just have a few minutes' quiet so that these people can appreciate the scenery, okay?'

'Humph,' says Tamsin.

They continue in silence after this, until the village sign appears. Grace concentrates on blocking the worst of the memories flowing around the car but she can't avoid a heavy sense of grief. Who is it coming from? Just Andy? Perhaps from all three. The road widens at last. Grace sees pavements either side and the drives to several imposing houses curling up the hillside to her right.

'This part of the village is known as The Level,' Andy says. 'There are some very swanky places here, but lots of ordinary terraced properties too. It's a good mix.'

Grace's ears prick up at the mention of Cassie Featherstone's address. So this is where May Rosevere lived before old age made her retreat to Memory Lane? She tries to catch a glimpse of the house numbers but they've already passed the biggest properties. There's a shop with old-fashioned bow windows that jut right out onto the pavement and a pub with several hanging baskets full of pansies. They're soon out of sight of The Level, turning down a steep cobbled lane.

'The sea! It's the sea ...' she gasps, as the glimpse of blue turns into the sort of view that features on calendars and jigsaws.

'We were kind of expecting that though, weren't we?' Robyn says. 'Being as we've come to the seaside?'

Grace looks over her shoulder and sees that the young woman is grinning at her.

'I know, I know ... you'll have to excuse me. I've lived in the middle of the country for too long, I reckon. Where are you from, Robyn?'

'We're just outside Manchester. I love the coast too, I'm not winding you up. It's gorgeous.'

The narrow roadway slopes dramatically and the beach stretches out to either side, deserted apart from a man walking two dogs down by the shoreline. To the right she can see weathered harbour walls, and the masts of a few boats. Andy winds his window down and Grace can hear the faint chink of their rigging. Something stirs inside her. It's half painful, half exciting.

'Yep. That's your outlook for as long as you're our guests,' Andy says, smiling across at Grace as he negotiates the twisty lane, only just avoiding a parked van. 'And that's Tristram over there with his dogs. You'll meet him later. He owns the restaurant at the end of the bay and as I said, he's part of the Curiosity Cottage creative team. We've been calling ourselves the CCCs. I think we ought to get T-shirts printed with a logo, personally.'

Grace is speechless for several seconds.

'It's amazing,' she says, eventually. 'The photos on your website didn't even begin to do it justice. We're never going to want to leave, are we, Robyn?'

'Well, *I'm* going to have to. I'm only here to see Gramps settled and then I'm off home. I'm at uni,' Robyn says.

'Ah. That's a shame. This view is stunning.'

'I can see there's going to be a fight for the bedroom that looks out over the beach,' says Andy.

James shrugs. 'I don't mind where I lay my head, so it's yours if you want it, Grace. I don't sleep much anyway, so I'll be awake half the night reading, most likely.'

Grace leans forward so she doesn't miss anything. She's going to find out everything there is to know about her mother here, she just knows it. Soon she'll understand what led up to the writing of that letter by a woman plenty old enough and surely financially stable enough to care for a child herself. She'll be able to dig deep to find the background details of where she comes from, who fathered her and why her mother dumped her, seemingly without a backward glance. A surge of anger leaves her breathless and she gasps. James taps her on the shoulder.

'You okay?' he asks.

'Grandpa, sometimes you don't need to ask that question,' says Robyn sharply. 'Give the lady some space, can't you?'

'I only said ... I didn't mean ...'

The fresh wave of sorrow in the memory that shoots from James into Grace's head hits her before she has time to put up her mental shield. She winces, blinking at its intensity. It's so blinding that she can't tell what he's thinking about, just that whatever it is, the pain is almost unbearable for him.

Glancing over her shoulder, Grace is amazed to see that James, although sitting very still and looking out of the window, doesn't look particularly sad. Come to think of it, his face is completely expressionless. He must be so used to this level of unhappiness that he can carry on as normal when the worst of it strikes. The thought is rather terrifying.

'Here we are,' says Andy. 'Welcome to the Cottage of Curiosities. I hope you find lots to spark your interest here. May Rosevere was a collector of odd items, and you're more than welcome to rummage in the cupboards and take things off shelves to look at. Nothing's out of bounds.'

'Like a sort of working museum?' Robyn asks.

'Exactly that. We've tried to leave as many of May's treasures around as we can without cluttering up the place. It's a way of keeping her memory alive. We all miss her.'

'And our house is next door,' says Tamsin, bouncing in her seat. 'Can I go over to see Julia now, Dad?'

'Emily's waiting, though. We need to introduce everyone, don't we?'

'You can do it.'

Andy sighs, and Grace wonders what the subtext of this conversation might be. She's already intrigued by the charismatic man and his lively daughter. Who is Emily and where does she fit into the picture? What's the friction all about?

The car rolls to a standstill in the parking area next to a long, single-storey granite building with large skylights in the steep roof. The beach lies ahead, with the tantalizing view of the harbour to their right. Andy's passengers open their doors just as a woman flings open the cottage door and strides towards them. Her hair is golden – long, wavy and flowing, like a Pre-Raphaelite model. She's wearing jeans, clumpy boots and a baggy checked shirt but she's feminine right down to her toes. The eyes that are fixed on the new guests are the bluest Grace has ever seen.

Andy clears his throat. 'And this is Emily,' he says. Grace glances at him as he goes around the back of the Land Rover to fetch their luggage for them. He's not looking at Emily and she's avoiding paying him any attention too.

Tamsin hops out of the car and heads across the narrow lane without a backward glance. 'Back soon, Dad,' she shouts.

Interesting, thinks Grace, *very interesting.*

Chapter Six

Emily has been watching for the Land Rover and rushes outside to greet the visitors, wanting to make a good impression. She watches with a familiar sinking feeling as Tamsin disappears round the back of Julia's cottage, but takes a deep breath and smiles.

'Welcome to Pengelly,' she says. 'It's great to see you all. Our very first visitors at the cottage.'

'Guinea pigs?' asks James, coming forward to shake Emily's hand.

'Not at all. Or I hope not, anyway. You must tell me if there's anything we've forgotten to put in your rooms. I think I've remembered everything.'

'Good job somebody can then,' says James under his breath.

Emily registers this comment but doesn't reply. When the new arrivals have been shown to their rooms and are unpacking, she turns to Andy.

'Thanks for fetching them,' she says, 'but I could have done it myself.'

'It's no problem. You wanted to get on with your writing, didn't you?'

She doesn't reply, concentrating on wiping a more stylish tray she's found for Grace's early morning tea. The one that's there seems too chintzy now that she's seen her guest.

'Em?' Andy prompts.

'Yes, I did. Thanks again.' It's hard to admit that although everything's now in place for her to blast out her long-awaited novel, it's just not happening. The brand-new loft conversion is perfect. When she sits down at her desk in the morning, the sun shines in through the skylights at just the right angle and there's plenty of fresh air. Her desk is ideally positioned to get all the available light even late in the day. Everywhere smells of new wood and furniture polish. Even so, this afternoon has passed by in a blur of indecision, screwed-up pages of notes and far too much coffee. Her nerves are jangling with the caffeine overload.

Wasted time. Emily could scream with frustration. How hard can it be to write a book? Everyone's doing it, or so it seems. She's got a treasure trove of inspiration right there at her fingertips too.

'How are you getting on with the letters?' Andy asks, as if reading her thoughts.

'I'm not. I can't seem to get a grip somehow.'

'In what way? You only have to read them and sort them, don't you? And then put them together into a story?'

Emily holds onto her temper with difficulty. As if it was that easy. It ought to be though, she supposes. Julia has generously passed on the heaps of family letters that came to light when Emily's grandpa died. He'd hoarded every last one of them right back to the fifties, and they're just asking to be made into a book. But how? Every angle she attempts seems trite or dull. There's got to be a way to bring the letters to life – to make the novel fresh and current but still keep the authentic flavour of a family sometimes at war but always interesting and sparky. And then there's the mystery of the opal ring. Where was it for all those years? Why did it suddenly reappear? Somebody must have known something about it.

'I'll get on with the writing again tomorrow. It might be easier now the first visitors are here. I've been a bit stressed about how they'd fit in, especially if they decide to stay for quite a long time.'

'You worry too much.'

The blithe words make Emily feel like hitting Andy over the head with the tray she's still holding. She takes a few deep breaths.

'Anyway, the visitors seem okay,' Andy continues when the silence gets uncomfortable, lowering his voice just in case they're still in earshot. 'Julia's expecting them for afternoon tea in about half an hour, to meet Tristram.'

'I'll make sure they're there.'

'And ... erm ... what about later?'

'You tell me. What about later?' She's finding it hard to look at him, feeling anger and disappointment battling for pole position as she thinks about the number of cancelled plans that have got in the way of their fledgling relationship lately. Tonight they were supposed to be going into Penzance to see a film, but apparently Vi, the babysitting neighbour who was going to entertain Tamsin and put her to bed, has cried off with a bad cold. He shrugs apologetically.

'You could come over to me instead? I'll cook if you like?'

'And wage war with Tamsin to see how long she can stay up so we don't get to be on our own? I don't think so, Andy.'

He gazes at her helplessly and she wonders, not for the first time, how such a lovely bloke can be so flaming irritating. Is it time to call it a day and try to find someone less complicated? It's getting harder and harder to know how to handle a motherless child, however adorable and funny Tamsin can be when she's in a good mood. Then there's the whole heap of sadness and guilt about his late wife that's never left Andy.

Emily sighs. Everyone has baggage, of course they do. She's growing to love this frustrating man more and more, and ... oh heavens ... she fancies him rotten. He's gorgeous, he's a great kisser and he can make her go weak at the knees without even touching her. Like now, in fact. Meeting Andy is the most exciting and heart-warming thing that's ever happened to Emily by far. And Tam's approval is worth fighting for, she's sure of it.

'I tell you what,' she says, giving in to the pull of those soulful brown eyes, and remembering that it's at least a week since he so much as touched her. 'Why don't you give me a call when Tamsin's safely asleep? I'll eat here and then I'll come round next door and we can open a bottle of wine and watch a film?'

'Brilliant! I'll do that. See you then. I'll get bedtime over as quickly as I can, promise.'

Andy grabs Emily by the shoulders, kisses her passionately and then lets her go suddenly as a door opens behind him. He raises a hand to anyone who's looking and heads for home.

Emily gives herself a little shake to get rid of the turmoil of steamy thoughts that come over her whenever Andy's around.

'Did I interrupt something?' Robyn says, coming into the room. 'I didn't mean to. He's lovely ... for an older person ...' she adds hastily.

Emily laughs. 'Thanks. I guess he's okay for a wrinkly.'

'I didn't mean ...'

'I know you didn't. It's fine, Andy was going anyway. Oh, here are the others.'

Grace leads the way into the kitchen, looking round appreciatively. 'It's a great cottage. I love the original features,' she says, 'and all the utensils and so on.'

'They were May's.'

Emily swallows a lump in her throat, watching as Grace picks up one of the solid weights that goes with the vintage scales on the worktop. She holds it in the palm of her hand, looking down. The older woman's face is set and pale now.

'Are you okay, Grace?' Emily asks, suddenly alarmed.

'Oh ... oh yes, I was just thinking about the person who owned these things. She sounds interesting.' She puts the weight down. 'When are we going to meet your grandmother?'

'Very soon. She lives across the road at number 60. She was big buddies with May. Tristram is Julia's fiancé and he's coming over too. It was his idea originally to open May's cottage as a kind of refuge. We did think to begin with that we'd market it as a place for people to come who were suffering from ...' Her words run out as she sees James's expression.

'Confusion? Memories disappearing without trace? The depressing inevitability of losing your mind?' James is smiling but his harsh words make Emily flinch.

'Well, I wasn't going to put it quite like that.'

Robyn puts a hand on her grandfather's arm. 'Button it, Gramps. You said you were going to try and be more positive about everything,' she reminds him, looking over at Emily apologetically.

'I did, didn't I? And I will. Anyway, it's just a bad patch, I expect. Sea air and a good rest is all I need. Sorry, ladies.' James goes over to the window and absorbs himself in watching a boat on the horizon, a mere speck in the distance. Emily half wishes she was on it at this moment.

*

'Right, well, we'd better be off to number 60, or Gran will be on my case. Come on, all of you, Julia Lovell's scones are said to be the best in the West Country,' she says, setting off towards the door and hoping they'll follow her.

Luckily they do, trooping obediently across the road like a school trip nearing the gift shop. The mention of scones has galvanized them all, and Emily guesses how tired they must feel, for different reasons. James looks travel-worn, and even Grace's glossy charm is less in evidence now as she negotiates the cobblestones.

Julia is waiting for them, and flings open the front door before Emily can take them round the back, which is her usual route to the warmth and cosiness of her grandmother's kitchen.

'Come in, come in,' Julia says, ushering them into

her sitting room and settling Grace and James in easy chairs either side of a crackling log fire before bustling away to fetch two loaded trays of tea and scones, clotted cream and strawberry jam.

The back door opens and Emily hears a deep voice shouting a hello. The cavalry is here. 'Oh good, here's Tristram,' she says with relief, standing up to give the newcomer a hug. 'Tris – these lovely people are Grace, James and Robyn.'

Tristram is dapper with a neat grey beard and the sort of clear-sighted gaze that is more used to looking out to sea than reading small print. He's wearing a long black overcoat and a trilby.

'Aren't you hot in that coat, dear?' asks Julia.

Tristram does a twirl, almost capsizing the teapot. 'Just a bit, but you've got to admit it's got class. I found it in a charity shop in Truro yesterday. It's my April image. I'm calling it my Spring Into Cornwall look.'

'You're so cool, Tris, you put us all to shame,' says Emily. 'Introduce yourself properly to the guests before they write you off as a poseur.'

'How rude. Hello, and welcome to you all,' says Tristram. 'I've just been saying to my daughter and son-in-law how good it is to have visitors. This village gets a bit claustrophobic sometimes. New blood is what we need, even if it's only for a short while at a time.'

James stands up to shake hands, fully in control of

himself again. Emily can see what an imposing figure he still is. The edges have blurred, that's all.

'Good to meet you,' he says. 'I've been a bit outnumbered by beautiful ladies so far today.'

Grace levers herself out of the low chair and comes forward too. She grins at Tristram. 'I didn't think James had even noticed I was female,' she says, 'but it's lovely to be here. What a beautiful village we've landed in. If I can ever tear myself away from the view from my bedroom, the beach looks very tempting too.'

'Let me know if you want to borrow a couple of crazy dogs,' says Tristram. 'They're always up for making new friends.'

'Hi, guys,' says Robyn, waving from the depths of the sofa. 'I can't get up because this kitten's sitting on me.' She looks down at her lap where a small tabby is curled up, purring.

'That's our Nancy, she sneaked in when I wasn't looking. She's got a thing about clotted cream. Just watch her like a hawk, or she'll lick the jam off your scone too,' Julia warns. 'She's one of the litter that Andy's cat had just before it was killed by a fox. Cassie up at Seagulls has got the black and white one and Andy kept the third for Tamsin, the big softie. Oh, and here's our visiting moggy. This is poor old Fossil. He was May's cat and I think he's still looking for her.'

A thin and rather bedraggled black cat slinks into

the room and goes to sit at Grace's feet, looking up hopefully. Emily is glad to see that their elegant visitor isn't too smart to make a fuss of the dust-covered new arrival. 'Fossil's been rolling in the dirt again. This cat likes to sleep in flower beds,' she explains. Emily winces as the ancient beast jumps up onto Grace's knee to avoid Buster's enthusiastic snuffling, but as Fossil settles down, purring loudly, Grace merely adjusts her position to make a more comfortable lap.

'Well, that's unusual,' says Tristram. 'Fossil's never been one for displays of affection. Except when May was around, of course.'

Reassured, Emily glances round the room as Julia dishes out cups and saucers and they all settle down to eat. It's going okay so far, she thinks. James already looks less stressed. But when she checks on Grace, the older woman's eyes are fixed on Fossil, and if she's not mistaken, they're full of unshed tears.

Chapter Seven

The rest of the evening passes peacefully and Grace can feel herself starting to relax for the first time since Harry died. When they go back across the road Emily asks the others if they mind eating fairly early and a couple of hours later produces a huge, bubbling lasagne with salad and garlic bread. She eats with them before excusing herself and heading next door after she's stacked the dishwasher. Robyn potters around the kitchen happily, wiping surfaces and humming quietly along with the radio.

James tells them he's going out to look at the sea for a few minutes, and Grace is drifting around in that peaceful, after-dinner limbo when thoughts are vague and woolly and even getting up from the table seems too much of an effort, when she feels a sudden wave of memories hit her. Robyn's standing still now, gazing out over the beach. She's got her back to Grace but her whole body is stiff with tension.

'Is something the matter, Robyn?' Grace asks, steeling herself to block the flow. When there's no immediate reply, she lets her mind relax again, so that she can pick up on the problem. Instantly, Robyn's preoccupation is clear. A picture of a much younger girl sitting on James's shoulders and laughing uproariously springs into Grace's head.

'Are you worrying about James?' Grace asks, knowing the answer before it comes but unable to think of any other way to find out why there's so much pain here.

'Yes, how did you guess? I can't help feeling like the worst person in the world for leaving him here. He's always been special to me. He'd never dream of letting me down like this.'

'But you're not letting your grandpa down, Robyn. You're trying to find a way forward for him, aren't you? And this is something you can't tackle on your own, as far as I can see, if he's having problems with his memory. Pengelly's going to do him good, and me too. I'm sure of it.'

'Really? You honestly believe this is the right thing to do?'

Grace just has time to nod before James comes back in bringing the scent of fresh sea air with him, and the moment passes. Robyn finishes her tidying and there are no more bursts of reminiscences, good or bad, although James appears to be trying to pin down a memory of his own. He's frowning slightly and biting his lip as they all go through to the sitting room and settle by the fire.

The jumbled memories fighting for a space in Grace's head on the train earlier in the day were draining. She yawns and stretches luxuriously, deeply weary, forcing herself to make small talk for a few minutes before she leaves Robyn and James to their own devices. This is the most socializing she's done since she was at work, and she's had enough of it for now. Meeting the ancient cat and then finding out that Fossil had belonged to May almost pushed her over the edge, and the whole day has taken more out of her than she could ever have predicted.

If Grace is going to interact with the others this much, she needs to work harder on her avoidance techniques, and practise summoning up the Italian idyll at a moment's notice. It hardly ever fails her if she's quick enough. That holiday in Umbria was the best Grace has ever had. Alone in Italy for three blissful weeks at the height of summer, she meandered from place to place by train, finally settling in the beautiful cathedral town of Orvieto for the last part of her stay.

Somehow, memories experienced in the musical language of Italy didn't seem to affect her as much, and by the end of her break, Grace had mastered the art of stepping into the virtual sunlit courtyard whenever necessary. All she has to do now is consolidate those skills. They're going to be vital here.

Soon ready for bed, Grace takes one last look at the

stunning moonlit view of the bay. She draws the curtains and switches on the bedside lamp with its pretty art nouveau shade featuring shimmering dragonflies, getting into bed with a sigh of relief. As she admires the amber wings of the beautiful creatures, her skin begins to prickle and an energizing warmth spreads right through her tired body.

The light glows, and a picture forms in Grace's mind of a fireside chair and a book open on someone's lap. It fades almost immediately but the warmth remains. Grace, stunned by this new development, stares at the lamp in amazement. She blinks a couple of times but the image has gone completely. Picking up vibrations from a living, breathing cat is one thing but this new development is odd, even in Grace's unusual world. Much too sleepy now to wonder how an inanimate object can possibly send her a memory, she decides to shelve the thought until morning. The room is cosy and welcoming, and her heap of downy pillows surrounds her with softness. The evening light fades as she reads for a little while before falling into the best sleep she's had since she found the letter.

In the morning, the wheeling and crying of the seagulls wakes Grace early and she lies quite still for a few moments, full of a sense of anticipation. Today she might discover something significant about her mother, or even her shadowy father. The information she's gathered so far has only served to whet her appetite for more. There are too many secrets here.

She slips out of bed, flinching as her toes touch the polished wooden floor, but the room is warm and cosy. With the curtains open, the wide expanse of sand beckons, but it's probably too early for a walk yet. Grace pads across to the dressing table and retrieves the letter from her bag, taking it back to bed to re-read for what feels like the hundredth time. She adjusts the pillows, props herself up against the carved wooden headboard and wraps her dressing gown around her shoulders.

Seeing the familiar words, Grace feels the same outrage this morning as she has done every time she reads them. How could any woman check out of her daughter's life so easily, without so much as a backward glance? Who's to say what sort of a mother May might have turned out to be? *Motherhood isn't one of my talents.* That sounds like a giant cop-out to Grace. So many questions, and no May here to answer them.

There's no information to point Grace to the mystery man, but surely if May came from Pengelly and had lived here for a long time, he must have been fairly local. When she'd eventually discovered that Harry and Audrey weren't her birth parents, Grace had often pictured her mother as a terrified young girl who couldn't care for her baby and was desperate to provide a secure start for her, as in the story that Audrey had reluctantly told her. If Grace hadn't needed to apply for her first passport for a school trip to France, she assumes she'd have been left in the dark for a lot longer. Audrey had at last been forced to produce Grace's elusive birth certificate, which she'd claimed for years to have lost.

'The poor soul had no family and she got into ...' Audrey lowered her voice at this point, '... drugs. I'd got to know her through volunteering at the YMCA. She died very soon after you were born and there was nobody to take you in. We wanted a baby so much and the girl knew we'd look after you well. It wasn't done officially, Grace. You might think that's wrong, but we were so afraid if the authorities were involved, we'd lose the chance of having you for our very own. At least you were properly registered.'

Grace supposes a fragile young woman without a loving family might possibly give her baby away to strangers, but why would a woman of May's age with a perfectly good home in a beautiful place like Pengelly farm out a healthy little girl? And why had she used only her middle name of Frances on the certificate if she'd actually wanted Grace to be able to come and find her at some later date? Grace reflects that this must have been Harry and Audrey's idea. It seems probable, as they did everything else they could to muddy the waters.

Unexpected tears prick Grace's eyes and she pushes

the letter back into its envelope. Nobody must know why she's here, at least for the first few days. If her birth mother and father turn out to have been callous and unfeeling, Grace wants no association with them, especially if the man in question is still alive, which seems highly unlikely given the timescale. Even so, the need to uncover every possible detail burns like a furnace in her soul. She gets out of bed again and collects what she needs from her travel bag, which is still only partially unpacked.

Stirring herself, Grace prepares to have a shower and leave the cocoon of her bedroom for the day, but just as she's sorting out her exploring clothes, she hears a wail from the corridor.

'Oh no! Pops? POPS! Where are you?'

Grace's heart sinks as she wriggles into her dressing gown and goes to investigate. It looks as if a shower and an early morning paddle will have to wait.

1968

*R*ecently back from an extended cycling tour of Southern Ireland, May sits on the harbour wall, sunning herself and listening to the cry of the gulls as they swoop to scavenge scraps from the latest fishing boat to arrive. The pungent smell of mackerel is in the air and May wonders if she should buy some for dinner. Charles loves them, and there's always a chance he'll choke on a fishbone.

'Hello, May,' a young man's voice shouts. 'Enjoying the weather?'

She looks up in surprise. The only men under sixty to be seen around Pengelly at this time of day are usually too busy working to have a chat. Sometimes she feels invisible. If it wasn't for her travels, she'd go mad with boredom.

'Goodness, Will, you made me jump,' May says, smiling up at the slim figure clad in flannels and a sports jacket. His shirt is open at the neck and his thin cheeks have already caught the sun. 'I didn't know you were coming to stay.'

'It was a surprise visit,' Will says. 'Don and Julia have been absolutely brilliant about it. I just had to get away for a while. Mother means well, but she can be ...'

'Controlling?' suggests May helpfully. 'Stifling? Generally bloody annoying?'

He laughs, but without much mirth. 'I didn't know you'd met her.'

'I haven't. I'm just good at reading between the lines,' May says.

Will lowers himself elegantly to sit next to May on the wall. In companionable silence, they watch a family making sandcastles on the beach for a while. A toddler with a shock of blonde curls is digging so exuberantly that she manages to throw sand in her brother's eyes, and he lets out an outraged wail.

'Cute, aren't they?' says Will. 'Have you ever fancied having kids, May? I guess you're a bit past it now. You must be pushing forty.'

'Cheek!' May clips him round the ear. 'If you must know, I'm actually fifty-nine though.'

'Never.' Will looks at May in astonishment. 'I was only joking. You definitely don't look it. What's your secret?'

'Sea air, lots of holidays, the odd glass of port and brandy, good food ... and just Pengelly life, really,' May hedges. There's no way she's telling Will that the only reason she looks so young is that she's a skilled memory harvester. Every memory she borrows from someone else's treasured *possessions provides her with a bit more life to live. Her father had the knack too. Sometimes the talent almost seems like a burden, but today, with the sunshine on her face and energy flowing through her veins, she wouldn't swap her unusual existence with anybody on earth.*

The only shadow on the day is the strange ache inside that she's getting from watching the little girl playing on the beach. Barbara ... or Grace, she hastily corrects herself ... must be about at this stage now. Has she also got plump little knees and wild curls? Does she know how to build a sandcastle yet? May forces her mind away from these painful thoughts and turns to Will.

'I've just come back from County Cork,' she says brightly. 'Have you ever been to Ireland?'

He frowns at her. 'Are you a mind reader? I've been making enquiries about going over there myself recently. I'm due some leave from work. But first, your good man has offered to give me a few sailing lessons. We're starting tomorrow, if the weather's not too bad. Today's wonderful but apparently big storms are forecast.'

'Charles is teaching you to sail? However did that come about?' May can't believe her husband would do anyone a good turn without either an ulterior motive or financial benefits, preferably both.

'My sisters clubbed together to buy me a few sessions,' Will says, shielding his eyes to gaze out to sea. 'I'm meant to be meeting him here, but he's late.'

May rolls her eyes. Charles isn't known for his punctuality. She tears her eyes away from the little girl on the beach and scrambles to her feet. 'I'm off to buy some fish now,' she says. 'I guess I'll see you around.'

Will gets up too and grabs May by both hands. He looks down at her fondly. 'I don't suppose we could ... I mean, obviously not now, but when Charles is busy sometime ...' he begins.

'No,' May says firmly. 'That was just a bit of fun, Will. It's not happening again. I never repeat my adventures. Pastures new, always. That's my motto.'

'I thought you'd say that. It was good, though, wasn't it?'

They smile at each other, but as May turns to leave, Will pulls her back. 'Hey, there was something I was going to show you. Look here.'

He digs in his jacket pocket and produces a small box. Flipping it open, he reveals a stunning opal ring, snug in its velvet nest.

'Oooh ...' breathes May. 'Where did you get that little beauty?'

Will taps the side of his nose. 'Ask no questions,' he says. 'What do you think of it?'

'It's gorgeous. It's not by any chance an engagement ring, is it? Because you know I'm already taken.'

They both chuckle but then May puts a hand over her mouth. 'Will, I've got an idea,' she says. 'Are you up for a bit of a joke?'

'Always. You know me. Explain.'

'Well, last time you were here, you said that drip Ida was getting on your nerves, mooning around and trying to make you ask her out?'

'Oh, good grief, yes. She was such a pain. Nowhere near as irritating as Tristram Brookes, though. Now there's someone I'd like to take down a peg or two. What a smug git he's turning into, eh?'

'Tris is okay. He's a good bloke, Will. What have you got against him? I've often wondered.'

Will grimaces. 'You don't want to know. I'm avoiding him now. I don't need the stress. I don't suppose young Ida means any harm, though.'

'Not harm exactly, but she can be really tiresome sometimes. Right, listen carefully and I'll tell you what we're going to do.'

They put their heads together as a small boat sails into the harbour. The man in it raises his binoculars and studies the couple standing by the harbour wall. He nods to himself. 'I thought as much,' he murmurs, as he reaches for his camera.

Chapter Eight

Emily, her mind full of the letters and her troubles with Tamsin, is awake much earlier than Grace, and ready for a walk before breakfast. It's shaping up to be a beautiful day and she's delighted to see Tristram walking his dogs along the beach. They often meet here and share their plans before everyday life gets in the way of the morning. As a step-grandfather, Emily can see Tristram is going to be a huge bonus in her life, even if he is a bit of a loose cannon sometimes.

'It's not going well so far, Em,' Tristram answers when she asks the regulation *how are you today?* question. 'First, Buster managed to get hold of an entire ham hock. The little bugger nosed the fridge open and ran away with it down the beach before I'd even had time to put the kettle on.'

Emily looks down at the unrepentant Puggle. He gazes back, small brown eyes sparkling.

'Then Bruno threw up in my wellies, and it turned out that he'd taken the opportunity while Buster was escaping to find half a trifle in the fridge and wolf the lot.' Bruno is Buster's sidekick, a normally sensible black Labrador. He, at least, has the grace to look slightly chastened.

'So now I'm late having my walk and that means I won't get down to the market until the best fish has all gone. Hey ho, it's no big deal really, and at least it means I've bumped into you. So how's your day panning out?'

Emily's about to reply when, as they approach the harbour wall, she sees a familiar figure standing right on the end of the jetty, leaning on the railings and talking to someone below.

'That's funny. I thought all the guests were still in bed,' she says. 'We'd better go and see if everything's okay.'

They climb up onto the stone walkway and hurry over to investigate.

'James?' Emily calls, feeling certain that exploring before breakfast isn't something that was on the cards for today, but the sea breeze blows her words away and before she and Tristram can get close enough to make themselves heard, James disappears down the slippery steps that lead to the harbour itself. Emily can hear the waves slapping against the weathered walls. The tide is high enough for the boats moored near the end of the jetty to still be afloat, and they hear the throaty roar of an outboard motor as they come closer. Sure enough, a small boat is heading out to sea. Sitting in the stern is James, waving merrily.

'James, where in heaven's name are you going?' Tristram yells, pointlessly, because the boat is now out of earshot of any amount of shouting.

They peer into the distance. 'Bloody hell, it's my mate Tom's grandson at the helm. You irresponsible young prat, Cameron, what do you think you're playing at?' shouts Tristram, making himself hoarse with the effort.

Emily knows Cameron has been a thorn in Tristram's side for years. He used to scrump Tristram's apples when he was smaller, once stripping the best tree completely bare on the day before the restaurant was catering for a huge party of WI members who'd all ordered in advance – most of them had gone for the roast pork with apple sauce and apple pie and cream to follow.

'He's still home, then. I thought he was going away to university?'

'Not him. He can't make his mind up what he wants to do so he's messing about in boats, as they say. Lazy young devil.'

Emily shields her eyes against the early morning sunshine and gazes out to sea. James is standing up in the boat and it looks as if he's flinging off what look suspiciously like his nightclothes. Tristram pulls out his bird-watching binoculars and trains them on the two figures. Cameron seems to be trying to restrain James, but before the boy can stop him, James, now naked, dives off the side into the sea.

'Are you mad, you idiot?' shouts Tristram. 'It's freezing in there. Cameron, get him out!'

Cameron can't hear this panic-stricken bellow, but luckily he has wasted no time in reaching for the older man, who has swum a lap of the boat at speed and is now trying to get back in without much success. With a huge effort, Cameron hauls him over the side and James disappears from view.

It's only then that Emily hears shouts from behind them, and her heart plunges even further into her wellies. Robyn and Grace, both in dressing gowns, are tearing barefoot across the beach towards them.

'Have you seen my grandpa?' Robyn gasps, as she comes near enough to be heard. 'He's not in his room, and the milkman says he thinks he saw him heading this way.'

Tristram waits until they're closer before breaking the news that James has taken an early morning dip but is now safely back in the boat.

'But what sort of pea-brain would take an old man out for a sail at the crack of dawn when they don't even know him?' Robyn asks, white with rage.

Grace says nothing, and even in the midst of all this angst, Emily notices that she's cool, calm and barely even out of breath after her dash across the sand.

'He's not an old man though, is he?' Emily says mildly, hoping to buy some time.

'Not at all, or if he is, then I'm an old lady,' Grace answers with a grin. 'But you've got to admit that probably wasn't the best way to start his holiday?'

'Let's go and meet him off the boat and you can see for yourself if he's okay.' Tristram leads the way to the jetty, just as the little boat chugs back to its moorings.

As soon as they dock, James bounces out, dressed in his damp pyjamas. His wet hair is standing up in spikes and his face is glowing.

'Morning, all,' he says, taking in the welcoming party. 'Well, that was an adventure. I haven't had so much fun since ...'

'Fun? You call worrying us all to death FUN? You could have drowned, Pops. And who the fuck are you?' Robyn turns on the soaking wet figure climbing the steps after James.

'Language, pet,' says James automatically, and then flinches as Robyn turns her glare on him.

'This is Cameron. I suppose you had to meet him sometime,' says Tristram wryly. 'He doesn't always think before he acts, do you, Cam?'

The boy is older than he appeared at first glance now he's on a level with them. He has the look of an off-duty vampire – skinny, with hollow cheeks and long black hair that's currently plastered to his skull and hanging in dripping strands over his shoulders.

'Chill, Tris. I don't see what I've done wrong,' he says.

'This guy just asked me if I was free to take him for a quick blast round the bay. How was I to know he was planning to practise his diving skills? I got him out again, didn't I?'

'It was fantastic,' enthuses James, very pink in the face. 'I never get to do anything off the cuff these days. You watch me like a hawk,' he says accusingly, glaring and pointing a shaking finger at Robyn. His teeth are chattering now and his lips have a blue tinge.

Robyn stares back, clearly battling with tears of relief, and Emily is delighted when her other guest steps in.

'Come on, let's go back and start the day again,' Grace says, turning to lead the way back. 'We could all do with a hot shower and a plate of bacon and eggs. Emily's stocked the fridge up for us and I don't mind taking first turn in the kitchen. Hurry up!'

James shakes Cameron warmly by the hand and follows Grace along the beach, not in the least chastened. Tristram and Emily turn to go after them. Emily is longing for coffee and warmth, but Robyn hasn't finished yet.

'You,' she hisses, poking Cameron in the chest, eyes blazing, 'are a complete waste of fucking space. You don't deserve to be in charge of a roller skate, let alone a boat. If I catch you even speaking to my grandpa again, I'll ... I'll ...'

'Don't worry, babe – I'm not about to risk tangling

with that fruit loop again,' Cameron replies, staring her down. 'Do you think I like getting soaked to the skin and freezing cold before breakfast? I suppose you'd rather I'd let him drown?' His jaw is set and he turns away from Robyn as if she's not worth the effort of saying more.

'He's not a fruit loop, it's just ... well, he can't always remember stuff any more. Don't you dare call him that.' Robyn takes a deep breath to carry on but she's overcome with shivering, and Emily takes her hand gently. 'Let's go and get warm,' she says, leading her in the direction of Memory Lane. 'You'll feel better when you're dressed and properly fed.'

Tristram takes one last look at Cameron, who's making sure his boat is safely tethered. 'You'd better have a good explanation for this,' he mutters. 'I'll speak to you later.'

Cameron doesn't answer, but the look he throws Tristram says he'll be ready for him.

Chapter Nine

Back at the cottage with breakfast out of the way, Emily throws another log onto the fire, releasing a shower of sparks. Even though the sun is out and the bright spring morning looks promising, she's decided this extra comfort is a priority for them all today. May hated her old gas fire with a passion but she couldn't manage logs and coal and refused to ask for help so it was the only option. Now, with the chimney opened up and swept, the old stone fireplace with its log stores either side is the focal point of the room.

Fossil's basket is in the best spot close to the hearth, and the skinny little cat is curled up in it snoring gently having polished off all the scraps of bacon that seemed to accidentally fall from Grace's plate. James is sitting in the most comfortable chair, flanked by Tristram and Robyn. Although it isn't long since they finished breakfast, they've all got large mugs of tea in front of them, and Emily's provided a plate of chocolate biscuits. Grace has tactfully gone for a walk, having set up a food kitty so that she can shop for lunch.

Emily sits down opposite James, relieved that Grace

is so practical. At this rate, the cooking and shopping will be dealt with efficiently every day and she might even get some work done later. That's if she can think of anything useful to write.

'Well, that was an interesting way to start the day,' says Tristram.

Robyn snorts. 'Interesting? He's lucky he's still here to tell the tale. Much longer in the sea and he'd have been suffering from hypothermia.'

'Oh, come on, love – let's not get carried away,' James says. 'I was perfectly safe. The boy gave me a hand but I could have got out of the water by myself easily enough. I might be forgetting a few things now and then but I'm not in my dotage yet, you know, and I've always loved swimming in the sea.'

'You're absolutely not in your dotage, or if you are I've got one foot in the grave and the other on the way after it,' says Tristram, 'but the thing is, in this village we're pretty cautious about the local currents as a rule and we always tell any visitors to Pengelly to check out the tides. You were too quick for us, that was the problem.'

James grins, but says nothing.

'I've got to set off in a couple of hours for the station. My taxi's coming at twelve. How can I go and leave you if you're going to do mad things like this, Pops?' Robyn says, biting her lip.

'Well, to be fair, you fuss about me just as much when I'm at home, so it doesn't really matter where I am.'

Emily decides it's time to bite the bullet. They need to know how James is going to cope without Robyn to watch over him if he's going to be staying long. 'Are you having a few problems, James? With your memory, I mean?'

There's a short silence. Robyn gets up and goes over to the fireplace, sinking down onto her knees to make a fuss of Fossil, who begins to purr loudly.

'Not really,' says James eventually. 'Or not in a big way. It's the others who keep flapping around saying I'm losing the plot. Robyn and her mother. Who, incidentally, is about as much use as ... as ...' he looks around the room for inspiration, '... as that little cat would be in running a home. She's always at work.'

Robyn leans forward, eyes blazing. 'We never said you were losing the plot, Pops. But you've got to admit you haven't been acting quite ...'

'Normally? So you all kept telling me. And what's that supposed to mean anyway? Who's to decide? Maybe this IS my normal now?'

James is just managing to keep his voice calm and even but Robyn's red in the face. Emily thinks she's bursting to spill the beans about how her grandpa has been lately but she probably doesn't want to let him down. Eventually she says, 'All we want is for you to be safe.'

'*Safe?*' All traces of calm are gone in an instant as James spits out the offending word. 'Who wants to be safe all their lives, eh? I had a nice, steady marriage with my childhood sweetheart for forty-three years. That should have been a steady enough bet, shouldn't it? But no. Just when we had time to spend together, planning to tour Europe or learn to ski ... or ... or go on a cruise ... she has to go and die on me.'

James is battling tears now, but he brushes them away fiercely. His granddaughter looks as if she's unsure whether to hug him or shake him.

'Pops! How can you say that? You're making it sound as if it was Gran's fault she got cancer.'

'No, I'm not. I didn't mean that, you know I didn't. It's just so bloody unfair. She was such a star, my lovely girl. I wanted ... we should have been able to ...' He bites his lip, glowering at them all. Robyn reaches a hand out to touch his arm and his shoulders slump.

'And now I've said way too much and lost my temper. None of this is your problem, Emily. Or Tristram,' he adds, as an afterthought. 'Anyway, I've got my own plans now. I can't keep wallowing like this. When we get back, I'm going to sell up and buy a narrow boat.'

Robyn stares at her grandfather in stunned silence as Tristram rubs his hands together.

'What a splendid idea,' Tristram says. 'If you fancied it, I could sort out a narrow boat trip for you while you're here? I'm sure there's some interesting stuff going on along those lines at Bude. And I'm so sorry to hear about your wife. We'll do whatever we can to take your mind off things while you're here, won't we, Em?'

James perks up for a moment but then slumps back into his chair. 'I don't know why I'm telling you all this,' he says. 'Hey, this isn't some sort of weird sect you've got here, is it? You're not just luring me and Grace in, are you? Acting all kind-hearted, we can check out any time we like and then we never get to leave, like Hotel California?'

Robyn looks horrified at his words but Tristram bursts out laughing. He stands up and wanders over to the window, hands in pockets. Emily's seen him do this before when he's been about to say something contentious. She holds her breath. *Careful, Tris,* she thinks, crossing her fingers for luck.

'James, I definitely like the idea of the narrow boat – always fancied one myself – but just bear with me on this, because I need to get something clear. If you're having problems remembering what you're supposed to be doing each day, and you're acting ... a bit randomly ... is now a good time to start something new? Being in Pengelly is hopefully going to help you to regroup. One step at a time.'

That wasn't as bad as it might have been. Tristram sometimes says a lot more than is wise. Emily's still holding her breath. She lets it out with a loud *poof* noise and everyone looks at her which takes the attention away from James for a moment, but she can see his face out of the corner of her eye even though she's trying not to look at him. He's still furious.

'Okay, so I've found this place to come to for some peace and quiet away from the fussing, and now you're telling me that I'm not allowed to go out on my own and explore but also that when I finally get to go home I might as well accept that the only new thing in my life might be a pair of zip-up slippers?'

'Not at all, I ...'

'Don't talk down to me me, you stupid old goat,' James yells, squaring up to Tristram, who's turned to face him.

Silence falls once more. It's not a good silence.

Chapter Ten

'Pops! That's so out of order.' Robyn jumps up, her face a mask of horror. 'You never used to be this rude. What's got into you?'

Tristram stands firm and looks straight back at James. 'I think we'd better make a deal,' he says. 'I won't tease you for being a bit forgetful or punch you on the nose when you're rude if you promise not to insult me for being long in the tooth.'

For a moment, James's face is blank, but then he starts to chuckle. He holds out his hand to Tristram. 'Let's shake on that,' he says. 'And I'm so sorry. You aren't old, and there's nothing at all goat-like about you. Even if you were, it'd be bad form to draw attention to it.'

Tristram pulls a face. 'Well, some of my ex-wives might take issue with the last part, but I certainly don't feel ancient yet.'

'*Some?* How many have you had?'

'Long story, for when we've got a beer in our hands, although I think Emily would love to tell it to you sooner.'

Emily holds up a hand. 'Excuse me, can I speak now?' she asks. 'It strikes me that what James needs from this holiday to begin with is a bit of space to get his breath back. It sounds as if the last few months have been full of change. Why don't you arrange to tell me roughly where you'll be, James, but there's scope for exploring within reason?'

'That sounds cool,' says Robyn. 'So long as it doesn't involve early morning swims?'

'There's a good leisure centre five miles up the road,' says Tristram. 'My old buddy Tom and I go three times a week and Ida Carnell often joins us when she's not off on one of her coach trips. If you want to get wet without throwing your granddaughter into a panic you're welcome to come too. I have to say Ida's an absolute picture in her rubber bathing cap covered in flowers.'

'It's a deal, for now at least. It's swimming in the sea that's the best thing in the world, though,' says James. 'But I really don't get why you two are being so supportive. I'm just a stranger paying for a B&B. You don't have to worry about me.'

Tristram smiles. 'Good question. Why the hell *are* we worrying, Em? Do you want to explain?'

'That's easy. It's all about the village. Ida's Adopt-a-Granny scheme got our lovely May back into being friends with my gran last year and stopped a lot of other older people in Pengelly feeling sorry for themselves.'

James waits, still looking puzzled.

'Everybody who stays with us is going to have different reasons for coming to Pengelly. We just want to help you to get the best out of it. Isn't that right, Tris?'

'In a nutshell, and well put, sweetheart. So, James, I guess the answer to your question is, that Julia and I are in our eighties and we don't know how much time we've got left to play with. While we're here and reasonably hale and hearty, we want to give something back. There's a lot of loneliness and sadness in the world. Maybe this cottage can be a bit of an antidote, in a small way. Or does that sound too cheesy?'

A log shifts in the fireplace and outside a seagull cries. 'No,' says James slowly. 'Not cheesy at all. I think I owe you a really big apology ... and probably a pint or two. But Emily, surely you're way too young to be troubled by the spectre of old age. Are you really sure you want to open your home to a string of random, unpredictable strangers?'

Emily looks at the three of them, all waiting for her answer. 'Absolutely sure,' she says. She looks over at the clock on the wall. Grace has been gone for quite a while now. She wonders why the other woman is here. Hopefully just for a holiday. Two people with complicated emotional problems might be a bit too much of a challenge.

There's a sudden clatter outside and they all jump. 'Hello, folks, does everyone like fish pie?' Grace shouts, entering the kitchen with two loaded carrier bags. 'I'll make a little veggie version for you, Robyn, if you've got time to stay for lunch.'

'I feel as if we've come full circle now,' says Tristram.

Grace comes into the living room. 'Why's that?'

'Well, May – the lady who lived here before Emily – was the absolute queen of the fish pie. She had a recipe that she'd developed over the years.'

'You wait till you taste mine,' says Grace. 'It's got coconut milk, lots of butter and parsnips in with the mashed potatoes and a touch of curry powder.'

'You're kidding. Really? I don't suppose there are prawns and salmon involved too?'

'How did you know?' Grace is looking at Tristram oddly now.

'It's just ... that's what May always used to put in hers. I know because I managed to get her to tell me how she did it so we could feature a version on the menu at The Seafood Shack. What a coincidence. Where did you get your recipe from?'

Grace frowns. 'Well, actually, it's not an old favourite – I made it up while I was making my list earlier. It just ... sort of ... came into my head.'

'Hmmm, May's sending you vibes somehow. She must approve of you,' says Emily, grinning, 'but whatever's in this pie, we'd better let you get on with it or it'll be too late for lunch and we'll have to call it dinner. Does that sound like a plan?'

The others all nod, and James excuses himself for a quick breath of fresh air on the beach while Robyn gets ready to leave. Emily goes into the kitchen after Grace to see if she can give her a hand and finds her staring out of the window, deep in thought.

'What's up?' she asks.

Grace gives herself a little shake. 'Oh, nothing. Do you fancy peeling me some spuds and parsnips?'

Emily rolls her sleeves up, gets out May's old peeler and a pottery mixing bowl and starts work. After a moment she senses Grace's eyes on her.

'NOW what's the problem?' she asks, trying to make a joke of it, but suddenly weary of being sociable.

'Are you remembering May while you're doing that?'

'Yes, I was, actually. I didn't know her as well as my gran did, but I've watched her work in the kitchen before when I was visiting in the holidays.'

'In this cottage?'

'No, it was a long time ago, when she was still up in the big house on The Level. My grandpa used to take vegetables for May when there was a glut in his own garden, and once she started to peel the potatoes while we were still there having a cup of tea.'

'You're using the same peeler? Can I see it?'

'I suppose it must be one from the old house, but what made you ask about May?'

Grace smiles. 'Oh, I don't know. Do you ever think memories can stay in a house after the person who made them has gone away?' She takes the proffered peeler and they both look down at it, where it lies on Grace's palm. The wooden handle is faded and worn, bound round with thick string to make it easier to grip, she guesses. The metal cutting edge is shiny and sharp. Grace wraps her fingers around it and closes her eyes.

'Are you okay, Grace?' Emily touches the other woman's arm and she jumps as if miles away.

'I'm fine. I was just thinking about the people who might have used this. I wonder if they've left some sort of ... traces?'

Emily considers this. She often has the sensation of her grandfather being around. She misses him dreadfully. As for May, she was such a lively woman that it wouldn't be surprising if she left shades of herself here, where by all accounts she was contented most of the time. But why would Grace care about any memories left hanging around in May's house? Emily hopes she isn't one of those intense people who think they can pick up on the atmosphere wherever they go.

She glances across to where Grace is poaching the salmon, humming quietly to herself. She's tied a pinafore around her waist and looks supremely contented. It's one of May's huge aprons from the back of the kitchen door, and it suits Grace very well. She seems very much at home here already. There's something unusual about Grace, and Emily's not at all sure what it is.

Before she can think any more about this, Robyn comes in carrying her rucksack.

'I think I've got everything,' she says. 'Did Emily tell you I'm going at twelve, Grace? I wish I could stay a bit longer, but I've already missed a week of uni getting a plan in place for Pops. Mum was busy working.'

'Yes, and I'm sorry not to have the chance to talk to you more,' says Grace. 'I can tell you're anxious about leaving James. We'll keep our eye on him though, won't we, Emily?'

Emily nods and tries to say something soothing in agreement, but Robyn hasn't finished yet. 'Pops isn't usually bad-tempered or insulting,' she says, fidgeting with a knife she's picked up from the table. 'Or he never used to be, at any rate. I couldn't believe it when he was so rude to Tristram. His personality's changed a lot since Nana died. That's no excuse, though.'

'Look, Tris and I are aware of the background now,' says Emily, 'and I'll fill Grace in when I get the chance. It's fine. You go and get on with your course. You can leave me your mobile number if you like, and I can keep you up to date?'

'Would you? That'd be so cool.'

'Course I will. Here's my phone, put it straight in and then you'll be able to relax a bit.'

'And mine's in my bag, if you want to go completely belt and braces,' says Grace. 'I can give my angle too, if it helps. I might be here for quite a while.'

'Brilliant. Oh, I can see Pops coming back. I'll go and have a quick word before the taxi comes.'

Robyn hugs Emily impulsively, and then hesitates for a moment. Emily isn't sure if Grace is the hugging type and she guesses Robyn is having the same thought.

'I'll just ...' she gestures towards the door and heads off to see James.

Grace carries on working in silence for a while as Emily brings her up to date with James's problems.

'We're all going to be living quite closely together for a while and I don't like secrets, do you?' she says when she's finished.

Grace doesn't reply, and the arrival of James and Robyn just as the taxi pulls up outside and begins hooting distracts Emily. It isn't until lunch is being served that Emily remembers Grace has never answered her question.

Chapter Eleven

When the kitchen is cleared, Grace joins Emily in the living room. James, after toying with a plateful of Grace's fish pie, has gone to his room for 'a bit of a lie down'.

'That was an amazing creation, Grace,' says Emily, leaning back in her chair and stretching her legs out. 'I'm definitely putting the recipe into my book.'

'Thank you. Will you be eating with us every day?' Grace isn't sure how she feels about having a chaperone hanging around. Emily's easy enough to get on with, but she could feel the younger woman watching as she worked, and weighing her up.

'Oh no, although I wish I could if today's lunch is anything to go by. I'll either be in London juggling my other life or up in the attic writing most of the time.'

'What do you do in the city? It sounds like a dream job if it lets you come back here in between times for a Pengelly fix.'

'Yeah, well, it's okay most of the time. I work for a publisher. I've only just cut my hours back and relocated from New York. I wanted to be near Gran and ... and other people ... so Colin – that's my boss – he said we could give it a try.'

'That was lucky.'

'Good timing more than luck, I think. He's reduced his own working time too – he was burning himself out. I expect you'll meet him at some point. He's got a bit of a thing for Andy's babysitter, Vi, but he's too shy to do anything about it.'

Grace has been looking around the room, taking in a few more details as Emily talks, and her eye falls on a pottery bowl painted in vivid blues and yellows, slightly chipped. She reaches out and picks it up. Emily smiles.

'Oh, you've spotted May's Sorrento dish. She used to keep lemons in it for when she had the odd G&T. I must remember to refill it. May loved to travel, and she'd pick up bits and bobs wherever she went. Sometimes I had my doubts if she actually paid for some of them.'

Grace gapes at Emily. 'You're joking, aren't you? May was a shoplifter?'

'Oh no ... not shops. And not really lifting, as such. It was just that I found out after she died, when I was clearing the cottage, that there were quite a lot of small things here that ... well, didn't belong to her originally.'

This is a new one for Grace. Her mother pilfered other people's possessions? What was that all about? 'But ... how did you know the stuff wasn't May's?' she asked.

Emily laughs. 'It was funny really. Gradually, people began to sidle up to me at different times when I was out in the village and ever so discreetly ask if I'd come across this or that ... a photo in a tiny beaded frame of someone's grandma, a battered paper knife with an enamel handle, some cigarette cards. Nothing that was worth much. They seemed to have guessed that May might have them stashed away.'

'Why on earth would an old lady want all those things, though?'

'I've no idea. I think she was something of a magpie. That was partly why I had the new sign made. That, and the secrets.'

'Secrets?'

Emily's cheeks are pink now. 'Oh, ignore me. I'm just making up stories. It's what I do. There probably weren't any. May was just a dear old lady. Stroppy sometimes, and didn't suffer fools gladly, as my gran says, but ...'

Grace decides to follow this interesting tack up another time. There's no point in making Emily uncomfortable. 'You haven't lived in this cottage very long, have you?' she asks.

'No, I'm still settling in. It's a perfect place to write, and I'm trying to get stuck into my book now. I was telling James earlier, it was a massive surprise when May left Shangri-La to me. She had no family of her own, and I think she wanted to give me a leg up. It just came at the right time, with Colin agreeing to the changes.'

'She actually told you she had no relations?' Grace shivers. It's one thing never to know your mother, but to imagine her denying your very existence is even worse, somehow.

'Yes. Why do you ask?'

'Oh, I don't know really. It's just odd to have no family at all, isn't it?'

'I suppose so, but everyone knew May was all alone. She was married years ago to a man called Charles. Apparently the village gossips had all heard that May's husband thought he was terminally ill. He went out in his boat when a storm was brewing and never came back. There was talk of suicide, Gran says.'

Grace pricks up her ears. This is more information than she was expecting at this stage. 'When did all this happen?'

'I'm not sure – it was ages ago. I tried to get her to tell me more about Charles but she always clammed up. You're very interested in May, aren't you?'

'Not really, just the villagers in general. I've always lived on the edge of a town. This is totally different in every way. What's your book going to be about?'

'I'm not sure. I still haven't found my hook, even though I've got the most amazing archive to draw on.'

'Have you? What's that?'

'Masses and masses of letters going right back to 1945. My grandpa kept everything his family in the Midlands ever wrote to him, and they took keeping in touch to a whole new level. They had no phone for a lot of those years, and no car, so they came down here on the train to stay with Gran and Grandpa whenever they could.'

'That must have been a bit hard on Julia? All those visitors?'

'Oh, she didn't mind. At least I don't think she did ... much ... Anyway, I want to use the letters as a base for my story but I still don't know where to start. There's so much in them. There are family arguments and secrets, and then there's the missing ring.'

Grace listens, fascinated, as Emily tells her about the cache of letters. Her mind races. Anything could be hidden in those pages. 'That sounds amazing. Tell me more.'

'I haven't seen all of them yet. The letters cover all sorts of subjects. There was some sort of feud at one point. I haven't even looked at that batch yet. Gran's got them tucked away somewhere. Mind you, some of them are so dull that nobody but me would want to read them.'

'*I* would.' The words are out before Grace can stop them, sounding over-loud.

'You would what?'

'I'd love to see them. Maybe I could help you to get

a fresh angle on the letters?' Grace's mind is racing. Will there be anything in them relating to her start in life? After all, May and Julia had lived in this village a long time together. It wouldn't be unreasonable to assume connections and references that might be revealing. That would be almost too much to hope for, but she can't help wondering.

Emily smiles at Grace. 'I'd love to work on them with you, but you're here for a holiday, aren't you? A rest?'

Grace doesn't answer.

'Grace, I don't want to take up all your time with this. You need to get around. See the area, and so on. If you're interested in finding out about Pengelly people you'd need to ask Gran or one of the older residents. Ida Carnell knows everything there is to know around here.'

'I'll do that. Where can I find Ida?'

'She lives on Silver Street, just off The Level. Number ten. You can't miss it. Just look for the fanciest curtains in the row. She's on holiday for a little while longer, though.'

'Thanks. I'll look her up when she gets back.'

Tristram breezes in just as Grace is thinking of her next question. Damn. She'll have to try again later. She plasters a smile on her face and prepares to make small talk. It's time to play the stress card. Emily is clearly going to keep probing until she gets a proper reason for Grace being here. Best to get it over with.

Half an hour later, by thinking on her feet and stretching her imagination to its limits, Grace has managed to sound both anxious and slightly bewildered by the fact that she's succumbed to work-related stress after so many years in a demanding profession.

'I never wanted to do anything else but teach art,' she says. 'I've loved passing on my skills and teaching the older ones about all the wonderful artwork out there in the world but I find smaller children a bit terrifying.'

'You're not kidding. Tamsin's ... anyway, you did well to stick it for so long,' says Emily hastily. 'There's no shame in taking early retirement. Is this a kind of in-between time for you, while you decide what's next?'

Grace nods. 'I'm feeling rather battered just now,' she says. This is no lie. Being here in Pengelly is already making it clear that she's been on very shaky ground for the past few months.

'It's not surprising you're finding life tricky. Losing both parents so close together must have been very hard,' says Tristram. His sympathy nearly floors Grace and she blinks back tears. This is mostly supposed to be a façade, not real distress. Her life is going to be just fine as soon as she's found out the truth about her origins.

'Yes, it was a sad time,' she says, reminding herself quickly of Harry and Audrey's deception. The sudden tears recede but Tristram's noticed them.

'Were you a close family?' he asks. 'You must miss them very much.'

'Close? I suppose we were ... well, kind of.' For a moment Grace allows herself to think of the two frail old people objectively; to remember them when they were young and lively. Caravan holidays and cricket on the beach, the three of them making up the rules as they went along. Picnics in the grounds of the local stately home. Her yearly birthday party that Audrey insisted on organizing even though Grace got more and more antisocial as the years went by and the guests dwindled each time. Those chocolate birthday cakes, though. They must have taken hours to make and decorate.

'Grace, it's fine to miss people you love. Don't fight it so hard,' says Tristram, passing her a handful of tissues. She's crying properly now, angry with herself for letting go like this. Audrey and Harry have been cruel and heartless, depriving her of May. Why should she miss them?

'Sometimes you have to let the past take care of itself,' says Tristram.

'Yes, you could be right.' Grace blows her nose noisily and hopes the subject of her parents is closed.

'Do you think you'll be staying here long?' asks Emily. 'Only, there are all sorts of things we can arrange for you to do if you need some ideas for how to spend your time? There's a car hire place in Mengillan if you want to explore further afield.'

'No!' The word comes out too sharply and Grace can see she's shocked the other two. 'I mean, I do drive, of course, but I sold my car before I came here. It was an expensive luxury and I don't need it any more. I just want to take some time to find out what it's like to live in a small village by the sea. Get some local colour, talk to people – you know the sort of thing? I'll mainly be wandering around, getting a feel for coastal living. And having a rest.'

A sudden wave of exhaustion washes over Grace. The effort of clearing her parents' house of years of belongings, dealing with the practical side of two deaths, the final classes at school with all the goodbyes involved and leaving her much loved art studio have taken their toll. A rest would be bliss.

'I would like to stay for at least six weeks,' Grace hears herself saying, in answer to Emily's question. She hasn't set even a tenuous end date up to now, but that seems a good long stretch.

The others nod, and Grace heaves a sigh of relief. She's jumped the first hurdles and it looks as if she's got away with it so far.

'I think I'll copy James and have a nap now,' she says, feeling her eyelids drooping.

'Good idea. Have you got any plans for later?'

'Yes, I have actually. When I was shopping I noticed there's an open meeting of the WI in the village hall tonight, and I think I'll go along. They've got a guest speaker telling them about life in Pengelly over the last hundred years. It'll be a good start to finding out about the area. I'll get a snack at the pub when it's over. See you all after breakfast tomorrow if that's okay? I've got the key you gave me.'

For a moment, Grace thinks Emily's going to offer to come with her, but she seems to think better of the idea and takes herself off upstairs to her writing desk.

Flexing tired shoulders, Grace heads for her room, feeling the peace of the lovely room enfold her as she flops onto the bed. She slips off her shoes and lies back. Her current book is on the bedside table, a fast-paced thriller with several seriously damaged characters. The thought of reading isn't tempting, and Grace reaches for the folded blanket at the foot of the bed. Wrapping herself in its softness, the scent of lavender soothes her. Grace's last conscious thought is of her childhood home, and of her adopted mum Audrey, who grew lavender especially to fragrance her lingerie drawers and linen cupboard. She breathes in the soft perfume and drifts off to sleep.

Chapter Twelve

Much refreshed after her long rest, Grace has a quick change and brush-up in her room and applies fresh lipstick and perfume. She enters the living room to find James sitting in front of the fire.

'Oh, hello,' he says, smiling up at her. 'I was just wondering whether to throw some more logs on or let it go out and have another walk. I've been asleep for ages, and if I don't do something, I'll nod off again.'

'It must be the sea air,' says Grace. 'I did the same.'

'Either that or we're starting to relax already. Emily's going round next door soon. Where are you off to? You look very smart.'

Grace battles with her conscience. She doesn't want company tonight but it seems mean to leave James here all alone. 'I'm going to drop in on a talk at the village hall about Pengelly's past,' she says. 'It probably won't be very interesting.'

'Oh, I'd like to try that. Can I come along with you? Or is it just for ladies?'

He sounds like an eager schoolboy, and Grace gives

up on her idea of a solitary walk and a seat at the back of the hall minding her own business.

'Of course you can. The poster said it was an open meeting,' she says. 'But you'll have to hurry up. I need to leave in five minutes.'

'No problem, I'm the king of speed when it comes to getting ready to go out, so don't leave without me.'

James is as good as his word and in just over five minutes Grace is by his side swishing up the lane in what she thinks of as her country clothes; the long camel coat swinging open, a black sweater and rust coloured cords tucked into her most comfortable boots – well-worn and polished brown leather with a low heel. She feels as free as she used to be on the first day of the summer holidays and has to restrain herself from giving a little skip like Tamsin does as they reach the top of the road. She catches James glancing at her appreciatively and reflects that his easy-going, somewhat crumpled style goes well with village life.

The hall is still in darkness – they're way too early for the talk – so Grace suggests a wander along The Level. She wants to peer at May's old family home from a safe distance. The *Seagulls* name plate is on one of the gateposts – a large blue ceramic tile, with the lettering picked out in white and a picture of two gulls in flight. It reminds her of the one at Curiosity Cottage so it must be another by the local artist Emily mentioned.

'This is an impressive pile,' says James. 'I wonder who lives here. It must cost a bomb to run a place this size.'

The drive curves up the hillside, and Grace imagines the fantastic view there must be from the front windows, right across the harbour and bay, although a thicket of trees in between probably blocks some of the scenery. Did her mother stand there looking out to sea? As they stand in the shadow of a fir tree, a pick-up truck turns into the entrance and pulls up beside her, engine running. A large man in a wax jacket leans out of the driver's window.

'You okay?' he asks. 'Lost?'

'Oh no, we're fine,' Grace answers, mentally kicking herself for being caught gawping. 'We're just exploring Pengelly.'

'Staying here?'

Grace looks at this man of few words more closely. His freckled face is friendly, she thinks, but he seems somewhat wary of this strange woman lurking by his fence.

'On holiday,' James chips in, following the other man's example of minimal speech. 'Beautiful place.'

'Here for long?'

'Maybe.'

'Enjoy.'

Their limited conversation grinds to a halt, and as

lights come on in the porch of the house, the man tips his cap and drives away. Grace wishes she had an excuse to follow him. She curses herself for her moment of weakness when she let James change her plans. If she'd been alone, she might have been able to somehow get an invitation to come up to Seagulls and meet Cassie Featherstone. This place must be bursting with memories of May.

'Are you okay, Grace? You seem a bit preoccupied,' James says.

'I'm fine. Come on, let's go and see if they've opened up yet. It's getting chilly out here.'

There are still no lights on in the village hall. 'How about a quick pint at the pub?' James suggests hopefully. 'We could see what the menu looks like. I'm a bit peckish. We could maybe go there for dinner later?'

This is all getting a bit too friendly for Grace's liking but she can't think of a good alternative. 'You should have eaten all your fish pie,' she says, as they turn towards the pub.

'I know. It wasn't because I didn't like it. I was just a bit choked up at saying goodbye to Robyn. I guess I haven't been very kind about her clucking at me lately.'

'Has it been awful?' Grace has never had anyone fussing over her so she can't imagine the problem. Audrey and Harry were always caring, but never demonstrative, and they tended to leave Grace to her own devices if she wasn't obviously doing anything risky.

James shrugs. 'I don't know why they go on about it so much. I'm not that bad. I forget everyday things but I can remember the names of all my old school friends and even their addresses.'

'Yes. That's not all that useful though, is it?'

They're at the pub now and entering the dimly lit lounge. Lamps are shining from all corners and a huge fireplace has a log fire at least three times as big as the one at Emily's cottage. Grace doesn't notice at first that James is cross with her. He orders their drinks and carries his beer and her wine over to a table in the window. It's not until she's taken the first sip and leant back in her seat that she registers the frosty atmosphere.

James is staring out at the quiet street, jaw set. He takes a pull of his pint and sighs.

'What did I say?' Grace asks, genuinely confused.

'You can be quite cutting, can't you? There was no need to be so blunt about it being useless to remember the old stuff when you can't think where you're meant to be later today.'

'I didn't say that.'

'Yes, you did, more or less.'

They sit in silence for several uncomfortable moments. Grace's heart is heavy. She's not used to socializing, especially with men. It's exhausting to be able to feel memories of potential lovers when all you want to do is have a quiet meal out or watch a film together. Every now and again she's tried to make a new connection work, but in the end has had to accept that she's not cut out for relationships. Female colleagues have fared no better. Grace doesn't do small talk. Her conversations with Emily and Tristram and the interaction at Julia's yesterday have added up to the most contact with other people that she's had for a very long time.

'I'm really sorry if I offended you,' Grace says, deciding it's best to be honest, 'but I'm no good at making polite chitchat. Never have been. I tend to say the wrong thing or I forget to join in when there's a crowd.'

'But you're the sort of person I'd describe as a woman of the world,' James says incredulously. 'You surely can't have a problem with being sociable. You were fine earlier.'

Grace feels the stab of a recent incident, bright and sharp, coming from James as he waits for her to explain. He's thinking about someone close to him. Maybe someone who has also been unnecessarily cruel about his problems. It's impossible to tell who it is. The thought occurs to her that this would be a good chance to have another try at giving James back one of his memories, but then she feels the sting again and decides that even if she could do such a thing, he's not going to want to relive this one if it gives him pain.

'Perhaps I'm learning to be more friendly. But I'm clearly not there yet.' She smiles at him, hoping he's the forgiving kind. It's going to be a tedious night otherwise.

'Why don't we start again?' James says, getting to his feet. 'I'll go and get a menu, we'll check it out, go and enjoy the talk ... or not ... and come back here for a slap-up meal. How does that sound? No offence taken. No more pressure to chat all the time.'

'Perfect. Let's do it.'

Half an hour later, her head swimming from the large glass of wine downed quite quickly, Grace is sitting next to James near the back of the hall, looking up at the stage. A slightly built woman with a shining curtain of chestnut hair is standing in front of them and holding up a hand for silence. Everyone stops talking almost immediately. Grace is impressed. This is a trick it took her a whole teaching practice to learn.

'Hello, everyone. Most of you know me, but I can see a couple of unfamiliar faces here tonight, so for your benefit,' she waves to Grace and James, 'I'm Cassie Featherstone, and I'm standing in for Ida while she's sunning herself in Marbella. Lucky Ida, is what I say.'

There are a few laughs, and Grace immediately warms to the younger woman. If she's approachable, it'll be a lot easier to find a way to meet her and ask if she knew May, perhaps even to look around her house. Cassie waits again for the noise to die down.

'As you all know, our resident artist, Angelina Makepeace, has agreed to give us a presentation tonight about Pengelly through the ages. We're all more than grateful to her and I'm sure you're all going to thoroughly enjoy sharing Angelina's memories.'

Grace has a momentary panic at this comment. She's been so focused on finding out about her mother that she hasn't given a thought to the fact that, during the course of a lecture about Pengelly's past, the audience will be flooded with memories of their own, which will make concentrating on the speaker difficult. Mind you, looking at the average age of the people around her, there must be some here who could do with having memories returned to them. If only she could find a way to make use of her gift.

There's a light smatter of applause, and a tall, thin lady tackles the steps up to the stage. Cassie holds out a hand to steady her, and whispers something in her ear that makes Angelina giggle. One or two people roll their eyes as a frail arm raises a small silver hip flask to the audience. Grace notices that there's a streak of vermillion paint in Angelina's short grey hair, and she's wearing a kaftan in a startling shade of green.

Without further ado, Cassie leaves the stage and an astonishing hour's talk begins.

'I hope I'm as sparkling when I'm her age,' Grace mutters to James. 'This lady's still got all her marbles.' He smiles but refrains from answering, and she realizes with a sinking feeling that she's been tactless again.

Her presentation over, Angelina proceeds to answer a whole flurry of questions until Cassie signals from the kitchen that it's time for coffee and cake.

Grace queues up at the counter and collects two brimming mugs of rather watery-looking brown liquid and a laden plate, leaving James to charm two elderly ladies who are pressing leaflets about forthcoming events onto him.

'This cherry cake's amazing, but please accept my apologies for the quality of the coffee,' says Cassie, coming out from behind the counter to talk to Grace. 'I've been wondering if you're Emily's guest? The one I wrote to? Oh, don't worry, I'm not psychic,' she continues, seeing Grace's startled expression. 'It's just that I know everyone else here, so I put two and two together.'

'Emily's guest? That's a nice way of putting it,' Grace says. 'Yes, I'm Grace. I'll be at Curiosity Cottage for a while, and so will James. Separately,' she adds, before Cassie has a chance to leap to the wrong conclusion.

'Have you met Angelina properly yet? If not, you should introduce yourselves. You'll love her. She made the house sign for the place where you're staying, and for my own home too. She's so talented.'

'We love her already. She was brilliant. No, I've only met Vera so far, when I went shopping earlier.'

They exchange glances and Cassie pulls a face. 'That's the issue with the coffee,' she whispers. 'Vera donated it and it tastes disgusting, but the rest of the WI ladies are too scared to bin it. There isn't another shop for miles and if you cross her, she makes sure you pay for it one way or another.'

Grace sees Vera watching her and smiles bravely, taking a big gulp of the insipid drink. The woman purses her lips. She has the sort of face that lends itself to attending funerals.

'I'm guessing that one gave you the full interrogation and maybe the sharp edge of her tongue?'

Grace says this is indeed the case. Vera made her earlier shopping trip seem more like an interrogation. The foraging expedition for the fish pie ingredients was an experience she's not in a hurry to repeat.

'You mustn't let Vera's nastiness bother you. She's a right misery, and mean too. She cuts her own fringe with the kitchen scissors. She asked me if I'd like mine doing last week.'

'I'm guessing you said no,' says Grace, looking at Cassie's glossy hair admiringly.

'Too right. I'd rather eat my own arm. She spreads gloom from that shop when she could be making the village a happier place. Ridiculous woman,' says Cassie, rather more loudly.

'Ssshh, she'll hear.' Grace glances over Cassie's shoulder to where Vera is sneaking an extra-large piece of Victoria sponge from an assorted tray of cakes and scones.

Cassie grins. 'No chance, she's too busy munching. I was sorry to have to tell you May had died. You said she was a friend of your mum and dad? Were they visitors here? It'd be before my time, I guess, if they came to Pengelly on holiday.'

Grace hesitates. It's becoming more and more obvious that unless she comes clean about the reason for her trip, she's going to have to tell a lot of lies, or at least be very evasive. This doesn't sit well with her. The longing to know more about May sweeps over her again.

'Are you okay, Grace?' Cassie says, putting a sympathetic hand on Grace's arm. 'What did I say?'

'I'm fine. It's just that ... look, Cassie, I can't tell you any more at the moment but I really do need to find out what May was like. I'll explain later, if you don't mind. I'm sorry to be so vague.'

Cassie grins. 'Ooh, I sense a mystery. Of course I don't mind. Was May a dodgy character then? I always thought she must have had hidden depths. We only met her once when we bought Seagulls because we were living in London at the time, but she struck me as a sparky woman, very much in tune with nature and her surroundings.'

'Really? Why?'

'A few reasons, but one in particular. She obviously adored the house and all the land that goes with it. When she showed us the garden, she pointed out a nettle patch in a dark corner and told us never to dig it up. She said it was a magnet for butterflies. She laughed when she said it, though. More of a cackle really. I wanted to ask her what was so funny but Dom got distracted by the frogs in the pond.'

'I wish I'd met her. She sounds ... interesting.'

'Yes, it's a shame you didn't come to Pengelly sooner. I was intrigued by the way she spoke of her husband too, although she didn't say much. There was no love lost in that relationship, I reckon. His name was Charles. Did your parents know him too?'

Grace remembers her cover story just in time, suddenly ashamed to be deceiving this friendly woman. 'Oh ... no, I don't think they met him.'

'They didn't miss much, by the sound of it. I tell you what, though, I'll send Dom down with the old photo album for you to have a look at as soon as he's free. May left it for me because she had no family. It's got a lot of pictures of the house over the years but there are others too. The funny thing is, there's a hole where I suppose her husband used to be in some of them, cut out very neatly.'

'Wow, thank you. That'd be great.' Grace is breathless at the thought of this treasure. 'Or I can collect it?'

'He'll be out and about tomorrow, if it's urgent. And if you want to know more about May, when Ida comes back, that's someone you'll *definitely* enjoy meeting. She's a human dynamo. She's made a big difference to life in Pengelly with her Adopt-a-Granny scheme, but there's still a long way to go. We need some new ideas.'

'Ah. I think Julia was involved with the granny project, wasn't she?'

'She was. Against her wishes, if what I heard was true. Julia was allocated May and they'd never got on in the past. They sorted out their differences after a while, though, and by the time May died they were as thick as thieves, as Julia would say. We got Angelina.'

Grace's mind is still on May and she doesn't take on board this last piece of information for a moment. When it sinks in, she says, '*Angelina's* your adopted granny? Really? She doesn't strike me as the type to take to being looked after. She's so full of energy and ideas.'

'Oh, you'd be surprised. There's an awful lot of loneliness in a village, when you scratch the surface. Angelina loves our boys. She can only cope with us all in short bursts but she's teaching them how to do the most amazing pastel pictures.'

Grace notices James waving madly and pointing to his mouth in mock starvation and reluctantly tells Cassie she needs to go. Back in her seat, she presents James with the now lukewarm watery coffee. He puts it on the floor with a grimace but polishes off the cake in three bites.

'Can we go and eat now?' he says.

'We can, with pleasure. What are you going to order?'

James looks down at his feet. 'Oh ... erm ... I couldn't decide earlier. I'll choose something when we get there.'

'Can you just remind me what's on the menu? I think I might have chef's choice of the day. Was it salmon?' As soon as the words are out, Grace wants to kick herself. James's face is a picture of misery.

'Not a clue. Not a bloody clue,' he says sadly.

1969

The garden is still sodden from an earlier deluge so May slips on her wellington boots before she ventures out. The summer downpours have been treacherous this year. The ferocious storm that took Charles away was the worst, and since then, the skies have been a uniform grey every day. Until tonight, that is. At last the evening sunshine breaks through the clouds and a few watery beams shine down on the row of ancient fruit trees in the orchard.

As she squelches through the long grass to the boundary hedge of copper beech, May's heart lifts in sudden joy. If she's lucky, she'll have a good half-hour before sunset to complete her task. Nobody will disturb her down here, which is a good job.

When she reaches the furthest point of her land May can't resist letting out a hiccup of laughter, quickly suppressed. She's wearing Charles's spare waterproof trousers so she's able to walk right into the middle of the prolific nettle patch. She pauses to admire a couple of butterflies, out past their bedtime, before sliding her hand into the surprisingly heavy carrier bag she's brought from the house. The canister is smooth to the touch, and when she pulls it out, she sees that it's tastefully decorated with a pattern of little boats and rainbows, presumably chosen by the funeral director, one of Charles's more long-suffering drinking buddies. Well, the boats are appropriate, but Charles never managed to find his pot of gold, did he?

Suddenly aware that it's usual to say a few words on such an occasion, May thinks hard, but nothing springs to mind apart from an extract from Othello that she had to recite when playing Iago at high school. There were no boys at May's school and she was always one of the tougher girls, so the Am Dram society never failed to cast her as a male character, to her chagrin. Oh well, it will have to do.

She clears her throat and stands up straight.

'It is merely a lust of the blood and a permission of the will,' May intones, in her best performing voice. 'Come, be a man. Drown thyself? Drown cats and blind puppies! I have professed me thy friend, and I confess me knit to thy deserving with cables of perdurable toughness.'

The words fall into the evening stillness and are gone. Even the birds are silent. Did Charles drown himself? May has no idea. He'd been convinced he was seriously ill but had never visited his doctor to discuss his worries. Lusts of the blood? Charles had plenty of those, most of *them inappropriate. And as for May pledging to be his friend, those days were long gone. Still, Shakespeare's words seem strangely fitting for this occasion.*

She eases the lid off the canister with hands that shake only slightly. Inside, the grey, gritty substance looks as if it could never have been part of a living, breathing husband.

'Right, Charles,' May says. 'You always said when the time came you wanted your ashes to be scattered at sea. Well, I don't give a fig for your wishes, you grumpy old sod. I'm sprinkling you here, where I throw my used tea bags and food scraps. And every time I do that, I'll stand here and laugh.'

May cackles loudly, the sound making a nearby squirrel jump and scamper away in alarm. She upends the canister and the ashes pour out in a steady stream, making a dusty layer on the fresh green leaves of the nettles. Underneath them, May can just see the remains of yesterday's potato peelings.

'Goodbye, Charles,' she says. 'I'm going to throw this container in the bin now and go and pour myself a port and brandy. We had some good times, but on the whole, as a husband you were a complete waste of space. You gave me endless anxiety about where you were in the evenings and which poor young souls you were damaging. The older you got, the less you cared for anyone else's desires but your own. Let's hope no one's permanently

scarred. I've given Will enough cash to get himself to County Cork. He'll not be the only one to be glad to have escaped your clutches.'

Without a backward glance, May ploughs her way back through the long grass and along the path between the runner bean sticks. She'll have to remind the gardener who comes in once a week not to scythe the nettles. The excuse of saving wildlife will be useful. And it's quite true, if May had the choice between spending time with Charles Rosevere and sitting watching butterflies flit around her garden, there would be absolutely no contest.

'Cabbage whites one, Charles Rosevere nil,' she mutters to herself as she enters the kitchen. The port and brandy bottles are waiting for her on the draining board, next to her favourite cut-glass goblet. Helping herself to a hefty slug of both, May raises the glass in the general direction of the nettle patch.

'To widowhood,' she says. 'The best thing that's happened to me for years.'

Chapter Thirteen

Julia crosses the cobbled lane to Andy's house as quickly as she can, avoiding the worst ruts. She's a little behind schedule for her babysitting mission tonight due to a surprise visit from Tristram, who takes his perks as a fiancé very seriously. Her cheeks burn as she relives the intense pleasure of being held in his arms. Goodness, Julia never imagined for a minute that life would take this turn after the shattering grief of losing Don. Their long marriage was as near perfect as it's possible to be, she reflects, with a mixture of wistful regret and joy at what the future holds.

What would her husband of so many happy years say if he could have seen her half an hour ago, eighty-six years old and with dodgy knees, but flushed with the passion of kissing a man who is clearly experienced in what makes a woman swoon? Half of Julia (the sensible part) thinks Don would be happy that she isn't still lost in the deep gloom that filled her soul after his death, but the rest of her can't help wondering if he'd approve of what went on this evening.

Tristram is eighty, but he's lost none of his youthful

enthusiasm for *smooching*, as he calls it. Six years older, Julia's aches and pains sometimes threaten to dampen her rediscovered ardour, but Tris can always take her mind off them.

Blushing, she lets herself into Andy's cottage, shouting a loud *hello* to reassure Andy that she hasn't forgotten.

'Hello, Aunty Ju,' Tamsin shouts, barrelling into the kitchen in green spotty pyjamas, a wild cloud of curls around her head. 'We did hairdressers tonight and Daddy dried it like this. I'm a pompom.'

She wraps her arms around Julia's slim waist, nearly flooring her with enthusiastic affection. Julia steadies herself with one hand on the kitchen worktop and bends to kiss the top of the little girl's head. She breathes in the delicate aroma of the baby shampoo that Andy still uses. Tamsin's mother laid in a store of the stuff before she died, not realizing she wouldn't be around to use it when her longed-for daughter was born. Seven years later, it's one of the traditions Tamsin's father can't seem to break.

'Dad's going out with Emily later,' says Tamsin, making a disgusted face.

'I know, that's why I'm here. We'll have fun together … and so will they,' Julia continues manfully, seeing the expression worsen into something of which a gargoyle would be proud.

'They do kissing. It's yucky. I saw them,' Tamsin says.

She makes vomiting noises, letting go of Julia to add the actions.

Julia shudders. Her cheeks flame again at the thought of Tristram. She gives herself a mental shake. This is worse than being a teenager.

'But grown-ups do like to kiss each other sometimes, my pet,' she says, groping for the right words. 'Your dad and Emily are really good friends.'

'Summer and me are friends, but we don't do THAT!' Tamsin's bottom lip is wobbling now and Julia can sense the night is going downhill at the speed of light.

'Right, let's go and make ourselves a nest of cushions on the sofa and get ready for them to go out. Then we can have stories,' Julia says, just as Emily lets herself in at the back door.

'Hi guys,' Julia hears her granddaughter call.

'Hello, love,' shouts Andy from upstairs. 'I'm just tidying up Tamsin's mess and I'll be down.'

'Want a hand?' Emily yells back, taking the stairs two at a time to join him.

'No, Em, that's not a good idea ...' Julia tells her silently, waiting for the inevitable reaction. She feels Tamsin stiffen. She's already snuggled up next to Julia, first story in hand, but she makes to slide off the sofa as she hears Emily's words.

'They're going to do kissing again up there,' Tamsin

mutters, wriggling to escape Julia's encircling arm. 'I'm going to tell them to stop it.'

'Don't be daft. Emily's only going to mop the bathroom floor. I know what a flood you make when you play hairdressers, I've seen it. All those soggy towels. We'll leave them to it. They might ask us to help if we go up.'

Julia waits, hoping she's said enough. Tam hates anything resembling housework with a passion.

'Okay. Read it now ... please,' Tamsin adds, seeing Julia's expression. The kitten jumps onto Tamsin's lap, and curls up in a ball.

'What did you decide to call this little fur ball in the end?' Julia asks, momentarily distracted. 'The last I heard, her name was Stripey Two after her mum, but your daddy says you changed your mind?'

'Her name is Allie. That was my mummy's name,' says Tamsin firmly.

When Emily and Andy enter the room, just as pink-cheeked as Julia was earlier, Tamsin has reached her fifth story.

'You were ages,' she says, glaring up at them from the comfort and safety of Julia's arms.

'Well, you made a very big mess up there tonight, Tam. I bet it was fun, though.'

Emily's words don't provoke a response. Tamsin is getting sleepy, despite her best efforts to stay awake.

'See you later, Julia,' says Andy, bending to give her

a kiss. His arm is around Emily's waist and he lets go briefly to hug his daughter. Emily takes a step forward as if unsure whether she should do the same, but the look on Tamsin's face almost stops her in her tracks.

'Yuck, yuckety yuck,' says Tamsin quietly to herself, but she allows Andy and Emily to hug her briefly, with only token resistance. They leave, and she turns to Julia.

'Why are they going out?' she asks. 'Emily was here last night. Why does Daddy need to see her again?'

Julia turns to look at Tamsin properly. She hesitates. The right words are very important here.

'Yes, Em came round last night to see your dad but you came downstairs as soon as she arrived, didn't you?' she asks gently.

'I was thirsty. I wanted a drink of water.'

'But then you wouldn't go back to bed, would you?'

'I ... I wasn't tired. And I needed the toilet.'

Tamsin's eyes are full of tears and Julia's heart aches for her, but this is too good a chance to miss.

'Why do you get so upset when Dad sees Emily, darling?' she says, cuddling Tamsin close. 'You and Em were friends, weren't you? You made some fantastic dens at my house and you played on the beach and ...'

Julia runs out of words when she sees the tears running down Tamsin's face. The little girl holds her stomach.

'I hate Emily,' is all she says. 'She gives me a pain.'

'That's a horrid thing to say, Tam. You don't hate her.'

'I do so too. And if she thinks she can come and live here with us and Stripey Two ... I mean Allie, well ... she just can't, that's all. There ... there isn't room.' Tamsin folds her arms across her chest and shivers. 'I wish May was still here,' she says.

'May? Why do you say that?'

'Well, because she would have told Emily to butt out, I just know she would. May used to stick up for me. I liked telling her stuff after school. I miss her ...'

The tears are flowing again now, and Julia reaches for a tissue to mop Tamsin's face, wondering where to go from here. The mention of May has pierced her own heart too.

'I miss her too, Tam,' she says after a moment. 'I didn't understand what a good friend she was until she'd gone and I have to admit I didn't always appreciate everything about her.'

'Did you love May?'

Julia would have hesitated to answer this question about her one-time adversary in the past but now she says, 'Yes, I did, Tam.'

'So did I. And she was the very best at looking after me. Apart from Dad. Oh, and I like being with you,' Tamsin says hastily, seeing Julia's face fall.

'Thank you, dear. And I agree it's very sad to lose a friend. But at least we knew her for a good long time.'

'*You* did. I didn't.' Tamsin's expression is mulish now. 'I'm only seven. And I'm lonely without her.'

'Me too,' says Julia, helping herself to another tissue.

They sit in silence for a while, and Julia holds Tamsin tighter. 'Do you think your daddy ever gets lonely?' she says carefully.

'No. He's got me.'

'But you go out quite often, to Brownies and school and to play with your friends. And when you've gone to bed at night, he's on his own for a long time.'

Tamsin considers this. 'He can go to bed too if he's bored,' she says. 'He's always tired when he's finished putting me to bed. I don't think he likes bath time very much. Another book?'

'Well, okay, but this is the very last story and then it's bedtime.'

'Noooooooo,' Tamsin begins to moan, and then sees the look on Julia's face and changes her mind. 'Okay then, just this one while we're down here, but we'll need another three for upstairs. That's what Daddy does.'

Yawning, Julia girds her loins. In her handbag, her mobile starts to ring.

'Leave it,' says Tamsin imperiously.

'I'll just check who it is, in case there's an emergency. They can probably wait, though,' she says, reaching for the phone. It's an unfamiliar number, and she answers even though Tamsin is now looking dangerously close to tears.

'Hello? Oh, it's gone to voicemail ... let me just listen, Tam, it might be important.'

Julia plays back the message and then switches the phone off.

'What's the matter, Aunty Ju? Why are you looking all funny? Was it a 'mergency?' Tamsin tugs on Julia's arm, jolting her out of her reverie.

'Not exactly. That was my brother-in-law, Will.'

'Uncle Don's brother? You told me about him. The thin man. Why don't I know him though, Aunty Ju?'

'He lives in Ireland, remember?'

'Oh, yes, he's the vicar one, isn't he?'

'Priest,' corrects Julia absently. 'He wants to come for a visit.'

Tamsin claps her hands and jumps up, starting to caper around the room. 'Uncle Will's coming to see us,' she shouts. 'Hooray. I needed a new uncle. That's fun, isn't it?'

Julia smiles. 'It just might be,' she says. 'It certainly won't be boring.' She looks down at the opals gleaming on the third finger of her left hand. There are a few questions about the ring that have never been answered and Julia has the strongest feeling that Will knows something about the time it went missing for so long. There wasn't a chance for her to talk to him before he went away so suddenly all those years ago, so soon after Charles drowned, but this time Julia vows to herself that she'll do better. She's wondered about it for far too long, and if anyone can solve the mystery, it's the enigmatic William Lovell.

Chapter Fourteen

The next morning, the unpredictable April weather takes a turn for the worse. When Grace first stirs, she can hear the rain pounding on her window. She snuggles down under her duvet and dozes off again, hoping it'll stop by breakfast time, but when she's showered and dressed by nine o'clock, the sky is still a sulky grey and light drizzle is falling.

'What's your plan for today?' she asks James as they sit round the table eating fruit and muesli.

'I've been invited to go mackerel fishing with Tristram and his friend Tom,' says James. 'I've never fished from a boat before. And then they're taking me over to Tris's restaurant to meet his daughter Gina. She runs it for him with her husband Vince, apparently. Tris has devised an experimental session of food tasting. It's meant to spark memories. If I catch a mackerel they say I can gut it and cook it myself, too.'

'That sounds fun. Who else gets to play?'

'It's just me today, but he says he's planning to make it into a session at the village hall. There are a lot of older residents in Pengelly, and losing track of memories is something they tend to panic about.'

'Can't understand anyone feeling like that, can you?' says Grace, grinning at him. No point in skirting around the subject if they're going to be living in each other's pockets.

'You can smile, but my daughter says I'm losing it, big time. I remember when she used to come to me for all the answers. I was her hero. She was such a sweet baby and an adorable child.'

As soon as his words are out, Grace is painfully aware of the sudden rush of pictures in James's mind. He's in a hospital ward and he's in a state of wild excitement. A baby is crying, a thin wail that goes straight to Grace's heart.

'James? What's the matter?' she asks, leaning forward to look him in the eye. His face is pale and clammy-looking.

'I was just thinking about the night Davina was born,' he explains, rubbing his eyes, 'and I was trying to remember the name of the wonderful midwife who delivered her, but it's gone. Davina was four weeks early and we thought she wasn't going to make it at one point. The midwife arrived on duty just as we reached the hospital and she stayed with us all the way through. It was a very long haul.'

The memory of Davina's birth is trapped inside

Grace's head now, bursting to get out and go back where it belongs. Well, there will never be a better moment to try to do something constructive with it. There's nothing to lose here, surely? James is struggling so hard to re-member details that his transmitted agony is becoming almost unbearable.

Grace takes both James's hands in hers, unsure why she feels so strongly that she wants to help him, but at the same time feeling a desperate need to soothe the turmoil in his mind. For goodness' sake, why not James and why not now? He's a sweet man and if she doesn't make the effort, Grace will never know if she has the power to give memories back. It's just not possible to ignore his pain any longer.

Focusing on James with all her strength, she lets the thoughts of the tiny scrap of humanity, born too soon but yelling lustily, trickle further into her mind. When she's got it all, she summons every available ounce of willpower and pours it back with all her energy.

James flinches, and then begins to visibly relax. 'What's happening to me?' he says, eyes wide.

'I'm returning a memory,' she says. 'Just let it happen, okay?'

Gradually, she feels the tension in his hands and arms soften even more. After a moment he blinks and says, 'Andrea.'

'Yes, that was her name. What did she look like?'

'Tall, with a long brown plait down her back. Freckles. Strong arms.'

'Good.'

He stands up shakily and goes over to the window. After a moment he says, 'Are you going to tell me how you did that?'

Exhaustion takes Grace's breath away as she tries to decide how to answer. After all these years, she's finally done something useful with her unwanted skill. The lump in her throat makes it hard to swallow.

'Well?'

She takes a couple of deep breaths and the room steadies. 'I ... I don't know, James. I'll try and explain some-time, but can we just leave it for now? You just go and enjoy your fishing and all the food tasting.'

'But I can't leave without knowing what you've done. This is all so weird. You must see that?'

Grace sighs. She's exhausted now, and the thought of stumbling through an explanation that she has no desire to give is making her want to cry. At that moment, they hear Emily coming down the stairs.

'Okay, I'll drop it for the moment, Grace,' says James quietly, 'but we need to talk about this. I'm off now, but I'll see you later. And ... and thank you ... whatever it was that you managed to do just then.'

He pats her on the shoulder and Grace watches him go, then Emily pops her head round the door.

'Oh, great – you're here,' she says. 'I was hoping to kidnap you to do some research on the letters with me upstairs. I'll probably have to go up to London again soon, so this is a good chance for us to make a start on sorting the letters properly and brainstorming some ideas, if you don't mind?'

Fighting off a huge wave of tiredness, Grace decides that the only other options are to go back to bed or to wander about the village and find someone prepared to discuss May without being able to give them a proper reason for wanting to know. At least she doesn't have to make a start on her enquiries in the rain. Emily will be a better person to talk to anyway. She was clearly important to May.

Rummaging in her bag for painkillers, Grace takes a swig of cold coffee to wash them down and follows Emily up the steep stairs to the loft apartment. Grace is intrigued to see what Emily's living accommodation is like. The downstairs rooms are still furnished in May's style, with a few modernizations for comfort. Tristram has said this is because neither he, Emily nor Julia can bear to change anything yet. May's belongings were so much a part of her that it seems all wrong to get rid of them or even to rearrange the familiar surroundings too much.

'Here we are, make yourself at home,' says Emily as they emerge into the wide, sunlit space under the eaves.

Grace gasps. The scent of new wood mingles with the subtle herbal fragrance from a scented candle on a low coffee table. A very comfortable-looking sea-green sofa sits in one corner and the opposite one is filled with a king-sized bed, covered with a patchwork quilt in all shades of green and gold. In the middle, underneath one of the enormous skylights, is an ancient oak desk and a matching chair with a cushion that exactly matches the quilt. There are yellow roses in a vase on a high shelf and so many books stacked beneath it that Grace's fingers itch to touch and examine them.

'Do you like it?' says Emily rather anxiously, when Grace doesn't comment. 'I've ordered some proper bookshelves but they haven't come yet.'

'Oh, Emily, it's perfect,' Grace breathes, her jaded feeling fading away as she looks around the room. 'This is just the sort of place I would love for myself.'

'You've got a flat in the Midlands though, haven't you? What's it like?' Emily says, gesturing for Grace to join her on the sofa.

'It's ... well, I guess if you saw it after living up here, you'd say it was very boring.'

'Why?'

The one word sets Grace thinking. Why indeed? During her working years, she hasn't spent many of the daylight hours in her flat, so its main function is to be cosy in the winter evenings or cool on summer nights.

There's a lot of white alongside all the shades of taupe and likewise, but the table lamps give a friendly glow and the carpets are thick and luxurious.

The spare bedroom, locked while her tenant is there, is kitted out as a studio with a laminate floor and work benches. Her oils and watercolour paints and her extensive collection of brushes are neatly arranged on shelves. It's all just how she likes it, but Grace hasn't felt like painting for quite a while now. Her heart hasn't been in it somehow. Grief and loss have left her floating in a sea of inertia. The pain of saying goodbye to Audrey and Harry has been waiting just around the corner, and Grace has been very much afraid that by losing herself in art, she might open the floodgates.

At weekends, Grace always cleans the place thoroughly but then tends to fill her time with outings to galleries at the quieter times, walks in the nearby countryside or late-night shopping trips when everyone else is heading home. She tries to explain this to Emily without adding her reasons for being so solitary, and the younger woman nods.

'My apartment in New York City was a bit like that. It was only when I came home that I discovered what my tastes were. I was lucky that Gran and Grandpa had stored all my books for me, and Gran gave me their desk and chair, so it felt homely straight away. Some of May's bits and bobs are here too – that lovely Turkish rug, for instance, and the tall green glass vase.'

Grace goes over to look at the vase more closely. She has an overwhelming desire to hold it.

'You can pick it up if you like. I don't think it's particularly valuable, but you could anyway – I don't believe in keeping precious things behind barriers,' says Emily, beginning to rummage in her desk drawer for a pen.

The vase is cool to the touch, pale green with deep swirls of a darker emerald colour. As she runs her fingers down its length, Grace notices a light tingling spreading up her arm and around her shoulders. It's like an embrace, but so delicate as to hardly be there. She holds her breath. Is this going to be another experience like the one with the dragonfly bedside lamp? Over the years, objects and animals have seldom transmitted memories, but with a stab of alarm, Grace registers that everything has been changing even in the short time since she came to Pengelly.

'It's beautiful, isn't it?' Emily says, looking up to see why Grace is so silent. 'May went on a lot of adventures. She and her husband didn't get on very well, Julia told me, and he never minded her going away, sometimes for weeks or months. That treasure was from Venice.'

'Yes, I thought it was probably Murano glass.' Grace's voice sounds odd to herself, as if it's coming from far away, but Emily doesn't seem to notice, carrying on talking as if nothing's happening.

'She collected all sorts of stuff, hardly ever new, but I think she made an exception with that piece because she wanted it so badly. I used to come and see her when I visited Gran and Gramps and she'd let me look at everything and tell me stories about her travels. I loved May.'

With an effort, Grace puts the vase carefully back on the shelf. The wave of tingling has receded but she feels strange and other-worldly. The image of a sunlit waterfront and a glass-blower's workshop is still in her mind. The experiences with the peeler and the lamp have unnerved her, and now the vase too. If this sort of thing is going to keep happening, nowhere will be safe. It's one thing dodging memories from people, but she can never begin to predict inanimate objects getting in on the act. If only May was here to talk to. This weird ability has surely got to be something they shared.

'The view from up here's amazing. Come and look.' Emily's at one of the skylights now, beckoning.

Grace drags her mind back to the present, with difficulty. This side of the room looks directly out to sea, and the tide is coming in. A couple of small children, wrapped up against the damp, splash in the shallows in brightly patterned wellies and the older girl with them is trying to stop a large red setter from shaking itself all over her. Their laughter reaches Grace across the beach and she smiles. 'It's blissful,' she says.

'Do you ever think about moving to the coast? I expect you've got lots of friends and family where you live, so it wouldn't be practical?' Emily asks, sitting down again and pulling a basket of letters towards her. 'Hey, I guess we should start work instead of me interrogating you.'

Grace can't tear herself away from the view yet. 'I haven't really got friends as such,' she says slowly. 'Well, there's Kat, I suppose. We worked together for years. But my teaching completely absorbed me and I'm fairly antisocial by nature, I guess. My parents are both dead and we didn't have any family, apart from a couple of cousins in the north who we never saw. I volunteered for various things at our local church now and again, but that was mainly to please my parents, and I didn't really get to know those people well either.'

In that instant, Grace knows she doesn't want to go back to her tidy, sterile flat. The lease runs out on it in two months, by which time her temporary tenant will have departed. Why shouldn't she relocate to the seaside? And where better than Pengelly?

Putting such whirlwind thoughts aside for the moment, she concentrates on the letters that Emily's spreading between them on the sofa. The envelopes and ancient stamps give off a faint, musty aroma. Grace can feel Emily's tension mounting as she flicks through them, and puts up as strong a shield as she can against the flood of her memories that's bound to follow. For a moment or two it's touch and go. Emily is experiencing a torrent of emotions now as she touches the faded envelopes, and the wave of feelings is getting stronger.

Grace takes a deep breath and does her best to remember the way the sunshine and shadows contrasted so sharply on the cobbles and the scent of the lilies growing in ceramic pots between the café tables. If she tries really hard, Grace can even envisage the young waiter who flirted with her so charmingly. Forewarned is forearmed, as Harry used to say.

'How do you want us to tackle this job?' she asks, slipping back into the Italian zone as a fresh wash of nostalgia threatens to swamp her. If Emily's going to get as upset as this every time the letters come out, it's going to be impossible to help. Grace can't maintain this level of defence for too long at a time, it's exhausting.

'Right, let's make a plan,' Emily says, squaring her shoulders. 'How about if you begin sorting them into date order – Gran and May already started that job, although I've got an idea they only scratched the surface, but you might find it's easier than it sounds – and I'll try and find some that mention the opal ring. It was lost for so long. There's something about the story that doesn't ring true.'

'How do you mean?'

'Hard to say until I can dig out more, but I can't help feeling that May knew more about it than she let on. Charles was blamed when the ring finally turned up again, but ... I don't know ... It was another area where she refused to comment. I loved May and she was a one-off, but she could be incredibly secretive.'

'In a bad way?' Grace is intrigued. The previously shadowy figure of May is already beginning to take shape in her head, but is she ready for this?

'Hmm, I'm not sure. There's no harm in keeping secrets so long as you aren't twisting the truth by keeping things hidden. Hey, we're getting into deep waters here and we've got work to do.'

Emily gives Grace a box of paperclips, folders and plastic wallets and carte blanche to catalogue the letters in whatever way she thinks best. She moves over to her desk and mercifully becomes totally absorbed in her task, leaving Grace free to get on with the job.

Always efficient and analytical for all her artistic leanings, Grace is soon finding her own methods of sorting the letters into categories. They work in silence, the only interruption coming when the old cat yowls at the foot of the stairs so plaintively that Emily is forced to go and fetch him.

'He's too old to get up here, but he seems to want to be with me,' she says, bringing Fossil in and settling him on a cushion which is clearly kept for his use, judging by the fur left on it. 'May asked me to look after him when she left me her cottage. Her exact words were, "He's not long for this world and he smells a bit, but he's a good soul in his way."'

Grace laughs and reaches out to stroke Fossil as he lurches off his cushion and ambles towards her. She's always resisted the temptation to have a cat, being in an upstairs flat and spending so much time at work, but as Fossil bumps his bony head against her hand and sets up a chorus of loud purrs, she begins to let herself imagine a different life in a cottage by the sea with her own cat, or even a puppy too, and a view of the bay.

'He likes you,' says Emily. 'That's a mixed blessing. The smell gets worse when he sits on your lap.'

As if understanding her words, Fossil scratches himself briefly and then makes a brave attempt to leap onto Grace's knee, but the sofa is too high for him and he lands back on the polished floor, yelping. She takes pity on the poor soul and picks him up.

'I hope he hasn't got fleas again,' says Emily.

Grace laughs. 'Me too, but then Hope is my middle name.'

'In that case, procrastination is mine,' Emily says, pulling a face as she looks at the heaps of letters.

'No, I really mean it, that *is* my middle name. Grace

Hope Clarke. My parents were very religious, as you might have guessed. They missed out Faith and Charity, so I suppose I should be grateful for small mercies.'

'Oh, but that's a beautiful name. What are *you* hoping for, Grace?'

That's a tough one. The answer isn't as straight-forward as it might once have been. Yes, she still hopes and longs to find out more about May and to discover who is or was the other half of the equation, but the goalposts are moving all the time and a part of her that has always felt frozen seems to be starting to thaw. She's already taken the first tentative steps into friendship with James and Emily, and even Cassie Featherstone has seemed interested in getting to know her. This place is getting under her skin. Now, a more burning question seems to be who actually *is* Grace Hope Clarke, and more to the point, where does she go from here?

2019

*M*ay *and Julia sit either side of Julia's fire, a plate of
scones on a coffee table between them and a letter
each on their laps. They've both decided to choose one to
read aloud, after a tiring afternoon of sorting them into
year groups. May is a little light-headed due to all the
memories that have been flooding into her mind, and
her eyes are very bright as she sips her tea.*

*'You look exceedingly well today, dear,' Julia tells her.
'Your hair is magnificent. The hairdresser really knows
how to make the most of white curls, doesn't she?'*

*May glances at her friend dubiously. Is she being
sarcastic? Julia's own smooth bob is unfeasibly dark,
without a single grey hair. May decided long ago not to
try and recreate her natural auburn because so often
she's observed a distressing orange tinge in ladies of a
certain age. She's inherited the early loss of hair colour
from her mother's side of the family. Her father died long
before he reached this stage but was youthful to the last
in every way.*

'I like to think I'm not letting myself go,' says May, giving Julia the benefit of the doubt and smiling at her graciously. They're friends now at last, after years of prickly avoidance, so the other woman isn't likely to be having a dig at May. 'I know you feel the same. We have standards to keep up, don't we? Did you see the dress Ida was wearing yesterday at the bring and buy sale?' May shudders. 'I thought they'd stopped making Crimplene.'

'I did. It wasn't good, was it? I think it's Lionel's fault. He begrudges every penny she spends on clothes. I don't know how she puts up with him. He's so gloomy, and the only things he really cares about are his pigeons. Anyway, let's get on with the letters. Will you go first?'

May nods, and swallows the last of her tea, replacing the bone china cup carefully in its saucer. She takes out the letter she's selected and begins to read.

'Dear Don,

I really had to write as soon as I returned home, first of all to say thank you for having me for such an enjoyable visit, but secondly to ask how you can put up with that absolute bore Tristram Brookes? Obviously I love staying with you and Julia, but this time it was all I could do not to punch the man on the nose, or worse. I'll telephone you later. It's wonderful that you've been connected at last, although it's a bit of a trek to our nearest call box. You have to remember to take the right change and I'm always getting cut off before I've finished talking, for some reason.

More later, oodles of love to darling Julia,

Your affectionate brother,

Will'

May looks at Julia with her head on one side. 'I've often wondered about the two men being at such loggerheads all those years ago. Do you have any idea why they didn't get on? Tristram has always been very cagey about it if I've asked.'

'I don't understand it either. I expect we'll find out one day. Anyway, here's mine. It's quite short.'

Julia unfolds her own letter and begins, her soft voice having its usual effect of relaxing May. What a joy this new closeness between the two of them has been. May can't understand why they let their old animosity rankle for so long.

'My darling Don, *reads Julia,*

If I have to wait any longer to see you, I think I will explode with excitement. Please tell me you can still be home in five days? Our digs are all ready for us. I've cleaned and cleaned until my hands are raw, just for something to do, because the rooms really weren't in a bad state, but I wanted to feel as if I'd prepared the nest myself for our first night there together. Can you believe we'll be snuggled up in that big feather bed so soon?

I'll go now, because I'm embarrassing myself with such thoughts, but my heart is with you, and I just can't wait to see your train pull into the station and for you to leap out and run down the platform to sweep me into your arms.

Ever yours,

Julia.'

'*That's lovely, dear,' says May, surreptitiously wiping away a tear. 'You're so lucky to have had that relationship with your husband. Charles wasn't much of a one for writing letters or for romance in general.'*

'*I'm sorry, May, I didn't mean to show off. I suppose I wanted to step back into that perfect moment for a little while. A time when anything seemed possible and everything you would ever need could be provided by just one man. Have you ever felt like that?'*

'*Oh yes,' says May, gazing into the glowing embers of the fire. 'Oh yes, Julia, I certainly have. But unfortunately, the man in question wasn't mine.'*

Chapter Fifteen

Two hours later, Emily's beginning to wonder how she ever thought she could complete this mammoth task on her own. Grace, fuelled with hot chocolate, is doing a sterling job, quietly sifting through the heaps of letters and methodically sorting them. She's much faster than Julia and May ever were because she doesn't waste time in reading much more than the dates and a few sentences that catch her eye.

'It's probably time we had a proper break, Grace,' she says, getting up from her chair and wiggling her shoulders. 'My back's aching and you must be ready to move too. Fossil's not easy to work around.'

Grace looks up, blinking as if she's been asleep. Her expression is hard to read, and Emily hopes she isn't bored silly.

'This is fantastic,' Grace says, putting Emily's mind at rest. 'What an amazing archive. I've never seen anything like it. How are you going to structure the book? Will it be their story, but in disguise?'

'No, that'd be lovely from a family point of view, but to be brutally honest, apart from the time when they were at loggerheads, they didn't do a great deal except talk about food rationing early on and clothes coupons, and later their social lives and more food. I've found the ones that talk about the ring but they're not much help. This one's about the best. It's from my grandpa's sister Elsie. Listen.'

Emily clears her throat and spreads one of the letters on her knee. It's faded and creased but she has no trouble reading it aloud.

'Dearest Don,

I'm at the end of my tether. You must be sick to the back teeth of me going on about this, and I know Kathryn's written to you too, but for pity's sake, where can that blessed ring have got to?

Will swears he knows nothing about it, and of course Mother believes him. When did she not swallow every last story he tells her? But Will isn't himself at the moment. He seems more and more distracted these days and he's always going off on his own. I don't know where he goes, and when we ask him, he just hedges around the subject.

Going back to the ring, I can't even find the leather box for it. When I think about that beautiful thing, those three perfect opals and the tiny diamonds all around them, I could weep, and you know wailing's not my style, Don. We've even had all the carpets up – what a dust storm that caused – but to no avail. It's gone for good, I reckon. Mother has never told us where she got it. I sense a mystery but she clams up when we ask her. I think it must be valuable, don't you?

I remember Julia once saying something interesting, when Mother first promised the ring to her at the time you were planning to get engaged. Julia said that it was a good job Mother wanted her to have it because if not it'd cause a rift between Kathryn and me when Mother finally … I can't talk about it, but you know what I mean. Well, at least we haven't got that worry now!

I must go. I've got my dress to press for the church social tonight and Mother wants Kathryn and me to take Will along with us. She says it's time he met a nice girl and settled down. Fat chance, I reckon. Anyway, he's very anti-chapel at the moment. He reckons all we've got going for us is weak orange squash and soggy biscuits. Rude, I call it. But it's the Catholic Club that draws him in these days, and not just for the whisky.

Anyway, love to you both and we'll see you soon, I've got my next leave sorted.

Best love, yours as ever,

Elsie. Xxx'

Emily leans back in her chair. 'I've decided what to do,' she says. 'I'm going to write a book with the letters as inspiration but not as the main feature. It's going to be all about the family ring. Gran's got it now. There's always been a big mystery about it and she says she doesn't know the full story.'

'And is that true?'

'Who knows? But opals are emotional stones. They've always been highly sought after and they're beautiful, whatever they mean. All those tiny points of colour that seem to move around. My story will be about a woman who goes searching for the one opal ring that can change her life.'

'Wow, go on, I'm all ears. What do you mean by that?'

'Some people, like my gran, think opals can help with memory loss. Maybe if a person finds the right one for them, it can help by hanging on to their memories. Wouldn't that be a great theme for a book? My story's going to follow the heroine of the novel and her search for the perfect stone. Fiction, but with the letters as background.'

Grace nods enthusiastically. Her eyes are shining. 'Tell me more.'

'That's as far as I've got yet. Gran says Uncle Will's planning to come and stay soon, a surprise visit, which is brilliant timing. He's been away for so long we thought he was gone for good. I'm sure he'll be able to give me some ideas. We've got our own story about a missing ring. I bet he knows more about it than he's ever let on. And I'd like to find out if May's husband, Charles, had anything to do with it all.'

'You mentioned him before. Why should he have been involved with your family and the ring?'

'He had his fingers in a lot of pies, by all accounts, some of them dodgy, and he was big buddies with Will. Gran once told me she and my grandpa tried really hard to put Will off the man but it was no good.'

'And Charles's story ended badly?'

'Yes. He took his boat out one night when a bad storm was brewing, which apparently wasn't like him. Even though Charles wasn't well-liked in the village, everyone respected him as an experienced sailor. Will disappeared to Ireland very soon afterwards and eventually became a Catholic priest.'

'Crikey! That's a bit of a drastic reaction to losing a friend.'

'I know. It seemed to work for him, though. Like I said, he never came back, or even wrote.' Emily clasps her hands together. She can feel excitement beginning to fizz through her veins as the characters from the past step into clearer focus. 'Grace, all these relationship tangles are starting to come together in my head. So long as I don't name names, I can weave some of these threads into my story, can't I? I wish May was here to help, though. Oh, you'd have got on really well with her. She'd have loved you.'

'Why do you say that?'

The sharp tone of the question seems to demand a more in-depth answer than Emily would have expected to give. She looks across at Grace, who is leaning forward slightly in her chair, still stroking Fossil but obviously waiting for something important. She thinks hard. Why did she assume the two of them would have hit it off? 'I reckon you're a similar sort of person,' she says, rather feebly.

'Go on, I'm intrigued.'

'Well, May was independent and a bit aloof. She kept her own counsel. She didn't have many friends, but once you knew her properly, you really warmed to her.'

'Is that how you see me?'

Grace's eyes are very bright, and Emily hopes the older woman isn't going to cry. She wonders why this all seems so important to Grace, but tries to be as honest as possible.

'Yes, it is. I feel as if you've fitted in here with us really well. You're kind and helpful and actually, even after this short time, I can tell I'll miss you when you go. You're welcome to stay as long as you like.'

Grace lifts Fossil gently off her knee and stands up. She goes over to the window and gazes out to sea. After a moment she turns back to face Emily.

'I can't carry on like this,' she says. 'I've lied to you all, Emily, and it's got to stop.'

Emily can't think of a reply to this unexpected confession. She already likes this calm, forthright woman. How can she be a liar?

'I've been trying to give the impression that I'm anxious and stressed. What I wanted from Pengelly was something much more serious.'

'Well? Don't leave me dangling.'

'I wanted ... no, I needed to find out about my birth mother,' Grace says, her face white now. 'The woman who dumped me on two people who were pretty much strangers and then cleared off to Cornwall to get on with her *own stuffing life.*'

The bald sentences fall into the space between them, the last three words much louder than the rest. Still Emily waits, somehow sure there's more to this than meets the eye. Grace rubs her eyes and takes a deep breath. Her next words confirm this in a big way.

'When my adoptive father died, I found some information. No, actually Harry gave it to me at last after years of keeping it secret. There was a letter that led me to find out that my real mother was May Rosevere.'

Emily can't take this in at first. May? Surely not, there must be a mistake. She does a few sums in her head. 'But that's ...'

'Impossible? That's what I thought, age-wise and

everything. But it's a lot more complicated than it seems on the surface.'

'You can't be May's daughter. You just can't.'

'But I am. The letter says so. She left it for me.'

'She'd have told me. Or at least Gran. May wouldn't have kept quiet about something as crucial as that.' But even as she says the words, Emily knows, with a pang of betrayal, that they're not true. May was a law unto herself. Other people's secrets were always safe with her because she didn't feel the need to gossip, and her own private affairs were just that. Private.

The rest of Grace's words are sinking in now. 'So you don't really need my cottage as a refuge at all?' Emily stands up and stalks over to the window. She's beginning to feel a burning rage building up now. She'd been convinced that with James and Grace, they had struck lucky right from the start. Two people who were struggling with their own pressures, and the cottage could help to make them feel better. A grand legacy for May.

Grace winces. 'It isn't actually as simple as that. I didn't *think* I was suffering from either anxiety or stress.' She pauses. 'Not in the way you see it anyway, but I reckon I've been kidding myself, because I'm showing all the signs of both those things, it turns out. I'm trying to juggle a lot of different issues all at once.'

Emily raises her eyebrows but can think of nothing

useful to say. She's been duped. And May? How could she keep such a huge secret from them all? Did she not trust Emily and Julia at all? Grace tries again.

'I really am sorry if I've upset you, but now I've met you all and settled into the cottage, I think I need to be here in this wonderful place as much as anyone else who might come. My problems with memories are a completely different ball game from the sort James is having.'

'What do you mean by that?'

'It's been a tough year but my whole life's been dominated by ... certain other problems. Look, I didn't mean to blurt all this out today. It's just that I hate to deceive you now we're getting to know each other.'

'And I hate being hoodwinked. I didn't think you were the sort of person to do that.'

Emily turns and leans against the windowsill, folding her arms. Fossil comes over to weave around her legs, nudging her with his bony little head, but Emily hardly notices him. It's almost as if she's losing May all over again. The pain bites deeply but she can see from Grace's face that she's not the only one suffering here. The tension in Grace's shoulders and the frown lines that aren't usually in evidence make that very clear.

'Actually, I think I was right in the first place. You're not someone who'd lie and manipulate without a good reason, are you?'

Grace shakes her head, apparently lost for words. They look at each other for a long moment and then Emily bends to scoop up Fossil and heads for the stairs.

'So, how about we start again from scratch? We've done enough work for one day and I'm starving. Why don't we go to the pub for lunch, find a quiet corner by the fire and you can tell me what's really going on?'

The relief on Grace's face is like the sun coming out. She follows Emily downstairs, they slip on their coats and they're out of the house and heading up the lane in five minutes flat. A fresh breeze ruffles Emily's hair. Today is turning out to be something of an eye-opener all round.

Chapter Sixteen

The next phone call from Ireland comes the day after the first and delivers an even bigger surprise for Julia. She flops down in her chair with the handset still clutched to her chest for several minutes after it ends, so shaken she can't think straight.

'Will's definitely coming home, and he's arriving tomorrow,' she murmurs to herself. 'What on earth would Don have said about that?'

The irony of the situation hits Julia as she thinks back over the years. Will has cut himself off completely and didn't even answer when she wrote to tell him that Don had died. Poor Don never stopped hoping his brother would come back, but for goodness' sake, why did Will wait until now? And what does he mean when he says he wants to make his peace before it's too late? Is he ill?

It's hard to take in this momentous news without someone here to share it. When her breathing settles and her heart rate's back to normal, Julia tries to ring Tristram to tell him what's happened, but as the call goes to voicemail she remembers he's spending the day with Tom and James. He's probably done his usual trick of leaving his phone by his bed. Julia's whole body is tingling with nervous excitement now. She clicks on Emily's number next but again gets only the request to leave a message.

Now what? She'll burst if she doesn't tell someone about Will coming back to Pengelly at last. As she begins to pace the floor, her phone rings.

'Emily, thank the Lord – I've been ringing you. What? You're in the pub at this time of day? Why? Oh, you're with Grace, I see. Anyway, I need to talk to you … right now. No, I can't come down and join you. Well … because …'

Julia thinks for a moment. Actually, why shouldn't she pop down to The Eel and Lobster? The idea of a sherry is suddenly very appealing. She glances into the mirror and decides a quick brush-up is all she needs to make herself presentable.

'Emily? Are you still there? Give me ten minutes and I'll be with you. Order me a large Tio Pepe. On ice.'

The unaccustomed outing puts a spring in Julia's step and she hurries up the lane. As the heavy oak door of the pub swings open, she sees the startled faces of a handful of locals as they turn in her direction, so she gives them a cheerful wave.

'We're over here, Gran,' Emily calls, and Julia spots her granddaughter sitting in the bay window with Grace opposite. Two pints of bitter are on the table between them, and Julia's sherry is waiting.

'We decided to blend in and drink beer today,' says Emily, seeing Julia's raised eyebrows. 'We've been working hard. Have a crisp?'

Julia settles herself next to Emily and accepts her drink but shakes her head at the proffered packet. There are limits. 'So what's all this in aid of?' she asks, gesturing towards the bar.

'We needed a break from the letters,' says Emily. Julia notices the glance that passes between the two other women and is momentarily diverted, but soon remembers why she's here. She pours out the gist of Will's phone call, taking a restorative sip of sherry between sentences.

'And I've got absolutely no idea why he's chosen this moment to land on us. I was sure he must be dead by now, to be honest, Em. I couldn't think of any other reason why he wouldn't respond to the news of your grandpa's passing.'

Julia feels tears prickle her eyes and reaches for her glass, but is dismayed to find it's empty. She peers into it, as if hoping it will magically refill.

'I'll get you a top-up,' says Grace, getting to her feet and making her way over to the bar. Every eye in the place is on her. Julia thinks it's something to do with the way Grace walks. She's straight-backed and elegant, with the sort of poise you only see when a person is either supremely confident with the way they look, or totally unconcerned about it.

'She turns heads, does Grace,' Julia comments, glad of the distraction from her worries. 'But then so do you, dear. Are you two getting to know each other nicely?'

'You could say that,' says Emily. She looks as if she's hiding a smile, but Grace is back before Julia can ask more questions.

There's a comfortable lull in the conversation as they all sip their drinks. The background music is soothing. Julia loves The Carpenters. She's always dreamed of hearing 'We've Only Just Begun' played at Emily's wedding one day. White lace ... promises ... She still hasn't given up on that idea, although it doesn't seem to be happening any time soon.

Grace clears her throat and Julia looks up, startled out of her reverie.

'Are you all right, dear?' she asks. 'Tickly cough? I hope you're not coming down with something.'

'No, I'm fine, thank you. Julia, I've been telling Emily a few details about myself and the reason I'm here. Do you mind if I fill you in too? Only, I think it's important that you both understand why it's so important for me to be in Pengelly. You've already been very kind and welcoming. I don't want there to be secrets between us.'

'Of course you can. Go ahead. I'm all ears.' She pats

Grace's hand and waits. As Grace's story unfolds, Julia opens her eyes wide and tries to stop her mouth dropping open. May's daughter? 'But ... surely that's ...'

Eventually, Grace stops. The Carpenters are singing about saying goodbye to love. Julia takes out a beautifully laundered handkerchief and blows her nose as delicately as possible. Goodness, what a revelation. It quite puts her own news in the shade.

'I'll need a bit of time to take all this in,' she says.

'I know the feeling,' Emily agrees. 'It gives us a whole new angle on May's character.'

'But I hope that'll help to jog your memories so you can tell me all about her.'

Julia purses her lips. That's all well and good, but there are quite a lot of things about May that nobody needs to dig up, least of all a daughter. A sudden horrified thought occurs to her. Grace must never find out what really happened to Charles.

Chapter Seventeen

The next morning, Grace dresses with more than usual attention to detail and applies her light make-up with care. The need to start her investigations properly has been weighing heavily on her mind, especially after the gruelling session in the pub with Emily and Julia.

'Morning, Grace,' says Emily breezily, as she approaches the breakfast table. 'I've made pancakes – are you interested? You can either have maple syrup or lemon juice. Excuse my pyjamas, I overslept this morning.'

Grace is relieved Emily isn't treating her any differently now she knows about May, but she isn't sure if she can face eating while the thought of what she might be about to find out fills her head. The sight of the stack of golden brown pancakes changes her mind, and she feels considerably more ready to face the day when she's eaten two and had a good strong mug of coffee. James joins them and eats silently, reading the newspaper he's arranged to have delivered.

'You'll have to excuse the lack of chat. Apparently,

he's sometimes like this first thing in the morning. Robyn did warn me,' whispers Emily, sitting down next to Grace with her own plate.

'I heard that. I might be a bit loopy but I'm not deaf,' James mutters, but Grace notices he's hiding a grin. Yesterday's outing must have done him good.

When they've cleared the table, James disappears quite sharpish and Emily heads upstairs, leaving Grace alone in the kitchen. It's Saturday morning, so she's not entirely surprised to hear Tamsin knocking at the door before letting herself in, followed by Andy.

'Is Emily around?' he asks Grace. 'We're meant to be going shoe shopping for Tam this morning.'

'Yes, we've just had breakfast. I heard the shower running a couple of minutes ago. Shall I shout for her?'

'I'll go,' says Andy, and is up the stairs before Grace can stop him. She gazes at Tamsin's cross face.

'So ... new shoes?' she says brightly. 'That's fun, isn't it?'

'I wanted to go just with Dad, not Emily,' says Tamsin, kicking the table leg.

'Hey, don't be cruel to Emily's table,' Grace says, wishing Andy would come back. Dealing with grumpy seven-year-olds isn't something she shines at.

'It's not Emily's, it's May's really,' says Tamsin, sitting down at the table and reaching for the last pancake.

She trickles maple syrup onto it, rolls it up and eats it in two bites.

'Oh yes, I'm hearing a lot about May,' Grace says, delighted to find a new person to sound out about her mother. 'Was she your friend?'

'Yes. She looked after me when I finished school some days. We had cake.'

Tamsin's face and fingers are sticky now and Grace wonders if she ought to find a cloth to clean her up before the others come back, but Tamsin hasn't finished talking.

'May liked collecting things,' she says. 'She had lots of them.'

'Really? What sort of things?'

'Oh, just stuff. Like that little mirror up there.'

Tamsin points to a heart-shaped mosaic on the wall with a small round mirror at its centre. 'That was my mummy's. Dad didn't notice it had gone. May wanted it. I saw her take it one day.'

'Did you?' Grace feels shivery now. 'Why didn't you say something?'

'Oh, I didn't mind. She wanted it very badly, I could tell. And I knew I could still come and see it here. We didn't have it on the wall at home and it looks nice up there. May used to take it down and hold it sometimes. It made her eyes go all funny.'

'How do you mean?'

Tamsin thinks for a moment, searching for the right words. 'You know when you're thinking about something else when you should be listening? My teacher calls it daydreaming but it's usually when I'm wondering what's for my tea. Like that. All misty.'

Grace has almost too much to think about now, but she can't get any more questions out before Andy and Emily appear, bright eyed and pink in the face.

'Right, let's go. Shoe shop here we come,' warbles Emily, smiling at Tamsin, who glowers back.

The shopping party leave, letting the door slam behind them. It's very quiet once they've gone, and Grace sits still for a few minutes, absorbing what she's heard. It only goes to underline what Emily's already told her. Being a collector of memorabilia is one thing, but surely this smacks of kleptomania? Why did May feel the need to take other people's possessions? It doesn't sound as if she was out to pilfer valuables, so what could the point have been?

Grace tries to shake herself out of this disturbing train of thought but the idea of her mother possibly having had a serious problem like this is mind-blowing. She'll need to discuss all this further with Emily, and anyone else she can find who's willing to speak frankly about May. She's about to make a move to explore the village in more depth and find someone else who might know of her mother's peccadilloes when Tristram arrives, kissing her on both cheeks and going straight over to put the kettle on.

'So, Grace, are you ready to have a proper chat with me or am I rushing things?' he says, as he waits for it to boil.

'Pardon?'

'It's fine if you want to shelve it for now, but I'm getting the strongest feeling you might need my help. Tell me to sling my hook if I'm wrong. I'm an interfering old bugger sometimes, or so Julia tells me.'

'Has Emily been talking to you?' Grace feels a painful lurch of disappointment at the thought that her new friend has spilt the beans so quickly when yesterday's revelations were meant to be in confidence, but Tristram looks surprised.

'No, what about?'

'Oh, nothing. What do you mean, then? I don't understand.'

He leans forward to pour the coffee. 'Grace, I'm eighty, I've been married four times and I'm well used to smokescreens. You're not suffering from the usual type of stress, are you? Although I do get the feeling there's a lot of tension here. So what's the real problem?'

Momentarily relieved that Tristram doesn't appear to know about her quest, it takes Grace a moment or two to register the last question. 'The real problem?' she repeats, playing for time.

He pulls a wry face and waits.

'You think I've got other difficulties?' Grace perseveres.

'I know for sure you have.'

'But ... how?'

'Apart from learning about life by making a lot of mistakes with my relationships, I've been in the restaurant business for a long time. I'm a people-watcher, Grace. It's the way I've always worked, learning what my regulars like, how their minds work, making each customer feel special.'

'And your point is?' The snappy tone of Grace's voice makes Tristram blink, but he carries on.

'I've talked about this from time to time with my friends George and Cliff who run the other local restaurant, Cockleshell Bay. They do the same. We can tell a lot about a person by the way they come into a room, how they sit, how quickly they order. We read them.'

'And you've read *me*? Really?'

He smiles. 'Don't be like that, Grace. Sarcasm doesn't suit you.'

The only sound is the seagulls crying and the rhythmic ticking of May's old clock. Grace mentally braces herself. There's no way she's telling this comparative stranger about the years of fighting off the tide of other people's memories, the disbelief of the doctors she's consulted, her reluctance to make close friendships in case she is forced to explain about her odd gift ... or curse. Her head is pounding unbearably now, with the effort of staying silent.

'I don't like the thought of you *reading* me against my will,' she says eventually. 'It's too weird.'

'I'm sorry, I honestly didn't mean to make you uncomfortable, but you're a fascinating woman, Grace, and whatever your problem is, I'm guessing it isn't going to go away overnight, however relaxing it is here for you. Have you got time to stick around in Pengelly for a good long time? I think you said you weren't on a deadline to get home? Will you stay with us for a while?'

Grace nods. At this moment, alone in her beige flat is the last place she wants to be.

Tristram sits quietly for a while and Grace at last begins to feel herself unwinding a little. She's almost falling asleep when the image of an elderly lady floats into her mind. Perfectly coiffed hair, styled in the way that many women of that age still have, suggesting the use of a lot of curlers and some time under an old-fashioned domed hairdryer. Grace has a feeling that this is someone she would love to meet, with her knowing eyes and the mischievous smile that melts Grace's heart with its shrewd kindness. Is it May? Can this really be her mother? She opens her eyes, suddenly alert. Tristram is staring into space.

'What are you thinking about?' she asks.

Startled, he looks across at Grace. 'Oh, nothing much,' he says, standing up. 'We'll talk again soon.'

He raises a hand in farewell and leaves the room without a backward glance. Grace's eyes close in exhaustion. Just as she's slipping into a light doze, she hears the door open again.

'One more thing,' says Tristram quietly. 'I want you to know that if you do decide to confide in me, of course anything you say will be treated with the strictest discretion. If I can help, I will. However serious the issue is. I don't judge, Grace, I've made too many mistakes myself.'

Grace looks up at him, seeing the warmth in the twinkling eyes. 'I don't think I've made any big mistakes,' she says. 'You seem to be assuming I've got a terrible skeleton in my cupboard. But thanks anyway. I appreciate your kindness more than I can say.'

'Oh, good.' Tristram looks surprised but gratified. 'I was afraid you were going to tell me to mind my own business.'

'Not at all. I'm beginning to figure that everyone shares their business in Pengelly.'

'That's true, and I can see that must seem a bit claustrophobic to you at the moment. Look, I must go now, but you know where to find me if you do want to talk. And remember, I'm completely discreet. When I need to be, that is.'

He grins at Grace and leaves the room for the second time. She lets out a long breath. Relief that she's escaped the inquisition mixed with a growing sense of purpose fills her soul. If that really was a glimpse of May drifting into her subconscious, she must be getting closer to discovering more about her mother. The journey is really beginning now.

Chapter Eighteen

By the time Julia gets a chance to tell Tristram about Will's visit, she's worked herself up into a state of high anxiety. There are too many subjects from their shared past that she would rather not revisit, not least the tangled set of events that led up to Charles's death and Will's sudden disappearance. She glances down at the opal ring on her finger. 'You've got a lot to answer for,' she tells it.

Her thoughts are briefly diverted when Emily texts to say the shoe shopping has been a complete disaster. It was going unexpectedly well, with the promise of an ice cream sundae afterwards, but then Emily felt honour bound to side with Andy when Tamsin chose a pair of strappy glittery sandals for school and now the little girl seems to hate her more than ever.

Julia heaves a deep sigh. As Tristram lets himself in and comes through to find her in front of the fire, she opens her mouth to pour out all her worries, but stops short when she sees the tortured look on his face.

'Whatever's the matter?' she gasps.

'I've had to cancel the food-tasting session. It's Ken.

He's had a fall in his care home up in Stockport and he's in hospital. Sounds as if he's at death's door. I'm going to have to go up there. He's got no other relatives alive now.'

For a few seconds, Julia can't think who Ken is, and then it comes back to her. The memory of the taciturn cousin who came to stay a few years ago isn't a pleasant one. 'Oh no. What's happened?'

'I don't really know, but it must be bad because he's in intensive care. I need to go straight away. You do understand, don't you?'

Julia doesn't. She nods as sympathetically as possible and refrains, with difficulty, from replying that Ken has only ever contacted Tristram when he wants something, usually money. The thought of Tris having to go dashing up north so suddenly makes her fume inwardly.

Tristram hugs her distractedly. 'And the other thing is ...'

He pauses, and Julia has a horrible feeling she knows what's coming next. 'The dogs,' she says wearily.

'Yes. It's hard enough to keep Buster away from the kitchen with me there on guard, but with the restaurant to run, Gina and Vince can't possibly keep an eye on the boys all the time and walk the pair of them too. Would you mind having them, darling? They'll be living with us after we're married anyway. It'll give you the chance to bond with them.'

'Of course I will. I'm sure Emily and Andy can help with the walking. Off you go, and give my love to Ken, if he's conscious enough to know you're there,' she adds, with an effort. How on earth is this going to work?

'Fantastic. I knew you wouldn't let me down and I wouldn't ask if you hadn't got the young 'uns as back-up. I'll get Gina to drop my lovely boys round later with all their food, and so on. I need to dash.'

Tristram leaves, with one final hug and kiss. Julia hasn't managed to tell him about Will's visit and now it's too late to bother him, with his packing to be done and last-minute arrangements to be made. It's a relief in a way because of Tristram's weird aversion to Will. Julia's never got to the bottom of it, and it hasn't been important before, but at least she'll be able to get her brother-in-law settled in before Tristram's back.

Julia has a momentary pang at the thought of Tris driving all that way up those motorways. At eighty years old, shouldn't he be slowing down by now? Taking a deep breath to stop the tide of worry, Julia reassures herself that her fiancé is the safest driver she's ever travelled with. He's virtually unflappable on the road, and his eyesight is as good as it's ever been. Even so, he'll be shattered by tonight.

She reaches for the phone to ring Emily, and then remembers her granddaughter's earlier text also said she was going up to London after the shopping trip for a few meetings with authors and wouldn't be back until tomorrow night at the earliest. Julia wonders at the writers' willingness to see Emily over the weekend, but they seem happy enough to fit in with her flexible schedule. As she wonders what to do next, Julia hears the front doorbell peal, and groans. Now what?

On the front step stand Grace and James, each carrying a large bag of potatoes. Grace's smile falters when she sees the look of exhaustion on Julia's face.

'I guess you know why we've brought these,' she says. 'Andy's friend at the garden centre dropped them off with Emily to get them ready for the Brownies' and Rainbows' social tonight up at the village hall, but she said you were expecting to do that job. Andy'll fetch them later, you don't need to get them there.'

Julia stands back and motions them inside. 'Will you both stay for a cup of tea? I'd forgotten all about the spuds but I can check them over and get them in the oven while the kettle boils. I could do with some company.'

They follow Julia into the kitchen and without preamble, sit down at the table and offer to help. Julia feels a weight lifting off her shoulders. James and Grace both seem so practical, and now she knows more about Grace's background, she can see May in her, very clearly. It's in the tilt of her head and the curve of her well-shaped eyebrows. Grace even chuckles like May. What a shame she didn't appear sooner. How May would have loved to meet her.

Julia sighs at the sadness of it all, but decides now isn't the time for gloom. She tips the potatoes out, gives both her visitors a sharp knife and instructs them to cut out any bad bits and make a slit round the middles. Within ten minutes, the potatoes are laid out in rows on baking sheets and safely in the oven, but before Julia can put the kettle on, the back door opens and they're suddenly swamped by a mass of wagging tails, delighted barking and licks to anywhere Buster and Bruno can reach.

'Hi, Julia, this is really good of you – although I'm guessing Dad didn't give you a lot of choice?' Gina's cheeks are glowing from her walk along the beach from Tristram's place and Julia thinks, not for the first time, what a glorious sight her soon-to-be stepdaughter is – curvaceous, cheery and full of energy.

'It's fine, I'm sure I'll cope,' Julia says, doing her best to sound positive. Gina hugs Julia, introduces herself to the other visitors and is gone again in a whirl of scarlet coat and black curls.

'Phew, she's a live wire, isn't she?' says James, trying without much success to stop Buster reaching the biscuits. 'Are these two beauties going to be living here for a while?'

'Do you like dogs?' asks Julia weakly, as she removes

the plate and closes the kitchen door, leaving a disappointed Buster on what he clearly sees as the wrong side of it.

'Love them,' says James. He's now on the floor making a fuss of Bruno while Buster has turned his attention to Grace. 'I had a Labrador much like this fella, broke my heart when he died. He was called ...' James pauses, gazing into space. 'Anyway, his name escapes me just now, but that's not important. It was the week after my wife died. Not a great time.'

Grace glances across at him but says nothing. She reaches for his hand and squeezes it. Julia thinks there's something very calm about Grace, as if life's whirling around madly but she's in the centre of it all, in some sort of limbo. What can she be waiting for, though? Julia dismisses the unusually fanciful thought and goes back to worrying about how she's going to cope with Tristram's two best buddies.

As if reading her mind, Grace says, 'We can help, can't we, James?' Buster makes himself comfortable under the table with his head on Grace's feet and Bruno does the same with James. Grace is still hanging on to James's hand, Julia can't help noticing.

He nods enthusiastically. 'Don't worry, Julia, that side of things is easily sorted. But how will you cope with their ... erm ... exuberance around the place?'

'I have absolutely no idea. Bruno's fine, it's just that

Buster does so love eating. He can't resist trying to break into the cupboards, and even the oven and fridge. I'm fond of the little chap, but I don't think my cottage is geared to keep anything edible out of his reach. And now Will's coming to stay too. He's my brother-in-law. I haven't seen him for years. Tristram doesn't know yet.'

Buster turns a mournful countenance towards Julia. A Puggle can say such a lot with just one troubled look. Bruno's tail is beating a happy rhythm on the hearth rug. Her heart melts. She can't let the poor souls down. Then a minor miracle happens.

'How about if we have Buster over at the cottage?' James says, leaning down to stroke Bruno's soft head between his ears. 'Would Emily mind? The kitchen door and the cupboards are old-fashioned and solid, and I can tie the handles together if necessary. Would that help?'

Julia feels such a surge of relief that she has to sit down suddenly. 'I'm sure Em wouldn't mind,' she says, 'but are you sure? This isn't why you came here. It seems an awful imposition.'

James smiles at Grace. 'I don't know about you,' he says to her, 'but I was talking to Tris's doctor friend Tom earlier when we went swimming. He's got a theory that tackling memory problems can be a holistic thing in some cases, and so has this paragon of virtue, Ida, who I keep hearing about.'

'I don't understand.' Julia frowns. She wants more than anything else for Tris to come home and take all this stress away.

'It's complicated. What it boils down to for me is that I've got to face up to this next part of my life instead of fighting it all the time, and the peace and quiet here is making me feel better already. Having Buster around will just be an extra part of the general therapy. I've missed having a pet very much.'

'And I'm more than happy to help,' says Grace. 'I was never allowed a dog when I was growing up because my parents were both allergic to them.'

James lets go of Grace's hand, stands up and stretches his arms out wide. His face lights up. 'Aha! His name was Gregory,' he exclaims, punching the air. 'My old dog, I mean. Grace, did you ...?'

Grace raises her eyebrows slightly and Julia senses a message has passed between the two of them, one that's made them both smile. She looks on admiringly – James seems very fit and strong, especially now he's happy again. His head is nearly touching the ceiling of Julia's cosy living room, and she notices Grace watching James too. Well, they're both single, perhaps there might be a holiday romance in the air? She gives herself a mental shake. Just because Julia and Tristram have found each other and are ridiculously romantic these days, there's no cause to try and pair everyone up.

'I've got an amazing idea,' says James suddenly.

Julia and Grace look at each other with identical alarmed expressions, and then giggle. 'I think we must have both had bad experiences of men saying those words,' says Grace. 'Go on then, hit us with it.'

'Why don't we – I mean you and me, Grace – have an expedition tomorrow with the dogs? The weather forecast's good.'

'A walk, you mean?'

'Well, yes, a walk, but more than that. There must be dog-friendly guest houses further down the coast. We could have a really decent ramble, book a couple of rooms for the night somewhere and either walk back the next day if our legs aren't aching too much, or get the bus home if they are. What do you say?'

Julia watches Grace as James's suggestion takes root. She guesses this is a woman who likes to keep her thoughts to herself. Grace hasn't got a particularly expressive face, but there's no mistaking the mixed emotions flitting across it.

'We don't know each other well enough to go on a jaunt like that, do we?' she says, after some thought.

'Of course we do. I won't talk at you all the time if that's what you're worried about. We can walk along appreciating the sea views and the sunshine, have dinner together later – we know we can do that already – and then have an early night, full of fresh air and ready to sleep. We can have a dog each in our rooms and Buster and Bruno will be out of Julia's hair for a day and a night, and some of the next day too. Tris might even be home by then, or at least not long after.'

Julia holds her breath. It's an odd plan for two almost-strangers, but oh, it would be so good to have the dogs looked after for a while. Grace gets out her phone.

'Oh, I forgot, I can't get on the internet on this. Let's go back and use Emily's laptop,' she says.

'What for?' asks Julia, still befuddled.

'To find some rooms. You're quite right. It's a lovely idea,' Grace says.

James does a brief victory dance, aided by Buster and Bruno, who frolic around him barking excitedly. Julia puts a hand to her forehead.

'Come on, Grace, let's take these two and their food and so on across the road. I think we've outstayed our welcome.'

'You speak for yourself,' says Grace, but she puts Buster on his lead and picks up a bag of dried food and a blanket. 'Right, beasts,' she says, 'looks like we're on the move. This holiday isn't turning out quite as I expected.'

'I feel awful about this,' Julia begins, but James holds up a hand to stop her.

'Ignore Grace,' he says blithely. 'She has an incredible ability to say things that offend people. It's an unusual talent, but you get used to it after a while.'

Grace tries to clip him round the ear but her hands are full. 'He's right though,' she says, 'I need to stop doing that. Honestly, this is fine, Julia. The expedition will be great. I'll take Buster out as soon as I've looked into accommodation for tomorrow night and James can walk Bruno in a little while.'

'Well, if you're sure?'

Julia watches them go with huge relief. She goes to the front window to see them safely inside Curiosity Cottage and notes, with a small smile of approval, that James holds the door open for Grace and takes charge of both dog leads so she doesn't get tangled up on the step. A true gentleman, like her Don had been, and like Tristram too, even if he is rather more fiery. Julia knows a good man when she sees one. She only hopes Grace does too.

Now to gird her loins for Will's visit, the thought of which is giving her butterflies again. At least Tristram isn't around to resurrect the old tension between the two men, but it won't be long before they come face to face. Julia resolves that whatever happens next, she'll dig out the root of the problem. Mercurial and occasionally quick-tempered, Tristram has always appeared to be magnanimously forgiving of anyone who annoys him and usually calms down as fast as he gets cross. This is the only time she's ever known him to bear any sort of grudge. What can have caused this long-drawn-out animosity? And even more interestingly, does Will still feel the same?

Chapter Nineteen

Grace clips Buster's lead to his collar an hour later and leaves the cottage with a difficult task achieved. Finding a dog-friendly place to stay hasn't been a straightforward matter, but she's finally managed to book two rooms in a seaside town about ten miles down the coast. She wonders what's got into her, agreeing to spend so much time with someone she barely knows, but it's done now, and James is so happy about his plan that she can't bring herself to be a wet blanket.

'I'll get Emily's maps out while you go for a walk,' he says, 'and when I've planned the route, I'll go out with Bruno. Shall I call for fish and chips on the way back?'

Grace thinks this is an excellent idea. Deciding what to eat later seems like a job she doesn't need. The visit to Julia's proved to be draining, to say the least. Giving James his memory of the long-dead Gregory needed a huge amount of energy, but the sense of achievement is still with her.

She catches sight of Buster's happy off-on-a-walk

face, tongue lolling and eyes bright, and she can't resist letting him loose and running with him right down to the water's edge. Skimming stones keeps Grace amused while Buster frolics in and out of the waves, barking at the breakers as they come in. Each new one seems to surprise him, and Grace begins to laugh, feeling a wild sense of freedom but at the same time, more peace than she's experienced for a very long time.

Maybe a puppy or, better still, a rescue animal is what she needs? But before that would have to come a proper home. A flat's no place for a bouncy dog. Distracted by the fresh breeze ruffling her hair, she rummages in her coat pocket for a bobble but when she looks up again, Buster isn't playing in the sea any more. Horrified, Grace turns to call him, realizing he's heading off at a gallop towards the far side of the bay. He ignores her, apart from a brief triumphant glance over his shoulder.

'Buster! Come back here, you crazy dog,' Grace bellows, jogging after him across the damp sand. Cursing her own stupidity, she remembers that Tristram's restaurant is in this direction, right on the headland. Buster's going back to base, of course he is. Chest heaving, Grace chases after him, only catching up when he finally comes to a halt by a picket fence. Luckily, the gate to Tristram's place is shut, which gives Grace time to get Buster safely back on his lead.

'Bad boy,' she tells him. The little dog looks up at her and nuzzles her hand. 'No, it's bad me, isn't it?' Grace says. 'You were just being sensible and going home for tea, weren't you?'

'Did you say you'd come for tea?' a voice asks, and Grace spies Tristram's daughter Gina coming across the yard, now clad in an all-enveloping pinafore. 'He's like a boomerang, this one,' she says, pointing to Buster. 'I should have warned you that he'd do this. Come in and get your breath back before you go off again, the kettle's on.'

Gina puts Buster safely in his run and she and Grace go into the warm kitchen. There's a wonderful smell of bread baking. Grace sniffs rapturously. 'Herbs?' she asks, 'Tarragon, maybe?'

Gina nods. 'Well done. You've got a sensitive nose. It's the speciality loaves for tonight's menu. I make them to sell in the village too. It's a shame one of my best customers isn't around any more to enjoy them.'

'Oh? Who was that?' Grace asks the question even though she thinks she can guess the answer.

'May Rosevere. She lived in the cottage where you're staying. I expect you've heard about her already. What a character she was. Dad and Julia miss her an awful lot, I think.'

'Yes, I got that impression. Did you know her well?'

Gina pulls a face. 'Yes and no. I knew her tastes in

bread, that's for sure. I once sent over a loaf that was slightly overdone, and she returned it right away and refused to pay for it.'

'She sounds a bit scary.'

'Not at all. She just liked things to be done properly. And also, she didn't like people to know it, but she had a full set of false teeth. Hard crusts were impossible for her to chew. I didn't make that mistake again. May was a character. There won't be another one like her, more's the pity.'

Grace digests this information, mentally adding it to her stock of snippets about her mother as Gina puts a steaming mug of tea in front of her and sits down opposite with one of her own. 'I can't have much of a rest because there's a lot to do yet. Vince has gone to the wholesale store, and with Dad away, I'm suddenly realizing how many little jobs he does around here every day. He never seems to run out of energy.'

She glances at the clock. Grace sips her tea and tries to decide what she can safely get away with asking, if there's only limited time before Gina bustles off again.

'You were talking about May Rosevere. Was she an energetic person too?' she finally comes up with. 'Only, there does seem to be a trend in Pengelly for lively older people. Your dad, Julia, Angelina ... Vera's still working in the shop and she must be heading for eighty? And

I keep hearing about someone called Ida who seems to hold Pengelly together all on her own.'

'Oh, you'll love Ida. Just don't let her sign you up for any jobs if you're planning on staying for a while. I think she runs on pure adrenaline. As for May, she always used to say she looked so young because of the Cornish sea air, and her hot buttered toast habit. Well, that and the port. She was a hundred and ten when she died. We honestly thought she'd go on forever, but she just seemed to decide she'd had enough after her heart attack.'

Gina doesn't appear to think Grace's interest is odd, so she risks one more question. 'That's sad. Did she die in hospital then?'

'Oh no, she was determined to be at Dad's birthday do. She wore a fabulous red dress, I remember. She'd easily have passed for seventy that night. Dad was in his element. All his friends turned up and we barbecued on the beach. It was the night he and Julia got engaged. The soppy old devil. I do love Julia, though. She'll be a great step-mum.'

'Did May have lots of admirers in her time, do you think?'

Gina looks at Grace rather oddly. 'Boyfriends, do you mean? Why do you ask that?'

'Oh ... I just thought ... she sounds such a ... a lively person.'

'She was that. Dad says she had an unhappy marriage but he reckons she amused herself other ways. Tom King – you know, the retired doctor, have you met him? – well, he had a bit of a walk-out with May, so they say, and so did the old chap from the pub, the current landlord's grandfather. She used to go off travelling too. Who knows what she got up to while she was away? And why not have some fun?'

This is almost too much information. All these possibilities, and her father might not even have been from this place. May could have met him anywhere. Even Venice, Grace reflects with plunging hopes, thinking of the green glass vase. There's no prospect of any more nuggets of information about May now because Gina's getting ready to start work again and Grace doesn't want to get in her way after she's been so kind.

'Right, I'll collect the wanderer and get him back to his digs,' she says. 'Next time I'll be more careful about where I let him off the lead.'

'Don't worry about it. If you're on the beach, there's not much chance of stopping him coming home. Just give us a knock and come and get him. There'll always be a pot of tea or coffee on the go.' Gina hesitates for a moment and then says, 'I don't want to sound needy, but I think we've probably got a lot in common, you and me. I don't have many friends my age around here. It'd be good to get to know you better.'

Grace feels ridiculously flattered. Is she getting the hang of making friends at long last? First Emily and James, then Cassie, Julia and now Gina. Maybe there's hope for her yet. 'That would be great,' she says. 'I guess my job's meant I haven't put nearly enough time into being sociable. But, Gina, I'm not your age, you know. I'm fifty-four. You can't be much more than late thirties, surely?'

'What? You can't possibly be fifty-four! I'm thirty-nine and I feel a lot older today. How come you look so young? I wish you'd known May – you'd have had a great time comparing beauty tips.'

Grace thinks long and hard about these words as she and Buster walk back along the beach. Regret at coming so close to having met her mother mingles with a fierce desire to find out everything she can about her. Not only that, but there must surely be someone here who knew May well enough to remember her being pregnant. Why wouldn't she want to keep a child? In the letter she just says she wouldn't be a good mother, but that seems a thin excuse for jettisoning her baby.

Grace mulls over the fact that May chose to give her child to a couple so far away from her own village. Her mother doesn't seem to have had family in that area, and Grace's home town, while reasonably attractive, could never be described as a tourist hot spot.

Her attention is caught by a small figure dressed in

grey school trousers and a red cardigan hurtling towards her across the beach. It's the sturdy figure of Tamsin.

'Buster!' shouts the little girl, almost falling headlong into the sand as she tries to stop running. The dog is delighted to see Tamsin, jumping up and attempting to reach her face. She kneels down to let him do this and Grace suppresses a shudder as Buster licks Tamsin's chin enthusiastically.

'You're getting your lovely trousers all wet,' Grace says, holding out a hand.

Tamsin lets Grace pull her upright and then starts to brush herself down, getting more sand stuck to her hands than she manages to dislodge.

'Hello, Grace,' she says. 'Dad's over there, he said I could come and see you if I don't go any further.'

Grace looks over to where Tamsin is pointing and sees Andy waving to her. He's perched on the sea wall near Curiosity Cottage.

'I left him there because he's got to read a boring letter from my teacher,' Tamsin says. 'I don't think it's going to make him very happy.'

'Oh. Have you got a day off today?'

Tamsin looks at her feet. 'No. Well, I didn't have this morning. I have now.'

'An unexpected day off? That's even better.'

'Dad doesn't think so. He had to fetch me home.'

'Goodness. Were you feeling poorly?'

'No.'

Tamsin doesn't seem to have any more to say on this subject, but when she sees Grace still looking at her enquiringly, she adds, 'I kicked someone again.'

There's a silence as Grace processes this information, particularly the *again* part. She's had very little experience of children under eleven. Surly teenagers are her speciality but the mutinous expression on this little girl's face reminds her strongly of some of her former charges. Tread carefully, she tells herself.

'Did someone make you cross?' she asks, bending to stroke Buster so she doesn't have to look at Tamsin.

'Yes. It was Storm.'

'Storm? That's never his real name?'

Tamsin giggles. 'I know, it's silly, isn't it? Why didn't they call him Drizzle? Or ... Wet?'

Grace is tickled too. 'How about Downpour? Raining-Cats-and-Dogs, maybe?'

'Or just Drip. That's what he is.' Tamsin isn't laughing now. She stuffs her hands into her pockets and kicks a stone, making Buster jump. 'Sorry, Buster,' she says. 'It's just ... he makes me want to say the baddest words I know.'

'Go on then. It might make you feel better. When I get angry I sometimes go into the middle of the park near my flat and swear and swear until I feel better.'

'Do you? Are you allowed?'

'Who's going to stop me? It helps. Do it. Buster won't mind and your dad can't hear us from over there.'

For a minute Grace wonders if this is a step too far. What right has she got to encourage Andy's daughter to be foul-mouthed? But the unholy glee on Tamsin's face reassures her and she waits for the explosion.

'Erm ... okay then ... BUM!' shouts Tamsin, covering her mouth with her hand immediately afterwards.

'That's the spirit. Keep going.'

Giggling again now, Tamsin whirls round on the spot. 'KNICKERS! PANTS! BOOBIES!' She holds out both arms as she spins. 'WILLIES!' she finishes triumphantly.

'Is that better?' Grace is laughing so hard her stomach hurts, tears trickling down her face. She sees Andy looking at them and waves, hoping he won't come over yet.

'Yes. Thank you, Grace,' says Tamsin, still hiccupping with delight.

'So, are you going to tell me why you kicked young Drizzle?'

Tamsin sniggers again, but then her face falls. 'He always says nasty things. He whispers them to me and Mr Norman doesn't hear him. Then he says he didn't say anything. Liar. That's when I kick him.'

'Just the one person making you cross, then? That's not so bad.'

'Well ... there's a lot of boys who do stuff that's annoying. I don't usually kick the girls, though.'

'Oh. Right,' says Grace, wondering where to go from here. 'What sort of things do they say?'

Tamsin's face crumples. 'About Dad. They say he's got a girlfriend and I'm going to have a new mum. Then they'll have lots more babies and they won't care about me. But you only get one mummy, don't you, and mine's an angel now, or that's what Ida Caramel says anyway. That's not her real name,' she says confidingly, 'it's just what I call her because she goes on a lot of holidays where it's hot and her face gets all brown like toffee.'

'Ah.' Grace feels as if she's slipping into even deeper water now. 'Well, I expect Ida Caramel knows all about that sort of thing.'

'She does. She's in the church choir.' Tamsin nods. 'So Emily can't be one, can she?'

'Can't be what?'

'A mummy. I know she can't because when I was at Summer's house last week I heard Candice say Emily's no angel, even if everyone thinks she is. Do you think Emily's an angel, Grace? She hasn't got any wings. She can't be my mummy, can she?'

'Erm ...' Grace is completely out of her depth now. The pain flowing from Tamsin is excruciating. 'Not the same sort of mum, no, but there are different kinds.'

She decides to really go for it. 'Both mine have died. My mum and dad, I mean,' she adds hastily.

'Have they? Are you sad?'

'Yes. But I'm starting to make some new friends in your lovely village. Like with you and Emily, things change.'

'Do *you* like Emily?'

The stark question surprises Grace and she thinks for a moment before answering, watching Buster barking at the breakers. 'I do like her very much, yes.'

'Why?'

'Because Emily made me feel very welcome when I got here and she's been kind to me. I can tell how much she loves Julia and your daddy and you. I don't think she wants to be another mum, more like a big sister for you, instead? How cool would that be?'

Tamsin looks up at Grace and the sudden hope in her eyes is disconcerting. How have they come so far so quickly? Has Grace said the right things? She holds her breath. 'Julia tells me you make great dens together and you both like playing on the beach?' she adds.

The little girl still says nothing. Grace can feel a memory floating towards her, as elusive as mist. This is one she'd like to experience, to know Tamsin better. She has a strong feeling of kinship with the little girl already, even though they are years apart. Grace concentrates hard instead of blocking the memory and gradually a picture appears in her mind of Tamsin and Emily paddling in the sea, shrieking with laughter as the waves splash their knees. The friendship between the two of them is clear to see, and Grace wonders at what point it soured.

'Just a sister?' Tamsin whispers.

'Yes, I think that'd be a very good start, don't you? I'd have loved a big sister to play with me when I was your age. I'd still like one, actually.'

'Would you? Haven't you got any?'

Grace shakes her head.

'Well then, I'm going to ask Dad if you can be my really big sister, and Emily's too,' Tamsin says, nodding her head decisively. 'Can you make dens?'

'I don't know. I don't think anyone's ever showed me how.'

'I might send Em a message to see if we can train you up next weekend,' Tamsin says. 'She's gone to Big London now but she'll be back by then. But she's not going to be my mum. No way. Okay?'

'Okay,' says Grace, weak with relief.

In unspoken agreement, they turn to walk up the beach towards Andy, calling Buster as they go. Tamsin slips a sandy hand into Grace's and her heart melts.

'Do you want to come to my house for a cup of tea?' Tamsin asks, as they reach the sea wall.

Grace smiles. 'Not today. I think you two have got a

few things to talk about, haven't you?' She looks up at Andy, so tall and muscular, with those amazingly warm brown eyes. Emily's a lucky woman, she thinks to herself, but she's going to have to play it very carefully because if Andy has to choose between Em and his daughter, she has a strong feeling she knows which way it'll go. 'I'd better be off now,' she says. 'Don't forget to text Emily, will you, Tamsin?'

Andy raises his eyebrows but Grace turns away. The rest is up to Tamsin.

Chapter Twenty

Grace peers out of the window the next morning and wonders if her trainers will be substantial enough for the job in hand or if she should try and borrow walking boots from Emily. It's never good going out for a longish trek in strange footwear, though, so she decides to stick with what's comfortable and just add thicker socks. Jeans and a hoodie complete the outfit, and she rolls up her raincoat with her other essentials for a night away.

'What time did you say we were going to set off?' Grace asks James. 'We'd better go as soon as we're ready, hadn't we? I hope we can manage to finish the walk before it gets dark.'

'Manage to finish?' James says in mock disgust. 'I'll have you know I've walked the Pennine Way and the ... something or other coastal path in my time, my good woman.'

'I bet the something or other coastal path was impressive. I haven't heard of that one, but it sounds great.'

He pulls a face at her and Grace reflects that that sort of comment wouldn't have been possible when they first arrived. James is relaxing a little bit more every day, even when his memory lets him down. Curiosity Cottage has a certain calm that's helping them both. Grace's own jangling nerves are soothed by being here and she's realizing that she has probably been suffering from a certain amount of stress and anxiety for years.

'So, do you want to help me remember the name of the path?' James asks, startling Grace just as she's about to share her thoughts with him.

'Erm ... pardon?' she says eventually.

'You did the same trick over at Julia's when I couldn't recall Gregory's name – the one you pulled off when I was struggling to remember the midwife who delivered Davina. I'm not completely daft, you know. Are you going to tell me what's going on?'

Grace chews her thumbnail and wonders what to do now. 'I will, but let's get on with the walk first,' she says, playing for time. 'I always feel more like talking when I'm out in the fresh air.'

'Hmm. Is that a promise?'

With relief, Grace hears the kitchen door open and Julia comes in, calling to them as she enters the sunny living room where they're still sitting at the table amidst a welter of croissant crumbs and sticky jam jars, with Buster lying under Grace's chair in case a crumb or two should fall.

'Hello, we weren't expecting you today. Have you

heard from Tristram?' says Grace, looking for signs of anxiety on the older woman's face.

'Yes, he's staying up in Stockport for a bit longer. My brother-in-law is arriving later today so I'm busy getting his room ready and so on. I almost wish I was coming with you.'

'How are you with map reading? I'm not sure Grace is up to the challenge.'

'For your information, my map reading skills are pretty stupendous,' Grace says. 'And we'll be fine because, don't forget, you've got the experience of the something or other coastal path behind you.'

James laughs. 'How could I forget a walk as memorable as that? Let's get going,' he says. He gives Julia a hug and Grace does the same. 'We'll be back soon to help you with the visitor,' he says.

Julia smiles at them both. 'Goodness, what would I have done without you two today? I think you must have been meant to come here.'

'You could be right,' says Grace, and her eyes meet James's. It's somehow hard to look away.

By mid-morning, having taken the local bus to the starting point of Crofters' Bank, Grace and James are striding down the road towards thick woodland with both dogs on their leads. Puffy white clouds race across the sky, and the morning sun is warm on their faces. James has insisted on carrying all their overnight gear and the dogs' food in his rucksack, so all Grace has in her smaller backpack is their bowls, water and a packed lunch, quickly rustled up after a visit to Vera's shop en route.

'It all looks fairly straightforward,' says Grace. She's folded the map neatly so it's small enough to manage, and James's earlier instructions seem clear. 'We need to head for that gap in the trees over there and then it's through Knight's Wood and onwards until we reach the sea. Then along the beach if the tide's out or the cliff path if not until we get to St Chad's. That's where the hotel is.'

James leans over to look at the map, and nods. 'Sounds perfect,' he says. 'I reckon a good long walk is just what we need. I used to go out for rambles every few days before Dot got sick, but since then I've not felt in the mood.'

They're matching their strides better now, James slowing down a little to allow Grace's shorter legs to keep up. She's a little breathless already. He seems so fit, the breeze bringing more colour to his already weathered cheeks. There's a sparkle in his eyes today that Grace hasn't seen before. As they walk through the opening between two huge oaks, Grace looks up in awe at the canopy of branches over her head. Dappled light falls through them making patterns on the packed earth, and the silence is all-enveloping.

'Unleash the wild beasts,' says James quietly.

Free at last, the two dogs bound away into the trees. 'Should we call them?' Grace wonders, peering into the gloom.

'No need, they need a run. We can just shake the food container and Buster will lead the way back. Let them explore, there's nobody else around.'

Only the sound of their footfall and the distant scuffling of the dogs can be heard as they follow the winding path deeper and deeper into the wood. Neither of them feels the need to speak. Grace thinks this must be her ideal way to spend a day. No noisy people, no chance of a babble of memories assaulting her mind. Then out of the blue she's stabbed by the agony of James's thoughts.

'What's on your mind, James?' she asks, desperate to defuse the painful memory. She conjures up her Italian vision, but somehow it's less effective when she cares so much about the person in question's feelings. This man seems so fragile at times and yet strong and protective at others.

He looks at her in surprise. 'I was just thinking about Davina again. Why do you ask?'

'I thought you looked sad,' she says, hoping the short answer will satisfy him. He seems to swallow this explanation.

'It's hard to accept we're not close any more,' he

says. 'Robyn rubs along reasonably well with her mum so long as they don't have to spend too much time together, but Dot always found Davina hard to deal with. She's kind of prickly, and she's so ambitious at work, you wouldn't believe. I used to be able to talk to her, though.'

'What does she do?' They're talking in low voices, almost as if they're in church.

'She's a vet, a very good one. She's got her own practice now.'

'Oh!' For some reason, Grace had been imagining Robyn's mum as a high-powered executive in a smart suit with a tight skirt and spiky heels. She changes the mental picture to a sort of female James Herriot in cords, wellies and a white coat. 'You must be extremely proud of her, in that case.'

'Yes.'

The one-word answer doesn't help. 'So what's the problem?' Grace persists.

It feels as if they're nearing the centre of the wood, and Grace can hear an unexpected buzz of voices coming from what looks like a clearing in the distance.

'I'm putting that question on hold,' she says. 'But I'll ask again later.'

James rolls his eyes but says nothing. They reach a gate in the fence that's separating their part of the wood from the next and find Buster and Bruno already there, looking hopeful.

'Did you pack their treats?' asks Grace.

James rummages in his pockets while Grace swings the gate open as far as it will go. It's a rustic affair, with a hinged part in the middle that means they'll have to weave their way through separately. James goes first with the dogs following, and as he emerges on the other side, Grace sees where the babble of noise is coming from. A group of men and women of a certain age are gathered around three bench tables, enjoying a picnic and quite a lot of beer.

'Get Buster on the lead quickly,' she hisses. 'You know what Tristram says happens when he sees food.'

James closes the gate behind himself and does as he's told with both dogs, looping the ends of the straps around a fence post.

'Hi guys,' one of the men shouts. 'How're ya doin'?' James turns to see who the owner of the voice is. An elderly man dressed in jeans and a brightly patterned kagoule is waving to them.

'Hello there,' James responds.

He's about to hold the gate open again for Grace to come through when the same voice booms, 'Hang on there, buddy. Ain't you forgetting something?'

Laughter echoes around the clearing. James frowns. 'I'm sorry, I'm not with you,' he says.

'It's a kissing gate. That means you can't go through it without *kissing* the beautiful lady. You hafta do it. We all did.'

'Yes, and I got the short straw,' bellows the woman by his side, nudging him so hard he almost falls off his seat.

'Visitors from across the pond,' murmurs James. 'I guess we're the local colour. What shall we do?'

Grace dimples at the small group and then reaches up to put her hands on James's shoulders, turning him around to face her.

'Just pretend,' she whispers. 'They can't see from there if you're actually doing it.'

He looks down at her for a moment and then, before she has time to sidestep, pulls her closer. Grace's eyes close automatically as she feels James's lips on hers, firm and warm. The kiss only lasts a couple of seconds, but when he lets her go, her cheeks are flaming and her heart's pounding.

Cheers ring out from the watchers on the benches. James ushers Grace through the gate with ceremony, collects the dogs and takes a bow, beaming.

'Thank you, gentlemen and ladies,' he says. 'I'd forgotten about the rules for approaching a kissing gate. That was a bonus to this already fine day.'

They cheer again and James and Grace get several high fives as they pass the picnic tables. Buster turns just as they pass the last one and lunges forward, nearly pulling Grace's arm out of its socket. Before she can stop him, he has half a pork pie in his mouth and is gulping furiously, eyes bulging with the effort of getting rid of the evidence.

'Oy!' The howl of outrage follows them as they hurry away.

'Sorry. Really sorry,' shouts James. Grace sets a cracking pace and at last they're out of sight of the group.

'Hey, it wasn't that bad, was it, apart from Buster letting the side down?' asks James. 'I know I'm out of practice, but I used to be known as quite an expert kisser in my day, I'll have you know.'

Grace doesn't reply, busy avoiding two cyclists and a large Alsatian coming from the other direction at speed. After a few minutes, James turns away from the main path and motions her to follow him up a steeper track. When they round a corner and are in no danger of being disturbed by other walkers, he stops and faces her.

'I didn't mean to upset you,' he says. 'I just couldn't resist. I'm sorry, Grace.'

'It's okay, I'm not bothered at all, forget it,' she says, very much aware of his nearness as he shrugs off his rucksack. She lets her own backpack drop to the ground and rummages for two bottles of water and the dog bowls. Giving them some each, she passes a bottle to

James. He takes it without comment and they both drink.

'Why have we come up here?' Grace says. 'This isn't on Tristram's plan.'

'I wanted to kiss you again but now I've realized that wouldn't be a good idea. Let's go, shall we?'

Grace is lost for words. It's been a very long time since any man has made her heart race, and the thought of it happening again is tempting. Maybe just once more wouldn't hurt. They can agree to put this behind them afterwards and carry on with the walk. They're grown-ups. It's not a big deal. She moves closer to him and slides her arms around his waist. He feels strong and wiry and when he bends to kiss her again, she breathes in the scent of Imperial Leather soap that mingles so erotically with the damp, loamy smell of the woods.

This time James doesn't hold back, and the passion in his kiss is scintillating, making her every nerve ending burn. Grace presses herself against him, letting go completely in a way she can't remember ever having done before. As their hips move together, an electric connection sears through her mind and body. She can feel his thoughts merging with her own. They're not memories this time, but fevered, sensual images of white-hot sex.

Gasping, she breaks the connection and stands back holding a hand against her chest.

'Did you feel that?' she gasps.

'I felt quite a lot of things,' he says, grinning. 'I've got to say that was easily the most dynamic kiss of my life. Could we do it again, do you think? Or failing that, I'll accept a few of your secrets in lieu.'

She shakes her head. This is too much to handle. 'Let's carry on with this lovely walk and get to the sea. The dogs are whining. We can have lunch and see how things go.'

The prosaic mention of food seems to be enough to convince James that this isn't the time to push his luck. He shrugs philosophically and helps Grace on with her backpack before wriggling into his own and leading the way back down the track.

Torn between relief and disappointment that he was so easily deflected, Grace follows, willing her face to stop glowing. That fierce connection with James and his thoughts has left her reeling. Why this man, and why now?

Chapter Twenty-One

Grace and James reach the brow of the hill and stop, both out of breath. The dogs are panting too, so Grace gives them another drink. The day is even warmer now, but the breeze across the wide open space lifts their hair and cools their cheeks. They gaze at the sweep of the sandy bay with delight.

'It was well worth the climb after all,' says Grace. 'I was beginning to curse you for picking the most difficult route, you sadist, but I'm so glad now that you brought us this way.'

She takes out her phone and takes a series of pictures of the view, plus several of James. Grace can feel the joy emanating from her companion. There's no trace of melancholy now, and he's grinning at her. The connection is still there between them, stronger now. Grace marvels at the feeling. This has never happened before. She's been aware of it as they walked, and the strange thing is that the closer she gets to James's thoughts, the less she seems to feel other people's. They pass two groups of hikers on the road to the coast, and each time, the onslaught of their memories is much slighter than usual, with James's sudden recollection of a route he'd taken with Dot coming out on top.

'Did you and Dot go on many walking holidays?' she asks him, as they let Bruno and Buster off their leads for a good romp and wander down towards some rocks that look like a good place to stash their bags and shoes.

James pulls a face. 'Occasionally, but not if she could help it,' he says. 'We usually went for package deals somewhere hot. Dot liked to lie by the pool and read, then go out for dinner and on to a bar every night to dance. It drove me almost insane. I like exploring in the daytime and then buying fresh stuff from local markets and cooking in the evening. Making the meal last, candles, wine, sitting on the terrace with the coffee and brandy ... you know the kind of thing. Maybe even a few games of cards.'

'Hmmm. It doesn't sound as though all that was very easy. Hard to compromise when one of you is off strutting their stuff on the dance floor and the other one's playing Patience.'

'True. What about you?'

'How do you mean?'

'Have you spent many holidays with partners? What do you like to do?'

'The short answer is no, and I like pretty much the same things as you. Gin Rummy's my game. I'm never beaten.'

'Is that a challenge?'

'Could well be, if you think you're up to it? I take no prisoners when I get going, I'll tell you that for nothing. Now let's paddle. Race you to the sea.'

They scramble out of their shoes and socks, fling them and the bags in a heap on the rocks, and pausing only to roll up their trouser legs as far as they'll go, tear down towards the waves. James wins easily, but he turns to grab Grace's hand as she splashes into the shallows and wobbles, dangerously close to losing her footing.

Laughing, they wade a little further out, still holding hands. Buster bounces along beside them in the shallows but Bruno sits just on the dry side of the shoreline, looking disapproving. The water is icy, but Grace feels the warmth of James's fingers interlaced with hers and has such an overwhelming burst of happiness that she has to stand still for a moment.

'What's up?' he asks, looking down at her with concern. 'Cold?'

Grace shakes her head, in need of a distraction. This is all too much, too soon. 'No, but I'm famished. Shall we go and sit in the dunes and have lunch?'

Backs against a marram grass-covered sandbank, Grace takes more photos and then she and James eat every single prawn sandwich, sausage roll and even the obligatory fruit that Vera insisted they buy. The dogs finish their own food in record time and Bruno lies down for a nap, but Buster sits bolt upright, ears cocked, in case any scrap of food is overlooked.

'Let's have a look at the map and the route again,' says James, brushing crumbs off his shirt. 'There's a pub marked on here just before we hit the town. I could murder a pint.'

'Come on then, it's starting to get a bit too hot out of the breeze. If I stay here any longer I'll have to have a nap.'

'Well, you can if you like, there's plenty of time. I'll lie down and you can curl up next to me, shall I? Bruno's in agreement.'

'No, let's press on.' The thought of snuggling up to James, warm and cosy and full of good food, is almost too hard to resist, but Grace isn't ready for that. It's hard enough to think of sleeping in the same hotel with only a couple of doors between them.

They pick up speed as they walk along the firm sand, jumping the odd small stream and pausing briefly for Grace to pick up shells and pretty stones now and again. The dogs are bounding along way ahead, running back and forth, torn between keeping James and Grace company and going off exploring all the new smells of this gloriously huge beach.

For once, Grace's mind is almost clear. It's a relief not to be thinking about May all the time, and it occurs to her that there's no rush to investigate her mother.

Might it not be better just to settle into Pengelly for a while and see how everything goes? She can play it by ear and ask people about May in a more natural way, if she lets herself relax.

This is the most free time Grace has had since childhood, and it feels good. James is quiet now and Grace isn't picking up any bad vibes from him at all. When they start to see wooden beach houses appearing on top of the cliff and pass groups of people enjoying the warm spring sunshine, Grace braces herself for the increasingly loud cacophony of memories. To her relief, once again the level is manageable.

Only one very elderly lady sitting in a deckchair near the promenade with a newspaper on her lap gives her a problem. She's wearing a battered straw hat and a dress covered in large poppies. Her lipstick is scarlet too. On the face of it, this is a picture of contentment, but underneath the calm surface, Grace can feel the woman's painful memories threatening to spoil her idyllic moment on the beach.

She waves to the lady and receives a half-hearted smile back. 'Lovely day,' Grace hazards, hoping she doesn't get her head bitten off. Bruno and Buster rush up to investigate, and Buster manages to steal a sandwich out of her bag before anyone can stop him.

'Don't worry about it, I couldn't eat them all. He can

have the rest if he likes,' the lady says, scratching Buster between the ears. He looks up at her adoringly.

'Don't encourage him,' says James. 'He's a terrible thief. Are you having a good day enjoying the sunshine?'

'Yes, but I just wish I'd got the energy of those young things.' She points to three children at the water's edge, jumping in and out of the breakers as the tide begins to come in.

'Fancy putting a toe in the briny? I'll escort you if you'll do me the honour, madam,' says James unexpectedly. 'Grace can mind the bags while we go, can't you?'

'Are you joking? Have you seen the state of my old legs? I can't even get my tights on any more to cover them up.'

James laughs. 'I'm way past the age where a woman's legs are the first thing I see. Come on, get your sandals off.'

She wastes no time in doing as he says, after a quick glance to see if Grace approves of this impulsive suggestion. 'I'm Harriet Poynton, but everyone calls me Hattie,' she says, as she and James make their stately progress down to the sea, arm in arm. 'And you are a very kind young man.'

'For that flattering remark I'll carry you on my back if necessary,' he answers.

Grace settles herself in Hattie's deckchair, watching their progress with delight. The dogs circle round them, barking excitedly. She can hear the old lady's squeals of joy as they all reach the sea. Kindness has always been the quality she admires most in others, and it's not often as much in evidence as this.

James and Hattie are both rocking with laughter now, clinging on to each other as the waves make an onslaught on Hattie's long skirt. She tucks it up into her knickers and whoops and the water nearly reaches her knees. Grace feels almost drunk with the happiness that's flowing all the way across the beach from the pair, and from a nearby group of teenagers playing volleyball over to her left. This is so much better than absorbing painful memories every time she's in a busy place, but what can have brought about the change?

When the other two return, still giggling and with the dogs acting as outriders, Grace stands up to make room for the older lady.

'That was terrific fun,' Hattie says, flopping down so hard the chair almost collapses. 'Thank you so much ... erm ...'

She looks up at James vaguely and he stares back. 'You can't remember my name, can you?' he says sorrowfully. Hattie shakes her head.

'Does that sort of thing happen a lot to you?'

Hattie doesn't answer, but her face gives her away.

'Well, I'll be honest, I can't remember your name

either, so we're quits. Do you live near here, Mrs X?' James asks.

Seeming baffled at the change of subject, she nods. 'I'm in the lodges on the edge of the town.'

'Is it on a bus route to Pengelly?'

She nods again. 'Why?'

'Well, I happen to know that there's a newish get-together type of group for people like us. It's at the village hall. I hear the cake's very good.'

'Really? For the oldies?'

'Yup. Well, it's for anyone who needs a bit of company, and we could all do with that. Do you fancy giving it a whirl? Look, I'll give you my number. Think about it and give me a ring.'

'I can do texting, you know,' Hattie says proudly. 'James!' she adds, with a delighted grin. 'That's it, isn't it? Now, I'll give you a clue, my name begins with H and it rhymes with batty.'

'Margaret,' James shouts.

'You silly boy. Guess again.'

'Erm ... it's not Hattie, is it, by any chance?'

They give each other a round of applause and Grace joins in, laughing at their joyful faces. Her heart feels as if it might burst. So much emotion in one day.

'Right, we'd better be off, but promise me you'll give it some thought ... Hattie,' says James, shaking the old lady by the hand.

'Indeed I will, James,' says Hattie. 'Thanks, both, for what you did today. I was feeling so very sad, remembering the good times with my Gerry and the children on this beach, and then you came along and made it better. I'll probably be just as miserable again tomorrow,' she says, with disarming honesty, 'but if I am, I'll give myself a mental slap and make myself remember today. Bye for now, I'm sure we'll meet again. God bless you.'

Grace and James head into the town with Bruno and Buster safely on their leads. They're both deep in thought and Grace hardly notices the crowds and the strings of brightly coloured bunting that garland the promenade, looping between each lamppost.

'Do you believe in all that?' Grace asks James, as they climb the steps that lead to the main road.

'All what?'

'Hattie said "God bless you." Do you believe in God, James?'

He hesitates on the top step, making a traffic jam of holiday makers. Several people crash into him and the leads start to get in a fearsome tangle. 'Whoops, let's keep walking. That's a big question, but yes, I do. That was part of the problem with me and Davina. Can we talk about it later? We missed the pub somehow. Let's go straight to our hotel and have a beer.'

They wind their way up the long, steep road that leads to where Tristram has marked The Queen's Head.

'Here it is, and look at that view,' says Grace, turning to see the wide arc of the bay spread out in front of them. 'I can't wait to have a bath and a cold drink, can you?'

The reception desk is deserted when they enter the lobby of the hotel. There's a sign next to a large bowl of water on the floor saying *Dogs welcome*, and Buster and Bruno waste no time in helping themselves. James rings the bell and he and Grace wait leaning on the desk, cheeks rosy, both overcome with weariness and fresh air.

After another ring and a good five minutes of nobody appearing, James shouts 'SHOP' as loudly as he can and bangs the bell three times. A door opens and a diminutive girl in a waitress's outfit slides out, saying, 'Sorry, I was loading the dishwasher. Can I help you?'

The girl's name badge says *I'm Naomi, have a nice day*. 'Are you staying here tonight?' the girl asks. 'Only, I don't usually do reception. Three people rang in sick today.' She rolls her eyes and seems about to enlarge on this, when James interrupts.

'We need two single rooms, and we need them now,' he says firmly. 'Could you just check us in, please? We've got a reservation.'

'Oh, right. Name?'

'Clarke,' says Grace. 'It was me who booked the rooms.'

Naomi clicks away on the laptop for a few seconds but then shakes her head. 'Nope. Nobody of that name here. When did you make the reservation?'

Grace gives her the exact time and date, and waits again, a creeping feeling of doom washing over her. Did she do something wrong when she phoned?

'I spoke to your receptionist,' she says. 'She said her name was Gloria.'

Naomi looks up and her eyes widen. 'Ah,' she says. 'That explains it. Gloria went home sick that day. She's not great at the job when she's well, to be honest, but when she's got one of her migraines ...' Her voice tails off as she sees James's expression.

'I hope you're not telling us there are no rooms available?' he says. 'Because I am going to insist that you sort this out immediately. It's your mistake, not ours.'

His voice is perfectly calm and even, but Grace can tell that Naomi is rattled.

'But there are no more rooms free,' she says. 'It's carnival week. Didn't you see the bunting and all the lights?'

James doesn't reply. He folds his arms and waits. Naomi blushes and busies herself on the computer again, clicking away rapidly. 'There's just one I guess you could have, but it's the honeymoon suite. It's only free tonight because the wedding party arrive first thing tomorrow. You'd have to be out by nine o'clock for housekeeping to come in.'

'But we need single rooms. We're not a bridal couple. This is insane.' Grace can hear the panic in her own voice but James puts a soothing hand on her arm.

'We'll take it,' he says. 'And we'll expect to have a large discount for this inconvenience. I don't suppose there's a sofa in the suite, is there, Naomi?'

'Oh yes, it's very comfy. It turns into a double bed.'

'Why would you need an extra bed in a honeymoon suite?' Grace wonders aloud. 'Surely that's a bit unnecessary?'

'Couples sometimes bring their kids,' says Naomi.

'Oh. Right.' Grace grins at James. 'I guess I'm just old-fashioned. I didn't think of that. Well, let's get this over with. Can we have the key?'

Naomi hands it over with obvious relief that they're going to leave her alone at last and James leads the way up a wide stairway. Grace follows, wondering how this is going to pan out. She's fighting a sick feeling of dread. Such close proximity with James is going to be very tricky to handle, surely?

James opens the door with a flourish and reveals a large room flooded with afternoon sunshine. There are two long windows, one of which opens onto a balcony. The view of the sea and the vast expanse of sand takes Grace's breath away. The door closes behind them and Grace flops down onto a small sofa just as Buster leaps onto the bed and attempts to devour both foil-wrapped chocolates. James groans and rescues the chocolates just in time, wiping a slobbery hand on his leg. 'You couldn't write it, could you?' he says.

'But James ... I don't ... I mean I don't like ... what are we going to do?'

'Do? We're going to have a lovely hot shower, or maybe a big bubbly bath, put on our complimentary dressing gowns and slippers and order some chilled prosecco. Then we'll feed the dogs, get dressed and go out for fish and chips. After that, who knows? Sometimes, Grace, you just have to let go and see what happens. And I'm more than happy to take the sofa.'

Grace hesitates for a moment and then comes and sits down beside him.

'Do you know what, James? You're absolutely right.'

Chapter Twenty-Two

As the evening draws on, Emily lets herself back into the cottage and revels for the moment in the peace and quiet. The only sound is of Fossil snuffling around the kitchen looking for food, and after she's fed the cat and put the kettle on there's only herself to think about for a change.

She heads for the stairs to her flat while the tea brews, quickly changing into comfortable sweat pants and a baggy T-shirt, then coming back downstairs to pick up a mug of tea and a blanket. It's been a while since she's had time to sit out on the veranda, and the sun was warmer today than it's been so far this year. Andy and Tamsin are out with the Sunday School for a picnic so they won't be back yet. Hopefully Grace and James have reached their overnight stop and Julia should have Will with her by now. She puts ticks by each name on her mental register, resolving to ring Gran in ten minutes. Everyone is accounted for.

Emily settles herself in May's old swing seat, wrapping the fleecy blanket round her knees and sipping her tea slowly while it's still hot. Fossil, hunger satisfied, jumps up beside her and lies down with a contented sigh. Coming home to Pengelly is wonderful, especially now she's got her own little house.

She debates starting on the proof of a novel she's been given to read but then decides to deal with messages first. Her phone has been on silent on the train home but it's constantly flashed with incoming texts and emails. None of them seemed urgent in her exhausted state but she's intrigued to see that there's a more recent email from Tamsin. This is new. Andy's been showing her how to use his computer and will have supervised any messages carefully, but the wording and spelling are all her own.

Hi Em I have bin to the bech and I sor Grays. We need to tork. See you soon, Tam

How puzzling. Emily reads the email again but it doesn't get any clearer. For one thing, it's been a while – much too long – since she's had any friendly communication with Andy's daughter, so that's got to be a positive development. There are no kisses although Tamsin's called her Em, just like she used to. But what's Grace got to do with anything and why do they need to *tork*?

Her other messages are much easier to understand. She's already dealt with the one from Gran saying Will's plane has been delayed but she's arranged a taxi for him, and Andy's text is brief.

Call you later. Love you madly, A. x

There are several more, and Emily works through them systematically as the sun goes down. She phones Julia, knowing she really should go over and meet her great-uncle for the first time, but her grandmother seems to be coping and says the visitor is so tired from the journey he's going to have supper on his lap in front of the fire, and then a bath and a very early night.

That's a relief. Emily is so comfortable she can hardly bear the thought of moving, but a rumbling tummy has almost persuaded her to stir herself when she hears the sound of footsteps and Andy and Tamsin come into view, hand in hand.

'You're home. Hooray!' says Andy, coming over to kiss her on the cheek.

Emily waits for the usual backlash from Tamsin which comes in a variety of forms when she sees her father making a fuss of Emily, but it doesn't happen. Instead, the little girl comes up to the swing seat and says, 'Have you had your tea yet, Em?'

'No, I was just thinking how hungry I am,' Emily answers, somewhat warily.

'We've got leftovers in our bag from the picnic and Dad said if I get my 'jamas on really quickly, he'll make hot chocolate, or he's even got some fizzy wine for you. It's your favourite. Do you want to come round? Fossil can come too.'

Emily doesn't answer immediately. Her eyes meet Andy's over Tamsin's head and he gives a faint nod.

'That'd be great,' she says, 'but Fossil had better stay here. I don't think your kitten – Allie, isn't it? – would really like him to come and steal her supper. I'll put him in the kitchen and give him some tuna for a treat.'

By the time Emily goes round next door, Andy and Tamsin have laid out the remains of their tea on the kitchen table.

'We were going to have a proper picnic on a rug in the living room but our kitten doesn't understand about not lying in the cake,' says Tamsin.

'Oh, and look, here's the youngest member of the family right on cue.' Emily drops to her knees to make a fuss of the adorable tabby that's just bounced through the cat flap. 'Hello, Allie.'

'She's not called that any more,' says Tamsin. 'I've christened her properly, with water and everything. She didn't like it much.'

'No, I guess she wouldn't. What's her new name then?'

'Bonkers.'

'Ah. Very apt.'

The little cat makes a quick run up the door curtain before dropping to the floor and galloping into the hallway. They hear her dashing up the stairs, meowing loudly as she goes.

'Sit down, Em. Would you like hot chocolate or a

nice glass of wine?' asks Tamsin politely. 'Dad says if you choose wine I can pour it, but he'll have to open it cos of the fizz and pop bit. I'll get your special glass, shall I?'

Emily feels as if she's stepped into some parallel universe where everything is lovely. It seems so long since she's been able to be around Tamsin without the air being thick with resentment. Tamsin places an elegant champagne flute with an emerald-green stem in front of her and carefully trickles prosecco into it, tongue out in concentration.

'Thank you, Tam,' says Emily. She wants to hug the little girl, but feels that might be a step too far.

They eat in a companionable silence with the radio playing in the background. Tamsin's eyes are heavy, and Emily steels herself for the inevitable bedtime battle, but when Andy says 'Time to go upstairs, love,' his daughter makes no protest, but comes round to Emily's side of the table.

'I want you to put me to bed, Em,' she says. 'I had a shower this morning so we needn't bother with all that.'

Emily nods, not looking at Andy, and follows Tamsin up to the bathroom. She supervises teeth cleaning and rudimentary face-washing and then sits on the bed as Tamsin collects her cuddly toys, lining them up next to her pillow.

'Do you want a story?' Emily asks.

'No, I need to talk to you. It's 'portant.'

'Right. Fire away then.'

'Fire what?'

'I mean, tell me what you want to talk about, sweetheart.'

'Oh. Okay.' Tamsin settles herself comfortably and says, 'It's about Grace. She's my new friend.'

Emily waits, totally mystified, while Tamsin adjusts the pecking order of teddies slightly.

'She's got no brothers and sisters,' Tamsin says, finally satisfied with the arrangement. 'And neither have you or me.'

'That's true. But why is that 'portant ... I mean important?' Emily remembers that Andy likes Tamsin to use proper words. She's got a tendency to revert to baby talk, which can be cute but sometimes gets a bit twee.

'She says you're like my big sister. Is that right, Em? You're not going to try to be my new mummy, are you?'

Light begins to dawn. 'No, you don't need a new mum, you've had one already and she'll always have that job.'

Tamsin nods. 'So you can be my big sister when you and Dad get married and Grace can be our big, big sister because I think she's lonely. I get lonely sometimes – do you?'

Emily's eyes are full of tears and she can't speak, but a voice from the doorway says, 'That sounds like the best plan ever. So, are you going to marry me, Em, and be Tam's big sister?'

Tamsin turns to Andy. 'Go and get it, Dad. Go on,' she urges.

Andy leaves the room. Tamsin whispers to Emily, 'I told him all this earlier and he was really happy. I think he cried a little bit. Boys do cry, especially if you kick 'em really hard – but I don't do that any more,' she adds hastily when Emily recoils.

There's a pause, and Emily can hear rustling coming from Andy's room. Finally, he comes back in holding a small turquoise gift bag with sparkly edges. He takes from it a leather box and opens it.

'Dad! Don't forget the other bit,' hisses Tamsin.

'Oh. Yes, the other bit.'

Andy drops to one knee in front of Tamsin's bed and opens the box. A circlet of opals glistens inside. Emily draws in her breath, speechless.

'Emily Lovell, will you do me the very great honour of being my wife and Tamsin's big sister?' Andy says, holding out the box. 'I know it'll fit because I borrowed one of your others. I wanted to get an opal one because you love Julia's engagement ring so much. I've had it ages, just in case ...'

He runs out of words, and Tamsin nudges Emily.

'You have to say yes after that bit,' she whispers loudly.

'Yes,' croaks Emily, reaching for the ring. Andy takes it from its black velvet nest and slips it onto her finger. It's a perfect fit. Of course it is.

'Hooray,' shouts Tamsin. 'Well done, Dad. I told you she'd say yes, but if she hadn't, I expect the shop would have given you the money back.'

Emily's laughing and crying at the same time now, and Andy's kissing her and Tamsin alternately. When they've all calmed down, Emily wipes her eyes.

'It must be way past your bedtime, Tam. I'm going to go and check Gran's okay. I feel bad about not going over to meet my great-uncle as soon as I got home, although I think he was quite glad I didn't by the sound of it. She's going to be so excited to see this beautiful ring, though. Then I'm off to bed too. It's been a long day.'

'A nice day,' murmurs Tamsin, already half asleep.

'And tomorrow, I'll make a celebration dinner for us all. Grace and James will be back by then.'

Tamsin opens one eye. 'Can we have veggie burgers?' she says.

'We can indeed. And a cake.'

'And sparklers?'

'What a good idea. Now snuggle down, my pet.'

Andy and Emily both kiss Tamsin and tiptoe

downstairs. 'You're not really going home, are you?' he says.

Emily sighs. 'I don't want to, but let's not push our luck. Have we really got Grace to thank for this about-turn?'

'I think so. I'm sure, knowing Tam, it's not going to be all plain sailing, but it's huge progress. You're going to marry me? Really? Promise, Em?'

They cling together for a moment, and his kisses are deep and warm. Emily can hardly believe this has happened after all the weeks of walking on eggshells around Tamsin.

'It's going to be all right, isn't it, Andy?' she whispers. 'Eventually, I mean?'

'It's going to be more than that, it'll be brilliant. We needn't wait long to get married, need we? Or do you want a big fancy wedding? I don't mind if you do, it's just ...'

'No big wedding, just something simple. And it can be as soon as you like.'

'In church? On the beach?'

'Why not a bit of both?'

Emily kisses her new fiancé goodnight and tears herself away with some difficulty. She reaches the back door of Julia's cottage on wobbly legs, but when she tries the door it's already locked and all the lights are off. Frustrated not to be able to tell her gran the wonderful news and show her the ring, she can't help being relieved that she hasn't had to see her mysterious great-uncle Will. He'll be safely tucked up in bed by now. Tomorrow is plenty soon enough.

Chapter Twenty-Three

Julia tries her best to wait until she thinks Tristram might be awake to make her phone call, but by seven o'clock she's too excited to leave it any longer.

'They're engaged at last, darling,' she says excitedly. 'I can hardly believe it. Emily texted last night to see if I was still awake and then phoned to fill me in on the details when I said yes. She did come round to tell me in person, apparently, but I ... went to bed early.'

Julia listens for a moment, happy to hear that Tristram is as pleased as she is. Then she frowns. 'Well, of course they want to get married as soon as possible, but why should *we* be in such a rush? It's not a race. No, I'm not even going to suggest that. A double wedding? The very idea. Every young couple want their day to be just for themselves, surely?'

Her shoulders slump as her fiancé responds.

'No, Tris, I won't even consider asking them.' She lowers her voice, conscious that the shower has stopped running and she might be overheard. 'I haven't managed to mention it to you yet because it was a last-minute arrangement, but we've had a surprise visit from Will. He got here last night. Isn't that enough to deal with?'

She listens for a moment or two, holding the phone slightly away from her ear.

'Yes, I know all that. Well of course he's staying with me,' she whispers. 'Where else would he go? I couldn't say no.'

The tirade at the other end of the line continues. Julia sighs. She's been expecting this but it's still very wearing. Eventually, she disconnects, exhausted both by her fiancé's outrage at Will's arrival and his passionate view of how soon they should be married. And how could Tristram even think that joint nuptials would be a good idea? It will take months of planning to get two weddings properly organized anyway. You can't rush these things. There'll be invitations to order, the guest lists to sort out, venues and, of course, clothes.

Julia's mind wanders along this last line of thought, blessedly distracted by the shopping aspect of the event. What does a bride of eighty-six wear if she wants to look glamorous without being mutton dressed up as lamb, as her own mother was wont to describe anyone over the age of fifty with flashy tendencies? Cream? Ecru? Oyster? A calf-length dress and jacket? A hat with a tiny veil, possibly. Low-heeled court shoes to match, definitely. She daydreams happily, almost forgetting her earlier panic, until she hears the sound of the back door opening.

'Gran?' calls Emily. 'Are you up?'

'Well, of course I am. I was so excited about your news I couldn't stay in bed a moment after six o'clock. I was going to come over as soon as I'd cleared the breakfast table.'

'Don't put everything away yet, I'm starving,' says Emily. 'Can I have a fried egg sandwich? I've run out of bread and Grace isn't here to do the shopping.'

'Help yourself, darling.'

'Where's Uncle Will? Isn't he up yet?' Emily says, getting out the frying pan and butter dish and going about the task with speed.

'The poor man was shattered last night. He's had a shower and he'll be down any minute. I was going to cook him a full English breakfast, but he says he's vegan now. He's as thin as a scarecrow. Much more glamorous, of course. He always was ...'

As Julia gazes into the past, eyes dreamy, they hear footsteps on the stairs. The man who enters the room is indeed painfully thin but also very elegant, dressed in a well-cut black suit and a snowy white shirt. He's wearing a cravat in various shades of blue and a matching silk handkerchief sticks out of his pocket, perfectly symmetrically.

Emily turns away from the cooker. 'Hello, I'm Emily. Your great-niece,' she adds unnecessarily, holding out her hand. Will takes it and raises it to his lips. The gesture somehow manages to be stylish rather than creepy.

'I'm so pleased to meet you, my dear,' he says, in a voice that has more than a touch of an Irish accent. 'You're just as beautiful as your grandmother described. You were bound to be, descended from such excellent stock, I suppose.' He smiles, and his pale face lights up.

Julia flaps her apron at him. 'Oh Will, you're such a flatterer.' She can feel her cheeks growing pink, and wishes her brother-in-law didn't still have this effect on her. She's always assumed he was gay, but his charisma works just as well with women as it ever did with men when he was a fey teenager. Years of celibacy as a priest must have sparked anguish in the hearts of a lot of his parishioners, Julia imagines.

'Sorry I didn't come over last night. I got engaged,' says Emily, waggling her left hand under Will's nose. He flinches and steps back.

'But that's Mother's opal ring. I … I mean, I thought … Julia must have had that one for ages, surely?'

'This one's new. It's Gran who's wearing your mum's ring.'

Julia holds out her hand too. 'We haven't had it for very long at all actually, Will, because it went missing for years and years. All very strange.'

She waits for a moment but Will makes no comment, so she continues. 'This one is the family ring. I'm engaged to Tristram. I expect you didn't notice it last night. Oh, of course I took it off because I'd been making pastry.'

Will is recovering himself now and a tinge of colour has come back to his cheeks. He sits down at the table. 'So you two ladies have ended up with almost matching engagement rings. How lovely. Congratulations, both of you. When will the happy day ... or should I say *days* be?'

The pre-wedding jitters are back in Julia's stomach again, flitting round madly. 'I expect Emily's got lots of plans already,' she says.

'Oh yes. Andy's completely over-excited about it all. He even suggested we have a double wedding with you and Tris. I thought it was a bit of a weird idea to begin with, but now I've had time to think, it makes total sense.'

'Does it?'

'Yes, it does.' Emily pauses to flip her egg onto a piece of bread, sprinkles it with salt and tops it with an even thicker slice. She slides the whole thing onto a plate and sits down at the table. 'Just imagine, Gran, you and me, floating down the aisle together, arm in arm. It'd cut out all that worry about who'd give us away.'

'But ... I thought ... your father?'

'You must be joking. When has Dad ever found time to come and see us or fit into our plans?'

'Don't talk with your mouth full, dear,' Julia says automatically, as Emily munches away happily. 'And what about your mother? Have you been in touch with her?' Julia has never warmed to her estranged daughter-in-law. Gabriella is back in Bavaria now, in her home town. Julia knows Emily keeps in touch and visits when she can, but it isn't a cosy relationship by any stretch of the imagination.

'Mum's got a lot on. Her husband isn't well and she's running the biergarten more or less single-handed. I told her she didn't need to come. And if Dad was here, he'd only mutter about why she hadn't made the trip. Worse still, imagine if they both came. I'm better off spending my wedding day with the people who make my life better.'

Will is listening to this interchange with interest, looking from face to face as if he's at Wimbledon. 'A double wedding. How marvellous,' he says. 'And Tristram, taking the plunge again. He's ever hopeful, isn't he, darling? Well, I know this time he's hit the jackpot. There's no doubt about that.'

Julia looks at Will sharply. 'I'll get started on your breakfast,' she says.

'No, no ... nothing to eat for me,' he says, waving away the offer. 'Just coffee will be fine.'

'But you're so thin ...' Julia begins, but Will is shaking his head.

'I never eat breakfast,' he says. 'I have a very light lunch, usually toast or some vegetable soup, and then my evening meal about five o'clock. After that, I fast until morning. It's the way I've always been. My house-keeper was very good at fitting around my routine and also keeping my shirts white. Her starching and ironing skills were out of this world.'

'You must be sorry to have left her behind,' says Emily dryly.

'She died, I'm afraid,' Will says.

'Oh, how sad.'

'Yes, it was. I couldn't get anyone else to take the job on, for some reason.'

'No, I meant sad for her, really.'

'Oh. Yes, for her too, of course. Anyway, that's what sparked my decision to come home. Although this isn't really home. I was brought up in the depths of the Midlands.' He pulls a face. 'So parochial, darling.'

Julia makes coffee without further comment. However is she going to manage her guest's routine with Tristram often appearing for dinner in the evening and randomly whisking her off for long, decadent lunches in either his own restaurant or his friend George's bistro along the coast? Emily seems to be thinking the same thing.

'I haven't had a chance to suggest this to Gran,' she says tentatively, 'but do you think it might be better if you stayed across the road with me at my cottage, Uncle Will? I run a B&B now and I have two guests staying already, but there's a third room free.'

'Why do you think that would be a good plan?' asks Will, as Julia prays inwardly for him to say yes. 'This good lady has a perfectly good spare bedroom, although the sheets are clearly not made of Irish linen. It's the best in the world,' he says to Julia. 'You should try it. Well worth the extra money, you'd find.'

Julia can't think of a polite answer to this. She puts the coffee pot down in front of Will with rather more force than is necessary. 'I don't suppose you take milk?' she asks, with icy politeness.

He shakes his head. 'I'm lactose intolerant and gluten free these days, but I follow a vegan diet anyway, so if I'm going to have milk in anything, it's usually of the almond variety. You can get that in the village, I presume?'

'Yes,' says Julia, holding onto her patience with some difficulty. 'We have moved into the twenty-first century in Pengelly. Vera even stocks tofu now. Emily, that's a very kind offer. Will is always welcome here, of course he is, but the routine of your cottage might suit him better. More freedom, and ... erm ... a bathroom of his own, and so on,' she adds vaguely.

'I thought so. You can get your own coffee whenever you wake up, Uncle Will, and make lunch and dinner as it suits you. Gran can't easily change her routine.

She's with Tristram a lot of the time so she wouldn't be available.'

Will shakes his head. 'But I can't cook for myself. I got into a terrible muddle after Mrs Dingle died. I did try,' he says sadly. 'I had to throw some of the saucepans away.'

'I think it's probably time you learned, in that case. When you go back to Ireland, you'll be needing to fend for yourself, won't you?'

'Yes, I suppose so,' says Will. He doesn't sound convinced.

'So that's settled. I'll help you take your luggage over after I've finished my sandwich.'

'Thank you, my dear.' Will glances at the remains on Emily's plate and shudders. He seems to be casting around for a new topic of conversation. 'So how is Felix these days, Julia? I remember Emily's father as a very handsome baby.'

Julia sighs heavily. Her only son is probably the most selfish person she's ever met. Charming, yes. Hard-working, most definitely, and generous to a fault with money – Felix is always more than willing to put his hand in his pocket when necessary. But sensitive of his family's feelings? Sadly, not at all. She goes back to the subject at the forefront of her mind – weddings.

'He's well. Very busy, as ever. But Emily, surely you should at least ask him if he wants to give you away?'

'I *have* asked. He's on a long business trip to the Far East, as he calls it, from the end of May until late October. Anyway, let's not worry about that now. Have you finished your coffee?' Emily asks Will. 'Right, let's go. I'll come upstairs with you and help pack your bag and we'll get you settled across the road. You'll love it,' she says, in bracing tones.

'I'm sure I shall,' he says, getting to his feet. 'I'm sorry my visit has put you out, Julia. That wasn't my intention.'

'Not at all, I don't want you to think you're in the way. It's just that, as Emily says, my own lifestyle is much more chaotic than it used to be.'

'And Tristram likes to have Gran to himself in the evenings, to be honest,' says Emily, grinning at Julia. 'They're a right pair of love birds.'

'How marvellous for you,' says Will, blanching slightly. 'Come on then, Emily, lead on. I'm putting myself in your capable hands.'

'And tomorrow evening you must come over here for dinner with Grace and James when they get back from their adventure. They're Emily's guests. Oh, but it might be too late for you to eat by that time. You'll probably want to get your own meal.'

Will winces. 'I can see I'm going to have to make some adjustments to my routine,' he says. 'So long as you don't mind making a meat-, fish- and dairy-free alternative, I'll be happy to join you. Do Grace or James cook at all, by the way?'

'You'll have to discuss that with the two of them,' says Emily. She exchanges smiles with Julia. 'I'm sure you can come to some arrangement together.'

Chapter Twenty-Four

Grace and James sit side by side on their balcony, wearing their fluffy white bathrobes and complimentary slippers. Both dogs are sleeping peacefully at their feet for the moment. Grace has washed and dried her hair and it's shining in the evening sunshine. She can see James looking at her admiringly out of the corner of her eye as he tops up her glass. The bottle is nearly empty, and a warm glow from the wine, the blissfully hot shower and the day's fresh air has made their faces glow with health.

'You are so beautiful, Grace, do you even begin to get that?' James says quietly, taking her hand in his.

For a while they sit in silence, revelling in the image of the sun slowly setting over a calm sea. There are still plenty of people on the beach, some playing cricket, some walking along the waterline, but most just doing what James and Grace are doing and watching night fall on this glorious day.

Grace turns to face James, disengaging her hand gently. 'I think it's time we got dressed and went to find some dinner,' she says, hearing her voice sounding unnecessarily chirpy.

'We could do that. Or we could ring for room service and just stay here, together?'

That last tentative word encourages Grace to bite the bullet and be honest with this kind-hearted, vulnerable man. She stands up, so that she's not tempted to follow her instincts and put her arms around him.

'I'm going to tell you something a bit odd now,' she says. 'You'll think this is very strange, I'm sure, but I've never spent the night with a man.'

He looks up at her, his face a picture of disbelief. 'You're kidding me? A stunning woman like you? You're surely not a ...'

She laughs. 'No, I'm not a virgin. I've had a few very brief flings, but nothing serious. And when it came to the crunch, I always went home. They never visited my flat. That's always been my refuge. I have certain issues with being in company for too long. I'm not what you think, James. I know I seem confident, and I am up to a point, but relationships aren't my thing.'

'Oh. Well, that may have been your past, but it doesn't mean to say it's your future, does it?' He pauses. 'Or is there more to it than that? Are you just worried about hooking up with a man who can't even remember what he read in the paper yesterday?'

'Don't be daft. It's not that.'

Grace retreats into the room and James follows, settling on the sofa. She puts her hands in the pockets of her robe and walks over to the far window. The view is of the distant hills, with rows of houses snaking up to the furthest point of her vision. Lights are coming on here and there, and there's smoke coming out of the occasional chimney as the evening chill begins to make itself felt. All those people, Grace thinks, all leading their own separate lives, happy with their families, or not, as the case may be, but none of them with my problem.

If only she could have found May and talked to her before it was too late. Just to hear her mother's voice would have been wonderful. Would she have sounded very Cornish? Well, of course she would, living down here for most of her life. You can tell a lot about a person from their accent and turn of phrase.

'Grace? Are you going to tell me more or do I have to guess what your "certain issues" are? I've got a few thoughts of my own about what makes you unique, of course, but I'd like to hear it from you.'

She comes back to join him on the sofa. The mood's broken now so she's quite safe. Should she come clean about why she's so different and why she's here in Pengelly? Suddenly, she knows she must. Instinct tells her that friendship with this man is probably going to be the best thing that's ever happened in her life, even if it never goes any further. He's damaged too. The hurt in his eyes isn't hard to see, and the mist of forgotten memories troubles him constantly. He deserves the truth.

'I tell you what,' Grace says, using the phrase her adopted father loved so much. 'In my view, the very best thing to do now is for us to get some clothes on, buy a bottle of wine and some fish and chips and go and sit on the beach. We can give the dogs a quick run so they sleep tonight. Then I'll tell you everything. I can't do big revelations on an empty stomach.'

James looks somewhat alarmed at the last sentence but they're soon dressed and out of the room, hurrying down the stairs as a frighteningly loud band strikes up their first song in the bar. Buster begins to yelp in alarm.

'I think we picked an excellent time to leave,' James says, pulling a face. 'Come on, we'll go to the chippie with the biggest queue, that's how I always decide. Then we'll be sure that the chips are fresh and hot if everyone else knows it's a good place too. You can wait outside with the beasts.'

Fifteen minutes later, they're sitting as far as they can be from the crowds and opening the wrappings of what Grace already knows will be one of the best meals of her life. Buster's nose is twitching but Grace tells him firmly that he's had his dinner already. The colours in the sky are fading gradually, soft apricots blending into indigo and violet. The night is much cooler now and she's glad of her hoodie. She sniffs rapturously, the sharp tang of vinegar setting off the comforting fragrance of perfectly cooked fish and chips.

They eat in silence, and as is happening more and more when she's with James, Grace is hardly troubled by stray memories from others around her. Sometimes, a passing couple's thoughts interfere with her peace but she's able to bat them away without too much effort. A deep sense of calm is emanating from James, overlaid with a tingle of anxiety. He knows she has difficult things to tell him.

Eventually, they lick their fingers and wipe their hands on the paper napkins provided by the efficient lady behind the counter at the shop and James hurries to the nearest litter bin before the dogs can delve into the leftovers. When he comes back, he pours red wine into two plastic cups he's begged from the off licence. Now there's nothing left to distract them, and James settles himself more comfortably on the sand.

'Go on then, let me have the secret, whatever it is. I can take it, love.'

The endearment, tripping off his tongue so naturally, makes Grace's eyes smart.

'Okay. I'll try and keep it brief.'

'No need, is there? We've got all night.'

She nods, and starts to speak. As the words begin to

flow and Grace pours out the bizarre story of her years of confusion about her strange gift, her consultations with doctors, all useless, her belief that her birth mother was dead, and then the later developments after May's letter. She ends with her decision to travel to Pengelly to find out as much as she can about her mother and solve the mystery of who her father might be. When she finishes, James says nothing for what seems like an age. Grace waits, not daring to look at him.

At last, he clears his throat. 'Well, that's a tale and a half,' he says. 'And now it's obvious why you were able to give me some of my memories back, I suppose. It was because you had them in your head already, wasn't it?'

'Yes, but you're the first person I've ever tried to do that for. I'm not sure if I can do it for just anyone, or ...'

'Or because you know we've got something special between us?' James finishes.

She turns to face him, and sees to her relief that he's smiling, but there are tears in his kind blue eyes. 'You poor love,' he says, holding out his arms.

Grace slides into them, and with her head on his shoulders, cries like she never has before, letting the years of pressure and uncertainty about herself melt away, at least for now. Both Buster and Bruno sidle closer and put their heads on her lap, licking her free hand. When Grace's sobs are settling down to the odd gasp and sniff, James passes her a perfectly ironed handkerchief and says, 'Right, I'm glad we've got that out of the way. I get the feeling a good old wail was just what you needed.'

Grace moves away from him slightly and dries her eyes, blowing her nose noisily on the soft folds of cotton.

'How romantic,' says James, smiling at her. His eyes crinkle when he grins and the lost expression leaves his face, she reflects, looking at him with deep affection.

'So you see, that's why I can't be anything but a friend to you, at least not until I've sorted myself out and found out who I really am,' she says.

'Have I asked you to be anything else?'

'No, but ...' she glances at him and sees that he's laughing.

'I'm joking. You know I'd like nothing more than to tumble you into that enormous bed and spend the night persuading you that my company in the bedroom is an excellent idea,' he says, 'but you're absolutely right, though it grieves me to admit it.'

'How do you mean?' Hope flickers. Does he actually understand?

'We're neither of us ready. I think we both know that there could be something pretty wonderful between us if we let it happen, that's if I can still remember who you are next time I see you.'

'Don't joke about that, James, it's the least of our worries.'

'Is it? I don't agree. But anyway, the most important thing is for you to come to terms with these *certain issues*, which I've got to say I find intriguing rather than off-putting. We'll need to concentrate on whatever makes that step easier. It's a long-term job.'

'I've been feeling that too. I'm seriously considering letting my flat go and renting somewhere down here for a while. Even buying a place, if it seems right. There's no hurry to find out about May. And as for the mystery man who got her pregnant, he's got to be long gone. I can make enquiries in my own time if I stay, and get to know the place where I began.'

James watches an elderly couple walk along the shore in front of them, hand in hand. It's almost dark now, and he puts an arm around Grace again. 'I thought Dot and I would be like those two over there, together forever, but my whole life's different now and it's time to accept it. I need to go home for a little while and sort the old house out, put it on the market and so on.'

'And then what?'

'Then I'm coming back here. As you say, rent or buy, it doesn't matter which. I want to be near you in Pengelly. Just as friends,' he says, seeing the alarm on her face. 'And to prove it, when we get back to the hotel, I'll make up the sofa bed and keep well out of your way. Trust me?'

'Absolutely.'

'Good. Best behaviour. Scouts honour.'

'Oh! You didn't get round to telling me about your problems with your daughter, did you?' Grace says. 'We got distracted.'

'Ah. We don't need to worry about all that, on this lovely night.' James is fidgeting now, making little heaps with his fingers in the sand.

Grace nudges him gently. 'Come on. I've dished enough dirt tonight. It's your turn.'

'Okay, if I must. Well, Davina came out to Dot and I, soon after her marriage broke up. It wasn't really a surprise. The marriage was a big mistake and we could always tell there was something badly wrong.'

'And?'

'Her first couple of new partners didn't come to anything, and she's always so busy with work that we hardly saw her anyway, but then, years later, she met Susanna. We love Suze and Robyn gets on well with her too, but they don't live together, so marriage was never mentioned. Then Davina told us that the two of them were planning to tie the knot.'

'And you weren't happy?'

'On the contrary, I was delighted. I'm a regular churchgoer and I had a vision of walking my only daughter down the aisle. I knew they'd do the official bit in the registry office but a blessing with our local vicar would be perfect. All our friends and family could be there. We could even have a marquee in the garden.'

'So what went wrong?'

'Susanna's parents refused to have anything to do with it. They were in complete denial about her relationship with Davina – still are. The wedding turned out to be a rushed job in the town hall with no party afterwards, and the girls both wore jeans. They didn't even really want us to be there – they were just going to have Robyn and Susanna's brother as witnesses, but Dot insisted we went.'

'Was it awful?' asks Grace sympathetically.

'No, not at all. The girls love each other, that was blindingly obvious on the day and it's what matters. But Davina knew how disappointed I was not to have been able to do the church part, and we quarrelled. It was silly, I should have held my tongue.'

Most of the other people on the beach are making their way home now, and Grace shivers. All this soul-searching is exhausting and she thinks they probably both need to rest. A little girl, up way past her bedtime, totters past carrying a bucket and spade, whimpering with tiredness. Grace watches as her father picks her up and hoists her onto his shoulders. Dads and their daughters. Such a precious bond. She feels the loss of

Harry keenly at that moment. He'd loved making sandcastles and had always carried her if she was tired. Then she thinks about the unknown father who didn't get to watch her grow up, and frowns.

'You can go and see Davina and sort it out, can't you? Now you've had a chance to think? Maybe the two of them could go to church with you one Sunday, just for a regular service? Would that help?'

He nods thoughtfully. 'It might. I could try.'

They lean together. Grace can hardly bear the thought of leaving this beautiful spot, tired as she is. She knows she's right to try living by the sea.

James gets to his feet, holding out a hand to help Grace up. 'From now on, I'm going to trust my own judgement. Pengelly, a new home and the chance to show off my home cooking to you. What more could a man ask for?'

'You can cook? Why didn't you say so before?'

James shrugs. 'Didn't want to show off.' He sees Grace looking at him with new eyes and laughs. 'No, I've got to be honest here. I've got three specialities. Bacon and tomato splash sarnies, scrambled eggs with a secret ingredient and Gloop.'

'Two questions. What's the secret ingredient and what's Gloop?'

'The secret ingredient is tomato, and Gloop is mainly tomatoes.'

'So your entire repertoire is actually quite tomato-based, in fact?'

'What of it? They're good for you. Got lots of ... something or other ...'

Grace hides a smile, grabs Buster's lead and heads for the stone steps that lead to the promenade. The future is looking better all the time, even if a bit full of tomatoes. All she needs to do now is relax. Easy. Isn't it?

Chapter Twenty-Five

Dusk is already falling when Grace arrives back at the cottage late the following afternoon. Footsore but glowing with health, she finds a stranger ensconced in what's already become James's favourite chair by the fire. Luckily, James is still on the beach with the dogs.

'Hello,' says Grace, trying her best to sound friendly but conscious of a desperate need for a bath and her pyjamas.

The man gets to his feet in one graceful movement. He's tall and willowy, beautifully turned out in his black suit, a starched open-necked shirt and a long cream trench coat. The whole effect reminds Grace of David Bowie in his Thin White Duke era. The newcomer has startlingly white hair, high cheekbones and a pale blue gaze that looks her up and down with obvious approval.

'You must be Grace. I was just going out for a stroll,' he says, holding out a hand for her to shake, 'but Emily said your arrival was imminent, so I waited. I'm Will, Julia's brother-in-law.'

'Oh, I see. We didn't know you were coming,' says Grace.

'Neither did I until last week, but nevertheless, here I am. A whim, you might say, but one that should have happened a long time ago. And now I appear to be staying here with you and your friend James.'

'Really?'

'You don't sound terribly thrilled. I'm getting the impression that my visit might have been a mistake. Emily has told me very firmly that Julia should have her privacy in case her intended wants to drop in, and now your face, delightful as it is, gives the hint that you feel the same.'

Will smiles self-deprecatingly as Grace falters out a denial. 'Of course I don't. This isn't my home anyway, it's Emily's. James and I are only paying guests. You're family, aren't you?' she says.

'Possibly on the black sheep side. Not even Prodigal Son material. I've been extremely bad at keeping in touch.'

Grace switches on the standard lamp to dispel the gloom and they settle opposite each other. In the soft lamplight Will's face seems all angles and his eyes are shadowy and mysterious. A startling picture is forming in Grace's mind. She hesitates. Her screening techniques are improving by the day and she has hardly needed them with James, but Will's memory is so powerful that before she's had time to decide whether to let it in, the intensity of it blasts into her subconscious. The shock is too much. Grace's whole body becomes rigid as the dark thoughts shoot from Will's mind into hers. Using every bit of strength available, she forces her shield up and the memory fades, leaving her trembling.

When she opens her eyes again, Will is staring at her.

'Grace, what just happened?' he asks. 'You looked, to coin a hackneyed phrase, as if you'd seen a ghost.'

'I ... I'm sorry, I think I've been overdoing it a bit lately. All that unaccustomed exercise and fresh air ...' she murmurs, taking a couple of deep breaths to steady her shattered nerves.

'Really? Are you sure that's all it is? You're very pale. Shall I go and find Emily?'

'No, no – I'm absolutely okay now. I'll make some tea in a minute. Probably just a bit dehydrated, that's all.'

'If you say so.' Will considers Grace for a long moment. 'Although I'd just like to remind you that I've spent many years as a priest and treated every confession with the confidentiality it deserves.'

'I'm sure you did. Why are you telling me this?' Grace can feel her hard-won composure slipping away. Will's gaze is way too sharp for her liking.

'Because you're troubled. There's something you don't want to tell me. I saw it in your face just then. What happened to you, Grace? For a little while, you'd gone away from this room, hadn't you?'

Grace doesn't reply, and Will says, 'Also, don't forget, for a very long time I've been part of an isolated community that still has no problem in believing in the impossible.'

'In God, do you mean?'

He laughs. 'God isn't impossible to me. No, I'm talking about the supernatural. People think of the fairy folk, leprechauns and suchlike, as the stuff of children's stories, but I've come to see that "there are more things in heaven and earth, Horatio, than are dreamt of in your philosophy."'

Grace is about to ask what he means when footsteps can be heard on the path and James enters the room. He's surrounded by what seems like a whole pack of dogs but is only two very excited ones. He stops in his tracks when he sees Will, and his mouth falls open.

'Ah, behold another person thrilled to see me,' says Will. 'I'm Julia's long-lost brother-in-law and you have got to be James. I'm also your new housemate. My name is Will. Until fairly recently, I was only known as Father Will Lovell.'

'Oh. Well, I'm very pleased to meet you, Father Will,' James rallies quickly. 'Are you staying long?'

'Who knows? Let's see how it goes. Call me Will, please. As it happens, I'm just off to see my old friend Angelina, she's promised to make a lentil curry for our dinner. Julia invited me to dine with you, but I like to eat early, otherwise the food tends to lie heavily, doesn't it? I'm not a good sleeper at the best of times.'

Will gets to his feet, brushes the creases from the knees of his trousers and heads for the door. Buster and Bruno follow him, barking energetically. 'See you later,' he calls. 'Don't wait up. Whose dogs are these? Are they like this all the time, James?'

'Like what?'

'Boisterous and loud?'

'They're dogs. That's what they do.'

Will seems to notice that he's gone too far. 'I'll see you both later.' He bends and tentatively pats both dogs. 'Goodnight, animals. We'll get used to each other eventually.'

'Who in heaven's name was that?' asks James, when the other man is well out of earshot. 'Julia's brother-in-law, did he say? Whoever he is, he really likes himself, doesn't he? And why has he got to stay here?'

Grace is wondering the same question. How can she avoid getting into this situation again? Whatever unsavoury experience Will was reliving just now, it's left her with a very bad taste in her mouth and it isn't something she wants to share. And the man is way too perceptive for her liking.

'You look exhausted. Go and have first bath. I'm going to start making Gloop,' James says, holding out a hand to pull Grace to her feet.

She goes to turn on the taps in the bathroom. Her mind is full of the passionate emotions she's been on the edge of experiencing through the window of Will's memory. Grace sighs. Perhaps a hot, bubbly bath will help.

'There's no rush, love,' calls James. 'Shall I bring you a glass of wine in there?'

She shouts out that she'd love some wine and switches on the old transistor radio on the windowsill, tuning it in to Radio Three. The family bathroom is fitted with an old-fashioned bath on legs, and Grace is touched that James has understood her passion for soaking in a tub of bubbles while they've been away.

James hands a glass beaded with condensation through the gap in the door as she opens it a crack, but doesn't try to come any further in. Grace takes a grateful sip of the chilled Sauvignon Blanc and steps into the foamy water as the tinkling sound of Chopin flows around her. Steam quickly fogs the window as the aches and pains brought on by the long walk and the stress of her encounter with Will's memories melt away. It's been a wonderful couple of days and her relationship with James is on a whole new footing now, but she's glad to be alone for a while.

Drifting away on a cloud of unusually peaceful thoughts, she hears James calling her again, his voice muffled by the bathroom door between them.

'Grace? Do you by any chance recall me telling you about Gloop?'

'The tomato thing? Yes. Why?'

'Only, did I tell you the whole recipe?'

'No. Are we short of something?'

There's silence for a moment and then he shouts, 'I can't remember how to make the bloody stuff.'

Her heart contracts with sympathy for him. He sounds so crestfallen.

'I'm guessing tinned tomatoes?' she calls back hopefully.

'Yes, and puree, I think, and ... onions ...'

'Maybe garlic? Is it a veggie dish?'

'Oh, no it isn't. Well done. Chorizo, chopped up small and fried in its own oil. And lots of garlic, you're right.'

'I saw some chorizo in the fridge, on the bacon shelf. Herbs? Just guessing, thinking Bolognese type sauce.'

'That's it, mixed herbs. The dried sort. Thanks, love, sorry to bother you. Thought it was going to have to be beans on toast.'

Grace tops up the hot water and slides down so only her head is sticking out. An idea is flickering at the back of her mind, not a new one, but something that needs addressing. She's just given James a memory jog. Nothing supernatural or odd about it, just lots of prompting that time. How can she access the people who need her services? The only answer she can come up with is the drop-in group that might be happening soon. Could she slide her way in there and work some of her magic in this village that's already starting to feel like home?

Chapter Twenty-Six

A week later, life in Curiosity Cottage has settled into a definite routine. It's not entirely convenient for any of the occupants, but it's working, up to a point. Emily has an early breakfast each morning and then either goes up to London or writes in her room. James and Grace eat together, following which Grace works on the letters or goes for a walk with James. Will has spent a lot of his time with Angelina, to Grace's relief, making it relatively easy to avoid being alone with him again, although part of her is still deeply curious to find out what his darkest memories hold.

Tristram is still away from home, as his cousin has faded away at last and he's in charge of funeral arrangements. This means the dogs are firmly in residence. Will is getting used to their bouncing but dislikes having to guard his food from Buster all the time, so he's taken to eating all his meals with Angelina. This suits them both very well.

'I need to find my way to the next village for Mass,' Will says one morning. 'I think Emily mentioned a friend of a friend who might take me? Failing that, a taxi will be fine.'

Grace wonders if Emily will want to take on this job for her uncle but James is already stepping in.

'No need,' he says, 'I'll come with you. I've been to the village church already. The young vicar's a live wire and he makes his services great fun, but I'm game for a shot of the old Hail Marys if you like? We can either get a cab or go on the bus.'

'*A shot of the old Hail Marys?* Is that how you describe the entire Catholic religion?'

James grins. 'I'm sorry, it's what my old ma used to call you lot. Shall we give it a go? You'll have to give me a nudge with the standing up and kneeling stuff. I don't suppose fun comes into it, but I'm game if you are.'

Will accepts graciously, and so begins an odd friendship. Grace notices that both men have very firm ideas about the merits of their chosen styles of worship, but she can tell that Will seems proud to be able to introduce James to his previous way of life.

'You must feel lost without all this routine, Will?' James says, as they arrive back later in the morning after their first foray to the church of St Mary Magdalene in nearby Mengillan. Grace looks up, sensing criticism, but James sounds as if he's genuinely concerned.

'Yes, I do. But sometimes, you have to stop and take

stock, don't you?' Will answers. 'Life isn't always about settling into a rut, however comfortable a rut it is.'

'How do you mean?'

Will goes to the sink to fill the kettle. Grace is relieved he's got the hang of coffee-making now, at last. He doesn't answer immediately, but when he's finished assembling the pot and cups on a tray, he says, 'I think for a long time I've been refusing to remember some of the more significant happenings in my past, if I'm honest, James.'

'Well, there's irony for you. *You're* refusing to let your memories in and I can't keep hold of mine. No coffee for me, I'm going back out to get a newspaper. I forgot about it when we were on the way home.'

'Yes. Some of my older blasts from the past might be better forgotten, I reckon. But I've spent so long blocking them out that I can't pin them down now I'm ready to remember. Does that make any sense at all?'

Will looks at Grace as he says this, and she watches James leave the cottage, aware that a significant moment is fast approaching. Will picks up the tray and motions for Grace to follow him into the sitting room. She sits down, about to make some sort of polite chitchat to defuse the situation that's building up, but before she can speak the wave of Will's memories is back, rushing into her mind before she can stop it.

The scene is a dark one. Grace can sense he's gone

back in time to somewhere moonlit and eerie. The night is bitterly cold. All around are shapes in the gloom. Low, rounded arches, and a few crosses. Some of the shapes are leaning drunkenly to one side. She registers with a start that Will is in a graveyard, and he's not alone. Somebody is laughing, and it's not a pleasant sound. A wave of pure lust floods her body and Grace flinches. Enough! She musters all her willpower to counter her Italian oasis against Will's fevered flashback. Gradually, the images fade and she's back in the present, eyes closed and breathing deeply to calm her shattered nerves.

'It happened again, didn't it? Whatever it was?' Will says quietly.

She nods. The game's up. But how much to divulge, that's the question. For a person who's spent a lifetime avoiding confidences, Grace reflects that she's now told James her deepest secret and only just stopped herself revealing it to Emily, Julia and Tristram. What's got into her? She hardly knows Will, and the impression she's gained from the letters is that he can't altogether be trusted. Still, Julia is clearly fond of him, and her gut feeling is that he may be capricious but he's got a good heart. She makes a snap decision.

'What happened to you in the graveyard?' she says.

Will stares at her. 'How did you know where I'd gone to in my head?'

'You were frightened ... and excited, weren't you?' Grace can feel herself blushing.

'I was torn between those two emotions for most of the time during that particular holiday. Sometimes, an inexperienced young man can choose the wrong ... friends,' he says.

They drink their coffee in silence until Grace can bear the tension in the room no longer.

'I expect you want me to fill you in on how I knew what you were remembering?' she says. 'It's not something I really understand so I can't explain, but sometimes, if a person is remembering a particularly emotional or important time – or in your case, passionate – I get a glimpse of it.'

'Second sight? Is that what you're saying?'

'Not exactly. Up to the time when I came to Pengelly, I only felt memories from people, but since I came here, a few objects have affected me too, and sometimes even passing thoughts can find their way into my mind. I can stop it happening if I'm quick enough, because I've practised a lot, but it isn't easy.'

Grace holds her breath, hoping with all her heart that this will be enough for Will. All this soul-searching is exhausting. He smiles at her and raises his cup in a kind of salute.

'An odd gift to have, although as I said before, during my time in Ireland I've experienced all manner of strange things. Learning to suspend disbelief is essential in my line of work, as you may guess. There's no need to say more.'

'But that was a very important moment to you, wasn't it, Will? The scene in the graveyard, I mean. Is it still troubling you?'

He grimaces, suddenly looking much older than his years. 'Yes, it was and is crucial to me, that's clear now. I need to address the problem because it hasn't gone away. That means my visit here might be interrupted at some point, but I have to make some calls first and do some digging of my own before I can set the ball rolling to put things right. The problem is that I don't know where to start. The vital details are lost in the mists of time, you might say.'

'That sounds very mysterious.'

'I don't mean it to be. To be perfectly honest, Grace, I want to get my full memories of that time back but I'm terrified of what I might remember.'

Grace nods, but says nothing.

Finally, Will takes a deep breath and says, almost to himself, 'I know what I have to do now, and where I need to go. Who knows how long it's going to take, though? Never mind, it's got to be done. There's no other way.'

Grace watches as he stands up and prepares to leave the room. At the last moment, he comes back to where she's sitting and bends to kiss her on both cheeks. He doesn't speak. Grace feels a sudden sense of loss. Has she done the right thing or just opened an unnecessary can of worms for Will? She hopes if he does go away, it won't be for long. Here is someone who needs her skills. To give Will back some of his memories would probably help him to find peace. Or would it?

Chapter Twenty-Seven

True to his word, Will leaves Pengelly without further ado. Brief notes for Emily and Julia say he'll be back as soon as possible but that he has urgent business in France. As soon as he's gone, Grace thinks of a whole host of questions she might have asked him if she'd known Will was going so soon and with every day that goes by she feels more annoyed with herself for missing the chance to dig out more information about May.

When the text arrives to say Will is passing through Calais and expects to be on the move for some time, Grace can't help a pang of envy. Justifiably proud of his photographic skills with his new smart phone, Will has sent a picture of a café in the town. Under a striped awning, a bistro table holds the remains of what looks like a feast of olives, bread and cheese, flanked by a half-full carafe of red wine. The evening sun is casting long shadows and Grace can almost smell the coffee in a carafe on the next table.

Fighting the sense of time lost, Grace tells herself to get a grip and be patient. He'll be back, she's sure of it. At least working with Emily on her book is giving the two of them the opportunity to get to know each other better, and surely now that Grace has diligently read and made notes on most of the letters from the earlier period over the last few days, she's justified in biting the bullet and asking Julia if she and Emily can have the rest; the ones that describe the famous feud in the family. So far there's been nothing at all to give any clues about the identity of Grace's father and not much that refers to May either. Maybe the final ones will hold the key. She heads across the road without telling Emily where she's going.

'Are you sure you need them?' Julia asks when Grace makes her request, pleating her skirt between fingers that Grace sees are trembling slightly.

'If we're going to see the big picture, we do. I'm discreet, Julia. This will go no further, but I think Emily should decide how important they are, don't you?' She crosses her fingers as she says this, hoping this subterfuge isn't too reprehensible. Julia looks so small and frail today.

'I suppose so, but they're not pleasant. I read them at the time but I've never wanted to repeat the experience. Don's sisters wouldn't leave him alone when it came to their squabbles. It got worse and worse. They seemed to think he had a magic wand to sort everything out.'

'They must have adored him.'

'Yes, I suppose they did. Don was their hero. And their mother adored him, of course. It's a wonder he wasn't spoilt and big-headed. He never was, though.'

'I'll only use them to add another layer to Emily's story, Julia, honestly.' Another crossing of the fingers. The end will hopefully justify the means, Grace tells herself, quoting Audrey. A pang of love for the woman who had a useful saying for every occasion takes her breath away for a moment. Audrey must have thought she was doing her best for Grace, keeping May's identity secret. There wasn't a scrap of harm in her, and it wasn't her adoptive mother's fault that Grace's growing up years were blighted by her odd talents.

'Yes, I can see that's the idea. And most big families have their arguments, don't they? Like this one, it's usually about money and who should have it.'

'I'm an only child, so I don't really have any experience of that.'

'No. You're lucky in some ways, I suppose. Don't quote from the letters, will you, dear? And don't say anything specific.'

Settled in Emily's flat with the younger woman absorbed in her first chapters, Grace makes sure the coffee table is spotlessly clean, and then slides the contents of the large, fat envelope onto it.

'What are you doing?' Emily's voice cuts into Grace's thoughts, and she starts guiltily.

287

'I ... I borrowed the last pack of letters from Julia,' she confesses, steeling herself for the reaction.

'Oh Grace, you didn't? Why on earth did you have to do that? They're way too painful, from what Gran's told me. I hate to think of Gran and Gramps being bombarded with all this vitriolic stuff. Why couldn't the girls have sorted it out for themselves instead of dragging innocent people into it?'

Grace lets Emily have her say, nodding sympathetically but saying nothing. She has an odd feeling about all this. Even clutching the big envelope that contains them has given her a sense of doom. When Emily finally stops talking and shrugs resignedly, going back to her own work, Grace reaches out and lays both hands lightly on top of the heap.

For a few moments, she sits in silence, absorbing the intense rush of pain that's pouring from the individual envelopes. This new ability to feel memories in objects has been happening so gradually, she's not fully understood until now how powerful it can be. It's more manageable in some ways, because she can walk away from inanimate objects more easily than people, but today the stabbing pain inside is sharp. Picking one out at random, she begins to read. It's very short.

My dear Don,

*And so it goes on ... and on ... and on. I don't
know how much more of this awful bickering I can
stand. Elsie never stops nagging and Kathryn seems
to think everything bad that's ever happened in the
world is my fault. As you'll have gathered from
the others, I'm coming down to see you very soon.
There are things we need to discuss. This family is
at war and I see no end to it – unless – but we'll
talk about that next week.*

 Your affectionate brother,
 Will

Grace longs to ask Will more about this letter and
why he'd needed to make the journey to Cornwall so
urgently, but there's no point in going down this road
again so she takes a deep breath and carries on. The
next letter is even briefer and makes her fingers tingle
painfully.

Don,

 *You, have to do something. Tell Will that if he
knows anything about the ring's whereabouts,
anything at all, he has to tell you. I'll never trust
him again. And while you're at it, ask May to
have another word with Charles. That's all I'm
saying.*

 Elsie

That opal ring again. Why was it so important to them all? And what had May got to do with anything? As she lets her eyes wander over the letters spread out in front of her, wondering if there are more references to her mother in them, something strikes her as odd. One of them, near to the centre, is different from the others.

She touches it with the tip of a finger, not wanting to make the agony worse, and then slides it away from the rest. This one is in a thicker, more expensive-looking envelope and it hasn't got an address on the front. Her heart seems to stop beating for a second as she reads the words:

For BARBARA – in case she ever comes searching.
Please keep safe.

Then underneath is written, in firm bold letters:

Grace Clarke

2019

*T*he letter isn't hard to write, but May can't decide how she's going to be sure her daughter will receive it. She supposes she could give it to Emily for safekeeping, but the thought of the explanations that will follow exhausts her.

Putting down her pen, May re-reads the words and then, satisfied that everything has been said, folds the letter and seals it into an envelope before she can tamper with it any more. A thought occurs to her, and she considers the packet on a side table. These are the ones that Julia won't read. The feud letters. Emily will get around to looking at them eventually, but it won't be until after May has departed this life.

Easing open the packet, May slips the new envelope right down into the middle and then closes it again, pressing down the flap to make sure it won't open again accidentally.

There. Now, she can go, with a peaceful heart. To see her child in person would have been perfect, but this is the next best thing.

'Forgive me, Barbara … Grace … wherever you are. You're in my heart,' she whispers, *'but then you always have been.'*

Grace stares down at her name, in black ink on the thick cream envelope. She tears the letter open in a frenzy of excitement and pulls out two large sheets of deckle-edged paper. The writing is achingly familiar, Steeling herself in case of shocks, she begins to read.

My dear Grace,

If you've found this, I'm afraid it means that we haven't been able to meet after all. I'm more sorry than I can say if that's the case, but I always vowed that I'd stick to the promise I made to Audrey and Harry not to try and get in touch with you, and they pledged they would keep their part of the bargain by letting you know about me, when the time was right. It's desperately sad that we will never now speak to each other in real life, but I'll try and tell you a little more of my story.

Audrey and I talked for hours on that long night in the hospital where we met. For a lot of that time she was crying, clutching a small white cardigan she'd knitted for her lost child. I wanted that garment very badly. Not for you, my own girl, but because it held so many of her memories inside it, and I needed them. Doing my disappearing act to conceal my pregnancy from Charles and the rest of Pengelly and going through childbirth alone had taken it out of me. I was weak.

Now, this is the difficult part to explain. My big mistake in those long-ago days was to assume my child-bearing years were over. I should have known better, because I've been aware since childhood that I inherited the gift from my father of being able to harvest other people's memories from objects they have treasured. That is what keeps me going. I was fifty-seven years old when you were born, but my body looked and felt so much younger than its actual years. It still does.

The memories I collect are like the fuel in a car, like logs for the fire, like food for my soul. Are you the same? I would so love to know whether the gift, if you can call it that, has been passed on. My dear Pa never got to find out how long his syphoning off skill would have allowed him to live. He was killed in the Blitz, so the end result is a mystery.

I expect you would probably have also liked to ask me who your own father was, Grace. Well, I am sorry, but I am not going to tell you. Enough to say that you couldn't have had a more wonderful man to make you happen. It isn't up to me to tell you his name. If one day you want to try and find him, that is up to you. Please be sensitive, though. His family may not understand how our relationship was. Joyful, brief, but not what anyone would have expected.

The other question I have no doubt you will ask is why I couldn't keep you. Part of the answer is that I didn't feel good enough to be a mother. My life had been largely self-centred up to the moment I knew for sure I was carrying you, and I'd always done my share of pleasure-seeking and globe-trotting. To settle in Pengelly to a life of nappies and feeding bottles wasn't a future I could picture for myself.

Far worse than that selfish admission was the problem with Charles. I couldn't think of a way to make him leave the house without triggering a messy divorce, and to do that I would have had to admit to adultery, which would have seriously damaged the only man I have ever truly loved. To bring a child into a home with such a cruel and twisted individual was impossible. I couldn't have put you through it.

So, my dear child, you and I had to go our separate ways. The desperately annoying thing is that not long after you and I parted, Charles drowned. Typical of the man to wait until then. Would I have kept you if it had happened sooner?

I like to think so, but it was too late by that time, and I'd made my promise to your new parents to leave any decision about contact to you when you were old enough. I fervently hope your childhood has been happy and you have had a good life so far. Honestly, I did my best.

Now, the time has come for me to say my final goodbye. I have decided enough is enough. To carry on purloining the precious memories of others is no longer the way I want to live, especially when it seems to be harming someone who has come to mean a very great deal to me in my last months on this earth. I'm ashamed to say I have stolen some of my good friend Julia's memories to extend my own life and I have no way of giving them back. I hope against hope that when I'm gone, she will recover them.

Go well, daughter of mine. I would have loved us to meet and talk, but wherever I am now, if I'm anywhere at all, I'll be thinking of you and being proud that I was half of a team that produced someone so beautiful. You were an enchanting newborn babe and I have no doubt you will make a most delightful child and a charismatic adult.

Much love always, from your mother,
May Rosevere

For a long time, Grace sits with the letter on the table in front of her. She reads it again after a while, and begins to cry silently. Her throat aches and her whole body tenses as the tears fall for the lost mother who *did* care after all, and at the news that she's not unique in her strange ability. So the talent, if indeed you can call it that, is a family trait, although it sounds as if May set out to take the memories she needed more deliberately. For Grace, there has been little choice in the matter.

Wiping her eyes, Grace gets up and goes downstairs without a word to Emily. She snatches up her coat, leaves the cottage and crosses the lane again to number 60, before she can change her mind. This is too big a deal to keep to herself and she knows instinctively that Julia is the one to share the letter with.

'I'm so sorry to be a nuisance,' she says when Julia opens the door, 'but I need to talk to you. It's very important.'

When she sees Grace's blotchy face, Julia ushers her in, clucking like a mother hen.

'Whatever's the matter, dear? I knew those horrible letters were bad news. You can see why I've avoided them. You're not even related to these people and they've managed to cause distress. Sit down. Tell me what's upset you.'

Grace takes May's letter from the envelope and hands it over. 'You'd better read this,' she says.

Julia sits down at the kitchen table, unfolds the pages and begins to read without another word. Grace settles opposite her and waits, resisting the urge to bite her nails. As Julia takes in the words, her eyes become wider and she glances across at Grace and back down to the pages several times, but she still doesn't speak. At last, she takes a deep breath, and says, 'Is it true?'

'Is what true?' Grace has slipped into that state of numbness that can happen after a big shock and a crying bout. She blinks at Julia, trying to pull herself together.

'All that about collecting ... stealing memories? Can you do it too? I knew May was different in some way, but I never dreamed ... and she says she stole some of my memories. She must mean from the letters. I was beginning to think I was going mad around that time. This is all so odd. I can hardly believe it.'

'Are you angry with her?'

'Yes ... no ... oh, I don't know. I loved May very much and it sounds as if she was trying to protect me in the end, doesn't it? Don't you think so?'

Grace nods, feeling more befuddled by the minute. There's too much to take in here. She begins to talk, pouring out her years of anguish to the older woman, her confusion about why she didn't fit in and her problems being in company or crowds. Julia listens, her head on one side, frowning.

'So you came here, to Pengelly ... why, exactly?' she asks eventually.

'To find out about May, and maybe my real father, and I suppose to see if knowing about them could give any clues as to how I am.'

'Yes, I can see that.'

'Imagine not having any idea what your parents are like? Not knowing how they look, or what their characters are or if you've got any inherited health issues or talents. It's unnatural.'

'But you had a kind couple to bring you up though, didn't you? It looks as if May chose carefully.'

'I did, and I can appreciate them more now I'm getting my head round May being my mother. It's hard, though, not knowing anything about your background. If you go to the doctor's, for instance, they often ask about your medical history. I'm rootless, Julia. I need to know these things. I'm halfway there now at least.'

'Oh, Grace, I'm so sorry you feel like this. What can I do to help?' Julia stands up rather shakily and comes round to stand by Grace's side, putting her arms around her and holding her close. Grace stiffens for a moment and then lets herself relax into the warm hug.

'I wish I could just hear May's voice,' Grace whispers. 'I want to know how she sounded. Cassie's promised me her photo album, but they've all been laid up with chicken pox since she made the offer and I haven't liked to nag.'

Julia lets Grace go and clasps her hands together. 'But you *can* hear her voice,' she cries. 'Or at least there's a chance of it.'

'What do you mean? You're not suggesting ...?'

Julia laughs. 'Don't look so terrified, I'm not planning a seance! No, I remember Ida Carnell saying that last year she was going to interview all the older residents as part of her Adopt-a-Granny scheme, so that she could hold a few sessions at the village hall to let us younger ones know how it was here in the past. She recorded them all on her old cassette player.'

'I've been meaning to arrange to meet Ida. I've heard so much about her but I just haven't got around to it yet. And you think she might still have the tapes? Really?'

'It's possible. She hardly ever throws anything away. Wait, though, Tom told me she's planning to move house and downsize. Oh no, let's hope she hasn't ...'

Julia leaves the sentence dangling as she goes over to the phone. When Ida answers, she makes short work of explaining her request. After a few hasty questions, which all seem to Grace to have long-winded replies, she disconnects.

'Well?' Grace can hardly bear the suspense. So close, and maybe it still won't happen.

'The short answer is, she doesn't know. Don't panic,' Julia holds a hand up to stop the flood of Grace's frustration, 'Ida's going to have a look in her cupboard under the stairs right now. She's only just begun the big sort-out so it's probably still there, unless her husband's got rid of it without telling her.'

'When will I know, though?' The words come out as a wail.

'She says you're to go round now. You heard my excuse, that you're researching for Emily's book. She's very keen to help. Off you go, I'll ring Emily and tell her I asked you to call on Ida on my behalf.'

Grace gives Julia a hug, surprising herself with how naturally it comes, and hurries out of the cottage and up the lane. She dashes along The Level, arriving in Silver Street out of breath and boiling hot.

The terraced cottage stands just around the corner from the main road through Pengelly in the centre of a row of five other bay-windowed dwellings. Grace pauses in front of the house, suddenly nervous. She's reassured by the secure feeling of Ida's home. It's a good, solid place. The windows are shining and the paintwork on the front door is gleaming too, although personally Grace wouldn't have chosen that particular shade of magenta. Even so, the house seems to welcome her. Heartened, she squares her shoulders before ringing the bell.

The door opens almost immediately and there

stands Ida, clad in a wrap-around pinafore, her tight curls almost covered by a scarf. She flings the door wide.

'You must be Grace, of course. Come in, come in – the kettle's just this minute boiled,' she says over her shoulder as she bustles away. 'Excuse the rig-out. My cleaning lady hasn't turned up today so I've had to set to and do it myself. Tea? Coffee?'

'Tea would be lovely,' says Grace, as Ida stops briefly for breath. 'But can we look at the tapes first? You ... you did find them?'

'Oh yes, they were exactly where I left them, which is a small miracle in itself. I'll put the kettle on afterwards, and I've got some rather tasty shortbread biscuits that I collected on the train from Dover after our coach trip. We always have a couple of nights at the port in a nice hotel and then travel home. We treat ourselves to first-class tickets, because Lionel says you get a better class of snack. He does love his food, bless him.'

Grace follows Ida into the large but over-furnished lounge, dodging a velvet-covered footstool and a couple of occasional tables before she reaches the safety of a fringed chaise longue. It turns out to be very uncomfortable, but she's so glad to be here she doesn't care. Her cheeks are burning with the effort of covering the distance between their houses so quickly.

'Goodness, did you run all the way?' Ida says, taking Grace's coat. 'I wish everyone was as excited about my recordings.'

Grace can hardly breathe as Ida reaches for the cassette recorder. 'I haven't seen one of those old machines for years,' she says, in awe. 'My mum had one. She used to listen to her Rosamund Pilchers and Miss Reads on it.'

'So did I,' says Ida, delighted. 'She was a woman with sense.'

'Yes, she was.' Grace is finding herself able to think about Audrey much more compassionately now, and the memory of the background noise of the gentle stories as her mum knitted in front of the gas fire is a happy one.

'You were lucky, dear – that cupboard was on my list of things to tackle today. Mind you, I'd have kept the tapes. They don't take up much room, do they? And I couldn't get rid of May's dulcet tones.' She laughs and pulls one of the cassettes out of the pocket of her pinafore. Grace reads the words written in black felt tip: *May Rosevere.*

After a couple of minutes of stopping and starting during which Grace's feverish anticipation almost gets the better of her, Ida finally finds the right place on the cassette. There's a bit of crashing and banging and then the first thing Grace hears is her hostess's voice asking a question.

'Sorry about that,' Ida-on-the-tape says, 'I dropped

the mike. So, here I am at fifty-nine Memory Lane, home of Pengelly's oldest resident, marvellous May Rosevere, who's one hundred and ten years young. How are you feeling today, May?'

Grace has been unconsciously holding her breath and lets it out slowly as the other person begins to speak. As she'd guessed, May has a rich Cornish accent. It's a no-nonsense sort of voice, warm but practical.

'I'm perfectly well, thank you, Ida,' May says briskly. 'But I do hate that phrase. One hundred and ten years young? Whoever thought that one up?'

'Oh ... well ...' Ida's floundering already. 'I ... anyway, let's start the ball rolling with your earliest memory, shall we? I know you've always lived in Pengelly. What's the first thing you can remember from your childhood?'

'Now, that's a good question, dear,' says May. 'I'd have to say it's being carried on my Pa's shoulders along the beach when the tide was out. I can remember hearing the sea birds crying overhead and Pa telling me that's why our house got its name – because his father before him had loved the sound of the gulls. There's some as hates that noise, but I've never been one of 'em. Those birds are the first sound I hear in the morning. Oh, and I do recall licking the cream and jam from the top of one of my ma's scones and getting a good ticking off for it. She was a gentle creature, was Ma, but nobody messed with her scones.'

Ida and Grace exchange smiles. Grace is totally captivated. She can't speak for the lump in her throat but Ida doesn't seem to expect comments.

'Tell us a little about your schooldays, May. What did you enjoy most about lessons?'

There's a creaky laugh. May says, 'Not much, to begin with. I was an outdoors kind of girl. I had no brothers and sisters to play with and Ma was glad to get me off her hands most of the time, so I was used to roaming free, exploring the sea caves when Pa was at work or climbing trees in the old orchard behind our house or the woods on the way down to the beach. I suppose you'd call me a tomboy. I didn't take kindly to being told to sit still and behave myself. I got the cane more than once for being cheeky, I must admit, but I still don't think that was fair. I was just expressing my opinion, when all's said and done.'

'But later? Did you get used to the routine?'

'I did, Ida. I had to. And then the love of learning got me gripped. Mathematics was my favourite but story time was the next best, right at the very end of the day. Pa was big on history and told me plenty of useful facts, took me to museums and suchlike at weekends, but stories had never been a big part of my life until then.'

'What were your favourites then, May?'

'Oh, too many to mention, dear. But one I came back

to time and time again was *The Secret Garden*. It taught me something about making friends, and I've always loved hiding places and secrets. Still do, although I don't get out much now. I'd dearly love another look at the old sea caves but these legs won't take me there any more. Secrets don't need much effort though, do they?'

'I'm not quite sure what you mean.' Ida-on-the-tape sounds as if she's getting somewhat out of her depth now, and it's a few moments before May answers.

'Can you keep a secret, Ida?'

'Oh ... well ... I hope my friends would all consider me trustworthy ...'

'Well, you're unusual then. Most folks round here love to tittle-tattle. I keep my cards close to my chest. Nice people, most of 'em, by and large, but gossipy. Some of my secrets would make your hair curl. Not that it needs it, dear, I can see you've had another perm.'

Grace reaches out and switches off the tape player. She's had about as much as she can take. The old voice echoes in her mind, taunting her with the fact that she'll never hear it in real life.

'Take it with you, pet,' says Ida, 'if you've not got time now. I've got no more use for it. There's not much more there, and she never did spill the beans about whatever it was that she was keeping to herself. Typical May. She was a bit of a tease at times. Would you like the other cassettes too?'

Celia Anderson

Grace nods gratefully, and Ida parcels them all up and gives Grace a sturdy carrier bag to put them in.

'You'd better take the tape player too,' she says, adding it to the pile. 'You won't find one of these old things at Shangri La, or Curiosity Cottage as we've got to remember to call it now. An apt name, I reckon. There are more curious objects in that little house than you can shake a stick at, in my opinion, but we won't go into where they came from. By the way, I'm all for this book of Emily's. It's good to keep memories alive, isn't it? Have you heard about the new drop-in group? It's starting soon, according to Tom King.'

'Yes, I'm very keen to join. While I'm here, at least. To help, not to get my memories back ... I mean ...'

Flustered, Grace stops talking and Ida eyes her shrewdly. 'You haven't told me why you were really so keen to hear these tapes, have you?' she says. 'I've got a feeling there's more to this than a bit of book research for Emily, am I right, dear?'

Grace struggles again with her life-long habit of keeping her own counsel. The kind but beady eyes fixed on hers are acting almost like a truth drug. The temptation to tell Ida everything is overwhelming. She's going to have to come clean.

'May was my mother,' she blurts out, waiting for the stock reply of *'But that's impossible!'* It doesn't come. Instead, Ida nods just once and waits for more.

'You knew her well, didn't you, Ida?' Grace says. 'She gave me away as a tiny baby to a couple she'd only just met. I have no idea who my father could have been. Can you give me any clues? Or even just tell me more about what May was really like?'

Ida lets out a shout of laughter. 'What she was like? How long have you got? And as for your father, I haven't got a clue. I'd tell you if I could, I would honestly, dear,' she adds, seeing Grace's face fall.

'But nobody even knew she was pregnant. How did she manage to hide it so well? Surely someone must have guessed, and the father would have found out somehow.'

'Oh yes, some people round here knew. May thought she'd managed to keep the whole affair secret by going off on one of her travels as soon as she started to show, but my mother wasn't fooled. She was the local midwife and you didn't get much past her, I can tell you.'

'And she told other people?'

'Only a small group. Don't make it sound so bad, Grace. Villagers love to gossip. We kept our inside information to ourselves. Same as we did when Charles went missing ...'

Ida breaks off, putting a hand to her mouth in such a theatrical gesture that Grace is tempted to giggle for a moment, until the words fully sink in.

'When Charles went missing? Ida, are you trying to say May was involved in his death?'

The other woman shakes her head. 'I'm not trying to say anything, dear. May was a good woman at heart. I'm sure if she gave you up, she thought about it long and hard. But there was a lot going on in Pengelly around that time. When my old friend Will comes home, you'll need to ask him a few of your questions about May.'

'I've tried, but ...'

'And while you're at it, ask him about that ring. Now, I must get on, I'm only halfway through bottoming the bathroom. This house won't clean itself, you know. We'll save the tea and biscuits until another time, shall we?'

Reluctantly, Grace picks up her parcel and leaves. Ida can't get rid of her quickly enough and has the front door closed before Grace has taken the two steps to the pavement. She hugs the tapes to her chest as she heads briskly along The Level towards the turn for Memory Lane. The more questions she asks, the more she seems to generate. May's voice echoes in her head. So the pregnancy wasn't such a well-kept secret after all? And if half the village knew, does that include her father?

Chapter Twenty-Eight

When Grace gets back from Ida's, still lost in the past, James is bursting with his latest news.

'Young Cameron's here – you remember him, don't you, Grace?'

Grace confirms that indeed she does, thinking back with a shudder to James's morning leap into the freezing sea. Where is this heading?

'Cameron's got a great plan,' James tells Grace, his eyes shining. 'Come and listen to this.'

Still feeling other-worldly after hearing May's voice, Grace does as she's told, flinching slightly as the boy with the long black hair jumps to his feet and starts pacing the room excitedly.

'I know James loves the open water,' he says, with a wide grin, 'so I thought of him first. I want to start an informal swimming club that meets on the beach for a dip every day. What do you think of the idea? There are people in the village and further afield who'd like the chance to swim in the sea but are a bit nervous of trying it on their own.'

James is clearly all for it, and looks to Grace for her approval.

'Every single day?' she asks weakly, shivering again at the thought of all those goose bumps on show.

'People can drop in and out of it as they like. I'm happy to be there most mornings first thing and I'm sure I can find a deputy if I can't make it for any reason.'

'I'm your man for that, and I'll join you as often as I can. Just don't tell my granddaughter,' James says.

'How is Robyn, by the way?' asks Cameron, casually.

'Fine. She's back at uni now. She texts me most days. Why?'

'Oh, no reason. It was just that I know I got off on the wrong foot with her that first morning. I hope she'll approve of this plan, though. I think it's going to be good for all of us.'

Emily clatters down the stairs from the attic and catches the tail end of the conversation. 'Plan?' she says. 'What's all this, then?'

Grace listens as Cameron repeats his idea. All this talk of the beach and swimming gives her the sudden feeling that she can't be inside any longer. As if reading her mind, Emily says, 'I've worked much too long today so I'm going to take the dogs out now. Julia's invited us for supper, so we don't need to worry about that. Will you join me, Grace?'

Leaping to her feet, Grace collects a warm sweater

from her room and is outside in less than five minutes. Emily leads the way down onto the sand, letting the dogs loose as she goes.

'So how did it go with Ida?' she asks.

Grace wonders how to answer this. She watches Buster and Bruno running in giant circles, accompanied by a Jack Russell belonging to a couple sitting on a rock.

'Okay, I guess.'

'But ...?'

'There isn't really a *but*. I've just got a lot to think about, that's all.' Grace outlines the visit as briefly as she can. The memory of May's voice is still very clear in her head and the whole situation is making her feel breathless and tingly, as if new revelations about her mother are just around the corner.

'How about you, Grace? Are you okay?' Emily asks. 'You look different today somehow.'

'What do you mean?'

'Oh, only that I've noticed you've stopped dying your hair blonde. It suits you, that bit of grey. Did you decide it was too much bother, now you've retired?'

Grace stares at Emily in puzzlement. 'I've never coloured my hair,' she says slowly. She raises a hand to her hairline. The roots do feel strangely coarse.

'I haven't been paying much attention to how I look recently, I've been too busy,' she says. 'Am I really going grey?'

Emily considers this, her head on one side. 'Yes, definite streaks,' she says. 'And all this talk of May has been stressing you out, I reckon. Do you feel anxious? There are shadows under your eyes that weren't there when you first arrived here.'

'Gee, thanks. No. The opposite if anything. The longer I'm down here, the better I feel. Let's round the dogs up in a few minutes and go back to the cottage. I need to see this for myself.'

In the harsh light of the downstairs cloakroom, Emily stands by Grace's side as she peers into the mirror on the wall. There's no mistaking the grey streaks now.

'How have I missed this?' Grace wonders aloud. 'Look at the state of me. There are even tiny wrinkles round my eyes. Is it all the fresh air? All of a sudden, I'm getting old.'

'No, you're not. It happens to everybody. And anyway, you look so ridiculously young, Grace – this doesn't matter at all. You're getting more beautiful every day. Your skin is glowing and your hair's as shiny as ever. It's probably because you're happier.'

'Maybe.'

Grace bites her lip as she peers into the mirror more closely. She accepts that she's started looking older since coming to Pengelly, but is it just a coincidence? Perhaps she's relaxing for the first time in years and letting her life just get on with its natural progress instead of working so hard to look good. Or is this something more sinister? And if, like May, she *can* control the ageing process, how far does she want to go?

Chapter Twenty-Nine

After the dinner guests have departed for Curiosity Cottage and an early night, Julia sits on her kitchen step listening to the birds making their own final preparations for sleep. Her thoughts are in turmoil again, following a conversation with Tristram on the phone. The double wedding arrangements are going full steam ahead. She's gradually coming round to the idea now, especially as it cuts out the problem of her son and his lack of family feeling. The only bugbear is when it'll happen.

Emily squeezes past her and goes over to settle on her grandfather's bench. 'I've loaded the dishwasher,' she says. 'Come over here and sit with me for a little while. We've got a lot to discuss.'

'I expect you're going to try and rush me into making plans again,' Julia says with a heavy sigh.

'I think you have to, Gran. There's a lot to think about if we're going to get married in September.'

'But why do we need to be in such a hurry? And I still think we should work around your father if we can.'

'You're making excuses again. Dad's already said he won't be free for months, unless he comes over in the next couple of weeks. It'll be like waiting for Christmas if we have to work around his schedule to book a date,' Emily says, taking hold of Julia's hand and patting it in what she seems to assume is a soothing manner. Julia withdraws her hand firmly.

'Well, that's not a problem, is it? It's only the end of April now.'

'Gran, I'm thirty-four and Andy's two years older. We're not teenagers who need to save up for a mortgage or get a bottom drawer together like you and Gramps did. We want to get married soon. Even so, before the end of May is a bit quick even for me. Or for all of us, if you and Tris definitely agree to have one big do.'

Julia is silent, willing herself not to cry. She loves Tristram with all her heart. This late-blooming romance has made her happier than she could ever have imagined possible after the loss of her life partner. But getting married so soon, even before the end of September? Where will they live? Might he agree to move in here and settle in Memory Lane? They haven't even discussed their future home yet. And he'll be with her all the time. All day ... and all of the night, as one of Felix's favourite songs from his teen years went. She remembers him playing it over and over again. The words didn't sound so ominous then.

'Gran, whatever is the matter with you today? I know you're pleased for me and Andy, so it can't be that.'

'Of course it's not. I'm delighted you've finally got engaged, of course I am.'

Emily holds up a hand. 'Hey, there's no need to snap. I'm just worried about you, that's all. You don't look as if we're talking weddings, more like planning a wake.'

Julia takes a deep breath. She can't say it.

'Gran, you're scaring me. What's up?'

'It's so embarrassing. I'm ... I'm afraid of sleeping with Tristram,' Julia blurts out. There, it's said. Her face is on fire. How dreadful to have to admit that shameful fact to your granddaughter of all people.

'Really? Is that all?'

'All? It's more than enough, thank you very much. It may seem like nothing to you, at your age, but I've spent all my adult life with one man. I've never been to bed with anyone else, Em. I was only fifteen when I began walking out with Gramps. I only ever even kissed one other boy and that was my cousin Tim, quite by accident under the mistletoe one Christmas.'

This revelation leaves Emily speechless. 'Wow,' is all she can say.

'So, do you understand now? I'm trying to get used to the idea of seeing Tristram's head on the pillow next to mine every morning, sharing a bathroom, and ... other things.'

317

Emily giggles, then puts her hand over her mouth. 'Sorry, Gran, I know it's not funny to you, but let's be sensible about this. Tris is eighty. He's hardly going to be expecting wild sex, is he? You're not going to be swinging from the chandeliers every night, are you?'

Julia, pink in the face now, can't help smiling at the image this conjures up, but soon sobers when reality hits home again. 'He's a very ... lively man, you know,' she whispers.

At this, Emily loses the plot completely and soon they're both laughing so hard Julia's worried she might have to nip to the loo.

'Stop it,' she says eventually, regaining control with difficulty. 'It's not in the least bit funny.'

Emily hiccups for a minute or two, taking deep breaths and wiping her eyes on her sleeve.

'Well, that's got your worries out of the way. Now we can really start making plans,' she says. 'And at least if we arrange the weddings for September we'll stand a good chance of Uncle Will being back. I don't want to get married without him there, do you?'

Julia shakes her head, but the longer he's away, the less sure she feels that her brother-in-law will ever return. The postcards addressed to *all at home* from France are still arriving on a regular basis, but Julia hasn't yet told Emily that she received a personal letter only yesterday from Will. It's in her pocket now but she doesn't need to re-read it. The message was clear and she can remember it almost word for word.

My darling Julia,

I'm feeling very lost right now and I could really do with a good long talk to you around that old kitchen table that's shared so many of our secrets. The trail I'm following keeps going cold on me, but I can't give up. When I've run to ground what I desperately need to find, I'll be home, but who knows when that might be? All I can say is that until I've achieved this, I'll never be at peace. The memories of the events from that stormy night so many years ago have chased me through the years. Don, Charles, May ... and the others who were in the pub before that odious man left for the harbour. It's all tied up with what I'm doing here in France. I promise to explain just as soon as I can.

Until then, I send my love to you and Emily. Also, please pass on my regards to James and Grace. I have the feeling that those two are going to be very important to us all in the future, in some way.

Yours,
Will x

'So are you saying I've got the go-ahead to book everything, Gran?' Emily persists. 'We can't leave it much longer if we want the church and cars and flowers and so on.'

An unexpected wave of excitement hits Julia. What is she making such a fuss about? Of course she wants this wedding. She adores Tristram, Emily and Andy are perfect for each other and it's high time she stopped being so feeble.

'Yes, dear, you're quite right. Full steam ahead from now on. And when you go back into the kitchen, could you pass me my shopping list? I'm going to need to make a very big fruit cake. Maybe two tiers? How about a carrot cake for the top one? Or chocolate?'

Emily hugs Julia hard. They sit together on the bench that Don built for his young wife all those years ago, deep in their separate thoughts and memories, as the birds settle down for the night and the sun begins to set over the bay.

Chapter Thirty

September

Grace sits in the kitchen of her new home, gazing out of the window as she watches three sparrows fight for mealworms on the bird table. She's never had a garden before, and feeding the birds is one of the pleasures of having her own space right outside the back door. Ida's house has proved the perfect place to settle, at least for now.

Renting a house for a while was Grace's first choice. Hedging her bets seemed a good idea, but when it became clear that Ida and Lionel Carnell's plans to move were happening more quickly than anyone expected, Grace had the overwhelming feeling that fate had taken a hand. They decamped to the empty bungalow at the top of Silver Street, leaving their substantial mid-terrace Victorian cottage free as soon as a buyer could be found, and Grace decided that she was that person.

Clearing her flat wasn't a wrench at all in the end. She packed up her books, her few pictures and ornaments and the best of her furniture and left the rest for the next tenants. A selection of new throws and rugs have added much-needed splashes of colour to her décor, and Ida's penchant for regularly having her house painted white from top to bottom means that, for now at least, there's no need to decorate.

Grace is happy to sit back and let the house tell her what it wants. Later she can add colour to some of the walls if she so chooses, but the white is restful. It's comfortable and quiet here, with thick, pale carpets that are quite at odds with what she saw of Ida's other, much fancier soft furnishings. Grace has splashed out on made-to-measure curtains in soft shades of moss green and grey, and hung large gilt-framed mirrors here and there to make the most of the light. There's a deep bay at the front of the house, with a chintz-covered window seat and a panoramic view of her new neighbours' comings and goings. At the other end of the long room are French windows that open outwards to reveal the tiny well-kept garden with its paved terrace and lush overhanging trees and bushes. It's like being in a woodland cave, thinks Grace, stepping out of the kitchen door to appreciate the warm September morning.

The only shadow in this peaceful new world of hers is Will's imminent return. Since moving out of Emily's cottage to make room for new guests, Grace has been aware of his return from France hanging over Julia. She knows how delighted Julia and Emily are that Will is coming back to see them married, but the thought of integrating Will into her life with Tristram and the challenge of coping with his routines and dietary needs has been worrying Julia considerably. And there's more to this anxiety, Grace is sure of it, but up to now, Julia hasn't offered to share her worries with Grace. It's a family matter, that's obvious.

The double wedding of Julia and Tristram and Andy and Emily is causing the most excitement that Pengelly has known for years. Everything else has been put on hold as wedding frenzy grips the two couples and their friends and families. Once persuaded the joint celebration is a good idea, Julia has gradually become even more excited than Emily about it all.

The stream of paying guests at Curiosity Cottage have luckily been forgiving of all this fuss, apart from one elderly gentleman who decided that staying in a place where there were constant deliveries of fripperies through the post and conversations based on hors d'oeuvres and flowers disturbed his peace. Emily has cut down her working hours in London even more and completely abandoned both the letters and her book, to Grace's intense disappointment.

She hopes once all the excitement is over they'll be able to get back to it. The thought of all those memories stashed away in Emily's flat is enticing. Her own investigations into her father's identity have ground to a halt. She's not been able to find a single shred of evidence to point to anybody, there's nothing in any of the letters to provide a clue, and as time goes on, Grace is becoming more and more convinced that some of the older villagers are actually ganging up against her to stop her digging any deeper into May's past.

As for other people's memories, mostly she blocks them out these days. Some are stronger than others, that's all. Is it her fault if she gets the occasional inadvertent energy boost from them? Grace tells herself it isn't. Her hair hasn't got any greyer, which could be a coincidence, but she doesn't think so. The drop-in group is proving to be a winner, and Grace has had a few moments here and there when she's been able to help a little in feeding a memory back to the person who's lost it, but on the whole, her progress has been disappointingly slow.

There's no reason to think that she's stuck in this limbo land because of her lack of success in uncovering her own past, but Grace can't help feeling the two are linked. If only she could find out who her natural father was, and how the mystery surrounding Charles's death relates to May, she somehow knows she'd be at a point where she could make proper use of her gift. It *is* a talent and not a curse, she can see that now, but at the moment it's going nowhere and benefitting nobody.

Going back to the thought of Will, Grace wonders if she's done the right thing offering to have him as her guest instead of letting him go to Julia's. Charming as she'd found him, not to mention intriguing, the idea of sharing her new space with anyone else is rather horrifying, but Julia's got so much on her plate, and Emily's home has its full quota of visitors. Andy's house will soon be bursting at the seams with his parents and sister who are travelling down from Yorkshire for the wedding. James and Robyn, plus sundry other guests are booked into the pub. Pengelly is filling up fast.

The invitation for Will to stay was blurted out on a whim, on a day when Julia was fretting about her brother-in-law's imminent arrival so close to the weddings, and Grace has regretted it ever since. She supposes this is all part of joining a community instead of living in a solitary state and tells herself for what seems like the hundredth time to stop being so precious about her home. He can't possibly want to stay with her for long, can he? All this will be over soon, and they can go back to normal life. And surely if he's under her own roof, an added bonus will be that there'll be ample opportunities to ask him a few more pertinent questions.

A patter of footsteps disturbs Grace's troublesome thoughts and she hears her name being called loudly.

'Grace, where are you?' yells Tamsin. 'Are you ready for the trying-on? I've had a bath specially.'

Tamsin and Andy have come along the narrow path that runs behind the terraced row, and now emerge through the gate at the bottom of the garden. Tamsin's hair is in a tight plait instead of its usual bush of wild curls and her face is shining from rigorous use of soap and water.

'Are we too early?' asks Andy, yawning. 'She's been up since the crack of dawn.'

'That's because it's all so special,' says Tamsin. 'Our dresses have got to be just right, haven't they, Grace? Are they here? Did the lady bring them?'

'Yes, she delivered them both early this morning, and no, you're not too early,' says Grace, submitting to a large hug from the little girl. The only dressmaker in the village has turned out to be Cassie Featherstone. It's her sideline while her children are small, although with her expanding waistline, getting near to the sewing machine has been a bit of a challenge. Cassie and Grace have become firm friends since Grace's move to Silver Street, and spending time at Seagulls for dress fittings has been soothing. May isn't there any more, but Grace can be in her mother's family home and absorb the atmosphere to her heart's content while Cassie pins, cuts and chats. Sometimes, it almost feels as if May is trying to communicate with her. The echoes in the house are very powerful.

'Imagine us both being bridesmaids,' says Tamsin. 'It's going to be awesome. You can go now, Dad, Grace won't want you to see her in her knickers.' She dissolves into giggles and Andy blushes.

'Yes, away you go,' says Grace. 'I'll bring her back later. I still think I'm a bit long in the tooth to be Julia's bridesmaid, and Matron of Honour sounds so boring.'

'You'll both be stunning. When's the famous Will arriving?' asks Andy, giving his daughter a kiss as he prepares to leave.

'Tomorrow.'

'Why is Will famous?' asks Tamsin. 'Is he on the TV? Is he on *Strictly*? Me and Dad like that, don't we?'

'He isn't really ... oh, I think I'll just go home,' says Andy. 'If you're sure you don't mind dropping her back when you're done?'

When he's gone, Tamsin and Grace look at each other, eyes sparkling. Tamsin claps her hands.

'Let's do it,' she says.

They go upstairs hand in hand to the big bedroom at the front of the house. Grace has kept this, her favourite room, as clutter-free as possible. The magnificent queen-sized bed covered in a vintage counterpane is in the centre of the back wall, but her two wardrobes and dressing table are in the boxroom next door. This just leaves one decent-sized spare room for visitors, which up to now has been vacant. Not for long, though.

Tamsin stands in front of the bed, her hands clasped together and eyes wide.

'Oooh,' is all she says.

The two dresses are spread out carefully on the bed to make sure they don't crease. Grace's is a delicate, lustrous mushroom shade and Tamsin's is the deep russet of terracotta flowerpots or autumn seed pods.

'It's nice they let us choose the colours ourselves, isn't it?' says Tamsin, stroking the silky fabric of her dress. It's ballerina length with a sash that is the same colour as Grace's. 'My dress is a bit like conkers, that's why I picked it. Have you seen my shoes, Grace?'

'Here they are,' says Grace, producing a pair of flat satin pumps dyed exactly the same shade of russet. 'Cassie did them for you.'

'They're lovely. Let's try everything on,' Tamsin says, ripping off her jeans and T-shirt. 'There's a thing for our hair each too. It's like a tiara.'

Grace helps Tamsin into her new frock and then slips into her own. As they look at themselves in the long mirror on the bedroom wall, Grace can't help thinking that she's never looked so good. Her green eyes shine, the newest recruit at the local salon has given her a gamine, pixie-like style for a change, and the long, hot summer spent largely outdoors has not only lightened her hair but given her a glowing tan.

When they've admired each other thoroughly and the dresses are safely hanging up out of harm's way in Grace's dressing room, Grace suggests an ice cream on the way home.

'It's only three days till the wedding now,' says Tamsin. 'I can't wait, can you? I hope Emily stops being cross before then.'

'Why is she cross?' asks Grace, as they weave their way over the busy road through the centre of the village and reach Vera's shop.

'I ... don't know.'

'Are you sure?'

Tamsin doesn't answer, but grabs Grace's hand and tows her over to the freezer.

They choose their ice creams and carry on towards Memory Lane, licking in silence.

'I think there is a reason why Em's mad at me,' says Tamsin in a very small voice.

Grace waits. When nothing else is forthcoming, she says, 'Is there?'

Tamsin stops walking and turns to Grace, her eyes flashing. 'I told her she isn't allowed to have a baby,' she says.

'Ah. And what did Emily say to that?'

'She asked me why. I think she was crying but she said she wasn't. Her eyes were all red and she kept sniffing. I didn't mean to make her sad.'

How to deal with this one? Grace is lost. 'But she was bound to be unhappy, pet. I expect she likes babies,' she says. 'Most people seem to.'

'Well, you haven't got any, have you? And you don't mind. Babies poo and wee and scream all the time. My friend Summer told me that. Her aunty just had one. And ...' she drops her voice in horror, 'it might be a boy baby if Em has one. With a willy, and everything.'

'Yes, boys tend to be made like that.'

They start walking again and Tamsin slips her hand into Grace's. 'I said Dad wouldn't want a screaming baby in the house making smells. Em didn't say anything. I wanted to ask her to promise not to have one, but I daren't.'

They've reached the top of Memory Lane now and they stop to look out over the bay. Tamsin's face is white and set. Grace wonders where to go next with this problem. There's no easy way to deal with it. She reaches down for a hug.

'They might love it more than they love me,' Tamsin says, and bursts into tears.

There's a bench where the view is most spectacular, and Grace leads Tamsin over to it and sits down, lifting the little girl onto her knee. The sobs are getting louder and a river of tears is dripping down Tamsin's cheeks.

'I don't want a baby,' she wails, burying her head in Grace's neck.

Grace wraps her arms around Tamsin and lets her cry until she's got no more tears left. Then she rummages for a tissue in her pocket and does her best to repair the damage.

'You'll feel lots better now you've told me why you were upset, Tam,' she says. 'Sometimes there's nothing we can do about a worry except tell someone else. If Emily and your dad decide to have more children, you'll be able to deal with it, I promise, and we'll all be here to help. James, me, Julia, Tris ... we all love you. Babies aren't so bad. But little girls who are seven and like reading stories and eating ice cream are more my style. You can always come and see me, don't forget that.'

'Can I?'

'Absolutely.'

'And sleep over?'

'Of course.'

'And if there was a baby, it'd be too small to come and see you, wouldn't it?'

'For a long time, yes. But it'd need a big sister to show it how to do everything, wouldn't it?'

The storm is over now with just a last few hiccups and a very damp jumper to remind Grace how devastating an idea can be when you're only seven.

'Let's go home,' she says.

Emily is in the garden when Grace and Tamsin reach 59 Memory Lane. 'Oh no, what shall I say?' whispers

Tam. 'I haven't thought of a plan yet. Can we hide? I bet she hates me now.'

'Too late. Hello, Em,' Grace says, smiling with more confidence than she feels.

'Hi Grace ... and Tam.' Emily isn't smiling back but her eyes are twinkling. Tamsin doesn't notice. 'You okay, love?' Emily asks.

'I'm ... I'm sorry about the thing I said about you not having a baby,' Tamsin says, so quietly that Grace can hardly hear her.

Emily holds her arms out and Tamsin goes into them. 'I don't suppose it'd be horrible *all* the time,' Tamsin mutters. 'Apart from the poo ... and the wee.'

Emily kisses the top of her head. 'It's not sounding very tempting. Let's just wait and see, shall we?'

Grace exchanges amused glances with Emily as Tamsin finally goes indoors. 'I think she was expecting a proper roasting about the baby issue – not an easy one.'

'No, it isn't, but thanks for whatever you said to Tam about the possibility of a brother or sister one day. It must have been something you thought up that made the difference. I've been dreading telling Andy what she said to me.'

Grace wonders if it would be tactless to change the subject to something less emotional now. She decides to bite the bullet. 'Em, do you think we'll be able to get back to sorting the letters and your writing after all the celebrations are over?' she asks.

'Oh, yes, I'm looking forward to it. On that subject, I wondered if you'd do me a favour?'

'If I can.' Are there still more random family visitors? If so, they'll have to have the sofa.

'I'm trying to make as much room as I can in the cottage for when we all get ready there before the ceremony. The last guests are going home today and then we're having a break from visitors. I've still got clutter and some has gone in Gran's loft, but there's a hamper.'

'You mean, as in picnic?'

'Much bigger. It's an enormous wicker basket full to the brim with all the letters. Could you store it for me? Just until after the honeymoon?'

'Of course. Send it round any time.'

Grace's mind races. All the letters just there for the reading, at any time – a treasure trove of secrets. The answers are coming closer. Maybe the vital clue will be in those faded pages. All Grace has to do is find it.

When she gets home to Silver Street, Grace decides to have a glass of very cold white wine in the garden and indulge herself in one of her guilty pleasures, May's photograph album. Dominic eventually arrived with it when his family were finally over the chicken pox outbreak. Grace had almost forgotten its existence, but when she held the red leather book in her hands for the first time, she experienced such a powerful rush of May's memories that she was amazed it hadn't called to her, even from Seagulls.

She sits down at the small bistro table in the sunshine, takes a large sip of wine and opens the album, with the now-familiar fizz of joy. The opening picture is a large black and white shot of Seagulls, taken from the bottom of the drive. It doesn't look too different, although the trees surrounding the house are much smaller and the car outside is some sort of vintage sports model that Grace has only seen in old films. There's a little girl standing on the front porch but she's too far away to see properly.

The following three photographs are set out in a vertical line. They are sepia prints but head-and-shoulders shots this time, so the features of all three family members are clear, and they look out of the pictures confidently.

The top one is a woman ... or is she still a girl? It's hard to say, but she looks around fifteen years old. Grace looks more closely. The caption underneath says *May Frances Rosevere, taken March 1937, aged thirty*. Grace gazes into the remarkable eyes of her mother. She's looking so amazingly young, like Grace did herself when she first started teaching. It was a problem to begin with when it came to discipline, and she had a few battles along the way.

May's expression is verging on severe but there's a slight smile trying to break out. Grace supposes having a portrait photograph taken in those days was a serious business. Her hair is wavy, in the style of the time. Grace experimented with afro perms herself when they were thought to be cool but has reverted to the straight hair she was blessed with. Not for the first time, she thinks May would have been better doing the same.

May's father, Bernard, has a direct gaze and a strong chin. His hair is cropped short and he has a small, neat moustache. His shoulders are broad, and Grace thinks her grandfather must have been a good man in a crisis. The name written underneath has been added using a different colour pen. *Bernard Hardcastle, born 1 June 1877, died 12 August 1941.* He must have been sixty when this was taken, and he has the appearance of a man half that age, with not a grey hair in sight. His wife Jessica, on the other hand, looks every bit of her fifty-five years, yet her own dates confirm that she was younger than her husband when all these pictures were taken.

Grace carries on flipping through the pages, and for once, pays more attention to the less impressive photographs further back in the book. Previously, she hasn't paused to study the smaller, more blurred black and white snapshots, preferring to concentrate on the ones where May and her parents look out of the pages and almost seem to speak to her.

Today, in the bright sunlight, Grace spots something she hasn't noticed before. In one of the later photographs, two people are sitting on the harbour wall. Their faces are in shadow but their bodies are turned to face each other, and now she looks more closely, Grace can pick up on an unmistakable closeness between the couple.

They're not touching but the woman's right hand is resting on the wall, very close to the man's left hand. The picture is underexposed and it takes a while for Grace, with the aid of a magnifying glass fetched from the kitchen oddments drawer, to identify May and a very young version of Will. Grace leans in closer and focuses the magnifying glass on the third finger of May's right hand. She's wearing what looks to be an exact replica of Julia's opal ring.

Chapter Thirty-One

Will's arrival is just as much an event as Grace expected it to be, given the build-up. He steps off the train in Penzance, debonair as ever, carrying a bulging holdall and a large carrier bag.

Julia rushes forward. Grace is surprised to see tears in the older woman's eyes. 'Will, darling. You've been away much too long.'

'Hello, Julia. Looking beautiful,' he says, and bends to kiss her on both cheeks.

'You or me?'

They both laugh quietly, and the others in the welcome committee shuffle their feet, probably feeling now, as Grace does, like intruders at this second reunion of old friends.

Tristram steps forward and the atmosphere changes. It's as if the sun has gone behind a cloud. Grace shivers, and holds her breath.

'So, we meet again at last, William,' Tristram says, his voice jovial. The smile doesn't reach his eyes.

Will grimaces. 'Nobody else but you and my mother

have ever called me that. It always makes me feel as if I'm in trouble.'

There's a short silence, and then Julia says brightly to Andy, Tamsin, Emily and Grace, all in a line like soldiers on parade, 'Right, let's get this show on the road. We're all glad to have you back and I bet you're dying for a cup of tea.'

Will's smile takes in the whole group, and is returned by everyone except Tristram. *Hmm*, thinks Grace. He shakes hands with them all, bending to speak softly to Tamsin, who giggles.

'Hello, Will, I'm happy that you're back,' she responds politely and Andy nods. Then she spoils it by adding, 'You're still very skinny, aren't you? You should probably eat more cake.'

When Will reaches Grace, she finds herself agreeing with Tamsin. She's shocked to find how thin his hand is, and how chilly. He doesn't feel quite real.

'Thank you so much for the kind invitation to stay in your new home, Grace,' Will says. 'I'll try to be the best guest ever. I'm a dab hand at washing up and so on, and I always make my own bed and dust my bedroom, as Mother taught us.'

His slightly self-mocking tone is as disarming as ever, but Grace can see Tristram out of the corner of her eye and he's visibly bristling. Julia is flushed and smiling, clearly much more pleased to see Will again than she was expecting to be. *Curiouser and curiouser*, Grace thinks, quoting *Alice in Wonderland* to herself. What can have gone on between these three in the past? Whatever it was, it hasn't gone away.

'Well, well, you must be exhausted,' says Julia, fluttering around Will in a most uncharacteristic way. 'Let's not stand around any longer. Shall we go back to my cottage or would you prefer to visit Tristram's restaurant first and have afternoon tea there?'

For an instant, Grace glimpses the utter weariness in Will's eyes before he plasters on a smile. 'Whichever is easiest,' he says.

'I think it might be best if I take Will home to my place so that he can unpack and freshen up, don't you?' Grace says. 'We can all meet up later for dinner. I know Julia's been cooking something amazing for us all.'

'Perfect,' says Will, and offers Grace his arm as they head for the car park. He doesn't seem to notice that he's left his luggage on the platform. Tristram rolls his eyes but takes charge of the battered holdall, so old as to be vintage, and Andy picks up Will's other bag. Tristram has borrowed the community minibus that Tom King has just finished raising money to buy, so they all pile in, with Tamsin at the centre, babbling happily now.

'What are you wearing for the weddings, Will?' she asks. 'I'm a bridesmaid and so is Grace, but I expect we can get you something nice to put on if you've only got that suit.'

'Tamsin,' hisses Emily, but Will only laughs.

'I like black, my dear,' he says. 'It's suitable for every occasion ... weddings, funerals, bar mitzvahs ...'

'What's a ...?' Tamsin begins, but Emily butts in to ask Will about his journey back from France, and the question is lost. Grace can see by Tamsin's face that she'll come back to it later.

Grace and Will are dropped off first, and Will waves to the others as they unload his belongings. 'Don't worry, I've got a fancy tie and a matching silk handkerchief, I won't let the side down,' he murmurs to Tamsin as he gets out of the car.

'What side?' Grace hears her asking Andy, but they're soon out of earshot and stepping into her quiet hallway. A light scent of furniture polish and freesias meets them and Will sniffs appreciatively. 'Flowers from an admirer?' he asks, as they jettison the luggage by the stairs. 'I hope it was James? If so, he has excellent taste.'

Grace isn't sure if he means James has good taste in flowers or women, but the freesias have indeed arrived that morning from him, so she makes no comment. She leads Will through into the cool sitting room. He flops into the nearest chair and leans his head back with a sigh.

'My darling, this is utter bliss,' he says. 'How did you know I wasn't in the mood for a family gathering?'

Grace sits down opposite him and studies the elegant figure, one long leg crossed over the other, completely at ease. Anyone less like a retired priest would be hard to imagine, although to be fair, she hasn't met many.

'I thought if I was in your shoes I would need a cup of tea and total quiet,' she says, 'and so that is what you shall have. Earl Grey?'

'Of course.'

'With lemon?'

'Absolutely.'

They smile at each other and Grace goes to the kitchen to put the kettle on.

Later, when they've both had three cups of tea and discovered that they are able to sit in silence without the need for small talk, Will says, 'I meant to say this to you before, Grace, but there was never the opportunity. You remind me of someone, but I can't put my finger on who. I'll get it eventually though.'

Grace feels the old familiar tingling running right through her body as a tide of memories flood into her mind. She's getting a very clear picture of the inside of Cassie's house, Seagulls. The kitchen ... the fire in the old range ... a woman standing at the kitchen table. It has to be May.

She takes a deep breath. 'I think you must have known my mother,' she says.

'Really? Was she from this area? I only visited my brother in Pengelly, I never lived here, you know.'

'Her name was May Rosevere.'

Will only just stops himself from dropping his teacup. He places it very carefully on the coffee table. There's a long pause. 'Are you sure about that?' is all he says.

'Yes.'

'But, and I'm not trying to flatter you here, my dear, you are far too young to be May's daughter. I heard she was a hundred and ten when she died and you must only be ...' He peers at her, 'Forty at the very most.'

'I'm fifty-four,' Grace says. 'May gave birth to me in secret when she was fifty-seven, and then I was adopted.'

'But surely that's ...'

'No, it's obviously not impossible, because here I am.'

The words come out more sharply than Grace intended, and Will flinches.

He uncrosses his legs and leans forward, elbows on knees, chin resting on his hands, like a very relaxed TV interviewer. 'Tell me more,' he says.

Grace finds herself pouring out her story again and once she starts, she's unable to stop the flow. 'I wanted to try to get to know May by living where she spent most of her life,' she ends eventually. 'I was just too late to meet her in person but I'm aiming to talk to as many people as I can, the older ones who knew her. People like you. I haven't really started in earnest, though. I've told James now, and Julia and Emily know, and I had to tell Ida Carnell. I bought this house from Ida, but I expect you know that.'

'Ida Carnell. Now there's a blast from the past, although she was Ida Cherrington-Smyth in those days. We always thought of her family as very grand, or at least they wanted to be. She used to follow me around like a lovesick puppy.'

'Really? Well, she was very helpful when I went to see her. She gave me a tape of May's voice. There's so much more to find out, though, I just know there is.'

She waits. Will is frowning now. 'What kind of things do you want to know about May?' he asks slowly.

'Anything. Anything at all.'

'Very well. I can only tell you about the May I knew. Your mother was a remarkable woman, Grace. Like you, she looked incredibly young for her age. She was sparky, full of life and brutally honest if you asked for her opinion on any matter. No sugar-coating. You know what I mean.'

'I do.' Grace has always prided herself on this last quality and secretly hopes the others might apply too.

'Her hair was more auburn than yours. Also, she didn't like me very much.'

'Yes, she did.' The words surprise Grace but she says them with complete certainty.

'How can you possibly know that?'

'I'm not sure, but I do.'

Will looks at Grace rather oddly. 'I wish I could believe you,' he says sadly. 'I thought very highly of May but I'm pretty sure she despised me.'

'No, she didn't.' This time Grace is even more certain. The memories that are still coming from Will are deceptive. He's viewing them one way, but Grace is somehow getting a different slant on them. Could she be getting May's angle? Is that even possible? But then, none of this is logical or sensible, so who's to say what can or can't happen?

'Why would you think that, Will? What did you do to make her despise you?'

He leans back again. 'This is a very strange conversation we're having, but we've come this far, so I might as well go on. I was ... close ... to May's husband Charles. The scene you somehow witnessed in the churchyard – well, I was with Charles that night.'

'Goodness.'

'I was very naïve, he was older and great fun to be with, when he was in a good mood. We went out on his boat a lot. I thought ... I assumed May suspected there was more between us.'

'You're gay?'

The stark question hangs between them. Grace wonders if she's gone too far, but after a while, Will's eyes meet hers.

'We didn't call it that in those days,' he says. 'The words people used were much less pleasant. And no, I didn't think I was, at the time. I was confused more than anything, attracted to both men and women. I entered the priesthood as an escape, in the beginning, but it's been a very good life, I have to say. God called me in an unusual way, and I answered.'

'So, you've never ...?'

'Oh yes, I dabbled with the affections of both men and women for a little while, before I made my final decision. My personality seems to fit better with celibacy, I've discovered. Putting my energies into my church life has been best for me all round, and I think I've been good at the job.'

'And are you happy now? Julia told me that you were ill off and on for years and that was why you didn't visit or keep in touch. That must have been hard to deal with alone?'

Will smiles. 'I've never been alone. I make friends easily and yes, I've been happy, in many ways. I'm not actually so unwell, to be honest, unless you count a nasty case of cold feet as a medical condition. The truth is, I was afraid to come back to Pengelly. There were memories here I would rather not have faced, and your timely intervention, whatever it was you did, certainly set the wheels in motion, but I do want to see dear Julia married. She deserves another chance. And there are other matters to discuss, before it's too late.'

The clock on the mantelpiece strikes six and Grace looks up in dismay. 'Oh no – we're meant to be at Julia's at half past and I haven't even showed you your room yet, let alone given you a chance to unpack and have a wash. One last question, and then we'll get ready to go out.'

'Let's have it.'

'Will, you've got to tell me. Do you know who my father is?'

Will blinks at her. 'I just assumed ... wasn't it Charles?'

'Apparently not.'

'Well, thank goodness for that. I did wonder how you'd turned out so well if that man had anything to do with your conception. I've been trying not to blacken his character too much but I'd hate to think he was related to you in any way.'

'Right. So in that case, Will, who *was* responsible?'

Chapter Thirty-Two

The morning of the joint nuptials dawns cloudy, but by nine o'clock the sun has burned away the early morning dew on Emily's lawn, and the prospect of a warm day lies ahead. The dragonflies are already out in force, which Grace always feels is a good omen. Harry loved them, and September was her adopted father's favourite month. He used to sit with her when he got home from work, counting the beautiful creatures as they flitted back and forth, iridescent and gauzy.

'A dragonfly is the symbol of change, my pigeon,' he often said. 'And September is a good time for that.'

For Grace, the only signs of change at the start of the autumn term were a bigger school uniform and a new pencil case, but she was willing to take his word for it. Now, so many years later, she wishes more than anything that she could have more time with the couple who had given her security and a safe base.

At last, it seems as if Grace is learning to remember Harry and Audrey with nothing but fondness. She knows they loved her, and her childhood was mainly happy, which is the most anyone can hope for. Letting go of some of the anger about their secretiveness has been cathartic. They had their reasons, no doubt about it. She'll never stop regretting the lost chance to meet May and is determined to discover everything she can about her, but there's no point in seething about it all. Finding out who her father was, on the other hand, is still very much on her mind, and Will has been completely unforthcoming on the matter.

'It's going to be perfect weather for you,' she tells Em. Grace has stayed over at Curiosity Cottage to make sure she's on hand to keep both brides and the small bridesmaid calm. Julia is in the shower and they're expecting Tamsin to appear any minute.

'Are you okay?' asks Emily, pouring more coffee for them both. 'You've been very quiet since Will arrived. How are you getting on with him? Must be difficult sharing your space.'

'He's an intriguing man,' says Grace. 'He knew May off and on for a long time. I ended up telling him about my reason for being here and we talked a bit, but when we got to a certain point, he clammed up.'

'Oh?'

'Don't worry, I'm not giving in. There's still Angelina to talk to, and Ida again if she's willing. They knew May pretty well, I guess. Even Vera. Now Tom's drop-in group's taken off properly, all those people will probably be under one roof every Friday afternoon. And we're getting on so well with Angelina's soup kitchen – that's got to be a great place to find people to chat to.'

The meet-ups at the village hall are proving very popular with the older residents. Ida makes most of the cakes and Tom provides top-quality tea and coffee. Hattie, the lady Grace and James met on the beach, has joined in enthusiastically, and Grace has been roped in to start a series of sessions for beginners who want to paint.

'I'm sorry I can't be more help with filling in the gaps about May,' Emily says. 'I only saw what she wanted me to see, I reckon. I can't help feeling that her legacy should be yours, though. This cottage, I mean.'

Grace thinks May's left her quite enough of a legacy to be going on with. She looks around at May's comfortable collection of kitchen equipment that Emily has wisely chosen to leave in place. They're old friends now – brass weights piled up on the chipped enamel of the kitchen scales, the tarnished metal mincer still clamped to the worktop, the blue and green pottery dishes that today hold plums and blackberries from the garden ready for breakfast, and the eclectic display of blue and white striped jugs and mugs on the dresser.

'She wanted you to have it all, Em, you know she did,' Grace says.

'But she didn't dare to believe you were out there, desperate to find her. I was a sort of last resort.'

'You were definitely not that. Everyone says how much May loved you.'

'But if you'd been here ...'

The unsaid words hang between them as they hear Julia coming downstairs and Tamsin bursting into the kitchen. 'Happy wedding day, you beautiful girl,' says Grace to Emily, while they're still alone. 'I'm completely happy where I am in Silver Street. May wanted you to carry on here, okay? You've given so much to James and me already, and to all your other guests. Let's say no more.'

The wedding machine swings into action. Nails are painted, hair is blow-dried to within an inch of its life. A make-up expert known only as Sylv makes Julia, Emily and Grace feel wonderful, and even Tamsin gets a slick of lip gloss. By eleven o'clock, kick-off is terrifyingly close.

'Will there be enough room in the church?' wonders Emily, for possibly the twentieth time that morning as Tamsin goes to stand on the front step, too excited to sit and wait with the rest of them.

'Of course there will.' Julia's attempting to reattach her circlet of flowers which fell off when Tamsin gave her a particularly enthusiastic hug. 'That's why we switched from our Methodist chapel. We'd never have fitted all these guests in there. The church is beautiful, too, and the vicar is a friend of Andy. His name's Kit, you'll love him, Grace. Better still, we'll really be able to spread out afterwards on the beach at The Seafood

Shack, just like we did for Tris's eightieth birthday bash.' She pauses. 'And for the wake after May's funeral.'

Grace's heart is full of sadness for the mother she's never had the chance to get to know. 'Did May have a good time at Tristram's party?' she asks.

'*Did* she? I'd say the word to describe her that night was magnificent,' says Julia. 'She had the most spectacular red dress ever and she spoke to everyone she liked. And some she didn't, for that matter. What a great lady she was.'

Julia's expression grows melancholy, and Grace knows drastic action is needed if this wedding isn't going to turn into a memory-fest.

'I wish Gramps was here to see me get married,' says Emily wistfully.

Oh dear. Grace has managed to stave off experiencing the worst of Julia and Emily's fluctuating moods as they think of what might have been this morning, but it's getting more and more difficult to block out their nostalgia. Weddings do that to a person, she guesses.

'It's a good job he isn't,' she says briskly. 'He'd be a bit surprised to find his wife getting hitched to someone else. And where would we put him? He could hardly be best man.'

For a moment, Emily and Julia stare at her in outrage, and then the corner is turned and they both start to giggle. Luckily, it's nearly time to go to church now.

'They're here,' shouts Tamsin. 'Come on, Grace, we don't want to be late.'

Grace hears the first of the cars approaching with relief, and checks her make-up in the hall mirror. James will be in church already, and she hopes she's looking her best, thanks to all the primping that's gone on today.

Robyn's there too, and not only that, James has persuaded Davina and Suzie to come to Pengelly for a visit. They're all staying at the pub, and James plans to rope them in to help him to decide where to live. He plans to rent somewhere that's big enough for Robyn too, when she eventually makes up her mind what she's doing next.

Grace and Tamsin pile into the first car, leaving Emily and Julia to follow in the next after a decent pause. Grace says a silent prayer to the God she hasn't spoken to since Sunday school. *Please let them get through these next few minutes without blubbing,* she whispers.

'What did you say?' asks Tamsin, busy smoothing her dress and admiring her bouquet. 'Dad says you shouldn't mumble.'

'Oh, nothing.'

'And that isn't true, is it? Dad says ...'

'Yes, yes, okay.' Grace looks down at her own flowers as they pull up outside the church. There's eucalyptus, smelling wonderfully herbal, frothy gypsophila, delicate sprays of an unfamilar cream flower with tiny bell-like blossoms, and roses almost the colour of Tamsin's dress.

'I love these bouquets, don't you, Tam?' Grace says, clutching at straws.

'Mmm. They're like little gardens, aren't they?' Tamsin takes a huge sniff of her flowers. 'Summer's going to be dead jealous when she sees the photos of me in my dress and everything. Oh look, Grace, they're waiting for us.' Tamsin's face is pink with excitement. 'Did you do a wee before we got in the car? I did. The toilets here are a bit spidery.'

They get out as elegantly as possible. Tamsin makes a huge effort not to rub against the car and Grace helps the smallest bridesmaid to arrange her dress and hold her bouquet properly. She gives the silky folds of her own dress a shake, squares her shoulders and takes Tamsin by the hand.

'This is it,' she says.

'Break a leg,' says Tamsin loudly. A couple of people near the back of the church turn and smile, and she tells them, 'That's what you have to say when you're doing a play. This is a bit like a play, isn't it? I ...'

Grace puts a finger to her lips as the bridal car pulls up outside the church. 'They're here, sshhh,' she whispers.

The vicar asks the congregation to stand and the organist plays the first notes of the music the brides and grooms have picked to start the ceremony. The joyful sound rings out through the church. It's an unusual choice – Grace has been to quite a few weddings over the years but never one that began with this lovely song. It was one of Harry's favourite tunes too, and she remembers him singing it to Audrey after they'd had one too many glasses of sherry at Christmas – 'True Love'. Bing Crosby and Grace Kelly, young and beautiful in *High Society*, Audrey's number one film.

Grace fights back tears and takes Tamsin's hand again as they lead the way up the aisle. She can see Andy and his best man, Emily's boss Colin, standing to the left of the altar, and Tristram and his best friend, a rather frail-looking George from the rival restaurant on the other side of the bay. Both grooms look as emotional as she feels.

'Hello, Dad,' mouths Tamsin, as Andy's eyes rest on his daughter. He gives her a little wave and blows her a kiss as they reach the front of the church and Grace and Tamsin peel off to the left to claim their seats.

As the two brides take their place, Grace can just hear a murmur from somewhere behind her. 'I see neither of them decided to wear white in the end,' the voice says, pure Cornish in accent. Vera is on form.

Fortunately the stage whisper is drowned by the vicar's welcoming words. The familiar words roll out, and Grace sends up another quick prayer. *Please don't let anyone spoil this lovely day.* God's going to be really surprised to be getting all these petitions from me after so long, she thinks. I hope he's listening.

Chapter Thirty-Three

Sitting bolt upright so as not to crease her dress in her pew right at the front of the church, Grace is very much aware of James, four rows back, in what would probably have been described by Audrey as the bosom of his family. She made sure she caught his eye as she walked up the aisle. On James's left-hand side is Robyn, and on his right, her mother Davina and Davina's wife Suzie who works with animals too. Grace was touched to see that today they've gone for glamour rather than practicality and pulled out all the stops. Davina's hair is as black as her daughter's and is loose on her shoulders, smooth and glossy. Both women are wearing shift dresses in jewel colours, Davina's emerald green and Suzie's sapphire.

Grace feels anxiety threatening to shatter her hard-won calm. If only James and his daughter understood each other better. Robyn texted Grace first thing today to say that when James got dressed this morning and he found to his horror that he'd left his suit trousers with the other items going into storage, Robyn had tried to make light of it, telling him that none of the wedding party would mind him turning up in his old grey cords, but Davina had been mortified for him, and made it worse by trying to think of a range of impractical solutions.

Grace knows in her heart that Davina meant well, but leaving James alone when he forgets things is always the best way. She makes a mental note to have a tactful talk to Davina and Suze about this later, wishing with all her heart that she could turn the clock back for him. This thick mist that descends is so debilitating. It's going to take patience and time to make him feel more like himself again, but maybe Grace can give him a few more precious memories back to help him along. She makes a silent vow to give it her very best shot, and to be braver about trying to help some of the other older residents too.

They stand for the first hymn. It's a harvest one, incongruous for a wedding but one of Tristram's favourites. The church is decked out in full harvest festival style, with sheaves of corn and huge vegetable marrows leaning against baskets of glowing red and yellow tomatoes and the ubiquitous piles of runner beans. The air is heavy with the evocative scent of chrysanthemums, and at the end of every pew, Emily has tied a huge sunflower flanked by long grasses and twigs.

'All is safely gathered in,' sings James, raising his voice as the hymn gets under way. Grace hears his mellow baritone and feels a sudden surge of joy. It's true. They're here in Pengelly, where James plans to stay for the foreseeable future. We *are* gathered in and welcomed, she says to herself. All I need to do is relax and let things happen.

The simple service continues, and Grace listens to the two couples making their vows, clearly and confidently. How can they be so sure of what they're saying? These are huge promises to make. All her life she's been daunted by the magnitude of the wedding service. Up to now, she's never been able to imagine being able to say these things with certainty. *Till death do you part?* Terrifying.

There's a heart-stopping moment at the point where anyone with objections is invited to state their case, but apart from the sound of Tamsin humming loudly to herself and asking Grace for a humbug, nobody blurts out anything embarrassing. Soon, everyone is on their feet ready to sing the next hymn, and Grace is pleased to hear James is in even better voice now as he belts out the traditional wedding choice, 'Love Divine'. She turns to see his eyes on her as she stands in the front pew, and as everyone sits back down, he gives her a thumbs up. It's time for Grace's big moment, and only James knows how nervous she's been about this.

The silky slip of a dress flows around her as Grace negotiates the two couples to reach the lectern. Turning to face the congregation, she takes a deep breath and puts her shoulders back. Then she sees the adoring look on James's face as he gazes up at her, and the tension ebbs away. She clears her throat.

'I'm new to Pengelly,' Grace begins, 'but anybody can see, even a rough-edged Midlander like me, that it's a place that looks after its own. I know these two happy couples are very important to you all, and they've come to mean a lot to me too, in a very short time. These people, this village – well, you've got everything going for you here, haven't you? The beach, the sea ... Vera's emporium ...'

A ripple of laughter runs around the church, and Vera nods graciously. James is beaming at Grace now and she can tell everyone is listening carefully.

'Sometimes, a new person on the scene can see things that the long-term residents take for granted, and it's clear to me that you've all got something very special in Pengelly. You care about each other in a way I've never seen before. I don't want to sound cheesy, but Andy, Emily, Julia and Tristram have all known tough times in their lives and the support and love of their friends here has pulled them through.'

Grace pauses, wondering if she's going to let herself down and cry, but instead takes a deep breath for her grand finale.

'So, good folk of Pengelly, my job here is to pass on

a big thank you from these four wonderful people to you, and to say that since arriving in your village, I've learned more about the true value of community than I've ever known before. And later, we're all going to raise a glass – probably quite a few glasses, if we're lucky – to old love, new love and grabbing happiness whenever and wherever you can. Pengelly, I salute you!'

There's a moment of silence when Grace finishes speaking, and then Will shouts 'Bravo' and begins to clap. Soon everyone is joining in, and Grace is being hugged with gusto by the newly married couples.

Even Vera is clapping quite enthusiastically now, and soon Grace is safely back in her pew, and the service continues with the signing of the register, a mercifully short and really funny talk from Andy's vicar friend, and a final hymn.

The two brides and their grooms lead the way out of the church to the triumphant sound of the organ playing the wedding march from Julia's favourite film, *The Sound of Music*. Grace poses for photograph after group photograph, her smile becoming fixed as she tries to keep warm. She wraps an arm around Tamsin, who's starting to shiver in the sudden cool wind that's sprung up. Autumn is in the air even in the shelter of the sunlit churchyard.

'I think it's time to go,' she whispers to Emily.

Emily waves to the drivers of the white limousines

and begins to herd everyone towards them. As they leave, Grace spots Robyn in deep conversation with Cameron, nose to nose in the shade of a yew tree. She smiles to herself.

'Is that Robyn's boyfriend?' Tamsin asks loudly.

'Quite possibly,' says Grace, 'but let's pretend we haven't noticed, shall we?'

'Why? Is it because boys are stupid and she won't want us to see her being nice to one of them?'

Emily and Grace exchange glances. 'No, I think Grace was meaning that everyone needs to be private sometimes,' Emily says. She smiles at Grace. 'Although sharing secrets is also good, to be fair.'

Chapter Thirty-Four

The wedding party is soon in full swing, with guests spilling out of Tristram's Seafood Shack and onto the beach, chatting and laughing as if they haven't seen each other for years. A fresh breeze from the sea sends some of them further across the sands to the marquee that Vince has hired, so there's plenty of room for everyone. This is just as well, thinks Grace, because absolutely everyone seems to be here.

She catches the eye of Emily's boss. Colin is Devon-born but lived in New York for years, where he met Emily in her more jet-setting days. He's cuddly, with shiny red cheeks, particularly today after three glasses of champagne.

'Grace,' he calls, 'come over here and let me get to know you properly. Em's told me an awful lot about you.'

'Crikey,' Grace says, accepting the brimming champagne flute he's offering. 'That sounds ominous.'

He laughs. 'No, only good stuff, I promise. She's very excited that you're helping her write her book.'

'It's all on hold. I don't know when we'll get a chance

to get stuck in again.' Grace thinks with longing of the piles of letters waiting in her house. 'That hamper she gave me is like Pandora's box. It's driving me mad. I hope we can go back to it soon.'

'Oh, I think you'll have plenty more time when the baby ...' He puts a hand over his mouth. 'Sod it. I'm such a big mouth. I've done it again. She'll throttle me. That was meant to be the biggest secret ever.'

'Emily's pregnant?' Grace is about to add 'Already?' but stops herself. Emily and Andy have got two houses between them and they're in love, married and looking towards the future. Why shouldn't they get cracking on extending the family as soon as possible? *But what about Tamsin?* a voice in her head whispers. *What's she going to say? Did I do enough to get her ready for this?*

'I don't think either of them expected it to happen so fast,' Colin says. 'But it's great news, isn't it? Unfortunately, I'll now have to kill you.'

'Yes, that is a shame. Could you wait until after we write the book? I won't tell them that you blabbed, honestly.'

'Well, okay, that does make good publishing sense, I guess. So, I've let slip my secret, and it was a pretty spectacular one if I say it myself – how about we swap? Where are they all going on honeymoon? I bet you know.'

Grace shakes her head. 'All I've been told is that

they're not going until tomorrow. Tamsin's coming to stay with me for a week. It's somewhere hot, though, because I saw Emily putting a bottle of factor fifty in her case. And Julia's bought a swimsuit. She says she hasn't had one for years.'

'They're never all going together? Surely not?'

'No idea. Buster and Bruno are going to stay with Tom and Cameron.'

They sip their champagne and watch the other guests mingling and chatting. The noise level is rising as the canapés are circulated and the glasses are topped up again. There are a few holidaymakers wandering along the beach and Grace can see their envious glances. She doesn't blame them, it's a fabulous party. A few months ago, this sort of gathering would have been a nightmare to her, with all the memories of weddings past, lost loves and heartache flying around. Today, it's manageable. Every now and again Grace feels a stab as someone has a particularly poignant thought, but mostly she can cope.

She sees James talking to Will, who's gesticulating wildly and laughing. James is grinning too, but his shoulders look tense inside the smart jacket. The incongruous cords seem to have gone unnoticed in the crush, but she can tell he's uncomfortable to have so obviously messed up. This is the downside of letting someone into your life and, she admits to herself for the first time, your heart. Being single and unbeholden to anyone can be lonely sometimes, but you never feel responsible for anyone else's pain, and you don't hurt as if you were in their place. How has she let this happen?

'You're miles away,' says Colin. 'Somewhere good? Although by the look on your face, I don't think so.'

'Do you ever get lonely, Colin?' Grace asks, emboldened by the champagne on an almost empty stomach. 'I know you've come home to England now. So was that why you moved?' She grabs a couple of cheese straws as a waiter passes by. To get drunk and fall over at this point would be very embarrassing.

He ponders this for a moment. 'That's a heavy one for a wedding party. I guess the answer would be yes and no. Yes, I do get lonely and no, that wasn't why I relocated. Wow.'

He stops talking and Grace follows his gaze. The lady in his eyeline is slim with short grey hair and very high heels. She's wearing a dress and jacket that, even from a distance, look seriously classy. 'Isn't that the babysitter Andy has for Tamsin? I hardly knew her without her jeans.'

'Yes. Her name's Vi. I've met her a few times when I've visited Emily.'

'Well, why don't you go and talk to her, then?'

Colin looks doubtful that this is a good idea, but

raises his glass to Grace and does as he's told. Alone for the first time today, Grace breathes a sigh of relief. The teacher voice and The Look are still useful sometimes. She slips her shoes off and is about to go for a little walk along the beach to get her own thoughts in order, when she feels a tap on her shoulder.

'Is it my turn yet?' asks James. 'I've come to escort you in for dinner, and after that, I'm claiming the first dance. So long as you don't mind being seen with a man who's only half smartly dressed, that is?'

He's making a joke of the situation but Grace can see the anxiety in James's eyes. She reaches up and kisses his cheek. 'I'd dance with you if you were wearing nothing but a grass skirt.'

'That's good. Because dancing's pretty much all I'm good for.'

'How do you mean?'

'Love, I've been doing a lot of thinking lately. I arrived in Pengelly without my trousers, I can't remember where I put my champagne glass down five minutes ago and I'm almost sure my daughter thinks I should be in a care home. All I can be is your best buddy, and that's only until I lose the plot completely.'

Grace looks at him steadily. 'We'll see about that,' she says.

*

By ten o'clock, the party's starting to wind down and Tamsin is flagging.

'I'm not tired at all,' she says, knocking over her lemonade glass and starting to cry.

'I'll take her home,' Vi volunteers, going to get their coats.

'And I'll walk you both back while there's still just enough beach,' says Colin, winking at Grace.

They set off together to take the shore route with Tamsin in the middle, holding a hand of each. Colin is beaming. Grace feels a pang of something indefinable. It can't be envy. She's going to be doing her stint having Tamsin staying with her for the next week, and Grace tells herself she'd better make the most of her last night of freedom. Perhaps it's something to do with the way they look a lot like a family.

James comes to stand beside her. 'How long are you staying at this do?' he asks. 'Only, Robyn, Davina and Suzie are leaving soon, and I wondered ...?'

As Grace ponders how to answer this, and indeed, what's actually being asked, Will saunters up with George and Cliff.

'Darling, these boys and I have got a lot of catching up to do, we haven't seen each other for years. Would you mind if I went back with them and stayed at their place tonight? I can call at Silver Street and get an overnight bag on the way there, if that's okay with you?'

'Of course. Lovely idea,' Grace says. She can feel James's eyes on her, and a tingling starts deep inside. She's getting, not a memory, but a picture of what could happen in her not-too-distant future. Her cheeks burn. 'Erm ... when do you think you'll be home, Will?' she asks, in what she hopes is a casual manner.

George laughs. 'Well, if we crack open the bottle of single malt I've been saving for when my hospital treatment finished, I doubt you'll see him before tomorrow lunchtime.'

All three men kiss Grace and shake James by the hand, then head towards Cliff's car, already planning their late-night snacks. 'I always say you can't beat cheese on toast and tomato ketchup sprinkled with fresh herbs at this time of night,' Grace hears George say, but Cliff's answering words are blown away by a sudden gust of wind.

The tide is coming in now, and James holds out an arm for Grace to take. 'Shall we go inside? I heard Tristram shouting something about bacon sandwiches for the last ones standing,' he says. 'Or ... are you ready for home?'

Grace turns to face him. 'I think I could probably make my excuses and go now,' she says. 'How about you?'

'Well, I've got my car here, now I'm here in the village for the duration, so I was going to head to the pub fairly soon. I could give the girls a lift back there and then drop you off home? I've only had half a glass of champagne because I never did find my glass and after that I wasn't in a drinking mood somehow.'

The air between them is crackling with unsaid words and the force of the feelings that are flowing from James. Grace shivers, torn between trepidation and excitement. She nods.

Half an hour later, they're sitting on the sofa at Grace's house in the soft light from two small table lamps, curtains drawn snugly against the velvety darkness. They're nursing large mugs of coffee and listening to one of Grace's ancient late-night compilation CDs. The mellow classical music slinks its way into Grace's mind, and the combination of that and the closeness of James make her giddy with possibilities.

James puts his coffee down carefully and takes Grace's mug out of her hand to do the same with it. He holds out his arms, and she moves into them as if she belongs there. 'You know what I said earlier about dancing being the only thing I was good for?' he murmurs.

She smiles, feeling the roughness of his chin against her cheek as he pulls her closer.

'And also that I could only ever be your buddy?'

'Yup.'

'Well, it turns out that was total bollocks.'

Grace laughs softly and he joins in, leaning down to kiss her very gently, then harder. Grace has the strangest feeling that they've slipped right inside each other's heads. His thoughts meet hers and there are no memories, only a joyful tide of anticipation.

'Let's go to bed,' she whispers, getting up and taking him by the hand.

He hesitates for a moment and she raises her eyebrows, afraid she's got it horribly wrong, but James says, 'But if I can't ...'

Understanding dawns. 'We're both a bit rusty,' she says. 'And if we can't, or even decide not to when it comes to the crunch, we'll have a damned fine cuddle instead, I'll tell you that for nothing. Deal?'

'Oh yes, most definitely a deal.' Solemn now, they shake hands on it.

'Come on then, or we'll have wasted the whole night on delaying tactics. I know you're nervous. So am I. But if you just trust me, James, and stop over-thinking everything, we'll be fine.'

The music ends as if on cue and they turn off the lamps and head for the stairs, still hand in hand. Outside on the moonlit street, a streetlight flickers and a cat yowls, but neither of them notice.

Much later, safe and warm in James's arms and almost asleep, Grace listens to the unfamiliar sound of someone else's night-time breathing right up close, so much more intimate than anything she's ever experienced before. As she drifts away on a tide of choices well made, at least for now, Grace makes a decision.

It's time to come clean to everyone about why I'm really in Pengelly, she thinks drowsily. *I'm not ashamed of who I am. And even if I never find my real father, I'm going to do everything I can to try. Somebody here knows something, I'm sure of it. And I'm starting with the letters, Emily or no Emily.* She yawns, wriggling out of James's reach to settle on her back for the night. There's only so much closeness a person can take.

Chapter Thirty-Five

James leaves Grace's house early the next morning. He hardly eats any breakfast. Grace guesses he's preoccupied with the thought that Will might arrive home sooner than expected and that Grace will be embarrassed.

'Relax, love. Will isn't the type to judge, as far as I can tell,' Grace says, but she isn't sorry to see him go. Last night was bliss, but she's going to have to ease herself in gently if they're going to be seeing each other as more than friends.

'I'll be in touch later,' James kisses her goodbye. She can tell his thoughts are already moving away, probably to what he's going to say to his daughter and granddaughter. He texted Robyn last night and received just a single smiley face and a thumbs up in reply, but James is still very much on edge. 'When will I see you again?' he asks.

'That sounds like a cue for a song,' Grace says, trying to think of the right answer. How can she set some ground rules without offending him? She hums the tune of the Three Degrees number under her breath, playing for time.

James doesn't return her smile. 'Shall we meet up for a drink later? What are you doing the rest of today?'

'Having another go at the letters, and then collecting Tamsin for her week-long sleepover.' Grace doesn't want to have to make excuses, but she needs some space. One eye is already on the hamper in the corner of the kitchen.

'Okay, just text me when you're free,' says James. 'If you're not too busy, that is.'

As soon as James has departed, the front door opens and Grace hears Will call, 'I'm home.' He comes into the kitchen, looking rather jaded and definitely paler than usual.

'You're making tea,' he says with relief, sitting down at the table. 'Just the ticket. Those boys certainly know how to drink. Mind you, they always did. And it's good to hear George is on the mend. Tough times for them. The chemo really took it out of him but he says he's had the all clear at last.'

'That's great news,' says Grace, dragging her thoughts back to the present with an effort. 'Toast?'

Will groans and shakes his head. 'Just builder's tea today, gallons of it, please, darling. Hot and strong. Anyway, I've got news.'

'Go on then, spill the beans.' Grace puts the teapot on the table and adds a jug of almond milk, sugar bowl and china cups. It's nice to have a house guest to spoil, she thinks, so long as he doesn't stay too long. A distraction is very welcome this morning.

'George and Cliff are selling their restaurant,' says Will, with the air of someone dropping a very large bombshell.

'No! But why?' Grace is mortified that she hasn't made time to visit Cockleshell Bay yet. She's heard such amazing reviews about the food, and now it's too late.

'They've had a kind of epiphany, I guess. Cliff's always in the kitchen, and the business side takes all George's time. Since his illness, George has decided he wants them to spend the rest of their lives relaxing and enjoying themselves.'

'That makes sense. You're a long time dead, as my mum used to say.'

'She must have been a cheerful soul.'

Grace laughs. 'She wasn't so bad really. She loved me and that's more than some people get.'

Will looks slightly puzzled at the way the conversation is going. 'Anyway,' he continues, 'George and Cliff have got a *mystery buyer.*' He lowers his voice as he says these last two words, and taps the side of his nose.

'Mystery buyer, as in, one person here knows, but it isn't me?'

'No. They wouldn't even tell yours truly, it's so secret.' The outrage on his face makes Grace laugh again.

'I'll really miss you when you go, Will,' she says impulsively.

'Why, where am I going?'

'Nowhere, I just meant ... oh, never mind. So Tristram will have the only decent seafood restaurant for miles around?'

'I got the impression that the buyer wants to keep Cockleshell Bay going in some other way. Don't quote me on that, though. And George and Cliff are talking about keeping part of it as an investment, like sleeping partners. It's hard to let go of something you love, isn't it?'

They drink their tea, each lost in their own thoughts. The September morning is warm and sunny and the back door is open, letting in the melodious sound of the many birds that flock to Grace's garden every day. A bee bumbles in and does a circuit of the kitchen, finally finding its way out again. The clock ticks slowly and the refrigerator hums. All is very peaceful. Will is the first one to stir.

'Can I talk to you, Grace?' he says.

'Oh. Yes, of course. Shall we go into the other room and be comfy then?' Grace stands up. She feels utterly exhausted at the thought of any more emotional soul-searching. Hasn't she done enough already today? But Will looks up at her, and the sudden desolation on his face catches at her heart.

'Come on then, top your cup up and let's go,' she says, leading the way.

When they're settled in the two easy chairs either side of the fireplace, Will leans forward. 'I have to tell you about something that happened a very long time ago. It involves your mother.'

Grace closes her eyes, wearier than ever. She's known this was coming, because Will's current memory of May is so strong that it's managed to burst through all the defences that have been forming inside her head since he arrived.

'Go on.'

'I was going to go to confession again to get this off my chest, and I still will, but I need to get your take on it too, if you don't mind?'

'Why?' The word comes out rather more sharply than Grace intended, and Will frowns.

'Because I value your opinion, Grace. Is that so wrong?'

She forces a smile. 'Of course it's not. I'm flattered. Tell me what the problem is.'

Will links his fingers together and stares down at them. 'It's about May's blackberry vinegar.'

'What?' This is the last thing Grace was expecting. Has she brought Will in here to talk recipes?

'Oh, I know it sounds odd, but May had a special way of making the vinegar, just for her husband.'

'For Charles?'

'Yes, for Charles.' Will says the name with such loathing that Grace flinches. She waits, and after a short pause, he takes a deep breath and continues.

'Charles had certain ... hobbies ... involving a few of the more impressionable young men of the area. He liked to take them out sailing by moonlight when the tide and the weather was right. May didn't approve.'

'No, I can see why that might have been the case.'

'Oh, not because of his sexual preferences. She wasn't prejudiced and she was happy to have the house to herself. An open marriage suited May very well. We talked about it,' he adds, in answer to Grace's quizzical expression.

'So what was the problem?'

'It all came down to Charles's character. Sometimes his friendships were innocent, and sometimes they weren't. People in rural areas like this were more judgemental in those days. May was before her time in a lot of ways, I think. Being gay wasn't something that was talked about and it certainly wasn't accepted, especially by some of the more dyed-in-the-wool elders.'

'But what about George and Cliff? Were they together then? You said you'd known them for years.'

Will smiles. 'Oh yes, their partnership was different in the locals' eyes because they were both so well-liked. There were a couple of local ladies in relationships, too, although it was never openly acknowledged back then. But Charles wasn't ... kind.'

He stands up and goes to the window. With his back to Grace, he says, 'I think May and I together ... well, there's no easy way of saying this – we murdered Charles.'

Chapter Thirty-Six

The old cliché of time seeming to stand still actually happens to Grace at that moment. She feels frozen. Even her eyes won't blink for several seconds. Then Will breaks the spell by coming to sit near her.

'I'll tell you the rest,' he says.

'I think you'd better.' Grace's voice sounds unfamiliar to her ears, like a distant echo of how it should be.

'I came into the kitchen one day at Seagulls, where May and Charles used to live. May had the radio on quite loudly and didn't hear me arrive. She was so shocked to see me that she dropped a funnel and some powder on the table. She'd been decanting her black-berry vinegar into small bottles and straight away I registered the labels on this batch. They were blue.'

'I don't understand.' Grace wants him to stop so badly that she's tempted to put her fingers in her ears, like a child avoiding a telling-off.

'The blue labels were meant to show that these particular bottles were reserved for Charles. He had bad asthma and he called it his elixir. He used to drink the vinegar diluted with hot water to ease his chest. May always marked them. She said it was to make sure she didn't give too many away to the neighbours and the church fund-raising stalls.'

'And you're saying ... what, exactly?' Grace is torn between defence of her mother, and total horror.

'She was putting ground-up sleeping tablets into Charles's bottles, Grace. She admitted it. She said it was to slow him down and stop him going on the prowl, as she put it. There had been a couple of occasions when the younger men of the district had been hounded by Charles.'

'But ...'

Will holds up a hand. 'I know what you're going to say. Somebody should have stepped in, reported him, or something. But people didn't seem so aware of possible abuse in those days. Or if they were, they often turned a blind eye.'

Grace sits in silence digesting all this. After a while, she says, 'Hang on, though. Charles must have been drinking the doctored stuff for years. How could it suddenly have killed him?'

'Ah. Well, on the night he died, I was with him earlier in the evening. He had a bad asthma attack in the pub and several of us warned him not to take the boat out. Some people said afterwards that he'd hinted that he was seriously ill, dying even, but there was no evidence of it. He'd already had several pints before he had the attack and there was a storm brewing too, but you never could tell Charles what to do. He went out to sea anyway.'

'But why is that anything to do with you or May? He was a grown man.'

'He was ... but I saw the bottle with the blue label sticking out of his pocket. You should never mix sleeping tablets with alcohol, everyone knows that, and so did May, but she'd given him a brand-new bottle even though he'd told her he was going to the pub. She knew he always drank more when he was in one of his black moods and that he would more than likely go out in the boat. That was how he let off steam.'

Grace's mind is whirling now. 'That can hardly be called murder though, can it?'

'Think about it, Grace. Surely you can kill someone by not telling them something they really need to know? The blackberry vinegar was harmless taken in moderation, properly diluted and without alcohol being involved. It just made Charles sleep soundly, safe at home in his own bed.'

'Yes, I get that.'

'But May was well aware, and so was I, what would happen if he had a fresh bottle when he was planning a bender. Charles loved the stuff. He'd swig it straight. He should never have been in charge of a boat that night, especially in bad weather. He either fell overboard and drowned, or he jumped. Either way, he wasn't in full possession of his faculties. I didn't try to stop him ... and neither did May.'

Grace wraps her arms around herself, chilled to the bone, and tries to be impartial.

'Perhaps May hoped Charles would feel drowsy after a couple of pints and come home instead of going out in his boat. Have you thought of that?'

'It's possible. She kept a close eye on him when she was around, and she liked to have the man where she could see him. Mind you, May was often away. She was an unusual woman.'

'Tell me more about her, Will. I need to hear everything. This is pretty awful.'

Will strokes his chin, eyes dreamy. 'She was a bundle of opposites. Generous to a fault but sometimes wary of giving too much of her time. A stern judge if you did something wrong but easy-going in other ways. An incredibly private person but occasionally ... more friendly than most women.'

'What's that supposed to mean?'

Will smiles. 'I suppose it can't hurt to say these things now. May took the occasional lover. I was very green in those days, pretty sure I preferred men, and she decided I should have the chance to look at the other side of the coin, you might say.'

'You ... and May?' Grace stares at him.

'It's not that unbelievable, surely?' Will says, pretending to be affronted. 'I was quite good-looking in those days.'

'It's not that, and you know it. You're still a charmer now. But you must have been so much younger than May. And a friend of her husband too.'

'One thing you'll learn if you're determined to find out more about this lady, Grace, is that May made her own rules. She set out to seduce me and it was a lovely experience, but in the end, I chose a different path. We stayed friends, though. There were no hard feelings.' He laughs. 'I could have worded that better, I guess.'

They sit in silence for a while, each lost in their own thoughts. Grace waits to see if there's more. Surely he's building up to a revelation. He has to be. If this gentle, elegant man is her father, she won't complain.

'Will,' she says in the end, running out of patience, 'I've got to ask. When did you and May ... I mean ... what year was it?'

Startled out of his reverie, Will jumps up, looking at Grace in horror. 'Oh no, I didn't mean to make you think that, darling. This was a good while before you were a twinkle in anyone's eye. I'm not your father, Grace. I told you before, I have absolutely no idea who has that honour.'

'Honour?' Grace's laugh sounds harsh even to her own ears. 'I don't think anyone can have had that view, do you? And if my mother was as generous with her favours as you're suggesting, it could have been most of the males in the village.'

Will settles himself again and leans forward. 'I certainly didn't mean to give you that impression. May was discerning. She occasionally indulged herself in a dalliance, from what I could gather, although never indiscriminately, and some of them must have happened further afield when she was on her travels. But you can be sure that whichever lucky man fathered you, he was someone she liked and respected.'

'I'll have to take your word for that. I'm going to find out, Will, one way or another. And I'll start soon, maybe at Angelina's lunch get-together in the village hall next week, when the honeymooners are back and Tam's gone home. That lady's really good at having the ideas and then getting everyone else to do the donkey work. I've been told to make enough vegetable soup to feed an army.'

'You've fitted in so well here, haven't you?'

Grace thinks about this before replying. 'Yes, I have, up to a point, but I haven't been honest with people. Only Emily and Julia, anyway. Oh, and James, of course. Talking of honesty, I want to show you something.'

She reaches for the red photograph album and opens it at the page where the youthful Will is sitting on the harbour wall with May. 'I found this, and I know it's you and my mother. But Will, why is she wearing Julia's ring? I know the picture's small, but I've scanned and enlarged it and I'm pretty sure it's the same one.'

Will peers at the snapshot, his brow wrinkled. 'She isn't. She's wearing ... Look, this is complicated, and I need to talk to Julia before I tell anyone else what I went to France to discover. I promise I'll come clean as soon as I can.'

'Right. I'll hold you to that. And I need to do the same, to tell you the truth. It's time to put my cards on the table. Or most of them.'

Will gives her a nod of approval but Grace shivers. Brave words, but how is it going to feel to be exposed to everyone here? To be revealed as May's daughter and some random man's son? What secrets are still lying in wait for her in Pengelly?

Chapter Thirty-Seven

The village hall looks cheery set out for lunch the following week. There are tables dotted around everywhere surrounded by chairs, each one laid with a pretty tablecloth, soup spoons and salt and pepper pots. Nothing matches, but it's a gloriously riotous sight. Grace breathes in the smell of freshly baked bread and heads for the kitchen with her giant pan of soup, struggling under the weight.

Tristram is already by the cooker wearing a bright green pinafore and Grace spies Robyn through the hatchway sitting in a corner of the hall, making sure all the spoons have had a polish. She comes into the kitchen to give Grace a hug.

'I asked if I could come along,' she says, as Grace raises her eyebrows. 'I know it's meant to be for the oldies but I haven't had home-made soup for ages. You don't mind, do you? Oh, but ...'

Robyn looks towards the door where Cameron is now hovering, seeming unsure whether to come in or not.

'Off you go, young 'un,' Tristram says to Robyn. 'I reckon that chap's come courting.'

Robyn reddens and looks undecided, but after a moment heads for the door.

Grace grins. 'I'm so glad I'm not Robyn's age any more,' she says.

'You're not joking. I couldn't stand being young again. This is the best part of my life by far.'

'With Julia, you mean?'

He nods. 'This marriage lark just gets better and better the more you do it.' He smiles at her. 'How about you? Are you and James an item yet?'

Grace doesn't answer, but goes to take over where Robyn left off with the table arrangements.

The room gradually starts to fill up and soon every table is taken. The hum of noise builds up until Grace is forced to retreat to the kitchen. Sometimes crowded places are still a problem, although her shielding techniques are getting better all the time.

She dishes out bowl after bowl of soup, while James, who's just appeared, hands round baskets of crusty bread. He gives her a brief hug, but Grace is now too keyed up to respond with more than a smile. Julia arrives with reinforcements of soup.

'Sorry I'm so late,' she says breathlessly. 'I told Tris to start without me. I had to wait for my apple crumble to be ready, Emily's bringing it. I'll do seconds, shall I?'

Eventually, everyone is fed and watered, and James comes in to tell Grace that Angelina wants a word with her. She follows him into the main hall and finds the old lady sitting in a corner wrapped in a rainbow-coloured shawl decorated with tiny mirrors and sequins.

'I wanted to ask you something, my dear,' Angelina says as Grace joins her. 'You remember when you called in to see me a couple of days ago and we chatted about May?'

Grace nods. Angelina was very forthcoming about May's somewhat bohemian lifestyle, but didn't come up with anything new. 'Yes, of course. Why do you ask?'

'It's just that ever since then, there's been something on my mind but I can't pin it down. I think it must be to do with that ring that caused so much trouble in Julia's family. I keep getting flashes of a memory but I can't grab it. Do you know what I mean? Did I say anything to you about a ring?'

Grace knows she didn't, but she can feel a mounting sense of anticipation. This is going to be important in some way. She takes Angelina's hand. The bones feel very close to the surface. 'Maybe you did,' she says. 'Let's have a go at remembering. If we both try, we can probably give each other a clue.'

They lean together with their eyes closed, and Grace picks up the scent of Angelina's patchouli oil and a faint whiff of turps. For a moment, nothing happens, but then a rush of pictures bombard Grace. Angelina's outside the pub in the dark. She's arguing fiercely with somebody. The opal ring flashes in a passing car's headlights and someone laughs.

Grace focuses on the scene and gradually, frame by frame, slides it back into Angelina's mind. The old lady shudders and then opens her eyes.

'That's it!' she says softly. 'I've got it. May was teasing Ida. She said she was going to divorce Charles and marry Will and that he'd given her a ring. Ida was furious. She always had a thing for Will. I told May not to be such a fool. I said she had to give the ring back. I thought it must be the one that Don's family were making all the fuss about.'

Grace can hardly breathe. She's done it again and it was relatively easy this time. There must be more that she can do with this gift now she's really controlling it. She drags her mind back to the subject of the ring before she can be distracted. 'And was it Don's family's ring?'

'May said it wasn't. She said it was a present to her and she wasn't giving it back because it made her feel like a queen, something that Charles had never bothered to do. And then she laughed.'

They sit in silence for a moment and then Grace notices that the room is also much quieter. One by one, the chattering locals stop talking and turn their faces to the front expectantly.

'What are they waiting for?' Grace asks Angelina.

'Oh, they'll be expecting me to say a few words. Come with me, Grace. You've done so much to help me get this idea off the ground, and with the drop-in too.'

For a moment, Grace's courage fails her and she longs for nothing more than to be sitting in her own little courtyard garden. Why is she putting herself through this? She follows Angelina to the front of the hall and they both perch on the edge of the stage.

Angelina clears her throat importantly. 'I just wanted to thank the team that have helped me to put this lunch party together. It took some arranging, I can tell you.'

Grace hears Tristram give an ironic cheer. He's the one that's done much of the hard work today, but she can tell he's more amused than annoyed at this oversight.

'The other thing I wanted to do was formally welcome Grace as a fully-fledged member of our little community. Pengelly is lucky to have her here on a permanent basis.'

Clapping breaks out and Grace climbs up onto the stage, heart pounding. It's time to take her courage in both hands. This next five minutes is going to be crucial to her mission. She needs to get it right. James looks at her with his head on one side, and she sees Will slide in and sit down at the back, having arrived late after his visit to St Mary Magdalene. Confession is by appointment these days, it seems.

'I want to appeal to you all for help,' Grace says. A sea of faces turns towards her. Even Vera's looks reasonably amiable. 'I need some of your memories.'

There's a ripple of laughter. 'You've come to the wrong place, love,' shouts an elderly man near the back. 'Most of us joined Tom's group because we've lost some of them. Memories, I mean.'

Grace smiles. 'Now, that's where we perhaps won't agree,' she says. 'Because I believe that all those experiences and recollections from our various pasts are locked inside us, hard-wired into our very bones. I don't accept they're ever lost. They just need finding.'

Everyone's eyes are on Grace now and the room is silent. From the kitchen comes the faint sound of the huge silver tea urn bubbling, and she hears Julia switch it off and then sees the other woman's expectant face peering through the hatch.

She stands up straighter, willing the watchers to be sympathetic. 'I've got to admit I came to Pengelly under false pretences,' she says. 'The story was that leaving my job and having looked after my ailing parents, who'd recently died, left me stressed and anxious, with no fixed plan for the future.'

'You mean you lied to Julia and the rest?' Vera says. 'Why would you do that? Why are you really here?'

Anyone having the urge to drop a pin would be able to hear it hit the floor very clearly, Grace thinks irrelevantly. This silence is unnerving now.

'Well, it turns out I didn't lie, Vera. When I started being honest with myself, I had to admit that was exactly how I *was* feeling. But I actually came here to find my mother.'

The words are out, and Grace can see the surprise on most faces now.

'I'll try and make this as brief as I can,' she says. 'My adoptive father, Harry, gave me a letter before he died that revealed my mother was actually someone most of you knew well. Her name was May Rosevere.'

Loud gasps and a rumble of conversation almost put paid to the rest of the revelation but Grace holds up a hand. 'If you could be really kind and let me get to the end, we can thrash out any questions later. This is quite a hard thing to do. I'm a private sort of person and I don't go in for baring my soul as a rule. The opposite, really.'

The babble dies down and Grace nods her thanks and continues. 'I have found out that May was unusual in many ways, and one of her ... features ... was that she seemed much younger than her actual years. She managed to have a child when she was the grand old age of fifty-seven. Yes, I know that sounds unbelievable, but trust me, it's true,' she says, when the noise level threatens to rise again.

'For reasons of her own, May decided not to keep her child and I think she was confident that nobody found out about her pregnancy, although I've found out since that at least one person rumbled her. She travelled up to the Midlands to have her baby and a random set of circumstances brought her into contact with Audrey and Harry Clarke who were desperate for a child of their own. They took me in.'

Grace steels herself for the next part. Is today going to be the start of a whole new kind of understanding of her past?

'I'm asking you today for two things. One is to share any memories you might have of May Rosevere with me. It doesn't have to be here and now, we can arrange to meet in private if you like. The other – more delicate – request is,' she clears her throat, suddenly terrified. 'I'm fifty-four years old. Does anyone here know who my father might be?'

Chapter Thirty-Eight

Safe in the sanctuary of her living room with James and Will later that evening, Grace cradles a brandy glass in both hands and stares into the fire, thinking back to her big revelation. There were so many people who seemed to want to share their memories of May that Grace has started a list, with phone numbers, so she can go and see them to talk properly over the next few weeks.

'But still no ideas about who your pa might have been,' says James, sounding almost as disappointed as Grace feels.

'The May Rosevere I knew was very discreet.' Will tops his own cognac up and offers the bottle to James, who shakes his head.

'Better not, my brain's bad enough without fuddling it any more,' he says. 'Are you still interested in coming to see Emily about the idea we had, Will? She said she'd be at home tonight.'

Grace frowns. This is the first she's heard of these two cooking up a plan. These last few days, they seem to have bonded, and Will's seen more of James than she has herself.

'It's no use looking at me like that, love,' James says, grinning. 'You'll hear about our idea soon enough if anything comes of it.'

'And she definitely knows you're coming?'

'Yes, I rang and asked if it was convenient. We shouldn't be too long, but I'll head straight back to the pub afterwards, because you look tired.'

'And I've got my key,' says Will, patting his pocket.

They both drain their glasses and head off towards Curiosity Cottage. Tired? What does that mean? It's usually just another way of saying you're looking rough. Grace hears them laughing as they amble down the road and feels an unexpected pang of loneliness. Will is a very easy guest to have around, but she hadn't banked on him taking James away. *What's wrong with me?* she asks herself crossly. *I've never minded my own company before. I've always loved being alone. I don't want to start being needy this late in the day.*

The doorbell rings just as Grace is contemplating going to bed ridiculously early with a good book and a hot chocolate. Half pleased at the diversion but apprehensive as to who would drop in without warning in the evening, which isn't at all a Pengelly habit, she goes to investigate.

Outside on the step is Tristram, holding an enormous bunch of yellow roses. 'I bought you these,' he says simply, handing over the bouquet.

Speechless, Grace motions her visitor in and they go through to the kitchen. 'The flowers are beautiful,' she says eventually, when she's made tea, 'but what have I done to deserve them?'

'I've told Julia they're to say a belated thank you for being such a beautiful and kind matron of honour, which they are,' he says. 'But when I get back I'll tell her the main reason, of course. I've never kept a secret from her before and it doesn't feel right.'

Grace takes the tray through so they can sit by the fireside, pours the tea and waits. There's a tension in the air that she hasn't experienced with Tristram before. It's as if someone's pressed pause on the room and every-thing is on hold. Tristram is as smartly turned out as usual, in a cord jacket and well-pressed chinos with a very fancy Fair Isle pullover over his shirt. He takes a sip of his tea and makes eye contact for the first time.

'I chose the flowers because yellow roses were May's favourite,' Tristram says. 'I haven't been able to stop thinking about what you said at lunchtime. Now I know who your mother is, I can see so much of May in you. I can't believe I didn't see it before.'

'In what way?'

'It's all there in the way you hold your shoulders and have such a straight back, your amazing green eyes, and now I know that you're actually fifty-four when you look so much less, so in that too.'

'You knew May very well then?'

Grace predicts the answer just before it comes. Her whole body tingles as Tristram says, 'I did indeed, sweetheart. In fact, I'm as sure as I can be that I'm your father.'

Grace stands up, but the floor seems to be about to rise up and meet her, so she subsides into her chair again with a thump. She hears Tristram's voice as if from a distance. 'Oh lord, now I've gone and done it. Are you going to faint? Stupid old idiot, I am. Should have broken it to you more gently.' She makes a huge effort to steady herself.

'I'm okay ... I think ...'

He goes into the kitchen and comes back with a glass of water. Grace drinks gratefully and begins to feel a little more normal. 'Can you tell me about it?' she says. 'About you and May, I mean?'

He nods, still watching her warily for signs of collapse. 'If you're sure you're ready?'

They settle themselves again and Tristram bites his lip, as if unsure where to start. 'I was twenty-six,' he says eventually, 'and what they called *a bit of a lad*, which in those days was a euphemism for being a terrible flirt. What nobody twigged was that I was all talk. I could do the chat, but I was petrified of admitting I'd never slept with a girl.'

Grace doesn't reply, but Tristram seems to take encouragement from her expression.

'I pretended to my friends – who at the time were a much wilder lot than me, I have to say – that I was a real Lothario. There were only two people who rumbled me, and one was May. The other isn't important,' he adds quickly, when he sees Grace about to ask a question.

'During one brief but very hot summer, she taught me everything I needed to know, with such love, such style, such fun ...' Tristram's voice tails away and he stares into space, lost in his reminiscences.

After a couple of minutes, Grace coughs discreetly and he comes back to the present with a start.

'She made it clear from the outset that this was just a joyful interlude with no strings attached, and it ended quite naturally with the start of the cooler weather. We used to meet in the dunes, you see, or in the sea cave along the bay.'

Grace thinks Tristram's about to drift off into a daydream again so she shuffles her feet meaningfully. He grins.

'Sorry. Soon after that I had to go up north to work for a few months, which was where I met the woman who became my first wife, Henrietta, or Hungry Hen, as Julia likes to call her. Still bleeding me dry, but that's another story. When I got home to Pengelly, May had gone off on her travels, as she liked to do. It was a while until we met again, and the summer fling was never spoken of, but we were always on good terms. I loved your mother very much as a friend and I think she felt the same about me.'

Grace can't speak. Her mind is so full of this new information that she feels as if it will explode.

'I know this is bound to be a shock to you, especially when you've been trying so hard to find out about May. The dates all add up or I wouldn't have said anything if it meant upsetting you with something that was doubtful. But Grace, I can't tell you how proud I am to be the father of such an intelligent, all-round lovely human being. I'll be here whenever you want to talk more. If you ever do?'

The last words are almost like a plea. Impulsively, Grace reaches forward and takes Tristram's hands in hers. 'Of course I do. This is fantastic. Incredible. I was starting to think I'd never find out. And for it to be you ...'

Their eyes meet again, and Grace is struck by the affection she sees on Tristram's handsome face. 'You must have been a very charismatic and persuasive young man,' she says smiling. 'You've still got it, haven't you? Oh!'

'What's the matter?' Tristram flinches at Grace's gasp, still very much on edge.

'What will Julia say? And Emily? Gina and Vince? They might not feel as happy about all this as you do.'

'They'll be delighted, there's no doubt about that. And Julia and Em have got a great distraction tonight anyway. Will and James are busy outlining their plans to rent the rooms at Curiosity Cottage on a long-term basis, at least until the spring when the holiday season starts again, which frees Emily up to concentrate on the coming baby ...' He sees Grace's expression and says, 'You did know, I'm assuming?'

'Yes, Colin let it slip at the wedding party. I was just thinking about Tamsin's reaction.'

'Ah. They haven't told her yet.'

Grace decides to worry about this one later. Tristram's gone back to the subject of the new tenants now.

'I can't say I'm overjoyed at the prospect of having Will across the road, but there you go, Julia and Em are pleased.'

'Why don't you like Will? I've been meaning to ask you, Tris, if it's not all too long ago to remember?'

'Oh, it's not a very nice story. I'll tell you sometime. I've got no problem remembering that part of my life. There are other memories that are getting more elusive, though. Since lunchtime, May's really been on my mind and I've been battling to remember the song we danced to at my eightieth birthday bash when she looked so fabulous. I've tried everything to jog my memory and Julia can't remember either. It was an amazing night.'

Grace is captivated by this challenge. She might feel

closer to her mother at the same time. 'I think I can help you with that one. Hold my hands.'

Tristram looks slightly alarmed but does as he's told, and they move closer so their knees are almost touching, intertwining their fingers. Tristram's hands are warm and dry, intensely comforting. Grace closes her eyes. For a while, nothing happens.

'I can't do it,' she whispers. The emotional punch of being with her father must be muddling her mind.

'Can't do what?'

'Give you your memory back. It seems to be a skill I inherited from my mother, although her take on it was ... different.'

'Aha. I knew she was special, but she would never tell me how. Go on, try again.'

They both close their eyes now, and Grace tries to tune out any background noise. The fire crackles, footsteps outside on the pavement draw nearer and then pass by, the clock strikes, but gradually those sounds fade away and she's somewhere even warmer. The smell of something wonderful to eat fills her nostrils. Is it barbecued chicken? A low hum of voices rises to a babble and then a cheer goes up and she's actually there in the Seafood Shack with all the partygoers, and she's watching Tristram approach a table in the corner.

He's dressed even more smartly than usual and he has a red rose in his buttonhole. As he nears the lady sitting at the corner table, he stops and bows low. 'May I have the pleasure of this dance, May?' he says with a chuckle.

Grace holds her breath. There is her mother, magnificent, as Julia said, in a long scarlet dress with her beautiful white hair perfectly styled and stiff with hairspray.

'You silly old fool,' May says, smiling up at Tristram. 'Can't you find somebody with a bit more go in them than me to drag around the floor?'

'Well, I could, but there's nobody here to hold a candle to you.'

'Don't tell Julia that,' May says, poking him in the ribs but beginning to haul herself to her feet.

Tristram helps her up and holds out an arm. May takes it and the crowd parts as they make their way onto the dance floor. The strains of the music aren't clear to Grace for a few seconds but then suddenly she's certain of the melody. It's another of Harry's favourites, from one of the Fred Astaire films he loved.

'Just the way you look tonight,' sings Tristram in a deep bass voice as he steers May gently around the floor. She twinkles up at him and whispers something in his ear that makes him blush. The song continues but the memory fades.

Tristram opens his eyes. 'Did you get anything?' he asks.

Grace nods. 'I did. It was beautiful. Now all I need to do is find a way of giving it back to you. Let's try again.'

The connection is still strong between them and Grace focuses all her energies on sending the magical moments back into Tristram's consciousness. She has no idea whether it's working and is beginning to flag when he suddenly gets to his feet and holds out a hand to Grace.

'Lovely, never ever change, keep that breathless charm,' he sings, twirling her round in the small space available. 'You did it, you clever sausage. It was "The Way You Look Tonight". How could I forget? May loved that song. What a brilliant daughter you are. The sky's the limit now. We'll have to think how we can make this useful. A planning meeting is called for. With wine! And cake!'

Grace smiles at him, exhausted now and still trying to take in all these amazing new developments, not least that she's got a brand-new father to get to know. 'We'll all be in Pengelly for the winter then,' she says happily, suddenly full of optimism for the future. 'One thing's certain, Tris – Christmas is going to be pretty spectacular this year.'

Chapter Thirty-Nine

December

Grace has been looking forward to the festive season in Pengelly with the sort of excitement she's not felt since she was a small child who still firmly believed in Father Christmas. The first sign that Pengelly is revving up for celebrations is the strings of fairy lights decking every possible place along The Level. This is done with the minimum of fuss, and is followed by an enormous fir tree being delivered to the church, a slightly smaller one to the chapel and a most spectacular display in the shop window.

'I do like to push the boat out in December,' says Vera, when Grace compliments her on her creation of a snowy mountainside dotted with traditional Swiss chalets, all with fully functioning lights. 'My late husband, may he rest in peace ...' She crosses herself and looks up to where Grace imagines heaven must be, in Vera's head at least. 'My Stan used to say, "There's nobody does Christmas like the missus," and it was true. After he passed on, I gave it all up for a few years, but I've decided it's time to bring the jollity back. You can't be miserable forever, can you?'

'No, you certainly can't. Or you shouldn't, anyway, if you can help it.'

Vera pats Grace's arm, which is the nearest thing to friendly she's ever managed. 'And I've got more go in me now I've got the nice little bungalow to go home to and no pesky stairs to climb. Young Robyn brings me a nice milky coffee down from the flat as soon as I get here every morning. She knows just how I like it – two sugars and piping hot. Not a bad lass, for a youngster. And what do you think about that boyfriend of hers setting up in George and Cliff's old restaurant? She says he won a load of money on the lottery one night when he was drunk. Can you believe it?'

Grace says she can indeed. Robyn has told her the full story of how Cameron bought a ticket for a bet and then nearly forgot to check the numbers when he sobered up. He's something of a socialist and the guilt of having so much money for no effort at all made him go wild for a short time. He was even on the point of giving most of it away when he met Robyn and decided there was a better use for it. They're both working as hard as they can to learn the ropes, enrolled on the same catering course at the college in Truro and loving every minute.

'Well, I'm glad I'm here to see the Christmas display happen,' Grace says, admiring the shelf of plum puddings, gourmet stuffing and tinned chestnuts, amongst other delights. 'I can't wait to see how you celebrate New Year.'

Vera sniffs. 'You *are* sticking around then?' she asks, looking over the top of her glasses at Grace. 'Only, some folks come here in the summer, decide to stay and then act surprised when the weather turns bad.'

'I think I've proved I'm not put off by a bit of dampness and a storm or two, Vera,' says Grace mildly. 'Ida's old house is about as cosy as you can get. I can't see me ever wanting to leave Silver Street.'

It's the first time Grace has put this feeling into words, but it's quite true. Pengelly has taken her to its heart. The insular, almost friendless Grace who arrived here in the spring seems like a different person now.

'Ah. Well, we've all rumbled why that is,' says Vera. 'You and him at Emily's cottage are thick as thieves, aren't you?'

'I'm not staying here because of James,' Grace begins, and then, seeing the knowing look on the other woman's face, shrugs and pays for her shopping without another word. Sometimes it's hard not to want to slap Vera. Best to remove herself from this place before the temptation becomes too great.

Grace picks up her loaded basket and sets off down

the street towards Memory Lane. Her mind is full of ideas for Christmas presents for her new friends. She's done quite a bit of online shopping, and she and Julia have visited various local markets and craft shops, but she still hasn't found the perfect gift for James. He's embraced downsizing with gusto and got rid of most of the possessions from his old home, happy to live with May's furnishings and just his favourite books and music system to make his room more of a bedsit.

James and Will share the living area quite amiably and Robyn goes round to cook for them some nights. When she's not available, they've begun to experiment with some very strange combinations of ingredients. Sometimes this is successful, others not so much. Grace shudders at the memory of being invited round to try out their new creation involving goat's cheese (Will seems to have relaxed his strict veganism), tomatoes, mashed potato and a mystery addition, which turned out to be dried apricots.

It's been a peaceful few weeks since the weddings. Grace has practised several times retrieving memories for Tristram and James and has managed a few tactful experiences with Hattie and Angelina. She's building up to making her skill more public at the drop-in group, but the thought of leaving herself exposed to scorn or disbelief is daunting. Not everyone is as receptive or kind-hearted as these four.

Grace spots Tristram coming up Memory Lane towards her and speculates, as she's done before without coming to a conclusion, why Tris still has a problem with Will. When they're forced to meet socially, they skirt around each other like angry dogs, but neither ever openly says anything to start an argument. Very strange. She decides to ask Will straight out about it next time there's an opportunity.

'Good morning, light of my life,' her father calls, as soon as he's within earshot. 'I'm just off to get a newspaper. Won't be long.'

He hurries up to her and enfolds her in one of his huge hugs. Grace breathes in the now familiar scent of the expensive, spicy balm he dabs onto his beard. He's wearing his long black overcoat and hat and looks particularly dashing today with the addition of a bright yellow cashmere scarf. He sees Grace looking at it and strokes it proudly.

'Charity shop bargain,' he says. 'Feel the quality.'

'Is Julia at home?' Grace asks, when she's duly admired the new purchase. 'I need to talk to her about arrangements for Christmas.'

'Yes, she's there, but I think things have got even more complicated now. Young Cameron's got ideas about having us all over at his new place. I'm trying to think of it as his gaff, and not George and Cliff's, but it seems strange not to have my old mates in competition with The Seafood Shack any more.' He sighs, and Grace pats his arm.

'I'll go down and have a chat about it then,' she says, giving Tristram a kiss.

As they part and Grace heads for number 60, she has an overwhelming sense of belonging. Her old flat and the town where she grew up were fine, but this is home now, and finding Tristram has been a complete joy. It's a strange and wonderful feeling to discover a father you didn't know existed, and in some ways, it's made it easier to respect the memory of Audrey and Harry.

'Hi, Julia,' she calls, as she lets herself in by the back door.

'Hello, dear.' The kiss is perfunctory this time. Julia is wrapped in an all-enveloping pinafore, busy making mince pies. 'Put the kettle on, would you? I'm gasping for a cuppa.'

Grace does as she's told and takes her coat off, settling herself at the table to watch. It's an art form, seeing Julia in action in the kitchen. Each little circle of pastry is carefully cut with the minimum of waste and tucked into greased tins before being filled with Julia's home-made mincemeat and topped with a pastry star. Her opal ring is in a little dish by the kettle, as usual, to keep it from being clogged up with flour.

'Do you want to test out one of the first batch?' Julia

says, putting the latest two trays in the oven as Grace deals with the teapot and finds a milk jug. Her newly discovered step-mother likes to do things properly even if it's only a quick elevenses in the kitchen.

They drink their tea and Grace has to restrain herself from whimpering with delight as she eats a still-warm mince pie, pastry crumbs cascading down her jumper.

'Is there a recipe for these?' she asks, through the last mouthful. 'They are amazing.'

'There is. I've got my old book back now.'

'Why? Where was it?'

'Over at May's, for some reason. Emily found it when she was sorting. I can't think how it got there.'

Grace considers this. She has a very good idea how Julia's recipes got into May's clutches. The temptation to purloin a whole lot of edible memories must have been too strong to resist. Unbidden, a clear picture of the white-haired old lady comes into her mind and she gasps. Julia is gazing into space and doesn't notice.

'What are you thinking about?' Grace asks, after a moment.

'Pardon? Oh, I was just remembering how May used to love my mince pies. You're very like her, you know,' she adds.

'Because I'm greedy and I love pastry?'

Julia laughs. 'Well, yes, there's that. But mainly, it's

more that you've got her confidence and calm. I do miss her, you know.'

'I wish I'd had the chance to meet her.'

The sadness that engulfs Grace when she thinks of all the lost chances of knowing May brings tears to her eyes, but she rubs them away and says, 'Tristram says Christmas dinner has taken a new turn?'

'Heavens, I have no idea what to do about that. Cameron says he wants to invite us all there. Will and James, too. Vince, Cameron and Robyn are planning to do the cooking, but it's all going to be vegetarian or vegan because they want to try out their new recipes on us.'

'It sounds wonderful, and we'll get to see the new layout before anyone else. What's the problem?'

'We can't have Christmas lunch without turkey!' The words burst out of Julia, startling Grace with their fervour. 'We just can't. It's not right.'

Chapter Forty

Grace ponders on the turkey problem. She's never much liked it and she really wants to go to the new restaurant. Her own memories of the big day are blighted by thoughts of dry meat and lumpy gravy. Cooking was never Audrey's strong point, and Harry always assumed the kitchen was a place meant for women only.

'Why don't we have an extra lunch later in the week at my house, just for you and Tris?' she asks. 'I bet James would help me. I don't mind having a bash at doing all the trimmings if it's just us four. I've never cooked Christmas dinner before.'

'Grace, you're fifty-four and you've not roasted a turkey?'

She shakes her head. 'I used to go abroad whenever I could as soon as we broke up for the holidays, often to Italy, as far south as possible. My mum and dad started going on those festive turkey and tinsel coach trips when I went away to uni, and after that, we never went back to the old routine. It was a relief, really.'

Julia looks at Grace pityingly. 'Poor soul,' she says.

'No, it was great. I had whatever I wanted to eat sitting in the sunshine somewhere, we did presents afterwards and they got to go ballroom dancing and eat sherry trifle with hundreds and thousands on it. Perfect.'

'So shall we say yes to Cameron? I must admit it'll be nice to have the day off. I'm usually in the kitchen from first light. The only problem is ... Will.'

'Oh. You mean him and Tris?'

'Yes. They can't really avoid talking to each other if they're sitting round a table.'

Grace hears Tristram coming back round the side of the house. She waits for him to come in, shed his outer garments and sit down, and listens to a tale he wants to tell them about Angelina's latest painting being sold to someone in America. 'The USA, Grace. She's going to be famous in her nineties. What a woman. You must show me some of your own paintings sometime. Maybe I've passed on something useful to you. Although mine are just daubs compared to Angelina's stuff.'

'Fantastic. But I want to ask you something,' she says, as soon as he draws breath and begins to eat a mince pie.

'Mmmph?' he mumbles, raising his eyebrows encouragingly.

'What have you got against Will?'

For an excruciating few seconds, Tristram chokes on

a pastry crumb, eyes watering as Julia pats his back and passes him a glass of water. She frowns at Grace but there's no point in backing off now.

'I want to know why two of my favourite people don't get on, that's all,' she says, when Tristram's recovered. 'We're all going to eat together at Christmas, and it's going to be really uncomfortable if you pair are pouting like schoolboys who've had a fight over their conkers.'

Out of the side window, Grace catches sight of the man himself heading up the lane. 'There's Will now,' she exclaims, jumping up. 'I'm going to fetch him in here to sort this out once and for all.'

Ignoring the loud protests of the other two, Grace rushes after the disappearing figure, shouting his name as loudly as she can. He pauses, looks back and begins to walk towards her. Shivering, and wishing she was wrapped up as warmly as Will, she tells him that Julia has a new batch of mince pies that need testing quite urgently.

'They're for the church coffee morning tomorrow,' she improvises, 'and she's insisting they're not good enough. I've told her they're fine, but you know Julia ...'

Bewildered, Will nevertheless follows Grace into the warm kitchen, recoiling when he sees Tristram.

'I rather think we've been set up,' Tristram says, standing up and motioning Will to a seat at the table. 'May I take your coat?'

415

Will is silent, but removes his vintage trench coat and hands it over. He sits down. When Tristram joins them all again, Grace says, 'This is down to me, I'm afraid. I'm sorry to drop this on you, but we've all been invited to have Christmas lunch at Cameron's new restaurant.'

'How pleasant,' says Will, his eyes giving nothing away. 'And your point is?'

'It isn't going to be in the least bit pleasant if you two can't get over whatever's bugging you, settle your differences and be grown up about it.'

Nobody speaks for what seems like an age, but eventually Tristram jerks a thumb towards Will and says, 'Ask *him*.'

Will smirks and Grace has the urge to shake him. Why can't he see how important this is?

'I suppose you're still thinking about that day at the sea caves?' he says. 'It was a joke, Tristram. I never meant to upset you.'

'Ha! A joke, you say? Writing *Tristram is a virgin* in yard-high letters on the sand for all the world to see? Very funny. How we laughed.'

'Not everybody saw it. I rubbed it out. Anyway, you *were* a virgin. Not for long though, if I recall.'

Tristram seems to feel this has gone far enough. 'Anyway, that's a minor issue. Let's cut to the chase. Where's your opal ring, Julia?'

Julia reaches for her ring and slips it on her wedding finger. 'Why?' is all she says, but Grace gets the feeling that she isn't totally surprised.

'Okay then, Will, as you've put me on the spot, explain to me how Charles managed to steal this precious thing, when it belonged to your mother and your family, not to you, and should have been safely in the Midlands until Don needed it.'

He leans back in his chair, for all the world like the counsel for the prosecution. Will's normally pale cheeks are flushed now. Grace winces. What has she unleashed here?

'I was going to come and see you both to talk about all this as soon as I got back from France,' Will says, in a low voice. 'I must admit I've been putting it off. Where shall we start?'

'You tell me. The ring went missing. The sisters always assumed you'd taken it. Why, I have no idea.'

They all look at the ring, sparkling gently. Julia twists it slightly, making the colours gleam, pearly and brilliant.

'We only found it by accident, just in time for us to get engaged,' says Tristram. 'And funnily enough, it was very carefully hidden inside the lining of Charles's fountain pen case. It had been missing for years. Ever since you legged it to Ireland, in fact.'

Will rubs a hand over his face. 'You're quite right. It

was me who gave the ring you're wearing to Charles. He promised me he'd get it to Don so you could have it, Julia.'

Julia covers Will's hand with hers, throwing a warning glance at her husband. 'You wanted me to have it all the time?' she says. 'But we thought you took it for yourself, and then Charles winkled it out of you to sell. He was always short of cash towards the end.'

'It wasn't quite like that. I *did* take it, but it was me who needed the money. It was a desperate situation. I knew you should have the ring by rights, Julia, so I had a copy made. It's a good one,' he adds. 'It wasn't cheap.'

'But ... but why?' Julia has withdrawn her hand now and Tristram is on his feet. 'The original ring wasn't worth that much, surely? Not enough to warrant you getting a copy made. There couldn't have been much left over after that.'

'Oh, but there was. Mother always knew how valuable it was. She didn't tell Elsie and Kathryn because they were getting so competitive about who should have it, but she made sure I knew. It was so precious because of who it had belonged to in the past. In the right hands, I was sure it would fetch enough for me to pay off my debts. I was being blackmailed,' he says sadly. 'I'd made a couple of bad mistakes with the company I was keeping at the time.'

Grace is so fascinated now that she's stopped worrying about the tension in the room. 'Who owned it?' she asks. 'It must have been someone really important.'

'It was part of a large collection left by Queen Victoria,' Will says, 'but it went missing soon after her death. She was fond of opals, so I found out.'

'Wow. But however did it come to belong to your mother, Will?' Grace is deeply impressed. 'I wish we could see the original.'

'I could never get the full story out of Mother about how it came into her family,' says Will. 'She was very secretive about the whole thing. And you *can* see the queen's opal ring. It's here.'

Will reaches into his pocket and brings out a small leather ring box. He places it on the table. Tristram sits down again with a thump and leans forward as Will clicks open the box. Inside, resting on a red velvet base, is the most beautiful ring Grace has ever seen. It's as near identical to the one Julia is wearing as possible, she guesses, but the precious stones set in this one glow with an inner fire that Julia's ring doesn't possess. The diamonds surrounding the three opals are slightly larger and more sparkly, and the opals themselves twinkle and shine with every colour imaginable in the sunlight from the window.

For a few moments, nobody speaks. Then Julia reaches out a tentative finger to touch the treasure.

'It took a lot of finding,' Will says. 'The trail had gone cold. I knew the ring had started off in Normandy, but my buyer had moved several times since I sold it to him. When I finally located him, he could only tell me the next person to own it. Of course, that was only the start of the hunt. That's why I was away so long over the summer.'

'But how did you get it back?' asks Grace, mystified. 'Surely it's worth even more now?'

Will shrugs. 'I've managed to amass quite a lot of savings over the years,' he says. 'A priest in Ireland has very few expenses, you know, and I've made a few good investments.'

'You must have had to spend every last penny to buy it back, though,' Tristram says. 'What are you going to live on now?'

'I'm fine. No need to worry. There's a small insurance policy ready to mature. Emily has been very generous with my rental arrangement. There probably won't be any spare for Christmas presents though, I'm afraid.'

'I think this is present enough,' Julia says shakily. Will pushes the box towards her and she takes the ring out. She slides the one she's wearing off her finger and replaces it with the original version. Holding out her hand to the light, she moves her fingers slightly to create even more of a sparkle. The others watch, entranced.

'Did anyone else know about this other ring?' asks

Grace, knowing the answer, but wanting to see what Will would say. She holds her breath. Please don't let him lie, she thinks to herself, I can't bear it if he lies.

Will grimaces. 'I was young and arrogant. I showed it to May and she cooked up a joke to tease Ida that we were engaged. She loved the ring. She said it made her feel like the queen who'd worn it first. May had the most wonderful quirky sense of humour but she could sometimes be a bit cruel, you know. Ida didn't see the funny side.'

Tristram seems about to argue with this statement, but then raises both palms to the ceiling. 'Yes, she was complicated. She loved with a passion but she also hated that way too. And she thought Ida was ridiculous, the way she moped around waiting for you to notice her and all the Cherrington-Smyths' ridiculous pretensions. You didn't help matters, Will.'

'I know I didn't. I'm not proud of any of my behaviour back then.'

Julia is still staring at Queen Victoria's beautiful ring as it gleams and sparkles on her finger. 'You stole this from me, Will,' she says slowly. 'It was meant to be mine. And all those years Don searched for it. You deserve to be punished for this. I don't see why any of us should forgive you.'

Grace is startled by these fierce words coming from gentle Julia, and from the faces of the others, they're equally shocked. 'But Julia,' she says, 'you can't mean that. I can see why you're angry, but it was all so long ago. A lot of bad things happened at that time. Surely Charles being murdered was worse.'

The stunned silence that meets these words makes Grace want to bury her head in her hands. Why on earth did she have to drop that bombshell into the conversation?

'Murdered?' Julia whispers. 'So the rumours were true? Was it May after all?' Tears begin to trickle down her cheeks and Tristram jumps to his feet to put his arms around her.

'You'd better explain what happened, Will,' he says heavily.

'You knew about this too, Tris?' Grace says. 'Was it some sort of weird conspiracy?'

Will swallows hard. 'We all thought it was May's fault, I guess, but I could have stopped it. So could you, Tris, and so could Ida, and Angelina and a handful of others. We let it happen. It seemed like a sort of Russian roulette. We all let fate take over.'

He goes through the whole story again for Julia's benefit, ending with '... but of course you were away at the time. Your mother was very ill.'

Julia listens, still looking at the opal ring. When he's finished, she says, 'And now it's over. May's gone, Charles has gone, and he was an evil man. I don't very often use that word, but he was, Grace. The ring's back where it belongs and Will's here with us, where he should be.'

Will clears his throat and blinks hard. 'So, am I forgiven, Tristram?' he says. 'Can we be friends at last? Julia, can we put all this behind us at long last?'

Tristram holds out a hand and Will takes it without hesitation. The handshake goes on so long that Grace begins to lose patience. Then Julia gets up and kisses Will on both cheeks.

'So what this boils down to is that we can all have Christmas dinner together without you two growling at each other? Because you've been tetchy too, Will, haven't you?' Grace says, weak with relief at this outcome.

Will looks at his feet. 'I might have been a bit offish,' he says eventually. 'I just felt so guilty. No amount of confession helped. I did a very wrong thing, all those years ago. I stupidly assumed Charles would hand the replacement ring over. I suppose I should have guessed he'd keep it really. I thought you'd never know and you'd enjoy the new ring just as much as you would have loved the original.'

Tristram grins. 'You're probably right, and there's absolutely no point in going over this any more. What's done is done and you've put it right as best you can. Let's have a mince pie to celebrate the return of this beautiful thing. I'll put the kettle on.'

Julia and Grace exchange glances. There's hope yet for a peaceful Christmas Day feast. Will refuses coffee, makes his excuses and goes to leave, looking exhausted. Grace follows him to the lane, ostensibly to see him off, but as she hugs him, she whispers, 'Well done, you've made Julia and Tristram very happy today. I still think there are a few things I don't know about my mother, though. More curiosities, if you like?'

'You could well be right, but be careful. You could end up finding out even more things you don't want to know.'

'I'm willing to take that risk,' says Grace.

Chapter Forty-One

There's a light sprinkling of frost everywhere when Grace wakes on Christmas morning. She lies in bed, luxuriating in the unusual feeling of being perfectly contented to be in her own home on this day. There's been no need to plan her escape to somewhere hot and far away. Although most of her Christmases have been spent abroad, the last two saw her well and truly grounded, unable to leave the frail old couple who depended on her for everything and refused point blank to have carers to help out. She regrets none of it, though. Their boundless love over the years has been paid back in full.

Grace takes a leisurely bath, gives the birds some extra mealworms and fat balls as a festive treat and eats breakfast watching the sparrows and robins fight over them. The kitchen is warm and cosy and there's no need to leave the house for another hour. She's arranged to meet James at church for the morning service, something she's never been tempted to try before.

'Are you sure you want to?' he asked as they said goodnight the previous evening. 'I don't expect you to do this for me. Davina and Suze are coming with me, if they get up in time, so I won't be on my own.'

Grace smiled. The two women arrived at the pub for a week's holiday only two days ago, having kept their visit secret from James, and he's still buzzing with the joy of it. 'I'll be there,' she said. 'And who says I'm doing it for you anyway?'

Dressed in a new red sweater and her smartest black skirt, Grace finds sparkly earrings and a necklace, pulls on her warmest boots and slips into her long camel coat which has been warming near a radiator. Adding a soft, crimson scarf and a spritz of perfume, both early presents from Robyn, she heads down Silver Street, soon catching up with Ida and her husband.

'I didn't know you were a churchgoer, dear?' Ida says. 'But it's lovely to see you. Happy Christmas.'

Calls of *Merry Christmas* can be heard from all sides as they near the old stone building, and Grace has such a lump in her throat from the strong feeling of belonging here in Pengelly, that she can't speak to James at first when she joins him in a pew near the back. She nods to Davina and Susanna, kisses James on the cheek and settles down to read the service sheet.

The manger filled with straw is centre stage near the altar and an elderly, rather battered plaster Nativity scene is set to one side, surrounded by candles. All around, villagers are murmuring to each other, but the chatter ceases as the vicar welcomes them and they all stand as the organ blasts out the first carol, 'Once in Royal David's City'.

When the final hymn ends, Grace follows a stream of people to the door, the stirring words of 'Hark the Herald Angels Sing' still ringing in her ears. *Born to raise the sons of earth, Born to give them second birth.* The carols seem to be all about love and giving. Grace has never listened to the words properly before. Second birth is what this new life in Pengelly feels like, and the varying kinds of love she's found here make her feel very humble on this Christmas morning. Maybe there is something in this church business. She resolves to have a proper talk to James about it all when the time is right.

There's a bottleneck forming near the door because everyone's queuing to say goodbye to the vicar. It's Kit, Andy's old friend, and as Grace reaches him, he leans in to hug her and whispers, 'Good turnout, eh? Nothing like Baby Jesus for getting bums on seats. Works every time. Nice to see you, my heathen chum.'

Grace digs him in the ribs and moves on, keen to scoop up her collection of elderly people to take to the lunch venue. Cameron has invited everyone he thinks would have otherwise been on their own, and James has added Grace to his car insurance so she can do some of the taxiing because Robyn has appropriated him to help with the cooking.

'Come on, gang,' Grace says to the huddle just outside the front porch. 'Let's get you to the restaurant before we all freeze. We need to pick Hattie up in ten minutes.'

She herds Angelina, Vera and an old gentleman by the name of Edgar towards James's sleek black car. Edgar is new to Pengelly but Vera seems to have adopted him. He gives the initial impression of being sweet and biddable, but Grace detects a flash of spirit in his eyes when Vera tries to fasten his seat belt.

'I've actually had an invitation to go across the road to Cassie and Dom's house for my lunch,' Angelina says, 'but I couldn't resist the chance to see Cameron's new place. It's been closed for ages now. Anyway,' she adds confidingly, 'I couldn't cope with all those little boys for too long. The new baby's due any day and they're completely over-excited.'

'And I asked Edgar if he'd like to join me for the day at my new place,' says Vera, not to be outdone, 'but in the end we decided we should support Cameron's venture, didn't we, dear?'

Edgar nods, but his eyes meet Grace's in the driver's mirror and she's sure she detects a very slight smirk on his face.

With Hattie safely on board, Grace drives the last couple of miles to the clifftop café with her carful of lunch guests warbling 'In the Bleak Midwinter' at the tops of their reedy voices, in a variety of keys. She's quite glad to reach the door with them and hand them all over to Tom, who's on welcoming duty.

'Well done,' he says to Grace under his breath, giving her a kiss and taking her coat. 'We're just waiting for Tristram's lot now. Will's already getting stuck into the egg nog.'

As he speaks, Andy's Land Rover rolls up. The back door opens and they hear Tamsin shriek, 'Happy Christmas, Grace. Have you seen the tree yet?'

Grace fields Tamsin's hug and they go inside hand in hand. The tree is just as magnificent as Robyn promised it would be. She waves to them from the long open hatchway to the kitchen. All the chefs are wearing white coats and black and white checked trousers, with their hair tucked into white caps bearing the motif 'The Vinery'.

'What do you reckon then, Tam? Is the tree cool, or what?'

Tamsin stands completely still, spellbound. The Christmas tree reaches right up to the high ceiling and is covered in twinkling white lights and frosted bunches of grapes. The vine theme is repeated all around the large room; leaves that look good enough to be real twined around candelabras on each table and decking every wall with more tiny white lights intermingled. The walls are painted in what looks like old-fashioned whitewash but Grace assumes must be something much more upmarket, and every table is laden with polished silver and glass sparkling in the candlelight. Soft Christmassy music is playing in the background, more carols and festive tunes.

'It's magic,' says Tamsin eventually, 'and Grace, I've got a secret, but Dad says it's okay to tell you. Just you,' she says importantly. 'Nobody else can know yet.'

'How exciting. Go on then, let's have it.'

'Em's not having one baby, she's got two in there. I'm going to have a brother and a sister, or two brothers, but I think it's going to be both sisters. That'd be best really because they can have my old clothes. I'm calling them Scarlet and Ruby. Or maybe Pearl and Peaches. Or ...' her voice tails away and she gives a little skip.

'How fabulous.' Grace sees Emily watching her and blows her a kiss, adding a thumbs up.

'We can have one each,' says Tamsin.

'I beg your pardon?' Grace has a sudden vision of Emily presenting her with the gift of a baby.

'Me and Emily, I mean. She'll be too busy to look after them both. I'm having first pick.'

'Well, that's lovely. A big sister is what everyone should have. I'll help too, if you need me.'

'Can you do nappies?'

'Erm ... no ... but I could learn, I expect.'

'I'll teach you. It's probably easy, although Emily's

bought the proper sort made of towel and you have to have pins. She says we're not having the plastic ones because we're wrecking the planet enough as it is. They just rot in great piles of ...'

Grace holds up a hand. 'I get the picture. Let's get out of the way of the door.' They both move forward to make room for more people coming in, and Tamsin links arms with Grace for a moment before hopping off to find Andy and Emily.

'This is heavenly,' Grace breathes to nobody in particular, gazing round the room as the excited guests seat themselves. There are no place names, so Grace joins Angelina, Ida and her husband at the nearest table, hoping there'll be room for James with them when he's freed from his duties.

'Thank you again for the lift,' Angelina says. 'Can I pour you a glass of wine?'

'Just a half. I'm driving,' says Grace.

Angelina tops up her own glass happily and drinks most of it in one go. 'I must say, Cameron's done us proud, and the extension looks very impressive.'

Cameron comes out of the kitchen at this point and claps his hands. His hair is cropped short now and he's clean-shaven. With his high cheekbones and dark eyes, this gives him the appearance of a very handsome forties film star.

'Just wanted to welcome you all properly to The

Vinery,' he says. 'And to say ... well, tuck in. You're our first official diners, but we're opening properly in the New Year and hopefully by the time the tourist season starts, you'll have all been our guinea pigs so often that we'll be absolutely perfect. Happy Christmas.'

He goes back into the kitchen to cheers, and the well-oiled machine that is Cameron's staff for the day swings into action. James brings Davina and Susanna to sit at Grace's table and is soon deep in discussion with them about ideas for a wedding blessing on their first anniversary.

'Kit says he'd love to do it, if you're agreeable to coming down here?' he says hopefully.

'It sounds perfect,' says Susanna, smiling across James at Davina. 'We've talked about it a lot lately. It'd be the icing on the cake. If my folks don't want to come, that's up to them.'

They carry on making plans, and under cover of the ensuing babble Ida leans towards Grace. 'I've been thinking about you, and what you said about wanting to know more about May,' she says quietly.

Chapter Forty-Two

Grace waits as the older lady tackles her starter of deep-fried seaweed with a vegan cheese fritter and fine slices of tomato. She munches appreciatively, and then says, 'I know lots of people have told you quite a lot already, but I've remembered something else.'

'Oh?' Grace can hardly keep from fidgeting. Lately, she's felt closer than ever to her birth mother, for some reason, and she's still greedy for as much information as she can get.

Ida swallows the last mouthful and drains her glass. 'It's about the blackberry vinegar,' she says quietly, looking Grace straight in the eye.

'Ah.'

Grace waits, painfully aware that the next few minutes will probably be crucial to the way she's always going to feel about May. Ida leans closer and lowers her voice even more.

'I was in the pub that last night. There were a few of us and we were all pretty merry. I ... I was aware of May's habit of making sure Charles was safely out of harm's way.'

'You were? How?'

'Oh, I see you already know about that? I wondered if you did. You seem the sort of person who ... knows things. Who told you? I suspected one or two other people had an inkling.'

Grace doesn't answer, and Ida shrugs and carries on. 'We were good friends, as much as anyone ever was with May. I'm much younger, of course, but May had friends of all ages.'

'And the night in the pub?' Grace prompts, when Ida is lost in the past for a moment. She glances around the table but the others are caught up in their own conversations apart from Ida's large and rather taciturn husband Lionel. He's very red in the face and seems to be on the point of sliding under the table.

'Sit up straight, Lionel,' Ida says sharply. 'And I think you've had quite enough wine for one day.'

He nods at her sleepily and she turns to Grace again, lowering her voice. 'Yes, the night at the pub. The others went outside to watch the firework display. It was the landlord's birthday and he was always a show-off, but I don't like loud noises so I stayed inside. Charles came back because he'd forgotten his cigarettes and started to take the mickey out of me for being a scaredy cat. It was then I saw the bottle sticking out of Charles's pocket and I asked him what he was doing with it. I knew May had recently ... adjusted ... a new batch and she never let him have any if she knew he was either going on a bender or heading out to sea, or both.'

'She didn't?' Grace feels the beginning of a great wave of relief stealing over her whole body. 'Go on.'

'Charles winked at me and put it on the table in front of us. He said he'd found the new bottles with the blue labels just as he was leaving the house. "What the eye don't see ..." he said. "Don't blab, Ida. My chest's bad. I need this stuff. She reckons the sugar rots my teeth the way I swig it down, so it's got to be well diluted, and if I go at it like mad it won't last the winter." I waited until he wasn't looking and then accidentally knocked the bottle onto the floor.'

'Oh, Ida. Really?'

'Yes, I did. It smashed everywhere. The barmaid was furious with me. I wasn't sorry. I always disliked the man but nobody deserves to die. Afterwards there was a lot of gossip but I kept right out of it, and it all worked out in the end. Nobody suffered. Well, except Charles, but he was so drunk he could barely have noticed he was drowning, the fool.'

Ida smiles at the memory and Grace's head spins slightly. She concentrates on breathing deeply and regularly. She's not going to faint. She mustn't. May is innocent. Grace says the words over and over again to herself as she drinks a glass of water. Ida's turned her attention to the main course now, a delicious-smelling nut roast studded with chestnuts and cranberries and surrounded by golden-brown roast potatoes, parsnips and carrots.

'Thank you,' Grace says. There are no more words. *Thank you* isn't nearly enough but it'll have to do for now.

Ida nods, mouth full, and Grace turns to James who's already finished his main course and is helping himself to extra vegetables.

'I'm just going outside for some fresh air,' she tells him. She weaves her way between the closely packed tables to the side door, waving to Julia and narrowly avoiding having to stop and chat to Will, who's looking almost as bleary as Lionel. Her coat is hanging in the lobby and she snuggles into it, grateful for the scarf as she steps out onto the decking.

The tide is coming in, and Grace watches a family walking along by the water, dodging the waves and laughing as they play tag. The father is carrying a baby in a sling on his back and Grace can just see the tip of its woolly hat.

She sits down rather suddenly on a bench as James emerges from the restaurant.

'What's the matter, love?' he asks. 'You've hardly eaten a thing.'

'Everything's perfect now,' Grace says. 'I'll explain when we've got more time. Something's been worrying me, but now I can look forward to the New Year. Settling into

Pengelly properly, carrying on with the soup kitchen and the drop-ins and everything, finding out how I can help in other ways. It's time to pull out all the stops at last.'

'You'll certainly be able to help Emily. I've just heard the news about the twins. Tamsin couldn't keep quiet any longer.'

'I don't know anything about babies,' Grace says doubtfully.

'But I do. We'll babysit together. I'm a dab hand at nappies,' James says. He shivers in his smart shirt and trousers. He didn't stop to find a coat before he came to look for her, which is typical of him, Grace thinks fondly. 'I do love you, Grace,' he says. 'You know that, don't you? No, I don't just love you, I absolutely adore you.'

He kisses her and Grace feels that fierce connection again. Her whole body fizzes with anticipation and joy. When they break apart, they smile at each other, a long, lingering smile that's full of promises. Grace gets to her feet, feeling the cold biting at last.

'Let's go back inside,' she says. 'I'm hungry now. I'm going to eat Christmas pudding and think about the future. We're going to be a great team, you and me.'

'But we don't even live in the same house. What are we going to do about that? And I'm sixty and I'm not sure how long I'll have what's left of my marbles. Some of them have already rolled away.'

'We'll worry about all that later. There's no need to

rush into living together. Some couples make it work having separate homes, at least to start with.'

James laughs. 'You're nothing if not an optimist,' he says.

'An optimist with a massive dose of curiosity thrown in,' Grace says. 'They're not bad things to be.'

They're just about to go in together, when the side door of the restaurant bursts open and Tamsin runs headlong into Grace's arms. She's sobbing so hard she can't speak for a moment or two, but as Grace hugs her, she blurts out, 'I've got to tell you something.'

'Could you fetch Tam's coat and tell Emily where she is?' Grace asks James, lifting the little girl onto her lap and wrapping her arms around her more tightly.

He hurries away, alarm on his face, but by the time he returns with a soft green throw from one of the bench seats, Tamsin is calmer.

'I couldn't see her coat but this is warmer anyway, and you can both cuddle into it,' he says. 'Do you want me to stay?'

Grace shakes her head and James goes back inside, with a last backward glance to check they're well covered up.

'Now then, my small chum, what's all this about?' Grace asks, when the sobbing has dwindled into a last few hiccups.

Tamsin takes the tissue that Grace has found in her

coat pocket and scrubs at her face. 'I thought of something horrible and I couldn't say it to Dad and Em,'
she mumbles.

'But you can tell me, can't you?'

'Yes. It's just ... when the sisters are born ...'

'Or brothers?'

Tamsin ignores this comment. 'When the babies
come out, the first thing they'll see is Em, and they'll
get bigger and bigger and they'll always be able to
remember what she feels like.'

Grace is lost for a few seconds and then she has a
flash of understanding. 'You mean, you can't remember
your own mummy?'

Tamsin nods. 'I was only really small when she went
away. I want to be able to remember her properly. I've
seen the pictures of her holding me in a blankety sort
of thing but I can't ... I can't ...'

She sniffs hard, trying not to cry again, and Grace
thinks fast. Dare she try to help? If she doesn't, this sad
scene will haunt her forever. What harm can it do?

'Tam,' Grace says, 'I don't believe memories ever go
away. Inside you, very deep inside, you're storing the
way your mummy felt when she cuddled you, right
from the moment you were born into this world, and
there are probably even some woolly memories in there
from before that, when you were still safe in her tummy.'

Tamsin's listening, her eyes big and trusting, and

Grace has one final misgiving. What if this somehow backfires? She's gone too far to stop, though.

'I think I can help you find those memories, or at least some of them, Tam.'

'Can you do magic then? Are you a witch? Or a fairy?'

Grace smiles, loving the way anything is still possible and believable when you're seven. 'No, but I want you to do something for me. Relax as much as you can and let your mind go free. Let it think about your mummy but not little details of how she looked in the pictures. More like ... I don't know ...'

'Her shine?'

'I don't know what you mean, love.'

'Dad told me that when my mum held me for the first time her eyes were shining so hard he thought she could light up the whole world.'

Grace gasps, almost floored by this beautiful image of new motherhood. She pulls herself together with difficulty. 'Yes, that's exactly it. Try for me, go on.'

They are silent for a while, wrapped in the fleecy throw, hearts beating together. Nothing happens for what seems like an age, but at last Grace feels the familiar energy flowing through her body. She prays that nobody else will come out here and break the spell, as the deeply buried echoes of Tamsin's first moments on earth begin to filter through into her brain.

'Keep going,' she whispers.

Tamsin's eyes are closed now and her expression lets Grace know the experiment is working even if she hasn't been able to tell from the buzz filling her own body. When the memories have become a trickle rather than a torrent, Grace concentrates as hard as she can, just as she did with the others, and sends them flowing back where they came from, but stronger.

'Grace, you did magic. You really did. You're so clever.' The little girl opens her eyes, rubs them with her fists and sits up, pushing back the folds of material.

'Can you feel your mummy now?' Grace hardly dares to ask in case she breaks the spell, but she already knows the answer.

'Yes! She smells like the brown stuff in the tiny bottle Julia puts in her cakes and her hair's all soft and warm. She holds me really gently and she calls me her little bird.'

'Vanilla essence?'

'That's it, and all sort of ... soapy.'

'Wonderful. That sounds perfect.'

'Are you crying, Grace? You mustn't. This is a happy thing. And it's Christmas Day. We're all doing presents back at our house later, remember?'

'I'm not crying.' It's only a small fib.

'I'll just go and check with Dad if the *little bird* bit's right, but I bet it is. Are you coming inside now?'

'In a couple of minutes. Off you go, I'll be in soon.'

Tamsin is back in the restaurant before Grace has

even had a chance to fold the blanket. She puts it on the bench beside her and gazes up at the perfect crescent moon that's just appeared from behind a cloud.

'Make a wish on the new moon, my pigeon.' Harry's words echo in her mind. She remembers him taking her outside to see it properly. Audrey always rolled her eyes at the daftness of this idea, but Harry was a great one for moonlit nights.

The words of the last carol that they all sang in church filter into her mind. *Love came down at Christmas. Love all lovely, love divine.*

'I wish all the love that's come down to us this Christmas will stay forever,' Grace whispers, to the moon.

She stands up just as the restaurant door swings open again.

'Are you ready to come in, Grace?' James says, holding out his arms to her. 'You must be freezing.'

'I'm ready for anything now,' she says, moving towards the light. 'I'm the memory keeper and the memory maker too. It's my legacy, and now I've got a job to do.'

James smiles at her. She can tell he doesn't quite understand what she means, in fact she hardly understands it herself, but does that matter? There will be time for explanations later. For now, love is more than enough.

2019

May sits up in bed, wrapped in a soft woollen shawl and surrounded by letters. The clock on the wall has a very loud tick and seems to be telling her that time is running out. It doesn't matter. May's had a good life on the whole, and she has very few regrets. Marrying Charles was a mistake, in hindsight, but there have been plenty of years since his watery demise to rejoice in widowhood, and to be fair, he could be amusing when he tried. If only he'd made the effort a bit more often.

The other big regret in May's life is, of course, Barbara. Could she have kept her daughter if she'd decided to put her heart and soul into saving her marriage? If only she'd known he'd be gone from this world so soon. Suddenly chilly, May snuggles further into her shawl and acknowledges that under the circumstances, she was probably right. Charles was sadistic and vindictive when he wasn't being witty, and Barbara is bound to have been far better off as Grace. If only May could have seen her just once before she sets off on her own big adventure. Death doesn't *frighten her in the least, but the prospect of leaving this earth without finding out how her child has fared makes her feel unusually melancholy.*

'Ah well,' May tells herself sternly, 'there's no use in crying for the moon. You've been a lucky old bird to have the gift of memory harvesting and to live to this ripe old age. It's almost time to call it a day.'

Soon, very soon, she'll take the action needed to speed herself on her way to who knows where. Perhaps Barbara – Grace – will come to look for her mother sometime in the future. May wonders if anyone will be around to tell the tale of the lady who for many years, never seemed to look any older. She hopes so. It will make an excellent story.

Cameron's Vegan & Gluten-Free
Christmas Roast

Ingredients
1 gluten-free brown seeded roll (roughly crumbed)
Juice of half a clementine (eat the rest while you make the loaf)
215g tin of chickpeas, juice included
180g pack whole cooked chestnuts, chopped/food-processed
75g dried cranberries
9 dates, chopped (dried prunes can be used instead)
2 hefty pinches sea salt & several generous twists of black pepper
1 red or green chilli, seeded and finely chopped
1cm fresh ginger, chopped or grated
2 spring onions, roughly chopped

Method
Mix all ingredients together in a large bowl and add extra seasoning if required. Optional extras are garlic, finely chopped peppers, nuts, red onion, dried chillies for more oomph, vegetable bouillon powder or anything else you feel like throwing in, within reason. I trust your judgement here ... (An egg also works well if the vegan part isn't vital.)

Bake at 180°C/160°C/gas 4 in a loaf tin for around 25 minutes or until the top feels vaguely crunchy. Leave to cool before turning out. Slices well hot or cold.

Audrey's Hearty Soup For Sharing

Audrey made this in vast quantities for her family, friends and neighbours, but here are some rough quantities to make a soup that will warm the cockles of your heart and do you good at the same time. Use any vegetables you like, just choose your favourites.

Ingredients
4 carrots
A large potato or 2 smaller ones
3 or 4 stalks of celery, depending on how strong a flavour you like
A medium-sized sweet potato
3 parsnips
A large onion, or 3 leeks, or both
Broccoli (especially the stalks)
Any leftover vegetables you find in the fridge
A cup of frozen peas (or a tin of processed, garden or mushy peas)
Stock flavouring (whichever sort you use – cubes, jar, stockpot, bouillon, home-made or a mixture of these)

2 bay leaves
Black pepper to taste
Meat-eaters' options: chopped raw chicken breast/
thighs or any tender cut of meat – small pieces, left-
over cooked chicken, lamb, etc.
Instant mashed potato or packet soup, to thicken

Method
Chop all the vegetables (making them as small or
chunky as you like) and put them in a pan large
enough to still be able to cover them with water. Add
peas and cover with boiling water. Add stock flavouring,
bay leaves and black pepper and stir well. If using raw
meat, add it now. If cooked, wait ten minutes. Put a
lid on the pan and simmer soup for half an hour (or
longer if you prefer a softer texture). When almost
ready to serve, thicken with either a couple of tablespoons of instant mashed potato or a packet soup
mix – one of the ones that make a pint (asparagus,
mushroom or thick country vegetable work well). This
soup can be blended but is more interesting left in
its chunky state. Take the bay leaves out before
blending or serving.

Serve with crusty bread and maybe a sprinkling
of cheese. The leftovers taste even better the next day
but will need thinning down a bit. This soup also
freezes well.

James's Gloop

Ingredients
Half a chorizo ring, chopped into small cubes (omit if this is to be a meat-free recipe)
Olive oil, 2 or 3 tablespoons (or cooking spray if you're being sensible)
2 medium red onions, chopped fairly finely
3 cloves of garlic (adjust to taste), chopped or crushed
400g tin of tomatoes
Half a tube of concentrated tomato puree
Salt, black pepper and dried chilli flakes, also to taste

Method
Fry the chorizo in the oil or cooking spray until crispy. Remove with a slotted spoon and place on kitchen paper, reserving the oil in the pan. Add the onion and garlic and fry until soft. Mix in the chopped tomatoes and puree, plus seasoning to taste. (Lovers of spicy food will throw in a few extra teaspoons of chilli flakes with glee.) Add the cooked chorizo. Cook all ingredients together until the consistency pleases you. Serve with spaghetti or other pasta of choice. Best eaten whilst watching reruns of *Downton Abbey* or similar, in front of a roaring fire.

Acknowledgements

Saying thank you is always a pleasure, even though in the strange times we are currently living in, I can't follow it up with a hug, some squidgy cake and a glass or two of bubbles. My family; Ray, Laura & Hakan and Hannah & Mark should be first on the list for their never-ending patience and great new ideas when I ramble about the story going on in my head, their constant humour and support and their lack of surprise at yet again finding me downstairs bashing the keys at 5am.

Ditto to all friends/cousins/sisters under the skin (including Jill, Rosemary, Liz, Kay, Sonja, Anne and Lynda,) the magnificently talented Romaniac girls (Jan, Sue, Debbie, Laura, Catherine, Lucie and Vanessa) and super-readers Mandy James and Christine McPherson – all fabulous and much loved, even though as I write this, we're not allowed to be anywhere near each other. They may have been secretly quite glad of this lately. Waiting for this brand-new book to be published has made me very excitable and not a little jittery, because ever since *59 Memory Lane* was completed, I have been desperate to go back to Pengelly and discover what happened next.

May's story was over in some ways by the last chapter, but her echo was still in my head, and Grace Clarke was waiting in the wings for her turn to be heard. Initially this continuation didn't seem to be on the cards, because it's not easy for a publisher to take on a sequel to a book that hasn't yet proved itself. Huge thanks, therefore, to the wonderful Charlotte Ledger who decided, in bright sunshine on a windy rooftop at the News Building, to give it a whirl. Her intuitive editing skills have been so very much appreciated, and I will always be grateful to her for seeing the potential in May and her mixed bag of acolytes. Thanks also to Sophie Burks who has seamlessly taken over the role of chief calmer-downer and all-round superstar from Charlotte. I look forward to working with Sophie as *The Cottage of Curiosities* emerges blinking into the sunlight.

With a great sounding of trumpets, my superb agent, Laura Macdougall, is a constant inspiration and support, with equally insightful editing skills and a strong dose of 'you can do this' and 'chin up'! Being a part of #TeamLaura at United Agents is a great thing. Knowing Laura constantly has your back is worth its weight in rubies/gold/scones (delete as applicable). She is a force of nature, and her lucky, lucky gang all love her very much.

In the end though, it's down to you, dear reader, to have a big imaginary bouquet of flowers, chocolate, gin and cake, because without you . . . well, you get the picture. I hope you enjoy/have enjoyed/might one day enjoy *The Cottage of Curiosities*. Thank you.

Book Club Questions

- Did Grace's initial lack of friends surprise you? In your opinion, could she have made more of an effort to fit in with her peers and colleagues in her growing up years?

- Was James right to uproot himself from everything that was familiar to him when he's at a point in his life when he may find change more difficult than usual?

- From the flashbacks, how would you describe May's character? Is she someone you would have enjoyed knowing?

- Did Emily approach her problems with Tamsin in a suitably sensitive way? Do you feel that Emily's relationship with her soon-to-be-stepdaughter progressed naturally, or could she have done more to help matters along?

- What would be the best and worse features of living in a place like Pengelly?

- How essential is it for an adopted child to find out about their birth parents? In your opinion, can it ever be said to be irrelevant or is it a basic human need?

- Do you ever wish you had a gift like Grace's? How would you use it?

- Did you feel Will to be essentially a force for good, or otherwise?
- Is it possible for old family feuds to ever be truly forgotten?
- Which character did you identify with most strongly, and why?

If you enjoyed
The Cottage of Curiosities,
don't miss Celia's novel
59 Memory Lane . . .

Available now in paperback,
eBook and audio!

Lost and Gone Forever

ALEX GRECIAN

PENGUIN BOOKS

UK | USA | Canada | Ireland | Australia
India | New Zealand | South Africa

Penguin Books is part of the Penguin Random House group of companies
whose addresses can be found at global.penguinrandomhouse.com.

Set in 12.5/14.75 pt Garamond MT Std
Typeset by Jouve (UK), Milton Keynes
Printed in Great Britain by Clays Ltd, St Ives plc

A CIP catalogue record for this book is available from the British Library

B FORMAT ISBN: 978–1–405–92236–4
A FORMAT ISBN: 978–1–405–92239–5

www.greenpenguin.co.uk

MIX
Paper from
responsible sources
FSC® C018179

Penguin Random House is committed to a
sustainable future for our business, our readers
and our planet. This book is made from Forest
Stewardship Council® certified paper.

For Christy,
as always

BOOK ONE

'Peter?' Anna could hear how frightened she sounded, her voice echoing back to her from the flat face of a curio cabinet that blocked the narrow path. She stood still and listened, but there came no answering cry.

She called his name again, louder this time, but with the same result. Or, rather, the same lack of result.

Perhaps, *she thought*, if I were to climb to the top of that curio, I would be able to see quite far along the path.

She approached the hulking cabinet and opened the doors at the bottom. There was nothing inside. She slid open a drawer and pulled it out, set it beside her on the grass. She pulled herself up, hanging on tight to the knurled trim along the side, and used the empty slot where the drawer had been as a toehold. Once begun, the climb was easy, shelves positioned at convenient intervals as if it had all been purposefully fashioned for small children to scale. At the top was an elegant pointed façade, and she clung to it and crouched low, willing herself not to look back down at the ground. I am not really so high up, after all, *she thought.* Were I to fall, I might not break my arms and legs. *But this thought was not so comforting as she had felt it would be.*

She looked ahead of her up the path, which wound around a dining set and through a great herd of French desk chairs, disappearing at the juncture of a Chippendale butcher block and a dollhouse cupboard. A small blue bird of some sort hopped from the base of a painted white sideboard, then flapped away to the top of a jumbled mountain of coatracks. Behind her, she could see that the sun was beginning to set, the sky bruised and livid.

She opened her mouth to call Peter again, but did not make a sound. All at once she felt utterly alone and afraid.

A grandfather clock chimed nearby. Startled, Anna lost her grip on the façade and nearly tumbled from her perch. She slid down the back of the curio and landed neatly on her feet on the packed dirt of the path.

Well, *she thought,* I suppose there is nothing for it but to find Peter and drag him back home in time for his supper. Otherwise, we shall both get the switch, and I should never forgive him if that happened.

And so she mustered her resolve and marched away into the ever-darkening wood without glancing back even once at the warm yellow lights of her house.

— RUPERT WINTHROP, FROM
The Wandering Wood (1893)

Prologue

He woke in the dark and saw that his cell door was open.

Just a crack, but lamplight shone through and into the room. He lay on his bed and watched that chink of yellow through his shivering eyelashes. But the door didn't open any farther, and the man – *the man Jack* – didn't enter the room. Had Jack forgotten to latch the door after his last visit? Or was he waiting to pounce, somewhere just out of sight in the passage beyond the cell?

He kept his eyes half-shut and watched the door for an hour. The sun came up and the quality of light in the room changed. The crack between the door and the jamb remained the same, but the lamplight behind it faded, washed out by the brighter gleam of the rising sun. At last, he threw his thin grey blanket aside and sat up, swung his legs over the side of the bed, and padded across the room to the bucket in the corner. When he had finished the morning's business, he scooped sand into the bucket and went to the table under the window. He splashed water on his face from the bowl, his back to the open door, ignoring it. He drank from a ladle and looked out through the bars at the narrow stony yard, all he could see of the outside world. Then he went back to the bed and sat down and waited.

His breakfast didn't come, but sometimes it didn't. Sometimes Jack forgot or was busy. A missed meal here or there was hardly the end of the world. So he sat and he waited. He began to worry when midday passed without any sign of food. His stomach grumbled. He checked the positions of the shadows in the yard, but they told him nothing he didn't already know. He had an excellent internal clock. He knew full well when it was time to eat.

When teatime passed with no tea or bread, he stood again and went to the door. He put his hand on the knob and closed his eyes. He concentrated on his breathing, calmed himself. He pulled the door half an inch wider and took his hand off the knob. He stood behind the door and braced himself.

But nothing happened.

Braver now, he touched the doorknob again, wrapped his fist around it, and opened the door wide enough that he could see out into the hallway. He put his head out of the room and pulled it back immediately. But despite his expectations, nothing had hit him or cut him. Nobody had laughed at him or screamed at him. All was quiet.

And so he stepped out of the room for the first time in as long as he could remember. He wasn't at all comfortable being outside his cell. His memory of the things beyond that room was vague and untrustworthy. He swallowed hard and looked back at his bed. It represented all he knew, relative security bound up with stark terror, the twin pillars that supported his existence.

He left it behind and crept down the passage on his bare feet, leaving the lantern where it hung on a peg outside the chamber. When he reached the end of the hallway there was another door, and he seized the knob without flinching. He stifled a gasp when it turned under his hand and the second door swung open, revealing a long wedge of wan afternoon sunlight. He had expected the door to be locked, had expected to have to turn around and retreat to his cell and his bed and his bucket. Had, in fact, almost wished for it.

He stepped out into fresh air. He felt the warmth of the sunbaked stones on the soles of his feet. When his eyes had accustomed themselves to the bright light, he looked around him at the empty street and turned and looked up at the nondescript house that had been his home for so long. He didn't remember ever seeing the front of the house before, and it occurred to him that he might have been born there, might never have been outside it. Perhaps his half-remembered notions of the world beyond his cell were only dreams.

A breeze stirred the hair on his bare arms, and he felt suddenly self-conscious. After hesitating a moment, he turned and went back inside, back down the passage, back into his room, to the bed. He picked up his grey blanket and draped it over his shoulders and left again.

Back outside, he looked up and down the street and smiled. He had a choice to make and he felt proud to have been given the opportunity. Jack was testing him, he was sure of it. He could go left to the end of the road where he saw another street running perpendicular to this one. Or he could go right. Far away to his right he could see the green tops of trees waving to him from somewhere over a steep hill. Perhaps a park or a garden. Trees. He could imagine how their bark would feel under the palm of his hand. He was certain he had touched trees before. He really had been outside his room. He nodded. The trees meant something.

Walter Day turned to his right and limped naked down the street toward the beckoning green.

I

Plumm's Emporium had for years occupied a large building at the south end of Moorgate, not far from where Walter Day spent a year in captivity and not far from Drapers' Gardens, where Day found shelter in the trees. Plumm's was bordered on one side by an accountant's office and on the other by that famous gentlemen's club, Smithfield and Gordon. In the winter of 1890, it had been announced that Smithfield would be moving to posher headquarters in Belgravia, and the renowned entrepreneur John Plumm purchased the club's building. At the same time, he made an offer to the accountant, who was only too glad to relocate. The Emporium then closed its doors for nearly four months. The great blizzard that hit London in March of 1891 slowed construction of the new building and caused much speculation about Plumm's financial stability. There were rumors that corners had been cut and cheaper materials used in order to get the place ready for the announced date. But when it reopened it was three times the size and four stories taller and had adopted its founder's name, John Plumm, though most shoppers continued to refer to it simply as Plumm's.

Beyond the cast-iron and glass storefront, the ground floor of Plumm's held two tea shops, a bank, three full restaurants, a public reading room, and a confectionery. There was an electric lift at the back, something most people had never seen, and this generated a fair amount of foot traffic, people coming in just to ride up and down. The first to third stories were supported by thick iron pillars and held a staggering variety of merchandise: toys and dolls, fabric of every variety, ready-made clothing, shoes and umbrellas and hats, groceries, baked goods and bedding, men's ties and cufflinks, coffee, books and maps and sheet music, jewelry, cutlery and crockery and cookware, rooms for lounging, rooms for smoking, and fitting rooms. At the top of the building was an enormous glass dome that was cleaned daily, along with the forty-three windows on the lower floors, by four men hired specifically for that purpose.

John Plumm himself gave a speech on the day of the opening and then stepped aside, gesturing wide for the gathered throng to enter. Men wearing white gloves held the doors open as hundreds of women (and more than a few men) hurried inside, and more staff waited within holding complimentary brandy and wine balanced on silver trays. These men, along with two hundred other Plumm's employees, were housed on-site in apartments that faced Coleman Street. In this way, as John Plumm explained, there was always someone in the store, and no customer would ever want for advice or service.

There was a workshop next to the apartments at the back, where skilled artisans created papier-mâché mannequins and display racks made of wood and brass.

John Plumm was rarely seen on the premises, but his lieutenant, Joseph Hargreave, who managed the daily affairs of the store, constantly patrolled the floor, adjusting scarves on the mannequins, resolving customer issues, and replacing the employees' soiled white gloves when needed. Hargreave had an eagle eye for imperfections among his workers and had shown three shopgirls the door before end of business on Plumm's opening day.

But he did not show up for work the second week after Plumm's opened its doors to the public, leading many of his employees to think that perhaps Mr Plumm had taken matters into his own hands and let his overzealous manager go. Joseph Hargreave was never seen alive again and was not missed by anyone except his brother, Richard, who decided to hire a private investigator.

2

On Monday, the evening after he left his cell, Walter Day hid, shivering, behind a stand of trees until Drapers' Gardens had emptied. When he was alone, he pulled up the grass beneath him and dug a shallow trench in the hard soil. He lay down and hugged his legs to his chest, waited until his teeth stopped chattering, and eventually fell asleep.

Tuesday morning, Walter kept himself hidden at the edge of the gardens until a vendor stepped away from his wagon long enough to scold a band of street urchins who were driving away customers. Walter snatched a loose cotton dress from the vendor's awning where it hung. He pulled it over his head, then, hungry and filthy and ashamed, but no longer naked, he scurried away. He clung to the side of the footpath, away from traffic, and tried to seem inconspicuous in his ladies' dress, his bare feet visible below the hem. He found half a fish pie discarded in the slush at the side of the road and ate it as quickly as he could, cramming the soggy mess into his mouth so fast that he could hardly breathe. He watched the shadows and the passing people while waiting for the man Jack to appear and take him back to his cell. When teatime had come and gone again and Jack still had not materialized, Walter began to cry.

Wednesday, as omnibuses rattled past carrying early-morning commuters, Day crawled out of the box he had slept in and joined the flow of pedestrians. When he came to a busy intersection, he watched a gang of children who rushed forward, one at a time, to assist people as they crossed the wet road, holding up their hands to halt the buses and taxis and private carriages, and collecting small coins in return. Hopeful, Walter caught a young woman's attention and held out his elbow for her. She looked away, her cheeks red with embarrassment, and a man standing behind Walter threatened to send for the police. It began to sleet and the foot traffic thinned. He took shelter beneath an oriel and sat on the ground, pulled his muddy dress down so that it covered his ankles, and waited.

On Thursday he returned to that same corner and watched the children more carefully, studying how they solicited pedestrians, and by afternoon had managed to help an elderly blind man cross the street. He earned a ha'penny in return and spent it on a cup of weak tea at a wagon across from the gardens. He slept in the trench again and used the dress as a blanket.

When he woke on Friday morning, he found a small pile of clothing had been left on the ground next to him. A pair of patched and faded trousers, a threadbare shirt, a thick wool coat, and boots with a hole in one toe. Next to the clothing was a walking stick with a round brass handle. He recognized it as his own from some long-ago time, like seeing a cherished toy he had played with as a child. There was little doubt about who had visited him in the night. He looked around, but saw no one, and so he put on the new clothes and buried his dress next to the trench so that it would not be stolen or discarded. More appropriately attired, he was able to help seven people cross the busy intersection that day and, for the first time since leaving his cell, he ate an entire meal. That night he slept well and was not bothered by any rumblings in his stomach.

The children were waiting for him at his corner on Saturday. Walter listened as they explained their position. This was their corner and, although he was much larger than they were, they outnumbered him and would cause him grievous harm if he continued to interfere with their ability to earn a living. He nodded and wished them well and wandered away in search of another intersection. He had no luck, but later that day he was struck on the back of the head by a cigar butt that was tossed from a passing carriage. He picked up the smoldering butt and carried it away with him. Over the course of two hours, he found nearly twenty more, an even mix of cigars and cigarettes. He took them back to his trench in the gardens and unrolled them all, using a piece of bark stripped from a tree to catch the precious bits of tobacco left inside them. It took some time, but eventually he was able to form two new crude-looking cigars from the leftovers. He took off his boots, put the cigars in the toe of the left boot, and slept on top of them so they wouldn't be stolen from him in the night.

On Sunday, he chose the two biggest and smartest of the children at the corner and made arrangements with them. He gave each of them a cigar and they shook hands. He spent the rest of the day combing gutters and alleyways, gathering butts and drying them in the sun. When he returned to the corner, his young business partners had sold the cigars and they each gave him half their earnings: four pennies. Walter ate another meal that night before getting back to work repurposing the used tobacco he had found. By the time he went to sleep, he had five new cigars hidden in his left boot.

3

The vast majority of London had failed to note Walter Day's disappearance and had gone about its business without marking his absence. But, even a year later, there were still people who woke up each morning with the expectation that they might see him again, perhaps that very day.

Among that select group was the former Sergeant Nevil Hammersmith, who because of his headstrong and reckless manner had been let go from Scotland Yard. He had opened his own detective agency, which he now operated in a headstrong and reckless manner. His offices were housed in a compact two-room suite in Camden, and a plaque outside the door read simply HAMMER-SMITH. Beneath that, in smaller script, were the words DISCREET ENQUIRIES.

The outer office lacked privacy, but the inner office lacked furniture, aside from a small table and a bedroll in the corner where Hammersmith often napped when sleep overtook him. Every other inch of floor space was occupied by stacks of notes and newspapers, sketches and blurry photographs, witness reports, location descriptions, and a record of every step Hammersmith had taken in the year since his closest friend and colleague had vanished.

One thick file folder was dedicated to the other cities and countries where men matching Walter Day's description had been seen. Hammersmith had traveled to Ireland and

France and even as far as New York in his search, but being cooped up aboard a ship for weeks on end had frustrated him and made him wary afterward of any leads that might take him away from London.

Hammersmith knew he was not the detective Walter Day had been and he felt he had to work twice as hard to make up for his lack of skill. For every dead end he encountered in his search for Day, he redoubled his efforts until his determination became an end in itself.

Hammersmith (the agency) had few clients, and they labored under the false impression that Hammersmith (the detective) worked for them. He did not. He worked for Claire Day only, and he cared about little other than finding her husband. He had two employees, both of them young women he had met in the course of a previous investigation.

Eugenia Merrilow sat behind a desk just inside the front door and screened potential clients. If a case was simple enough and if she judged that the agency was close to running out of oil for the lamps and therefore needed money, she would take down pertinent details and promise to pass the information on to Mr Hammersmith. In fact, she gave nearly all their new cases to Hatty Pitt.

Hatty had become a widow when she was seventeen years old. A murderer called the Harvest Man had escaped prison, tied Hatty to her bed, and butchered her husband, John Charles Pitt. She had been unhappy in her marriage and was pleased to have got her freedom back (a selfish thought that never failed to cause a twinge of guilt and sorrow for poor John Charles).

Hatty had no training as a detective, no training in

anything else, either. But she had been interested and available when Mr Hammersmith had announced he was opening his own detective agency. When he had taken her on, she'd assumed she would be his secretary or clerk and the thought had been acceptable, but not really very exciting. She had a new lease on life, and she had decided early on that she didn't want to do the same sorts of things her friends were all doing, the same sorts of things she surely would have done if she'd remained married to poor John Charles. ('Poor' was beginning to seem like John Charles's first name.) And so she had persuaded Mr Hammersmith to hire Eugenia Merrilow as well, suggesting that it might take more than two people to manage the task of finding anyone in a city the size of London. It was her way of paying Eugenia back for taking Hatty in when she had first lost John Charles and had nowhere else to go. Eugenia had not asked for a salary (she was wealthy and bored), but wanted interesting work, which meant Mr Hammersmith could afford her. With Eugenia to take up the secretarial duties, Hatty had been free to begin insinuating herself into Mr Hammersmith's investigative work. He had been too distracted to object or even to notice what she was doing. Within a few months she had created a satisfying occupation for herself.

The cases Eugenia gave her were simple enough: follow a wandering husband on the train and note where he disembarked, deliver a note of foreclosure to a small business, hunt down a missing pet, etc. She thought the fact that detective work was not commonly performed by women actually gave her an advantage. No one suspected her of following them, no one viewed her inquiries as suspicious.

She was nearly invisible. Eugenia did not accept cases that involved any hint of serious danger, and Hatty consulted with Mr Hammersmith, who seemed always to be under the impression that Hatty was asking hypothetical questions. He would generally give her an hour of his time before she could see his attention wandering back to the case of the missing Inspector Day. She was often frustrated by his single-mindedness, but admired his sense of purpose and his dogged determination.

She also admired his long eyelashes and his long fingers and the way his uncombed hair flopped down into his eyes at inconvenient moments. She suspected Eugenia Merrilow harbored similar feelings, but the two of them had never discussed the matter.

Most days, when Eugenia unlocked the door and brought the post to the desk, Hammersmith would emerge from the inner office rubbing his red-rimmed eyes. He would greet her absently, take his hat from the rack, and leave. Some days he would go to Scotland Yard and pester Inspector Tiffany or Inspector Blacker. They were sympathetic, but never had any new information for him about Day's disappearance. The men of the Murder Squad had finished moving to a new headquarters on the Victoria Embankment, and their search for Day was necessarily interrupted by the minutiae of daily life, by other cases, by other crimes.

Some mornings Hammersmith would visit Claire Day and they would discuss the investigation. Walter Day's wife was now caught up in her own routines and distractions, the demands of four children, a busy household staff, and a new career. It was a poorly guarded secret that Claire had written a popular book of children's rhymes under the pen name Rupert Winthrop. But a series of unfortunate events in the previous year had traumatized her to the extent that she rarely went anywhere in London alone. She still wrote her poems and had begun to think she might like to write a prose story for children. In the evenings after the dishes had been cleared, she would compose a new rhyme and read it to her adopted boys, Robert and Simon (they had been orphaned by the Harvest Man, the same madman who had widowed Hatty Pitt), before tucking them into bed. Then she would work until dawn, or sometimes she would lie in her bed and watch shadows move across her ceiling. She did not sleep much, and her eyes were generally as bloodshot as Hammersmith's. The sales of Claire's poems, and the advance she had received for her next book, had paid for the Hammersmith Agency's office.

The blizzard of that March had kept most people inside, where they didn't get into the sorts of trouble that might require detecting of the private variety. But the sun had begun to come out sporadically and snow had melted and become slush, which was now beginning to disappear as well. People were leaving their homes and, after being pent up for so long, were getting into all manner of mischief, both minor and calamitous.

On the first warm day of spring, fog had lifted off the Thames and invaded the neighborhoods north of the river. Hatty stood in the outer office, watching grey nothingness roll by outside the window, obscuring the fish-and-chips shop across the street. She held a pencil and a small notebook of the sort preferred by her employer. Eugenia sat behind her desk, sorting papers into piles that Hatty suspected were entirely random. Eugenia had provided (and was prominently posed in) the many framed photographs of tableaux vivants that lined the agency's walls. Across the desk from her, draped across the client chair like an empty suit, was a bespectacled older man with a silver fringe of hair and an untidy mustache. He had carefully arranged two long hairs across the gleaming pink expanse of his scalp. Hatty felt pity and a touch of admiration for the futile vanity of her new client.

'I would like to speak directly to Mr Hammersmith,' the man said. 'This is a matter of some importance to the family, as you may imagine.'

'I'm afraid,' Hatty said, 'that Mr Hammersmith is busy elsewhere at the moment, but he will review my notes the moment he returns.'

'I'll wait for him.'

'It may be some time.'

'Then I'll find another detective.'

'You should certainly feel free to do so, sir, but Mr Hammersmith asked me to tell you how much he appreciates your confidence in him. He wanted so very badly to meet you himself.' In fact, Hammersmith had said no such thing. He had probably forgotten all about the meeting and the potential client, who was now drawing himself up in the chair and adjusting his waistcoat.

'Then why isn't he here?'

'He's with the commissioner of police,' Eugenia said. 'You can't very well say no to the commissioner of police when he sends for you.'

Hatty frowned at Eugenia, but Eugenia didn't notice, didn't even look up from her busy work. It was the standard lie they always gave and it made Mr Hammersmith seem very important indeed, but Hatty didn't care for it. As far as she was concerned, the business of the Hammersmith Agency was the uncovering of lies, not the propagation of them. When Eugenia didn't note her disapproval, Hatty gave up and turned her attention back to the client.

'Mr Hammersmith had to go immediately to see about the details of another case.' It was not entirely a lie.

'Called on by Sir Edward himself?'

Now the client was impressed and Hatty knew they had him on the hook. She just wished she'd been able to impress the man herself, instead of invoking Sir Edward's reputation in order to secure this new piece of business. She glanced at the first page of her tiny notebook.

'Your name is . . . ?'

'I never gave my name when I made this appointment,' the man said. 'I didn't want the family's reputation to be jeopardized.'

Hatty made an impatient gesture at Eugenia, who glared at her for a moment before rising and retreating to the inner office. Hatty took her chair and set the note-book on the desk in front of her. She couldn't very well stand against the wall and question their new client.

'Surely you don't mind telling me your name now that you're here, sir,' Hatty said.

'I'd rather —'

Hatty interrupted him. 'Then what is the nature of your trouble?'

'My brother is missing. I wouldn't say he's disappeared so much, only that I don't know where he is.'

'Of course. Well, you've come to the right place. We specialize in looking for missing people.' True enough, although Hatty didn't mention their lack of success in actually *finding* missing people. 'But we can't begin to search for your brother unless we know his name.'

'I don't doubt it, but see here, young lady, this is a very delicate situation.'

'A business matter hinges on his availability?'

'Something like that.' He sat up even straighter now. 'In fact, his position has been given to someone else in his absence, and I have every hope that the situation might still be reversed. But how did you know?'

'I told you. We do this sort of thing all the time.' Hatty had made an educated guess based on the client's pomposity. She leaned forward over the desk and lowered her voice. 'Anything you tell us will be held in the strictest of confidence. Just as it says on the sign outside. We are extremely discreet.'

The man cleared his throat and looked around the tiny room as if to assure himself that they were alone. His nostrils needed to be trimmed, and Hatty noticed a dried yellow nugget clinging for life to the wiry grey hairs. She absently rubbed her own nose. It had been broken a year before and had healed with a slight bump halfway down the bridge. She thought it gave her a worldly appearance and she took perverse pride in this exotic imperfection.

She waited, her pencil poised over a blank sheet in the notebook, and finally the man cleared his throat and spoke. 'If . . . I mean to say, once you find my brother, I would like all notes and records of your inquiries turned over to me so I may burn them.'

'As you wish,' Hatty said. First, get the man to talk, then worry about keeping promises.

'Good. Well, then . . . I say, this is awkward.'

'How so?'

'I've never had occasion to employ your sort before, you know.'

'Ah. My sort.'

'It feels a bit . . .' The man left off as if there were too many adjectives to choose from.

'Your brother's name?'

'Yes. Just so. His name.' A deep sigh, and the man straightened his shoulders, ready to take the plunge. 'His name was – pardon me, his name *is* Joseph Hargreave.'

Hatty wrote this down. 'And your name?'

'You need my name as well?'

'It would help us when it comes time to make out the bill for services.'

'Of course. My name is Richard Hargreave. *Doctor* Richard Hargreave.'

'And what's happened to your brother?'

'He left the flat – we share an apartment in the city – three mornings ago very early, straight after breakfast, and was headed for the store, but he never arrived. The first day he was gone I became mildly concerned, because he usually tells me if he has an engagement and needs me to allow for his absence. By that evening I was distraught and have remained so ever since.'

'You say he sometimes has engagements? Business affairs?'

'He manages the bulk of our parents' estate, which keeps him just busy enough, I suppose, in addition to his duties at Plumm's. Occasionally he has to meet with a banker or with our solicitor about one thing or another having to do with our investments. I don't trouble myself with all that, but he's quite capable.'

She had written the word *Plumm's* in her notebook and underlined it, but she decided to wait a moment before following up. She didn't want the client to lose his train of thought. 'And you think he would have told you if he had a meeting of that sort? With an investor? Is it possible he's had to leave town for some reason and it slipped his mind that he hadn't informed you?'

'No, no, no. His money is also my money, after all. He always keeps me up to the minute about everything. He wouldn't have . . . Well, he would have told me, that's all.'

Hatty looked up from her notebook. 'You're afraid he's met with foul play?'

'I certainly hope not. But the thought has occurred to me, and I don't know what to do about it.'

'I'd say you've done it already. You've come to us and put the matter in our hands.' She smiled at him, and he managed some sort of a sneer in return. 'Now,' Hatty said, 'I need details. Tell me everything you can about his habits, his appearance, his acquaintances, everything you can think of that might be helpful.'

'And you'll relay this information to Mr Hammersmith straight away?'

'Absolutely.'

'Very well.' Dr Richard Hargreave cleared his throat, adjusted his spectacles on his nose, and began to talk about his brother. The nugget of snot dropped to his lap, and Hatty looked down at the desk and wrote as fast as she could.

4

A two-wheeler pulled up to the mouth of a narrow alley
in Saffron Hill. Two people alighted, a man and a woman,
both dressed head to foot in black. Their fashions indicated they were not native to England. The man took a
bag from the floor of the cab and tipped the driver, who
sped away as fast as his horse could move. The couple in
black stepped into the alley and walked slowly along,
looking all round them at the stalls of stinking fish and
yesterday's vegetables. The man held his elbow out to
the woman, who slipped her arm in his. A pickpocket
circled and came up behind them but the man in black
casually swung his bag, without looking, and the pickpocket went down in a heap. They walked on as if they
hadn't noticed him.

The alley wandered on, and they followed it through
the fog, their boot heels clacking on broken stones, awn-
ings above them dripping on the woman's umbrella, held
above them both. They did not speak, nor did they look at
each other, but they stopped together when they reached
a small home with no garden and a stinking garbage pile
against the front bricks. One shutter was painted with the
notice: LOGINGS FOR TRAFFELERS.

The man led the way to the front door and, without
knocking, opened it for his companion. She nodded to
him as she passed over the threshold. Inside, the place

was small and damp and reeked of old sweat and gin. A tiny old woman came rushing from some back room to greet them.

'Yer in luck,' she said. Her voice was thick, both with liquor and a Cockney dialect. 'I've two beds left.'

'We'll take a room to ourselves,' the man said.

'Oh, you'd be wantin' a posher place 'n this, then. We goes by the mattress here, and you'll be furnishin' yourselves when it comes to linens.'

'A room,' the man said again. His companion did not speak, nor did she look at the landlady. She stared straight ahead and worried her thumb along the handle of her umbrella.

'That'd come dear, sir,' the old woman said. 'I can't be givin' out a whole room to just two people, can I?'

Now that the matter had come down to money, the man seemed to relax. He smiled for the first time, and when he did, the landlady shivered.

'We'll give you forty a week for the room. Two weeks in advance. And we'll take our meals elsewhere.'

'Forty? A week?' The old woman leaned toward him and shook her head. 'I hate to say it, I do, but you can get a better place 'n this for forty a week, sir.'

'Yes.'

'Well then, I'll take yer money. What name would you like on the register?'

'None. If we wanted a name on the register, we'd stay somewhere that didn't smell of rat piss.'

'Gotta put sumpin' down for the inspectors.'

'Very well, put down Parker.'

'Mr and Mrs, then?'

'If it suits you.'

'Gimme an hour or so to clear out a room.'

'Clear the mattresses off the beds, too, or the floor if there are no beds.'

'We got proper beds here, like.'

'Good. Send a boy round for new mattresses. Clean mattresses. We'll pay for those, too.'

'New mattresses?'

'And linens. New. Never used. Have them on the beds when we return.'

'New mattresses, new linens. That'll cost, sir.'

The man smiled again, and the old woman backed away from him. He reached into his pocket and drew out three coins. He took the landlady's hand, turned it over, and laid the coins on her palm. 'I trust that will suffice.'

The old woman drew in a sharp breath through her nose and nodded. The man nodded in return.

'Never seen a lady wear a man's clothings before.' The old lady jerked her thumb in the woman's direction. 'Don't she talk?'

'Oh, you wouldn't want her to talk,' the man said. 'I'm the polite one.' He took his companion's arm, and the two of them left the house without another word or a backward look. The man pulled the door quietly shut behind them.

When she was sure they were gone, the old woman clutched her wrist where the man had touched her. It felt icy cold.

Nevil Hammersmith stood in the middle of his flat and looked round, expecting to see a thick layer of dust and cobwebs coating the familiar mantel, the table under the window, the single wooden chair, and the hot plate. He had always lived a monastic existence, but had spent the majority of his time lately in the cluttered office, eating fish pies and tea and sleeping on the floor when his eyes grew heavy from poring over the same witness reports and news articles again and again, looking for some previously neglected clue that might lead him to Walter Day. But the flat was neat and tidy. There was a flowerpot on the table, and a green plant stretched upward toward the window above. Hammersmith peered at this new addition to the flat and blinked twice, not sure what to think about it. He leaned slightly forward on his toes, his hands behind his back, as if in unconscious competition with the plant for sunlight.

He heard footsteps on the stairs, and a moment later the door opened and Timothy Pinch entered, bringing with him the mingled scents of chocolate and sugar and lemon rind from the confectionery downstairs. Timothy paused when he saw Hammersmith, then grinned and crossed the room to him.

'Nevil,' he said. 'Good to see you. It's been weeks, hasn't it?'

Hammersmith nodded. 'I stayed here last Tuesday night, I think. Maybe Wednesday.'

'Sorry to have missed you. It's been so lonely, I had to get some company for myself.' Pinch pointed to the plant. 'A maidenhair fern. It's almost as talkative as you are.'

Hammersmith grimaced, then tried to turn it into a smile.

'Sorry,' Pinch said. 'What brings you?'

'I left a file here,' Hammersmith said. 'At least, I think I did. Can't remember where I put it.'

'Ah, yes, I've tidied up a bit here and there. Anything that looked like it might be related to your work I've put in the top drawer of the desk.' Pinch pointed to the small rolltop in the corner where the hallway narrowed and led back to the two bedrooms.

Hammersmith nodded his thanks and rummaged through the drawer. The file he wanted was beneath a report on the weather conditions the evening Walter Day had disappeared.

'Perfect,' he said.

'Tea?'

'No, thank you,' Hammersmith said. 'I really ought to get back to the office. Unless you . . .'

'I was going to have some myself.'

'Well, then, I suppose I'd be glad of it.'

'Good.'

Pinch busied himself at the fireplace while Hammersmith waited, feeling like a stranger in his own home, which he decided he probably was. Once a fire was going and a kettle had been put on to boil, Pinch stood and rubbed his hands together. He grinned again and clapped.

'Now,' he said, 'tell me everything.'

'About what?'

'You know. Cases. Investigations. That sort of thing.'

'Ah, no, nothing much to report, I'm afraid.'

Pinch clicked his tongue and frowned, disappointed. He was two or three years younger than Hammersmith, and two or three inches shorter, but he gave the impression of greater height, as if he only needed to straighten out his gawky frame and unkink his limbs to throw off the shackles of adolescence. Under slick fawn-colored hair, his eyes were the clear blue of an undisturbed pool, and a family of squirrels might have comfortably sheltered in the shadow of his nose. He vibrated with nervous energy. Hammersmith glanced at the complex pattern of chemical burns and stains on Pinch's laboratory coat, which he never seemed to remove, except for dinner.

Hammersmith looked away, back at the intruder houseplant. 'And what about you? How go the studies?'

'Fascinating,' Pinch said. 'Really just fascinating. I can't tell you. Dr Kingsley is ahead of his time. I'm just incredibly lucky to be able to work with him.'

In addition to his duties at University College Hospital, Dr Bernard Kingsley was the official forensics examiner for the Metropolitan Police. The busy doctor had been in need of a capable assistant for some time, and Pinch was his most promising student. Pinch squatted before the fire again and launched into a one-sided discussion of the migratory habits of maggots within a festering corpse. Hammersmith nodded and sat at the table, watched as thick tendrils of fog brushed against the windowpanes.

He missed his previous flatmate. Charming, funny, proudly superficial Pringle. He and Colin Pringle had not been much alike, but he had trusted Colin, depended on him. He sniffed the air as if he might still catch a phantom whiff of the hair tonic Colin had worn or the sprig of mint he had chewed. But the act of conjuring Pringle's memory made his absence more acute. Hammersmith blinked, grimaced, focused on Timothy Pinch and his wide, guileless face. Pinch was a friendly sort, but Hammersmith was in no mood to feign friendliness.

Hammersmith understood that he was becoming more reserved lately, that he sought out the company of others with decreasing frequency. He had never been a particularly outgoing person, had always been dedicated almost obsessively to his work, but he was getting worse. It seemed to him that the murder of Colin Pringle had been the first link in an ugly chain that stretched back over a year and a half: the formation of the Murder Squad, the discovery of Jack the Ripper in a cell under the city, Jack's escape from his tormentors and Walter's abduction, Hammersmith's ouster from the police force, the new detective agency.

He wondered what Pringle might have thought of it all.

'I say,' Pinch said. 'You look pale. Awfully sorry, old man. I forget most people don't have the same affinity for maggots that I do.'

'More's the pity.'

Pinch grinned at him and brought the kettle to the table, where he poured out two steaming cups of tea and added lemon. Hammersmith stood, and they both sipped while watching the variations of grey move beyond their window.

6

The fog embraced Claire Day, cradled her as she moved along the street, protected her from the gaze of her fellow travelers. She carried an umbrella, but didn't open it. The fog wasn't wet or cold; it didn't oppress. She saw nothing but grey in its many shades and variations, but she knew that there were other people around her somewhere, other streets ahead. Somewhere. Given enough time, she would stumble upon them, and given more time the fog would burn away and everything would be made clear.

Horses clopped along beside her, but Claire stayed on the path, unseen and self-contained. Today was a day for walking, and for once she didn't want companionship. She strolled slowly, watching for the shapes of children and call boxes and tall thin gas lamps when they materialized in front of her.

She sensed movement and stopped, watched the rolling greyness, and waited for someone to appear, but no one did. She took a tentative step, then another, and saw a shape cross the path ahead. Another shape, a man, followed, and another, this one a woman connected to a smaller shape, a child holding her hand. Two men carried a huge box, a dark grey square punched out of its surroundings. Claire moved to the side of the path and stopped, reluctant to try navigating through the ragged parade. There was comfort in being unnoticed, but she didn't want to surprise anyone. After a moment, as the queue of people marched past her and into the unseen street, she felt for the wall of the building behind her and sidled along it until she came to the corner. The quality of the fog changed. The spots and patches of light, of dark, of density and thinness, disappeared, the grey no longer adopting the characteristics of the doors and windows of the buildings around it. Here, there was only a swirling sameness. She stepped into an empty lot, weeds reaching at her through the dirt and fog.

There was no way to know how large the lot was or where the next building might be hiding. She shuffled forward, swinging her umbrella gently back and forth in front of her. Sounds – muffled voices, faraway footsteps, and hooves against cobblestones – drifted at her from somewhere, seeming remote and unimportant. She looked down just in time to stop herself from tripping over a chair.

It was a plain wooden chair set down in the middle of nowhere, and yet perhaps ten feet away from the street. Beyond it was another chair, and another, dark shapes squatting in the mist. She counted twenty of them, placed in haphazard rows, facing nothing. The queue of fog-bound drifters had been some sort of impromptu audience for . . . for what? A preacher? A balladeer? One of the many science shows that had sprung up without a head-quarters, traveling from post to post in a coach, demonstrating the latest electrical advances to passersby?

She gathered her skirts and sat in the chair closest to her. One leg of the chair was resting on a pebble or per-haps in a hole, and it rocked under her weight. The soft sound of her own breathing echoed back from faraway nearby walls. She listened and heard, too, shuffling footsteps coming from somewhere behind her, or in front of her, or even above her (for all she knew, there was a walkway of some sort up there), and yet she knew that nobody could see her, nobody would find her there unless they literally stumbled over her.

In a way, she thought, she was as lost as Walter was. She had never faltered in her conviction that he was alive. More precisely, she would have known if he were dead. She didn't need evidence that he was out there somewhere in the fog. She only needed to know where. He might even be sitting in another chair in the same empty lot with her, only an arm's length away and yet unreachable.

She imagined she might snap some make-believe reins and the chair under her would take off at a trot, lead her to her husband, the other chairs following behind. Poor Walter astonished but overjoyed to see her arrive at the head of a galloping wooden herd. They would ride away together, gather the boys and the twin girls on chairs of their own, and leave the city behind with all its wretchedness and mystery.

'If you don't mind, miss.'

She started at the sound of the voice and jumped up off the chair, holding her umbrella like a weapon.

'Didn't mean to frighten you.' She still couldn't see the man who was talking, but his voice was quiet and gentle.

'I suppose I'm a bit nervous,' Claire said to the nothingness. 'Have you been standing here all along?'

'Thought I'd give you a minute to yerself. Looked like you might need a rest.'

'How could you know what I look like? You must have eyes like a bird.'

'Aye, that I do. You'll excuse me I hope, but I've gotta get this last chair on the wagon soon or the horses'll leave without me.'

'Last chair?' She peered around her and realized that the other squat shapes were gone. She was standing in front of the only chair left in the lot. 'I didn't even hear you take the others.'

'I'm a quiet sort when I need to be. Like I say, you looked like you needed the rest.'

'Thank you for letting me sit for so long.' How long had it been? 'Do you mind if I ask, why were the chairs here? A meeting of some sort?'

'Puppet show, ma'am. Like for the children. Not many showed today, though. Too gloomy to see the show. Mostly we just done the voices and left the puppets in the box. Let them children imagine what they don't see.'

'A puppet show. How lovely.'

'Well, thank you. Next time, when it's cleared up some, you bring yer own young ones and they can watch the play for nothin'. You tell the ticket taker Jim said it was all right.'

'Very kind of you. I suppose I should get out of your way.'

'Not at all.' A small man detached himself from the fog and limped past her. One of his legs was short and twisted. He tipped his hat at her, bent and picked up the chair, and was almost instantly gone, faded away. She strained to hear his footsteps, but there was no sound. She turned her head back and forth and felt a small spike of panic in her throat.

'Wait,' she said. 'Wait, sir. I don't know which direction to walk. Where's the street?'

There was no answer. Claire raised her umbrella so that it was parallel to the ground and took small steps until she felt the umbrella touch a wall. She scraped the point of the umbrella along bricks until it encountered empty air and then thrust forward, almost making her stumble.

'Oi! Watch it.' Someone marched past her, and she followed. Now she could once more hear the horses and the cries of vendors and the happy shrieks of children playing in the mist. She smiled and took a deep breath and made her slow way along the path, hoping she was headed in the direction of home.

As soon as she got there, she shut the door to the parlor, sat at her writing desk, and began to compose a new story about furniture that returned to the wood where it had once stood tall as trees. She did not hear the governess knock at the door or see the sun set. Everything disappeared for her except the scratching of her pen on paper, and she wrote well into the night.

7

Day woke and brushed a leaf off his face. The sky was completely dark and it took him a moment to realize that there was someone hovering over him. Day waited, tensing himself and wondering whether the cigars in his boot were still there. Somewhere he heard a fox rustling in the brush.

'I know you're awake, Walter Day.'

Day took a quick shallow breath. He recognized the voice. It was him. It was the man Jack. He reached for his walking stick, but Jack put a hand on his arm.

'Why are you lying in a trench in a park, Walter Day? Why are you here in the mud, instead of . . . Well, you confound me. Why haven't you gone home? Why aren't you doing what I told you to do?'

Day swallowed hard. The words made little sense, but the voice filled him with fear. His mouth was dry and his eyes stung and he felt his bladder trying to give out. He closed his eyes – there was nothing to see anyway – and concentrated on maintaining his dignity.

'You should answer me now.'

'I don't . . . I don't know what you mean.'

'I gave you a task, Walter Day.'

'I don't know who that is.'

'You don't know your own name?'

'I don't know my name. Am I . . . Did you say my name? Just now, was that my name? Is that who I am?'

'Fascinating. In retrospect, I suppose I should have experimented with someone else before mesmerizing you.'

'Mez . . . ?'

'To be truthful, I was growing bored with you and I may have rushed things.'

'I don't understand anything.'

'I know. What a shame. To think I once admired you. It's my own fault, really. I've gone and broken my favorite toy.' Jack sighed, and Day heard him shift, leaning away. He kept his eyes closed. 'I see you're wearing the clothes I left for you,' Jack said. 'Are they warm enough?'

'Yes. Thank you.'

'We can't have the great Walter Day wandering about in a woman's dress. It's remarkable you haven't become sick. How awfully hardy you are.'

'What name did you say?'

'Remarkable. I suppose I'll have to fall back on my secondary plan now. A shame. It would have been so much more fun if things had worked out with you. But perhaps I'll give you a bit more time.'

'Time for what?'

'Go home, Walter Day. Go home to your wife and her adorable children.'

'Home? I don't know . . . Where is my home?' Day waited. 'Jack?'

There was a long silence, and when Day opened his eyes, the shape had gone.

8

He did not hear from Jack again and, after enough time passed, he stopped having nightmares. He threw out the cotton dress when it became too filthy and too threadbare to keep him warm at night and bought a second shirt, which he washed and wore every other day while his primary shirt dried. He traded his boots, along with eleven recycled cigarettes, for another pair that fit him well. They were also secondhand, but in better repair, and they did not blister his feet and ankles as badly as the old pair had. He left money for the vendor who had unwittingly provided him with a dress in that first difficult week outside his cell. He also purchased a shallow wooden tray that folded over on itself and fastened with a simple clasp. At night, he stored his cigarettes and cigars inside it to keep them dry. During the day, he opened the tray and displayed his wares, taking a corner at the busy junction just north of London Bridge.

He worked there seven days a week, from six o'clock in the morning until just past four in the afternoon, then closed whatever remained unsold inside the tray, along with a small hand-lettered sign that read REASONABLE TOBACCO.

He would walk to Finsbury Circus and around its perimeter, scanning the ground for discarded butts, then up Moorgate to the Artillery Ground, or sometimes back down to Trinity Square and the Tower. He bypassed the end of Moorgate, where a new department store had recently opened. Traffic there was terrible and cigarette ends were hard to find.

Once, on Featherstone near Bunhill Fields, a stranger shouted at him. He turned, and the man yelled, 'Walter! Walter, is that you?' and jumped up and down, waving his arms. Day hurried away, and the stranger followed after him for a few minutes, trying to get his attention. Eventually, the stranger shrugged and turned back, and Day slowed his pace. Within minutes he had forgotten about the man, but he unconsciously avoided Featherstone after that.

He retained a slight limp, the result of an old injury that he could no longer recall, but his leg didn't cause him pain until late in the day and he rarely leaned on his cane.

By now he was well known, and the local boys would often scout the streets in advance, hoarding butts that they traded to Day in exchange for a smoke from his left-over stock in the folding tray. He learned the names of the most talented scouts and saved cigarettes back for those boys. Soon he had a network of children searching out tobacco for him, and he would retire early in the afternoon, receiving them in a short queue outside the warehouses of the East India Company on Seething Lane. Each evening he returned to Drapers' Gardens by various circuitous routes, always careful that he wasn't followed.

Within a few weeks of opening his Reasonable Tobacco business, itinerant though it was, he was doing well enough to rent a room above a shop that overlooked the gardens. For sixpence a night he was able to look out of his window at the trees and shrubbery he had slept in during the first and most difficult days of his freedom.

He began stockpiling the butts that were brought to him, sorting the used tobacco by color and collecting it all in three jars. He rolled new cigarettes and cigars on Saturdays, never leaving his room except for tea with his landlady, Mrs Paxton.

She was a kindhearted young widow, and she picked out a new wardrobe for him, allowing him to pay for it over time with the small addition of a penny a night on his room. Sundays he would help Mrs Paxton press the blouses and skirts to hang in the window of her downstairs shop. Her wares were strung on a thin wire across the bay window that faced the gardens. Before dawn each day he swept the path to her door and filled the gas lamp above it. She told him that she enjoyed having a man about, but she continued to be troubled by his lack of memory.

One Sunday she was folding a petticoat when she stopped and let it hang from her hands. She looked across the room at him, frowned, and bit her lower lip. 'What if you have a family somewhere?'

He shrugged. 'If so, there's not a thing I can do about it.'

'Why haven't you gone to the police?'

The question troubled him. He wasn't sure why he'd avoided the police. He shook his head and tested the iron that was heating over the fireplace. A drop of water sizzled on its surface, but he left it where it was for a moment. 'I think the police would put me in the workhouse,' he said. 'I couldn't stand it. I prefer to be my own man. I value my freedom.' But he knew it was a lie as he said it.

Or, rather, it was a half-truth. He did enjoy his freedom, but there was another reason he avoided the police, some compulsion. Even thinking of it brought a deep feeling of doom. He knew he must stay far away from New Scotland Yard and he must not think about the possibility of a family waiting for him somewhere.

But his answer was enough to satisfy Mrs Paxton. She finished folding the petticoat and placed it atop a stack on the window seat. 'And what about your name? Do you enjoy not having a name as well?'

He shrugged again and picked up the iron by its blackened wooden handle. 'I have a name. But call me whatever you like. I don't care.'

'Don't you want to know your full name?'

'Someone told me my full name. It was some time ago and it may even have been a dream. I don't remember it well. I was half-asleep.' He thought perhaps he didn't want to remember.

'Maybe if you thought hard about it. Maybe if you say your first name over and over, your last name will occur to you.'

'Walter, Walter, Walter . . . No, nothing seems to come after Walter.'

'Nothing?' She put a finger to her lips and smiled. 'And what if I need to introduce you to someone? Shall I refer to you as Mr Nothing?'

'Why would you introduce me to anyone? Besides, I hardly need a name to press this skirt.'

'I could say that you're a cousin of my husband's. I could call you Mr Paxton.'

'Did your husband have a cousin?'

'Several, but he was never terribly close with them.'

'What was his name? Your husband, I mean.'

Another long pause, long enough that he had time to realize how much the memory of her husband might hurt her and to regret giving her reason to return to that memory.

'I'm sorry,' she said. 'I'd rather not talk about my husband.'

'Of course. I apologize.' He turned and got to work. After a moment he heard the rustle of fabric and knew that she had returned to her own chore, folding clothes.

It was some time before she spoke again. When she did, he was pressing a white cotton jacket. The work was somewhat delicate, and he did not turn around to look at her.

'His name was Ben. Benjamin Paxton.'

'Ben is a good name.'

'He was a good man.'

'He must have been very good indeed if you chose to marry him. But I'm sorry I made you think of him just now, Mrs Paxton. I didn't intend to upset you.'

'I'm not upset. Perhaps a little sad, but that has nothing to do with you.'

'I think it might not be a good idea to tell people I'm his cousin. I think for now we can leave my full name a mystery and simply call me Walter. When you need to call me anything at all.'

'Walter it is, then,' she said. 'And you must call me Esther.'

'I couldn't,' he said.

'I wish you would.'

He finally turned and looked at her. Their eyes met, but her face immediately flushed and she took a step farther away from him. He nodded and stared down at the jacket, at the iron in his hand. The thought of calling Mrs Paxton by her given name stirred the same feelings of wrongness in him that the idea of the police did. And yet, he had nothing, he had no reasons for anything he felt, no memories of anything before his cold cell and the sun shining on a narrow courtyard. Now he was free and alive and he could not bear the notion of shutting himself away again, of giving up the things that life had to offer. If he could not remember his old life, how could it be wrong to build a new one?

'Very well,' he said. His throat felt very dry. 'Very well, Esther.'

9

'Of course I feel for you. You're a woman trying to get by on suspect employment, and with four small children, with no man to help her and no future prospects so long as she remains in this city. You can't accuse me of not understanding your life when I'm up late every night thinking only of you and the mess you've made of things.'

'That's . . .' Claire stopped and calmed herself before speaking again. 'Father, you have to know how cruel that sounds.'

'I think you should watch your tone of voice when speaking to me,' Leland Carlyle said. 'I know women these days are encouraged to speak before they think, but you ought to be grateful to me. Lord knows I've been patient with you.'

'Yes, thank you,' Claire said. She was so angry she could barely see, but she knew that any outward sign of her feelings would only be used against her.

'Before you launch into another of your unwarranted attacks against me, I was only agreeing with you,' Carlyle said. 'I was telling you I genuinely understand your position. It can't be easy. That man left you with four children. Although, of course, there's no real reason for you to burden yourself with half of them.'

'Robert and Simon are my children just as much as Winnie and Henrietta are. And my husband didn't leave me. I never said that.' But her father had struck a nerve, and she hoped the doubt she felt didn't show on her face. She didn't want to believe that Walter might have left her on purpose, and she tried not to even think about the possibility, but it was there.

Carlyle snorted and crossed the room. He poured himself a drink from the decanter of brandy that Claire kept filled for the day Walter returned home.

'You've adopted children when you can't even care for your own children.' He took a drink. 'Claire, perhaps I've loved you too much, indulged you too much. You must have some perspective, some logical sense of responsibility, rather than tripping gaily about on your feelings. Do you want the boys to go to an orphanage? Of course not. I confess I find them charming. I want what's best for them, too. I simply don't agree that you and this situation are what's best for them.'

'I love them, I feed them, I clothe them. They have a roof over their heads.'

'And they have no father. They are boys without a father.'

'That's not their fault. They lost their parents, and then they lost Walter. Would you have me abandon them, too?'

'So you admit Walter's abandoned them? Abandoned you all?'

'That's not what I said. You keep twisting my words.'

'I'm doing no such thing. You continue to evade my points. What kind of men will those boys become when they have no father in their lives?'

'When Walter comes home –'

'I'm tired of hearing about Walter Day. Of all the men

you might have married, it escapes me why you would choose that one.'

'I did choose him. And I choose to stay here until he comes home to me.'

'The wiser choice is to come back to Devon with me. Your mother and I will see to your needs, and the needs of your children. Make the better choice, Claire.'

'Between you and Walter? I will always choose Walter over you. Always.'

Carlyle raised his hand to hit her, but then took a deep breath and lowered it. He closed his eyes and sipped his brandy. When he opened his eyes again, he smiled at her. 'He has no intention of coming home. I know that's a harsh truth, but you need to hear it.'

'He will. He's been hurt or imprisoned somewhere.'

'Would it shock you to know that Walter is alive and well? And that I saw him?'

'Saw him?' Claire's heart swelled and seemed to fill her, to squeeze her lungs. She couldn't breathe and she couldn't see. Her father's words rang like bells in her ears.

'I debated whether to tell you, but now I think it might be best for you to face the truth.'

'What do you mean you saw him?'

'I was leaving the club, and he was on the other side of the street, walking along just as daring as you please. Someone called out to him and he darted away.'

'What street? Where were you?'

'Oh, I don't remember. As I say, I was near my club, so it must have been somewhere near the bridge.'

'London Bridge?'

'Yes, the bridge.'

'What was he doing?'

'Walking.'

'What were you doing?'

'I was also walking. There was nothing remarkable about any of it except that he turned and ran when he heard his name.'

'Walter can't run. His leg injury prevents it. You saw someone who looked like Walter.'

'I know my son-in-law when I see him.'

'That's the first time you've ever called him that. You've never acknowledged that he's a part of your family, and you only say it now to hurt me.'

'Not at all. If I've kept my distance from him, it's only because he makes his life more complicated than it needs to be. And he complicates the lives of everyone else around him. I honestly don't think you can deny that.'

Claire sat on the arm of a chair and threw her hands up in frustration. 'I need to know so much. Was it really Walter? Did he see you at the same time you saw him? Did you chase him away? I believe, if it really was Walter, you must have said something awful to him to drive him further from us.'

'I assure you that's not the case.'

'Well, why *didn't* you say anything? Why didn't you call out his name? Or follow him? You say you watched him as he disappeared again. Why wouldn't you try to bring him home?'

'As I say, he didn't see me, and I didn't wish to make a scene in the middle of the street.'

'I need to be alone, Father. Please.'

Carlyle drained his glass and set it on the table. He put

his hand on Claire's shoulder, and when she tried to move away from him, he tightened his grip.

'I understand,' he said. 'But you deserved to know the truth. Your husband isn't missing. He simply doesn't want to be with you. It's hard to hear, I'm sure, but I think you'll thank me some day for my honesty.'

'Please just go.'

'Do you need any money?'

'I don't need anything from you.'

'Very well. I'll ask your mother to look in on you tomorrow.'

He grabbed his hat and went to the door. He turned back, and he looked as if he might say something more, but then changed his mind and left, closing the door quietly behind him. Claire sat for some time, staring at the door as if it might open again and Walter might be standing there. She knew her father had meant to hurt her with his words, to unmoor her and make her more willing to leave London, to return home with him to the estate in Devon. But he had made a mistake because he didn't understand the depth of her love for her husband. Leland Carlyle had given his daughter renewed hope.

IO

The boy's name was Ambrose and he was fourteen years old. He was a clever lad and full of energy, and Day had put him in charge of some of the other boys. Ambrose worked many jobs. Every morning he scouted for cigarette and cigar butts in the streets. He coordinated the efforts of the other children involved and helped to make sure nobody covered the same ground twice in a day. In the evening, after their findings had been given to Day and the other boys had gone, Ambrose took his chess set and sat in Trinity Square, playing all comers for money. He did well. The square was close enough to both Tom's Coffee House and the George and Vulture Tavern, where London's most enthusiastic chess lovers regularly met, so Ambrose's table attracted those players who were not members of chess clubs or who couldn't get in on a game at those reputable establishments.

His board was handmade from grooved and fitted boxwood, and he had fashioned the pieces from materials he had found while scavenging. The white king was made from the bowl of a broken ivory pipe, while the black king was an ebony organ key that he had stolen from a church, then sanded into shape and polished.

He played anyone who sat down across from him and only collected if he won. He usually made enough from three or four games to pay for a room in one of the houses across the bridge. When he lost, or when he couldn't get anyone to play against him, he slept in nearby alleyways or on rooftops.

But whether he was in a room or on a roof, he got little sleep. The rooftops were safer, but he tended to move a lot while dreaming and sometimes came perilously close to rolling off the edges of buildings. It was better when there was a skylight. The boxy frame of a skylight gave him something to anchor himself against. And it gave him a thrill to peek down inside businesses and warehouses. He often wondered about the businessmen who met in top-floor offices, wondered at how their lives had been arranged for them so that they never had to sleep out in the cold. He imagined they had all grown up with parents and families and opportunities that Ambrose would never know.

He had been chased away from the roof of the East India Trading Company and so found himself in the alley behind Plumm's. Two washerwomen passed Ambrose without seeing him in the shadows and entered the department store through a back door. Ambrose waited a few minutes, then tried turning the knob, but the door had been locked behind the women. Too bad. Finding an out-of-the-way corner in a storage room would have been ideal. Instead, he found an access ladder that was semi-concealed in a niche at the back of the building and climbed up. It was a new building, without the customary coat of grimy black soot that covered the bricks of more established stores in the neighborhood. Ambrose was able to hug close to the wall, out of sight of the alley below.

He pulled himself over the edge of the roof and stepped out, testing the boards and shingles beneath him before putting his whole weight on them. From his new vantage point above the fog he could see far in every direction, all the way past Drapers' Gardens to the Thames in the south. He took a deep breath of the cool, clean air and smiled up at the stars. He tiptoed to the enormous domed skylight and peered down into a room below. It didn't occur to him that he might be violating anyone's privacy. Finding things was a big part of his job.

In the room, oblivious to the boy on the roof, eight men sat around a scarred table and talked business. A ninth man, a large fellow wearing white gloves and tails, circulated a box of cigars, and each of the other men took a smoke. The man with the gloves punctured the tips of their cigars and made another circuit of the table, lighting them. The businessmen sent tendrils of smoke upward toward Ambrose, but their gazes did not follow the smoke. They talked together about the day's business, about personnel and shelf space and displays. The man with the gloves took the box of cigars away and set it on a side table that already held four other boxes of cigars and cigarettes and pipe tobacco. There were larger boxes and crates stacked all round the room, marked with symbols that Ambrose could barely make out: alcohol, guns, ammunition, lamp oil, all the most valuable or dangerous goods that the store had to offer, kept on the top floor where they couldn't be easily pilfered.

If he could only find a way into that room, he could take away big handfuls of tobacco, boxes of it, all of it new, none of it found on the street and dried out and reused. It would cost Ambrose nothing, and it would be a boon to his employer.

Reasonable Tobacco, indeed.

He watched as the men smoked and talked for the better part of an hour, and his mind turned over ways to lower himself into the room and get back out. It seemed impossible. Perhaps it would be better to follow the women through the back of the store one night and hide until the place was empty. But he didn't think he could do that. The alley was too narrow for him to go unnoticed. Perhaps he could pay the women to look the other way or leave the door unlocked.

His musings were interrupted when one of the men pushed back his chair, stubbed out his cigar, and stretched. The others followed suit and, in small groups of two or three, the men left the room and closed the door behind them. Ambrose hurried across the roof and watched the fog moving slowly along the street below. In due course, he heard the men exit the building and go their separate ways, creating eddies in the mist and hollering 'good night' back and forth.

Ambrose went back to the skylight and looked down into the darkened room, empty but for those crates of volatile merchandise. He felt along the outside of the wooden casing for a lock or a catch and, when he didn't find one, tried pulling upward on it. He heard something creak and felt the frame give. There was the sound of splintering wood and the big pane of glass cracked, a fine silvery thread zigzagging away from Ambrose toward the far edge of the roof. At that moment, below him, the door opened and the man with the white gloves entered the room. Ambrose froze, still clutching the skylight's frame, afraid to let go for fear it would make further noise or, worse, come apart and crash inward. The man with the gloves held the door open for the two washerwomen, who entered behind him. One of them held a rag and a bucket; the other carried a mop. Ambrose could hear their voices as the three people talked, but they were too far away and the cracked glass muffled the sound. Below, the man closed the door and turned a lock. Neither of the women looked up as he removed his gloves, folded them, and put them in his pocket. From another pocket he took a folding razor and opened it. As Ambrose watched, the man stepped up behind one of the women, grabbed a handful of her hair, and snapped her head back. In a flash, he had pulled the razor across her throat, releasing a spray of blood that glistened black in the wan light. Ambrose gasped. The other woman started to turn around, but the man let go of the first woman and stepped over her body as she dropped to the floor. He moved gracefully, like a dancer, and grabbed the second woman's arm before she had a chance to move. Ambrose forgot himself and pounded on the skylight. The silvery crack in the glass widened, but didn't separate. The man below him slashed the razor downward, in one practised move, opening up the second woman from her throat to her pelvis, and her insides splashed out at his feet.

Then the man looked up and saw Ambrose. He was still holding the arm of the second woman, who had gone limp and lifeless. In his other hand he held the razor. His right shirtsleeve was drenched in dark blood. Ambrose held very still. *He can't see me,* he thought. *It's dark and the glass will obscure my shape against the sky,* he thought.

But the man smiled at Ambrose and saluted him with

the dripping razor, and Ambrose could no longer hold himself still. He reeled backward, pushing away from the skylight, and almost fell off the roof. He ran trembling to the access ladder and made his way down to the alley floor so quickly that his feet only touched every third or fourth rung. He ran as fast as he could to the mouth of the alley and didn't stop, but pelted breathlessly down the street.

Behind him, he imagined he could hear the door open and quiet footfalls as the man stepped gracefully out into the grey mist.

Surely, Ambrose thought, *surely he didn't get a look at me. Surely he could never find me again.* But somehow he knew that the man had seen him and would find him, no matter how fast or how far Ambrose ran.

The draper's shop was closed for the night, the doors locked, the shutters bolted over the display windows that faced the park. Day woke up from a dream about a whispering shadow and leapt out of bed. Someone was pounding on the door. He lit a candle and threw a dressing gown (made especially for him by Esther Paxton) over his nightshirt before taking the back steps to the ground floor. The pounding continued, growing louder as he moved closer. Through the small window in the back door he saw a boy's face against the pitch black of the trees, an ivory cameo on black velvet. He put down his walking stick and unlocked the door, pulled it open, and Ambrose stumbled in.

Day led him to the parlor and left him there to catch his breath. He padded back upstairs and used his hot plate to heat two cups of gunpowder tea, which he brought back down the stairs. Ambrose had already got a cozy fire going and took one of the cups from Day.

'What, no ale?'

'Sorry,' Day said.

'It'll do,' Ambrose said.

'Are you quite all right?'

'I'm good, yeah,' Ambrose said.

'It looked like you were being chased.'

'Just in a hurry. Ran over here. I don't sleep so good anyway and thought I'd take a chance you were about.'

'I was sleeping.'

'Sorry then.'

'But nobody's trying to harm you?'

'I dunno if he even saw me. No, that's not true. He saw me, all right.'

'Who? Who saw you?'

Ambrose stared at the fire and sipped his tea. He opened his mouth as if about to talk, then shuddered and took another sip. Day let him be, and after a few minutes the boy straightened his shoulders and spoke quietly, watching the flames. 'He kilt them two women. The man with the gloves did it after them others was gone for the night.'

'You saw this happen?'

Ambrose nodded.

'A man wearing gloves. But he didn't see you? Are you sure?'

Ambrose shook his head. 'No. 'M not sure.'

'Did he chase you?'

'No, guv, he looked right at me, he did. Like he was lookin' right into me and knew everything about me.'

'This man. Describe him for me.'

'Can't. He was in shadows the whole time. Like he stayed in the shadows without even tryin'. Like they followed him round, like they was his dog and stayed at his heel.'

'Dark, wavy hair?'

'Yes.'

'Tall?'

'Couldn't tell. I was lookin' down on him.'

'How did he kill the women?'

'Wiff a razor, like. Calm and collected as he could be, like he was guttin' a fish is all. They didn't hardly stand a chance. They was dead before they even knowed it was happenin'. He didn't have no reason for it; they was just doin' they jobs.'

Day set his tea down on the table between them. He sat back and frowned at the boy. He thought he knew who Ambrose was talking about, who the man with the gloves must be. 'Where is he? I mean, where did you see him?'

'At the new store. I think he works there.'

'Plumm's?'

'That's the one. Ever been in there?'

Day swallowed another mouthful of his green tea. 'No.'

'Neither me,' Ambrose said. 'But it's got a window in the roof. A big one, round and beautiful.'

'And you've been spying on the goings-on there?'

'Not spying, no. Not me. But I like to sleep up high when I can. Keeps the tearaways offa me. So I was up there on top of the place, like, and just so happened to look down in, and there's gennulmens of leisure, don't you know? And they got a smoking room in there.'

'An office on the top floor?'

'Right.'

'Is he there now?'

'I dunno. Maybe. He mighta chased me.'

Day stood and went to the door. He pulled the curtain aside on the tiny window and looked out into the night. There was nothing to see. Only the dark shapes of trees and bushes. He drew the lock across, then went around the ground floor and checked the shutters on all the windows.

'You'll stay here,' he said. 'I can't very well turn you out at this time of night. You can sleep here on the sofa.'

'That's kind of you, guv.'

'But you must be gone by the time Mrs Paxton arrives in the morning. I don't think she'd care to find a . . . Well, I don't think she would appreciate my taking the liberty of lending out her sofa. I'll fetch you a blanket from upstairs.' Day started toward the staircase, then stopped and turned back. 'And, Ambrose . . .'

'Yes, guv?'

'Don't steal anything.'

'What, like a ribbon or somethin'? What would I do that for?'

'Just don't.'

Ambrose grinned. 'Don't worry none, Mr Tobacco. Your lady's ribbons is safe from me.'

Mr and Mrs Parker had a table at the back of the coffee-house, where the lights were dim. It was early, and foot traffic was minimal. The high judge entered and removed his coat and hat, handing them over to the gentleman at the door before passing under a low arch and scanning the room. His business brought him to London on a regular basis, but he never seemed to have time to enjoy all that Mayfair had to offer. He thought he might stroll down to Piccadilly after tea to buy souvenirs for his family. He spotted the Parkers at their table, recognizable from the description they had sent him, and gave Mr Parker a discreet nod. Parker waved him over and an abrupt feeling of dread washed over him, dispelling pleasant thoughts of long walks and frivolous purchases.

The couple stood as he approached, and the judge saw that the woman was wearing trousers. He shook his head, but decided to say nothing to her about it. Perhaps it was the custom in whatever place they called home. If they wished to travel inconspicuously about the city, though, she would need to update her wardrobe sooner rather than later.

Before he had even taken a chair, the high judge began talking. 'I shouldn't be seen with you,' he said. 'You know I can't. This place is quite out in the open, isn't it?' He glanced around him at the nearly empty room, its tables laid out with latticework napkins and bone china.

'The hour is unusual, and you English are good in the area of staying out of each other's business,' Mrs Parker said. Her grammar was stilted and her accent was unplaceable. The high judge flicked his gaze to Mr Parker, but the man didn't seem the least put out that his wife had spoken for them both. There was something unsettling in the woman's expression. Her eyes were flat and dull and regarded him the way he thought he might regard an insect or a bit of soot on his collar.

He smiled at her, but when she didn't smile back, he gave up and turned his attention to the man instead. 'Be that as it may,' the high judge said, 'a less public place might have been better.'

'No,' Mr Parker said. His voice was low and soft, and the judge leaned forward to hear him. The accent made it difficult to pick out his words. 'A less public place makes people wonder.'

'I don't know about –' the judge said. But Mr Parker cut him off.

'This is where we are now,' Parker said. And that seemed to end the matter. The judge would talk there, or nowhere. His prospective employees would simply return to their home country, where he knew their services were in great demand. He wondered where they had originally come from and whether they felt any native sympathies for anything.

'I understand.' The judge sighed. A woman wearing an immaculate apron approached. 'I don't care for coffee,' the judge said. 'Do you also serve tea?'

They did, and he ordered Imperial with strawberry cakes and brown bread for the table. He shot a glance at the Parkers, and Mrs Parker nodded back. She was satisfied with his choices. When the woman had left, the judge leaned forward and whispered. 'I have news.'

'Don't whisper,' Mr Parker said. 'It draws attention. Pretend you are speaking of something mundane . . . What? Anything English is mundane enough, I suppose.'

The judge sat back, mildly offended. The insult was hardly merited. He took a moment, wondered if he shouldn't stand and leave and forget the entire affair. But he had set this in motion, had wired a coded message to these vulgar people, and they had traveled all this way. And what did it matter if they were vulgar? Of course they were. One had only to look at what they did for a living. They killed people, without compunction or shame, and with no thought for the justice behind any of it. They were hired to do a job, they were nothing more than tools, and tools did not have manners. He pulled down on the bottom of his waistcoat, straightening it, and cleared his throat.

'No need for that sort of thing,' he said. He felt he was displaying admirable restraint.

Mr Parker nodded. 'Apologies,' he said. 'We are tired from the traveling and are not looking forward to our, how do you say it here? Our accommodations tonight.'

Mrs Parker smiled, and the high judge felt something cold and wet run up the length of his spine.

'I could arrange . . .' he began, but Mr Parker held up a hand to stop him.

'No,' Mr Parker said. 'Thank you, but we make our own way. You do not need to know where we are staying. No one needs to know that.'

'I see. Trust no one, is that it?'

'I think I would say it more as "be careful whom you trust." '

'Just so.' The judge was warming to the whole thing. He was sitting across the table from hired assassins and he controlled them. At least for the moment. 'I have urgent news. It may change everything.'

'Tell us.'

'Walter Day is alive,' he said. He didn't whisper, but he kept his voice low. 'I saw him in the street.'

The Parkers exchanged a glance. Mrs Parker shrugged, and Mr Parker spoke. 'We don't know who that is.'

'He's a detective with Scotland Yard.'

'And you wish us to make him go away?'

The judge took a second to realize what the killer meant. He shook his head. 'No. It's only that Walter Day complicates the matter.'

'In what way?'

'It's . . . Well, it's a bit much to explain.'

'Then don't.'

'No, I . . . No, it's just that Day is tied up with everything else, and it's hard to see why.'

'He's alive, we visit him,' Mrs Parker said. 'Then he is no longer alive. Very simple. Although to deal with a policeman in this way will be costing more money than we agreed upon.'

'No, not Walter,' the judge said. 'And he's not . . .' He could hear a note of panic creeping into his voice, but was relieved to see the woman with the apron approaching with a big silver tray. He hadn't prepared well enough for the meeting. He was used to working with people who shared his point of view. He was used to being a leader, being listened to and obeyed, but here he was being forced into a subservient position. He sat back and let the woman set out the tea and cakes and bread, along with butter and cream and lemon, small chocolate biscuits that he hadn't asked for but must be a speciality of the house, jam and honey. She smiled at them and walked away. Neither of the Parkers made a move toward their cups or the food, so the judge helped himself before speaking again. 'Walter Day is no longer a policeman, and he is not, not precisely at this moment, the objective.'

'What is the objective?' Mrs Parker poured some tea and then swirled in a dollop of cream. The judge was gratified to see that she knew what to do with a cup of tea. Perhaps that same expertise extended to killing people.

'The objective . . .' And here the judge could not help himself. He leaned forward and whispered. 'The objective is Jack the Ripper.' He leaned back and sipped his tea. It was very hot. He waited for a reaction from the Parkers, but was disappointed. They concentrated on their own cups and did not appear to take any special notice of what he had said. He took a bite of chocolate biscuit and raised his eyebrows. 'Jack the Ripper,' he said again.

Mr and Mrs Parker exchanged a look. Mrs Parker picked up a bit of bread and smeared it with jam. She took a delicate bite. Mr Parker watched her, then turned to the judge. 'The Ripper is already dead. Or gone. One or the other.'

'He is neither dead nor gone. He's alive and he's still causing mischief. It's only that the sort of mischief he causes has changed of late.'

'So you know where this person is, then, this Jack person?'

'No,' the judge said. He had felt a bit of fire banking in his belly, and now it sparked out and died.

'Of course not. The biggest mystery ever in your city, maybe in your entire country, and you expect us to solve it for you now? Like this?' Mr Parker snapped his fingers and two elderly men several tables away looked over at them.

The high judge turned his head so the men wouldn't recognize him if they saw him later and waited until they went back to their own conversation before he spoke. 'If I knew who he was, I wouldn't need you.'

'And why do you need us?'

'To kill him, of course. To kill Jack.'

Mr Parker looked again at Mrs Parker. As one they pushed back from the table and stood. Mrs Parker reached down for another slice of bread.

'You can't leave,' the judge said.

'You've wasted our time,' Mr Parker said. 'You will get a statement of charges from us shortly. Our traveling expenses. I suggest you pay it with all quickness.'

'Wait,' the judge said. He stuck out his hand, as if warding off an approaching carriage. 'One minute. Hear me out.'

'Why?'

'I'm paying you for your time, aren't I? We are, I mean, the Karstphanomen are. I speak for them. Look here, you might just as well finish your tea.' He could hear a note of desperation entering his voice and he fought to control it. He hoped the next time he opened his mouth that wheedling tone would be gone. 'You've come all this way; why wouldn't you at least finish your tea?'

After a moment Mrs Parker sat, and Mr Parker followed suit. Neither of them looked at the judge, but he took their continued presence as an invitation to speak. 'We caught him,' he said. 'Two years ago. We're the ones. The police couldn't do it, the press couldn't do it. We did it. The Karstphanomen.' He smiled at them, proud, but they ignored him.

'Another spot of tea, love?'

Mr Parker nodded, and Mrs Parker poured for him. He sipped without acknowledging her or the judge.

'Well, you see,' the judge continued, 'we did it. But we couldn't very well just . . . We couldn't just end him. He'd done so much, done so much to them poor women.' He stopped and caught himself. His grammar was slipping. It wasn't like him at all. He hadn't even touched a drop.

'So you let him go again? For the sport?' Mrs Parker licked a spot of cream off her upper lip.

'No,' the judge said. He felt very warm. 'No, we kept him. And we showed him what he'd done. We did the same things to him, over and over, that he'd done to the women, in hopes that we could make amends for some of it, maybe for all the things men have ever done to women.'

'Not possible,' Mrs Parker said. 'Not even a thing to think about.'

'But we meant well.'

'The road to hell is paved in that sort of rubbish,' Mr Parker said. 'Isn't that what they say? Rubbish thinking?'

'Very well to say now,' the judge said. 'But he got himself free, Jack did. And Walter Day helped.'

'Walter Day is the fellow you say is alive now.'

'Right. We thought he was dead. We thought Jack had got Walter.'

'You say this Day fellow avoided you?'

'He did.'

'Then what is there to fear from him?'

'What if Jack told him something?'

'What if he did?'

'Walter Day will be found. There are many people looking for him. My own daughter is . . . But if Jack told him who we are, and if Walter tells the police who we are . . . well, things are likely to get a bit hot in London.'

'So I repeat myself: You want us to remove Walter Day.'

The judge sat back in his chair. The back was high and padded, and he heard a gasp of air as his weight hit it. 'No,' he said. 'No, at all costs you must not harm Walter Day. But you must eliminate any and all things that Walter Day might disclose. If there is no Jack, there is nothing for the police to investigate, do you understand? If Jack is dead, the trail ends with him, and I can deal privately with anything that Walter knows.'

'You know this Day person well?'

'Well enough.'

'Perhaps Jack has fled. Perhaps he's no longer in London.'

'He's here. He's killing us. He's killing the members of the . . . He's killing the ones who tortured him. He's out for revenge, and there are damn few of us left now.'

'Ah.' Mr Parker leaned back, a bite of cake held halfway to his mouth. 'Now I begin to see.' He turned to Mrs Parker, and she pursed her lips. She nodded, and he turned his gaze back to the high judge. 'You are afraid of this Jack because he is going to kill you and you wish him to be dead before he does so. Why did you not say as much at the very beginning?'

'It's a complicated situation.'

'In our experience, most situations can be made to be less complicated. It is our speciality.'

'You don't understand,' the judge said.

'Then tell us.'

He did. He left out everything that he thought the Parkers might use against him, but he told them about finding Jack asleep, sprawled across the body of poor Mary Jane Kelly, about taking Jack and clapping him in irons and leaving Mary there on the bed, her guts spilled out across the mattress. He told them about the year they'd spent, he and the others, cutting Jack, cutting him in every place that he had cut his victims, but keeping him alive so they could cut him again. And again. And he told them about Inspector Walter Day, who had stumbled across their dirty secret, the secret they kept deep underground in abandoned tunnels, how Saucy Jack had somehow changed places with Walter Day, tortured the detective, damaged him physically and mentally, then spirited him away.

When he had finished, Mr and Mrs Parker waited, as if there might be more to tell. They polished off the cakes and the tea, and Mr Parker excused himself. He stood and walked away. When he had gone, Mrs Parker fixed the judge with a contemptuous stare and smacked her lips. 'So,' she said, 'that was a long story, but it only means this: You thought Walter Day was dead, but now he is not, and his being alive is a problem for you.'

'We thought we could stop Jack. Find him and kill him,' the judge said. (Why was she speaking to him in this manner when her husband wasn't even there? The man ought not involve his wife in business matters. But there was no use trying to make sense of foreign customs. People from other countries were often like animals.) 'He keeps killing us, Jack does. There are bloody few of us left.'

'So you say, but we still don't understand why you want this Jack dead and not Walter. Finding and killing Walter Day is the simpler task.'

'It's too much to go into.'

'There must be something personal, some other reason you —'

'Don't you dare.' The judge slammed his fist against the table. 'I've been patient with you, I've allowed you to speak to me as if . . . as if we were somehow equals, but don't you dare question me or my motives.' He shook his finger at her. 'You just watch your tone with me. Do you know who I am?'

To his surprise, Mrs Parker smiled again. And the longer she smiled, the bigger her smile became. The judge looked around for Mr Parker and was glad to see the man returning to the table. He stood and grabbed Mr Parker's chair for him. His hands were trembling.

Mr Parker looked at them both and settled a hand on Mrs Parker's arm. He shook his head and waited a moment before addressing her. 'What has happened? Our host looks likely to piss himself.'

'I've been good,' Mrs Parker said. 'I haven't hurt him. We have been discussing the work we are to do.'

'Ah,' Mr Parker said. 'Very well then.'

'And the . . . I'm sorry, what do you call yourself? Within your silly gentlemen's club?'

'It's not a . . .' The judge paused and wiped his face with a napkin. 'It's not a club. It's a society. And I am the high judge because I am responsible for the final decisions as regards the ultimate fates of our subjects.' He raised his cup and sipped, trying to regain his composure.

'The judge, then,' Mrs Parker said. 'The judge of the Karstphanomen. Isn't that what you call yourselves? He has decided to pay us double our usual amount.'

'But that's not . . .' The judge aspirated a mouthful of his tea and went through a brief coughing fit. The Parkers watched calmly. No one around them seemed to notice or care. The elderly men had already left, and the waitress was nowhere to be seen. When he could breathe again, the judge continued. 'I never,' he said. It was the best he could do. His throat burned now.

'You have brought the fee we asked for?'

'It's here.' The judge pushed an envelope across the table, and Mr Parker made it disappear. 'It's all right there. The entire amount you said.'

'Good,' Mr Parker said.

'But this is sufficient for only one half of the job you require,' Mrs Parker said. 'This is the amount you will pay us to find Jack the Ripper. And when we do, you must pay us the same amount again to kill him.'

'What?'

'We don't care to solve international mysteries. It is not what we do. We do a single job, a job most people, for whatever reason, do not care to do for themselves. You ask us to find this person who is unfindable and then also to put an end to his doings, is that not right?'

'I thought you would —'

70

'There is no point in thinking about what we do,' Mrs Parker said. 'You have asked us to do two things, so you should pay us two times. Is that not fair? You will pay us and we will do it and then you will sleep like the babies all night long, is it not so?'

'Mr Parker, surely you won't allow your wife to speak to me –'

'If you haven't noticed, Mr Carlyle, I don't allow or disallow my wife anything. She tends to speak her own mind. Is that the phrase? And you are a lucky man if all she does is speak.'

They knew his name. His real name. Perhaps they knew more. Where he lived? The membership of the Karstphanomen? He took a deep, shuddering breath and thought of Claire and the babies. Then he nodded.

'Good,' Mr Parker said. 'Then it's settled. Thank you very much for the tea and cakes. We'll get on with our business now.'

Leland Carlyle, the high judge of the Karstphanomen, sat quietly as the killers left the coffeehouse. Carlyle averted his eyes as Mrs Parker walked away. Her trousers left little to the imagination. On their way out, Mr Parker gave the woman in the apron a coin. He smiled and nodded at her just as if he were a human being.

There was a small stack of books on the mantel, and Ambrose pointed to them. 'That what you use for cigarette paper? Roll tobacco up in the pages and people get clever when they smoke the words?'

Day chuckled. 'No, I don't think I could do that.' He picked up the top book, blew a film of dust off the cover. 'I like books. Do you know how to read, Ambrose?'

Ambrose shook his head. 'I mean, I know a bit from the ragged school, but only barely enough. Books'r hard, and we didn't need to know readin' to make a living.'

'You should try again. You're a clever lad, and reading's easy once you've got the hang of it. You could go far with a little education. Do more with your life.'

'Like you? Sellin' old leavings on the street?'

Day turned the book over and opened it to a random page.

'I'm sorry,' Ambrose said. 'Didn't mean nothin' by what I said. What's that book about?'

'I've read it before,' Day said. 'It's by Lear.'

'What's that mean?'

'The author. Edward Lear. It's a book of his poems. My . . . I knew a woman once who liked them. She wrote poetry, too.'

'Can't figure the meaning in poems. Thanks, but no thanks.'

'Suit yourself,' Day said. 'But these poems are funny. Do you know the alphabet?'

'Some. I know the shapes.'

'Here's a nonsense alphabet. You might like that.'

'I appreciate the thought, guv, but I'm only smart about some things.'

Day sat on the sofa beside Ambrose. 'Here,' he said, 'do you know this letter?'

'Oh, I seen this before.' Ambrose pointed at a small illustration of a cat. 'That letter means *cat*, and it means *cigar*, too. But it should mean *moon*, 'cause that's what it looks like, right?'

'"C was a cat who ran after a rat; but his courage did fail when she seized on his tail. Crafty old cat!"'

'That is a bit funny. That's a way to go about teaching a thing. Make it so it's not boring. Lemme see.' Ambrose took the book from Day and leafed through it. 'That don't look right, that picture.'

'Why not?'

'I mean, that letter looks all wrong to spell the word *shrubbery*. Ain't what I remember.'

'Because that letter is a *Y*, and the illustration there is of a yew. A yew tree. "Y was a yew, which flourished and grew by a quiet abode near the side of a road. Dark little yew!'

'Dark little you?'

'Exactly right.'

13

'We can't turn him away,' Hatty said. 'We can't afford to.'

'What does . . .' But Hammersmith suddenly decided it wasn't worth arguing with her. He closed his mouth and waved his hand at her, hoping she'd leave his office and go bother Eugenia instead.

She didn't. 'We have one client and we haven't made progress in a year on that case, and he was your friend and I'm sorry, I'm truly sorry to put it so bluntly, but we need more clients and we need more work and I'm sure we need more money coming in.' She paused for breath, but before Hammersmith could say anything, she started again. '*I* need more work. I'm as good as any man at all this; I just need the chance to actually do something.'

Hammersmith waited to be sure she was finished. After a moment of strained silence, he nodded. 'He was my friend. He *is* my friend. This agency, such as it is, exists for only one reason, and that's to find Walter Day and return him to his family.'

'For all we know he's dead.' Hatty's eyes widened, and she swallowed hard. 'Oh, no, I'm sorry. I didn't mean to say that. Sometimes I just talk and things come out that I didn't ever intend.'

'No, you're right. He may be dead.' Hammersmith looked away at the stacks of papers that dominated his office. 'He may be.' He looked back up at her. 'But we have no evidence that he is dead, and so we must assume that he's alive and needs our help. And if he's dead, if he's really gone, then we need to find that out and settle the issue for Claire. She has four children, and the uncertainty is hard on her.' *It's hard on all of us,* he thought.

'May I begin again in some way that isn't so rude?'

'No, I understand your frustration and I appreciate your honesty. Just as I appreciate your help here. But I can't handle more clients. I have to think about Walter right now. Anything else would be . . .' He broke off again and waggled his fingers in the air, this time dismissing all the hypothetical cases he couldn't deal with. 'Go back to his home and look again for more clues.'

'I've been there a hundred times. Or at least a dozen. And I've been to the pub he used to frequent, and I've been to Scotland Yard so much that they don't even talk to me any more there. There's nothing I can do, and you don't have time to work on the Hargreave case. So let me keep at it, let me do the investigation.'

'This is more involved than the usual sort of thing you do,' Hammersmith said.

'Yes, it is,' she said. 'But it's nothing I can't handle, I promise.'

'And if I need you here?'

'If you need me, I'll drop everything, I'll let the other case go and be right here to do anything you ask.'

He could already see that he'd lost. She was now framing the debate in such a way that it was a foregone conclusion. And he couldn't muster the energy to steer things back the way he wanted them to go. She was probably right. If they hadn't found Walter in a year of looking . . . Well, Walter was probably dead. Or it was even possible he didn't want to be found. Before he'd gone missing, Day had seemed overwhelmed by the prospect of fatherhood, and his career prospects hadn't been good. Some men in that situation might leave their families and start again somewhere else.

Hammersmith shook his head, dispelling the unworthy thought, but Hatty misunderstood the gesture.

'Fine,' she said. 'I'll go back to 184 Regent's Park Road and I'll look for clues that aren't there and were never there. And then I'll do it all over again tomorrow.'

'No,' Hammersmith said, 'it's not you. I was reacting to a thought I didn't like.'

'Thinking what?'

'Something else. Something shameful and unfair. Walter Day was a good man, and he'll be found. But there's no point in combing over his house again. There's nothing there.'

'Does that mean . . . ?'

'Tell me about your case. What is it?'

'A missing man.'

'We seem to be specializing.'

'It's all very mysterious. He works for the new store — you know, the one that opened up where Plumm's used to be, only it's still Plumm's, I suppose, only much larger and with more things to buy.'

Hammersmith shook his head. He had no use for stores.

'Well, in any event, it's there,' Hatty said. 'And this man, Joseph Hargreave, works for the place. Only he didn't come to work one day and he hasn't been seen since.'

'Happens all the time.'

'I suppose it must, but this time someone came to us about it. His brother is mad with worry and wants you to investigate, only he doesn't know that it's me doing the investigating, not you.'

'We should tell him.'

'Oh, no, you mustn't. If he knows, he'll hire someone else and won't pay us.'

'Hatty, you've never really investigated anything before.'

'But I have. I've done it all along, only you didn't hear me properly when I talked to you about those cases and you didn't know what I was doing, Mr Hammersmith. But I've never hidden the truth, not precisely. And I'm really quite capable. You'll see.'

'A client ought to be able to expect a certain level of —'

'How old are you, Mr Hammersmith?'

'I have no idea.' (He really didn't have any idea.)

'Well, you look quite young to me. And how many years did you work as a detective for the Yard?'

'Well, none, I suppose. But I —'

'You were a sergeant, and I know all about that, but you weren't a sergeant for a terribly long time, were you?'

'I don't know. A few months, perhaps?'

'And before that you were a constable. How long was that?'

'Two years, perhaps?'

'So before opening this agency, you had no detective experience and virtually no experience beyond that of a common bobby.'

'There's no such thing as a common bobby. It's a very hard job, and those men put their lives at risk for the safety of their fellow Londoners.'

She went on as though he hadn't spoken. 'But people like this Dr Hargreave, all our clients, believe you're up to the task, and why?'

'Because –'

'Because you're a man.' She stopped, and her shoulders sagged. She suddenly looked tired. Hammersmith wondered where she lived and whether she had anyone to take care of her.

'I'm sure it's not only that,' he said. She opened her mouth, but he put up a hand to stop her. 'You've had your say. Now let me talk. Yes, I'm a man, and there are certain responsibilities that go along with that. But I'm not the sort who thinks women aren't as smart as men. That's ridiculous. Only I don't like to see you put yourself in any sort of danger, that's all.'

'Asking questions here and there won't cause any danger.'

'That's precisely what does cause danger. Be quiet and let me think.'

He looked again at the Walter Day case files, none of which contained anything useful. He wondered what might become of him if Hatty Pitt left. He would be alone in this office every day, obsessing further and deeper over an unsolvable mystery, caring less and less about everything else in the world. The fog would drift in through the doors and the windows and would envelop him. And he would disappear as surely as Walter had, only his body would still inhabit this office and he would still shuffle about as if he were actually contributing something to society. With no one to interact with him, to contradict him and challenge him, he might very well go mad.

'All right. Take the case.' He held up a finger to cut off her excited response. 'But every day, at the end of the day, you and I will discuss this case of yours, along with any other case you decide to take into your own hands, and I will be involved in all ways I deem appropriate. You will take no action that is not approved by me. Is that agreeable enough?'

'Yes.'

'Good.' He scowled at her. 'Well, go on, then.'

She turned and went, but stopped in the doorway and looked back. 'Thank you,' she said.

'You're welcome.'

'And I promise I won't be in any danger.'

'That's not a thing you can promise. Just say you will try to keep yourself out of danger.'

'I will.'

'Then it's settled.'

'You're very kind to care about my well-being.'

He blinked at her, unsure of what to say.

'But,' she said, 'you would be much more attractive if you'd cut your hair back away from your eyes.'

She left, and Hammersmith stared, confused, at the door. What did his hair have to do with anything?

Esther Paxton pressed Walter's suit, and she picked out the finest merchandise from her shop window for herself. She would be careful with the dress and put it back in the window when they returned from Plumm's.

It had taken a great deal of persuasion on Walter's part to get her to visit the department store, but he had finally won her over by suggesting it might be a good thing for her to be seen there. She would be an ambassador of sorts, welcoming Plumm's in its new glory back to her neighborhood. Far from seeming weak or frightened by the competition, she would be perceived as a confident merchant making a goodwill appearance.

Privately, Day was worried about Esther's financial future. It occurred to him that she might be better off relocating to some smaller shop farther away from the massive competition.

And the midnight visit from Ambrose had left him shaken. Was it possible that Jack was at Plumm's? Did he work there or had he broken in? If it even was Jack. Perhaps Day was inclined to see Jack's hand in everything. But he remained nervous about taking Esther there, and his concern was only ameliorated by the fact that it was broad daylight. Or the closest thing London had seen to broad daylight in the past month.

As the weather grew warmer and the slush evaporated

from the streets, fog continued to swirl in, rolling down the roads and pooling in low-lying areas. Esther took Walter's elbow, and he escorted her up Throgmorton Street, listening for oncoming traffic and steering her around puddles in the path ahead. Plumm's seemed to rush at them, pushing its bulk through the fog, and they paused to admire its immensity. In the lower windows, a family of mannequins was picnicking by a stream made of shimmering blue fabric. A gentleman offered a lady a parasol under the light of a gas globe that was meant to evoke the moon. A stuffed horse trotted through a fabulous wood constructed of coatracks and armoires. Above them, in the windows of the next floor up, an Egyptian queen glared down from a throne that was decorated with costume jewelry. Cat-headed mannequin servants ranged outward from the throne, each holding some different item from Plumm's many speciality departments.

'So much glass,' Esther said, her voice muffled by the fog and so soft that Day barely heard her.

'The windows?'

'Imagine,' she said. 'Imagine the expense. Why would anyone be so ostentatious?'

'It attracts people,' Walter said.

'But what sort of people? My clients are more tasteful than this.' She looked up at him and squeezed his arm. 'Aren't they?'

'Vastly,' he said. 'Shall we?'

She squeezed his arm again (he felt uncomfortable with the intimacy, but couldn't bring himself to tell her so), and he led her across the street. A man with white gloves held the door for them and they entered. Inside, the spectacle of so much sheet glass was dwarfed by even more glass set into the wooden frames of counter after counter, by hanging displays and live models and walkways that led away in every direction through a labyrinth of wares. Esther gasped and turned to leave, but Walter held her there.

'It's no wonder,' she said. 'Of course my clients would rather shop here.'

'Not all of them. Not everyone is so easily won over by this sort of shallow display. Your clients know the difference. They understand the value of quality and of tradition.'

'Not all of them. Not enough of them.'

'Don't be silly. This is a fad. This sort of thing will never survive. It can't. It'll collapse under its own weight.'

She smiled up at him, but he could tell she wasn't convinced. They walked on, past a tea shop and past racks of ready-made dresses, past the shelves full of shoes and the cabinets full of crockery.

'Perhaps this wasn't such a good idea,' Walter said.

'No, you were right. I needed to see this. I ought to know what the future looks like.'

'You could incorporate some of this into your own business.'

'How? Look at this.'

They were on the gallery now, high above the sales floor. The framework of an enormous cube was perched atop a pole. Wires ran from beneath it in a thickly braided cord, and workmen scurried about, constructing a globe that was apparently meant to fit inside the cube. Day guessed the sides of the box would be glassed in to represent the

82

store itself and the wires might make the globe revolve. 'Plumm's Brings the World to You' or some such puffery.

Walter grimaced. 'Just emphasize what makes you different, Esther.'

'What do you mean?'

'Look at it all. It's impressive, I grant you, but it's impersonal and, really, it's a bit much, isn't it? They might fit me for a suit, but they don't know my name.'

'I don't know your name, either.'

'I mean to say that you know your clients, you understand them. That's a commodity.'

'Do you think they understand that?'

'They might. If you do.'

'You mean if I make them understand.'

'You have to believe it first.'

She nodded, and he let the subject drop. But it seemed to him that she perked up a bit. At one point she took his arm and guided him quickly away down another aisle, and he shot her a questioning glance.

'A client. I didn't want her to see me.'

'She should see you. She'd be ashamed.'

'And?'

'And she should feel guilty.'

'No, if she feels guilty and ashamed, she'll never come back to me.'

He smiled. 'Ah. Human nature. That ugly beast.'

They continued, touring the various departments, though Esther paid more attention to the fabric selections than anything else. After two or three hours, Walter suggested they have tea at one of the many shops throughout the store. They settled on the smallest tea shop on the first-floor landing, and they took a table near the window so they could look out through the grey at the street below.

'I don't really think this is so bad,' Walter said. 'I think this place does something completely different from what you do, and you could easily capitalize on that difference.'

'I agree,' she said. Day saw that the sparkle was back in Esther's eye. 'It's completely different, as you say. I think I could change a thing or two, bring in some new fabrics, some new patterns, and my clients will be satisfied. They want modern things, but they don't necessarily want substantial changes.'

But Walter had stopped listening. Across the room a man had entered the shop and he stood there now, watching them with a puzzled expression. Esther had her back to the man and didn't see, but Day felt chills up and down his spine. The man caught the arm of a staff member and whispered something in her ear. He handed the shopgirl a slip of paper that was folded in half, nodded to Walter, and left. A moment later, the girl brought the slip of paper to Day's table.

'Are you Walter Day?'

'I don't . . .'

'Walter Day?' Esther leaned forward over the table. 'Is that your name?'

'I'm not . . .'

'If that's you, I'm supposed to give you this,' the girl said.

Walter reached out his hand and took the note from her. It felt very heavy. He unfolded the paper and read.

Met me here tomorrow. Noone. Bring the woman if youve groan tird of her.

'What does it say?' Esther reached for the note, but Day pulled it away.

'Nothing,' he said. 'Just something about a special price they have on clocks.'

·'Clocks?'

'Something like that. Timepieces of some sort. We should leave.'

Esther looked round the room, but it was empty of anything menacing, only a handful of customers and white-gloved staff going about their business. 'What's going on? Is Walter Day your name?'

'It's not. I don't know. Can we leave now?'

'If you want to.'

'I do.'

They abandoned their tea and their seedcakes. Walter dropped a few coins on the table and they left. Day watched the crowds in Plumm's, but the man was nowhere to be seen. He propelled Esther down the stairs and out by the front door. An attendant saluted them and invited them to come again, but Day didn't hear him. Pushing Esther ahead of him, he rushed out into the fog and didn't slow his pace until they had turned the corner and were on their way back to Drapers' Gardens.

Esther stopped walking and, when she had caught her breath, scowled at him. 'Walter, will you please tell me what's going on? Who was it in there, and how do you know those people?'

'Not people. One person. If you can call him a person.'

'Who? What's his name?'

'I don't know his real name,' Day said, 'but he calls himself Jack.'

He shrugged off her further questions and lapsed into a brown study until they had returned to the shop. Once there, he hurried up the stairs and locked his door and refused to answer when Esther knocked later in the day.

I should never have gone out in anyone's company, Day thought. *I should never have allowed myself to be seen with someone.*

He curled up in the corner of his room with his back to the wall and watched the shadows move across the ceiling until night came and the room was plunged into darkness. Even then sleep didn't come for a long time. He kept his eyes open and listened for footsteps on the stairs until the sun came up again.

He knew he would have to return to Plumm's at noon. Otherwise Jack would find him and would hurt him. Worse, Jack would hurt Esther. Day felt trapped and alone, with nobody to turn to and no recourse. His life would never be his own as long as Jack was free in the city.

15

Hammersmith paused in the open door of a large room. He recognized many elements of the Murder Squad as he had known it: the sprawl and bustle, the men huddled in twos or threes, their heads down, murmuring to one another, occasional words like *dismembered* and *mutilated* echoing off the high ceiling and differentiating the atmosphere from that of a gentlemen's club. But there was more of it, more of everything. In the year that had passed since Hammersmith had last worked with these men, the squad had doubled in size. Their desks filled a room that would once have seemed cavernous. Hammersmith recognized Michael Blacker, Tom Wiggins, and one or two other of the inspectors, their jackets hung along the wall below their hats, their shirtsleeves rolled up and their braces let down. But there were many new faces, too.

Sergeant Kett was working behind the desk at the door and he waved. He got up and came around and shook Hammersmith's hand, but he wasn't smiling. Above his bristling red mustache his expression was sombre and his clear blue eyes were watery.

'What brings you today, Nevil?'

Kett was the centre of the entire Murder Squad, coordinating the movements of his constables and facilitating all communications between the detectives. Hammersmith was certain that without Kett, the Yard would long since have fallen into disarray. When Hammersmith was a constable, Kett had taken special interest in him, had paired him with Day in hopes that they would complement each other's strengths. Hammersmith had always thought of the burly sergeant as a mentor.

'I'm still not used to the new building,' Hammersmith said. 'It's . . . Well, it's imposing.'

'It's already too small,' Kett said.

'And the Murder Squad? How is everyone?'

'We've expanded. Twenty detectives now.'

'Twenty?' Hammersmith sighed. 'At least I still see a man or two I know. I thought it might be worth checking in again to see if there's been progress. Any clues or . . . well, anything at all.'

'Don't you think we would've sent for you?'

'I know everybody's busy. It's possible there's been some small thing and nobody's had time to send for me.'

Kett sighed and put a hand on Hammersmith's shoulder. 'Aye. Everybody's busy. Listen, son, it's time.'

'Time?'

'Time to move on, put this thing behind you. I admire the way you've stuck to it, but Walter Day is lost. He's gone, maybe gone for good. And no amount of runnin' round on your part's gonna get him found again.' Hammersmith shook his head, but Kett squeezed his shoulder. 'Nevil, he's gone. He's gone.'

'If it's all the same to you, I'd like to talk to Tiffany, or maybe Blacker. Maybe they've found something they haven't passed along to you.'

'You know better than that. Anyway, I can't let you in. Tiffany's got three new cases today all by himself, not to mention what everybody else has to deal with. You'll stir things up and keep 'em from workin'.'

Hammersmith looked away, out at the room of busy men. Blacker looked up and nodded to him, but he didn't stop what he was doing, didn't come over for a chat.

'Right,' Hammersmith said. 'Very well. I'll go.'

'One of these days we'll hoist a pint and tell stories about Inspector Day. We'll do it soon.'

'Sure we will.'

'We will,' Kett said. But his attention had already wandered. Hammersmith saw the sergeant's gaze returning to the work waiting for him at his desk. He shook Kett's hand again and turned back to the door.

Outside, he glanced up at the invisible sky. 'Walter, where are you?' Hammersmith was completely isolated. He might be the last man on Earth, standing there in front of the Yard, surrounded by layers of nothingness. 'Walter, I'm losing you, man. Do something to get their attention or I won't be able to help you. Reach out if you can.'

As if in answer, a stranger unfolded from the blanket of grey and passed by within inches of Hammersmith. 'Talkin' to yourself? You'll go mad doin' that, you know.' The man chuckled and then was gone, swallowed back up by the fog.

Hammersmith stuck his hands deep in his pockets and walked away in the opposite direction. 'Wasn't talking to myself,' he said. 'Not my fault if nobody was listening.'

16

Day woke from a dream within a dream. Someone was chasing him, but he was underwater, moving slowly, pushing himself forward. When he had awoken the first time, he was still underwater, but now he was on his bed in his cell. The beams of sunlight that stabbed through his barred window, through the green water, were bars themselves, solid yellow, hot and sharp. He swam around them, straining to get to the window, but the sun kept cutting him, burning him, the water cooling his skin so that he would try again. The second time he woke, he lay there for a long time, his skin still tingling, listening to the quiet. At last he rose and crossed the room and looked outside. There was no sun to cut him or burn him, and the air was diffuse, grey and comforting, a mist that hugged the ground, hiding all the evil and fear that Day knew was there.

He brushed his teeth and splashed water on his face from the basin beside his bed. Within ten minutes, he was dressed and on the path in front of Esther's shop, closing the door behind him. Drapers' Gardens was larger in the fog, bounded on all sides by nothing except his imagination. He could hear horses clop-clopping along Throgmorton Street and he turned in that direction.

'Where are you going?'

Day wheeled, his cane raised and ready, and saw Ambrose

standing in the shadows of the shrubbery, blinking sleep from his eyes.

Day lowered his cane. 'Did you sleep here in the gardens last night?'

'I meant to be gone already,' Ambrose said. 'I usually wake up with the sun, but there ain't no sun, is there?' He looked up at the sky, inviting Day to see for himself. 'I thought it might be safer for you if I was nearby.'

Day smiled and nodded. The boy was still frightened. Day realized he should have found a place for him to sleep out of harm's way. He knew all too well how cold and hard a trench beneath the trees could be. But he had been distracted by other worries.

'So where are you going?'

'Just taking a walk, I suppose,' Day said. In fact, he wanted to think a bit before his noon date with Jack, turn the situation over in his mind and try to find some advantage for himself.

'Gimme two minutes.' The boy darted into the shrubbery, and Day stood, watching the fog roll at him and away, pushing the air ahead of it, kneading the gardens like so much bread dough. He snapped to attention when Ambrose spilled out on to the path, combing his hair down with his fingers. 'Weren't even two minutes, were it?'

'Fast.'

'That's me.'

They walked in amiable silence, each wrapped in his own grey thoughts. There was almost no traffic yet, and they passed no other people. Then Plumm's rose out of the fog ahead of them. It seemed to vibrate there, humming with kinetic current. Day paused on the path, and Ambrose stopped beside him. They watched the building for a long while, and Day thought he might not be surprised if it uprooted itself and lurched toward them.

Ambrose grabbed his wrist. 'Someone's coming.'

Day listened. Through the fog came the sound of a man's footsteps, approaching from the direction of the gardens. He knew in an instant who it was. Without a word, Day took Ambrose by the arm and hurried him across the street toward the department store. A white-gloved man exited the front of the store and glanced at them. Day nodded politely but steered the boy diagonally away. The black maw of an alleyway presented itself, and Day ushered Ambrose into it. Behind them, the sound of steady footsteps clocked off the flagstones. When he glanced back over his shoulder, Day saw nothing but swirling grey.

'What's happening, guv?'

'Shh.'

He couldn't see anything in the alley. Strange things crunched under his boots, and something furry brushed against his ankle. Ambrose tried to jerk away from him, but Day tightened his grip on the boy's arm and kept him marching forward. A minute later, they came to a wall and Day turned the corner to his left, feeling along the bricks. At last they reached the end and there was nowhere else to go.

'Dead end,' Ambrose said. 'You think that bloke's still comin' along? You hear him?'

Day could not hear him, but he could sense him circling in the dark. Jack was drawing near, he was somewhere just round the corner, coming closer to them with every panting breath they took. Day felt along the wall and found a knob and tried to turn it. A locked door. He raised his walking stick and rapped on the door with the brass end, but there was no answer, no sound from within the building.

'Quick, Ambrose, feel around the ground here and find something thin and flat, something metal, if possible. A collar stay or hairpin will do.'

'What for?'

'Just find me something now.'

He heard the boy scrabbling around on the stones, sifting through the filth that accumulated on every square inch of London's streets and alleys. Day felt along the door next to the lock for a keyhole and ran his index finger over it, seeing the shape of it in his head. When he reached back, Ambrose dropped four wet objects in his palm.

'Any of those do, guv?'

'Yes, Ambrose. Perfect.' One of the objects seemed to be a flat strip of thin metal, perhaps a rib from a lady's corset. (Day tried not to think about how a corset had come to be torn to pieces at the back of a dead-end alley in Cornhill.) Another was a bit of bent wire. He dropped the other two objects at his feet and went to work on the keyhole, inserting the flat rib and working the bit of wire in next to it, listening all the while for those footsteps behind them. He maneuvered the wire until he heard a click and he smiled, licked his lower lip, and reached for the knob. In a matter of seconds he had ushered Ambrose inside and closed the door behind them. He turned the lock and breathed a sigh of relief.

'Where'd you learn to do that?'

'I don't remember where I learned it,' Day said.

'Well, I'm glad you remember the doing of it. You ought to use that little trick of yours to do better than old tobacco leavings. You could clean out a place before nobody knowed you was ever there in the first place.'

'But that would be wrong, Ambrose. We must survive, but we must also observe the law at all times.'

'All times?'

'Well, perhaps the law might be bent when your life depends on it.'

'I'd say. Like now.'

Ambrose produced a small box of matches from his pocket, and they rummaged around until they found a lantern hanging from a hook on the opposite wall of the room. Once lit, the lantern revealed that they were in a small storeroom with large double doors. 'To bring in big things like furniture,' Ambrose said. These interior doors weren't locked, and so the two of them went through and into the vastness of Plumm's main floor. Day immediately ducked down behind a counter and pulled Ambrose down beside him. People were bustling about all round them, preparing the store for opening, laying out fabrics and jewelry, and lighting gas globes. Day waited, but nobody approached their counter; nobody had seen them enter through the storeroom.

'Can't go back that way,' Ambrose said, and Day put a finger up to his lips, warning the boy to keep quiet. Ambrose lowered his voice to a whisper. 'How're we gettin' outta here, guv?'

'Carefully,' Day said. It seemed to him that the safest

course of action was to wait where they were until Plumm's opened for the day's business and then leave when there were shoppers about. But there was always the possibility that Jack had a key to the outside door and could pop up behind them through the storeroom.

Was Jack even there? Had Day imagined the familiar cadence of his step? No, Ambrose had heard it, too, and he'd been terrified.

Day reached out and patted the boy's shoulder. It seemed ineffectual, but Ambrose smiled up at him. Whether he was comforted by the gesture or humoring Day, the smile was welcome. Day smiled back.

'Look,' he said, 'we can't stay here or we'll be discovered. I think the only thing to do is go back into that room and wait.' He pointed at the storeroom, and Ambrose nodded.

Together, they crawled along behind the counter and dashed back into the room. They were visible again for perhaps half a minute, but there was no hue and cry. Nobody came to investigate the trespassers, the man and the boy who were hiding from a monster in the fog. And so they sat there in the dark and watched the door and listened for the expected crowd of morning shoppers, when they might slip out unobserved and make their escape.

17

Claire had made a careful inventory of every wooden item in her house: furniture, toys, knickknacks, utensils. She had a list on the table next to her on the porch and she referred to it as she wrote. She had used the word *armoire* five times now. She stood and brushed her hair behind her ear and walked into the kitchen. There was the sideboard and the butcher block counter. There were chairs and giant spoons. She walked on down the hall to the sitting room where there was a gliding rocker and an end table and there were several paintings in wooden frames.

She had used them all.

Claire wondered if she wasn't making an enormous mistake. She hadn't told anyone yet, but she was running out of money. Her book of rhymes had sold well, but she didn't feel like writing more rhymes for publication. Her publisher had refused to give her an advance on anything but more poems, and she simply didn't feel she had enough of them in her to make a book. Her babies were getting older and they'd want real stories. She wanted to write about the things that interested them: dolls and toys and playing outside on a clear blue day.

It amazed her that a stray thought had become a full-fledged story in a matter of a day or two and now it was coming along nicely. In her new book, a forest had been razed and the wooden things had all returned to their birthplace, the place where they had been simple trees and known nothing but the green and the rain and the lemon rays of the sun.

The sun that hadn't touched London in months.

The fog that covered the city seemed also to have covered Claire's mind. She worried that she wouldn't be able to keep Nevil's office open and his staff employed, wouldn't be able to keep him from becoming a dustman and abandoning the search for her husband.

She knew she could still take money from her father, but she would rather die. She shook her head and scolded herself for indulging her miserable thoughts. Perhaps it would help to get out of the house.

The governess wandered into the room, saw Claire's dour expression, and turned to leave, but Claire grabbed her arm.

'Dress the children to go out, won't you?'

'An outing, mum? Today?'

'Yes. It's . . . Well, we ought to enjoy the last of the cool weather while we can, don't you think?'

'The cool weather, mum?'

'Yes, it's still a bit cool out, isn't it?'

'If you say.'

'I do.'

'Of course. Shall I tell them where we're off to?'

'I thought we might step out to the new store. Look at the wares, the furniture and such.'

'Furniture? The store?'

'Yes.'

'Graham's?'

'No, I was thinking Plumm's.'

'Ah. Because Graham's doesn't have furniture.'

'No, it doesn't.'

'Only groceries.'

'Yes.'

'But why there? Why Plumm's?'

'Oh, why not? Will you get them ready or won't you?'

'Of course, mum.' The woman, Tabitha, scurried off, and Claire sank back against the wall. Everything was a chore. And Walter wouldn't have helped her one bit, really. He would have run off at the first sign of trouble with the governess. But he would have made her laugh about it later. He would have given her a hug and whispered something pleasant in her ear. He would have been sweet. He would have been kind. He would have put the whole rest of the world in perspective somehow.

She tried to think of what Walter might say to her now. She wasn't exactly a match girl, he would have told her. Money was tight, corners had to be trimmed, pennies pinched, but her children had a fine home and food to eat. It wasn't as bad as all that. Was it?

She pushed herself off the wall. Plumm's would have lots of the kinds of things she wanted to see. All sorts of wooden items for sale, and she would be inspired just seeing them all. She would finish her new book and then maybe she would write more rhymes after all. It occurred to her that she ought to invite Fiona Kingsley to come along with them.

What they all needed was a splendid outing to lift the doldrums.

18

The case of the missing Hargreave brother was much bigger and more important than the usual sort of inquiry Hatty Pitt undertook, and she saw it as an opportunity to prove herself in Mr Hammersmith's eyes. She'd wasted no time in getting to work on it and had made a list of the places she thought Joseph Hargreave might be hiding. He lived his life as many London gentlemen of decent means did. He had an apartment in the city that he shared with his brother where he spent the bulk of the week. He and his brother also owned a cottage in Brighton, where they whiled away the weekend hours. Hatty thought she might be able to gain access to both places. Hargreave had his club, of course, and Hatty had no chance of getting in there, so she had drawn a question mark next to that item on her list of locations. Lastly, he had his place of employment: Plumm's. That would be the easiest place to get into, and so she had underlined it on her list, but decided to save it for later in the week when she would be more tired and might need something relatively simple to do.

She did not worry about the fact that she didn't know what she was doing. Nobody, after all, knew what they were doing when they started a new job. They learned. And Hatty was a quick learner.

A man gave her his seat on the train to Brighton and she fell asleep, and so felt groggy and bad-tempered when she arrived. She followed a family on holiday off the train, and a solemn woman handed Hatty a pamphlet about the new clock tower. Hatty took it and smiled at her, but the woman didn't smile back. The sky was a dusty blue color, and she could taste salt on the air. No fog to be seen in any direction. The breeze was a bit chilly, but Hatty wasn't the sort to complain. She avoided the taxi rank outside the station and oriented herself before setting out, shading her eyes with one hand (the sun wasn't visible anywhere in the sky, but it was still brighter than anything she'd been accustomed to of late), while in her other hand she clutched a torn piece of notepaper on which she had written Hargreave's address.

She walked south down Queens Road and stopped to admire the clock tower, referring to the pamphlet the woman had given her. The tower was tall and all of polished stone, with decorative arches and little statues guarding little nooks at all the corners. Hatty thought it looked nearly as solid as the woman with the pamphlets. A pair of troubadours sang 'Mr and Mrs Brown' while strolling round the square. 'Dear Mistress Brown, your clock is fast, I know as well as you . . .' The man played violin, and the woman held out a hat. Hatty dropped a ha'penny in, pretending to herself she was on a seaside holiday.

After the clock tower the road changed to West Street, and she turned left on to Duke and followed that along to the end of Prince Albert Street, where she found the small detached cottage. The home shared by Joseph and Dr Richard Hargreave was in need of a coat of paint and a new roof. The garden needed tending, and the black wrought-iron fence along the street was missing several rails. But through a break between the houses behind it, she could see Kings Road and, beyond that, the endless grey haze of the sea.

A woman came out of the house next door, at the end of a queue of terraced homes, and stood framed in the open doorway. She was perhaps ten years older than Hatty, but her face was lined and she wore the shadows under her eyes like badges.

'They don't want any,' the woman said.

'I'm sorry?'

'Those brothers don't want any of whatever it is you're selling. You needn't waste your time.'

'Oh, I'm not selling anything,' Hatty said. 'They're not at home, are they?'

'What do you think, I watch this entire street? I wouldn't have the slightest idea if they're home.'

Puzzled, Hatty hesitated with one hand on the gate. She thought she might be able to ask the woman a question or two about the Hargreaves, but she wasn't sure where to begin or how to break through the woman's hostile front. She tried on her best and brightest smile and shone it on the woman. 'May I ask your name?'

'I am Mrs Ruskin. Ruth Ruskin. And that's all you'll get from me. I'm not any more interested than my neighbors are in buying from you.'

'Again, Mrs Ruskin, I'm not selling anything. I don't suppose your husband's at home?' Perhaps, Hatty thought, Mr Ruskin would be easier to talk to.

'My husband has not been with us for some time now.' Ruth Ruskin's frosty exterior cracked, and before she could break entirely, she turned and fled back into her house, slamming the door behind her.

'What an odd woman,' Hatty said. 'I hope everyone here's not like her.' She shrugged and let herself through the gate and marched up the path to the door of the Hargreaves' cottage. She knocked and waited and, when nobody came to the door after a minute or two, she knocked again, keeping one eye on the house next door in case Ruth Ruskin decided to come back out and cause trouble.

She didn't have much of a plan worked out. She thought she might question the servants and perhaps they'd let her have a look round inside. At the very least, she'd be able to verify that Joseph Hargreave was not, in fact, simply away on holiday, which seemed to be a sensible first step in the investigation. She was surprised when Dr Richard Hargreave opened the door wearing a dressing gown and slippers. His hair was disheveled, tufts of silver sticking up in every direction, and he hadn't shaved. He had a book in his hand, a finger holding his place halfway through. Hatty tilted her head to read the title. *Venus in Furs*.

'What are you doing here?' His breath reeked of gin.

'Well,' Hatty said, 'what are *you* doing here?'

'I live here.'

'I thought you'd be in the city, at work.'

'I took some well-deserved time away from my practice,' Hargreave said. 'I find I have too much on my mind at the moment.' He turned and walked away, leaving the door open. 'Might as well come in, you made it this far.'

Hatty stepped over the threshold and looked around. It

was a small cottage with no hallways, each room leading to another, and she guessed she was in some sort of sitting room doing double duty as a study. She held a finger up to her nose to help mask the odor in the room and hoped Hargreave wouldn't notice or take offense. The windows were shuttered, and the single lamp at the back of the room didn't illuminate much, a sharp contrast to the delicious sunlight outside. Green wallpaper was peeling away at the corners, and a lazy cobweb drifted in Hargreave's wake as he showed her in. There were three deeply cushioned chairs in the room and a table that was heaped with dirty dishes. Newspapers littered the floor beside one of the chairs. Hargreave bent and tore a piece from one of them, using it as a bookmark. He set *Venus in Furs* on the arm of the chair and looked around, as if seeing the place for the first time.

'Let the staff go a week ago now,' he said. 'I think they were stealing from us.'

'I see.'

'I suppose I'll have to find someone to come in and clean, though, won't I?'

'That might not be a bad idea.'

'Well, have a seat, if you like.' He waved a limp hand in the direction of the other two chairs. Hatty examined the nearest one and flicked a few crumbs away before sitting down. 'Got no tea and no coffee, but if you want gin I have that. Maybe some rye. And there's milk, I think, but I wouldn't touch that if I were you. Smelled a bit off yesterday, and I doubt it's got better overnight.'

'I'm fine,' Hatty said. 'Thank you.'

'So, you thought maybe Joseph had gone on holiday

and forgotten to tell me,' Hargreave said. 'Is that it? For-got to tell Mr Plumm, too, hadn't he? Just shimmered off to the sea and not a care in the world, eh?'

'I thought . . .' Hatty said. She cleared her throat and started again. 'Mr Hammersmith suggested I come and have a look round here.'

'Ah. So Hammersmith's handling the likely stuff and leaving the odd tidbits for you.'

'Something like that.'

'Has he got any clues yet? No, I suppose not, or you wouldn't be nosing round here, where you're not needed, would you?'

Hatty smiled. 'You say you've spoken to Mr Plumm?'

'Told him I'd be forced to take legal action if he sacked Joseph. My brother's not been gone so very long, has he? No reason to replace him just yet. Let the detective do his work, I say. And he says back to me that the store's got work of their own needs to be done and no worker to do it, has they? And I say, "Well then, you'll be hearing from my solicitor unless you're willing to give the matter more time to sort itself." And Plumm says, "Very well." Just like that. "Very well, Dr Hargreave, I've got solicitors of my own, don't you know?" And before I have a chance to say anything else, the door's hitting me on the backside and I'm out in the street without so much as a fare-thee-well. Is that right? Does that sound right to you?'

'It sounds rather uncaring,' Hatty said. 'I'm sorry.'

Hargreave took a small shuddering breath and smacked his lips and looked down at the book on the arm of his chair. He frowned and turned it over so that Hatty could no longer see the title. 'I might eat,' he said. 'Would you care for anything? I think I've got half a pudding, maybe the remains of a roast. Almost certainly there's a cheese, if it hasn't turned.'

Hatty hesitated. She was hungry, but suspicious of anything that might be found in Hargreave's pantry. Still, she wanted to take a look round the place, and a detective's work wasn't always meant to be easy, was it? 'Yes, please,' she said.

'Well, come along, then, and let us see what there is to see.' He led the way through a door at the back of the room, which Hatty discovered led to a dining room. The table was heaped with financial papers. Through another door and she found herself in a grubby kitchen. Food-encrusted crockery filled the basin and every surface in the room was covered with butcher's paper, shriveled ends of sausages, puddles of beer and gin and clotted cream, half an apple, brown and withered, a bowl with something that had formed a skin, a knife embedded upright in a hard barm cake. A cloud of insects, tiny pinpricks in the air, hovered over some sort of gelatinous substance on the wall. Hatty's heart sank.

'This isn't all my own mess,' Hargreave said. He seemed embarrassed, which Hatty took as a good sign. It was the sort of room that called for embarrassment. 'As I say, we let the servants go, and Joseph and I forgot to clean up after ourselves last weekend. Besides, there's dishes here I know we didn't use. They must have snuck back in here while we were in the city and helped themselves to our provisions.' He drew himself up in a pose of indignity. 'They bloody well deserved the sack, didn't they?'

'Do you have a broom?'

While Hargreave looked for a broom, an activity that involved standing in the middle of his kitchen and turning slowly round and round while peering at the skirting board, Hatty found an apron hanging on a hook inside the pantry door and put it on. She decided to tackle the goo on the wall first and rinsed a rag in a pitcher of water that was only slightly yellow. She discovered that the goo had cleaned the wallpaper beneath it, so that once she had wiped it all away there was a bright spot on the wall, but she wasn't committed enough to the task to keep going. The bright spot would have to remain isolated there until Hargreave spilled more of whatever the goo was and dealt with it himself.

Hatty was reasonably certain that housekeeping and cooking weren't in the average detective's job description, but she wasn't the average detective. Besides, she was still hungry and she wasn't about to eat anything that came out of Hargreave's kitchen until the place was properly cleaned.

After the muck was washed off the wall, she tackled the dishes, wiping them down with more rags and leaving the pots and pans to soak in more yellowish water. She gathered the garbage in a pile on the counter and caught Hargreave's attention.

'Where's your rubbish?'

'My rubbish?'

'I need to toss all this or you'll have more bugs and other vermin even nastier.'

'Oh, the bin is . . . um, I think right outside the door there. At least, I think it is.' He pointed at an outside door next to the pantry, and Hatty unlocked it, stepped out, and took a deep breath of clean sea air. Sure enough, there was a big bin, swarming with flies, resting against the back wall of the cottage. She would have to cart the left-over food out to it, rather than bringing it in.

She stepped inside and realized how bad Hargreave's home smelled. She decided she must have grown used to the odor, but the cool breeze outside beckoned her, and she decided she'd much rather find a vendor and buy a meat pie on the way home than try to cook something edible in that particular kitchen. She would get the old food out of the house and then be done with it all. Richard Hargreave hadn't hired her to clean his house, he had hired her to find his missing brother.

She scowled at him as she walked back past, but he didn't seem to notice. Nor did he help her gather the garbage and take it out. So she didn't bother to try to salvage the dirty knife or the bowl. She tossed them along with the rest of it.

The bowl was heavy, though, and it sank quickly to the bottom of the bin, causing layers of refuse to topple in on top of it, upsetting whatever delicate ecosystem had begun to form. Something grey and pink and strange caught Hatty's eye as it was uncovered in the process. She held her breath and leaned in for a closer view, then ran back inside the kitchen for a rag. She took it to the bin and reached down inside, wrapped it around the pinkish grey thing, careful not to touch anything with her fingers, and fished it out.

Dragged into the light it wasn't nearly as odd-looking, but still she stared at it, trying to understand what it might be. It seemed harmless, if disgusting: wilted and tough, but not like any cut of meat she had seen before. She brought it closer to her face and licked her lower lip while she thought, then thought about the fact that she was licking her lip and suddenly recognized the thing wrapped in the rag. She dropped it in the dirt.

She leaned against the house and waited until she was calm again. Back inside, she stalked through the kitchen, leaving the back door open, and sat down at the dining room table. She found a pencil and used the back of one of the financial documents to take notes. (She was going to have to remember to carry round one of those little notebooks Mr Hammersmith always used.) When Hargreave followed her into the room, she indicated that he should sit across from her.

'Are you going to finish cleaning in there?'

'No,' Hatty said.

'Well, it needs cleaning.'

'Then hire someone whose job it is to clean. Or do it yourself. Meanwhile, I'd like some information from you.'

'What sort of information? I've told you everything I know.'

'I want you to remember exactly when you let the household staff go and when you and your brother were last here.'

'I can try to remember, but I'm not sure –'

'Just do your best, sir. Anything you can tell me might be of help.'

'Well –'

'And when we're done here, I'm going to have to head back to London to share this information with Mr Hammersmith, but I want you to fetch the thing on the ground beside the rubbish bin, if you would be so kind, and keep it safe here until the Brighton police arrive.'

'The police are coming?'

'They will be as soon as I alert them.'

'Alert them? Alert them to what?'

'I believe you had a human tongue in your bin. It's entirely possible there are other bits of your brother in there, too. Now, let's focus on that timetable.'

Of course, Hatty had no evidence that the tongue had ever belonged in Joseph Hargreave's head, but it gave her great satisfaction to shock Richard Hargreave and it made her feel very much like she imagined a detective ought to feel. The best part was that Hargreave became immediately cooperative and gave her no more arguments.

19

Day woke and sat up. His hair was damp, his collar limp with sweat, and his mouth tasted stale. For a moment he thought he was back in his cell, but then he felt a wave of relief as he recalled his experiences of the past weeks. The relief was tinged with a sense of dread. He would be meeting Jack again today, and Jack might take him back to that cell.

But Day no longer wanted to return to his little bed with its rough grey blanket, or to his tiny window that looked out on stones and snow.

He struggled to his feet in the cramped space and cracked open the door to the storeroom. People bustled this way and that, but nobody looked his way. He glanced back at Ambrose. The boy was sprawled in what seemed to Day to be a very uncomfortable position, his neck bent awkwardly, his mouth wide open. But his chest was rising and falling steadily. Day left him there in the dark, where he was safe for the time being, and stepped out, shutting the door behind him.

He was on the main floor of the department store, all shining wood and glass and a black spiral staircase that ran up through the centre of the room to the gallery, where he and Esther had sipped their tea and eaten their seedcakes and looked down on the other shoppers. The whole place smelled of perfumes and talcum, mixed with wood polish and body odor.

Day drew his watch (another gift from Esther) from his pocket and was astonished to see that it was already half past eleven. He had slept for three hours on the floor of the storeroom. Did he still have time to get back to the draper's shop and change his collar, comb his hair, splash a little water on his face? There was certainly no time to nose around the store, as he'd wanted to, to try to find some advantage over Jack before their meeting, but he at least wanted to look presentable, to seem confident. Jack sniffed out weakness in other men and exploited it. And he knew all of Day's weaknesses, had already exploited every one of them.

On thinking about it, Day decided a fresh collar probably wouldn't change anything. All he could do was brace himself and face whatever was coming his way, whatever Jack had planned for him.

As if on cue, Day looked up and saw the man himself at the gallery rail. Jack smiled and waved at him, gestured for him to come up.

No time any more to do anything except climb those steps. His decisions were all made for him. He put his watch away and trudged to the spiral stairs and went up. His leg suddenly hurt, and he had to use his cane to push himself off each step. Along the way he passed several shoppers, all of whom gave him nervous glances and sidled as far to the other side of the steps as they could. He thought he must reek of doom.

Jack was waiting for him at the top and took his arm.

'You're early,' Jack said. 'How lovely.' He led him to a little table with a lacy cloth draped over it and he pulled out a chair for him.

*

'It's incredible.'

Fiona Kingsley had been available to accompany the Day clan on their outing to Plumm's. She had brought a sketch pad and a small case of pencils, paints, brushes and charcoals. Everything there seemed false to her, designed to evoke some feeling or response, but she still felt a little thrill as she looked round at it all.

There was a giant globe in a box above her being glassed in by men who reminded her of busy ants.

'It is very big,' Claire said. 'And there're so many things. How can they sell all these things?'

'Who would buy some of them?' Fiona was looking at a brooch shaped like a butterfly, with mother-of-pearl inlays and antennae made of thin wire with beads on the ends.

'You could illustrate some of it,' Claire said.

'I think they'd expect me to buy something if I tried to draw it. But I'll do a quick sketch of some wooden things to help the book if we find anything new or different. Do you think we ought to try the furniture department or the – Oh, Claire, we should look in the books department and see if they have yours.'

'Do you think they do?'

'Why wouldn't they?'

'Surrounded by all of this? That would be . . .'

'It would be incredible.'

'That is the word.'

'Miss Tinsley!'

Fiona jumped and turned. A small round fellow was hurrying toward them. Fiona blinked and tried to remember where she had seen him before, but he was on them before she could place him.

'You remember me,' the man said. He was perhaps fifty years old, and his face was red all over and beaming with pleasure. She could not help herself and broke out into a huge smile despite herself.

'It's me,' the little man said. 'Alastair Goodpenny. You do remember me?' He stopped short and his face changed; his smile disappeared and his forehead creased with wrinkles.

She did remember him. She had consulted with him the previous year on a case her father and Hammersmith had been involved in. He was the proprietor of a kiosk in the Marylebone bazaar and had advised her on a pair of cufflinks that had been owned by a murderer.

'Her name is Miss Kingsley, not Tinsley,' one of the boys said. She thought it was Robert, but she didn't turn round to see.

'There's no need to shout,' Goodpenny said. 'I can hear you. Miss Tinsley and I have known each other longer than you've been alive.' He softened then and bent down, and Fiona turned to see which of the boys he was talking to. It was Simon. 'What's your name, little boy?'

'My name is Simon.'

'How unusual. Jemima is commonly a girl's name. From the Bible, isn't it?'

'Simon. My name is Simon.'

'Just so. And you should be proud. Though you might also want to strengthen your upper body. With that name you'll be forced to defend yourself often enough, I should think.' Goodpenny straightened back up and beamed at Fiona. 'How are you, Miss Tinsley? How is that boy you were so fond of? Mr Angerschmid?'

'Thank you, Mr Goodpenny. I believe Nevil is fine, although I don't see much of him these days.'

'Oh, what a shame. He seemed in need of a woman's attention, don't you think?'

Fiona blushed. 'Have you met my friend? Mr Goodpenny, this is Mrs Day.'

Claire offered her hand, and Goodpenny leaned over it, his manner courtly and endearing. 'My great pleasure, Mrs Dew.'

'The pleasure is mine,' Claire said. She gave Fiona a knowing smile that Mr Goodpenny failed to notice.

'What are you doing here, Mr Goodpenny? Are you shopping?'

'No, no, Miss Tinsley. I'm employed here now. They need good people who know how to judge a piece of silver and who understand what a man needs in the way of accessories. You're not after such a thing today, are you?'

'No, thank you. We're here to look for things made of wood.'

'Of course I would. You have only to tell me what you need.'

Fiona glanced round at Claire, who looked puzzled, and whispered, 'He can't hear a thing.' Claire hid a smile behind her hand.

'Shall I give you the grand tour? We've only been open a short while, and I'm still learning the place myself.' Mr Goodpenny seemed proud and happy, and Fiona felt glad for him.

'We'd be delighted,' she said.

'Well, let's see if we can find the thing you're after,' Mr

Goodpenny said. 'I wouldn't be surprised if Plumm's carries it.'

They had no idea what he had in mind, but he led the way down a narrow path between two counters and Fiona followed. Claire and the boys and the nanny with her double pram all came along.

Ambrose crawled out of the storeroom and crept along behind the counter. He had awoken as the latch clicked shut, and his boss was walking away from the room by the time Ambrose rubbed the sleep from his eyes and peeked out of the door. He'd been abandoned there.

He knew he'd be thrown out of the store as soon as anyone of authority saw him. He didn't look like he had money or a reason to be there. The only way he could think to explore Plumm's and catch up to the guv was to pretend he was running deliveries for someone posh. He stood up and straightened his threadbare jacket and tried to look like he imagined a delivery boy might look. He marched past a grouping of chairs and tables and sofas, then along in front of the cabinets of jewelry and scarves without paying attention to any of the fineries on display. *These things,* he thought, *don't impress me. I see finer things all day long at my employer's home.* He kept this silent mantra going, in hopes that if he thought a thing, however false it might be, it would manifest itself in his face and his bearing. His real employer barely had a home at all and didn't seem to care about much of anything except tobacco leavings, but thinking about that was of no use in this situation. He passed several shopgirls and not one of them stopped him, so he imagined he was carrying off the internal disguise well. His manner was almost regal.

But he couldn't keep himself from looking upward, past the huge installation that was being constructed. Somewhere up there was a skylight, on beyond the vaulted ceiling and the shops and offices. Somewhere up there Ambrose had watched two women being murdered.

And the man who had murdered them was right there, standing in plain sight above him!

Ambrose actually gasped when he saw him and ducked down behind a display of silk trousers. The murderer was taking the guv's hand, escorting the boss of Reasonable Tobacco to a little table as if they were going to have tea together right there in front of God and everybody.

Like they was friends.

Was his employer going to turn him over to the killer? Had Ambrose been lured to the store on purpose so they could do away with the only witness to the murders? But no, if the guv planned to betray Ambrose, surely he wouldn't have left him sleeping in a closet with the door practically open. He would have locked Ambrose in until he could make his arrangements. At least, that's how Ambrose thought *he* would have done it if he were that sort of person.

So it wasn't a trap for him. But it might be a trap for his employer. He'd told the guv all about it, and now the killer was saying something to him up there, telling the guv something, and the guv didn't look none too happy about it, either. The killer was threatening him.

And then Ambrose understood: His employer was protecting him by hiding Ambrose and diverting the killer's attention.

Ambrose wasn't the bravest boy on the streets, but he was loyal. He'd never let anyone down, so far as he knew. He had to do something and he had to do it fast.

'Excuse me, young man, but you're blocking the aisle.'

Ambrose turned and saw a nasty old nanny pushing a pram that held two babies. Behind her were two more children, boys who were maybe a little younger than Ambrose himself. There was a slender girl with her nose in a sketch pad and a fat little clerk who was jabbering about something. And behind them all was the most beautiful woman Ambrose had ever seen, with golden hair that shone brilliantly under Plumm's yellow lights.

'Well, get a move on, why dontcha?' The nanny raised her hand as though she meant to swat at Ambrose from three feet away and with a pram between them.

The beautiful woman frowned at her governess. 'Tabitha, be nice.' Then she smiled at Ambrose and said, 'This place is amazing, isn't it? I've never seen a store so large.'

Ambrose managed to nod at the beautiful woman, stunned that she had spoken directly to him. She was the nicest posh lady he had ever seen.

Before he could find his voice and answer her, the nanny said, 'Yes, Mrs Day.' And all eight of them swept past Ambrose and into the furniture department behind him.

Tabitha was simply not going to work out. Claire scowled at the nanny's back and tried to figure out how to let her go when she had no one to take up the slack. Tabitha was the third governess the babies had been through in the past year. And none of them had worked out. The first had left them because there always seemed to be a killer of some sort prowling about the house. (Claire couldn't blame her.) The second had hit one of the boys. And now Tabitha was acting willfully awful.

Imagine! Talking to a poor delivery boy as if he were street scum.

She rolled her eyes and noticed something familiar at the outside edge of her vision. Her attention was drawn by two workmen having a row over something they were building, a huge globe, perhaps fifty feet around, in a glassed-in box. She ignored them and focused on one of the men taking tea at the gallery above.

The big gas lamps behind them shone down through a mass of dark hair, and it only took her a moment to place the man. She had once met Jack the Ripper. He had even come into her bedroom. And the man sitting above her, having tea like any other ordinary person, was that same man. She was certain of it.

'Missus?'

Claire came to herself and shook her head.

Tabitha touched her arm. 'What is it, ma'am?'

'Can't you leave me alone for a single moment and let me think?'

'Yes, ma'am.'

'Watch after the children. Isn't that your job? Isn't that the whole of your job?'

'Yes, ma'am.' The nanny hung her head and hurried after the boys, who had taken the pram and were pushing their way into the books department. Mr Goodpenny and Fiona had disappeared together around a bank of tall wardrobes with double doors. Claire could hear the cheerful little gentleman going on about the quality of the wood finish.

Claire made a mental note to apologize to poor Tabitha. She looked up again at the tea shop near the railing. And Jack was still there. He was sipping from a cup and he was . . . He was looking down at her. He saw her. His features were sketched out in grey upon grey, like the mist outside, but she could see a smile crease his face. He was smiling at her. He set down his cup and raised his hand, touched his forehead in a salute.

Claire looked away and closed her eyes. She heard a train racing through the department store and she nearly jumped before realizing it was her own heavy breath. Her heart was racing, her lungs were laboring. She opened her eyes and looked up again. The devil was sitting across from someone, and Claire finally turned her gaze on him. His back was to her, but she had known him most of her life and she knew him now. She knew him like she knew the freckle on the back of her ring finger, knew him like she knew the strawberry birthmark on the small of Winnie's back.

Walter Day did not turn around and look at her, but she knew him. Oh, she knew him! And he was alive. And he was taking tea at Plumm's with Jack the Ripper.

Claire Day felt the room rush at her from all directions, and she fell unconscious at the feet of a mannequin.

Ambrose had moved on, humiliated by the angry governess, but he turned back when he heard a loud thump. Her companions were gathering round her, so it took Ambrose a minute to realize that the beautiful woman had fallen. Several people had already noticed, and a commotion was in its beginning stages. Shopgirls were coming from every corner of the store now, and an officious-looking manager-type with a waxed mustache popped his head up over a partition across the main floor, craning his neck to see what was going on. Ambrose hurried and got to the beautiful woman right away. He bent over her, pushing the nasty nanny away. He heard the nanny squawk, but he didn't care. He was in love. He patted the beautiful woman's cheeks. Gently. And her eyelids fluttered.

'Danger,' she said.

'Yes, missus?'

She raised one tremulous arm and pointed above them. She pointed at the gallery, at the killer, who was smiling down at them. She knew about the killer the same as Ambrose did. They had something in common. The guv, sitting up there with his back to them, started to rise at the sound from below, but the killer pushed the guv back down, physically turned his head so that he wouldn't see what was below him. Ambrose wanted to call out, wanted to shout at the guv, tell him to get away. But the beautiful woman grabbed his arm.

'Walter,' she said.

'Ambrose, mum,' he said. 'My name's Ambrose.'

'He's up there,' she said. 'Save him.' She tried to point again, but failed and fell unconscious once more.

It didn't matter. He understood. This beautiful woman had seen Ambrose's employer and she loved him as Ambrose did. She somehow understood the danger the guv was in. And Ambrose knew that he had to save his employer if he wanted this woman, this angel, to ever look at him again. If she had fallen for the guv, then Ambrose might have to give her up, but he still wanted to win her favor.

He let the awful governess take his place at the beautiful woman's side and he rose and hurried away. He picked up his pace and elbowed his way through the other shoppers that had gathered round, through the gaggles of shopgirls and the officious managers like green-headed mallards, went to the spiral staircase, and took the steps two at a time to the top.

20

'We have to move on,' Jack said.

'Wait,' Day said. 'I didn't come here to be manipulated by you.'

'Yes, you did.' Jack took Day's arm and almost bodily lifted him from his chair. Day looked to his left and right, embarrassed, wondering if anyone saw, but no one reacted. At this time of the late morning, people were not quite ready for their lunch and had long ago finished their breakfasts. There were only two other occupied tables, and the old ladies at both of them were rising now, approaching the railing, curious about some sort of row that had broken out below them.

He glanced over the railing and saw that a blond woman had collapsed. He opened his mouth to call her name, but then closed it and looked away. He didn't know her. She was a stranger to him.

'Tut tut,' Jack said. 'It won't do if you and I are seen together at the moment you're discovered.' He leaned in closer. 'We'll have to get this done another way. Work first, play later.' And he ushered Day up and away, past a phalanx of workmen in canvas trousers who were wrestling with sheets of glass bigger than they were, along the queue of tables, to the back of the floor, where there was a long hallway lined with heavy oak doors.

'What do you mean? What do you mean when you say

"discovered"?' But Day allowed himself to be led. If Jack was concentrating on him, he wasn't killing anyone else, he wasn't exploring the other floors and finding the urchin in the storeroom. He wasn't hurting the unconscious woman with blond hair. If Day could keep Jack distracted, then Jack would continue to be Day's own private monster.

'Never you mind. Come in here.' Jack opened a door and led Day into a quiet office, really nothing but a small room with a desk and two chairs. A typewriter and a telephone sat atop the desk, next to a blotter arranged with a pen, a letter opener, a small stack of plain envelopes, and an inkwell.

Jack was breathing hard and he moved round to the other side of the desk. He sat with a grunt and winced. 'I shouldn't have exerted myself quite so much,' he said. 'Listen, do you trust me?'

'No, of course I don't trust you,' Day said. 'You're horrible and you'll most likely kill me once I stop providing you with amusement.'

Jack leaned forward in his chair. Day could smell his breath, all copper and rot. Jack moved from the waist, his shoulders straight up and down, as if he were one of those wind-up automatons that swiveled back and forth, performing some simple task over and over. In this case the task was murder. Back and forth, again and again, until Jack's rusted gears wound down.

'I could never kill you, Walter Day,' Jack said. *(That name again.)* 'You're my mirror image, the flip side of my spinning coin.'

'You're not the other side of my coin,' Day said.

'No, I'm the edge of it. And I circle round and round and never stop, so don't think that I will.' Had he read Day's thoughts about the declining automaton? Day almost believed that he had, that he could. Nothing seemed impossible where Jack was concerned.

'Whose office is this?'

'You know, I don't remember his name,' Jack said. 'I call him Kitten because he makes a lovely soft animal noise when I hurt him. Like a pleading cat. I'd have you in sometime so you could hear it for yourself, but I don't know how much longer poor Kitten can hold out.'

Day shuddered.

'I went to your house,' Jack said. 'Except it's not your house any more, is it? And I'm not talking about that new place your wife's moved to. That was never your home. You've never even seen it. No, I went to the house with the blue door, the one where we had so many adventures. I knew you weren't there, but I've missed you lately and I wanted to bask in the air that you'd walked through so many times.'

'I don't know the place you're talking about.'

'If you ever go back, you'll have a surprise waiting for you. I left something there.'

'Left something?'

'It wasn't easy, either. Cost me more than a little.'

'What do you want?'

'Ah, yes, to business, then.' Jack picked up the letter opener from the desk. He poked the tip of his finger with the dull blade and frowned. 'Not as useful as one might wish,' he said under his breath, as if he were talking to himself, not to Day. 'Anyway, let's be done with all this silliness. I'm a patient man, I really am, but you've drawn it all out to the point that it's no longer much fun, I'm afraid.'

'I've drawn what out? You talk in riddles, in maths I don't understand. If you want to take me back there, back to that cell, you can try, but I won't go quietly and I'm no longer afraid of you.'

'Ah. That draper woman, the one with the little shop in the gardens, she's influenced you, hasn't she? Turned you against me.'

'You leave her out of this.'

'That's just it, you see,' Jack said. 'I didn't include her in the first place. You did. I let you go free and you should have gone home, should have returned to your employ- ment, but you didn't. And you didn't return to me, either. I would have taken you back in, cared for you as I always have. But instead of coming back to me, or doing any- thing at all useful, you took up with this slattern –'

'Don't say that,' Day said. He felt his face getting warm. 'Don't you dare say that about her.'

'Oh, it wasn't meant to be an insult. She's quite my type. Yes, my type indeed. You've good taste in female flesh, Walter Day.' He closed his eyes and seemed to gather himself, his shoulders hunching and his fists clenching, unclenching. Then he opened his eyes and smiled. 'But regardless of how you'd describe her, you brought her into this, and so I should leave it to you to get her out of it.'

'Get her out of what? I don't know what you mean.'

Jack sighed and waved his hand at a cabinet on the opposite wall. 'I wonder if you wouldn't help me out and fetch some gauze from the top drawer there.'

Day opened a door in the top of the cabinet and Jack snapped at him. 'The drawer, I said. It's in the drawer. You never listen to me!'

Startled, Day slammed the door shut and slid open the drawer, found a roll of gauze, and tossed it over the desk to Jack.

'Thank you. The scissors, too, if you'd be so kind.'

Day found a pair of surgical scissors and laid them on the desk, slid them across. He wondered if Jack planned to use them on him, to stab him to death.

'Now sit,' Jack said. 'Let's pretend we're adults discussing something of importance.'

Day stepped forward as if in a dream, everything moving in half-time, his limbs heavy, and he was reminded of his underwater dream. Jack was like some unceasing, irresistible tide. Day sat and laid his cane across his lap.

Jack smiled. He pulled off his jacket, leaning forward to tug on the sleeves, then unbuttoned his waistcoat and removed it. The front of his white shirt was soaked in blood. He untucked it and pulled it up, revealing a nasty gash under his ribs on the right side of his torso. 'I'm afraid they may have nicked my liver,' Jack said. He smiled again and winked at Day, then unspooled some of the gauze and began wrapping it round himself.

'What happened?'

'Those Karstphanomen are getting tricky. They laid an ambush for me. But don't worry, I took care of them.'

'You killed them?'

'Four of them. They're waiting for you. Oh, but I've ruined the surprise.'

'I don't think I care for any more surprises.'

'Walter Day, I must admit something. There is something about you, some stolid . . . justiceness. Is that a word? You look exactly like justice. You need only a scale and a blindfold. And perhaps a surgical alteration or two. You are Lustitia, the symbol of fair play. Lust. Lustitia. We want what we see and we take it, the basis for all our modern ideas of justice. Might makes right? It was always so, and I may be misappropriating the words of our cousin in the colonies. But it doesn't matter.'

'I don't understand anything you say,' Day said.

'Of course, your intelligence is not what attracted me to you. It's, as I say, your solidity. You are a marble slab of sheer goodness.'

'Please just . . . Will you tell me . . . What about Esther?'

'Yes. Esther. She is disposable, I'm afraid.'

'No!' Day stood quickly and the chair fell back, smacking against the floor.

Jack scowled at him and held a finger to his lips. He tucked the loose end of his bandage under itself, then rose and went to the door and looked out, up and down the hall, shut it softly, and returned. 'Pick up your chair, Walter Day. And lower your walking stick. What do you plan to do? You can't hurt me and you don't want to. Let's not pretend to be other than what we are. And let's not bring passion into this. Lust and passion are not the same things at all.'

Day shook his head, but picked up the chair. He sat down and waited, but he kept his fist gripped tight on his cane. He might get one chance to swing, and he didn't want to waste it.

Jack crossed behind him and went to the cabinet. He

found a clean white shirt and took his seat across from Day. 'You have much to learn, and we've only begun our journey.' He pulled the shirt on, and Day noticed again how strangely he moved. Jack was clearly in a great deal of pain. 'I think perhaps you didn't have a strong father figure in your life. Was Arthur Day too busy valeting to teach you about the world? Or have I asked you that before? I get confused.'

'You keep bringing other people into our discussion.' Day fixed Jack with what he hoped was a steely glare. 'Leave Arthur . . . you leave my father out of it. Leave Esther and everyone else I know out of it. It's you and me.'

'It has ever been thus. But you miss the larger point. I genuinely don't care about anyone else, but you do, and that makes you vulnerable. So I am going to have to harm Esther Paxton to get my point across to you. I ask you, is that fair to her? Is that justice, Walter Day?' Day started to rise again from his chair, but Jack waved him back. 'Be calm.'

'I told you. This doesn't involve her.' Day could barely speak.

'It didn't, but now it does. And that's your fault.' Jack looked down at the blotter. 'I'm still so . . . All you had to do was go home, live your life, and go back to work. Why didn't you do that?'

'Is it too late?'

Jack raised his fist and brought it down in an arc that would have ended with the blotter, but he pulled his arm up at the last minute and opened his hand and laid it atop the other and took a deep, shuddering breath. Then he smiled again, but it was not a real smile at all; it was nothing Day had ever seen on another human being's face. 'I unlocked your door. I left your clothes where you would find them at the end of the hall –'

'I never saw them. I was out in the cold, naked, with nothing. You left me with nothing.'

'I gave you everything, even money. Certainly enough to hire a cab to take you anywhere you might have wished. It was all right there, great detective, and you walked past it.'

'I never saw any of that,' Day said. 'I never saw it.'

'I asked so little of you. Only the smallest favor in return for months of my hospitality.'

'Why? Why did you let me go?'

Jack's eyes narrowed. 'I think you've deliberately forgotten. And you've somehow made yourself unable to see things around you. Even today, you didn't seem to recognize your own ... Well, Walter Day, you are turning backflips to avoid going home.'

'I'll go home now.'

'And where is that? Where is your home? Tell me.'

Day said nothing.

'You see? You are determined to forget,' Jack said. 'Perhaps your forgetting begets a deeper strength than I knew you had. Your ability to trick yourself and to build a new life indicates a bottomless capacity for rightness within you. As I say, one coin, two men, you, me. I learn from you, you learn from me, and we both benefit, don't we? But enough. Here.' Jack turned the telephone around, swiveling it on its post so that the receiver hung nearer to Day. 'Ask for Scotland Yard.'

'Scotland Yard?'

'Ask for the commissioner, and when he accepts the call, tell him where you are. Ask him to send someone for you. Have him send that ass Tiffany. Or Blacker, or even Wiggins. It doesn't matter. If you value Esther Paxton's life, do it.'

Day picked up the telephone receiver and held it to his ear. When the switchboard responded, he was able to choke out the words Jack had told him to say.

'Tell them who you are,' Jack said.

They waited in silence in that anonymous office, Day and Jack, and the space seemed to Day to grow smaller and more uncomfortable as each minute passed. He could hear the operator and other voices in the background like distant birds, other women connecting other calls, and he wondered what those people had to say to each other, what might be important to them, whether there were other lives depending on other calls. When Sir Edward Bradford's voice finally came on the line, Day couldn't remember what he was supposed to say.

'Hello,' he said.

'Walter? Is this Walter Day on the line?'

'Please,' Day said, 'help me.'

Sir Edward continued to talk, but Day could no longer hear him. He looked up and into Jack's eyes, and the room seemed to spin round him. He dropped the receiver and fell sideways off his chair, dragging the telephone with him. As darkness crept in from the edges of his vision, he heard Jack say (kindly, as if talking about a particularly troublesome but much-loved child), 'Oh, Walter Day. What am I to do with you?'

21

When Claire Day opened her eyes again, Robert and Simon were kneeling beside her on the floor. Simon was holding her hand, and Robert bore a worried expression that Claire would have done anything to erase. Behind them, Fiona was shielding the pram, keeping the babies from seeing what had happened, and Mr Goodpenny was turning in circles, hollering for help. She felt ashamed that she was the cause of so much concern and embarrassed that she had fainted. After everything she had been through in the past two years, she felt she ought to be made of sterner stuff than that.

She smiled at Robert, but he didn't smile back. That wasn't a surprise. Robert and Simon had seen their parents murdered and had barely escaped the same fate. Claire had tried to give them some semblance of a normal life, but the boys rarely let her out of their sight. They were convinced she would die, too, or disappear the same way Walter had, leaving them alone again.

'I'm all right, Robert,' she said. 'Everything's fine.'

He nodded, but put his small hand on her forehead. Two shopgirls and a floor manager were hovering nearby, clearly not sure how to deal with the situation. Claire nodded at them, trying to convey that she was fine, no harm done, everyone could go about their business in the usual way.

She looked up at the gallery. The table where Walter had been sitting was empty now. Had she really seen him there? Or had she been searching crowds for her husband for so long that her mind was now playing tricks on her?

'I'm not ill,' she said. She held out her hand, and the floor manager stepped forward to help her up, but Robert waved him away. He and Simon pulled at her arms with all their might. If she let go of Robert's arm, she thought he would fly backward into a display case.

She smiled again, this time at the floor manager.

'Please, ma'am, are you sure you're entirely well?' he said.

'It's this place. It's so huge and lovely. I'm afraid I was overwhelmed.'

The manager finally smiled back at her, relieved and flattered. 'It is a bit much, isn't it? Please, we have an automatic lift at the back, just this way; won't you have a cup of tea? It's courtesy of Plumm's. You can relax and catch your breath and look around while resting your feet.' He glanced down at Robert and Simon, who were now clinging to her skirts as if they intended to prop her up in the event of another fall. 'And cakes for these brave little boys,' the manager said.

'Thank you,' Claire said. 'Perhaps I should sit down. Please give me a minute to catch my breath, won't you?'

The manager clapped his hands once and turned to show them to the lift. The customers, disappointed that the drama had ended so bloodlessly, resumed shopping, and the staff returned to their duties.

It seemed impossible that the man on the gallery had been her husband. If she claimed to have seen Walter, she would be raising the boys' hopes, and what if it was a case of mistaken identity?

And if she wasn't wrong, if she really had seen Walter? Why hadn't he seen her? He hadn't even looked. He wasn't a cruel or insensitive man, and she couldn't believe, couldn't allow herself to even think, that he didn't love her any more, that he had decided to leave and never look back.

'Robert,' Claire said, 'and Simon, would you boys check on the little girls for me? I don't want them to be worried.'

Robert clearly didn't want to leave her side, but he allowed Simon to lead him a few feet away to where the governess was walking slowly along behind the manager, cooing at the babies. Claire moved closer to Fiona.

Fiona whispered, 'Are you quite sure you're all right?'

'I am,' Claire said. 'But tell me . . . Did you happen to look up there, at the tea shop right there, a bit ago? A minute ago, when I fainted?'

'No, I was sketching the furniture for ideas to help with your book. Is it the book? The pressure of it, I mean. Is that why you passed out?'

'No. At least, I don't think so. It's . . . Well, you're going to think me mad.'

'I won't.'

'Oh, please don't, Fiona. You're the only one I can tell, and if you give me that look, that pitying look that says you're only humoring me, then I think I shall scream.'

'I wouldn't do that. Not ever. Not even if you really were mad.'

Claire smiled and shook her head. 'I saw him.'

'Saw who? You mean Mr Day? You saw him here?' Fiona gasped and stood on tiptoe, turning her head this way and that. 'Where is he?'

'Stop that. We don't want to attract any attention to ourselves. He was at the tea shop up there.'

'But where is he now?'

'So you do believe me?'

'Of course I do.'

'He was right there, sitting at a table there.'

'And you didn't call out to him?'

'He wasn't alone,' Claire said.

'Not . . .'

'Not what?'

'Not another woman.'

'No, of course not.'

'Then who?'

'I'll tell you later. It's too complicated to tell you here.'

'But do you think he's still here? In the store?'

'I hope so. Surely we would have seen him leave, unless there's a back way.'

'We have to tell Nevil,' Fiona said. 'I mean Mr Hammersmith. We have to find him and get him here right away, before it's too late and Mr Day disappears again.'

'Oh,' Claire said. 'Oh, of course. Nevil will help us.'

She hadn't even thought. She wasn't alone. She had so many people around her who loved her and who loved her husband. And if Fiona believed her, then Nevil Hammersmith would believe her, too. He would search the place from top to bottom as soon as he arrived. Nevil would search the entire neighborhood if need be. She had to talk to him right away. She could send a runner to his office later in the day, but she knew he had gone to Scotland Yard today to check once more on any progress that might have been made. If he was still there . . .

She raised her voice. 'Excuse me.'

The manager turned around and raised his eyebrows at her.

'I wonder if you might have a telephone somewhere here.'

Jack hung up the receiver and set the telephone upright on the desk. He checked Day's pulse, which was strong and regular. People were such fragile things, full of delicate organs and unbalanced humors.

'Well,' Jack said, 'I can't simply leave you here, can I?' He squatted and got his hands under Day's arms, lifted him into the chair, then stepped back and pressed his hand to his abdomen. The gauze wrapped around his torso was already spotted with fresh blood. He gave the unconscious man a black look. 'This would have been so much easier if you only did what was expected of you, if you only acted like any other ordinary human being.'

But of course, if Walter Day had been any other ordinary human being, Jack might have killed him months ago. Walter Day seemed ordinary enough, but there was something about him, some special quality, that drew Jack to him. Jack wished he understood what it was so he could cut it out of the detective and move on.

He shook Day and, when there was no response, slapped him across the face. Still, Day didn't wake up.

'Walter Day, I can't decide whether you're the strongest person I've met or the weakest,' Jack said. 'I've never seen anyone so thoroughly hiden away inside his own head.'

The office door opened and Jack looked up, surprised to see a child standing there, a boy perhaps thirteen or fourteen years old. The boy's face was full of fear and anger, and Jack smiled. He heard the distant rumble of the electric lift.

'Please,' Jack said, 'come in. I've been expecting you. Close the door, would you?'

The floor manager knocked on the door and, when there was no response, he jiggled the knob. He shrugged at Claire. 'The new fellow has a lot of work to catch up on. We've had some minor staffing problems recently. Not to worry, all smoothed over. I suppose Mr Oberon doesn't want to be disturbed just now. But come, there's a second phone in Mr Plumm's office. He's out at the moment, and I'm sure he wouldn't mind.'

He led the way down the passage toward a door at the end, but Claire hesitated. She touched the doorknob and quietly twisted it, thinking perhaps it might magically open for her where it hadn't for the manager. But it was indeed locked, and after scowling at it for a moment, she turned and followed along in the manager's wake. She rubbed her fingers against the fabric of her dress. The doorknob had given her a slight shock when she'd touched it.

The murderer took his hand off Ambrose's mouth and held a finger to his lips.

'There's a good lad.' His voice was barely more than a whisper, rasping against Ambrose's skin. 'Be quiet now. There will be big trouble for us all if my friend is found here.'

Ambrose nodded. He was trembling, and his nose was running.

'You seem frightened,' the murderer said. 'Don't be. As long as we're quiet, we won't have any trouble. Do I know you, boy?'

Ambrose shook his head.

'Well, I could swear . . . But if not . . .' He frowned down at Day. 'My friend's had a bit too much to drink, I'm afraid.'

'Guv?' It was the best Ambrose could manage under the circumstances, but there was no response from the motionless man in the chair.

The murderer looked back and forth between Ambrose and the guv. 'Oh, you know him! For how long?'

'A few . . . A week or three.'

'What has he told you about me?'

'Nothin', sir, I swear it. I don't know nothin'.'

'He's never mentioned me? Never mentioned old Jack?'

'No, sir.'

'I'm wounded.' There was indeed a patch of blood creeping up Jack's belly. He was literally wounded, and Ambrose wondered if the guv had done it. The man calling himself Jack stared at Ambrose until he could feel the hairs on his neck creeping. 'I have seen you somewhere,' the murderer said.

'What did you mean you was expectin' me? What you said before.'

'Providence always provides. I can't move our mutual friend by myself. I need help, and so you've happened by in the nick of time.'

'I need to . . .' Ambrose's voice trailed off, and he turned toward the door.

'Don't leave, little boy.'

'But I —'

'I said don't leave. Now be quiet until they've passed back by again. After that, we'll talk.' The murderer sat on the edge of the desk and smiled at Ambrose. Ambrose felt very cold.

'Is he dead?'

'No. Not in the least.'

'You gonna kill him?'

'Now why would you ask me that?'

'I don't know.' Ambrose realized he was panting, as if he'd run a long distance.

'Be quiet now,' Jack said. 'They're coming back through.'

Ambrose nodded and swallowed. He could hear footsteps and a lady talking outside the office door, but he couldn't make out what she was saying. Whoever she was, the murderer didn't want her to find him here. Ambrose knew that Jack was going to kill him and would probably kill the guv, too, and his only chance was to speak up, to scream and holler and make the people outside in the hallway break down the door. If there were enough people round them, the murderer wouldn't dare do anything. They could catch him. Ambrose would tell them about the two dead women, and they would put Jack in prison, and there would be no more worries. He opened his mouth, but before he could utter a sound, Jack's hot, dusty hand was suddenly clapped over his lips again. He hadn't heard Jack move up behind him. The voices in the passage were fading as the woman and her entourage reached the lift and the door closed behind them.

The murderer's lips touched Ambrose's ear. 'Now we can talk.'

The hand disappeared from Ambrose's mouth, and Jack was already sitting again on the corner of the desk when Ambrose lifted his head.

'What's your name, boy?'

'Ambrose.'

'Good. Did I already say you can call me Jack if you want to? Some people do.'

'Is it your name?'

'Sometimes. But I have many names and I have no preferences among any of them. Now.' Jack clapped the palms of his hands against his thighs and looked round the office as if he'd only now arrived there. 'I've had a chance to think our situation over and I've decided there's no polite way to proceed. Don't you agree?'

'No, sir. We can be polite.'

'My advice to you, Ambrose, is to embrace the moment. Of course, you must be polite if you can, but there are times when a small amount of rudeness is unavoidable. And there are times when outright savagery is required.'

'Savagery?'

'Indeed. And if we shrink from the occasion, then we miss our chance to enjoy the savagery for itself. For the marvelous change of pace that it is.'

'What are you going to do?'

'It's not what I'm going to do, Ambrose, it's what you're going to do. You seem to feel some regard for our friend here.' He waved a loose, languid hand at Day's slumbering form. 'And so you will run a small errand for me and come right back here.'

Ambrose shook his head, but couldn't speak.

'Yes,' Jack said. 'If you do not, or if you tell anyone

about me or bring anyone back to this office, I will kill our friend while you watch. And I will kill anyone else you've brought here. And then I will kill you. Only I will kill you very slowly. Very slowly indeed. And I will enjoy it so much more than you will. Do you understand?'

Ambrose shook his head again, then gasped and nodded.

'Good. Do you believe I will do what I say?'

Another nod.

'Wonderful. We're getting on splendidly, aren't we?'

Ambrose cleared his throat and licked his lips with a dry tongue. 'What is it that you want me to do?'

Mr and Mrs Parker had waited outside the coffeehouse and followed Leland Carlyle when he emerged because, as Mrs Parker had rightly pointed out, 'The best way to find our man is to track his man.' Jack the Ripper was claiming the lives of the Karstphanomen. They had no clue to his identity, but they did know the identity of the high judge of the Karstphanomen, and it stood to reason that Jack would, sooner or later, get round to murdering Leland Carlyle. So they followed him and waited for someone to make an attempt on his life.

Carlyle and his wife had taken Hardwick House for the summer months. It was situated on Brook Street near Grosvenor Square, and after leaving the coffeehouse, Carlyle returned there. Mr and Mrs Parker waited outside, across the road in the mews, for hours, but the high judge did not reappear.

'I'm terribly bored,' Mrs Parker said.

'You're speaking English.'

'When in England ... It's good practising. But I'm bored.'

'Yes,' Mr Parker said. 'This job of work is less straight-forward than I would prefer.'

'It's all tangled up in itself.'

'Anything involving Jack the Ripper is bound to be. We're tasked with discovering the whereabouts of a fellow who escaped the police and a whole club of gents that've been trying to find him for a year now.'

'And killing him. That's the fun part, of course.'

'Of course. That's always the fun part.'

'It's just, there aren't usually so many dull parts before the killing.'

'But it's worth it, wouldn't you say? We'll be the ones to finally put an end to this whole Ripper business.'

'You know he plans to have us killed in turn. Carlyle does.'

'You think so, too?'

'I do. We'll do his dirty business for him, and then he'll do away with us and put it all behind him.'

'Well,' Mr Parker said, 'I don't plan to let him do that.'

'I didn't think you did. But forewarned is forearmed.'

'I am always armed.'

Mrs Parker laughed, a light tinkling sound that always reminded Mr Parker of chimes in a gentle breeze. Part of what he enjoyed about the act of murder was the way it made Mrs Parker laugh. It reminded him of her childhood in the country, of watching her ride horses and playing with her in the wood behind the estate, where she had tortured small creatures for fun.

'Let's go and come back tomorrow,' Mrs Parker said.

Mr Parker could rarely deny Mrs Parker anything, but now he frowned. A deep crease appeared between his eyes. 'He may not be coming out tonight, but it's still possible Jack the Ripper might make an appearance while we're gone, and then we'll have lost the only means we have for finding him.'

'He won't come tonight,' Mrs Parker said.

'And you know this because?'

'Because he's no doubt off doing something more fun than watching a boring old house. Something gooey, like slitting open a serving wench and turning her on a spit over a crackling fire. Watching the fat roll down the skin of her thighs and sizzle on the coals.' Her eyes were closed, and she licked her top lip.

He watched the tip of her pink tongue. 'And if he's not? If he's waiting for us to leave so he can kill our client before we do?'

'Then I will most sincerely apologize to you,' she said.

'Don't you want to find our target quickly?'

'We're not going to find him tonight.'

He felt he had pushed her as hard as he could. Any more and she might become dangerous. 'Very well,' he said. 'What would you prefer?'

'That place,' she said. 'That place he told us about.'

'He,' in this context, could mean only one person: an old man they had killed in his bedroom in Alsace. His death had taken several days to play out, and Mr Parker's daughter had spent the entirety of that time at his side. Mr Parker had slept on and off, but Mrs Parker had never slept; she had listened to the old man's ravings as his body had fed on itself and his fluids had soaked into the mattress beneath him.

'That place is in France, my dear,' Mr Parker said. 'He was talking about Paris, I think.'

'And where are we now?'

'London.'

'And they are different?'

'They are some miles apart from each other.'

'Can we go to Paris tonight?'

'Not if we want to fulfill this contract.' She was tugging her earlobe and tapping her finger against her throat and, watching her, Mr Parker began to feel nervous himself. Without realizing he was doing it, he began to rub the two-inch scar on his left temple. One of many reminders he carried of Mrs Parker's temper. 'Very well,' he said. 'We need to stay in London if we're to make any money this trip, but perhaps we can take the rest of the evening off and find something fun to do here.'

Mrs Parker instantly relaxed and lowered her hand from her throat. Mr Parker smiled at her. She really was quite lovely when she wasn't screaming or hurting him.

'Nobody old this time,' she said. 'I want to find someone young and healthy. It's so much more satisfying when they start out strong.'

'Yes, my darling,' Mr Parker said. He reasoned that they might find a suitable distraction for her in Hyde Park and gestured for her to walk ahead of him down Brook Street. There was no way he would have her at his back. Never again.

Esther Paxton was worried. She had taken down the wire
from across her front window and folded and put away
the display clothes. She had shuttered the windows, but
she'd left the globe above the door lit. She had not seen
Walter all day. Normally he would have returned before
she closed up the shop. He would have walked her home,
and perhaps they would have shared a light supper along
the way. Then he would go back and lock up the shop and
get busy rolling cigarettes and cigars for the following
day's business. He was unfailing in his routine. But today
he had been gone before she arrived and there was still no
sign of him.

Of course, he was free to leave, to find another place to
live, though Esther would miss the extra income. But
surely he would have told her, would have given her
proper notice, would have been more considerate than to
simply disappear. There were unresolved issues between
them, at least she felt there were, and Walter would not
have left her alone without warning.

She had just resolved to stroll about the neighborhood
and look for him when there was a knock at the door. She
peeked out the small inset window and saw a tall man
with dark wavy hair smiling back at her. He was quite handsome, but there was something unusual about his smile,

like it had been painted on, like he was a mannequin made up to look human. She banished the thought and silently chided herself for being so ridiculous. She was just worried about Walter, that was all.

'I'm afraid I'm closed for today,' she said, loudly enough to be heard through the door. 'Please come back in the morning.'

'Oh,' the stranger said, 'but I have a message from Walter Day for you.'

'Walter Day?' (Was that Walter's full name?) 'A message?'

'It's a note from him. He's sorry to be so late this evening, but wondered if you'd wait for him. There's more, but he wanted me to give it to you myself.'

'Please slide it under the door.' That mannequin smile still bothered her. She was watching the man through the window, and his mouth barely moved as he spoke. He was like a puppet being worked by invisible strings and rods.

'There's also a small box here,' from the unmoving grin. 'I'm afraid it won't all fit.'

'Oh, very well,' Esther said. She threw the bolt and opened the door.

The man stepped across the threshold and removed his hat. He was carrying Walter's cane, with the bright brass knob at the top. He bowed to her, too low and too formal, making a show of it. 'Thank you, madam.'

'Where is it? The box?'

'Oh, that.' The man turned and shut the door behind him. 'I'm afraid I lied about the box. But I do have a message for you from Walter Day. Or rather, it's about Walter Day. He didn't send it personally.'

'Who are you?'

'Didn't I introduce myself? Please, call me Jack.'

He raised Walter's walking stick high above his head and brought it down in a glimmering arc.

25

Leland Carlyle woke in the wee hours with a dreadful realization that felt physical, like some enormous toad sitting on his chest, crushing him, sucking the breath out of him. The girl at the coffeehouse, the one with the apron, she had heard everything. Carlyle couldn't remember what he'd said, what the Parkers had said. He had been careful, hadn't hinted at any impropriety while the girl had been within earshot, but now he felt convinced that she had listened in. Why wouldn't she? Carlyle was clearly a gentleman of means, and girls like that were always trying to better themselves. She would have listened to their conversation. She might, even now, be planning to blackmail him, might be writing a note to his wife or to the authorities. He should have known, should have been more careful.

He snorted and rubbed his eyes. They were tearing up, and he felt a lump in his throat. It was so hard to be strong, to remain resolute in all situations, all day every day. Sometimes a man struggled to bear up under it all. Especially when there were so many people around him who would take advantage if he showed weakness, who were waiting for an opportunity to turn things around, to work against him.

He had been strong once, much stronger than he was now, but a year of being hunted like a damn fox had begun to wear him down. He jumped at every shadow now, distrusted every new person he met. It was impossible to be too careful when Jack was lurking somewhere nearby.

If the girl had heard anything – had she? He felt certain, but he'd also felt certain he was being careful – if she had heard him use specific names or heard him mention the killing specifically, then she was a danger to him and to the entire Karstphanomen. The thought of disappointing those worthy men was somehow worse than his fear of Jack.

He turned over on to his side and stared at the wall, glad Mrs Carlyle slept in another room. Perhaps the girl hadn't heard him order a murder. And perhaps, if she had heard, she would applaud him for hiring the murder of Jack the Ripper. Surely nobody wanted that madman running around free.

But if she had heard, and no matter what she thought of it, she could implicate Leland Carlyle, she could ruin him.

He would have to do something about her.

Perhaps he could add her to the task he'd given the Parkers. One more body would be nothing to them. They could dispatch her easily. But, of course, in doing so they would have a certain power over him. They would know that he was frightened of a girl. And what would they charge him for it? Whatever the amount, it would be difficult to hide any more money from his accountant. No, he couldn't ask them to take care of any more than they already were.

He would have to do it himself.

And, satisfied that he had arrived at the proper conclusion, Leland Carlyle turned on to his back again and fell instantly asleep. Within moments he was snoring.

At the back of the Whistle and Flute, in a corner where there were no lamps and the light from the street failed to reach, was a large round table with four chairs. Blackleg was not always to be found sitting at this table, but when he was gone nobody else sat there. It was his table. And anyone who had the second chair, across from him, should be bearing good news if he wished to be seen anywhere again.

Hammersmith entered the pub and waited for his eyes to adjust. *How strange,* he thought, *that the gas lamps outside are so much brighter than the light inside.* The table in the corner was occupied. The chair opposite Blackleg was empty. The burly criminal was reading a newspaper, and there were two glasses of beer in front of him. Sometimes Hammersmith had seen men pull chairs over from neighboring tables and play games of Happy Families with the powerful criminal, but this was not one of those times. Hammersmith snaked his way around the other tables, which were set about in no discernible pattern, and pulled out the empty chair. Blackleg folded his newspaper and slid one of the two glasses across to Hammersmith.

'You're on time,' Blackleg said.

'I always am.'

'I took the liberty of ordering for you.'

'Thanks.' Hammersmith raised the glass and drained

half of the murky liquid, then wiped his lips on his sleeve. He noticed a suspicious yellow stain on his cuff and frowned at it. He couldn't remember eating or drinking anything yellow recently.

'This about your missing mate again?' Blackleg gestured for another two glasses, and a woman across the room nodded to show she'd seen him.

'It is,' Hammersmith said.

'I been lookin'. Like I told you I would. And had my girls lookin'. Everybody else, too.'

'You know what he looked like?'

Blackleg smiled. He knew whatever he wanted to know. He had started as a common criminal, crossing picket lines at the docks, but had worked his way to the centre of certain crime rings in London. He controlled all the illegal activities that his warped moral code told him were necessary to society, which meant in practical terms that he avoided anything that might harm children. And unnecessary murders.

What he considered 'unnecessary' seemed to change from moment to moment.

'And there's no sign of him in any of your . . .' Hammersmith broke off, not sure how to phrase the rest of the question.

'Naw, none of my people have seen anything,' Blackleg said.

Hammersmith took another pull from the glass and stared off at the back wall of the pub, which was streaked liberally with rust and mildew.

'Don't take it bad,' Blackleg said. 'One good thing is there's no sign of any bodies or nuthin', either.'

Hammersmith turned his gaze on the criminal and scowled.

'What I mean,' Blackleg said, 'is I done questioned everybody I know might've done your friend bodily harm, might've had it in for a peeler and taken matters in their own hands, so to speak. Nobody knows nuthin'.'

'Nothing they're telling you.'

Blackleg sat back and smiled. The woman appeared and set down two more glasses, foam sloshing over her hands and across the tabletop. She flicked her fingers at the wall and hurried away.

'They'd tell me,' Blackleg said. 'The one thing, the *one* thing, is they don't lie to me. Most other problems I can help with or forgive, but lying destroys trust, and without trust . . . well, what do we have?' He spread his hands wide, then clapped them together and lifted his glass.

'So there's no body,' Hammersmith said. 'No body after a year of looking. Then someone hid his body very well, don't you think?'

'No. No, I don't just mean there ain't a corpse. I mean nobody kilt him.'

'I mean no offense, but isn't it possible someone else harmed him, someone you don't know or doesn't work for you?'

'No, it's not possible without my knowing. A body's a big thing, it is, if it's a grown man. You can chop it up, you can melt it with certain things, but then you've got pieces or chemicals, you've got evidence. That's the sort of evidence you lot, you police, look for. But that's the evidence the rest of us hide from you, and I know about hidin'' better than you or anybody you know. Nuthin' stays hidden from me if I want it found.'

Hammersmith frowned and sipped his beer.

Blackleg leaned forward and clasped his hands atop his folded newspaper. 'Sumpin's odd about all this, I'll grant you that,' he said. 'But what I'm givin' you here's good news. If he's dead, he died in another city, maybe a different country entire. But he didn't die here. Not in my city.'

Hammersmith nodded. He had inquired in other cities, other countries, spent time in Paris, in America and Canada. All of those places were dead ends.

'We been lookin' for Jack, too, you know,' Blackleg said. 'Made it hard for him to operate, hard to get about easy. If he's still in the city, he's had to go to ground somewheres. Like a rat in a hole. Ol' Blackleg's been a busy man lately.'

'It sounds like it.'

'Just so long's you know I'm doin' what I can. We'll find one or the other, and we'll do it soon. And if I don't, you will. Then Jack'll lead us to your mate or he'll lead us to Jack. And then we can go on about our business like old times.'

'I hope you're right.' Hammersmith finished his second beer and set the glass down, took a deep breath, and stood. 'Thank you.'

'You owe me now,' Blackleg said. 'And you know I won't ask nothin' bad, like, but you'd best be ready to pay if I do ask it.'

Hammersmith felt his scalp tingle, but he nodded. 'I know.' He had gone to the Devil for a favor and had been well aware of the price when he did it. There had been nothing else he could do.

'You're a good man, Nevil.' Hammersmith wasn't sure how to take the compliment coming, as it did, from the worst criminal in London. 'If anybody can find this bloke, it's you. Keep at it.'

Of course he would keep at it. What else was he going to do? He'd opened an agency for the express purpose of keeping at it. He had employees now who depended on him to keep at it. And, of course, his closest friend was out there somewhere, probably in terrible trouble, and counting on Nevil Hammersmith to keep at it.

He left the pub and stepped outside. The air was cool and wet, and he coughed, a deep booming sound that cleared his lungs and surprised him. He stepped off the kerb and sat down and rested his arms on his knees. He stared out into the dark street. It stretched in both directions away from him, disappearing into the fog.

Which way to go? Was there anywhere he hadn't already looked for Walter Day?

Hammersmith put his head down on his arms and closed his eyes. If only he had Day there to help him look for Day. He was only one half of a team, after all. It shouldn't all be on his shoulders.

'Oi! Are you Mr Hammersmith?' Hammersmith looked up to see a boy on a bicycle approaching him. The boy stopped against the kerb and stood there with one foot on the ground and his head tilted, breathing hard and blinking at him. 'I said, are you Hammersmith, sir? Do you know him?'

'Um. Yes, I'm Hammersmith. But what —'

'Oh, thank God, sir. I been all over since this afternoon. Practically all night. To your flat, to Scotland Yard, to your office. Everywhere. Your lady at the agency opened up and said you might be here, and thank God again, 'cause you are and now I can have a rest. My legs are done and gone.'

'What is it? Do you have a message for me?'

'Right.' The boy patted his jacket pockets and found a folded piece of notepaper. He handed it over.

'Who sent this?' Hammersmith took the note and stood, angling the paper so it caught the dim gaslight from a globe above him.

''Nother lady name of Day, sir.'

'Claire.' Hammersmith opened the note and dropped it. He bent and picked it up, wiped it on his trousers, and read it again.

'Sir? Is it good news?'

Hammersmith looked up at the boy, who was holding out his hand for a coin. He smiled. 'It's the best news,' Hammersmith said. 'Walter's alive!'

BOOK TWO

Somewhere between an array of water closet cabinets and a jumble of upside-down daybeds, Anna had got herself turned around and stepped off the path. Confident that she knew the way back, she had circled around an enormous bath and shower combination, had turned left at a washstand, and had stumbled over a pull toy shaped like a frog. She had sat for a moment, waiting for her skinned knee to stop hurting quite so terribly much, and when she stood up again she realized that she did not at all know the way back. Nor did she know the way forward. The path was completely obscured in both directions by wooden things of every type and sort.

'Well,' she sniffed. 'This is a fine situation you've got yourself into, Anna.'

She almost answered herself but did not want to appear mad, and so she set her shoulders and chose a direction that seemed promising and marched off, expecting at any moment to rediscover the path.

When the sun set somewhere behind an enormous stack of church doors, Anna stopped.

'At least it isn't terribly cold,' she said. 'But I wonder if anything lives in this wood and whether it is friendly. That is, if there's anything here at all.'

'I have wondered the very same thing,' said a voice behind her.

She turned and saw a perfectly formed little girl made of wood, holding a wooden cross that was nearly as big as she was. She was no more than two feet tall and she balanced the cross on one end in the dirt. Long tangled strings stretched from the four corners of the cross to the girl's wooden arms and legs, which were each jointed at the middle with stout wooden hinges. Her head was a smooth polished ball attached to her body by a broomstick, and her quizzical little face and glossy hair were painted on.

'Why, your dress is painted on as well, isn't it?' Anna asked.

The girl looked down at herself and then looked back up at Anna, but her expression did not change. 'Of course it's painted,' she replied. 'I'm a puppet.'

'Are you really?' Anna said. 'It's only that I've never seen a puppet speak all by itself.'

'And I have never seen a puppet without any strings.'

'But I'm not a puppet. My name is Anna, which is a very proper name for a girl. And my dress is made of cotton, not paint. But I do wish my clothing were painted on. It seems ever so much more convenient.' She held out her hand, and the puppet girl steadied her cross before taking it. 'And what is your name?'

'I do not have a name,' said the girl. 'I have never met my puppeteer and so I have never been named.'

'But what do your friends say when they wish to get your attention?'

'I have no friends.'

'How awful.'

'But I have only been alive for a single day and haven't met anyone else.'

'Well, now you have met me and I will be your friend. Now we must have a name for me to call you. You must have something you call yourself. When you are thinking about what to do next, whether to have a bit of something to eat or a spot of tea with milk or perhaps you would rather play a parlor game with another little puppet who lives down the lane and so you say to yourself, "Well, so-and-so, I will go to the kitchen and see what Cook's preparing for luncheon before I decide what to do." What do you say instead of "so-and-so" when you think to yourself?'

'What is a luncheon?'

'Oh, this is no good at all. I can see that I shall have to name you.'

'How kind of you.'

'What are puppets usually called? Punch or Judy, I suppose.'

'I do not think I would like to be called Judy. And especially not Punch. Perhaps you might simply call me Marionette Puppet, since that is what I am.'

'Then it's settled. It's a pleasure to make your acquaintance, Mary Annette. May I call you Mary for short?'

'If it makes you happy to do so,' the girl said.

'It's only that Annette is so close to being my own name, and I wouldn't want to get us confused.'

'Do you think you might?'

'No, I don't think so, but it's always best to err on the side of caution, don't you think?'

'I cannot think. I have a wooden head.'

'But you only just now said that you were wondering something. It's the very first thing you said to me. And wondering is much the same as thinking.'

'Is it really?'

'I believe so. Is your head entirely wooden?'

'Through and through.'

Anna leaned forward and peered at the girl's shiny golden hair. 'That must be quite helpful whenever you fall down and don't get a knot on your head. Knots are ever so painful.'

'I am sure I wouldn't know about that,' said the little wooden girl, 'but I do worry about cracking it.'

'Well, if you can't think, then you shouldn't worry, either. You're only getting the worst of it that way.'

The girl stood still and didn't reply. Anna hated to have to carry the entire conversation herself, but she supposed she ought to set a proper example in manners for the puppet. 'Are there more like you?'

'Puppets, you mean? If there are, I have not encountered them yet,' Mary said.

'Yesterday this was a plain empty field with nothing in it except grass and dirt and old stumps and bugs. Before that it was a huge place filled with trees, and Peter and I played here every day with a little boy who was our best friend. But then men came with saws and wagons and took all the trees away to make other things out of the wood. I suppose you must be made from one of the trees that was here before. All of the wood must have become homesick and come back again to the place it was born.'

Mary looked all round her at the furniture and tools and flooring. 'But I wasn't born. I was made. Who made me?'

Anna shrugged. 'I don't know.' She looked up at the sky. The moon had risen above the coatracks, and stars were visible in the deep blue overhead. 'I do miss Peter,' she said. 'I'm trying to find him, but I'm afraid he's lost.'

'I will help you,' Mary said.

'Oh, will you?'

'Yes. You are my first friend.' Anna imagined she could see her smile, but her painted face did not move. 'And perhaps we will find the puppeteer along the way.'

'The puppeteer?'

'The one who made me. I need someone to hold this.' Mary hoisted the joined beams of her cross on to her shoulder.

'I'm sure we shall find them both,' Anna said. She slipped her hand under Mary's elbow, and they walked together into the darkness of the wood, Mary dragging the tail end of her cross, which left a long, ragged mark in the dirt behind them.

— RUPERT WINTHROP, FROM
The Wandering Wood (1893)

Sir Edward Bradford had been up before the sun and had dressed quietly in the dark, careful not to wake Elizabeth. She hadn't been sleeping well lately. He swiped imaginary dust from the surface of his mahogany desk. It had been difficult to get the desk moved from Great Scotland Yard, but Sir Edward could not imagine his office without it. Still, it was much too large for the cramped room, and his visitors' knees were smashed up against the other side of the desk. Claire Day and Inspector Jimmy Tiffany were clearly uncomfortable, but were doing their best to appear at ease.

'Are we waiting for Mr Hammersmith?'

As if on cue the door opened, slamming into the back of Claire's chair, and Hammersmith poked his head into the office. 'They told me I was expected.' He had purple smudges under his eyes and Sir Edward wondered whether the lad had slept.

'Come in, Nevil,' Sir Edward said. He waved his hand as Hammersmith navigated the end of the desk. 'Watch the corner there.'

Hammersmith bowed slightly in Claire's direction and shook Tiffany's hand before sitting and placing a slim file folder on the desk in front of him.

'Good, we're all here,' Sir Edward said. He raked his fingers through his white beard. The empty left sleeve of his jacket was pinned to his shoulder, and the head of the tiger that had taken his arm was mounted on the wall above him, a constant reminder to others that the commissioner was still quite capable despite his loss.

'Claire has good news,' Hammersmith said. He was fidgeting in his seat with barely controlled excitement.

'I don't mean to be rude,' Tiffany said, 'but your news should wait a minute or two.' He smiled at Claire. 'We have some good news of our own. Commissioner, you should tell them.'

'Yes, of course,' Sir Edward said. He indicated the telephone on his desk. 'Yesterday I received a call. It was . . . um, it was Walter Day on the other end of the line. Walter called me.'

'Are you sure?' Claire stood up and leaned over the desk as if she might hear him better. 'Are you positive it was Walter?'

'I believe it was. He didn't say his name, but I recognized his voice.'

'What did he say?'

'He asked for help.'

'Did he tell you where he was? Was he calling from the department store?'

Hammersmith cut in. 'Why did he need help?'

'He didn't tell me,' Sir Edward said. 'He rang off almost immediately. But the point is, he's alive.'

'I knew that he was.' Claire felt behind her for her chair and lowered herself into it. 'I always knew.'

'Why did you ask about a department store?'

'That's our news, sir,' Hammersmith said. 'Claire saw him.'

164

'You saw him?' Tiffany's eyes widened. 'He was at a shop somewhere?'

'Yesterday,' Claire said. 'He was at Plumm's. On an upper level, talking to someone.'

'Who? Who was he talking to?'

'Where is Plumm's?'

'One at a time, please,' Claire said. 'Plumm's is the new place on Moorgate. I went there to research my new book and he was there. I was certain it was him, but I only saw him for the briefest of moments. I'm afraid I . . .' She trailed off, embarrassed.

'Is there a way to . . .' Hammersmith motioned at the telephone. Inspector Tiffany nodded. He reached out and tapped the phone's receiver.

'I've already talked to Sarah, the girl at the exchange. Twice. She doesn't remember where the call originated. A dead end, I'm afraid.'

'I receive one telephone call in a month and that girl can't remember anything about it,' Sir Edward said. He sighed and shook his head.

'Would you mind if I talked to her?'

'Nevil, I already said I –' Tiffany broke off and waved a hand at Hammersmith. 'Do what you want.'

'I don't doubt you,' Hammersmith said. 'I only meant –'

'It's our first real clue in a year,' Sir Edward said. He smiled at Hammersmith. 'You want to follow it. I understand, and so does Inspector Tiffany. Isn't that right, James?'

Tiffany nodded, but his jaw was clenched.

'You may speak to Sarah,' Sir Edward said. 'But it's not necessarily a good use of your time.'

'We have to do something,' Claire said. 'You have to keep looking. Go to Plumm's. Walter's alive.'

'Of course, Mrs Day. Nobody's proposed that we stop looking. If anything, this prompts us to redouble our efforts. I'm putting the entirety of the Murder Squad on this case today. Most of the men knew Walter well and will recognize him on sight. I apologize to you, Mrs Day. We've let the search dwindle over these past few months, and that's regrettable.'

'Sir,' Tiffany said, 'with all due respect, and you know how much I've wanted to recover Inspector Day, but we have so many other cases, we're already worked to the bone.'

'I'm afraid that will always be the case, Inspector.'

'I didn't mean to imply that I was unwilling or that I haven't already spent long hours searching.'

'Of course not. Nobody here thought you were unwilling to help.' In fact, Sir Edward was sure everyone else in the room disliked Tiffany and questioned his willingness to do anything other than the letter of his job, but he was a good policeman. 'But with the certainty that Mr Day is still very much alive, now is the time to strike, to bring to bear all of our expertise, all of our manpower, all of our determination to recover our missing comrade, don't you think?'

'Of course, sir.'

'Good. That's settled.'

'How can I help? What can I do?'

'You, Mr Hammersmith, in addition to having been a very good policeman yourself, were Mr Day's closest ally here. You've stayed with the case all this time and have the most knowledge of it. My men are at your disposal.'

Tiffany jumped to his feet. His chair tipped backward, but didn't fall. The space was too narrow, and the top of the chair wedged against the wall and pushed against Tiffany's knees so that he had to bend forward and lean against the desk, undermining his dramatic gesture. He pointed at Hammersmith.

'He's not . . . He's not Scotland Yard. He's not . . . I'm sorry, Hammersmith, but you're not a policeman now. I don't even know what you are or what you do with yourself. You have a shopfront somewhere. You don't command . . . Well, sir, he can't hold a command.'

Sir Edward smiled and paused long enough for Tiffany to sit back down and compose himself.

'He can hold any command I give him, Mr Tiffany. Unless he would prefer not to. I know it's unusual, so I'll leave it to you, Nevil. All I want is to see Mr Day back here, safe and sound. Whatever gets us that result.'

Hammersmith stood, carefully, and paced around the scant two-foot-square area of the office that wasn't filled with desks, chairs and people. He looked like a dog chasing its tail. 'If it's all the same to you, sir,' he said, 'I'd rather Tiffany have the command.'

'Very well. But I'd like you to share your files and any findings with him, if you're willing.'

'Of course, sir.' He placed a hand atop the file folder on the commissioner's desk. 'I've summarized my findings of the past year. I'm afraid it's not much.'

'Every little bit, my boy. And, Tiffany, let's make a plan to divide the city up so we can start the search as soon as possible. We'll start with this department store at the centre. I don't want Day slipping through our fingers again.'

Tiffany nodded and stood, more carefully this time. He motioned to Hammersmith, and the two men left the office. Sir Edward asked Claire to stay behind for a moment.

'I owe you an apology, Claire. We should have looked harder. Damnit, we practically gave up on Walter. Pardon the language.'

'I know you did your best. As Mr Tiffany said, my husband wasn't your only concern.'

'No, he wasn't. But he was one of our own.'

'Was?'

Sir Edward shook his head. 'No, you're right. You're right. He *is* one of us. And we'll find him now.' He leaned forward and spoke more quietly so that Claire could barely hear him. 'We will find him. I promise you that.'

Claire opened her mouth, then closed it and smiled at the commissioner. She turned and left the office and shut the door behind her.

28

Mr Parker woke up late and cursed himself for a fool. He couldn't afford to be careless. Ever. He turned his head and saw nothing, then sat slowly up and looked all round the room. Mrs Parker was gone.

His sense of unease was tempered by his pleasure at discovering he was alive to experience another day. He placed his bare feet on the floor, careful to avoid the wire that ran between the legs of the bed. He disengaged his snares and padded barefoot across the room to the door. The alarm there had been disengaged and the key was missing.

He breathed a deep sigh of relief and busied himself with the morning routine. He washed his face and removed the wooden form that kept his mustache in its proper shape overnight, then brushed his hair and his beard until they glowed. He worked a little Macassar oil into his mustache and beard and sculpted them into sharp points that stuck out from his face at right angles. His fingers were a bit greasy, and he rubbed them dry on his eyebrows, taming the stray hairs there. He examined his handiwork in the polished metal mirror on the vanity and smiled. He had always been a handsome devil. It was no wonder Mrs Parker had fallen for him.

By the time she returned to their rooms, he was fully dressed and all the traps had been disabled. They were free to move about the room without injuring themselves. As long as he remained alert, Mrs Parker posed no danger to him. But they both knew that there would be a day when he let down his guard or forgot to set his snares and that would be his last day. Until then, they had resolved to enjoy each other's company and make the best of their situation.

'I brought you something,' Mrs Parker said. She checked once more for wires and blades before she sat on the edge of his bed and held out a plain paper sack for him.

'What is it?' He kept the bag at arm's length while opening the top, but to his extreme relief there were no human body parts inside.

'Biscuits,' she said. 'I was passing a cart and remembered which kind you liked.'

'How kind of you.' He sniffed one and took a bite. It was not in Mrs Parker's nature to poison him. 'Have you breakfasted?'

'I ate without you. I'm sorry.'

'No, no, that's quite all right.' He suppressed a shudder.

'You were sleeping so soundly, and I found the key to my shackles. You shouldn't leave it where I can reach, you know. Anyhow, I let myself out and decided to explore a bit while I had the time to myself.'

'I thought I'd left the key well out of reach,' he said.

She gave him a knowing look and waggled one eyebrow. He smiled. She was able to stretch and contort herself to the most unlikely extremes. She was a marvel, truly.

'I did have to dislocate my left arm, but it's back in place now,' she said. 'This city has so many interesting things to see.'

'How long were you out?'

'Oh, three or perhaps four hours. I wasn't able to sleep well.'

'Sorry to hear it.' If she had been out by herself for three or four hours, there would be at least one item in the newspapers. But he knew that nobody had identified or followed her. She wouldn't have betrayed the location of their rooms by returning if there had been the slightest chance. She read his expression and smiled again.

'We'll pick up a copy of *The Times*,' she said.

'Will I be able to infer what you've been up to?'

'If you read closely.'

'Not front-page stuff, I hope.'

'You wound me. Nothing so spectacular. We haven't finished our work in London. You know I don't soil the nest before the job's done.'

'I apologize.'

'I do hope Mr Ripper makes his move today. I'm growing anxious.'

'If nothing happens today, we'll find another way,' Mr Parker said.

'Oh, good.' She sat back and stared out of the window. 'The sun's finally out. I do hate how dreary this city can be.'

They had divided the duties that defined their unusual occupation, and Mr Parker was the strategist. Mrs Parker was rubbish at planning, but she carried out other aspects of the work with great gusto. She was also the prettiest woman Mr Parker had ever seen. He loved her with every fibre of his being, and the only thing he feared more than her presence was the possibility that she might some day leave him.

He polished off his last biscuit and checked the mirror again. Upon removing a crumb from his mustache, he crossed to the door and opened it wide. He picked up his case (heavy with saws, mallets, scalpels, three revolvers, a stout length of rope, and a pair of manacles) and gestured for Mrs Parker to lead the way out.

'Come,' he said. 'Let's find our pigeon again.'

Mrs Parker leapt from the bed like a cat and stopped in the doorway for a kiss before bounding out the door. Mr Parker watched her walk away, his eyes wide and his nostrils flared. He still considered himself the luckiest man in the world.

29

'Well,' Tiffany said, 'come along if you're coming.'

He led the way to a cluttered desk in the far corner of the Murder Squad's room. It was, in its way, isolated, pushed up against the wall as far from the other men's desks as it could be. Piles of paper existed in a sort of precarious détente, threatening at any moment to slide off each other to the floor. Tiffany pulled out a chair and gestured for Hammersmith to sit. Before Hammersmith could demur, Tiffany plopped down on the corner of the desk, toppling an avalanche of papers behind him. He tossed the file folder Hammersmith had brought on top of the mess and it somehow stuck. Hammersmith took the offered chair.

Tiffany tapped the file. 'Save me time. What's in it?'

'Not a lot, actually,' Hammersmith said. 'I did the usual sort of follow-up, went over Walter's old house half a dozen times or more without seeing anything amiss. Fiona Kingsley drew up a terrific picture of him and I took it around, showed it to everyone on that street so many times, I thought they might stone me if they saw me coming round again. Took it across the park, too, and showed it on the other side. Nothing came of it. Quite a few people there knew him; most avoided his house. Too many bad things had happened there, and none of the neighbors wanted a killer visiting them in the middle of the night. Only the one of 'em saw Walter that night.'

'The old woman.'

'Aye. Talked to her two or three times, but she's not all there. A bit mad, I think. She says she saw Walter get in a black carriage. Right after that, she saw the Devil himself stroll away down the street, laughing, she says.'

'The Devil.' Tiffany rolled his eyes. 'Helpful.'

'Couldn't give a good description of him. Wavy sort of dark hair, she thinks. Tall, thin. And evil.'

'Right. Evil's, what, a physical trait?'

'I have no idea.'

Tiffany sighed. 'So I know most of this already. Anything new? Anything in the last month or so?'

'Nothing.'

'The old woman, did she say if Day had his hat? Did he have his cane? The one with the brass knob at the end?'

'He had them both. At least as far as she can say. But I wouldn't rely on her for much.'

'No.'

'I've gone over everything again and again. I've talked to every cab driver, every private carriage owner I can find in the vicinity. I'm at my wits' end. No, I was at my wits' end eight months ago. The trail is dead.'

'And yet Walter's alive,' Tiffany said. 'Or so Sir Edward believes.'

'I'll talk to the telephone dispatcher.'

'I said I've talked to her.' Tiffany ran a hand through his hair and stroked his mustache with his fingertips. It looked to Hammersmith like a nervous tic. 'You're welcome to do it again, but there's nothing there. I feel like we're being played with.'

'Oh,' Hammersmith said, 'we are. We quite definitely are.'

'By the Devil?' Tiffany chuckled. 'Well, there's strength in numbers, I suppose. If we're working together now, however much that's actually practical – which it ain't – but if we're putting our heads together maybe something will finally fall out.'

'I know you can't be pleased,' said Hammersmith.

Tiffany shook his head and frowned. 'I don't care. Not really. It's not like I don't want to find Walter.'

'Good. That's good.'

'Yes, yes. But I've also got a woman clubbed her husband to death and took the kids off away somewhere. I don't find her, who knows what she'll do with 'em. And that's a case I could use Walter's help with, but of course I ain't got him. And I've got three men who took a woman into an alley and done horrible things to her. She's alive, but I want those men, and I want 'em now. Those are just since yesterday, never mind everything else I ain't got to yet.' He waved a hand over the reams of reports on the desk behind him. 'So I'll give you what I got and I'll do what I can, and so will every other man in this room, but I'll not answer to you, no matter what Sir Edward's got to say on the matter. I can't. I just ain't got the time and I can't go back to that poor woman or to that dead man's mother and tell them I was busy with summat else, can I?'

Hammersmith nodded, then shook his head, unsure of how to agree with the inspector. 'I understand,' he said.

'Then you tell me what you need and I'll do my best.'

'I don't . . . I don't really know what I need.'

'What? Men? Guns? I've precious few of either. Same with information. You're welcome to our files, but if we'd found anything out, we'd have let you know by now.'

'I've got used to acting alone. Walter was always the one –'

'Right. Well, no sense in that now you've got something real to go on. Take Jones. He's a good fellow.'

Hammersmith and Tiffany both looked up at the sound of approaching footsteps. A man as big around as he was tall moved between the queues of desks as if he owned them. And in a way he did. Hammersmith stood and shook Sergeant Kett's hand.

'Good to see you again, boy,' Kett said. 'Inspector Tiffany, I couldn't help but overhear.' (Hammersmith hid a smile. The sergeant had been across the room, but had ears like a bat.) 'If it's all the same to you, I'd like to offer myself in place of Jones. I might've said some things to young Hammersmith here that were uncalled for, and I'd like to make up for it.'

Tiffany shook his head and frowned. 'We need you here, Kett.'

'Sergeant Fawkes can handle my duties along with his own for a few days if it comes to that.'

'I'd still rather send Jones along than lose you here,' Tiffany said.

'Day was a good lad. He was one of my boys, and I don't sleep so good at night since he's missing. Been a long time without a good sleep now.'

Tiffany leaned forward, away from his desk. His hands were clasped above his knees and his head was down. He resembled a grief-stricken man in prayer, and

Hammersmith wondered how long it had been since Tiffany had slept. How long since any of these men had slept.

At last, Tiffany straightened up and slipped off the corner of the desk. He leaned back against it and crossed his arms over his chest. He nodded. 'We'll make do with Fawkes for a day or two. But, gentlemen, let's find Walter fast. Find him fast and bring him home and maybe we can all put this nasty business behind us.'

Hammersmith stood. 'I suppose we'll tread the same ground again. With two of us at it, we might be able to circle farther out, talk to more people.'

'Wait.' Tiffany tapped the folder again. 'You said the Kingsley girl drew a picture of Day for you?'

Fiona Kingsley worked as an illustrator of children's books, but she had grown up assisting her father, Dr Bernard Kingsley, London's premiere forensic examiner. She had accompanied him to crime scenes and sketched them for the police. Lately, she had used witness descriptions to sketch criminals, giving the detectives of the Murder Squad a visual aid in tracking and catching them.

'She's a good artist,' Kett said. 'I'm sure it was a good likeness.'

Tiffany waved at Kett, irritated. 'Of course. But did you ask her dad?'

'Ask him what?'

'For help.'

'What could he do?'

'He does that thing of his. Puts powder all over and finds fingerprints.'

'What good would that do? And you don't even believe in that, anyway.'

Tiffany leaned forward and scowled up at Hammersmith. 'I believe in anything that solves a case.'

'But you said —'

'I say a lot of things. What does it matter what I said? Seek out the doctor and take him along, if he'll go. He's smarter than the rest of us put together. One way or another, he might figure something out.'

Dr Bernard Kingsley stood at a table in his laboratory and stared down at the body of an infant. The baby girl had been neglected, left too close to the hearth, and her cotton dress had caught fire. It looked to Kingsley as if the child had actually rolled into the flames. Burns covered three quarters of her tiny body, her dress had grafted itself to her charred skin in places, and her arms and legs had shriveled to stumps. Kingsley bent and kissed her forehead before pulling a sheet up over her. There was no need for an autopsy in this case. The cause of death was obvious. And horrible. He hoped her negligent parents had been burned as well.

'Father?'

Kingsley turned around, startled, and smiled at the sight of his youngest daughter, Fiona, who hesitated at the open door. He wiped his hands on a towel, crossed the room, and took her in his arms.

'Father, are you all right?'

Kingsley sighed and stepped back, looked around at the room he spent so much of his time in. Twelve burnished wooden tables stood in a row, each of them slanted just enough so that fluids could run off them into a drain in the centre of the floor. Months before, electric lamps had been installed above the tables, and now the room was brighter, more clinical and less intimate than it had been under the old gas globes. Five of the tables were occupied by the dead. In addition to the baby and one of her siblings, there was a man who had choked to death on his dentures and a woman who had died of pneumonia. Only the fifth body posed any mystery regarding cause of death, and Kingsley had been waiting to get to it, dealing with the easier cases first.

'I suppose I'm a bit melancholy today,' he said. 'I've a bad feeling.'

'Well, of course you do,' Fiona said. 'You've two children on your tables. The dead always affect you this way, children especially so.'

'That must be it.' He smiled at her. 'What brings you round here today?'

'I wanted to visit you.'

'Well, I'm glad of it. Come, let's get out of here.'

He turned the knob that shut off the electric lights and ushered his daughter out into the passage, shutting the door behind them. There was a small window at eye level, and Kingsley imagined he could see the bodies on his table glowing slightly, as if they'd absorbed some of the light in the room. He wondered if the baby had been afraid of the dark.

They climbed the stairs to the ground floor, and Kingsley let his daughter lead him through a maze of hallways to his office. He stopped short of the door. It was halfway open and light spilled through into the hallway. He could see a shape moving on the other side of the frosted glass. He moved ahead of Fiona and pushed the door open.

Nevil Hammersmith jumped and turned around from the desk, where he'd been writing something on a slip of paper. He grinned and ran a hand through his dark mop of hair before stooping to pick up his hat. To Kingsley's eye, the former constable looked as if he'd lost weight in the months since he'd last seen him, and Kingsley wondered how that was even possible.

'I was just leaving you a note,' Hammersmith said. 'Thought maybe I'd find you downstairs in your laboratory, but just in case . . .'

'I was indeed down there. Good to see you again, Nevil. It's been too long.'

'It has.'

Hammersmith seemed ill at ease, averting his eyes, and Kingsley looked around, confused. Fiona seemed similarly uncomfortable. Kingsley frowned.

'To what do I owe this honor?'

'Ah,' Hammersmith said. 'Well, Tiffany, Inspector Tiffany . . . By the way, good to see you as well, Fiona.'

Fiona mumbled something Kingsley couldn't make out. She curtsied and backed out of the door and was gone. The two men listened quietly until her footsteps had faded away down the hallway.

'That's odd,' Kingsley said. 'Perhaps she left something in the laboratory. I'm sure she'll be right back.'

'Yes,' Hammersmith said. He seemed relieved. 'I'm sure she will. Um, about the . . . Inspector Tiffany thought you might be able to help us out with a little thing.'

The doctor moved around and sat behind his desk. He indicated for Hammersmith to take the only other chair, but there was nowhere else to put the books that were stacked there, so Kingsley stood back up and they both leaned against the desk.

'Is it a new case?'

'Rather an old one, I'm afraid,' Hammersmith said. 'It's Walter Day.' Kingsley listened as Hammersmith filled him in on the fresh developments: the phone call, Sir Edward's renewed determination, and the fact that Hammersmith was working with the police again. When Hammersmith had finished talking, Kingsley sat back down and stared at a corner of the ceiling, pursing his lips and moving them in and out, chewing over the information.

Finally he focused his gaze on Hammersmith, who had waited patiently. Kingsley was impressed. Patience was not one of the younger man's best qualities. 'I've quite a lot to do here,' Kingsley said. 'Five people on my tables right now. They deserve my attention.'

'Of course,' Hammersmith said. He backed toward the open door. 'I knew you were busy, but thought it would be foolish to pass up the opportunity to work with you again, however slim the chance.'

Kingsley held up a hand to stop Hammersmith. 'As I say, I've a lot to do, but none of it is as important as finding Walter. I'm ashamed to say I'd given him up for dead. If he's alive, of course I must do anything I possibly can to help.'

'Oh, that's wonderful news. I haven't made much progress over the last few months. Hell, I haven't made any progress at all. I could use another pair of eyes, especially yours.'

'What can I do?'

'Well, on that point I'm not entirely sure. Inspector Tiffany is available to us in an advisory capacity, and so is the entire Murder Squad, I suppose. And Sergeant Kett, you know him?'

'We've met.'

'He's waiting for us. Well, for me, but I hoped I'd be bringing you along. He's at the house. The house where Walter disappeared.'

'His old address.'

'Yes,' Hammersmith said. 'Just so. Kett's going over the place again. Not as if it hasn't been gone over.'

'One never knows. Even a hair found along the skirting might be the one clue needed to break through.'

'A hair.' Hammersmith sighed. 'What about finger marks? Fingerprints? Whatever you want to call them, do you think they might be useful?'

'I did think so,' Kingsley said. He closed his eyes. 'When Walter disappeared, I went to that house and I looked for fingerprints. I looked for hair against the skirting, for blood, for footprints. I found nothing.'

'I had no idea you'd even been there.'

'Of course I was there. Walter was my . . . is my friend.'

'Why didn't you tell me you'd investigated?'

'Why would I have? I didn't find anything that might have helped you.'

'Well, I suppose . . .'

'Yes?'

'I suppose it would have been good to know I wasn't alone in the search.'

Walter Day had been awake for hours, staring at a dusty orange wedge of sunlight that reminded him of an earlier time. He was in the bottom of a large cart that had a steel frame and canvas sides, and his only view was of high roof beams and dust motes and that wedge of sun. He had no energy, and his vision refused to clear, so that when he held his hand up in front of his face he saw three versions of it. The light, however feeble, pierced his brain, the smell overpowered him, and the thought of what must have happened to bring him to this place was unbearably painful.

He had delivered himself once again to Jack, and Jack had easily stripped him of his independence. Nothing Day did made any difference. Jack always won.

The room was quiet and dim, despite that single orange wedge, and eventually Day gripped the metal frame of his ineffectual cage and pulled himself up. It was awkward, and he fell two or three times to the bottom of the loose canvas sling before he was able to throw his weight the right way to tip the cart over. He landed badly, crushing the fingers of his right hand between the frame and the hardwood floor. He flopped out and stuck his fingers in his mouth and looked all round him to see if anyone had heard and come running. But no one had. He was alone.

Or at least he seemed to be alone. Jack might be hidden somewhere, watching him. But Jack might be anywhere at any time, and there was no longer any sense in fearing that. If the man wanted to show himself, he would, and there was nothing Day could do about it.

In the wan half-light, Day could see that he was in some sort of combination workshop and warehouse. He assumed the canvas cart had been used to remove him from the Plumm's office. The space was a large rectangle with a high ceiling, and each of the long walls was lined with benches and tables. There were bins beneath the tables, and the handles of saws and mallets were visible from where Day crouched, his throbbing fingers still in his mouth. Chisels and picks and short serrated knives hung from nails in the walls, and the floor was mottled with dark stains that had been bleached and mopped, and bleached and mopped again. A machine Day didn't recognize was bolted to one end of the nearest bench. At the far wall was a stack of wooden blocks and planks, and a few of the benches held chunks of wood that were still in the process of transformation: into heads and hands and polished boxes complete with glass tops cut from enormous sheets that leaned against the sturdiest table in the corner. There were other canvas carts, perhaps a hundred of them shoved in random clusters round the tables, and a queue of dozens of silent female mannequins stood at attention behind Day, some of them missing hands and arms and heads, items still in progress, still waiting to be revealed within the big blocks of wood.

He wondered what time it was. Despite the sunlight, nobody was at work; the half-finished carvings had been abandoned.

The room was utterly quiet except for Day, who panted

and sniffed and shuffled in place. Dust motes swam through the air around him like curious fish. Beneath the scents of sawdust and iron there was a subtle burnt odor caused by the friction of tools against heavy materials. And there was another scent, too. Fetid, sweet and coppery. Day recognized it immediately. There was a dead body in the room with him. He hoped it was an animal, a squirrel or rabbit that had burrowed in and died there, unnoticed beneath a bench. But he knew better. Jack didn't murder rabbits.

He lowered himself to his hands and knees and crawled over to the wall. He peered down the queue of benches behind the bins. It was too dark to see all the way to the far wall, but there were no shapes that reminded him of a human body. He pulled himself up and sat on the end of a bench, waiting for his fingers to stop aching, waiting for his head to stop aching. He watched the orange wedge advance toward him from the high windows, dispelling the shadows. Eventually, he stood and walked slowly to the canvas carts jumbled in the corner. He rolled them out one at a time, pushing them away behind him, until he came across one that felt heavier than the others. He took a deep breath and looked down into it. It was filled at the top with a mass of loose bald mannequin heads, and he moved them to another empty cart. Under the first layer of heads was a shock of hair. He moved more heads until a woman's face came into view. Her eyes were open and staring, her grey lips drawn back from her teeth in a hideous grin. His knees felt weak, and he braced himself against the cart's frame until he could trust himself to walk, then he rolled the cart over near the benches and left it there. He went back to the corner and began again, moving one cart at a time until he found another heavy one. This one was filled with wooden hands and feet, and he didn't bother to remove them but instead dug down, pawing them aside until he found a hand that gave under pressure from his fingertips. He pulled on it, and the wooden parts fell aside, revealing a second woman. Her torso was split open, and he could feel her ripping apart as he pulled. He stopped and moved her cart to the benches, parking it beside the first one.

He rested then, and took short breaths through his nose, staring down at his knees. When he was sure he wouldn't vomit, he went back and began searching the canvas carts again. There was only a handful of them left, and he entertained a sad, small hope that they would all be empty. And they were. All but the last one, which was fitted perfectly into the corner, where Day was sure Jack had left it. There for him to find at the very end, a special surprise, a parting gift.

There were no mannequin parts covering this body. Perhaps there hadn't been time to cover Ambrose after transporting Day to the workshop. Or perhaps Jack had wanted to make sure Day didn't overlook the boy's body.

Day didn't realize he was crying until he saw moisture on Ambrose's face. A single tear splashing on his cheek and rolling down, absorbed by the canvas side of the cart, as if it were the boy crying. Alive again for an instant.

Day slumped against the wall and sank down. He buried his face in his hands and did not move until long after the orange wedge was swept away under a fresh yellow carpet of daylight.

When Hammersmith and Kingsley arrived at 184 Regent's Park Road, they were astonished to see three police wagons and at least a dozen uniformed bobbies moving in and out of the house through the familiar blue door. A small crowd of neighbors had gathered at the periphery, and Hammersmith pushed through them, motioning for Kingsley to follow him. Sergeant Kett must have been watching for them because he immediately came bounding down the steps, still barking orders at the constables behind him.

'One of you men get down here and control this lot.' Kett waved the back of his hand at the crowd, as if to push them away. 'Move along,' he said. Nobody moved. Kett turned toward Hammersmith. 'Good, you brought the doctor. We're going to need him in there.'

'What's happened?'

'Ugly stuff, I'm afraid.' He was almost out of breath, and Hammersmith wondered whether it was from exertion or shock. 'Just come on and you'll see.'

An angry buzz circulated through the crowd as Hammersmith and Kingsley were led up the steps and into the house.

'As if they've got a God-given right to see everything for themselves,' Kett said.

A constable lifted a length of rope that was strung across the open front door, and the three of them scuttled beneath it into the house.

'I see you're using the kits I supplied,' Kingsley said, 'to help keep the scene intact.'

'Always do these days,' Kett said. He patted a pair of rubber gloves that were tucked into his belt. 'Ain't seen you much, though. Always that fellow Pinch who comes round.'

Kett led the way through the entry and past the staircase. An aggressive cloying odor filled Hammersmith's nostrils. The scent of decaying meat seemed to coat his tongue. He smacked his lips and nearly gagged. Across from the stairs, on their left, was the parlor, and Hammersmith peeked in as they passed the open door. He caught a glimpse of a man lying naked on the floor, his arms and legs spread. There was something wrong with the body, but he instinctively pulled his head back and kept walking, following Kett down a long passage to the kitchen. Behind him, he heard Kingsley gasp. Whatever had happened to the dead man in the parlor, it was enough to make the seasoned doctor uncomfortable.

'Yeah,' Kett said. He didn't turn around. 'That's bad enough in there, but the real show's in here.'

With that, they entered the kitchen. The room was dominated by a heavy burnished metal table. The six chairs around it had all been moved aside, and four of them were pushed up against a sideboard. A second dead man lay facedown on the table. His wrists and ankles were tied to the table legs, and the flesh of his back had been laid open, exposing his spine. The table was bowed beneath him, and a dry yellow puddle of plasma flaked in the breeze from the open back door. The bodies of two more men sat in the remaining chairs against the far wall.

Their hands were raised above them and nailed to the wall, and their feet were nailed to the floor. All three men were nude, their clothes folded neatly and stacked on the sideboard. Next to the back door, above the two men in the chairs, four circles had been drawn on the wall in blue chalk. Beneath the circles was a message, also in blue chalk:

Exitus probatur Mr Hamersmith

> *Thees ones neerly did me, but faled*
> *I left you the kidnes but for the one I ate.*
> *All karsts who wer there have pade now but 2*
> *The crow an the white king.*
> *They wil rue the day they do me as they did.*

Kind regards
Your frind Jack

Hammersmith took it all in quickly, then moved past Kett to the door and stepped through into the thin mist of the back garden. An ash tree loomed out of the fog, its branches hanging heavy over the tops of four pale chairs and a tiny round table. A veneer of lilac smothered the dead meat odor that followed Hammersmith out of the house. He sat in one of the chairs without bothering to dry it off and felt the accumulated moisture soak into the seat of his trousers. He didn't move. After a moment, Kett joined him.

'Rough,' Kett said.

Hammersmith nodded.

'You've seen it rough before, son.'

'I have,' Hammersmith said. 'But I still don't like it. And there's the message, too. The writing on the wall.'

'Someone copying the Ripper's work, you think?'

'No,' Hammersmith said. 'I think it is the Ripper. And I'm worried he's trying to tell us that he's killed Walter. That he's been torturing Walter for a year and . . . Is he saying that Walter's dead?' A sudden thought made Hammersmith jump up from the chair. 'I saw the three men there, but the one in the parlor . . . I didn't see his face. It wasn't . . .'

Kett shook his head. 'Not one of them in there's Walter Day. I checked that first thing.'

'So this was all here . . .'

'These dead men have been here for a week or two, I'd say. Few days, at least. Up to the doctor to say for sure, though. He's workin' on 'em right now. Set right in on 'em while you came out here.'

'I should go back in.'

'Do like I do and breathe into the cuff of your sleeve. Filters it out a bit.'

'I'll go you one better,' Hammersmith said. He pulled his shirt up over his mouth and nose. His sleeves snugged up under his armpits and he couldn't lower his arms all the way, but he could breathe well enough. He followed Kett back into the kitchen.

Kingsley looked up from the table where he was examining the second body. 'I thought we'd lost you, lad.'

'Needed a moment's all,' Hammersmith said. He was breathing hard now, warm air gusting down across his chest.

'Ah,' Kett said, 'the private sector's been too easy on

you.' He grinned, then made a face and stuck his nose into the end of his sleeve.

'Let's get some more windows open in here,' Kingsley said.

'On it,' Kett said. He hurried away, shouting at his men as he went.

Hammersmith kept his distance from the table. 'What do you think of this?'

'There's a lot to deal with,' Kingsley said. 'A lot to try to put into some kind of context. I'm trying to piece together how many men were here. You've been in this house and examined it, and so have I. How long do you think the killer had to do his work here?'

'It's been at least two months since I was in here,' Hammersmith said.

'Aye, more than that for me. It makes me wonder if whoever did this was watching us, waiting to make sure the place was empty. Unless it's sheer chance. It's possible someone came upon the abandoned house and seized on an opportunity for mischief.'

Hammersmith pointed to the message on the wall. Kingsley looked up at it and nodded.

'Fair point. That's clearly directed at you, even if your name's been spelled incorrectly. The men who did this — I'm assuming they were men. Or maybe one man. Women tend to be less messy when they kill — they knew you visited here on occasion and they wanted to get your attention.'

'I think we both know who did this. There was only one killer here.'

Kingsley straightened up and stepped back from the table. 'You mean . . .'

'Of course it was him. Of course it was Jack.'

Kingsley stared at the message for a long moment. He nodded and turned away. 'I believe it.'

'You do?'

'Of course. The evidence is too great to ignore. The hard part is figuring out how one man was capable of overpowering four others.'

'But Sir Edward doesn't believe Jack exists.'

'Sir Edward knows he existed, but he doesn't like to think about Jack. He's a military man. The concept of evil is too huge for him to conceive of. He thinks of murder as an exercise in motivation and reward. In his philosophy, people only kill because they want something.'

'Jack wants revenge. That's motive, don't you think?'

'It's more than that. There are things in the air and under the dirt and even dwelling within our own bodies, things that will kill us if we aren't constantly diligent. But we can't see them. They're invisible predators.'

'Jack the Ripper isn't invisible.'

'He may as well be. He operates on society like those germs and bacteria do on our bodies. You can't go after him the way you do every other criminal.'

'I can,' Hammersmith said. 'I really can. You romanticize him, I think. But I'll treat him like any ordinary criminal because he doesn't deserve better than that. I'm going to find him. Because he's a man, not some demon or figment. I'll find him just as soon as I find Walter.'

'You may be able to do both things at once.' Kingsley

stepped away from the table and walked to the kitchen's back wall, where he stared up at the message there. 'It's no accident that he's left these men here for us to find, rather than dumping them in some Whitechapel alley. He's taunting us. Well, he's taunting you, actually.'

'Telling us he has Walter,' Hammersmith said.

'Perhaps. Or maybe just telling us he knows something we don't. Each line of this thing is a separate jab.'

'The spelling is —'

'The spelling's a ruse, I think. Meant to make it seem like he's not as smart as he actually is. He's used Latin in the first line, so he's more educated than he'd like us to think. And there are other inconsistencies here. A study in misdirection.'

'Do you really think he ate someone's kidney?'

Kingsley pointed to the splayed corpse on the table. 'That one's missing his left kidney. But there's no indication that anyone ate it. If he cooked anything here, he cleaned up after himself. And if he ate it raw, there are no signs of it, no bits of it dropped on the body, no extra blood left on the outside of the clothing or on the table itself. Nothing on the sideboard. If he consumed any part of this man, he's not a sloppy eater.'

'Then where is it?'

'I think he took it with him.'

'But he wants us to think he ate it? Why?'

'Perhaps he only means to disgust us, to throw us off our game. He's taken all their tongues as well. That seems to be his calling card.'

'All right,' Hammersmith said. 'In the second line of his poem —'

'You think it's a poem?'

'I'm more versed in literature than poetry. He makes it sound like they surprised him. Or maybe even hurt him. I'd guess by the fourth line he's talking about the Karstphanomen.'

'That seems like a safe assumption. Which would indicate that these four men were all a part of that secret society. But it's hard to say whether he's randomly depleting their ranks or is only attacking the men who were directly a part of his incarceration. Does his revenge extend to all of them or only those few that had a hand in torturing him?'

Hammersmith pointed above the message to the row of four circles. 'Four zeroes, four victims. This looks angry to me. I think these must be the specific men who tortured him. Or some of them. There can't be many more of them, can there?' He sniffed and looked away. 'Do you think it's a coincidence that Walter's been missing for a year? The same amount of time Jack was held prisoner?'

'It's hard to say what's a coincidence in all this mayhem.'

'If he's telling the truth, I'm sure he means to kill again before he's done. It's all he ever does. It's all he's good at. "The crow and the white king." What do you suppose they are?'

'I don't know.'

'People? His next victims?'

'Or chess pieces,' Kingsley said. 'He may be talking about the rook. When he says *crow*, I mean. *Rook* is another word for a crow, and a white king is, of course, one of the two objectives in chess.'

'So either he's referring to a game – he sees all this as some sort of gambit and we're supposed to figure out his next move, or maybe make the next move ourselves – or these are references to people and this is some sort of riddle. The white king could be the leader of the Karst-phanomen. Who do you suppose that would be?'

'It's a secret society for a reason. I recognize two of these three men, though.' Kingsley indicated the dead men lined up under the message, but he didn't look directly at them. 'One's a very successful solicitor. He's backed a number of enterprises lately.'

'Enterprises?'

'Oh, a small string of tea shops, a haberdashery, I hear he's even got some money invested in Plumm's. I don't know them, but I'd wager the other men here are also prominent in their fields. Once we identify them, we might have a better idea of the circles Jack's stalking.'

'Whoever their leader is, he'd best be wary.'

'For all we know, he may already be dead. For all we know, one of these men is the Ripper's "white king."'

'No,' Hammersmith said. 'I don't think so. Jack's leaving clues. He wants me to search for him, he wants me there when he does it, when he claims his last victim, doesn't he?'

'What makes you think that?'

'Otherwise, why tease me, why write this here in this way so he can be sure it'll get brought to my attention?'

'Why you?'

'I've been after Walter for a year. Jack's not stupid. He's been watching me.' Hammersmith pounded his fist against the palm of his other hand. 'He might have been right there the whole while I was looking for him. But why act now?'

'Why does he do any of this? You're trying to make sense of pure chaos.'

'If I don't catch him, do you think he'll go back to his old ways after he's had his vengeance? Don't you think he'll start up again, killing women?'

'I don't think he'll ever stop,' Kingsley said.

'Nor do I,' Hammersmith said.

'Don't let him distract you. Find Day. I'll do everything I can to help.'

33

Day came blinking out into the morning sun and rested in the shade of the department store while he got his bearings. He was so used to the smothering fog that the city looked new and bright and innocent to him. The workshop was behind Plumm's, and so, once he realized where he was, he jogged up Moorgate and through Great Bell Alley. His leg hurt and he couldn't go as fast as he needed to, but there was a part of him that was afraid of what he'd find when he got to Drapers' Gardens and Esther Paxton's little shop.

If I hadn't spent so much time discovering the bodies in the workshop . . . But no, he stopped that thought before he could finish it. If Jack had paid a visit to Esther, he had done it in the night while Day was at the bottom of a canvas cart. If Esther was dead, she had been dead for quite some time already.

He bypassed the shrubbery where he had spent his first days of freedom and limped down the stone path to the door. The wire was not across the window, Esther's wares were not displayed, and the globe above the door was still lit, even though it was broad daylight. Esther would not have wasted expensive oil. Day found that he couldn't swallow and he had to lean over and spit. He caught his breath and knocked at the door. There was no answer. He tried the knob and it turned easily. He swung the door open and stepped inside, careful and quiet, conscious of the fact that Jack might be near.

It was dark inside the room. Day listened and thought he heard a small sound somewhere far away at the back of the house. He left the door open and took a step forward. Something crunched under his foot and he drew back. After a moment's hesitation, he went to the window, keeping close to the wall as he moved, and unlatched the shutters, threw them back. The room was immediately awash in bright sunlight, and Day blinked. He turned around.

Esther's rug was heaped against the wall, and all the furniture that had been on it was scattered about. A table with a pretty glass inlay was upside down, the glass crushed and pebbled. Two chairs were on their backs, one missing a leg. A lamp had broken, adding its glass to that of the table, and a puddle of oil had spread to the bounds of its ability, soaking one corner of the rug. Most alarming was a hole in the wall next to the door, an ugly gash, the wallpaper around it torn and tattered.

Day drew a ragged breath and licked his lips. 'Esther,' he said. Softly, but the sound of his own voice gave him courage and he called again, louder this time. 'Esther!'

There was an answering cry, but he couldn't tell if it was her. The sound was high-pitched but muffled, and there were no words, only a senseless animal sound. Day thought of Jack's victim, the man he had called 'Kitten,' and he shivered.

Day moved quickly now. Someone was alive in the draper's shop, and that gave him hope. He hurried across the room as well as he was able, avoiding the glass and setting a chair upright as he passed. There was an inner door and he pushed it open, his fist raised in defense. Nothing. Only a short passage that he knew led to a tiny parlor at the back and a staircase that led to the rooms upstairs where he kept his meager belongings: his change of clothing, his jars of tobacco and rolling papers, a small decanter of brandy. He called out again.

'Esther? Esther, are you here?'

He listened and heard the animal sound again coming from the parlor.

Day bounded past the staircase and through the last door into the room at the back. Esther Paxton was propped up against the far wall. Her legs stuck straight out from her body, her skirts hiked too high for modesty and her hair falling in tangled ringlets round her face. It was not bright in the room, but a window was open and Day could see that she had a black eye. It looked to Day as if her nose might be broken, and blood had crusted around her mouth and chin. The front of her dress was dark and wet, and a long smear of blood trailed down the wall toward her body.

But her chest was rising and falling. She was breathing. She was alive.

He went to her and knelt in her blood, which had pooled beneath her. He stood and opened another window to get more light in the room and knelt again, examining the wounds in her stomach. She had been stabbed at least twice, but not deeply, and her dress was already going stiff as her blood dried. He had no way of knowing how long she'd been lying there, and now he cursed himself for taking so long in the department store workshop. He was always a step behind Jack, and the people around him paid the price.

He took off his jacket and balled it up, lifted her head, and laid it back down on the jacket, hoping it might make her more comfortable. 'Don't stop breathing, Esther. Just keep breathing. That's all you have to do now.'

He left her there and ran back through the shop to the front door and pelted out on to the street. He dashed up Moorgate as fast as he could, ignoring the pain in his leg. The usual gang of boys loitered at the intersection near Finsbury Circus, waiting to help pedestrians. He recognized one of them, a lad who occasionally scouted tobacco for him.

'How fast can you run, Jerome?'

'Pretty fast, sir.'

'Get to a telephone. Do you know where the nearest telephone is? Go to it and call University College Hospital. Ask for Dr Bernard Kingsley. Tell him Walter Day needs him to come straight away. Can you do that?'

'Yes, sir.'

'Do you know Paxton's shop off the gardens?'

'I do.'

'Tell him to go there. Tell him to send his best people there. Someone's badly injured and may be dying, may be dead already if he doesn't hurry.'

'There's nearer doctors to here, sir, if it's a hurry you're in.'

'Yes. That's a good lad. After you make the call, find the nearest doctor and get him over there, too. Get two doctors. Get three. Bring whoever you can muster. Go now.'

Jerome nodded and went back to his cluster of friends. Day grew anxious as he watched the boys talk, but in an instant three of the boys had peeled off and were running in different directions. Jerome had delegated his errands to some of the others. He hoped it would be Jerome himself making the call to Kingsley. Trusting that the boys could move more swiftly than he could, Day returned to the shop and checked again on Esther. She was still breathing, steady but irregular.

He wondered at the fact that Dr Kingsley's name had come into his head at the moment he needed to remember it. Now that things were unraveling, there was a lot that was coming back to him. Like a fog being lifted.

The light from the window glinted off something metallic beneath Esther's legs, and Day recognized the brass knob at the end of his cane. He pulled the walking stick out from under her and scraped a few drops of dry blood off the shaft with his thumbnail.

Had Esther used his cane to protect herself or had Jack left it to taunt Day?

He moistened his cuff with spit and used it to clean some of the blood from Esther's face. He willed her to open her eyes, and when she didn't he stood and turned the knob of the cane until it clicked. Apparently neither Jack nor Esther had realized it was a sword cane. He drew a two-foot dagger from the stick and tested the blade against his thumb.

Then he left the shop again, confident in the knowledge that the best doctor in London would save Esther's life. He marched back to Moorgate and west to Plumm's. He had determined that, one way or another, his long war with Jack the Ripper was going to end.

34

Timothy Pinch swept into the kitchen and dropped his black bag on the table next to the body. Dr Kingsley looked up and raised an eyebrow, then returned to his work, probing the incisions in the dead man's back.

'Took you long enough,' he said.

'Well, you know, Fiona came round, and I thought you'd want me to give her the details.' Pinch removed his jacket and folded it lengthwise, draped it over the back of a chair, and smoothed out the wrinkles.

'Why would I want you to tell my daughter about a murder?'

'She's a curious girl.' Pinch stopped rolling up his sleeves for a moment in order to peer over Kingsley's shoulder at the corpse.

'That she is,' Kingsley said. 'And you're a curious fellow.'

'What's that?'

'Never mind.'

'What are we doing?' Pinch clapped his hands together and rubbed them. 'Are they ready for transport? I've got a wagon waiting at the curb.'

Kingsley grunted and poked tweezers deep into one of the wounds. He pulled out a long dark brown hair and straightened up, holding it to the light that streamed in through the back door. Pinch leaned in for a look.

'That hair doesn't belong to this chap here,' he said.

'No,' Kingsley said. 'Nor does it belong to any of the other gentlemen we've got in here.' He gestured at the two dead men sitting with their hands nailed to the wall.

'What about the man in the parlor?'

'I don't think so. I haven't got to him yet, but –'

'I looked in on him before I came in here,' Pinch said. 'He's got yellow hair. Unless the head in there doesn't belong to the body in there.'

'Good point. Let's make sure the bones match up in the spine. It's entirely possible he brought another head with him and took that poor fellow's.'

'Who would do such a thing?'

Kingsley raised an eyebrow again, but didn't respond.

'So much anger,' Pinch said.

'Not necessarily. Have you got a pouch for this?'

Pinch produced a pouch from his waistcoat pocket and Kingsley dropped the hair into it.

'I think it's possible our murderer has finally made a mistake,' Kingsley said.

'What, the hair? It's not much.'

'No, but it's more than we had.'

'What's all that mean?' Pinch pointed at the writing on the wall, and Kingsley gave it a glance.

'Not sure,' Kingsley said. 'Chess pieces are the obvious inference. Rook and white king. The rest of it's mostly nonsense.'

'Doesn't say rook. Says crow. Could mean a doctor.'

'How's that?'

'Crow. Another word for doctor, you know? On account of the black robes we all used to wear. Made doctors look like big black birds to some people, I suppose.

Of course the reference is a bit outdated at this point, but maybe if the age of the fellow who wrote this –'

'A doctor?'

'Well, I don't know,' Pinch said. 'No need to look so ashen and all. Thought we were playing a guessing game.'

Kingsley took a deep breath and nodded. 'Yes, indeed. Hadn't thought of that, is all. A doctor. And if it's a doctor, what would that make the white king?'

'Haven't the foggiest.'

'Hmm.'

'All right, then,' Pinch said. 'Best get this fellow out of here, right? You get his legs and I'll take the torso?'

'Not yet,' Kingsley said. 'I haven't dusted.'

'Oh, that.' Pinch turned away and looked at the counter and the sideboard. 'Do you think it'll do much good?'

'Perhaps.'

'Never has.'

'It did once. That was before your time, lad, but it's worth putting the effort in.'

'If you say so.'

'I do say so.'

Pinch lowered his head and cleared his throat. 'Apologies, sir.'

'No harm done. You're young, that's all. And you're intelligent. I was much the same at your age, sorry to say. Anyway, I've already taken the ink on these men's fingertips. It's over there on the counter, if you'd be so kind.'

'Of course, Doctor.' Pinch straightened his spine, and his eyes darted over the countertop until he saw a slip of parchment. He picked it up and gazed at it, his tongue rolling over the inside of his cheek. After a moment, he went to his bag and rummaged within until he found a magnifying lens. He held the parchment up so that it got full benefit of the light and went over it with his lens. Kingsley watched him, a smile touching the corner of his mouth. 'I see,' Pinch said.

'The differences.'

'Yes, quite pronounced, especially here.' Pinch pointed with the end of the lens's handle. 'And here.'

'You've got your powder?'

'Of course, sir.'

'Let's dust every inch of this kitchen, and the parlor, too. If we're lucky, the killer will have left some impression behind him.'

'It's amazing, really. If all the fingerprints are different, then what about toe prints? Or earwax? Someday we'll be comparing blood and saliva and urine. Do you suppose one criminal's mucus is different from every other? Or perhaps the pattern of the growth of his hair?'

'Let's not get ahead of ourselves.'

'But aren't you at all fascinated by how similar we are, one to another, but how many invisible differences we have?'

'It does make one wonder.'

Pinch opened his mouth to reply, but at that moment a boy pelted into the kitchen, followed by a frustrated constable.

'I'm looking for Dr Kingsley,' the boy said.

'Apologies, Doctor,' the constable said. 'The boy got past me at the door.'

'It's all right.'

'I know how you like a place to be undisturbed and whatnot.'

'I said it's all right. Let's hear what the young man has to say.'

'You Dr Kingsley then?'

'I am. What's your name?'

'Jerome, sir.'

'Jerome, you have a message for me?'

'It's from Walter Day, sir. I rang the hospital like he told me, and they said you was here, so I came straight over, I did.'

'Walter Day? Did you say you've got a message from Walter Day?'

'It's what the gentleman said, sir. I never knowed him by that name, but it's what he said.'

'Well? What *did* he say?'

'You're to go to the Paxton place, the draper's. It's in the gardens. Someone's hurt, and he needs you quick as you can get there. You coulda got there quicker, too, if I hadn't taken so much time to find you.' The boy scowled and kicked the floor.

'Not your fault, lad. But I don't know this place you're speaking of. Can you lead me there?'

'You know I can, sir! Let's go!' And with that, the boy ran from the room.

'Wait!' Kingsley turned and grabbed his bag, shoving his tape measure, magnifying lens, and tweezers back into it in a jumble. He snapped it closed and turned to Pinch. 'You can finish up here, Timothy? Get the fingerprints and compare them to those on the parchment?'

'Of course.'

'Good. Prepare the bodies for transport. It seems I've been left behind. I'd better see if I can catch up. Good Lord, Walter Day himself. After all this time.'

He stuck his hat on his head and, holding it there, ran from the kitchen.

35

There was a knock on the wall next to the open door, and Sergeant Fawkes stuck his head into the office.

'Sir?'

Sir Edward looked up from his book and smiled. 'What can I do for you, Sergeant?'

'The door was open.'

'Indeed. And you have rescued me from this.' He took off his spectacles and waved them at the book. 'Slow going, but our Dr Kingsley seems to feel it would be good for me to read it.'

'Medical whatnot?'

'Of a sort. Forensic case studies from France, of all places. The good doctor is catholic in his choices.'

'I see, sir.'

'Was there something you needed, Fawkes?'

'There's a gentleman says he wants to talk to you and won't have no truck with anybody else.'

'A police matter or something personal?'

'Says it's a bit of both. His name's Carlyle.'

'Leland Carlyle? Well, send him in, then. I'd best put this away.' Sergeant Fawkes disappeared from the doorway and Sir Edward scanned the desk for a bookmark, then shook his head and closed the book, unmarked, and hid it from sight in a drawer. He folded his spectacles against his chest and slipped them into his breast pocket.

A moment later, Carlyle hove into sight and bustled into the office, all nervous energy and breathless arrogance. He turned and shut the door and sat across from Sir Edward before the commissioner could invite him to do so.

'Did she tell you I saw him?'

'Ah,' Sir Edward said. 'You're here about Inspector Day. Yes, it's exciting news, and we're acting with all haste.'

'But you talked to Claire. Did she tell you I actually saw Walter the other day?'

'She did not tell me that. But it's good news. Between that and the telephone call, I'd say we're just round the corner from finding him at last.'

'That's exactly what I'm here to talk about. It really is a matter of time. And that could be a problem, depending on what he's learned during the past year.'

'What are you afraid he's learned?' Sir Edward slumped back in his chair and rubbed the bridge of his nose.

'The membership.'

'The membership?'

'Of the Karstphanomen. He might know who we are.'

'You mean who *you* are.'

'You can't deny you were once –'

'I am not a member of your cult, Mr Carlyle.'

'Cult?'

'I don't care what you call yourselves.'

Carlyle looked down and shook his head. 'We've been over this time and time again. Let's not repeat ourselves now. This is a matter that requires serious attention or there will be dire consequences.'

'How do you think Walter's learned your membership rolls?'

'Jack knows.'

'Jack?'

'Jack the Ripper.'

'Oh, piffle.' Sir Edward fished his spectacles from his pocket and, ignoring Carlyle, found his book again. He thumbed through the pages until he found the spot he wanted and began to read. Carlyle watched him all the while without saying a word. After a moment, Sir Edward looked up and frowned. 'You're still here?'

'You're not going to help?'

'Help with what? Good God, man, you've gone completely round the bend. Jack the Ripper has told Walter Day sensitive information about your secret society, and you want me to . . . well, what? Order Walter to keep mum about it? Am I to pretend I believe Jack the Ripper's still gallivanting about London, despite the fact that his murders stopped two years ago and have not recommenced? Jack is gone. You fear a ghost, a boogeyman. I'm frankly tired of hearing about this myth. Even my own men have tried to bring the spectre of Jack back, despite an overwhelming lack of evidence. Go away with your ridiculous children's stories. Go away and don't come back.'

'He does still exist. He does. He's killing us. Do you know how many are left? A handful, that's all, and we cower behind locked doors at night, jump at every creaking floorboard, every knock at the window by a tree branch. Have you any idea what it's like to live that way?'

'No. At the end of the day I go home to my wife and have a good meal, a glass of port, and then to bed for a solid night's sleep. I do not burden myself with fairy tales and ghost stories. You may indulge yourself if you like, but leave me out of it.'

'You won't do anything?'

'I still don't know what you would have me do. Listen, Mr Carlyle, my men are going to bring Walter Day home. God willing, he'll even return to work. He was a good detective once, and I have every hope that he will still be a good detective. Your daughter will have her husband back, you will have your son-in-law, all will be right with the world, and I may very well enjoy a second glass of port that evening, but I will certainly not bother Walter with your brand of silliness. I would advise you to restrain yourself in the matter and not bring it up with Walter. He's had a rough enough go of it, I think, and could probably do with a return to normality, if that's at all possible.'

'I have taken certain measures. I wondered whether I was doing the right thing, but now I see that I was right to do it.'

'What have you done?'

'With luck, you'll never know.' Carlyle stood and put on his hat. 'Good day to you, sir.'

'Leave the door open on your way out,' Sir Edward said.

Carlyle stomped away, and Sir Edward returned to his book. After reading the same page three times, he leaned back and sighed. 'Lord save me from Frenchmen, Karstphanomen, and other assorted asses,' he said.

Fawkes stuck his head back into the office. 'What's that, sir?'

Sir Edward jumped in his chair. 'Did you hear our conversation, Fawkes?'

'No, sir. Thought you said something about Frenchmen.'

'Here, Fawkes, read this book and tell me what it says.' Sir Edward handed the book over to the reluctant sergeant.

'I'm not much of a reader, sir,' Fawkes said. 'What's it all about?'

'To be perfectly honest, Sergeant, I haven't a clue.'

Hammersmith had two clues to work with.

The words *crow* and *king* written on the wall indicated that the killer might be a chess player.

And one of the dead men in the murder house was a backer of Plumm's.

Adding one and one together, Hammersmith reasoned that Plumm's might sell chess sets. He hadn't figured out what to do if they did or what that might have to do with multiple murders. But it was a place to start.

He had lost a year in the hunt for his friend and he couldn't afford to lose any more time. Walter was alive and needed help. Sleep and food had always been secondary concerns for Hammersmith, but now he pushed them further back, out of his mind entirely. Day had come into his life just when his father had left him. Day was close to his own age, but wiser somehow. Greater, he felt, than Hammersmith could ever be. He needed that in his life, needed Day to give him guidance. He would never find a friend like that again. He needed, for Claire's sake and his own, to find Walter Day.

Plumm's wasn't open yet when he arrived, and he stood in the shelter of an awning across the way, staring out at the street. A light mist still clung to the ground and to the walls around him, and yesterday's drab grey cobblestones were today a mottled rainbow of natural tones in the new sunlight. A tall man with thin hair slicked back along his scalp passed without seeing him and unlocked the front door, slipped through, but no light appeared inside the department store once he was in. Hammersmith waited. Eventually another person appeared, then another. Then lights did come on inside. A white-gloved man came out and sniffed the air. The man stepped forward and rolled a gate back from the doors.

As Hammersmith watched, a young woman appeared at the end of the street and walked slowly toward the department store, hugging the wall. Light shimmered through her hair, which was drawn up at the back of her neck. As she drew near, she noticed Hammersmith and crossed the street toward him. He pulled back in the shadows and motioned to her.

'What are you doing here?'

Hatty Pitt rested her hands on her hips and scowled up at him. 'I'm doing my job, Mr Hammersmith. What are you doing here?'

'I'm confused,' he said.

'That's not really an answer, you know. More a state of mind.'

Hammersmith shook his head. 'Now wait a minute. You work for me, not the other way round. How did you know I'd be here?'

'I didn't. And it seems to me you've no right to tell me where I can and cannot be when you've been gone and I've been the one –'

Hammersmith held up his hands and put his head down. He sighed. 'Hatty. Why are you here? Why have you come to Plumm's this morning?'

'I've been working on my case for a whole day and a half now. I've made real progress.'

'Is it to do with Walter Day or the Karstphanomen or the murders of those four men?'

'What four men?'

'So it has nothing to do with any of that?'

'It's that missing person, Hargreave. He was a floor manager here. The supervisor.' She hooked her thumb over her shoulder to indicate the store. 'He's disappeared.'

'Interesting,' Hammersmith said.

'Mildly so,' Hatty said. 'But not terribly. Men disappear all the time. What makes this case especially interesting is that someone wants to pay us. And with our detective missing from his own detective agency for weeks on end, and with charges coming in left, right and centre, a paying client is very interesting indeed.'

'I could swear I told you to consult with me on every development.'

'I couldn't find you. Time is of the essence in a missing person case, Mr Hammersmith.'

Hammersmith was surprised by her forthrightness. He gave her a rueful smile. 'Yes,' he said. 'Yes, of course.' She was, he thought, very much like himself: headstrong and too honest for her own good. He admired these qualities in her, but wondered if he irritated others as much as she was irritating him. 'Tell me,' he said. 'Tell me about the case.'

There was little to tell, and Hatty caught him up within five minutes. He made her go back over the bit about how she had found a tongue in a rubbish bin and he admonished her about traveling to strange places by herself. Meanwhile, foot traffic around Plumm's had increased and the shutters on all four stories had been opened. Elaborate displays were barely visible in the windows of the ground storey and the floor above it. Gossamer mist moving over glass gave the mannequins behind it an eerie energetic quality.

'So,' Hammersmith said, 'your client's brother – or rather, *our* client's brother – was employed here.'

'Yes. I thought I'd talk to his coworkers.'

'Good. And have you talked to his household staff?'

'Not yet,' Hatty said. 'I'm starting here at his work. He was the floor manager, so he must have interacted with dozens of Plumm's staff every day. It seems to me there might be clues here.'

Hammersmith nodded and pursed his lips. 'Good.'

'Thank you. But you never said why you're here, Mr Hammersmith. Is it something to do with finding Mr Day?'

'Yes. I've only now come from a murder scene. One of the victims was a backer of this store.'

'Oh, he might've known my missing person.'

'Hmm. Maybe. But he might never have set foot in here. Might be it's just money moving about and no connection at all.'

'What does the murdered man have to do with Mr Day?'

'He was found at Walter Day's old address.'

'On Regent's Park? But it's been a year since he was there.'

'Well, obviously. It's been a year since anybody was there. Anybody besides us and the police.'

'So it might not be related to his disappearance.'

Hammersmith shook his head. 'It's related, all right. What say we go inside and see what there is to see.'

*

Hammersmith had once visited a bazaar, and he had been inside mammoth train stations, but he had never seen a space so big devoted solely to selling things. Everyone in Plumm's department store was there to buy something or to entice someone else to buy something. Everywhere he looked, Hammersmith saw wooden mannequins and busts made of wax and papier-mâché, he saw flat wooden forms draped with dresses, festooned with necklaces, and pinned with brooches. Counters were set in diagonal clusters, topped with globes of light that accentuated the sparkle of jewelry and the richness of fabric. A wide spiral staircase with a wrought-iron rail led to another floor, where Hammersmith could see an array of women's shoes and boots. Workers struggled across the gallery above, leaning against the rail, carrying huge panes of glass for an upper-storey display in progress. An enormous blue globe spun slowly inside the framework of a brightly lit cube that was tipped up on one corner.

'It's beautiful,' Hatty said. 'It's all beautiful.'

'Welcome to Plumm's.' A small, officious man with a pencil-thin mustache hurried toward them. 'How can I help you?'

'We'd like to speak with Mr Plumm,' Hammersmith said. He worked to put some authority in his voice.

'Mr Plumm? Why, I'm afraid he's in a meeting right now. But I'm Mr Swann. Please, I'm sure I can help you with anything you might —'

'Mr Hargreave said we might be able to see Mr Plumm,' Hatty said. 'It's dreadfully important.'

'Mr Hargreave?'

'Joseph,' Hatty said. 'Joseph Hargreave.'

The prim man drew himself up as if there were some invisible thread attached to his head that extended to the high beams above, through them and to the heavens. 'Joseph Hargreave is no longer employed by us. And his brother is not welcome here, either. Not at the moment. There has been some irregular behavior, and at Plumm's we pride ourselves on professionalism and decorum. No shopper shall ever be —'

'Then who's managing the floor now, Mr Swann?'

'That would be Mr Oberon,' the man said. 'But he's quite busy now, supervising the new installation.' He pointed up and back, and Hammersmith looked at the railing above him, where a tall man with dark wavy hair had joined the workmen struggling along with their sheets of glass.

'Mr Hargreave has been replaced?' Hammersmith could hear a note of surprise in Hatty's voice, but his attention was fixed on the man above him. 'Already?' There was something about that man on the gallery, something familiar in his movements, the tilt of his head, the halo of light from the window overhead. The man – Mr Oberon – looked down, and a slight smile twisted his lips.

'Mr Angerschmid?' Hammersmith tore his gaze away from the dark man on the gallery. Another man, small and round, was hastening toward him from the far side of a cabinet that displayed cufflinks and flasks. 'I thought that was you!'

The little man was beaming from ear to ear, waving his hands wildly, and it took Hammersmith a moment to place him. Then he remembered. 'Ah,' he said, 'Mr Goodpenny, isn't it?' An old acquaintance from another case.

'It's been too long, Mr Angerschmid!' Goodpenny was still moving toward him, but as he spoke, his eyes rolled up toward the gallery and the smile began to slide from his face. 'But where is – Oh, my!'

And then the immediate surroundings were a deafening jumble as Hammersmith was toppled off his feet by a rushing weight and he hit the ground hard. A ripple of sound passed over him then was gone, and all he could hear was his own pulse pounding in his temples. Cold pinpricks showered him in a wave from head to foot, followed immediately by an overall itching sensation.

Hatty rolled off him. He sat up and looked around. The shoppers and staff of Plumm's were milling about in slow motion. A handful of them were approaching what appeared to be a large skinned fish in the middle of the sales floor. Hammersmith, Hatty, and half of the hostile Mr Swann were on a small island in a spreading red expanse, which was oozing toward the base of the nearest jewelry counter. A pane of display glass, which had looked so heavy and formidable when up above them, was now strewn everywhere, broken into more manageable sizes, a few of the larger chunks stuck in the mannequin busts at odd angles. Mr Goodpenny was on his knees, holding Mr Swann's wrist as if checking for signs of life, but that was a foolish hope, and he might have been better off tending to his own arm, where an apple-size piece of glass had embedded itself. Across the room, Mr Oberon was descending the spiral staircase, a prince of some golden realm that moved at another speed. The air sparkled with glass dust that was slowly settling over everyone and everything below the gallery.

Hatty had saved his life by pushing him out of the way of the falling glass.

Hammersmith could see Oberon gesturing to the sales force to get the milling women and children away from the grisly sight of Mr Swann's bisected body. He could see Hatty shouting at him, asking him if he was hurt. He could feel the vibrations as small bits of glass continued to plunk down around him and on his clothing and in his hair. He could smell urine and blood.

But he couldn't properly hear anything. Everyone was mouthing words and there was a distant incoherent monotone as noises mashed together into a low groan, as if he were deep underwater.

He got to his feet and ran his fingers through his hair, wincing as a thousand bits of glass bit into his hands. Looking around him again, he could see that there was nothing he could do for anyone. The efficient staff had already ushered everyone who was unharmed away somewhere. He suspected they would be receiving free tea and cakes, at the very least. Aside from himself, the only people left on the floor were Mr Oberon, Mr Goodpenny, at least two sizable pieces of Mr Swann, and Hatty. He gestured for Hatty to turn around. She twirled, and he satisfied himself that she was unharmed.

Hatty pursed her lips and stepped forward. She reached up and touched Hammersmith's neck. He drew back, puzzled, but she shook her head and held up her hand, showing him. Her fingers were smeared with blood. He rubbed his palm across his ear and didn't like the amount of fluid he saw when he held his hand out to look at it. He wiped his hand on his trousers and pressed the cuff of his sleeve against the side of his head, hoping pressure would staunch the bleeding.

He pointed at his ears and shook his head. 'I CAN'T HEAR!'

She shrugged and nodded and pointed to her own ears. She couldn't hear, either. At least, when he leaned in to take a closer look, her ears weren't bleeding. He was afraid he'd punctured his eardrums and was glad to think that she hadn't.

He found her lack of reaction remarkable and reminded himself that she had seen her husband murdered in a similarly gruesome fashion. He took her elbow and helped her maneuver over the pool of Swann's blood, tiptoeing across some of the larger chunks of glass. He saw that many of the dresses and bolts of fabric on display had been ruined and he briefly wondered how much money the store had lost in that one clumsy, disastrous moment.

Then Mr Oberon arrived and waved Hatty on, guiding her past the wreckage. He handed her off to a matron, who took charge of the young woman, steering her away from the horror show. Another man had arrived and was tending to Mr Goodpenny's arm. Goodpenny shouted something at Hammersmith from across the room, but Hammersmith shook his head and pointed to his right ear, indicating again that he couldn't hear. Goodpenny smiled and nodded. He'd never been able to hear.

Hammersmith turned and caught the fading expression on Mr Oberon's face. It was immediately replaced by a comforting smile, but for one moment, Hammersmith might have sworn the other man's eyes were full of hatred and anger. He was struck again by how familiar the man seemed, but he couldn't place him. Oberon leaned forward and put his lips near Hammersmith's ear. His breath tickled and he smelled like metal and fish and old rope. Hammersmith heard nothing more than a cavernous rumble. Oberon pulled back and cocked his head, smiling in an expectant sort of way, one eyebrow arched. Hammersmith shrugged at him. Oberon seemed disappointed, but nodded. He took Hammersmith by the arm and led him away from the scene of the accident.

37

The coffeehouse opened before lunch, and Leland Carlyle was there early. He wasn't sure when the staff would show up to begin preparing, but the place was empty when he arrived, so he stationed himself behind a tree across the street from the front door. He was surprised by how boring it was to simply stand and wait for someone else and regretted that he hadn't brought a newspaper or book to look at.

Just after midmorning, a sour-looking old man unlocked the shop and went in. He propped the door open and drew the shutters. He disappeared somewhere inside and a moment later emerged again with a broom and a dustpan and began sweeping the path outside the shop. Within a few minutes, an old woman arrived and entered the shop without stopping or saying a word to the man. Carlyle could see her passing back and forth in front of the windows, donning an apron and laying cloths on the tables. The old man went back inside and carried his broom to the back of the shop, out of sight. Carlyle waited longer and soon saw the girl who had served him the previous day. She walked down the street, in no particular hurry, looking up at the tops of trees and clearly enjoying the feel of the sun on her face. Carlyle could identify with her. After the blizzard and the slush, the rain and the heavy fog, the sun was a welcome visitor. The girl's skirts dragged behind her on the ground, and he wondered how well the old man had swept, whether the girl was carrying cigarette butts and dog shit around in her hems.

He stepped out and hailed her, watching the door of the shop from the corner of his eye in case the old couple came back outside.

'Do you remember me?' The girl looked at him and frowned. 'No? I was here yesterday with a couple. You remember?'

'I'm sorry,' the girl said. 'Did you leave something behind?'

'No, no, nothing like that.' Carlyle hesitated. The girl actually didn't remember him. She hadn't listened to his conversation with the Parkers. 'I just . . .' He glanced over at the door of the shop. 'I had a wonderful time and wanted to know when you would be open today.'

Now the girl smiled, and he realized she'd been afraid he would proposition her. He felt a moment of deep embarrassment, but shook it off.

'We'll be open at half past the hour today,' she said. 'Mum and Dad should have the tables ready by now, though, if you'd like to come in early. I'm sure we could accommodate you.'

It was a family business. Suddenly Carlyle saw her as someone's little girl, and he thought of his own daughter and was ashamed of himself. 'Oh, no, no,' he said. 'I wouldn't want to impose. I'll come back later. I've been away from the office too long as it is.'

She looked confused, but smiled again at him and nodded. 'Any time. We're open seven days a week.'

'Here.' He took out his coin purse and handed her a

coin. 'For your good service yesterday.' And without waiting for her to respond, Carlyle trotted away down the street as fast as he could go.

'Oh, my,' Mr Parker said. 'What's he gone and done?'

'He's reminded her of himself, is what,' Mrs Parker said. 'And now she'll remember him forever. Maybe us, too.'

They were loitering round a stall at the far intersection, pretending to look through an assortment of paper fans. They'd had no intention of buying anything and were only using the vendor as a convenient place to conceal themselves, but Mrs Parker had found three fans that she liked, and the proprietor was trying to haggle with Mr Parker just at the moment he felt they ought to break away to discuss their plans. Mr Parker overpaid him and beckoned for Mrs Parker to come away before she found another fan she fancied.

'She's watching him as he goes,' Mrs Parker said.

'We did nothing remarkable yesterday. There was no reason to come back.'

'He thought he was going to cover his trace, didn't he?'

'Yes, my darling.'

'And instead he made himself stand out from the crowd.'

'That he did.'

'Amateur.'

'Well,' Mr Parker said. 'They're all amateurs, aren't they?'

'It's why they need us,' Mrs Parker said.

Mr Parker sighed. 'I suppose we'll have to do something about it.'

'Oh, let me. Do let me take care of it.'

'Discreetly.'

'Of course. I'm always discreet, dear heart. Aren't I?'

'Have you forgotten the Belgian ambassador, darling?'

'But that couldn't be helped. He was so enormously fat. And so loud. Like a squealing pig, he was.'

'We led the gendarmes on a merry chase that evening.'

'It was exciting, wasn't it?'

'But would not have been so exciting had we been caught.'

'That might have been dreary,' Mrs Parker said. 'But you know I would never have allowed us to be caught. Not alive, at any rate.'

How well he knew it. 'Yes,' Mr Parker said. 'You take care of this little mess the high judge of the Karstpha-nomen has created.'

Mrs Parker stood on tiptoe and gave him a kiss on the lips. He felt dizzy at her touch. She pressed her new fans against his chest, and when he took them from her she scampered away from him down the street.

The shopgirl looked up expectantly when Mrs Parker approached her, and Mr Parker caught the fan vendor's attention. He engaged the man in a discussion of his wares, and when he looked up both women had disappeared from sight down an alley next to the coffeehouse.

Day stopped abruptly when he reached the junction of Prince and Lothbury. People were streaming out of Plumm's, many of them shouting and waving their hands, trying to attract the attention of passersby. Several men were carrying unconscious women, trying to juggle the women and their hats, struggling toward the opposite curb.

Day held his cane down along the side of his leg and moved through the crowd to the front doors, where he was met by a stern man, his white-gloved hand held out.

'There has been a mishap, sir. Please come back on the morrow.'

'I need to get inside,' Day said.

'No one is to go inside at the moment. Please come back on the morrow.' Clearly he had been given a script.

'I'm an inspector with Scotland Yard. I've been sent to deal with the trouble.' Day had no idea what the trouble was, but he was certain Jack was at the centre of it and was equally certain that he was the only person capable of dealing with Jack.

The man with the white gloves looked him up and down and stuck his nose in the air. 'I have received no notice, sir, if you are indeed who you claim.'

'You doubt me?'

'I did not say that, sir.'

'You have a telephone on the premises?'

'Of course, sir. This is Plumm's.'

'Call the police commissioner, call Sir Edward Bradford at the Yard and tell him that you won't let me in. He'll put you on notice right enough.'

The guard coughed and looked down the street, gathering his thoughts and his dignity. 'Do you have a badge of some sort?'

'Inspectors don't carry badges. Only constables.'

'This is true?' The guard's expression changed. He was alarmed by the idea that there was something he didn't know.

'Of course. Why would I carry a badge? I'm not arresting anyone. I tell the constables who to arrest. They're the ones need the badges.' Day had been hiding deep inside himself for so long that there was no trace of emotion on his face, no way for the guard to tell if he was bluffing.

'Ah, of course. This makes perfect sense.' The guard stepped aside and waved Day through, but then followed him inside. 'It's . . .' The guard stopped with his mouth still open and waved his white gloves at the enormous ground floor space.

Day stopped, too. Peering over the first queue of low display counters, he could see a man lying on the ground. His eyes were open and one arm was thrown over his head, a white glove spotted with red reminding Day of his new companion. A step farther and the man's waist became visible, his intestines spread out over the floor, a pond of congealing effluvium keeping him afloat. Day turned away.

'It's a bit much, isn't it, sir?' The man with the white gloves (pure white, no blood) patted Day on the back. 'I suppose even you must be taken aback by a thing like this.'

'What's your name?'

'Gregory, sir.'

'Gregory, what happened here?'

Gregory glanced down for the first time at Day's cane. 'Don't policemen carry guns, sir?'

'Most do. I'm with the special branch.' He twisted the handle and drew the blade out far enough that Gregory could see it. 'The swordsmen. You've heard of us.'

'Oh, yes, sir,' Gregory said. 'Of course, sir.'

'What happened?'

'A most unfortunate accident. A windowpane that was being installed fell from up there.' Gregory pointed at the gallery. 'There was no time for him to move, sir. Or so I suppose.'

'Did you know him?'

'Mr Swann, sir. I will admit he was not well-liked, but I can't believe it was murder. If that's why you've come, I would have to say –'

'Who was up there at the time? Up there on the gallery when it happened?' Day squinted up at the milling people above. It looked as if someone had ushered everyone in the store out through the front doors or up the stairs, away from the blood. The problem with the latter choice was that women and children might glance down and see the whole grisly mess from above. He hoped the staff were keeping everyone distracted and looking the other way. 'I assume not all of those people were up there.'

'I was there, on the door.' Gregory pointed back behind them. 'I didn't see. The installation was a favorite of Mr

229

Hargreave. He ordered that glass last week, and it was very expensive. They wouldn't have risked having it jostled.'

'Hargreave, you say? Where is he now?'

'Oh, um, he's gone, sir. Got the sack, as it were.'

'But somebody's still putting it together. The installation.'

'Well, his replacement has that task, I suppose.'

'And who is that?'

'Mr Oberon, sir.'

Day squinted at him. 'You don't like Mr Oberon, do you?'

Gregory pulled away from him and looked down at his shoes. 'I didn't say that, did I?'

'And why don't you like Mr Oberon?'

'He's . . . Well, he makes me uncomfortable. I believe he hates me.'

'He hates you?'

'He has no reason, I assure you, but he wants to harm me. I see it in his eyes. When he smiles I . . . He's a cruel man, and I've seen my share of cruel men.'

'Why would he single you out?'

'Oh, he doesn't like anyone. The girls all see it in him, too. We stay well away from him. I have no idea how he won his position.'

Day nodded. 'Thank you, Gregory. Your candor is much appreciated by the Yard, and I'll see to it that you get some sort of commendation. You'd better tend the door now. We don't want any women seeing a thing like this.'

'Of course, sir. As you say.'

'And call more police. Get more men here right away.'

Gregory nodded and hurried away. There was a sense

of relief about him, as if he'd been lowered from a meat hook and set free.

Day realized too late that bringing more police would only complicate things for him. He needed to find Jack and deal with him before anyone could try to stop him. He took a step forward and saw the other half of the poor dead man. One shoe had come off and the leg of the man's trousers was split open at the seam, leaving his shin naked and unguarded. Day grimaced. Dignity was a fragile thing, and the dead were so often robbed of it.

He looked up again and two figures above caught his eye. They were moving rapidly across the gallery, one of them steering the other by the arm as they maneuvered through the crowds toward a back hallway.

Day felt his face flush and his stomach dropped. He pulled the sword free of the cane's shaft and ran forward. He slipped in Mr Swann's blood and caught himself, nicking himself with the sword in the process, but he ignored the sudden flash of pain in his arm.

'Nevil!'

The two men on the gallery did not stop moving, but one of them looked over the railing and saw Day. He smiled and gave a little wave with his free hand, then Jack and Hammersmith were lost from view behind a wide marble column. Why hadn't Hammersmith turned around?

'Nevil, stop! It's him!'

Day made it to the stairs and bounded up them. His weak leg took his weight and Day knew that he would suffer later for the exertion, but it was still bearing up for now and that was all he cared about. The stairs bounced beneath him, and he could see screws working loose at the juncture where the steps met the railing. All the people on the gallery must have rushed upstairs in a panicked knot.

At the landing he pushed his way through a mass of milling customers and white-gloved staff. It was early in the day and the store hadn't been very busy yet, but there were still at least five dozen people crowded at the top of the steps as if debating whether to try to skirt the body downstairs and leave. A woman was lying propped against one of the columns and another woman was gently shaking her, trying to wake her. A third woman was screaming, her hands trembling at her face. A man was wandering alone in a daze, blood spattered across his jacket. Everyone around the man was giving him a wide berth. Someone had taken a stack of blankets from a display shelf and was passing them out. Day had once been called to the scene of a traffic accident. Two omnibuses had crashed into each other, killing one team of horses and a driver. Although no one traveling inside had been killed, they had all looked like these people: numb and lost and somehow snapped free from the normal orbit of life around them.

Day did not stop to help anyone. He did not ponder the fact that yesterday his own name had been a mystery, but today he remembered that long-ago carriage wreck. He kept his pace, shoving people aside, ignoring the screams and cries around him. He had one objective and he kept himself focused on it.

Through a break between people he saw the top of Jack's head, dark wavy hair, unfashionably long, and he picked up the pace. Someone grabbed at his arm and he turned. A small round man smiled at him and held out a blanket. Day shook his head, but the man adopted a pity-ing expression and pressed the blanket against his chest.

'Your arm's bleeding, sir,' the man said. 'Let me look at it.' The man's own arm sported a thick bandage.

'I can't,' Day said.

'I represent the store, sir, and I can assure you we wouldn't –'

'I don't –'

'You needn't shout, sir. I can . . . Oh, my, I just realized I really can't hear you. You were speaking, weren't you?'

Day pushed past him and ran on. The top of Jack's head was still visible, and he launched himself through an opening between customers.

The world slowed down. He thought he could hear a tune playing in the background, a high-tempo melody that only served to charge him further. As he moved slowly forward he watched Jack turn, a grin on his face, that same wooden, unfeeling grin that charmed people who didn't know him. Jack brought his arm up at the same speed with which Day was moving and pushed up off his toes, and he was laughing as he hit Day full in the chest.

Day staggered backward into an installation. It was a globe bigger than a four-wheeler carriage, and when Day hit it the framework of the box around it buckled. He put his weight on it and kicked Jack in his wounded abdomen. The monster bellowed and fell to one knee. With a great wrenching sound, the globe tore loose from its perch and toppled to the floor. Day was pulled off balance and stum-bled backward. Time froze for one fleeting instant as the great spherc quivered, then slowly rolled away, picking up speed, people jumping out of its way as it moved. It slammed into the railing, and the loose screws of the balustrade gave way. Day followed it, windmilling his arms, unable to get his feet back under him. The wrought iron yielded under the pressure, sending a shock wave back along the metal frame to the stairs, which promptly removed themselves from the landing, bending the footing at the bottom. The entire piece of ironwork dragged itself out into the air, followed by the globe and then by Day's fragile body.

The last thing he saw as he plummeted toward the ground floor of Plumm's was a look of alarm on Jack's face. Day had never seen any sincere expression there before, never seen anything that wasn't meant to reflect malice or authority. The killer scrambled forward on his hands and knees, reached out, tried to catch Day as he fell.

But it was too late.

Day closed his eyes and surrendered himself to gravity. It was the first time in more than a year that he had felt at peace.

Mr Oberon dropped down and disappeared in the crush of people. There was a great deal of commotion, and Hammersmith was pushed back toward the wall. He couldn't see over the bobbing heads of frantic men around him. He couldn't hear anything except a low pulsing noise, and he felt confused, slightly panicked, missing one of the primary tools he used to navigate the world around him.

Someone grabbed him by the hand and pulled, and Hammersmith looked down to see Hatty Pitt. She was leading him through a break in the mob, and he gladly followed her. Her hand was warm and dry, and the pressure reassured him that he wasn't completely lost; he was tethered to this strong little person and he would not float away just yet.

She dragged him to the lift at the back of the gallery and let go of his hand. He could see her speaking to the operator, who cowered behind the gate. The operator gripped the curved bars and leaned down to hear Hatty better, and Hammersmith surmised that the gallery must be noisy. Hatty gestured, and the operator shook his head, shouted something at her. Hatty shouted back, gesticulating more wildly and pointing back toward where Hammersmith stood. Evidently she wanted to get on the lift and the operator wasn't obliging her. Hammersmith tried to look engaged and aware of what was going on, but he wasn't sure whether Hatty wanted him to appear friendly or authoritative. He settled on an expression he thought might convey some sort of stern kindness. It was the sort of look his father had often given him when he was a boy, and a look he had seen many times on Sir Edward's face.

The operator glanced in his direction and shrugged, pulled the gate open. Hatty grabbed Hammersmith again, hurried him onboard. The gate shut and the operator worked a lever next to a high stool, and Hammersmith felt his stomach lurch as the lift slowly descended toward the sales floor below. He looked out through the gate at the shins of Plumm's customers who were standing on the gallery, then at their feet, and then they were all gone and he was looking at a massive broadside that advertised C&J Clark beaded evening shoes for women. The advertisement featured a woman who seemed to be able to walk on clouds in her new shoes, and she was followed by a gentleman in laced-up black Clark boots and three children all queued like ducklings wearing patent leather Clark shoes. The image doubled and tripled as it slid past and he blinked to get it back in focus. He assumed the broadside's primary job, other than selling shoes, was to cover the joists and ductwork that might otherwise be visible as the lift moved up and down. He wondered if a third benefit of the happy family in the illustration was to make customers feel a bit more at ease as they moved through the air between floors. With the proper shoes they could walk on clouds, never mind the electric lift.

He checked his ear and saw no fresh blood on his

fingers, but the back of his hand was smeared with wide brown streaks that he couldn't wipe away. His blood had dyed his skin, and he thought again of his father, whose tanned brown hands had once laced his boots tight and mussed his hair. Hammersmith wondered what his father would have said about lifts and telephones and men who killed each other for sport. He could not remember his father's voice and he thought it was possible that he would never hear anything again. How long before he would no longer remember what anything sounded like, and how did his life always seem to circle back to death and injury?

There was a slight jolt as the lift thumped to the ground, and the operator leapt from his stool and pulled the gates open as a cloud of plaster dust and powdered stone rolled into the tiny chamber. Something registered in Hammersmith's peripheral vision, a shadow somewhere he didn't expect to see shadows. He put out an arm to hold Hatty back as she began to step out. An instant later, a man's body slammed into the floor in front of them and Hatty jumped, surprised.

The lift operator pushed past them and rolled the man over. A splintered bone protruded from the man's arm and the operator reached to touch it, perhaps to try to put the bone back where it belonged in the man's arm, but then pulled his hands back and looked up at Hammersmith, his face pale. Both men were wearing white gloves, the uniform of the Plumm's employee, and Hammersmith realized that the operator knew the injured man. Hammersmith knelt next to the body and felt for a pulse, then nodded to the operator and gave him a smile he hoped was encouraging. If they could get a doctor there soon, the man would live. Until then it was probably a good thing he had been knocked unconscious by the fall. The pain would be intense when he woke up.

Hammersmith looked out across the sales floor where twisted black metal was strewn over the hardwood and embedded in the bright glass counters. The staircase had wrapped itself round several displays, and a phalanx of wooden mannequins lay crushed beneath a marble column. The brilliant blue globe from the installation, bigger than Hammersmith's flat, rolled lazily to and fro over the ironwork and rubble, crushing wooden forms and demolishing crockery. As Hammersmith watched, it bounced over a segment of the iron stairs, bounced again and again and seemed to pick up energy before bursting out through the front of the store in a silent rain of glass. He watched it bump down off the kerb and gain a jolt of momentum before it disappeared from sight down the street.

He looked up and nudged Hatty, who followed his gaze to the gallery above, where a woman was being pushed dangerously close to the edge of the drop-off, no railing there to stop her or hold her weight.

'HEY!' Hammersmith knew he was shouting, but he couldn't judge how loud he was. A man looked round at the sound of his voice, reached out, and grabbed the woman before she could fall, pulling her to safety.

Satisfied that everyone above was reasonably safe for the moment, Hammersmith turned and lifted the unconscious man under his arms and pulled him away from the lift. It was still dangerous there, where anything might fall from above. The operator moved a length of railing to make space, and Hatty stacked bolts of fabric to make a temporary gurney. They laid the man there. As Hammersmith straightened back up, the room spun round him and he put out both arms to keep his balance.

Hatty tugged on Hammersmith's sleeve and pointed. He squinted and saw fingers, a sleeve, partially hidden behind an upended counter. Someone else had fallen or had perhaps still been on the ground floor when the railing came down. He climbed toward the prone figure, moving cabinets and rubble, throwing wood and iron to the side, making a path so that Hatty and the operator could follow.

There was a man lying atop a table on a wrecked display of wicker baskets and carriage blankets. The legs of the table had given out and it had collapsed, but the man moved as Hammersmith approached. As Hammersmith drew nearer, the man lifted a sword and waved it in the air, fending him off.

Hammersmith stopped and moved carefully round the fallen man so that he would be visible. He stumbled and grabbed the edge of an overturned cabinet until he felt steady enough to walk again. The man's torso came into view. As Hammersmith moved, he raised his hands and held them up, palms out at shoulder level. 'I MEAN YOU NO HARM!'

He had no way of knowing whether the man responded. He had to trust that he wouldn't be run through if he tried to help. He took another step and now he could see the man's face. The man lowered his sword and smiled.

Hammersmith stopped and stood for a long moment without moving, unaware that Hatty was calling to him or that policemen had begun to stream through Plumm's broken front doors. At last he rushed forward and dropped to one knee and scooped the battered form of Walter Day into his arms and held him tight so that he wouldn't disappear again.

After a moment, Hammersmith raised his head and shouted. 'IT'S HIM! HE'S HERE! WALTER'S OVER HERE!' He realized he was crushing his friend and he pulled away. Day's lips moved, and Hammersmith squinted, trying to read what he was saying. 'WHAT? I CAN'T HEAR!' Day spoke again, emphasizing his words carefully, and this time Hammersmith understood.

'It's good to see you, Nevil.' He closed his eyes and the sword dropped from his hand, clattering unheard to the floor.

BOOK THREE

The two carriages sat facing each other from a distance of perhaps twenty yards. The larger of them was hitched to a team of eight stick horses, all of them champing at the bit, dragging their blunt ends back and forth in the dirt. The smaller carriage, a two-seater, had a team of two rocking horses that moved to and fro, cutting parallel gashes in the path under the runners. The drivers sat up top. The Jack-in-the-box had thrown back his lid, and he swayed gently at the end of his spring and hurled insults at the other driver, who did not appear to notice him or react to his words. As for the other driver, Mary Annette's painted-on face was calm, her rosy cheeks were little red circles, and her smile a droll black bow. Her cross had been made to fit into the seat beside her so she did not need to carry it and could instead hold her lance out in front of the carriage in a straight line that pointed at Jack.

'Oh, I do not like this,' Anna exclaimed. 'I do not like this one bit. Oh, oh.'

'It is a hard world,' said the Kindly Nutcracker. 'And this is the way of it.'

'What do you think, Babushka?' asked Anna. 'Isn't there anything we might do to save poor Mary Annette?'

The Russian doll shook herself all over and split in half, as she so often did when she was thinking. Her shiny black hair tipped back and she rolled over and her inner self hopped out on to the path. This version of Babushka had hair that was painted yellow, and her lacquered violet dress was decorated all over with flowers and pretty

243

bulbs. 'Perhaps if we were to talk to Jack, he might take back what he said and they would be friends after all.'

Anna clapped her hands together. 'Oh, let's do!' she said. But then a terrible thought entered her mind and she frowned. 'Oh, but he never will listen. He is a scoundrel through and through.'

Babushka shook herself again, this smaller part of her that had spoken, and the top of her yellow head popped off. She rolled over again, and an even smaller version of her tumbled out at Anna's feet. This tiny, perfect replica of her outer shell was painted blue with angry red streaks slashing through her painted-on costume.

'No,' this miniature Babushka declared. 'Jack will never listen to anything that is right and good. We shall kill him and be done.'

'Oh, no, we mustn't kill anyone,' said Anna. 'That would make us every bit as evil as Jack is.'

While they were debating this point, Jack removed the wooden cigar from his mouth, which was cut into his face so that he appeared constantly to be grinning but with quite a malicious gleam daubed in his eye. He looked every bit the naughty little elf. He spoke very loudly so that everyone could hear. 'I am going to run you through with this lance, Mary Annette, and split the wood that you are made of into two pieces, and then I will do the same to any of your friends who would dare to take up your quarrel with me.'

Anna gasped, of course, for this was a truly awful thing to say to anybody, and especially to her dearest new friend in all the wood. She began to wonder if perhaps Jack was too evil to be allowed to live, after all.

'We should burn him,' the smallest Babushka said. 'No matter if he wins or loses, we should unstick him from his spring and break him into all his pieces and burn them all until he is gone and can cause no more trouble for anyone.'

Anna began to nod, but then she caught herself and reminded

herself that she was really a very good little girl and that good people did not break other people into parts and burn them, even if they said cruel things to others.

'If he wins,' said the Kindly Nutcracker, 'I will bite him very hard indeed. On the nose.'

'Yes,' Anna agreed. 'Perhaps he does deserve a good solid bite on the nose. But I do not think we shall burn him.'

'But what if he does split Mary Annette into two pieces as he has threatened to do?' asked the largest piece of Babushka. Anna thought it was quite odd that Babushka should be so concerned about it when she was accustomed to being split into pieces herself.

Anna thought very hard for a moment, and then she smiled. 'If Jack breaks Mary Annette into two pieces, why then, we shall glue her back together. And if he breaks her into twenty pieces, then we shall glue those back together just the same, and it will be as if she was never broken.'

'I do not have any glue,' the Kindly Nutcracker said. 'Do you?'

'No, I do not,' said Anna. 'But we are already on a quest to find Peter, and once we do find him, then we will have to embark upon yet another quest to find a pot of glue like the one that my father keeps in his workshop.'

'Why, then we will all be able to remain together for a while longer, and you will not go home to your family and leave us behind,' said the middle Babushka.

'I will never leave you behind, no matter what happens,' said Anna.

'Unless Mary Annette wins the joust,' the Kindly Nutcracker said. 'If she wins the joust, then Jack will fall off his carriage and break and we will not need any glue at all.'

'We will still need glue,' said Anna. 'If Jack should break into even a thousand pieces, we will find glue and we will put him all back *together in a different way so that he will be good and kind to every-one from this day until the last.'*

'That is a wonderful plan,' said the Kindly Nutcracker.

'Yes,' said the middle Babushka.

'I do not like that plan,' said the smallest Babushka.

But it was too late for Anna to argue with the angry little Babushka, for just then Jack cracked the reins of his carriage and said, 'Hah!' and the stick horses jumped forward, and at the same time the two rocking horses slid on their rockers, pulling Mary Annette's carriage forward, and the joust was under way.

— RUPERT WINTHROP, FROM
The Wandering Wood (1893)

40

The great department store that had tried to reinvent the very notion of shopping was no more. The windows had been broken out and displays removed by police in order to allow easier access, so that now Plumm's façade resembled a toothless skull glaring down the street at anyone who approached. The falling balustrade had rent huge gashes in the walls on either side of the ground floor and had pulled at least one support beam away, causing parts of the ceiling to cave in. The opulence and luster had been scraped away, revealing the poor naked bones of the place. Volunteers pitched in, along with the police and fire brigades, to help bring out the dead and injured. Many men worked well into the night, searching for anyone who might be trapped inside, and women bustled to and fro, bringing blankets, food, light and comfort to both the workers and the victims.

In the wee hours of the morning, a halt was called to the work. The doors were secured and the windows boarded up, leaving a solitary guard inside. When the last volunteer had trudged homeward, the dregs of the city crept out of the shadows and alleyways nearby. The new boards were pried from the broken windows and, ignoring the ineffectual guard, looters busied themselves clearing the store of anything that could be salvaged.

As the sun rose, the street was quiet again. Plumm's was little more than a dark blotch on the terrain, a stripped and empty husk with no dreams or promises left on offer.

41

The library of Guildhall on Aldermanbury was turned into a makeshift ward for the injured that had been carried out of the Plumm's wreckage. But the Print Room was reserved for two very special patients.

Nevil Hammersmith had succumbed to exhaustion and passed out after finding Walter Day. Immediately after waking up, he had taken a post at the foot of Day's gurney and had not moved since. He was watching Timothy Pinch at work, plastering the inspector's broken ribs, when Fiona Kingsley knocked softly on the double doors that connected the room to the library.

'How is he?'

'Sleeping peacefully,' Hammersmith said. He stood aside so she could see Day.

'Oh, hullo, Miss Kingsley.' Pinch perked up and smoothed his hair, accidentally rubbing plaster into his scalp.

'Mr Pinch. Please go on with what you were doing. I only wanted to check in on Mr Day.'

'Oh, I'm getting him fixed up proper, no worries on that front.'

'Yes, I'm sure you are. And, Nevil, how are your ears?'

'Your father looked me over just a bit ago. He says I've ruptured my eardrum.'

'Oh, my. Oh, Nevil, can't you stay out of trouble?'

Hammersmith ducked his head and grinned. 'It doesn't seem so.'

'Oh, he'll be fine,' Pinch said. 'His ear will heal itself, given time.'

Fiona nodded, but didn't even look at the young doctor.

'I can hear out of my other ear,' Hammersmith said. 'And the ringing's stopped now. So it's not all bad.'

'It's nothing,' Pinch said. 'Doesn't even require treatment.'

'That's good,' Fiona said.

'I hope you've notified Mrs Day.'

'There was a great deal of confusion,' Fiona said. 'So many people were injured and my father had me running round like a madwoman organizing the Hall. I meant to send somebody to fetch Claire, but I simply lost track of time and nobody else thought to send for her. When I realized, I had a boy sent right away with the message, but I'm afraid she's going to be cross. I feel awful about it.'

'We could tell her we only found him this morning,' Hammersmith said.

Fiona smiled and brushed a stray hair out of her face. 'You'd do that for me?'

'No, I'm sorry,' Hammersmith said. 'Much as I'd hate Mrs Day to think we never considered her, I don't think I could lie.'

'Of course.' Fiona's smile disappeared and she nodded. 'Good old Nevil. Well, I suppose I should go and wait for her. She'll want to know where we're keeping Mr Day.'

'I'll walk you out,' Pinch said. 'Give me a minute to

rinse my hands.' The plaster was drying in his hair, sticking it straight up at odd angles.

'Please don't bother,' Fiona said. 'I'm fine on my own.' She glanced at Hammersmith as she said it.

'Perhaps you should finish with Walter,' Hammersmith said.

'No, no, this will wait a bit,' Pinch said. 'He's not in any pain while he's asleep, now is he? Miss Kingsley, do wait for me. I wanted to ask you something.'

'Oh, no, Mr Pinch.'

'No?'

'I mean to say there's so much going on right now, I don't think I could possibly answer any questions.'

'Ah.' Pinch looked round the room and ran his fingers through his hair again. 'Yes, well, I seem to be running out of linens in here. Be right back.' He made a faint squeaking sound, as if someone had stepped on his toes, and hurried out of the room.

'What was that all about? There's plenty of linens in here,' Hammersmith said.

'Oh, Nevil,' Fiona said. 'Why don't *you* ever ask me anything?'

'I just did. I asked you what was wrong with Pinch.'

'But you never ask me anything meaningful.'

'That's meaningful enough, isn't it?'

'Nevil Hammersmith, it would serve you right if I married Timothy Pinch.' Fiona spun on her heel and marched out of the room.

Hammersmith took a deep breath and frowned at the door, wondering if she planned to return and explain herself. When she didn't, he sat back down at the foot of the bed. He didn't understand what he had to do with Fiona and Pinch, but if she wanted to marry the young doctor, Nevil didn't intend to get in the way.

He thought he ought to be happy that she had found someone, but something about it all sat strangely in his stomach. He wasn't accustomed to thinking about romantic matters; they made him uncomfortable. It occurred to him that he might be lonely and he thought he might ask Fiona about that, if she was so determined that he should ask her things.

He had just made up his mind to follow her and demand an explanation when Walter Day opened his eyes. Hammersmith immediately put all thoughts of Fiona Kingsley out of his head and breathed a sigh of relief.

The things Walter Day talked about usually made some sense.

42

Dr Kingsley saw his daughter rush from the Print Room, her hair flying, her hands covering her face, and he was reminded of the girl she'd once been, running through the grass, her skirts flitting about her ankles. Nostalgia for those simpler times threatened to cloud his mind, but he snorted and brushed it away. The past hadn't really been any easier, and while Fiona was indeed more complex now, at her core she was the same sweet child she had always been.

'Nurse, take over for me here,' Kingsley said.

He didn't wait for a response, just trotted after his daughter. She was in the parlor, sitting with her back to the library. He hesitated at the threshold, wondering whether he ought to interfere, wondering how she had turned from that little girl to this beautiful woman on her own. Should someone have asked him if he was ready for that? Just as he was about to turn back, she looked up and gave him a teary smile.

'I'm sorry,' she said. She seemed about to say something else, but then shook her head and buried her face once more in her hands.

Kingsley patted his pockets until he found his handkerchief. He checked it for blood before handing it over to her. She didn't look up as she took it.

'I'm such a . . .' But her voice broke and she couldn't finish.

Kingsley pulled a chair over and sat next to her. He reached out and put his hand on the arm of her chair, there if she needed him, but not ready to intrude. He sensed that he ought to stay there, but he didn't know what he was supposed to do, so he settled on being a presence.

Fiona wiped her eyes with his handkerchief and blew her nose. She put a hand on his, and he was glad he'd stayed.

'I'm a fool, father. All this time.'

He had some idea of what she meant. 'You're not a fool. You're a good person. And so is he. Perhaps it simply wasn't meant to be.'

'Then there is no one else. I shall be a spinster.'

He couldn't help it. He smiled, and she turned away from him again.

'Oh, I know you think I'm a silly little girl.'

'I've never in your life thought you were silly. You have taught me as much as I have taught you. And I'm not at all the person you need when there are matters of the heart to discuss. I have only felt romantic love for one person in my life.'

'You never talk like anyone else does, even at a time like this.'

'I talk like I talk.'

'Of course you do. I'm sorry. I'm just all . . .' She broke off and waved her hands in the air, but one hand fluttered back down to rest on his again.

'You have no idea how proud I am of you,' he said. But he saw that she was about to start crying again, so he felt he ought to change the subject. 'You know, young Pinch seems to be quite fond of you.' He knew right away that it was the wrong thing to say.

She took her hand back.

'Damnit,' he said. 'I don't know what's so appealing about Hammersmith. He's a decent fellow, but he's so focused on his work that he doesn't even notice anything else.'

Fiona took the handkerchief away from her face and looked up at him, her eyes rimmed red and her nose moist, but a smile playing across her lips. 'You think Nevil is too focused on his work? You?'

'Ah, yes. I am perhaps not the right person to point out that flaw, am I?'

'Father, I didn't mean . . .' She looked away again.

'No, no, you're right. Maybe that's why the boy's so appealing. It's what you grew up with. You think it's normal.'

'I don't know what's normal, and I don't care what's normal.'

'He's what you want?'

'I don't want to want him. Or anyone else.'

'Fiona, look at me. Have you told him how you feel?'

'Of course not.'

'Well, then all of this is for nothing. How can he know if you don't tell him?'

'I've practically thrown myself in his path. I'm sorry, Father, but I have.'

'You were a child when he met you.'

'I'm not a child now.'

Kingsley smiled a sad sort of smile and looked carefully at the laces of his shoes.

'I know you still see me as a child, Father, but I'm truly not. At least three of the girls I went to school with are married already. I'm practically a spinster. I really am a grown woman.'

'Then make him see that. If he's worth all this, then do something about it. You can't simply bat your eyes and hope for the best. Go after what you want, Fiona, because life is too short to do otherwise. Before you know it, you'll be old and you'll have no idea where it all went.'

'You're not old.'

'What makes you think I was talking about myself?'

She laughed and he smiled. He took the handkerchief from her and wiped her eyes and dabbed at her nose.

'Now come on. I need help out there, and as we've established, Mr Pinch is woefully inadequate.'

'Oh, Father!'

But she stood and took his arm, and together they walked back to the library. He felt the slightest bit bad for Nevil Hammersmith. The boy apparently had no idea what was going on, and if he wasn't careful he was going to lose the best person he would ever have the opportunity to meet.

43

When Day awoke, the first thing he saw was Nevil Hammersmith sitting dutifully at the foot of the bed like an old Labrador. Hammersmith jumped up and grabbed the inspector's hand. He seemed incapable of speech, and Day smiled.

'How long was I asleep?'

'All night. I was beginning to worry you'd never wake up.'

'Where am I? The hospital?'

'Guildhall.'

'Oh,' Day said. 'Posh.'

'Indeed,' Hammersmith said. 'Nothing but the best. Let me get the doctor. He was just here.'

'No need. I'm fine.'

'Well, he'll want to see you. And not to worry, Claire knows and she's on her way here. We all want to hear everything that's happened with you.'

'Oh, is it Kingsley? The doctor, I mean.'

'His assistant was plastering your ribs. But of course Kingsley's here. He's tending some of the others who were hurt, but now you're awake I imagine he'll take over your treatment himself.'

'Hold off, would you, Nevil? Don't fetch anyone just yet. In fact . . .' Day struggled to sit up. 'Keep everyone out. Do those doors lock?'

'I don't . . . Well, let me . . .' Nevil hurried to the double doors that connected the room to the library beyond it, but they opened outward and there was no way to barricade them properly. He shook his head and returned to the side of the bed.

'Where's my cane?'

'On the chair over there,' Hammersmith said. 'You drew the sword on me, you know.'

'But I didn't kill you, which is not only a huge relief, but it means I can trust myself around you. I don't know that I could guarantee the same about anyone else at the moment.'

'What's going on? What's wrong?'

'To be honest, I don't know,' Day said. 'Not entirely. You must think I'm mad.'

'Yes, of course I do. A complete nutter.'

Day broke into laughter. He couldn't help himself. After all he'd been through, the constant stress and anxiety, it was good to know he could depend on Nevil Hammersmith to be utterly honest. Pain lanced through his torso, and he clutched his stomach.

'You're not supposed to move,' Hammersmith said. 'Doctor's orders. You're busted up a bit inside from the fall.'

'How bad?'

'Fractured ribs.'

'Lucky I'm not dead.' Day gritted his teeth and took a shallow breath.

'I think what happened when you fell, you hit a table and the table collapsed under you. Could be worse, though. One chap out there . . .' He nodded in the direction of the library. 'He's got to have his arm off.' He made a sawing motion with his hand.

Day waited until he had caught his breath and waved Hammersmith closer to him so they could speak quietly. 'All right,' he said, 'so maybe I am mad. Who wouldn't be? I barely remember anything of the past year, but it's coming back to me in bits and pieces, and more and more with every passing minute. I remember snatches of conversations I had with that creature, things that he told me.'

'Jack, you mean?'

'Yes. Jack.'

'So you've been with him this whole time, while everyone's been tearing their hair out searching for you?'

'Not the whole time. But, yes, most of it.'

'How have you survived?'

'Because of something I think he wants me to do. It's why you've got to keep everyone away. And, Nevil, it's why you've got to help me get out of here right away.'

'I don't understand.'

'Jack wants me to kill someone close to me.'

44

Leland Carlyle retreated to his club. Not the secret society, not the underground chambers of the Karstphanomen, but rather the gentlemen's club he frequented while in the city. There he could rest and think, free from the concerns of family and business. He had nearly killed someone that morning, had gone to a coffeehouse specifically to murder a young woman, and the fact that he might even entertain such a notion shook him to his core.

He handed over his hat and coat and retired to the public room, where he took a seat by the fire. He sank into a wide leather chair, ordered a Scotch and soda, and closed his eyes, enjoying the feel of quiet privilege that he no longer felt he deserved.

He had always been able to rationalize the activities of the Karstphanomen. Murder was not the order of the day for that group of men. They championed justice. They taught murderers a valuable lesson about the cost of a human life. But today Carlyle had reduced himself to acting like a common killer.

He wondered when he had lost track of the line that separated the civilized man from the predator. And he wondered when he had crossed that line.

More, he had hired mercenaries to act on behalf of the Karstphanomen. But he had done so at the bidding of the members, and so he didn't feel personally responsible for that miscalculation. He realized they had done it from fear, from a sense of self-preservation. But he understood now that the Karstphanomen could not be personally responsible for murder or they were no better than the men they judged. What they had done flew in the face of everything they professed to believe in, everything they had set themselves against.

They had invited judgment upon themselves.

'Sir?'

Carlyle opened his eyes, a smile at the ready, thinking his drink had arrived. But the valet, Potter-Pirbright, was standing at the side of his chair with a look of concern draped over his normally receptive features. He was holding Carlyle's hat and coat.

'What is it?'

'Your guests are causing a minor sensation, if you don't mind my saying. It might be best to ask them to move along. Or perhaps the gentleman has an errand elsewhere.'

'I believe you're mistaken,' Carlyle said. 'I have no guests.'

'My apologies, sir.'

'No need. A mistake, that's all.'

'Indeed.' But Potter-Pirbright didn't move from the side of the chair.

'Was there something else?'

'They arrived at your heels, sir, and have not stirred from the front of this establishment since you entered.'

'I told you, they're nothing to do with me.'

'As you say.'

'Then what is it, man?'

'They are disturbing some of the others, sir. In particular, the young lady wearing trousers has caused a bit of a stir with some of the older gentlemen of the club. Those of us in the younger generation are more open-minded, I'm sure.' (Potter-Pirbright was eighty years old if he was a day.) 'If she would stop leering at everyone who enters, perhaps her presence would be more easily overlooked.'

'But I tell you, they're not – Did you say the woman was wearing trousers?'

'Indeed, sir. And fetching trousers they are.'

Carlyle knew of only one woman who wore trousers in public. And if she had followed him here, to his club, perhaps she had followed him elsewhere. Carlyle stood, and Potter-Pirbright helped him on with his coat. He took his hat and, without a word to the valet, left the public room and went out by the front door. He paused and looked back at the club, the heavy oak doors and the marble columns of the porte cochere. He knew he would not be welcomed back.

He turned and looked up and down the street, but the Parkers were nowhere to be seen. He raised his hand and hailed a two-wheeler, hopping in as soon as it rolled to a stop. He gave the driver Claire's address and settled back into the seat. He thought longingly of his Scotch and soda, which had surely been prepared already. What would they do with it? He snorted, a sad, abrupt sort of chuckle. The valet would probably drink it, congratulating himself all the while for having disgraced Carlyle. That sort was always looking for an opportunity at the expense of their betters.

If Mr and Mrs Parker had followed him to his club and seen him inside, perhaps they had turned their attention elsewhere. He had, after all, set them an impossible task.

He had asked them to find and kill Jack the Ripper. Who would blithely undertake such a thing? Unless they had planned all along to do away with Carlyle himself and keep that portion of their fee they had already collected. It made perfect sense.

If they had followed him to his club, perhaps they had followed him to his daughter's home. Perhaps they thought she knew something or was an accomplice. He knew he wasn't thinking straight, but he thought perhaps that was a good thing. It showed he wasn't like them. He was a caring human being, a man who had stopped himself from committing violence. A good man.

Leland's wife, Eleanor, was surrounded by servants at all times (and no doubt making them miserable), so he wasn't unduly concerned about her.

But he needed to look in on his daughter before he could think any further. It occurred to him that the Parkers had purposefully drawn him out of his club for some reason, but he didn't care. If Claire was all right, then he hadn't completely ruined his life yet. She was the best of him, and they couldn't take her away. He wouldn't let them.

45

Claire Day ran through Guildhall to the library and spotted Fiona Kingsley talking to her father. Sunlight through the high windows illuminated a ghastly scene, with a dozen or more men and women on gurneys and a handful of doctors and nurses flitting about among them, bringing towels and water and instruments to their bedsides.

'Fiona! Dr Kingsley!' Claire bustled up to them, and the doctor set down a bone saw, wiped his hands on a rag tucked into his belt.

'Claire,' he said. 'Really, you shouldn't be in here. This isn't something you ought to –'

'Where is my husband? Where's Walter?'

'Ah, of course. He's in the other room. But he's sleeping right now.'

'I don't care. Which room?'

'Father,' Fiona said, 'you can't keep her away from him after so long.' Fiona's eyes looked red.

'Yes, yes, I see. If you can be quiet and let him sleep, I'll show you in.'

'I'll wake him if I damn well want to wake him.'

Kingsley's eyebrows flew up, but he sighed and motioned for her to follow him. He led the way to the huge doors of the Print Room, and Claire averted her eyes as she passed a man who was lucky to have passed out.

She looked away too late to avoid seeing the bones of his arm protruding from the flesh.

Kingsley pulled open a door and stuck his head in the room, then rushed inside. Claire and Fiona followed him. The room was empty.

'Where is he?'

'I don't know,' Kingsley said. He turned around and shouted. 'Pinch! Get in here!' To Claire he said, 'Young Pinch was treating your husband.'

Kingsley didn't wait for his assistant. He went to the doors at the other end of the room and through them, down a short passage to the art gallery. It, too, was empty, but a window at the far end of the room was standing open, a slight breeze blowing the curtains.

'He's gone,' Kingsley said.

'And Nevil's gone with him,' Fiona said.

Pinch trotted up behind them. 'Well, he won't get far with those ribs,' he said.

'You don't know my husband,' Claire said. 'And perhaps I don't, either.'

46

'Slow down, Nevil, would you?'

Hammersmith stopped and waited for Day to catch up to him. 'I'm sorry. I wasn't thinking. Your leg?'

'No . . . Not at all . . . It's only . . .' Day shook his head and held up a finger, asking for a minute. He leaned on his cane, and when he'd caught his breath he started again. 'It's hard to breathe with this plaster on.'

'We're well away from Guildhall now,' Hammersmith said. 'But where are we going?'

'I need to check on someone at Drapers' Gardens. Just need to make sure she's all right.'

'You mean Esther Paxton.'

'How did you know?'

'She's back there in the library with the Plumm's casualties. We've left her behind.'

Day turned and put a hand on his chest. 'She was there?'

Hammersmith nodded.

'Is she well?'

'Not bad. The doctor moved her there so he could keep an eye on her injuries while he tended the others, but none of us knows who she is. I mean to say, who is she to you?'

'Until yesterday I thought she might represent a new life for me.'

'A new life? Is that where you've been the last year?

266

Taking up with some woman while the rest of us were worried sick about you?'

'It's not . . . Here, let's get off the beaten track so we can talk.' Day hobbled down Mason's Alley and ducked into the doorway of a restaurant. Hammersmith followed, and they stood out of sight of the main thoroughfare.

'Well?'

'Nevil, it's not what you think. I was held prisoner for months. By the time he let me go, I thought maybe everyone had moved on without me.'

'You fool.'

'Yes, well, I am that. But Nevil, I couldn't go back to my life as I knew it. And at first I didn't even know my life. I didn't remember who I was. It's come back to me gradually, and more yesterday than ever before. But I can't trust myself near anyone but you. And it's because I didn't try to kill you already, don't you see? Esther wasn't a part of my old life, and so I could be with her. At least, I thought I could. Only it didn't work that way. He wouldn't let me be.'

'None of that makes even the slightest bit of sense, you know.'

'Oh, I know.'

'Why don't you try telling me again.'

'Let's keep walking,' Day said. 'But slowly. I'll talk along the way.'

They walked east toward Drapers' Gardens while Day filled Hammersmith in on everything that had happened to him in the past few weeks. When they reached the gardens, Day pointed out the shrubbery where he had slept during his first few days of freedom. A minute or two later, they arrived at Esther Paxton's shop and Day dug out his key. He opened the door and Hammersmith followed him in. The furniture had been righted since Day had last seen the place and the broken glass swept up.

'The neighbors must have pitched in,' he said.

'Neighbors?'

'This was practically demolished.'

'It still doesn't look like much.'

'I have a room upstairs. She was very good to me. Here, sit down – watch there's no glass there – and I'll tell you the rest. Tea?'

'Please. Unless you plan to poison me.'

'Why would I do that?'

'I have no idea. You're acting odd. Talking about killing people.'

'If I were planning to kill you, I certainly wouldn't use poison. In the past you've proved immune to the stuff.'

'Immune or not, I don't much care for it.'

'Fine. I won't poison you. Give me a minute.'

Day climbed the stairs and Hammersmith went to the window. He watched people passing by, children running to join their friends, women paying social calls on one another or heading out for the day's shopping trip. The beat constable hove into view down the street, and Hammersmith glanced at the stairs before slipping out the front door. He left the door open and raised his hand, hailing the constable, who strolled over to him.

'Help you?'

'I'm hoping you can do something for me. Is there a telephone nearby?'

'Got my call box next street over.'

'Is there any chance you'd be willing to ring Guildhall?'

"'Fraid it's meant for official police business, sir. If you're looking for a telephone for yourself, I can direct you to –'

'No time. I need a doctor here right away.'

The constable perked up and turned his gaze on the open front door of Paxton's Drapery. 'Someone hurt? Not that same woman got roughed up yesterday?'

'No, no, nothing like that.' Hammersmith stopped and scowled at the constable for a moment, trying to figure out how to explain that his friend had become a raving madman, without seeming to be disrespectful of Day or raising any alarms. At last he reached into his pocket and pulled out a half crown, which he held up so that the constable could see it. 'Just this once, maybe you could break the rules?'

The constable nodded slowly, then reached out and took the money. 'Guildhall, you say?'

'Yes.' Hammersmith breathed a sigh of relief that he'd run into a reasonably corrupt policeman. 'The doctor's name is Kingsley. Give him this address and tell him to drop everything and get right over here. It's about Day.'

'Today?'

'No. Inspector Day.'

'Inspector Day? Has he been found?'

'Oh, um, well, yes, actually he has. But he needs help.'

The constable handed the half crown back to Hammersmith. 'You keep this, then. Day was always good to me. Keep your eye on him and I'll fetch that doctor.'

With that, the constable turned and hurried away. Hammersmith put his half crown back in his pocket and went back inside, quietly shutting the door. He crossed to the sofa and sat, and in another minute Day reappeared, holding two teacups by their handles in one hand.

'Here we are,' he said. 'Were you outside just now?'

'Took the air a bit.'

'Hmm. It is stuffy. Here, I don't seem to have any milk.'

'It's all right. Just fine as is.'

'Good. I put an extra dollop of poison in yours, though, so don't take the wrong cup.'

'Right.' Hammersmith managed a wan smile and took the offered cup. He stared at it dubiously, then blew across the steaming surface and took a sip. 'Funny,' he said. 'I hardly taste it.'

47

Hatty was feeling a great deal of pressure. Now that Inspector Day had been found, she took it for granted that Mr Hammersmith would finally assume the proper duties of a detective and would begin to investigate other cases. Which was all well and good, but Hatty was afraid it would mean the end of her freedom. Would Hammersmith allow her to keep investigating cases on her own? More likely, she would be relegated to a clerk's position at the agency, and she didn't think she could bear that.

She had helped move Mr Day and some of the other victims of the Plumm's collapse to the hall and had seen to their comfort as well as she was able, but as soon as she'd had the opportunity she'd slipped away. Even if she never got a chance to investigate another case, she wanted to finish the one she'd started, she wanted to find Joseph Hargreave and prove, if only to herself, that she was capable of the work.

Success begat success. Perhaps Mr Hammersmith would see how good she was and allow her to help in some manner more substantial than just taking notes and filing paperwork. He was a good man, Mr Hammersmith, and she clung to the hope that he might be a progressive employer. But she couldn't prove herself unless she solved the case. She had to move quickly.

The three obvious places for Hargreave to be hiding were his cottage, his place of employment, and his flat in the city. She had ticked those off in the past few days, but there was one more place to check before she hit a dead end. Plumm's kept small apartments behind the store for certain employees, in order to keep their commute short and keep them on the job longer each day. One had been reserved for the floor manager's use. It seemed to her that it would be hard to hide for very long in a flat behind a department store, but she was desperate and therefore willing to turn over any rock available to her.

The street in front of Plumm's was quiet, people passing by and stopping to stare at the magnificent wreckage. But nobody was going in or coming out. The injured had been moved, and the staff had been dismissed. The police had secured the main doors, but windows had been broken out at the front and sides of the building, and no attempt had been made to board them up again. There was nothing left worth stealing. Tomorrow workers would come and begin tearing everything out, hauling away the rubble. Hatty wondered if they would rebuild or give up and sell the lot. Would anybody still be willing to shop there, knowing what had happened?

She skirted the main building and went around to Coleman Street, where there was a door set into a recess. She knocked on it, and when there was no answer, she knocked harder so that her knuckles tingled. She heard no sound from within. She looked all round, then tried the knob. To her surprise, the door was unlocked, and she opened it and went inside.

She was facing a long passage with doors on either side and a staircase that led up the right-hand wall. All was quiet. The staff had been temporarily relocated. She walked to the first door and opened it without knocking. The small room was furnished with a table, a chair, a bed and a lamp. All of it looked cheap to Hatty; none of it looked like the sorts of things that were actually sold by Plumm's. The table held a small collection of toiletries and cosmetics, and there was a cardboard wardrobe standing in the corner next to the bed. Inside hung three identical white blouses and three identical black skirts. She left that room and went to the next, where she found similar furnishings and similar clothing hanging in another cardboard wardrobe. Hatty decided that the female staff of the store must be housed on the ground floor, and she went back to the staircase and climbed up.

There was a locked door at the landing of the first floor up, so she kept going. When she reached the next floor, she paused and listened, glad that her loss of hearing had been temporary. She wondered what she would do if she found Joseph Hargreave and he was dead. She had seen dead bodies before, but she didn't care to see another one if she could help it.

The door at the far end of the hallway swung slowly open, an invitation, and her breath caught in her throat.

'Hello? Is someone there?'

Hatty heard nothing but the return echo of her own voice, and so she crept forward until she was just outside the room. There was no light inside and no one emerged into the passage.

'Mr Hargreave?'

'Please come in.' The voice was soft and low with a pleasant rumbling quality. 'Forgive me for not standing. I'm a bit indisposed.'

'Mr Hargreave, is that you?'

'No, indeed,' the man inside the room said. 'But come in. I'd like to talk with you. You may leave the door open behind you if that puts you at ease.'

'No need. If you aren't Mr Hargreave, I'll be on my way.' She turned to go, but the voice called out to her again.

'Which one are you? I'm afraid I get you all mixed up, one with the others.'

'What do you mean?' Hatty did not turn toward the door, but nor did she continue down the hallway. She stood, tense and ready to run, with her back to the dark room.

'I know you're not Eugenia Merrilow. She's quite distinct in my mind. You're either Fiona Kingsley or Hatty Pitt. You two are rather similar to each other, if you don't mind my saying, and I haven't bothered to pinpoint which of you is which.'

Now Hatty turned and faced the man she couldn't see. He was somewhere far back in the room, and she felt confident she had enough of a head start if he came after her. 'How do you know us?'

'Oh, our friend Nevil Hammersmith likes to surround himself with pretty little females of the species, doesn't he?'

'I don't know.'

'Why do you think that is?'

'I don't know.'

'You don't know much. You might at least venture a guess. I'm going to do just that and guess that you are Hatty Pitt. Ah, by the change in your posture I see that I'm right. Very good to meet you, Hatty Pitt. Please, don't be so rude. Come here where I can see you better. You're silhouetted in the light and I can only see your form.'

'I think I'm fine where I am.'

'Shall I sweeten the pot for you, then?' Hatty heard the creaking wood of a chair as someone shifted his weight and then a muffled cry of pain. 'Did you hear that, Hatty Pitt? That was Joseph Hargreave. Just the man you wanted to see.'

'Mr Hargreave?'

'Oh, he can't answer you. Cat's got his tongue. Or something's got it, but he certainly hasn't.'

Hatty felt a creeping warmth along her scalp and her throat. She knew where Mr Hargreave's tongue was.

'Did you know Joseph Hargreave and his brother were members of a secret society that tortures people like me?'

'Of course not.'

'It's true. I can tell you, this is a man who needed his tongue out, and more besides.'

'That's horrid.'

'Hatty Pitt, you and I have something in common, did you know that?'

'What have you done to Mr Hargreave?'

'I asked you a question. You can't answer with a totally unrelated question of your own. That's not playing by the rules of proper conversation, now is it?'

She raised her voice, calling out to the other man in the room. 'I'm going to bring the police, Mr Hargreave. Please just wait a few minutes and I'll be right back.'

'Tut, tut, Hatty Pitt. If you leave here before we finish our conversation, I will kill Mr Hargreave outright long before you return with the constabulary.'

'What do you want from me?'

'An answer, to start. Do you know what we have in common?'

'No.'

'We have both saved Nevil Hammersmith's life at different times. Isn't that interesting? I stopped his bleeding to death once when there was no one else to do it.'

'Why would you do that? You seem ghastly.'

'Hurtful of you to say. I did it because I had no reason not to. I didn't wish Nevil Hammersmith any harm at the time. Of course I changed my mind some time later and tried to drop a great gob of glass on him, but you saved him from that. According to Oriental custom, we now share an obligation to Nevil Hammersmith's well-being.'

'You're Mr Oberon, aren't you?'

'It's what I've been calling myself.'

'You took Mr Hargreave's place.'

'Hatty Pitt, I have spent the past weeks pretending to be someone I am not while occupying this shithole of a flat and that stupid wee cottage by the sea with only this dolt for company. He's a terrible conversationalist, owing in part to the fact of his missing tongue. But he wasn't of much use even before he lost that. If it isn't too much to ask, I'd like to have a civil chat with a nice young lady.'

'"Come into my parlor, said the spider to the fly."'

'Did you call me a spider, Hatty Pitt? Are you afraid of spiders? No need to be. Spiders rid the world of filthy vermin. Do you think you're filthy vermin? Is that why you're afraid to converse with me? And would you place Mr Hargreave in mortal danger simply because you're afraid? You seem like a brave girl to me. You wouldn't do that to Mr Hargreave.'

'You'd kill us both anyway as soon as you got your hands on me.'

'Hmm. You know, you're probably right.'

Hatty gasped and took a step backward, but something in her refused to let her leave. The man inside the room was clearly some sort of monster. But she did not want to be cowed by anyone, not man or woman or the Devil himself. 'I'm not afraid of you.'

'Well, perhaps you should be, after all. I sometimes have the best of intentions, but then my nature gets the better of me anyway. I'll tell you what: I promise not to touch you once you are inside this room. To be quite honest, I could use some assistance. But if you back away any farther, I shall rush at you no matter what the cost to myself, and then I will touch you a great many times and in ways I do not think you will appreciate.'

'You may threaten me all you like, but there are people who know where I am. I told Eugenia where I was going.'

'Are you lying to me, Hatty Pitt?'

'No. No, I'm not lying to you.'

'I believe you. So you see, you're doubly safe. You have Eugenia Merrilow's knowledge of your whereabouts and you have my word that I will not touch you.'

'Your word isn't worth anything to me.'

'Oh, but it should be worth something at least,' Mr Oberon said. 'I almost never break my word.'

'You won't hurt me?'

'I said I wouldn't touch you and I won't.'

'And you won't hurt Mr Hargreave, either?'

'Oh, I've said no such thing. I've harmed your Mr Hargreave on a near constant basis these past weeks, both here in his flat and at his cottage. It was the only thing to keep me occupied, really. I've been so very bored.'

'You won't harm him any more than you already have, then?'

'Oh, I'd hate to promise you a thing like that.'

'You must or our conversation has ended.'

Mr Oberon laughed and she heard the clapping of hands. 'Delightful. So very brave. Yes, Hatty Pitt. Come and sit with me and I promise I shall leave Mr Hargreave alone for the time being.'

Hatty considered for a moment, then breathed deeply and stepped across the threshold into the room.

'Wonderful,' Mr Oberon said. 'Now please, call me Jack.'

48

'He thinks he's mad,' Hammersmith said.

'He might very well be mad,' Dr Kingsley said. 'Who knows what he's been through this past year? Has he told you much?'

'Very little. When we were talking he focused more on the past month than the past year. I don't think he remembers a lot of what happened to him.'

'Strange. Amnesia is quite rare. I wonder if he's suffered some sort of head trauma.'

'There's one way to find out.'

'Yes, of course,' Dr Kingsley said. 'Let's have a look at him.'

Hammersmith opened the door of the draper's shop and followed Kingsley inside. It seemed darker than it had mere moments before, and he realized Day had rehung the curtains in the windows.

'Walter?'

'Back here.' Day's voice traveled down the passage from the back rooms. 'Out in a moment.'

Kingsley set his bag on a table and sat on the sofa, straightened the creases of his trousers. Hammersmith had never seen the doctor act nervous before.

Day entered the room, holding a curtain rod. 'I managed to bend this back into –' He stopped when he saw Kingsley and dropped the rod, shrank back against the wall. 'Nevil, no! What have you done?'

'He's here to help,' Hammersmith said.

Kingsley stood and opened his arms to Day. 'Walter, I wish you no harm.'

'I don't mind whatever you wish for me. It's what I might do to you, don't you see?' Day disappeared, his footsteps pelting away to the back of the house again.

Kingsley shot Hammersmith a confused glance and went to the doorway. 'Walter?'

'Go away, Doctor! I can't guarantee what I'll do if you stay here.'

'Walter, you won't hurt me.'

'I don't know that.'

Hammersmith still wasn't sure how loud he was talking or whether he ought to yell. He cupped his hands around his mouth and shouted in a way he hoped wasn't too forceful or unfriendly. 'I won't let you hurt him, Walter. Don't you trust me?'

'Of course!'

'If you try to harm Dr Kingsley, I'll stop you.'

'What if you can't?'

'Walter,' Dr Kingsley said. 'I don't believe you'll hurt me. Don't you trust my judgment? Don't you trust Nevil's judgment?'

They were quiet then and waited. Eventually Day shuffled back into view.

'If I make one move to hurt the doctor, Nevil, you've got to do whatever it takes to stop me.'

'That won't happen,' Kingsley said. 'You won't hurt me any more than you would hurt Nevil, would you?'

'I may not be in control of my actions.'

'It doesn't matter, Walter. Let me explain something. Come here and sit.'

Day obeyed, perching uncomfortably at the edge of the sofa as if he might flee. He looked terrified, and Hammersmith pitied him, imagining his friend sleeping in a ditch to avoid endangering his friends and family. It was hard to imagine what a year in the clutches of Jack the Ripper might do to a person's mind.

Kingsley settled into a chair across from Day and smiled. 'Mr Hammersmith says you think you've been mesmerized?'

'Yes,' Day said. 'That's what it was. He did that to me. Jack did that.'

'It's a popular parlor trick. But the popular conception of it is surrounded by a lot of mumbo jumbo, and most people don't really understand how it works. I don't think you're going to harm anyone, Walter, no matter what you've been told by that lunatic.'

'He's ordered me to kill someone, I know that much. As soon as I see that person, I'll lash out. He's done something to my brain to ensure that I've become his weapon against his enemies. Against my friends.'

Kingsley smiled. 'I see. And you thought I might be Jack the Ripper's enemy.'

'The crow,' Hammersmith said. 'Or the white king.'

'I don't know who it is,' Day said. 'I don't remember that part. He hid it from me. I only know that it's someone close to me, which is why he's done this, why he's used me. I think maybe he can't get close to the person himself, but I can. Or perhaps it's simply his perverse sense of humor to make me do it. To ruin me. I couldn't live with myself.'

'He certainly is perverse,' Kingsley said. 'I'm just not sure he's as smart as you seem to think he is.'

Hammersmith cleared his throat. 'Can you fix this, Doctor?'

'Fix it? Certainly, if I knew the commands Jack used to do this. Without that knowledge, it might take some time.'

'Which is why,' Day said, 'I've got to stay away from everyone I love.'

'Well, it would seem Dr Kingsley and I are both safe from you,' Hammersmith said. 'What if we introduced you to each person you know, one at a time, and we'll stop you if you try to kill them?'

'Don't be ridiculous,' Kingsley said.

'I was being serious,' Hammersmith said. 'What's wrong with that plan?'

Kingsley sighed. 'I'm not prepared to become Mr Day's personal attendant. Walter, you're not a madman. As far as I can see right now, talking to you here, you're as normal as you ever were. Somewhat indecisive, as you have always been, but a sincere and caring individual. Now, if Jack's done something, if he's mesmerized you as you seem to think, there are very real limitations to that. He can't have suggested to you that you murder someone you care about and then really expect you to go through with it. You simply wouldn't do it.'

'I wouldn't?'

'No, Walter, you can't be made to do something under hypnosis that you wouldn't have done otherwise. It doesn't work that way. In other words, if you have a strong compunction against harming me or Nevil or anyone else, why then, you'll stop yourself, even without the intervention of Mr Hammersmith or myself. No matter how much you've been told to kill someone, you'll balk at the task.'

'Is that true?'

'Well, I'm no expert in mesmerism, but from everything I've read, yes, you are perfectly safe from killing your friends and family. I can promise you that. You're not likely to kill anyone else, either. In fact, given your facility for understanding other people, I'm surprised you would think such things about yourself.'

'I was afraid.'

'Of course you were. You've been under this person's influence long enough, he might have got you to think anything. I can put you back under hypnosis fairly easily and I might be able to poke around in your head and see what's been done, but it's not necessary at the moment and I hate to do it without knowing more. And I'd like you to be a bit more calm before we make the attempt. Meantime, you're quite safe from becoming a murderer, I assure you. It's this memory loss that's got me more concerned.'

'Things are starting to come back to me. I think I can remember nearly everything.'

'He remembered I'd been poisoned,' Hammersmith said.

'Good. Tell me, what did he do to you? Did Jack strike you on the head or otherwise do anything that caused you pain or headaches?'

'I don't remember.'

'Would you allow me to examine you?'

'If you like.'

'Thank you.' Kingsley stood and approached Day, his hands held out at his sides.

'You seem wary, Doctor.'

'I am a bit.'

'But you said I won't hurt you. You were certain of it.'

'What I meant was that Jack cannot have compelled you to hurt me. But you might still be a danger.'

Day sat very still, his hands in his lap, while Kingsley moved around to the back of the sofa and bent down to look at the top of Day's head. 'I'm going to touch your head.'

'All right.'

'Don't be alarmed.'

'Thank you. I won't be.'

'Good.' Kingsley probed Day's scalp with the tips of his fingers, moving Day's hair this way and that. 'Hammersmith, bring that lamp over here, would you?'

'What is it?'

'Get that light over here. Look at that. Do you see it?'

'I don't know,' Hammersmith said.

'Feel it. Scars. Many of them. Mr Day, have you suffered any head injuries before?'

'I was hit in the head with a shovel. But that was years ago.'

'Hmm. More than once?'

'Only the one time. It was enough to put me off the experience.'

'Indeed.' Kingsley sniffed and nodded to Hammersmith. He moved back round and sat across from Day. 'Not so bad, was it?'

'No. But you say I've got scars on my head?'

'I'm afraid so. Quite a few. More than might be explained by your encounter with the shovel. This fellow Jack was unkind to you while you were in his care.'

'Is that why I don't remember?'

'I don't think it's that simple. Walter, I think you don't remember because you don't *want* to remember. Sometimes, when a person has experienced something profoundly traumatic, he can sort of choose to forget. I've seen it once or twice in my practice and I believe that's what's happened with you.'

'I don't want to remember what he did?'

'Exactly. And because you don't want to remember, you're burying those thoughts and memories deep in your brain somewhere.'

'Then can you help me remember?'

'I don't know,' Kingsley said. 'I don't think so. Nor do I think I ought to. Sometimes the psyche protects itself this way. It might actually cause you harm if you were to remember.'

'But I need to know what Jack wanted from me or I won't ever feel at ease around anyone again.'

Hammersmith had been standing against the wall, watching them. Now he crossed between them and sat next to Kingsley. 'Figuring out what a criminal's after? It's only the sort of thing we do all the time, isn't it?' He leaned forward so that he was looking Day directly in the face. 'Why did the man kill his wife? What did the burglar want? Jack is a criminal, and we question criminals all the time, both directly and indirectly.'

'Right,' Walter said. He perked up a bit and edged closer

to them, his hands gripping his knees. 'Do you think we can?'

'Yes. Absolutely. Doctor, what was the rest of the rhyme on the wall in Walter's house?'

'In my house?'

'Your old house on Regent's Park. Jack left a message there.'

'It wasn't a rhyme,' Kingsley said. 'At least, not like any rhyme I've ever seen. It started with a Latin phrase. *Exitus probatur.* It means –'

'It means "the ends are justified,"' Day said.

'Something like that,' Kingsley said.

'No, that's exactly what they mean when they say it. The Karstphanomen, those shadowy men that Jack hates so much.'

'So that was a warning to them, not to me,' Hammersmith said.

'Jack mentioned Mr Hammersmith in his message,' Kingsley said.

'I think he's proud that he saved your life,' Day said. 'He's responsible for you.'

'He'll regret that when I find him.'

'What else did the message say?'

'A lot of poorly spelled nonsense,' Hammersmith said. 'The point is that he's still focused on the society, the Karstphanomen. That's who he's after.'

'And that's who he's sent me after, too,' Day said.

'Has to be. So someone you know is a Karstphanomen.'

'I don't know any of them. Not any more. Inspector March is dead now and I can't think of any others.'

'But you do still know another one, you must. It's why

he needed you. You can get close to one of them and he can't. But why can't he do it himself? Why send you?'

'Perhaps it's as Mr Day suggested. Jack could kill that man himself if he wanted to, but finds it more amusing to send our friend to do it,' Kingsley said.

'To hurt me, even as he hurts someone else.'

'Or to break your will even further.'

Hammersmith ran his hands through his hair and stood and paced back and forth. 'We have to draw him out somehow. We have to end this. If we can figure out who that evil bloody bastard was trying to get at through Walter, maybe we can get him to make a mistake.'

'I might have some idea,' Kingsley said. 'Something Mr Hammersmith said a minute ago.'

'How so?'

'That writing on the wall. He said he was after some-one he called "the crow." It's been pointed out to me that the word *crow* might sometimes be specific jargon mean-ing a doctor.'

'I hadn't heard that before.'

'Possibly before your time, Mr Hammersmith. But Jack may be targeting a doctor, and I might know who that is.'

'Who?'

'Me,' Kingsley said.

49

Fiona followed Claire through the front doors of the Hammersmith Agency. The young woman behind the desk didn't look up.

'What can I do for you?'

'My husband is missing,' Claire said.

'Oh, dear, Mrs Day.' The woman jumped up and came around, moved the paperwork off a chair, and gestured for her main client to sit. 'What brings you here today?'

'Eugenia,' Claire said, 'this is my friend Fiona Kingsley. Fiona, this is Miss Merrilow.'

'Pleased,' Fiona said. 'We don't need to sit down. We're looking for Mr Hammersmith. Is he here?'

'I haven't seen him at all today,' Eugenia said.

'Do you know where he is?'

'I'm afraid I don't. I'm alone here or I'd try him at home.'

'Do you think he's there?'

'No.' Eugenia leaned back against the front of her desk and bit her lower lip. 'Really, he's rarely at home, anyway. He's out somewhere looking for Mr Day, if that helps matters, Mrs Day.'

'He's found my husband already,' Claire said. 'And now he's run off somewhere and so has Mr Day, and I don't know where they've gone.'

'He found him? He finally found him?'

'For a minute or two,' Claire said. 'But now they're both gone.'

'Oh, dear,' Eugenia said again. 'A cup of tea?'

'No, thank you. You've no ideas?'

'Even Hatty hasn't been in and she usually checks in with me.'

'Hatty?'

'Yes,' Eugenia said. 'I'm sorry, what did you say your name was?'

'Fiona.'

'Yes, Fiona. Hatty is the other investigator here.'

'She's an investigator?' Fiona had no idea why, but she felt a hot pang of jealousy at the base of her neck.

'Well, she fancies herself one.' Eugenia pushed herself off the desk, went round to her chair and sat back down. 'She usually checks in with me in the morning, but she wasn't here today.'

'Do you think she's with Nevil?'

'No, they rarely cross paths.'

Fiona felt a wave of relief pass through her. 'Well, we've got to track Mr Hammersmith somehow. Do you think Hatty knows where he is?'

'I would have no idea. The last I heard, she was going to investigate the department store. The new one, you know? She's on her own little hunt for someone. It's awfully ambitious.'

'Do you mean Plumm's?'

'Yes, that's the one. The gentleman she's looking for works there. Or worked there. Perhaps he's dead. Exciting! At any rate, he worked there, he lived there. And Hatty's got some kind of list of places to look at.'

'If she was going there, then we should go there, too,' Fiona said.

'It collapsed,' Claire said. 'Isn't it completely gone? That's where Mr Hammersmith found Walter.'

'Wait,' Fiona said. 'What do you mean he lived there?'

'I can't believe he found Mr Day,' Eugenia said. 'How long have we been looking? Months!'

'What do you mean he lived there? Lived at Plumm's?'

'Yes, they have apartments at the back,' Eugenia said. 'Or so Hatty said. Keeps the workers there longer hours.' Her eyes flicked to the clock against the wall.

'At the back? Behind the store?'

'Somewhere back there. I don't know. Nobody tells me anything. I'm quite undervalued.'

'I'll tell Mr Hammersmith to give you an increase in pay,' Claire said. 'Thank you.'

They were already out of the door when Fiona heard Eugenia's voice. 'Does this mean you're no longer a client?'

50

'I was old enough to know better,' Kingsley said. 'But I still allowed my emotions to get the better of me. My wife had just died, and I was angry and I had two young daughters.'

They were walking down Moorgate toward Plumm's. Day was leaning heavily on his cane, and Hammersmith was leaning forward, trying desperately to hear what Kingsley was saying. Kingsley's voice was a soft foghorn noise drifting across to him from some faraway place. He could make sense of the words, but the conversation was getting ahead of him.

'They approached me,' Kingsley said. 'Catherine had died of consumption, and Fiona was at an age when she needed a mother. I wasn't of much use to her any more.'

'I'm sure that's not true, Doctor,' Day said.

'Fiona's a wonderful person,' Hammersmith said.

Kingsley shot him an arch glance. 'So you've noticed that, have you?'

While Hammersmith tried to parse the meaning of that, Kingsley continued.

'I don't think you've met my older daughter. She's been away at university. She didn't come home for the funeral, didn't answer my letters. After a while, I stopped trying to reach her. I felt her disappointment so keenly and I thought she blamed me for her mother's death. I blamed myself. And I blamed this damn city with its horse shit in the streets, the germs and the dirt.'

He lapsed into silence as they reached the department store and Day led them around to a tall outbuilding with huge double doors that stretched two stories high. He pulled a handle and one of the doors swung open on well-oiled hinges. The three of them stepped through into the dusk of the warehouse. Yellow light poured through windows that were set high under the roof. Hammersmith marveled at the size of it. A game of cricket might comfortably have been played inside. Much of the vast space seemed to be wasted. The chamber was sparsely filled with construction equipment, lumber and building materials, workbenches, wheeled carts, and a congregation of mannequins in one corner. He imagined the life-size wooden people hushing one another, startled by the three men who had entered their hall uninvited.

'They're over here,' Day said. He walked to where a number of the carts, perhaps a hundred of them, had been haphazardly collected and he started to roll them away from one another, checking inside each one. He stopped and stood silently. Hammersmith and Kingsley joined him and looked down into the open top of the cart.

'I knew him,' Day said. 'Not well, but he was a good lad. He wanted to learn to read. He would have grown to be a good man if anyone had given him the chance. He deserved better than this.'

The inspector's eyes welled up, and Hammersmith looked away, pretending not to notice.

'This city doesn't nurture its children,' Kingsley said.

Hammersmith leaned forward. 'What did you say?'

'I tried to make things better here after Catherine died,' Kingsley said. 'I did. I moved the morgue into the hospital, I set guidelines for cleanliness, and I looked for new ways to do the same old things, ways to improve on our methods. My methods, police methods, hospital methods. I was trained to think of everything in terms of how it was done, the methodology. It's why I gravitated so easily to helping Scotland Yard. But it wasn't enough.'

'There are two others here,' Day said. 'Two women. Strangers to me, but someone will know them.'

'We'll bury them properly,' Kingsley said.

'The Karstphanomen came to you?'

'They offered me membership,' Kingsley said. 'Of course, this was after they'd vetted me, taken me to dinners, studied my reactions to their veiled ideas during long conversations and good Scotch. Some of them seemed to be as angry as I was. Some had suffered losses or worked in positions where they saw firsthand how often bad men got away with their crimes. Some of them were hungry for power or were simply the sort of men who enjoy hurting others. I didn't see that at first. I was blinded by loss and pain and idealism. I feel ashamed now.'

'How could you know what they were?'

'I should have paid better attention. We both should have. The clues were there, plain to see.'

'Who do you mean?'

'Hmm?'

'You said "we both should have paid attention." You're one.'

'Ah, yes. I really shouldn't tell tales, but you may need to warn Sir Edward about this man's agenda, too, if he doesn't already know. We were both courted. He was new to his current appointment and would have been a prize recruit for them.'

'Sir Edward is a Karstphanomen?' Day took a step back and almost stumbled. Hammersmith leapt forward, but Day caught himself by stabbing the ground with his cane. He waved his friend away.

'No,' Kingsley said. 'No, of course not. In fact, Sir Edward took certain precautions to protect us from the more zealous elements of the club when we refused membership.'

'So you didn't join them,' Hammersmith said. 'Of course you didn't. But in that case why would Jack be after you now?'

'Oh, I don't know for a fact that he is after me. I know very little, really. It's taken me a long while to realize how little I know.'

Day seemed to be ignoring them. He was rolling carts back and forth, checking each one for weight before looking inside them. At last, he turned around and nodded. 'They're both here. In these two carts.'

Kingsley passed his hand over his face, then moved forward and looked down into each of the carts in turn. Hammersmith followed him, but he didn't recognize either of the women.

Kingsley sighed. 'Whoever did this was no doctor. Some say Jack the Ripper must be a surgeon. They say he must have a physician's knowledge of the body in order to do what he does. But they've mistaken passion for knowledge. There's a glee on display here, a monstrous pleasure at work, not a surgeon's technique. He's simply learned by doing, and who knows how long he's been at it?'

'You think they're prostitutes?'

'No. Look at their hands.' Kingsley reached in and lifted one woman's hand. Neither Day nor Hammersmith leaned in to see. They both waited for the doctor to tell them what he had observed. 'They were menial workers of a different sort. Their nails are short and their fingertips are calloused. The skin is bleached from contact with chemicals. These women worked as maids or housekeepers of some sort. I don't say their lives were any better than you assumed them to be, Mr Hammersmith. Life is hard.'

'Ambrose said they were in an upper room at the store,' Day said.

'Perhaps they found something Jack didn't want them to,' Hammersmith said. 'Or saw something incriminating. If he's gone to ground here with all the pressure from the police and Blackleg's people hounding him, maybe he was protecting his refuge or his identity.'

'Or perhaps he could no longer resist the urge to kill,' Kingsley said. 'Some of these creatures simply need to kill, and woe betide anyone who crosses their line of sight at the wrong moment.'

'Was it really so wrong that the Karstphanomen did what they did?'

Kingsley stared at Hammersmith down the length of his nose, then turned his head to the ceiling high above them. He drew a long breath and blew it out through his mouth. 'I'm not sure it's up to you or me to determine that sort of thing. But perhaps I've spent too many evenings discussing theology with my daughter.'

'Did you ever see him? Did you ever see Jack after he'd been captured?'

'I did see him,' Kingsley said. 'It was only the one time. It was a glorious occasion for the Karst. They had come across him while he slept. Or so we were told, Sir Edward and I. We were roused from our beds in the middle of the night and ferried by private carriage to a room in Whitechapel, where he lay stretched out across his most recent victim. I gave him a sedative, stabbed the needle so deep in his neck I might've gone through and hit what was left of the girl under him. I was aiming for his spine, hoping to paralyse him, but I wasn't precise enough. He lived, and he is obviously mobile.'

'You helped them.'

'That one time. I came to my senses after and haven't had any dealings with them since. I have seen one or two of them in passing. They're unavoidable, really. Some of them are very powerfully connected in this city. And in others. But we spent that night, the commissioner and I, discussing what had happened and what was to be done. We lacked the influence to stop them, not without causing ourselves a great deal of grief. Perhaps we should have pushed harder, maybe even arrested them all. But we would have lost our appointments, him with the police, me with the hospital, and we both felt we could still do some good. I would do things differently now. As I say, it was a confusing time for me.'

'They have that much power?'

'Yes, Mr Hammersmith, they come from all walks of life. There are members of parliament, there are lords and judges.'

Hammersmith thought he saw Kingsley shoot an inquisitive glance at Day, but the inspector didn't notice or react.

'I should say they *were* powerful,' Kingsley said. 'Our friend Jack has whittled them down to the bone, I think.'

'There can't be many of them left.'

'I wouldn't think so.'

'What about Sir Edward?'

'We have never spoken of it since. I believe he has blotted the entire thing from his mind, much as you have avoided all thought of your own life, Mr Day. Our minds defend themselves by going dim, the way you might close the shutter on a lamp.'

'Why did I do that?'

'You thought you were protecting the people you loved. You loved them so much that you gave up your own life in order to save them. It's not common, but I've read about similar things.'

'Jack made that happen?'

'You say he mesmerized you, but that's not what your memory loss was about. You forgot because you needed to forget.'

Hammersmith put his hand to his ear. 'What about Jack?'

'He's wounded,' Day said.

'He's dangerous,' Kingsley said.

'He's somewhere nearby,' Hammersmith said. 'Right?'

'He was losing blood,' Day said. 'I don't think he could have gone far.'

'Where? Where was he wounded?'

'Somewhere in his belly.'

'That doesn't tell me much,' Kingsley said. 'How much was it oozing?'

'It seemed like a lot of blood, but I was disoriented. I feel like I've been disoriented for so long.'

'Yes, yes, but was there visible pus? Or anything brown coming with the blood? Specifics, son.'

'It was seeping steadily, but not fast. There was pus. I didn't see anything brown. No, I did, but it might have been dried blood. I don't know how long he was bleeding.'

'How was he moving?'

'With difficulty, but when there was need, he was quick.'

'He's mad,' Hammersmith said. 'The mad move quickly.'

The other two looked at him and he smiled at them, but Kingsley turned away and addressed Day again. 'Was he sweating?'

'I don't remember,' Day said.

'I'd guess he has gone to ground here. Not in this place.' He waved his hand at the high ceiling, the walls that faced each other across the vast distance. 'But he might be at Plumm's.'

'The store is a wreck,' Hammersmith said. He hoped he was keeping up well enough with the conversation.

'So there's this warehouse we're in,' Kingsley said. 'There's the store proper. What else? Is there a place on the premises where someone might hide away?'

'I don't know,' Day said. 'He has an office. He stole it from someone. Probably someone he killed.'

'You think he could be there?'

'He'd be foolish to go there now.'

'Except the store's deserted. Who would look for him there?'

'You could be right.'

'Let's look,' Hammersmith said. 'We're prepared, he's not. Let's find him.'

'You lads go,' Kingsley said. 'I'll join you in a few minutes. My priority is doing right by these poor victims.' He nodded at the carts and thought of the boy there.

Hammersmith wondered how well Day had known Ambrose, how much that tiny death had hurt him. He wondered if that might be worse than a year of forgetfulness.

'How long will it take the police to get here?'

'Not long,' Kingsley said. 'Sir Edward will have a lot of questions. We're all going to be observed carefully after this.'

'Then we'll hurry. If Jack's still here, Nevil and I will do our best to deal with him quickly, before he has another chance to get away, to kill more innocents.' He indicated the bodies in the carts.

'I'll find a telephone,' Kingsley said.

'See if you can't get Inspector Tiffany to come out here,' Hammersmith said. 'And Sergeant Kett. They may not believe the Ripper's about, but they'll come just the same, and we could do with their help.'

'I'll do my best to persuade them,' Kingsley said. 'And I'll get a wagon on its way for these bodies. Then I'll find you.'

51

Mr and Mrs Parker had drawn Leland Carlyle out from his club and followed him to his daughter's house, to Guildhall, and then to a shabby detective agency. He went in while his driver waited, then came rushing back out, and the cab rolled away once more down the street with the Parkers trailing after.

'It's quite a cortege we make, dearest heart,' Mrs Parker said.

'They're going to want results soon,' Mr Parker said. 'How patient can they possibly be?'

'Who?'

'Whoever they are. That club that's so secret, we're not supposed to know their name.'

'The Karstphanomen.'

'Them, yes.'

'Have they paid us yet?'

'Not entirely.'

'We should get them results then,' Mrs Parker said.

'It's a problem. I'm afraid we've taken an impossible case. We can't actually find Jack the Ripper, no matter how formidable we may be. That gentleman has slipped through every trap ever set for him and taunted the newspaper and police into the bargain. Our only real hope was to be in place when he acted.'

'But he doesn't appear to want to act against Mr Carlyle, darling.'

'So far as we know, Jack doesn't even know Mr Carlyle exists.'

'What if he doesn't attack Carlyle?'

'Our reputation will suffer.'

'And we won't be paid for more work?'

'We will have trouble getting more work.'

'Husband?'

'Yes?'

'Who knows that Mr Carlyle has hired us?'

'I don't know,' Mr Parker said.

'Do you think he was acting on his own, or do you think others know about us?'

'I shouldn't think very many others do.'

'And none of them have met us. None of them can verify that he actually employed us, am I right?'

'I believe you are, light of my life.'

'What I mean to say is . . .' The carriage rumbled over a hole in the street, and Mrs Parker grabbed Mr Parker's arm to steady herself. He caught his breath and tried not to look at her. 'What I mean to say,' Mrs Parker said, 'is what if Mr Carlyle were to disappear?'

'We would be in a very bad place. He's our only way of finding Jack.'

'No, my cabbage, what if he disappeared and we went home?'

'Oh, you mean . . . ?'

'I mean what if we were the instrument of disappearance, if you insist on making me say so?'

'We would not be paid the full amount agreed upon,' Mr Parker said. 'We like to be paid.'

'We would eventually be paid by someone else for something else. This all seems so pointless, doesn't it?'

Mr Parker nodded. 'It's not really the sort of thing we customarily do.'

'Not at all.'

'In fact, it's rather more work than usual.'

'I don't like it to be so much work.'

'Of course.' He tensed while patting her hand, but she seemed to welcome the gesture. 'Let's give it the afternoon. Imagine if we were the ones to bring Jack the Ripper down.'

'The afternoon, then,' she said. She let go of his arm and moved away from him, and he wondered if he'd said the wrong thing to her. 'We'll follow Mr Carlyle for the rest of the afternoon, and if nothing interesting happens, we'll go home.'

'Agreed,' Mr Parker said. 'Not such a big commitment of time after all, is it?'

'But, Father, what if we do meet Jack?'

'There are two of us to his one. I shouldn't think he'd be too much trouble.'

'That's not what I meant.'

'What then, turtledove?'

'What if I don't want to kill him? What if I admire his work and find him to be . . . Well, what if we like him? As a person.'

Mr Parker smiled at her. 'Then we shall invite him to tea and Mr Carlyle will still disappear.'

But Mr Parker was not at all sure he wanted to have tea

with Jack the Ripper. He would be surrounded and out-numbered by dangerous animals in human guise. He realized that his time with Mrs Parker was coming to an end, and he didn't think their parting would be pleasant for him. He wished he were capable of walking away and leaving her, and he cursed himself for a fool because he knew he could not do that.

52

'There's a lamp beside the door,' Jack said. 'Reach over to your right and you'll feel it.'

Hatty took a moment, wondering if there really was a lamp or if she might encounter something awful hanging there instead. But, *In for a penny, in for a pound,* she thought, and felt along the wall in the dark. To her great relief there was indeed a lamp. She detected an earthy mix of odors in the room, sweat and musk and something else she couldn't place.

'Matches are on the table there,' Jack said. 'Be careful, don't burn the place down.'

Hatty fumbled the lamp off its hook and shuffled around until she bumped into a table. She patted along the surface and found a wooden box, opened it, and struck a match. When she'd lit the lamp and slid back the shutter, the room flickered into view around her. It was just like the rooms on the floor below: there was the bed, the chair, the table and the wardrobe. The men and women did not live noticeably different lives. But in many subtle ways, this room was more comfortable than the others, reflecting Joseph Hargreave's better position within the Plumm's hierarchy. The wardrobe was not made of cardboard. The bed was canopied, with thick mattresses that set it higher off the floor than the others she had seen downstairs. There was a figure on the bed, obscured by heavy blankets and pillows. The chair was upholstered in leather, with bright brass studs glowing along the seams.

The man sitting in the chair was surrounded by a mane of dark wavy hair, thick and unfashionably long. He smiled at Hatty, but he didn't rise to greet her. He was slumped over, leaning heavily on his left elbow, and his face looked pale to her. She recognized him from the gallery railing of the store, from the moment before a sheet of glass had sliced one of Plumm's staff in two.

'Mr Oberon,' Hatty said. 'Are you quite all right?'

'Good of you to inquire, Miss Pitt,' he said. 'The best answer I can give is that we shall see.'

Hatty kept her eye on him and went to the bed, keeping it between them in case Jack suddenly leapt from the chair. She thought she might be able to reach the door again before he could reach her. She wondered how much damage a swinging lamp might do to a man if she aimed it properly and hit his face.

'I promised I wouldn't touch you,' he said, as if he could read her mind. 'Don't you trust me?'

'No.'

'I should stop asking that question. I never get the response I want.'

Hatty leaned over the bed and had to look away again. She closed her eyes, then realized she was leaving herself vulnerable. She snapped them open again, but Mr Oberon had not moved.

'What did you do to him?' She was certain she was going to vomit, but didn't want to give him the satisfaction of seeing her do it.

'I did many things to him,' Mr Oberon said. 'It would

305

take some time for me to describe them all to you, but I will if you like.'

'He's dead,' Hatty said.

'Don't look so put out about it. I believe in the end he welcomed death.'

'He looks like he's been dead for days.'

'Oh, no,' Jack said. 'If he'd been dead for days, I would've moved him. I moved all the others. Can't draw attention with a stink. No, he was alive when I left for work this morning.'

'You went to work every day? While you were pretending to be a Plumm's employee?'

'Oh, but I am a Plumm's employee. The old man kept me on when Smithfield and Gordon moved away. Mr Hargreave's disappearance was a boon for me. I was promoted like a shot, if it's not immodest to say.'

'You wanted Mr Hargreave's position?'

'I wanted his apartment. Or perhaps I wanted his cottage at the sea.'

'That's where you took him.'

'Joseph and I had some fun there before we decided to return to the city. His brother was a bit too nosy.'

'Why not kill him, too?'

'Who says I didn't? Oh, but I did enjoy Joseph so very much. There are few of these Karstphanomen left, and I like to savor their last moments when I can.'

'I heard Mr Hargreave cry out. When I was outside the room just now, he made a noise.'

'Oh, that was me. I thought it might get you in here, and I wanted to cry out anyway. It served two functions. I do like to be efficient whenever possible, don't you?'

'Why did you want me here? What will you do now?'

'You are convenient, that's all. No greater design this time. And you look like a kind sort of a person. There's a stack of clean linens in the wardrobe, and a corset in there, too. Hargreave was a vain man, but I think the corset might work to my advantage, keep my guts where they belong. I was rather hoping you would help me dress this.' He opened his jacket and showed her a dark wet stain on his shirt.

She glanced at the closed wardrobe and wondered what surprises Mr Oberon had waiting inside it. 'You've been wounded,' she said.

'There were four of them there, and I only expected two. They got me in the end.' He lowered his voice to a fierce whisper and bared his teeth at Hatty. 'But I got more of them, didn't I?'

Hatty moved back toward the door. She held the lamp up high in front of her, hoping Jack couldn't see the fear she felt. 'Is it fatal, then? The wound?'

'There are things I know that no one else knows, Miss Pitt.'

There was a long silence, and Hatty stood still, waiting for him to talk again. If he had answered her question, she couldn't understand the meaning of it. At last he grunted and began to speak again, but his voice was lower and weaker.

'Quite often people decide to die because it's the easier choice than living. I've seen it, Miss Pitt. Time after time, I've watched their eyes as they make that decision, and then I watch the light leave them. And I've never really understood. Wherever they go when the light leaves, is there still blood?'

'I don't think anyone knows the answer to that,' Hatty said. 'Not for sure.'

'So much of what men do is undertaken only to avoid humiliation. That is what makes yours the stronger sex, Hatty Pitt. You are able to bear up under constant humiliation, to turn it slowly to your advantage. We men wither and beg to be killed, while you bide your time.'

'So you're the champion of my sex, Mr Oberon?'

'Why not me? Who knows more about women than I? The linens. Fetch them, would you? I'm afraid the wardrobe's a bit far for me to reach at the moment.'

'No,' Hatty said. 'I will not help you. It's time for you to think about making that decision you mentioned. I urge you to make the proper choice.'

She backed out of the door and down the passage to the stairs, but he did not chase her. She thought she heard him chuckle quietly in the dark, but she couldn't be sure. She dropped the lamp at the landing and turned.

Behind her there was a great *whomp* as oil hit the flammable carpet and exploded outward, but she didn't turn round or slow down. She pelted down the steps and kept running.

Let it burn, she thought. *Let it all burn to the ground.*

BOOK FOUR

A dozen sets of miniature farm animals, all carved from soft pine and stained dark brown, stampeded out of the smoke, and Anna leapt to the side of the path. There were twelve little sheep and twelve little cows and twelve little goats and twelve little horses, along with a hundred or more chickens and geese and ducks, all of them running as fast as they could and making a tremendous noise. One of the little pigs broke one of its legs off and it stumbled. Anna reached out to pick it up and rescue it from being crushed, but the pig grunted and turned on its side and rolled away, disappearing amongst the other creatures.

Anna coughed and wiped her watering eyes. The sky was obscured by billows of smoke and ash, and all round her the furniture and toys and carriages and statuary were ablaze.

'All of this from a single match,' Anna said. 'Oh, why must matches also be made of wood?'

She was alone again, her friends having run away at the first sight of fire. She did not blame them in the least. They were all quite flammable.

'It is becoming quite hot now,' Anna said.

'Then you should leave.' Jack appeared out of the smoke, hopping toward Anna on his spring. The tip of his false cigar was alight now and it glowed a bright rosy red. 'You are not made of wood as the rest of us are, and so you do not belong.'

'But I can't leave until I find Peter,' Anna said. 'He must be very scared now, as he has never stayed outside during the night alone,

except one time when I went in to dinner and forgot he was with me and accidentally bolted the door and left him.'

'Peter will burn here, and so will you, Anna,' Jack said. He bounced all round her in a circle as the fire drew closer to them.

'And you will burn, too,' Anna said. 'I do not believe you have thought this through well enough. You are made of wood just as Babushka and poor Mary Annette are, and also the Kindly Nutcracker you so cruelly broke apart.'

'I know that I will burn,' Jack said. 'And that is what I want.'

'I don't understand,' Anna said.

'The workmen would have come and taken all of the things here away,' Jack said. 'The wood will never be allowed to be together as we were when we were trees. And so I have decided to burn us all away and leave our ashes here where there was once a vast forest, and where for a single day and a single night we were able to return.'

'But you are the only one who has decided such a thing, and it is not your place to do so,' Anna said.

'It is my nature to surprise others, and that is what I am doing,' said Jack. 'You should not expect me to be anything other than what I am.'

'What you are, you nasty little Jack, is a man in a box,' said Anna. 'And in a box is where you shall go.'

And with that, Anna plucked Jack off the ground by the top of his head and pushed him back down into his case, which was painted all over with colorful circus scenes that were now bubbling and melting in the heat from the fire.

'I do not want to go into my box any more,' Jack said. 'It is dark in there and lonely.'

He struggled mightily and his spring was very strong, but Anna pushed until he was packed away tight, and then she closed the lid and latched it.

'You might have thought of that before you struck that match,' said Anna. 'That was not a pleasant surprise in the least.'

She put the box under her arm, holding it closed so that Jack could not open the latch and pop out, and she marched away from the flames in what she hoped was the right direction. She had very little time now before everything would disappear and her childhood playground would be reduced to ash, as Jack had threatened.

'Oh dear,' she said. 'I wonder if the fire will spread to my house. That would be bad indeed. I must find Peter so that we can put out the fire with buckets of water. I know he will help.'

And with Jack bumping and thumping inside his box, Anna began to run as fast as she could, all the while calling Peter's name.

— RUPERT WINTHROP, FROM
The Wandering Wood (1893)

53

'Everything's ruined,' Hammersmith said.

Day whistled long and loud and looked round them at the deserted department store. 'It's been picked clean.'

Much of the metalwork had been disassembled and carted away, the electrical wires pulled from the walls, and the plumbing and much of the wood paneling taken, leaving great mounds of plaster and dust and ruined carpeting. A box fell to the floor in the toy department, causing Day and Hammersmith to jump. They turned and watched as a startled fox ran past them and vanished among the shattered remains of cut crystal glassware.

'How'd that get in already?'

'I'm just glad you saw it, too,' Day said.

'The office you say Oberon was using . . .'

'Up there.' Day pointed at the crumbling gallery at the back of the store. 'He can't possibly be using it now. There aren't any stairs.'

'I don't see a ladder, either,' Hammersmith said.

'Unless he's using that,' Day said. He pointed at the lift, which stood open, the iron gates ripped from their hinges some time in the night.

'I don't know how that thing works and I'm not gonna gamble on it,' Hammersmith said.

'Neither me. I doubt there's any electricity left to power it, anyway.'

'Don't understand electricity. Never seen any.'

'You can't see it, but it's all round us.'

'What, inside the walls?'

'Wires and cables.'

'Then how do they keep the walls from catching fire? I don't see it letting off any steam or releasing pressure.'

'We'll ask Dr Kingsley. I'm sure he knows,' Day said. 'But this is a dead end. Even if there were a ladder, I doubt I could climb it.'

'How's your leg?'

'Not at my best, but not at my worst, either. I'm not as bad off as you remember me. I exercised well this past year and got a good bit more mobility out of it. It's these ribs bothering me at the moment. Can hardly breathe without it feeling like I've been stabbed in the chest. Oh, sorry, Nevil, I forgot.'

'What, my chest? I've still got a horrible scar over my heart, but it doesn't bother me any more. It's a miracle, really.'

'You have an uncanny knack for healing. Your ear seems to be functioning now.'

Hammersmith put a hand to his ear. 'Not so much. I still can't hear from this one, but if I stand on the right side of you, it seems I do all right. The other ear compensates.'

'We're a fine pair, aren't we?'

'Hullo!' They turned at the sound of the voice. An old man clambered over a distant mound of splintered wood and glass and picked his slow way toward them. 'Hullo, I say!' He held up one arm, waving a rifle over his head.

'Oh, no,' Hammersmith said.

'You know this fellow?'

'I'm afraid so. His name's Goodpenny. He means well.'

'I say,' Goodpenny said. He had found a clear path that wound round through the remains of toiletries and sundries and now he trotted up to them, breathing hard. 'If it isn't young Master Angerschmid. Good to see you, lad.' His hair stuck straight up, one lens of his spectacles was broken, and he was bleeding from a minor scratch on one cheek. He smiled and held up a finger, turned his back to them and tucked in his shirt before turning back and pumping Hammersmith's hand vigorously. 'Long night here, lads, but I did my best, I did.'

'Your best?'

'Looters, my boy. Looters. Got the trusty Martini-Henry from the back room, but no ammunition for it. That's all on the top floor, and I couldn't get at it. Most called my bluff, but I stayed the course and scared off a man or two.'

'Mr Goodpenny, that's terribly brave of you.'

'Was it?' He looked around them and sighed. 'I've lost everything now, Mr Angerschmid. Sold off my stall at the bazaar to buy a piece of this, and now it's gone, isn't it?' He sniffed and pulled himself up, offered them a wan smile. 'I've forgotten my manners. Terribly sorry, long night, as I say. My name's Goodpenny.' He stuck out his hand and Day shook it.

'Mine's Day. Walter Day. And isn't that a pleasant thing to be able to say after all this time?'

'Well, I'm sure, except that I can't remember ever saying it before,' Goodpenny said. 'No, I take it back. I've recently met a lovely young woman of that same name. What a startling coincidence. It's a pleasure to meet you, Mr Dew. You're friends with young Angerschmid then?'

'It's Day.'

'Indeed, and I'm glad of it after such a long night. Did I mention I haven't slept? Not one wink.'

'I mean –'

Hammersmith put a hand out and shook his head at Day. It wouldn't help to correct Goodpenny. He leaned in close and murmured, 'Goodpenny can't hear.'

'No,' Goodpenny said. 'Nobody else here. I say, how is your young lady friend? Miss Tinsley. I saw her just a day or two ago. I do hope she was nowhere near when this happened.'

'Who's Tinsley?'

'He means Kingsley's daughter Fiona. You'll remember her. He seems to think there's something between us.'

'And is there? I've been away long enough, she must have grown up a bit.'

'No, she's not interested in the likes of me. Got eyes for her father's assistant, Pinch.'

'Don't know him,' Day said.

'He was taking care of you this morning, before you woke up. Young fellow, well dressed, large nose.'

'I'm sorry, Nevil,' Day said. 'Good Lord, but that girl fancied you.'

'Did she really?'

'She certainly did,' Goodpenny said.

Day shook his head. 'How could you not know that?'

'She never told me.'

'You're supposed to notice that sort of thing without being told,' Goodpenny said. 'Not everything needs to be said aloud to be understood.'

'Well, it's a little late now.'

'Win her back,' Goodpenny said. 'Go after her and declare your love. It's never too late.'

'I never said I loved her. She's a little girl.'

'My wife was fifteen when I married her,' Goodpenny said.

'Different times, sir. Anyway, whoever she might have fancied at one time or another, right now she fancies Pinch. She said so.' He shook his head. 'Mr Goodpenny, you say you were here all night?'

'No,' Goodpenny said. 'I was here the entire night through. Never left.'

Day and Hammersmith exchanged a glance. 'Was there anyone else here you thought might be especially menacing? Tall fellow, dark wavy hair?'

'Everyone was at least mildly menacing, my dear boy.'

'You must have met him. Went by the name of Oberon.'

'Doberman? A German fellow? Don't recall. Perhaps if you described him more.'

'I can't,' Hammersmith said. 'But Mr Day might be able to. Walter, you must have seen a great deal of him.'

'I . . . I can't describe him. I try to think of him, but the image is hazy in my mind, as if there's a constant fog surrounding him.'

'No one like that was in here,' Goodpenny said. 'Only normal folks fallen on hard times, looking for free wares. Come to think of it, I'm glad this wasn't loaded.' He hefted the Martini-Henry and all three of them jumped back as it fired. Immediately a sofa that had already been torn nearly in half exploded in a cloud of cotton batting and wooden splinters. Goodpenny gave them a halfhearted smile and bit his lip. 'Well, it's not loaded now.'

'Bloody hell,' Hammersmith said. 'Even if I could've heard proper before, I'm sure I can't now.'

'At least you didn't shoot anyone,' Day said.

'No, I've never shot anyone,' Goodpenny said. 'Nearly did just now, though. Frightfully sorry, gentlemen.'

'No harm done.' Hammersmith looked at Day and suddenly couldn't help himself. He burst out laughing. Even Day cracked a smile.

'That would be quite a homecoming,' Hammersmith said. 'You disappear for a year and then suddenly . . . shot dead before you've even seen your wife. Welcome back, Walter Day!'

Day's smile disappeared. 'Nevil, we've got to find Jack and make him undo whatever it is he's done to me before I can go home or see Claire.'

'I understand. I'm sorry. We'll find him.'

'Well, he's clearly not here. That shot would have brought anyone out. This place is deserted. He's not in his office.'

'And he's not in the workshop.'

'Which leaves . . . what?'

'There are flats round the back,' Goodpenny said. 'Some of the staff live there, on and off. I never did. Got my own place. But the rooms were all cleared out after this happened.' Goodpenny swiveled his head to take in the mess all round them. 'They'd be empty now.'

'Be a perfect place to go to ground if he's injured, as you say he is,' Hammersmith said. 'Beds, fresh clothing.'

'Let's go,' Day said. 'Is there a street entrance? Or a way in through the store?'

'Both,' Goodpenny said. 'You can go round by the

outside or straight across there. There's a passage behind the lift.'

'There's an alley,' Day said. 'But it dead-ends at a storeroom. It's how Ambrose . . . Anyway, we'd have to circle wide.'

'He might see us coming from the street.'

'I don't fancy the idea of all that collapsing on us.' Day nodded at the gallery.

'Then you go by the street and I'll go through there and we'll have him trapped.'

'I'll stay here,' Goodpenny said. 'There's still a possibility I might discover some of my own merchandise under all this. The stationery will be lost, of course, but I had many fine items of silver and teak. An ivory piece or two. They might have survived.'

'You be careful, Mr Goodpenny,' Hammersmith said. 'That thing's not loaded any more.'

'Nobody knows that but us, lad.'

Hammersmith nodded and turned to watch Day, who was already picking his way back across the littered sales floor, but Goodpenny grabbed his arm and leaned in close. 'If you've got any feelings for that girl, Mr Angerschmid, you've got to do something about it before it's too late. I miss my wife every day now, but I still wouldn't trade our years together for anything, though they surely led to heartbreak at the end.'

'It's not –'

'Whatever it is, don't make it so you're lonely, lad. Don't wait until it's too late. A man's not a man unless he's got someone to share his life.'

'Um, right. Thank you, Mr Goodpenny. I'll be off.'

'Watch yourself. If you run into that foggy gentleman, you ring for the police straight off. Don't try to be a hero. You don't have the constitution for it.'

Hammersmith saluted and trotted away, jumping over a ruined credenza. He didn't look back, but he knew Goodpenny was watching him go. The man was kind, but completely addled. Still, he wasn't wrong in his warning about Jack, and Hammersmith suddenly wished he were armed. He bent and picked up a length of iron pipe. He swung it in a low arc and thumped it into the palm of his hand.

Almost as good as a truncheon.

54

Hatty was halfway down the stairs when a long shadow stretched across the floor below her. A man turned the corner and looked up at her, and in the split second it took her to recognize him, Hatty panicked and stumbled.

Hammersmith bounded up the stairs and caught her as she fell. The impact caused him to take a backward step down, but he held on to her. When she looked up, he was frowning at her.

'Hatty? What are you doing here? It's not safe.'

'I know it's not safe. Let go of me.' She pushed him away and they stood awkwardly mashed together in the narrow stairwell. She felt embarrassed for having tripped and ashamed for snapping at him when he had helped her. She wished he hadn't seen her lose her balance. She was certain he thought she was nothing more than a silly little girl.

'Hatty, there's a dangerous man somewhere around here. You can't be –'

'He's upstairs,' she said. She could already hear the crackle of flames behind her. Soon, the fire would be visible and the stairs would become unpassable. 'You're talking about Mr Oberon, right? I don't think that's his real name. He's killed Mr Hargreave, so we're not going to be paid for that case, I don't think.'

'I don't care about that. I need you to get far away from here. But where is he up there?'

'There's a room at the end of the passage on the next floor up. He's injured, and I don't think he can move.' She grabbed Hammersmith's arm as he stepped around her. 'Mr Hammersmith, I set it on fire. He's going to burn up there. Leave him.'

'You have no idea what this man is capable of.'

'How do you know him? He mentioned you to me.'

'We have a history. I'll tell you about it if we survive until tomorrow.'

As they spoke, the landing above them had grown gradually darker and smokier. The wallpaper at the corner of the stairwell began to peel away, curling toward them in long strips.

'Go!' Hammersmith pointed the way down and out, then turned away from Hatty and ran up the stairs, two at a time. He disappeared in a billow of dark smoke.

Hatty looked down, then up, then shrugged her shoulders and followed Hammersmith back up toward the room where she knew Mr Oberon was waiting.

Sir Edward Bradford grabbed his hat and stopped at the door, looking back at his office and trying to think of anything he might need. He had learned long ago never to rush into anything without first considering what might happen. The price of that lesson had been his left arm, and he had determined that the loss would only strengthen him. He went back to the desk and took his Webley from the top drawer, stuffed it into his belt.

He rushed down the stairs with Fawkes at his heels and he pointed at Inspector Tiffany, who stood at his desk with a sheaf of papers in his hands. Tiffany was in his shirtsleeves and had the rumpled look of someone who had not slept.

'Inspector Tiffany, you're with me,' Sir Edward said. 'And I want Inspector Blacker, too. Sergeant Kett, you can come. Fawkes, you'll coordinate from here. Kett will relay anything that needs doing.'

'What's happening, sir?'

'That damn telephone again. And every time it rings, it's always something about Inspector Day.'

'What,' Tiffany said, 'he's been found yet again?'

'Indeed. We're off to that new department store. Plume's.'

'Plumm's, you mean,' Kett said. 'But, sir, there's nothing there. The place is a ruin and everyone's been cleared out. If Mr Day was there, he ain't any more.'

'I have just received word from Dr Kingsley that our man Day is indeed at that store. And I'll be damned if I let him slip away from us again. I'm going out there myself this time, and I'll grab him by the scruff of his neck and drag him back to the land of the living if I have to.'

'As you say, sir.'

Tiffany dropped the papers on his desk and grabbed his jacket. Blacker saluted and grinned, and they both hurried after Sir Edward, practically running in order to keep up with the determined commissioner.

'It's eerie,' Claire said.

'It is very quiet,' Fiona said. 'Where are all the shoppers?'

People were, in fact, passing by them on the cross streets, but the space in front of the store was being avoided. 'It amazes me how something can go from overcrowded to abandoned in the blink of an eye,' Claire said. 'Do they all think the building will fall on them?'

A man passed by them, watching them from the corner of his eye, but he said nothing. Claire and Fiona stood on the street and watched him until he had crossed over and walked away round the corner. A carriage drew up to the kerb opposite them and stayed there, the driver up top making a point of not looking their way.

'Should we tell him the place is shut down at the moment?'

'I think that's obvious.'

'Well, what's he waiting for?'

The four-wheeler sat there unmoving, but a curtain was pulled aside at the edge of one window and then closed again.

'Go over there,' Claire said. 'Ask him if he's waiting for someone.'

'I'm not going over there. You go over there.'

Claire had just made up her mind to cross and rap on the carriage door when it opened and her father stepped out into the street.

'Claire,' he said, 'how lovely to run into you here. What a coincidence.'

'Father, are you following me?'

'Not at all. I was . . . Your mother sent me to Plumm's. She wants something for the house.'

'What does she want?'

'I've got a list here.' Carlyle made a show of patting his jacket pockets and even grabbed the brim of his hat as if the list might be tucked in his hatband. 'I seem to have misplaced it.'

'As you can plainly see, the store isn't open for business today, Father. It's been wrecked.'

Carlyle looked up for the first time at the broken windows, the litter in the street, the lack of pedestrian traffic. 'What's happened?'

'I'm not entirely sure, but Walter was involved somehow.'

'Walter did this?'

'Well, I don't think that's even possible, but he was here. He may be here again. Fiona and I are looking for him.'

Fiona raised her hand in an awkward greeting.

Carlyle shook his head as if clearing it and swiped his hand through the air in front of him, dispelling the lies between them. 'Look, Claire, I want you to come with me. Your friend, too. There's great danger. I can't explain, but –'

'What are you talking about?'

'I said I can't explain. But there are people about who might wish to harm you. Or harm Walter. I'm not sure any more what they intend, but we should leave here, get out of the city, maybe back to Devon, and wait until we hear from your husband.'

'Why would I leave with you if my husband's in as much danger as you say?'

'Because, for once in your life, you could simply choose to obey your father. I don't think that's too much to ask.'

'I'm here to find Walter. Fiona and I both are. Help us and I'll go with you afterwards. Then you can explain yourself. Right at this moment, nothing matters to me except that after a year, I'm finally close to being with my husband again. Nothing, nothing else matters.'

'Walter.' Carlyle's eyes were wide, and he spoke in a whisper.

'Yes, Walter,' Claire said.

'No, I mean, look. It's Walter.'

Claire turned and saw her husband climbing out through the smashed front window of Plumm's. Walter was gaunt and had the beginnings of a dark beard. His eyes were shadowed, and he was dressed like a pauper, in a torn and tattered suit with no hat. But it was undeniably him, and he was alive and he was only a few feet away from her, clambering over the remains of a window display.

For a moment, Claire couldn't breathe and the world seemed to hold still, but for the struggling form of her husband. She thought she could hear Fiona saying something, perhaps her father continued to speak, but everything receded and became unimportant.

Then she caught her breath. 'Walter!'

She ran toward him, her arms out, her skirts dragging behind her on the ground, as he looked up. But she stopped when she saw his eyes. There was no recognition there. He wasn't even looking at her. He stared past her and his eyes flashed with hatred and anger. She heard a click as the handle of his walking stick disengaged. He drew the blade from his cane and pushed past her. She stumbled and gasped and fell to the ground, looking up just in time to see her husband lunge at Leland Carlyle and impale him on his sword.

Mr and Mrs Parker stood in the shadows of an apothecary down the street from Plumm's. Mr Parker's mind had begun to wander when Mrs Parker grabbed his arm and pointed. They watched a man run out of the abandoned store and stab the high judge of the Karstphanomen.

'That's him,' Mrs Parker said. 'That's our quarry. Jack the Ripper's finally made his move.'

'But we're too late. He's killed our client.'

'Can't blame him for that. We considered the same thing ourselves. Anyway, Carlyle's not dead yet.' With that, Mrs Parker leapt forward and raced down the street with Mr Parker fast at her heels. They separated in front of the store. Mrs Parker chased the attacker, who had dropped his sword, while Mr Parker stopped to check on Leland Carlyle, who was breathing but was quickly losing blood. Already a crowd had begun to form, as if from nowhere. The street had been virtually empty, and now people sprang up in twos and threes, gathering around the man on the ground.

'Don't hurt him,' Carlyle's daughter said, but she wasn't looking at Mr Parker or her father; she was addressing Mrs Parker, who had stopped to pick up the fleeing man's sword and the barrel of his cane. Mrs Parker didn't seem to hear the woman. She ran on, pushing her way through the onlookers and, now doubly armed, chased the man into an alleyway.

Mr Parker got the daughter's attention. 'You know him? The one who did this?'

'It's my husband. I don't know what's going on, but he's not himself. He's a policeman. He must have meant well.'

Mr Parker shook his head, unable to believe their bad luck. Jack the Ripper was related to their client? *And* he was a policeman? Things were getting entirely too complicated. He put pressure on Carlyle's wound and turned his gaze again to the young woman. 'What's his name?'

'Leland Carlyle.'

'Here, let me help. My father's a doctor.' The other girl squatted next to Carlyle, and Mr Parker took the opportunity to back away, bumping into the people behind him.

He stood and fixed Carlyle's daughter with his best glare. 'I asked the name of the other one. Not this one. I know this one. What's the name of the man who stabbed him?'

'Oh. That's Walter Day.'

'Walter Day,' Mr Parker said. They had been specifically told not to kill Walter Day, but was it possible Carlyle didn't know Day was the Ripper? There was something strange going on, but Mr Parker couldn't figure it out and he was suddenly afraid they had been played for fools. He needed to find his daughter, his partner, and take her away, leave this country. He turned and ran down the same alleyway he had seen Mrs Parker enter.

By the time Dr Kingsley returned, there was a crowd gathered on the street in front of Plumm's. He recognized Claire Day, who stood alone, leaning against the brick façade of the wrecked store, but few of the others. A man jumped up from the ground and ran down an alley beside the store. Others watched him go, but no one else moved.

Kingsley went to Claire and gently touched her hand. 'Claire? Claire, can you hear me?'

She looked up at him, but she didn't act like she knew him. He waved a hand in front of her, but her glazed eyes didn't follow the motion. He checked her pulse and smoothed her hair out of her face. He took her arm and walked her back to the wide window ledge outside the store. He brushed the broken glass from it, then took off his jacket and laid it down so she could sit on it. He had smelling salts in his bag, but he wasn't sure they were necessary.

Kingsley pushed his way through the rabble, rolling up his sleeves as he went, hoping he wouldn't see Walter Day or Nevil Hammersmith dead on the ground. Instead he saw his daughter leaning over a stranger. Fiona was pressing a cloth against the man's abdomen, but blood pulsed out through her fingers and soaked the street beneath them. Kingsley knelt beside his daughter and moved her hands out of the way so he could see what he had to deal with.

She looked at him with tears in her eyes. 'Can you help him?'

'You did the right thing, Fiona. If the wound had been just an inch away from where it is, the pressure you put on it wouldn't have been enough to save him.' He ripped open the man's shirt and peeled the fabric away from the wound, then rooted through his black bag for bandages, alcohol, a needle and thread.

'Then he won't die?'

'I'm making no promises, but you've given him a chance.' Fiona shivered, and Kingsley wished he had his jacket back so he could drape it over her. 'The police are on their way and they'll be able to provide transport for him. Who is he?'

'It's Claire's father. Walter stabbed him. Mr Day tried to kill Mrs Day's father right in front of her. Why?'

Kingsley blinked hard and rocked back on his heels. He shook his head. 'He didn't kill him. If we can keep this man alive, then Walter Day isn't a murderer.' But he knew that time was of the essence and he hoped the wagon he'd ordered was on its way already. The bodies in the workshop could stay where they were an hour longer so the police could get Claire's father to the hospital for proper care.

Kingsley shook his head again and sighed. He had left Walter Day to his own devices, knowing full well the man might be a danger. He hadn't counted on the Ripper's enemy being someone who had made himself Day's enemy as well. He continued stitching, not looking up from his work as he talked. 'Fiona, you must think very carefully. Did Mr Day say anything? Anything at all? Did he mention a crow or a white king when he did this?'

'He didn't say a thing. He just did it. It happened so fast. I don't understand.'

'It's all ridiculously complicated.'

He finished and cut the excess thread away, pressed bandages around the wound, and taped them securely in place. He checked the victim's pulse again and was gratified to find that it was weak but steady. He stood and helped Fiona up, wiped her hands with his handkerchief, and walked her over to where Claire still sat in the open window of the fabulous department store.

'Fiona, you've done a great deal to help already, but I need you to take care of Claire. She's had a shock, and so have you, but you've got to be strong for me a bit longer. You've got to watch over Claire. Can you do that?' Fiona nodded, and Kingsley smiled at her. 'That's my good girl. I'm very proud of you.'

He glanced behind him at the crowd, which had begun to break up, people wandering away now that the entertainment had ended. Kingsley was disturbed to see that some of them were only children.

'Tell me where Mr Day went,' he said. 'Did you see?'

Fiona nodded and pointed at the mouth of the alley.

'Fiona, was Mr Hammersmith . . . was Nevil with him?'

'No. I don't know where Nevil is. Oh, do you think he might be in danger? Do you think Mr Day might –'

'No.' Kingsley patted her hand and smiled at her. 'Don't worry now. It will all work out. I can fix everything.'

But his words sounded hollow to him. He hoisted his bag and took a deep breath. It was, he thought, possible to fix everything, to reverse the terrible mistake he'd made in leaving Walter Day in an unstable mental condition, but in order to do that he would have to find Day before the police did.

55

Hammersmith took off his jacket and ripped the left sleeve off. He discarded the rest of the jacket and wrapped the sleeve around his mouth and nose, tied it at the back of his neck. It made his face hot, but he could breathe a little more easily. He crept forward, gripping the length of pipe tight in his fist. The end of the hallway was a wall of flames and smoke, but Hammersmith needed to see Jack's body for himself. He needed to know that the monster was finally and truly dead.

'Mr Hammersmith!'

Hammersmith turned and saw Hatty Pitt at the landing behind him. She was obscured by smoke and was coming slowly toward him. She reached out to steady herself against the wall, but pulled her hand back. The wallpaper was bubbling in the heat.

'Hatty, what are you doing here? Go back downstairs.'

'You'll die up here,' Hatty said. 'You need my help.' Her voice was low and hoarse, and Hammersmith realized his own throat burned when he tried to talk.

Hammersmith reached down and picked up his jacket, ripped off the other sleeve, and tied it around Hatty's mouth. He shook his head at her, but he didn't have enough air to try to speak again, unless he absolutely had to. He waved Hatty back and proceeded once again toward the source of the flames. At least he could keep her behind him.

The fire reached the ceiling and began to crawl across it. Hammersmith knew there wasn't much time left, but he couldn't turn back now. He put his arms over his face, steeled himself, and ran forward, jumping through the flames and through the open door into the room. A moment later, Hatty barreled into him from behind and knocked him forward into the bed. His hand brushed against cold flesh. He pushed himself back away from it and adjusted his grip on the iron pipe, his only weapon. He shook his head again at Hatty, reached past her, and closed the door to keep out the smoke, then checked her arms and face for burns.

Somehow the air felt cooler and relatively smoke-free. The fire was out in the hallway, but soon, he knew, it would consume the doorjamb and make its way into the room. They had a few moments at most to look around. Not much time for detective work.

Hatty pulled the sleeve down off her face and pointed at a chair in the corner of the room. 'He was there. Sitting right there. Mr Hammersmith, I didn't think he could even move.'

'Well, he must have found the strength.' Hammersmith nodded at the corpse in the bed. The man lay in a dried pool of blood and his jaw was missing, the flesh torn back halfway down the length of his throat. 'Is this Joseph Hargreave?'

'I believe so,' Hatty said. 'At least, that's what Mr Oberon told me.' She shuddered and looked away. 'He does resemble his brother. At least . . .' Her voice trailed off. Hammersmith understood. Hatty was strong, but some things were not meant to be seen.

'Stand back,' Hammersmith said. He moved round the foot of the bed and approached the wardrobe that stood between the bed and the window. He took two deep breaths, raised his iron pipe, and pulled the door open.

A second body, stiff with rigor, fell out at his feet. Hammersmith gasped and took a step back, then leaned forward and pushed the body over on its side. It was not Mr Oberon.

'That's Richard Hargreave,' Hatty said. 'The doctor. He was this one's brother.' She pointed at the dead man in the bed. 'He's killed both brothers. I mean, he made it sound as if he had, but I was holding out some hope.'

'Hope isn't much of a defense against Jack,' Hammersmith said. The crackling of the fire had grown much louder, and over the top of the closed door he saw a tongue of flame lick the ceiling of their room. 'Wait, Hatty, did you say this man was a doctor?'

'Yes, Dr Richard Hargreave. Mr Hammersmith, I'm afraid we're trapped in here.'

'The crow. This was the crow in the message he left at Walter's house. Not Dr Kingsley at all. Dr Kingsley is safe from harm. We need only worry about the white king, whoever that is.'

Smoke began to seep into the room, causing Hammersmith's eyes to sting. He looked at Hatty and saw that her eyes were watering, too, tears streaming down her face. She coughed into her fist. 'Mr Hammersmith, I think we're going to die in here.'

'I certainly hope not. We've got a case to finish.' He went to the window and pulled back the curtains, his pipe raised and ready to smash the glass out of the frame. But the window was already broken, and a knotted length of linen hung from the sill, fastened around the window's latch. Hammersmith leaned out and peered down into the narrow alleyway behind the store. He couldn't see far enough into the shadows below the window, couldn't see whether the makeshift rope ladder went all the way to the ground, but decided a broken leg was better than burning to death. He banged away at the bits of broken glass still stuck in the frame. Behind him he heard Hatty yelp and turned to see that the fire had entered the room, eating away at the door all round the jamb and peeling back the wallpaper.

Hammersmith ripped the sheet from the bed, exposing the rest of poor Joseph Hargreave, and grabbed Hatty's arm. She tried to pull back, but he gripped her harder and looped the sheet round her waist. She nodded her understanding and sat on the windowsill, rotated so that her legs were kicking free in the air outside, then pushed off without even waiting to see that Hammersmith had braced himself. He could feel the fire at his back as he strained to support Hatty's scant weight. She turned and grabbed the knotted linen rope, and as he watched her lower herself down the outside wall of the building, it belatedly occurred to him that Jack the Ripper might be waiting for them below.

Sir Edward's carriage pulled up outside Plumm's, and the commissioner jumped out and scanned the street, taking in the diminishing crowd and the injured man at its centre. A moment later, a second, larger carriage stopped behind his. Tiffany, Blacker and Kett piled out, along with three constables, and they ran to catch up to Sir Edward.

'There's a man down,' Sir Edward said. 'Blacker, see to him. Tiffany, Kett, catch these people before they run off. Get statements from them. You others, cordon this off. Dr Kingsley will want to look the area over.'

He spotted Claire Day and Fiona Kingsley sitting against the building. Fiona stood and approached him.

'Miss Kingsley,' Sir Edward said. 'Your father summoned me here by telephone. He said Mr Day was to be found in the vicinity, but clearly a great deal has happened since then. What can you tell me?'

'Mr Day stabbed Mr Carlyle and ran away down that alley.' She pointed. 'Several people have already chased after him. Mr Carlyle needs immediate attention.'

'Yes, I see.'

'There are wagons coming to take away some bodies in a warehouse, but my father said to tell you that Mr Carlyle should be taken first.'

'Of course. And we needn't wait for the wagons. They won't be in any hurry to get here if they think it's not an emergency. Dead bodies are sadly all too commonplace, especially round here these past few days.' He waved his arm at Inspector Blacker. 'Blacker, use my carriage. This man is Inspector Day's father-in-law. Get him to hospital right away, and make sure the doctors understand he's to be a priority.'

'I'll tell the driver,' Blacker said.

'Go with him. I want it understood that I'm taking responsibility for this man's well-being and will be quite cross if he's not taken care of.'

'Yes, sir.'

'And, Blacker, none of your jokes. I want the hospital staff to take this seriously.'

'I never joke with doctors, sir. They're not known to be humorous people.'

'Away with you.' Sir Edward turned back to Fiona. 'How is Mrs Day holding up?'

'She's had a shock, sir. It's been a difficult year, and this only adds to her hardships.'

'I don't believe Walter is responsible for this.'

'I saw it, sir, with my own eyes.'

'I don't mean that I disbelieve you. I mean there are circumstances neither you nor I can currently understand. Your father explained a bit of it when we spoke on the telephone, but I'm hoping for more details from him.'

'He's gone with everyone else, chasing after Mr Day.'

'Then that is where I must go as well. Thank you, Miss Kingsley. Look after Mrs Day, and we'll get this sorted. I promise you that.'

He watched her go and sighed again. They had so many problems to deal with from outside the Murder Squad. And yet there seemed to be no end of problems within the squad itself, most of them centering on Walter Day. But he was fond of the lad and was determined that he could be a steadying influence in Walter's life.

Provided he could catch up to him.

56

'Walter Day, what a pleasant surprise.'

Day stopped and squinted at the shadowed end of the alley. His leg ached, which was often the case when he tried to move too fast. He looked about for a weapon, but saw nothing he could use. He wondered what had become of his walking stick. He remembered having it in his hand and didn't recall setting it down anywhere, but it was gone.

'It's all right,' Jack said. His voice echoed weakly back and forth between the brick walls, making it impossible to pinpoint his exact location. 'I won't bite you. Or stab you, or cut out your liver and eat it. Unless you promise to remain very still. I don't think I'm in any shape for a fight.'

'You don't sound good, Jack.'

'The pain is rather exquisite. I'm afraid I overextended myself climbing down.'

Day glanced up at a hazy square of light, a window overhead. A rope of some sort hung down from the ledge, and a shape hung there in the dark. The smoke moved above and Day thought he could pick out a familiar figure at the window. He took a step forward.

'That's close enough, Walter Day. You look confused. Is something bothering you?'

'You can't see my face any more than I can see yours, Jack. The light's wrong.'

'I see more than you do. And I hear more than you do. I hear confusion in your voice. What's happened?'

'I don't know.' Day took another step forward. If he kept Jack's attention on him, the Ripper might not look up.

'Oh, my,' Jack said. 'You did it, didn't you?'

'Did what?'

'You finally did me that favor you promised.'

'Favor?' But now fragments of memory exploded in his head. Images of blood and anger, a man on the ground at his feet, bleeding and unconscious. 'Jack, what did I do? What did you make me do?'

'An interesting fact about mesmerism, Walter Day. The public believes you can make a man do anything when he's under your spell, but it's not true. You can't force someone to do something he wouldn't do anyway. It's what makes mesmerism such a limited tool for murder.'

'I know that now.'

'You could only have killed someone you already wanted to kill. That's what makes it delicious.'

'I never wanted to kill him.'

'But of course you did. I helped you discard your inhibitions for one glorious moment. And in return you've eliminated the last of those dreadful Karstphanomen for me. Or at least of them what held me in that cold, dank prison and did things to me. I did the crow myself, and his body's burning even as we speak. And you've done the white king. Congratulations, and thank you.'

Now Day took a step back. 'You've sealed my fate.'

'I've set you free.'

'What else have you set me to do? What other surprises are waiting in my head?'

'Nothing. That was the only thing. Oh, well, I did leave a little suggestion in there that you mustn't ever harm me or stand in my way. That was only to make things easier for me with my comings and goings. I promise, other than that, you're your own man once again.'

'I can never go back.'

'You can go wherever you please. And now I set you free from me. I don't think we need each other any more, do you? If you'll stand aside, I think I can make it to the street. From there, the world is my murky oyster stew.'

'I'm not letting you go.'

'You have no choice. Oh, but Walter, look out behind you. That young lady has stopped listening to us and I think she intends to do you harm.'

Day turned just in time to see a strange woman, wearing trousers and brandishing Day's own sword. The blade came slashing down at him, and at that same moment, he heard a shot ring out down the length of the alley.

57

'Ah, Miss Tinsley,' Goodpenny said. 'And Mrs Dew. What a delight to find you here.'

Goodpenny climbed down from the display box inside the window and sat on the sill beside Fiona. He laid a rifle across his lap and took a moment to catch his breath, watching as two constables picked up the unmoving body of Leland Carlyle. The policemen crab-walked the unconscious man to Sir Edward's private carriage and laid him across the seat inside, folding him at the knees so he would fit.

'It looks as if exciting things have been happening out here,' Goodpenny said. 'What have I missed?'

'I don't think I can bear to repeat it all, Mr Goodpenny,' Fiona said.

'A bear, you say? How terrifying. I'm quite frightened of bears. They have a nasty habit of eating people.'

Fiona sighed, but didn't bother to correct the well-meaning little man. They sat in silence for a long moment, and then Goodpenny uttered a cry of delight and reached inside his jacket. He pulled out a small horn, brown and translucent, ridged like an oyster's shell, with a leather fitting at one end and a leather strap round the middle.

'Look what I found,' he said. 'It's a horn.'

'I can see,' Fiona said. 'It's very pretty.'

'No, no, for hearing. The horn has been fashioned into an ear trumpet, you see? It's an aid in hearing. Look at what I do.' He held it up and jammed the leather tip in his ear. 'People speak and the sound goes right in here.' He pointed to the flared end of the horn. 'It goes all the way through and is amplified during its journey to my ear, like so.' He swiped his finger down the length of the horn and ended with a flourish at his ear.

'You'll finally be able to hear, Mr Goodpenny.'

'Oh, it's not for me. My hearing's still sharp. It's for your young man, Mr Angerschmid. He's hard of hearing now.' He removed the device from his ear and presented it to Fiona.

'Thank you, but he's not my young man,' she said. She shook her head and laid the trumpet on the sill beside her.

'Give it time. Give it time. I say, that bear's not still about, is it? We should really get you young ladies to a place of safety. I'm afraid this rifle's of no real use since I have no bullets for it.'

'The bear has gone. They took it away to the circus.'

'Oh, thank goodness.'

'But the bear is quite the least of our problems, Mr Goodpenny.'

'Bears are enormous problems.'

'Yes, I can see that they might be. But Mrs Day's husband has tried to kill her father. That's him in the carriage.'

Goodpenny looked up as the driver cracked his reins and the carriage rolled away, revealing Inspector Tiffany, who had been standing on the other side of it talking to an old woman. Tiffany looked up and nodded at them, then bent his head to hear what the woman was saying.

'What a friendly fellow,' Goodpenny said. 'Tell me, did Mr Dew succeed? Did he kill the man?'

344

'No. Claire's father is still alive. For the moment, at least.'

'Well, then. Many's the man who's tried to murder his father-in-law. I'm not sure it's even a crime these days. I've been tempted myself, from time to time. It's that bear we ought to worry about. If it escaped the circus once, it's liable to do so again.'

'Oh, Mr Goodpenny! You're impossible!'

'Now, now, dear. I don't mean to make light.' He turned and smiled at Claire. 'Mrs Dew, where are your delightful children?'

Claire looked up and seemed to notice Goodpenny for the first time. 'My children?'

'Young Jemima and his brother, and those two darling babies.'

'They're with their governess.'

'That horrible woman? You mustn't neglect them for long. They'll need you about. And they'll need their father, too. Unless I'm very much mistaken, I've recently made your husband's acquaintance.'

'He's gone.' Claire's eyes welled up and she buried her face in her hands.

Goodpenny put an arm around her and fished a handkerchief from his waistcoat pocket. 'Forgive me, my dear.'

'He's been gone forever and now he's going to prison. He won't ever come home again.'

'Going to prison? Oh, I shouldn't think so. I've met your husband, and he seems like a good man, a capable fellow. A bit lost, perhaps, but that's why he has you, isn't that right? Someone who will always bring him back home.'

'You don't know us.'

'I know people, Mrs Dew. And just looking at you, I

can tell that you're a strong person, and that you and your husband need each other very much. Where there is love, there is always a way.'

'You must love your wife.'

'I did, my dear.' He nodded and smiled, but it was a sad sort of smile. 'Yes, I do love her.'

Fiona clapped her hands and stood up. 'Mr Goodpenny, you've given me an idea. But I wonder if you will help me with a small matter.'

'Anything for you, Miss Tinsley. You know that.'

'Might I borrow your rifle?'

'Oh, but it's not mine. It belongs to the store, I suppose. But with all the loss Plumm's has sustained, I suppose they won't miss it for a time.'

'I don't think they'll be getting it back.'

'Yes, as long as they get it back. Here you are.'

'You don't want to know why I need it?'

'You need it, dear. That is all I care to know.'

'Oh, thank you, Mr Goodpenny!' Fiona bent and kissed him on the cheek.

Goodpenny rubbed his cheek and watched her run across the street, where she handed the rifle to Inspector Tiffany. Tiffany took it from her, and they stood talking for quite some time. Goodpenny chuckled and patted Claire's hand. 'She's a good girl,' he said. 'Whether Mr Angerschmid realizes it or not, our Miss Tinsley is a prize.'

'I do wonder what she's doing,' Claire said.

Goodpenny picked up the ear trumpet from the sill where Fiona had left it. He lifted it to his ear and leaned forward. 'Listen, my dear. Do you smell smoke?'

58

Hammersmith looked back and saw that the bed was on fire, the ceiling above it a roiling inferno. Advance scouts of flame, like ant columns, stretched outward across the floor, edging ever nearer his left foot. His back and his feet were uncomfortably warm, beginning to itch with heat. Hatty still hung below the window, dangling from the knotted linen rope.

'Hurry,' he said. He could barely make out her shape against the dark floor of the alley below.

'Mr Hammersmith, there's someone down there.' Her voice was hoarse and quiet, and he had to lean farther out to hear her. 'I think it's him. I can hear him. Someone else, too.'

Hammersmith strained to hear. There was muffled conversation below, the clanking of metal on brick, the scuffle of shoe leather on stone. More than one person, and possibly a fight. He pulled his head back in and examined his options. There were none. The door was completely obscured by fire and smoke, and he knew that the hallway outside the room would be impassable. His eyes burned and he was having difficulty breathing. He leaned out of the window again, enjoying the feel of the cool breeze on his face.

'Hatty, you're going to have to go all the way down. I'll be right behind you.'

'They're below me. Mr Oberon will catch me.'

'When you're close to the ground, push off from the wall and jump as far as you can. Get as far away as you can, Hatty, and run. You'll only have to worry for two minutes, I swear it. I won't let anything happen to you.'

He couldn't hear her response. The flames were licking his ear. His trouser leg was suddenly on fire, and Hammersmith dropped his iron pipe. It hit the floor with a low thud, and at the same moment he heard a gunshot from the alley outside. He leapt out the window, clung to the frame above him, and stood silhouetted against the room, using one hand to beat at his smoldering leg. He knew he was an easy target now if Jack was indeed waiting below them with a gun. The fire crackled at his good ear and he shook his head, trying to get the muffled ringing sound to fade long enough that he might hear whatever it was Hatty was trying to say to him. At least she was still there below him. She hadn't been shot. But she was vulnerable, a sitting duck for whomever was shooting, and her arms had to be close to giving out. He doubted she had the strength any more to climb down. At any moment, she would lose her grip and drop.

'Stay,' Hammersmith said. 'Just hang on there.'

He eased himself down, hoping the makeshift rope would hold them both and that it wouldn't burn before he reached the alley floor. He grabbed the inside of the frame, ignoring the searing pain in his fingers, rested his weight on the ledge, let go with one hand, reached down, and grabbed the rope. Then he let go with the other hand and dropped down so that he was directly above Hatty. Carefully, he maneuvered over her, pushing her with his body so that she was up against the outside wall of the building.

'Don't let go,' he said. She nodded, her eyes closed, and he could feel her breath on his cheek. Her hair smelled of smoke and strawberries, and he noticed how long and slender her throat was, how gracefully her head tilted.

He crawled slowly down, hand over hand, alert to where his hands were in relationship to her torso, her waist, her legs. Finally he was past her and the flames were far enough above him that he no longer felt the heat from them. He reached the end of the rope and let go.

'Doctor!'

Kingsley turned and saw Sir Edward running toward him. 'Commissioner, be careful. I don't know what kind of weapons these people may have.'

Sir Edward drew up alongside Kingsley and stopped, panting lightly. 'Everything's come home to roost, hasn't it, Bernard?'

'I'm afraid it has,' Kingsley said. 'But this isn't the time to fret over it. Walter's somewhere ahead of us there, along with someone who's gone chasing after him. This is no place for a doctor or an old soldier.'

'Did you see Walter?'

'I did. He seemed fine to me. At least physically. But I made a mistake. I let him –'

There was a deafening explosion as the domed skylight above Plumm's burst open, raining glass down on the street. The cobblestones under them bucked and shuddered, and the two men fell back just as a chunk of the department store's brick-and-mortar wall ploughed into the ground where they had been standing.

'My God,' Kingsley said. 'Are you all right?'

Sir Edward staggered to the kerb and sat down. 'The world seems to be spinning,' he said. 'I just need to –'

'You're bleeding. Let me –'

'No, I think I'm all right. Get going. Get to Walter before this whole place comes down round our ears. I'll be there as quickly as I can.'

Mr Parker was flung backward against the opposite wall of the alley as a tall, thin man dropped out of the air above him and knocked both Walter Day and Mrs Parker to the ground. Mr Parker looked up and saw that there was another person, a girl, hanging in the air above him. People were falling out of the building. Mr Parker realized he somehow still had the gun in his hand and he raised it, intending to hit his target this time.

Mrs Parker groaned and raised her head. 'Darling,' she said, 'did you shoot at me?'

'I missed,' Mr Parker said. 'I was aiming –'

'You never miss. I believe you were trying to –'

'I'm with the police! Please put down your weapon.' An older gentleman ran toward them, carrying a black medical bag. 'Good Lord! There's a girl up there,' he said.

The building beside them exploded a second time in a shower of glass and metal and brickwork. Something heavy smashed into Mr Parker's neck and he fell backward again, but concentrated on keeping the gun in his hand. The policeman was unconscious on the ground, but Mrs Parker was still moving, trying to extricate herself from the tangle of bodies and bricks. Mr Parker shook his head and leaned against the alley wall. He couldn't breathe, and everything seemed to be moving in slow motion.

He was surprised to see that the young woman was still dangling out of the window. The window itself was gone, but the rope had held fast, and so had the girl. The doctor dropped his bag and positioned himself under the woman.

'Let go, dear,' the doctor said. 'I'll catch you.'

Mr Parker raised his gun. He felt panicky, as if he might vomit, and the world seemed to swim in and out of focus. He fired a second time, not sure where the gun was pointed. The doctor staggered forward, but stayed on his feet, his arms out, ready to catch the girl. Mr Parker fired again, then turned at the sound of something moving toward him. A big man with dark wavy hair erupted from the shadows, and Mr Parker felt his abdomen burning. As the man took his gun from him, he looked down and saw a large sliver of broken glass protruding from his stomach. The man yanked and a gusher of blood followed the glass out of Mr Parker's body.

Hatty couldn't feel her arms any more, but her shoulders quivered with the strain of hanging on to the knotted linens. She heard the man beneath her urging her to let go, but she wasn't sure she could. Her hands were made of stone. She couldn't see or hear Mr Hammersmith below and she wondered if he'd been hurt or even killed.

The two explosions had knocked her about, banged her into the wall and disoriented her. Blood trickled into her eyes from a scalp wound delivered by a flying brick. But somehow she hadn't been knocked off the makeshift rope.

At last she steeled herself and focused on her numb fingers. She forced them to open one at a time and felt lancing pain shoot up her arms as her petrified knuckles unlocked. She immediately plummeted into the arms of the waiting man.

He staggered forward under her weight and they hit the wall hard. He fell to his knees and gently set her down before toppling sideways on the alley floor. She sat up and looked at him, recognizing him at last. He was the doctor from Guildhall who had helped so many injured Plumm's customers.

'Dr Kingsley? Are you all right?'

He rolled over on to his back and smiled up at her. 'Give me a moment, will you?'

'Sir, you've been shot. I'll get a doctor. I mean another doctor.'

'Too late, I think. You . . . you hurt?'

'I don't know. My hands hurt, but I'm all in one piece, thanks to you.'

'You look a bit like my daughter.'

'What should I do? I can't tell where the blood's coming from.'

'Just talk to me for a minute, would you? It's quite cold down here.'

'Help will be coming soon,' she said. 'Very soon, I'm sure.'

Hatty looked round and saw the unconscious body of Mr Hammersmith. There were other people, but she didn't call out to them for help. They were shouting at one another, ignoring Hatty and Dr Kingsley. One of them (she was certain it was Mr Oberon) stabbed another, and the injured man screamed. Hatty screamed, too, and fought the urge to run. Dr Kingsley needed her help.

She still had Mr Hammersmith's jacket sleeve hanging

loosely around her throat and she pulled it off over her head. She probed Dr Kingsley's chest with her aching fingers, and he winced.

'Fiona . . .' He coughed and a bubble of blood burst from his open lips, freckling Hatty's face and arms.

'My name is Hatty, sir. If I can find where the blood's coming from, perhaps I can make it stop.'

'Be good to each other,' Kingsley said. 'Nevil's a fine boy, but he needs you.'

'You mean Mr Hammersmith?' Dr Kingsley's breathing had become shallow, and with each breath he made a gurgling sound that alarmed Hatty.

'What time is it? I'm late,' he said.

'No, sir. No, sir,' Hatty said. 'Stay awake.' She found a hole in his waistcoat and pressed the soot-covered jacket sleeve into it, hoping that would staunch the flow of blood.

Dr Kingsley smiled at her. His lips were a ghastly red, rimmed with blood. 'That's it,' he said. 'You're doing a fine job. Proud of . . . Tell Fiona.'

He closed his eyes.

'No!' Mrs Parker pulled herself up and grabbed the sword from the alley floor.

'Tut tut,' the man Jack said. 'Let's not be hasty.'

'You killed him,' Mrs Parker said.

'He's not dead yet. Look at him. He won't last much longer, but who knows? I have a similar wound and I've managed to do a great deal despite it. Was he your lover?'

'Yes.'

'Well, this must be heartbreaking for you.' He pointed Mr Parker's gun at her and pulled the trigger. There was an audible click, but nothing happened. 'Oh,' Jack said. 'Well, that puts me in a rather difficult situation.'

Mrs Parker stepped forward, the sword raised high. 'Are you really him?'

'Him? Do you mean God? Yes, I suppose I am.'

'Kill him,' Mr Parker said. His voice was a liquid whisper. 'Help me. We can still get away.'

'Yes, one of us requires your assistance,' Jack said. 'I suppose you have a choice. Him or me. I'm really in no position to blame you either way.'

The sword slashed down and Mr Parker's eyes grew wide. A thin red line appeared on his throat, then opened, and blood cascaded over his collar. He slumped, lifeless, to the alley floor.

'Oh, what a pleasant surprise,' Jack said. 'Now, if you wouldn't mind, I'm not at my best, and we should move quickly if we're to get away.' He held out his hand, and Mrs Parker hesitated. At last, she lowered the sword and took Jack's hand.

'Lovely,' Jack said. 'But we can't go that way, my sweet. There will be more people coming.'

'Then . . .'

'We'll go back in. Through this door is a storeroom.'

'But the store is on fire. It's falling down.'

'What is life without risk?'

He put his arm around her, and she helped him walk to the door. He produced a key and, as Hatty Pitt worked to keep Dr Kingsley alive, the two monsters entered the inferno and were gone.

AFTER

At last they came upon a clearing in the wood, and there, sitting on a footstool in the centre of the clearing, was Peter. The Kindly Nutcracker's head shouted, 'Halt!' and the Rocking Horse skidded to a stop. Anna jumped out of the carriage and ran to Peter and lifted him high in the air. Peter's little body made of rag and dowels was limp, and one of his legs had broken at the joint so that it swung awkwardly about in the air.

'Why doesn't he say anything?' asked Mary Annette.

'I don't know,' said Anna. 'He is very limp. I hope he is not taken ill.'

'I know why,' said the Babushka. She rolled out of the carriage and hopped over to Anna. She shivered and quivered and split in half. Then she shivered again and quivered again and split in half once more, and the angriest Babushka jumped out into the clearing.

'I do not like breaking open,' said the angriest Babushka. But then she did break in half, and an even smaller Babushka was revealed. This one wore tiny painted-on spectacles, and her hair was drawn up into a flat glossy bun at the top of her head.

This new Babushka said, 'Peter cannot talk to you, Anna, because he was never truly a part of our wood. When we were chopped down to become toys and furnishings and matches, we wanted to come back to see you again. But Peter was not made from the same wood we were. He was already a little doll of rag and wood when you used to play here. And so he remains a doll, but without the spark of life that we have.'

357

'But what made you come alive?' Anna asked. 'If it isn't this place that has the magic, then what has done it?'

'You did it, Anna,' said the Babushka.

'You missed the wood,' said the Kindly Nutcracker's head. 'And you wanted us to come home to you.'

'You were sad and wanted to play in the wood one more time,' said Mary Annette.

'And so we came to see you,' said the Kindly Nutcracker's head.

'If I could bring you all to life, then surely I can bring Peter to life as well,' said Anna.

'Perhaps you do not want him to be alive,' the Babushka said.

'Nonsense,' said Anna. She wagged her finger at her doll as if she were scolding a bad little boy. 'Peter, I command you to wake up and do a dance for me.'

'But he cannot,' said Mary Annette. 'His leg is broken, don't you see?'

'The Kindly Nutcracker is broken, but he is still able to talk and to steer the carriage,' said Anna. 'And, Mary, your strings have all been cut, but you are able to walk and talk just like anything.'

'Anna, soon you will be an adult and you will not wish to play with dolls any more,' said wise little Babushka. 'What will happen to Peter then?'

'Why, I will give him to my own children to play with,' Anna declared.

'Perhaps,' said the Kindly Nutcracker's head. 'Perhaps you should fix Peter's leg and enjoy him as he was meant to be enjoyed, until such time when you no longer wish to play with him. That would be kinder than making him a living thing that will be sad when you are no longer interested in him.'

Anna lowered her arms and let Peter sit in the dirt while she looked at her new friends. 'What will happen to all of you when I am too old to frolic in the wood any more?' she asked.

'But we all have new homes already,' Mary Annette said. 'My puppeteer will miss me if I am not there in the morning. He is creating a new story for me to act out.'

'I was going to be on the mantel of a family's fireplace at the holiday home so that I could break open tough nuts for them to eat.' The Kindly Nutcracker's fuzzy white beard bristled in the breeze. 'Perhaps they will fix me.'

'I am on display at a fabulous department store,' all of the Babushka's heads said at once. 'Soon, a child will convince his mother to purchase me and I will provide amusement for that child. That will be a fine life for me.'

The Rocking Horse rocked back and forth in the grass as if nodding in agreement, and Anna wondered if it already belonged to a child or if it was waiting for someone to come along and discover it.

'But if you are all meant to be somewhere else, then why are you here?' she asked.

'We are here to say our good-byes and to have one last great adventure,' said the Kindly Nutcracker's head. 'By morning we will be gone again, and it will be as though we were never here.'

'Oh, oh, but I will miss you so,' said Anna.

'And we will miss you,' the smallest and wisest part of the Babushka said. 'But everything must change, and we must go to our new homes and have many more adventures of a different sort. And you must do the same.'

Anna looked down at Peter, who hung from her hand the way he always had. In the dim light of distant fires, he looked somehow different. But she knew that it wasn't him at all. He had remained the same, while the world all round her had changed.

'When will you go?' she asked.

'We will be gone when you wake in the morning,' said the wise Babushka. 'This place will be as it was when you went to bed last, nothing but stumps and brown grass and the sad little creek that now runs through a field.'

'And I will never see you again?' Anna asked.

'No, but you will remember us,' the Kindly Nutcracker's head said. 'And we will still have the rest of this night to be together.'

'Then there is time for glue,' Anna said. 'We must go to my house at the edge of the wood, where my father keeps glue in a drawer in his workshop. He also keeps nails there, as well as the sort of nail that winds round itself.'

'You are talking about wood screws,' the Rocking Horse said.

'Why, Rocking Horse!' Anna exclaimed. 'I did not know that you could talk!'

'Neither did I,' said the Rocking Horse. And those were the last words he ever spoke.

'It would be kind of you to glue me back together,' said the Kindly Nutcracker's head. 'I am glad you were able to find all the parts of me that were broken apart by that rascal Jack.'

'Is it possible for you to mend my strings?' asked Mary Annette.

'I am sure we can,' Anna said. 'Now we must hurry before dawn breaks and you all must leave. I will make you all whole again so you will look proper for your new homes.'

Anna clambered back up in the carriage after helping the Babushkas in first and putting all her parts back together into a single egg shape. The Kindly Nutcracker's head yelled, 'Haw!' and the Rocking Horse plunged forward.

When they had arrived at Anna's home, she ran to her father's shed, where he kept glue in a drawer and nails in a box, and she put the Kindly Nutcracker all back together, except for one small piece that she could not find. But the hole where that piece belonged was on the bottom of his feet, which were all fashioned from the same chunk of wood that had been painted blue and did not separate. She did not think anyone would notice the missing piece if the nutcracker stayed in his place on the mantel and did his job, which was to crack open nuts. Then she nailed Mary Annette's strings back into place on her cross.

And she glued Jack's box shut to keep him from springing out and surprising people. While her friends watched, she put Jack's box at the bottom of her toy chest so that the other toys could all keep an eye on him and keep him out of trouble.

When she woke in the morning, she ran to the window. The sky was a light blue color smudged with grey, and silhouetted against it were queue after endless queue of stumps where there had once been trees. Her friends were gone, except of course for Peter, and except for Jack, too, because he had been given to her as a gift.

Many years later, when she had children of her own and they had children, too, Anna asked for her old toy chest to be brought down from the attic, and she took Peter out and gave him to her littlest granddaughter so that she might have a new playmate and so that Peter would have a new friend, too.

Her eyes were not good any more, and so she did not notice that Jack and his box were missing from the chest.

— RUPERT WINTHROP, FROM
The Wandering Wood (1893)

59

In the spring of 1891, Plumm's department store burned to the ground after a top-floor storeroom full of ammunition and lamp oil exploded. Hundreds of thousands of pounds' worth of merchandise was destroyed, and seven bodies, burned beyond recognition, were later found in the rubble. John Plumm was traveling in France at the time and he stayed there until the London press moved on to other, fresher stories and his creditors had been dealt with.

Plumm's had been touted as the biggest and most extravagant experience to be had in London since the Crystal Palace, and many years passed before another enterprise of its type was attempted.

But in that same season, the city produced two other momentous events, neither of which received the sort of notice that Plumm's did: Inspector Walter Day resumed his life, and Dr Bernard Kingsley, late of University College Hospital, passed away quietly in his sleep.

60

For the first weeks after Dr Kingsley's death, his daughter visited his grave every day. Sometimes she would see Timothy Pinch there, and twice she saw Hatty Pitt. She did not speak to either of them. On her fifth visit she found Walter Day at her father's grave, standing next to a rather pretty young woman whom she hadn't met. She ignored Walter, but the woman intrigued her, and so she introduced herself.

'I'm very sorry, Miss Kingsley,' the woman said.

'Did you know my father?'

'Not well, I'm afraid. I was injured and he helped me. I should introduce myself. My name is Esther Paxton.'

'Oh,' Fiona said. 'You were the one . . .' Her voice trailed off and she made an effort not to look at Walter, who stood awkwardly nearby holding a bouquet of flowers.

Esther saw the expression on Fiona's face and she flushed. She looked at the tops of her shoes. 'I just came to say good-bye.'

'To my father?'

'Yes, and to Mr Day. I never knew Walter's name or that he had a family. I hope you'll believe that.'

'Of course.'

'I should have known, I should have thought . . . But I was happy just to have someone there with me again. I would never have –'

'No, I know. Nobody thinks less of you. You helped him when he needed help, and everyone is so very grateful to you.'

'That's kind of you.'

'Perhaps you could visit some time. I'm sure Claire would be delighted to meet you.'

Esther made a small noise and smiled at Fiona. 'No. I have my shop to look after, you see. Business is quite good lately, since the fire. My customers are returning.'

Day took a step closer to them and fiddled with the flowers in his hand. 'I'm so glad to hear that, Esther. I mean, Mrs Paxton.'

'Thank you, Walter.' She didn't look up at him. 'Miss Kingsley, I'm glad to meet you. From what little I knew of him, I'm sure your father was a good man.'

'Thank you.'

'If you'll excuse me, I have another grave to see this morning. My husband is buried over there.' She pointed. 'He's in that copse of trees, and it's been too long since I visited him.'

She left them there, and they watched her walk away. After some time, Walter laid his flowers on Dr Kingsley's grave and reached out, touched Fiona's arm, then walked away in the opposite direction.

Fiona remained at the grave that entire morning, as was her custom. It was peaceful there, and quiet. Eventually she took out her sketchbook and began to draw a bird that had perched on her father's stone.

61

Nevil Hammersmith packed away his documentation of the Walter Day case and put it all into storage. With the clutter gone, his office seemed bare and forbidding, and so he moved back into his flat and learned to enjoy the company of his new fern.

Walter Day slept in Hammersmith's office, taking advantage of the empty space and the unused bedroll. He made daily trips to Finsbury Circus, teaching the boys there to sort leftover tobacco by color and age, and to roll new cigars. He gave his folding tray, along with his Reasonable Tobacco sign, to Jerome, who seemed to be the most responsible and resourceful of the lads.

They did not talk about his friend Ambrose.

And Day did not return again to Drapers' Gardens.

One evening, in the second week after his return, Claire Day came to visit him at Hammersmith's offices. Fiona Kingsley accompanied her, but Claire left the children at home with their new governess.

Hammersmith, Fiona and Hatty Pitt waited in the outer office while Claire talked with her husband, and Hammersmith sent Eugenia Merrilow out to fetch tea for them all.

'It's time for you to come home,' Claire said.

'You know I can't do that,' Walter said.

'So you plan to live here, in poor Nevil's office on the floor?'

'I'll find another place to live.'

'Oh? And will you return to that woman?'

Day knew she meant Esther Paxton. 'I never . . . Claire, I wasn't myself.'

'That's not an answer.'

'I cared very much for Esther, but she was only a friend, and never anything more than that. Somehow, I always knew in my heart I was a married man.'

'And that's all that kept you from her bed?'

'Of course not,' he said. 'And, no, to answer your question properly, I have no plans to ever see her again. Nor do I believe she wishes to see me.'

There was a long silence before Claire spoke again. 'I think I can live with that,' she said. 'I do trust you, Walter. But . . .'

'But I stabbed your father.' Walter smiled. 'You know, I've always wanted to stab your father, but I regret doing it in front of you.'

Claire looked away and smiled. 'It's not that. He'll live. I've spoken to Sir Edward, and he explained that you'd been manipulated somehow, that you didn't know what you were doing. I can't imagine what you must have gone through.'

'I'd rather you never know.'

'But I hope you will tell me sometime, when things have settled and you feel comfortable.'

'If it's not your father, there must be something else troubling you.'

'Why didn't you come back?'

'I didn't . . . I didn't remember.'

'But, Walter, why didn't you remember me?'

His eyes filled with tears, and he put his arm up so she wouldn't see. He turned away from her and she waited, without going to him or touching him. When he spoke, his voice was like the fog that had lifted from the city. 'I did remember. I did, but I lied to myself. I couldn't lead him back to you. I couldn't bring that to our house again. I thought I had to start anew and let you go on to live a better life.'

And then she did go to him and put her hand on his arm, and he turned toward her.

'Oh, Walter, I can't live any sort of life without you.'

'At some point, once the police conclude their investigation, they're going to take me to prison, Claire.'

'So you've continued to stay away.'

'I've only tried to shelter you.'

'The men in my life are constantly trying to shelter me, to protect me from themselves and from each other, deciding what's best for me at every turn. I'm quite sick and tired of it all. I don't want everything to be hidden away from me. I'm a grown woman and I'm perfectly capable of making my own choices.'

'I don't want you or the children to see me behind bars.'

'As I say, I've spoken to Sir Edward and I don't believe he has any such plan.'

'I'd like to hear that from him.'

'Then we'll pay him a visit today. I want our life back. My bed is cold, and the children need their father.'

'Are you sure you –'

'As I say, I can make my own decisions, Walter. And it seems I need to make yours for you, too. So it's settled. You're coming home with me, and I won't hear another word about it.'

62

When Walter and Claire emerged from Hammersmith's office, they were holding hands.

'Does this mean I get my bedroll back?'

'Yes,' Day said. 'Thank you, Nevil.'

'Don't mention it. I'm just glad things are back to normal at last.' He glanced at Fiona and shook his head. 'No, not normal. I'm sorry.'

'I know what you meant,' Fiona said.

'Timothy Pinch mentioned you yesterday,' Hammersmith said.

Fiona wrinkled her nose, but before she could respond, the door opened and Sir Edward Bradford strolled into the office. There was a small bandage on his scalp, just above his temple.

'Ah, everyone's here,' he said. 'Good. Saves me some time.'

Hammersmith poured another cup of tea and set it at the corner of the desk where Sir Edward could reach it. 'Did you find Mr Oberon's body?'

'It's hard to say,' Sir Edward said. 'Three of the corpses found there were women, and one was a child, probably a boy.'

'His name was Ambrose,' Day said. 'I never knew his full name. Just Ambrose.'

'Ah. Yes, Ambrose then. Of the three men who were dug out of that ruin, it's impossible to say anything about them. Mr Pinch is working to find identifying marks of some sort, but I've seen the bodies and I don't hold out much hope.'

'I was only now on my way to see you,' Day said. 'To turn myself in.'

'Turn yourself in for what? Surely Mrs Day has told you I have no interest in arresting you.'

'Someone ought to pay for stabbing Leland Carlyle.'

'Oh, that. No. That was clearly self-defense. Fiona was kind enough to pick up Carlyle's rifle, a Martini-Henry, from where he'd dropped it in the street. Inspector Tiffany examined the weapon, and it had recently been fired. We're just pleased that the round apparently missed you.'

Day looked at Fiona, who made a show of fixing her hair in its chignon. 'Self-defense?' he said.

'Indeed. I've pieced together what must have happened, based in part on knowledge I have of Mr Carlyle's recent activities. Mrs Day, you may not wish to hear some of this.'

'It's all right. I can bear it.'

'Very well. Your father seems to have been engaged in a sort of private war with this Oberon person, and Oberon apparently thought it was clever to use Carlyle's son-in-law as a pawn. So he captured and manipulated Inspector Day. In return, Carlyle hired a soldier of fortune to pursue Oberon, and Plumm's became their battleground. We found the hired killer's body in that alley, and it turns out the fellow was wanted in several other countries. He's suspected of murdering an ambassador. Honestly, we're all lucky Mr Day escaped with his life.'

'Then I'm really free to go home again?'

'By all means, do. You've had a long holiday, Walter, and

it's high time you went home and got back to work. That boy Simon is going to be a policeman when he grows up and he needs some instruction. Take the rest of the week, relax. I'll see you first thing Monday morning at your desk.'

'My desk? I'm back at the Yard?'

'I never sacked you.' He frowned and turned his gaze on Nevil. 'Now, Mr Hammersmith, I did make the mistake of sacking you. In light of your single-minded work in bringing Mr Day back to us, I've re-examined that decision. I'd like you back Monday morning as well, if you're willing.'

'I thought you —'

'I always worried you'd get yourself killed as a policeman. But you haven't stopped putting yourself in the way of danger and you're not dead yet. I might as well make use of your particular talents if I can. And we need someone to mind Mr Day so this sort of thing doesn't happen again. He gets into an extraordinary amount of trouble himself. I think more than when the two of you are together.'

Hatty put down her teacup. 'What about this place?'

'If you close the Hammersmith Agency, I will have nothing with which to occupy my days,' Eugenia said. 'I quite like it here.'

Hammersmith sighed. 'I do, too, but we've lost our biggest client.' He nodded at Claire. 'I don't think I can afford to keep the doors open now.'

'You could,' Hatty said, 'if you had a sergeant's salary.'

Sir Edward stood quietly watching them, stroking his beard. Hammersmith looked from Hatty to him, and Sir Edward shrugged his shoulders.

'I can't do both things,' Hammersmith said.

'I'll run this place for you,' Hatty said. 'You know I can do it. I'll bring in new clients to replace Mrs Day, and the agency will practically pay for itself.'

'You can't call it the Hammersmith Agency if Nevil isn't even here,' Fiona said.

'Actually, I do have an idea along those lines,' Hammersmith said. 'Something your friend Mr Goodpenny told me, Fiona. He made me realize I shouldn't be alone all my life. And seeing Mr and Mrs Day back together again only reinforces that.'

'Oh,' Fiona said. She took a step forward.

'So if she'll have me, I'd like to ask Miss Pitt to be my wife. Then she'll be a Hammersmith, too, and the agency can remain as it is.'

'Oh,' Hatty said. She looked round at the shocked expressions on her friends' faces. 'I had no idea.'

'I've been considering it these last few weeks. It seems like a sound notion. Practical.'

'Then, yes,' Hatty said. 'Yes, I will marry you, Mr Hammersmith.'

She was about to say something else, but the front door slammed and, through the window, they all watched Fiona Kingsley run away down the street until she was swallowed up by the unceasing traffic.

Hammersmith frowned at Day. 'I wonder what's got into her,' he said.

Day leaned close and spoke so that no one else would hear. 'I'm afraid you have created a situation, Nevil.'

Epilogue 1

The giant blue globe had rolled down Prince Street, causing innumerable traffic accidents. At the corner of King William Street and West Cannon, it bounced off Monument Station, crushing a dog against the west wall of the building, and rolled south along King William to London Bridge. The globe hit the eastern side of the three-foot-high balustrade, breaking the rail and twelve posts, then caromed away to the other side, where it launched itself high into the air.

It went down with a splash and floated away downriver.

It eventually came to rest at the East India Docks, where it bobbed in the water for weeks, slowly losing its color. Boys from the area made a game of throwing rocks at it, trying to spin it or sink it, but despite the shoddy workmanship used in the construction of the Plumm's building, it's centerpiece installation proved to be surprisingly sturdy and watertight.

John Plumm eventually had it hauled from the water, and a wide hole was cut through it. He furnished the inside as a foyer and attached it to the front of his renovated building, but he no longer had any interest in running a department store.

His new venture, called the Globe, introduced cosmopolitan culture to the neighborhood, but at affordable prices. A rotating mural of foreign lands and people was painted, at great expense, along the spherical inside of the foyer, which whetted the public's appetite for the sorts of unusual cocktails served inside.

The nightclub was a success and remained open for many years, until a second fire on the premises ruined Plumm and prompted him to leave London for good. The globe was detached, the remains of the building torn down, and a small emporium was built in its place.

The first stall to open there was Goodpenny's Fine Stationery and Supplies.

Epilogue 2

In the summer of 1891, a man and a woman who claimed to be married moved into a cottage at the end of Prince Albert Street in Brighton. Their name, they said, was Oberon, and the man said he was a cousin of Richard and Joseph Hargreave. He also said the brothers had lent him their home so that he could take the salt air while convalescing from surgery. He moved slowly and rarely left the house, but those neighbors who visited found him charming, even courtly. His wife was not as agreeable, and so, before long, the couple was left alone.

No one had been particularly close to the Hargreaves, and so no one bothered to write to them in London to verify the couple's story. In fact, neither Richard nor Joseph Hargreave was ever seen in Brighton again.

It was during this same period that the number of unsolved murders and unusual deaths began to increase in East Sussex, and the constabulary was kept busy. The couple who were staying in the Hargreaves' cottage stopped receiving visitors, and their windows were hung with black crepe. Neighbors were told that Mrs Oberon's sister had taken ill. Mr Oberon was often observed on the beach and he was always polite but distant. He walked slowly with a cane that had a distinctive brass knob at the handle. It was rumored that Mrs Oberon had left in the night to care for her sister, but she never returned.

In the spring of 1892, Mr Oberon reported the news of his wife's untimely death. She had fallen from a horse in Provence and had been instantly killed. Many residents of the area thought it strange that the crime rate fell back to routine levels after Mrs Oberon's departure. It was unthinkable, however, that anyone would bring the subject up to Mr Oberon, who appeared quite distraught.

Three months later he took a second wife, a young widow with a son. He took his new family away, claiming that there were too many memories for him in Brighton. He left no forwarding address or clue regarding his destination. The cottage on Prince Albert Street was shuttered and abandoned.

A week after that, two detectives arrived from London. One of the detectives was tall and uncommonly handsome, though his clothing was stained and creased. The other man walked with a slight limp. They carried with them a sketch of Mr Oberon and asked about him in all of the local establishments. They spent some time walking up and down the beach, observing crowds at the racetrack and talking to the beat constable on Prince Albert Street. They did not answer anyone's questions about themselves.

There was much speculation after the detectives had gone, but soon life returned to normal. Every once in a while someone would see a silhouette on the beach at twilight and think, *There goes Mr Oberon for his after-dinner smoke*, before remembering that he had moved on.

Many years later, when the cottage was torn down to make room for new terraced housing, the body of a woman was found behind the plaster of a pantry wall. No one living in the area was able to identify the badly decayed corpse, and there were no fingerprints left. She was buried in an unmarked grave, and her clothing, including her torn and tattered trousers, was burned.

He just wanted a decent book to read ...

Not too much to ask, is it? It was in 1935 when Allen Lane, Managing Director of Bodley Head Publishers, stood on a platform at Exeter railway station looking for something good to read on his journey back to London. His choice was limited to popular magazines and poor-quality paperbacks – the same choice faced every day by the vast majority of readers, few of whom could afford hardbacks. Lane's disappointment and subsequent anger at the range of books generally available led him to found a company – and change the world.

'We believed in the existence in this country of a vast reading public for intelligent books at a low price, and staked everything on it'
Sir Allen Lane, 1902–1970, founder of Penguin Books

The quality paperback had arrived – and not just in bookshops. Lane was adamant that his Penguins should appear in chain stores and tobacconists, and should cost no more than a packet of cigarettes.

Reading habits (and cigarette prices) have changed since 1935, but Penguin still believes in publishing the best books for everybody to enjoy. We still believe that good design costs no more than bad design, and we still believe that quality books published passionately and responsibly make the world a better place.

So wherever you see the little bird – whether it's on a piece of prize-winning literary fiction or a celebrity autobiography, political tour de force or historical masterpiece, a serial-killer thriller, reference book, world classic or a piece of pure escapism – you can bet that it represents the very best that the genre has to offer.

Whatever you like to read – trust Penguin.